MW01182268

Writings From Sir Arthur Conan Doyle

Sherlock Holmes, Hound of the Baskervilles, and The Lost World

Arthur Conan Doyle

Red and Black Publishers, St Petersburg, Florida

Library of Congress Cataloging-in-Publication Data

Doyle, Arthur Conan, 1859-1930.
[Works. Selections]
Writings from Sir Arthur Conan Doyle : Sherlock Holmes, Hound of the Baskervilles, and The lost world / Arthur Conan Doyle.
pages cm
ISBN 978-1-61001-029-0
1. Holmes, Sherlock (Fictitious character)--Fiction. 2. Private investigators--England--Fiction. 3. Challenger, Professor (Fictitious character)--Fiction. 4. Detective and mystery stories, English. 5. Adventure stories, English. 6. Fantasy fiction, English. I. Doyle, Arthur Conan, 1859-1930. Adventures of Sherlock Holmes. II. Doyle, Arthur Conan, 1859-1930. Hound of the Baskervilles. III. Doyle, Arthur Conan, 1859-1930. Lost world. IV. Title. V. Title: Adventures of Sherlock Holmes. VI. Title: Hound of the Baskervilles. VII. Title: Lost world.
PR4621 2013
823'.8--dc23

2012051801

Red and Black Publishers, PO Box 7542, St Petersburg, Florida, 33734
Contact us at: info@RedandBlackPublishers.com
Printed and manufactured in the United States of America

Contents

Editor's Preface

Arthur Conan Doyle was born in Edinburgh, Scotland, in May 1859. While at the University of Edinburgh studying medicine, he published several short stories. After serving as a ship's doctor on a voyage to West Africa, he moved to Plymouth, partnered briefly with a friend from medical school, then set up his own practice. He never had very many patients, however, and in his spare time he again began writing short stories. In 1887, he published a short story titled "A Study in Scarlet", featuring a meticulously logical detective named Sherlock Holmes. "The Sign of Four" followed in 1890, and in 1892, Conan Doyle wrote a number of stories that he collected together into a book-length work, titled *The Adventures of Sherlock Holmes*. It was a huge success. *The Memoirs of Sherlock Holmes* was published in 1894, followed by *The Hound of the Baskervilles* in 1902. In all, Conan Doyle wrote four books and 56 short stories featuring the Sherlock Holmes character.

In 1912, Conan Doyle, beginning to tire of the Holmes character, introduced a new hero with *The Lost World*, featuring Professer George Edward Challenger. The Challenger character appeared in two more novels and several short stories.

In addition to the Holmes and Challenger books, Conan Doyle wrote a number of historical novels, as well as nonfiction books on the Boer War and on the recent history of the Congo Free State in central Africa. He ran for Parliament twice on the Liberal Unionist ticket, but wasn't elected.

Unfortunately, the man who created the supremely evidence-gathering and deductively-reasoning Sherlock Holmes, also fell for several things he should not have fallen for. In 1906, Conan Doyle's wife Louisa died, in 1918 his son Kingsley, who had been wounded in the Battle of the Somme, died from complications, and in 1919, his brother, General Innes Doyle, died from pneumonia. In his grief, Conan Doyle turned to spiritualism, and canvassed a number of mediums and psychics in an attempt to contact his dead family members. Although an agnostic from a young age, Conan Doyle now embraced spiritualism and supernaturalism wholeheartedly.

In 1921, he was convinced by the stories of two little girls who claimed to have seen (and produced photographs of) winged fairies in their backyard in Cottingly, and published a book defending their claims—the girls later admitted the stories and photos were all faked. In the 1920's, Conan Doyle became friends with the magician Harry Houdini and, despite Houdini's own reputation for debunking fake spiritualists, convinced himself that Houdini actually had supernatural powers. Houdini ended their friendship when Conan Doyle stubbornly refused to believe that all of Houdini's stunts were just ordinary magician's illusions. Conan Doyle wrote several books about spiritualism and supernaturalism.

Conan Doyle died in England of a heart attack in July 1930.

The Adventures of Sherlock Holmes

Adventure I. A Scandal In Bohemia

I.

To Sherlock Holmes she is always THE Woman. I have seldom heard him mention her under any other name. In his eyes she eclipses and predominates the whole of her sex. It was not that he felt any emotion akin to love for Irene Adler. All emotions, and that one particularly, were abhorrent to his cold, precise but admirably balanced mind. He was, I take it, the most perfect reasoning and observing machine that the world has seen, but as a lover he would have placed himself in a false position. He never spoke of the softer passions, save with a gibe and a sneer. They were admirable things for the observer—excellent for drawing the veil from men's motives and actions. But for the trained reasoner to admit such intrusions into his own delicate and finely adjusted temperament was to introduce a distracting factor which might throw a doubt upon all his mental results. Grit in a sensitive instrument, or a crack in one of his own high-power lenses, would not be more disturbing than a strong emotion in a nature such as his. And yet there was but one woman to him, and that woman was the late Irene Adler, of dubious and questionable memory.

I had seen little of Holmes lately. My marriage had drifted us away from each other. My own complete happiness, and the home-centred interests which rise up around the man who first finds himself master of his own establishment, were sufficient to absorb all my attention, while Holmes, who loathed every form of society with his whole Bohemian soul, remained in our lodgings in Baker Street, buried among his old books, and alternating from week to week between cocaine and ambition, the drowsiness of the drug, and the fierce energy of his own keen nature. He was still, as ever, deeply attracted by the study of crime, and occupied his immense faculties and extraordinary powers of observation in following out those clues, and clearing up those mysteries which had been abandoned as hopeless by the official police. From time to time I heard some vague account of his doings: of his summons to Odessa in the case of the Trepoff murder, of his clearing up of the singular tragedy of the Atkinson brothers at Trincomalee, and finally of the mission which he had accomplished so delicately and successfully for the reigning family of Holland. Beyond these signs of his activity, however, which I merely shared with all the readers of the daily press, I knew little of my former friend and companion.

One night—it was on the twentieth of March, 1888--I was returning from a journey to a patient (for I had now returned to civil practice), when my way led me through Baker Street. As I passed the well-remembered door, which must always be associated in my mind with my wooing, and with the dark incidents of the Study in Scarlet, I was seized with a keen desire to see Holmes again, and to know how he was employing his extraordinary powers. His rooms were brilliantly lit, and, even as I looked up, I saw his tall, spare figure pass twice in a dark silhouette against the blind. He was pacing the room swiftly, eagerly, with his head sunk upon his chest and his hands clasped behind him. To me, who knew his every mood and habit, his attitude and manner told their own story. He was at work again. He had risen out of his drug-created dreams and was hot upon the scent of some new problem. I rang the bell and was shown up to the chamber which had formerly been in part my own.

His manner was not effusive. It seldom was; but he was glad, I think, to see me. With hardly a word spoken, but with a kindly eye, he waved me to an armchair, threw across his case of cigars, and indicated a spirit case and a gasogene in the corner. Then he stood before the fire and looked me over in his singular introspective fashion.

"Wedlock suits you," he remarked. "I think, Watson, that you have put on seven and a half pounds since I saw you."

"Seven!" I answered.

"Indeed, I should have thought a little more. Just a trifle more, I fancy, Watson. And in practice again, I observe. You did not tell me that you intended to go into harness."

"Then, how do you know?"

"I see it, I deduce it. How do I know that you have been getting yourself very wet lately, and that you have a most clumsy and careless servant girl?"

"My dear Holmes," said I, "this is too much. You would certainly have been burned, had you lived a few centuries ago. It is true that I had a country walk on Thursday and came home in a dreadful mess, but as I have changed my clothes I can't imagine how you deduce it. As to Mary Jane, she is incorrigible, and my wife has given her notice, but there, again, I fail to see how you work it out."

He chuckled to himself and rubbed his long, nervous hands together.

"It is simplicity itself," said he; "my eyes tell me that on the inside of your left shoe, just where the firelight strikes it, the leather is scored by six almost parallel cuts. Obviously they have been caused by someone who has very carelessly scraped round the edges of the sole in order to remove crusted mud from it. Hence, you see, my double deduction that you had been out in vile weather, and that you had a particularly malignant boot-slitting specimen of the London slavey. As to your practice, if a gentleman walks into my rooms smelling of iodoform, with a black mark of nitrate of silver upon his right forefinger, and a bulge on the right side of his top-hat to show where he has secreted his stethoscope, I must be dull, indeed, if I do not pronounce him to be an active member of the medical profession."

I could not help laughing at the ease with which he explained his process of deduction. "When I hear you give your reasons," I remarked, "the thing always appears to me to be so ridiculously simple that I could easily do it myself, though at each successive instance of your reasoning I am baffled until you explain your process. And yet I believe that my eyes are as good as yours."

"Quite so," he answered, lighting a cigarette, and throwing himself down into an armchair. "You see, but you do not observe. The distinction is clear. For example, you have frequently seen the steps which lead up from the hall to this room."

"Frequently."

"How often?"

"Well, some hundreds of times."

"Then how many are there?"

"How many? I don't know."

"Quite so! You have not observed. And yet you have seen. That is just my point. Now, I know that there are seventeen steps, because I have both seen and observed. By-the-way, since you are interested in these little problems, and since you are good enough to chronicle one or two of my trifling experiences, you may be interested in this." He threw over a sheet of thick, pink-tinted note-paper which had been lying open upon the table. "It came by the last post," said he. "Read it aloud."

The note was undated, and without either signature or address.

"There will call upon you to-night, at a quarter to eight o'clock," it said, "a gentleman who desires to consult you upon a matter of the very deepest moment. Your recent services to one of the royal houses of Europe have shown that you are one who may safely be trusted with matters which are of an importance which can hardly be exaggerated. This account of you we have from all quarters received. Be in your chamber then at that hour, and do not take it amiss if your visitor wear a mask."

"This is indeed a mystery," I remarked. "What do you imagine that it means?"

"I have no data yet. It is a capital mistake to theorize before one has data. Insensibly one begins to twist facts to suit theories, instead of theories to suit facts. But the note itself. What do you deduce from it?"

I carefully examined the writing, and the paper upon which it was written.

"The man who wrote it was presumably well to do," I remarked, endeavouring to imitate my companion's processes. "Such paper could not be bought under half a crown a packet. It is peculiarly strong and stiff."

"Peculiar—that is the very word," said Holmes. "It is not an English paper at all. Hold it up to the light."

I did so, and saw a large "E" with a small "g," a "P," and a large "G" with a small "t" woven into the texture of the paper.

"What do you make of that?" asked Holmes.

"The name of the maker, no doubt; or his monogram, rather."

"Not at all. The 'G' with the small 't' stands for 'Gesellschaft,' which is the German for 'Company.' It is a customary contraction like our 'Co.' 'P,' of course, stands for 'Papier.' Now for the 'Eg.' Let us glance at our Continental Gazetteer." He took down a heavy brown volume from his shelves. "Eglow, Eglonitz—here we are, Egria. It is in a German-speaking country—in Bohemia, not far from Carlsbad. 'Remarkable as being the scene of the death of Wallenstein, and for its numerous glass-factories and paper-mills.' Ha, ha, my boy, what do you make of that?" His eyes sparkled, and he sent up a great blue triumphant cloud from his cigarette.

"The paper was made in Bohemia," I said.

"Precisely. And the man who wrote the note is a German. Do you note the peculiar construction of the sentence—'This account of you we have from all quarters received.' A Frenchman or Russian could not have written that. It is the German who is so uncourteous to his verbs. It only remains, therefore, to discover what is wanted by this German who writes upon Bohemian paper and prefers wearing a mask to showing his face. And here he comes, if I am not mistaken, to resolve all our doubts."

As he spoke there was the sharp sound of horses' hoofs and grating wheels against the curb, followed by a sharp pull at the bell. Holmes whistled.

"A pair, by the sound," said he. "Yes," he continued, glancing out of the window. "A nice little brougham and a pair of beauties. A hundred and fifty guineas apiece. There's money in this case, Watson, if there is nothing else."

"I think that I had better go, Holmes."

"Not a bit, Doctor. Stay where you are. I am lost without my Boswell. And this promises to be interesting. It would be a pity to miss it."

"But your client—"

"Never mind him. I may want your help, and so may he. Here he comes. Sit down in that armchair, Doctor, and give us your best attention."

A slow and heavy step, which had been heard upon the stairs and in the passage, paused immediately outside the door. Then there was a loud and authoritative tap.

"Come in!" said Holmes.

A man entered who could hardly have been less than six feet six inches in height, with the chest and limbs of a Hercules. His dress was rich with a richness which would, in England, be looked upon as akin to bad taste. Heavy bands of astrakhan were slashed across the sleeves and fronts of his double-breasted coat, while the deep blue cloak which was thrown over his shoulders was lined with flame-coloured silk and secured at the neck with a brooch which consisted of a single flaming beryl. Boots which extended halfway up his calves, and which were trimmed at the tops with rich brown fur, completed the impression of barbaric opulence which was suggested by his whole appearance. He carried a broad-brimmed hat in his hand, while he wore across the upper part of his face, extending down past the cheekbones, a black vizard mask, which he had apparently adjusted that very moment, for his hand was still raised to it as he entered. From the lower part of the face he appeared to be a man of strong character, with a thick, hanging lip, and a long, straight chin suggestive of resolution pushed to the length of obstinacy.

"You had my note?" he asked with a deep harsh voice and a strongly marked German accent. "I told you that I would call." He looked from one to the other of us, as if uncertain which to address.

"Pray take a seat," said Holmes. "This is my friend and colleague, Dr. Watson, who is occasionally good enough to help me in my cases. Whom have I the honour to address?"

"You may address me as the Count Von Kramm, a Bohemian nobleman. I understand that this gentleman, your friend, is a man of honour and discretion, whom I may trust with a matter of the most extreme importance. If not, I should much prefer to communicate with you alone."

I rose to go, but Holmes caught me by the wrist and pushed me back into my chair. "It is both, or none," said he. "You may say before this gentleman anything which you may say to me."

The Count shrugged his broad shoulders. "Then I must begin," said he, "by binding you both to absolute secrecy for two years; at the end of that time the matter will be of no importance. At present it is not too much to say that it is of such weight it may have an influence upon European history."

"I promise," said Holmes.

"And I."

"You will excuse this mask," continued our strange visitor. "The august person who employs me wishes his agent to be unknown to you, and I may confess at once that the title by which I have just called myself is not exactly my own."

"I was aware of it," said Holmes dryly.

"The circumstances are of great delicacy, and every precaution has to be taken to quench what might grow to be an immense scandal and seriously compromise one of the reigning families of Europe. To speak plainly, the matter implicates the great House of Ormstein, hereditary kings of Bohemia."

"I was also aware of that," murmured Holmes, settling himself down in his armchair and closing his eyes.

Our visitor glanced with some apparent surprise at the languid, lounging figure of the man who had been no doubt depicted to him as the most incisive reasoner and most energetic agent in Europe. Holmes slowly reopened his eyes and looked impatiently at his gigantic client.

"If your Majesty would condescend to state your case," he remarked, "I should be better able to advise you."

The man sprang from his chair and paced up and down the room in uncontrollable agitation. Then, with a gesture of desperation, he tore the mask from his face and hurled it upon the ground. "You are right," he cried; "I am the King. Why should I attempt to conceal it?"

"Why, indeed?" murmured Holmes. "Your Majesty had not spoken before I was aware that I was addressing Wilhelm Gottsreich Sigismond von Ormstein, Grand Duke of Cassel-Felstein, and hereditary King of Bohemia."

"But you can understand," said our strange visitor, sitting down once more and passing his hand over his high white forehead, "you can understand that I am not accustomed to doing such business in my own person. Yet the matter was so delicate that I could not confide it to an agent without putting myself in his power. I have come incognito from Prague for the purpose of consulting you."

"Then, pray consult," said Holmes, shutting his eyes once more.

"The facts are briefly these: Some five years ago, during a lengthy visit to Warsaw, I made the acquaintance of the well-known adventuress, Irene Adler. The name is no doubt familiar to you."

"Kindly look her up in my index, Doctor," murmured Holmes without opening his eyes. For many years he had adopted a system of docketing all paragraphs concerning men and things, so that it was difficult to name a subject or a person on which he could not at once furnish information. In this case I found her biography sandwiched in between that of a Hebrew rabbi and that of a staff-commander who had written a monograph upon the deep-sea fishes.

"Let me see!" said Holmes. "Hum! Born in New Jersey in the year 1858. Contralto—hum! La Scala, hum! Prima donna Imperial Opera of Warsaw—yes! Retired from operatic stage—ha! Living in London—quite so! Your Majesty, as I understand, became entangled with this young person, wrote her some compromising letters, and is now desirous of getting those letters back."

"Precisely so. But how—"

"Was there a secret marriage?"

"None."

"No legal papers or certificates?"

"None."

"Then I fail to follow your Majesty. If this young person should produce her letters for blackmailing or other purposes, how is she to prove their authenticity?"

"There is the writing."

"Pooh, pooh! Forgery."

"My private note-paper."

"Stolen."

"My own seal."

"Imitated."

"My photograph."

"Bought."

"We were both in the photograph."

"Oh, dear! That is very bad! Your Majesty has indeed committed an indiscretion."

"I was mad—insane."

"You have compromised yourself seriously."

"I was only Crown Prince then. I was young. I am but thirty now."

"It must be recovered."

"We have tried and failed."

"Your Majesty must pay. It must be bought."

"She will not sell."

"Stolen, then."

"Five attempts have been made. Twice burglars in my pay ransacked her house. Once we diverted her luggage when she travelled. Twice she has been waylaid. There has been no result."

"No sign of it?"

"Absolutely none."

Holmes laughed. "It is quite a pretty little problem," said he.

"But a very serious one to me," returned the King reproachfully.

"Very, indeed. And what does she propose to do with the photograph?"

"To ruin me."

"But how?"

"I am about to be married."

"So I have heard."

"To Clotilde Lothman von Saxe-Meningen, second daughter of the King of Scandinavia. You may know the strict principles of her family. She is herself the very soul of delicacy. A shadow of a doubt as to my conduct would bring the matter to an end."

"And Irene Adler?"

"Threatens to send them the photograph. And she will do it. I know that she will do it. You do not know her, but she has a soul of steel. She has the face of the most beautiful of women, and the mind of the most resolute of men. Rather than I should marry another woman, there are no lengths to which she would not go—none."

"You are sure that she has not sent it yet?"

"I am sure."

"And why?"

"Because she has said that she would send it on the day when the betrothal was publicly proclaimed. That will be next Monday."

"Oh, then we have three days yet," said Holmes with a yawn. "That is very fortunate, as I have one or two matters of importance to look into just at present. Your Majesty will, of course, stay in London for the present?"

"Certainly. You will find me at the Langham under the name of the Count Von Kramm."

"Then I shall drop you a line to let you know how we progress."

"Pray do so. I shall be all anxiety."

"Then, as to money?"

"You have carte blanche."

"Absolutely?"

"I tell you that I would give one of the provinces of my kingdom to have that photograph."

"And for present expenses?"

The King took a heavy chamois leather bag from under his cloak and laid it on the table.

"There are three hundred pounds in gold and seven hundred in notes," he said.

Holmes scribbled a receipt upon a sheet of his note-book and handed it to him.

"And Mademoiselle's address?" he asked.

"Is Briony Lodge, Serpentine Avenue, St. John's Wood."

Holmes took a note of it. "One other question," said he. "Was the photograph a cabinet?"

"It was."

"Then, good-night, your Majesty, and I trust that we shall soon have some good news for you. And good-night, Watson," he added, as the wheels of the royal brougham rolled down the street. "If you will be good enough to call tomorrow afternoon at three o'clock I should like to chat this little matter over with you."

II.

At three o'clock precisely I was at Baker Street, but Holmes had not yet returned. The landlady informed me that he had left the house shortly after eight o'clock in the morning. I sat down beside the fire, however, with the intention of awaiting him, however long he might be. I was already deeply interested in his inquiry, for, though it was surrounded by none of the grim and strange features which were associated with the two crimes which I have already recorded, still, the nature of the case and the exalted station of his client gave it a character of its own. Indeed, apart from the nature of the investigation which my friend had on hand, there was something in his masterly grasp of a situation, and his keen, incisive reasoning, which made it a pleasure to me to study his system of work, and to follow the quick, subtle methods by which he disentangled the most inextricable mysteries. So accustomed was I to his invariable success that the very possibility of his failing had ceased to enter into my head.

It was close upon four before the door opened, and a drunken-looking groom, ill-kempt and side-whiskered, with an inflamed face and disreputable clothes, walked into the room. Accustomed as I was to my friend's amazing powers in the use of disguises, I had to look three times before I was certain that it was indeed he. With a nod he vanished into the bedroom, whence he emerged in five minutes tweed-suited and respectable, as of old. Putting his hands into his pockets, he stretched out his legs in front of the fire and laughed heartily for some minutes.

"Well, really!" he cried, and then he choked and laughed again until he was obliged to lie back, limp and helpless, in the chair.

"What is it?"

"It's quite too funny. I am sure you could never guess how I employed my morning, or what I ended by doing."

"I can't imagine. I suppose that you have been watching the habits, and perhaps the house, of Miss Irene Adler."

"Quite so; but the sequel was rather unusual. I will tell you, however. I left the house a little after eight o'clock this morning in the character of a groom out of work. There is a wonderful sympathy and freemasonry among horsey men. Be one of them, and you will know all that there is to know. I soon found Briony Lodge. It is a bijou villa, with a garden at the back, but built out in front right up to the road, two stories. Chubb lock to the door. Large sitting-room on the right side, well furnished, with long windows almost to the floor, and those preposterous English window fasteners which a child could open. Behind there was nothing remarkable, save that the passage window could be reached from the top of the coach-house. I walked round it and examined it closely from every point of view, but without noting anything else of interest.

"I then lounged down the street and found, as I expected, that there was a mews in a lane which runs down by one wall of the garden. I lent the ostlers a hand in rubbing down their horses, and received in exchange twopence, a glass of half and half, two fills of shag tobacco, and as much information as I could desire about Miss Adler, to say nothing of half a dozen other people in the neighbourhood in whom I was not in the least interested, but whose biographies I was compelled to listen to."

"And what of Irene Adler?" I asked.

"Oh, she has turned all the men's heads down in that part. She is the daintiest thing under a bonnet on this planet. So say the Serpentine-mews, to a man. She lives quietly, sings at concerts, drives out at five every day, and returns at seven sharp for dinner. Seldom goes out at other times, except when she sings. Has only one male visitor, but a good deal of him. He is dark, handsome, and dashing, never calls less than once a day, and often twice. He is a Mr. Godfrey Norton, of the Inner Temple. See the advantages of a cabman as a confidant. They had driven him home a dozen times from Serpentine-mews, and knew all about him. When I had listened to all they had to tell, I began to walk up and down near Briony Lodge once more, and to think over my plan of campaign.

"This Godfrey Norton was evidently an important factor in the matter. He was a lawyer. That sounded ominous. What was the relation between them, and what the object of his repeated visits? Was she his client, his friend, or his mistress? If the former, she had probably transferred the photograph to his keeping. If the latter, it was less likely. On the issue of this question depended whether I should continue my work at Briony Lodge, or turn my attention to the gentleman's chambers in the Temple. It was a delicate point, and it widened the field of my inquiry. I fear that I bore you with these details, but I have to let you see my little difficulties, if you are to understand the situation."

"I am following you closely," I answered.

"I was still balancing the matter in my mind when a hansom cab drove up to Briony Lodge, and a gentleman sprang out. He was a remarkably handsome man, dark, aquiline, and moustached—evidently the man of whom I had heard. He appeared to be in a great hurry, shouted to the cabman to wait, and brushed past the maid who opened the door with the air of a man who was thoroughly at home.

"He was in the house about half an hour, and I could catch glimpses of him in the windows of the sitting-room, pacing up and down, talking excitedly, and waving his arms. Of her I could see nothing. Presently he emerged, looking even more flurried than before. As he stepped up to the cab, he pulled a gold watch from his pocket and looked at it earnestly, 'Drive like the devil,' he shouted, 'first to Gross & Hankey's in Regent Street, and then to the Church of St. Monica in the Edgeware Road. Half a guinea if you do it in twenty minutes!'

"Away they went, and I was just wondering whether I should not do well to follow them when up the lane came a neat little landau, the coachman with his coat only half-buttoned, and his tie under his ear, while all the tags of his harness were sticking out of the buckles. It hadn't pulled up before she shot out of the hall door and into it. I only caught a glimpse of her at the moment, but she was a lovely woman, with a face that a man might die for.

"'The Church of St. Monica, John,' she cried, 'and half a sovereign if you reach it in twenty minutes.'

"This was quite too good to lose, Watson. I was just balancing whether I should run for it, or whether I should perch behind her landau when a cab came through the street. The driver looked twice at such a shabby fare, but I jumped in before he could object. 'The Church of St. Monica,' said I, 'and half a sovereign if you reach it in twenty minutes.' It was twenty-five minutes to twelve, and of course it was clear enough what was in the wind.

"My cabby drove fast. I don't think I ever drove faster, but the others were there before us. The cab and the landau with their steaming horses were in front of the door when I arrived. I paid the man and hurried into the church. There was not a soul there save the two whom I had followed and a surpliced clergyman, who seemed to be expostulating with them. They were all three standing in a knot in front of the altar. I lounged up the side aisle like any other idler who has dropped into a church. Suddenly, to my surprise, the three at the altar faced round to me, and Godfrey Norton came running as hard as he could towards me.

"'Thank God,' he cried. 'You'll do. Come! Come!'

"'What then?' I asked.

"'Come, man, come, only three minutes, or it won't be legal.'

"I was half-dragged up to the altar, and before I knew where I was I found myself mumbling responses which were whispered in my ear, and vouching for things of which I knew nothing, and generally assisting in the secure tying up of Irene Adler, spinster, to Godfrey Norton, bachelor. It was all done in an instant, and there was the gentleman thanking me on the one side and the lady on the other, while the clergyman beamed on me in front. It was the most preposterous position in which I ever found myself in my life, and it was the thought of it that started me laughing just now. It seems that there had been some informality about their license, that the clergyman absolutely refused to marry them without a witness of some sort, and that my lucky appearance saved the bridegroom from having to sally out into the streets in search of a best man. The bride gave me a sovereign, and I mean to wear it on my watch-chain in memory of the occasion."

"This is a very unexpected turn of affairs," said I; "and what then?"

"Well, I found my plans very seriously menaced. It looked as if the pair might take an immediate departure, and so necessitate very prompt and energetic measures on my part. At the church door, however, they separated, he driving back to the Temple, and she to her own house. 'I shall drive out in the park at five as usual,' she said as she left him. I heard no more. They drove away in different directions, and I went off to make my own arrangements."

"Which are?"

"Some cold beef and a glass of beer," he answered, ringing the bell. "I have been too busy to think of food, and I am likely to be busier still this evening. By the way, Doctor, I shall want your co-operation."

"I shall be delighted."

"You don't mind breaking the law?"

"Not in the least."

"Nor running a chance of arrest?"

"Not in a good cause."

"Oh, the cause is excellent!"

"Then I am your man."

"I was sure that I might rely on you."

"But what is it you wish?"

"When Mrs. Turner has brought in the tray I will make it clear to you. Now," he said as he turned hungrily on the simple fare that our landlady had provided, "I must discuss it while I eat, for I have not much time. It is nearly five now. In two hours we must be on the scene of action. Miss Irene, or Madame, rather, returns from her drive at seven. We must be at Briony Lodge to meet her."

"And what then?"

"You must leave that to me. I have already arranged what is to occur. There is only one point on which I must insist. You must not interfere, come what may. You understand?"

"I am to be neutral?"

"To do nothing whatever. There will probably be some small unpleasantness. Do not join in it. It will end in my being conveyed into the house. Four or five minutes afterwards the sitting-room window will open. You are to station yourself close to that open window."

"Yes."

"You are to watch me, for I will be visible to you."

"Yes."

"And when I raise my hand—so—you will throw into the room what I give you to throw, and will, at the same time, raise the cry of fire. You quite follow me?"

"Entirely."

"It is nothing very formidable," he said, taking a long cigar- shaped roll from his pocket. "It is an ordinary plumber's smoke- rocket, fitted with a cap at either end to make it self-lighting. Your task is confined to that. When you raise your cry of fire, it will be taken up by quite a number of people. You may then walk to the end of the street, and I will rejoin you in ten minutes. I hope that I have made myself clear?"

"I am to remain neutral, to get near the window, to watch you, and at the signal to throw in this object, then to raise the cry of fire, and to wait you at the corner of the street."

"Precisely."

"Then you may entirely rely on me."

"That is excellent. I think, perhaps, it is almost time that I prepare for the new role I have to play."

He disappeared into his bedroom and returned in a few minutes in the character of an amiable and simple-minded Nonconformist clergyman. His broad black hat, his baggy trousers, his white tie, his sympathetic smile, and general look of peering and benevolent curiosity were such as Mr. John Hare alone could have equalled. It was not merely that Holmes changed his costume. His expression, his manner, his very soul seemed to vary with every fresh part that he assumed. The stage lost a fine actor, even as science lost an acute reasoner, when he became a specialist in crime.

It was a quarter past six when we left Baker Street, and it still wanted ten minutes to the hour when we found ourselves in Serpentine Avenue. It was already dusk, and the lamps were just being lighted as we paced up and down in front of Briony Lodge, waiting for the coming of its occupant. The house was just such as I had pictured it from Sherlock Holmes' succinct description, but the locality appeared to be less private than I expected. On the contrary, for a small street in a quiet neighbourhood, it was remarkably animated. There was a group of shabbily dressed men smoking and laughing in a corner, a scissors-grinder with his wheel, two guardsmen who were flirting with a nurse-girl, and several well-dressed young men who were lounging up and down with cigars in their mouths.

"You see," remarked Holmes, as we paced to and fro in front of the house, "this marriage rather simplifies matters. The photograph becomes a double-edged weapon now. The chances are that she would be as averse to its being seen by Mr. Godfrey Norton, as our client is to its coming to the eyes of his princess. Now the question is, Where are we to find the photograph?"

"Where, indeed?"

"It is most unlikely that she carries it about with her. It is cabinet size. Too large for easy concealment about a woman's dress. She knows that the King is capable of having her waylaid and searched. Two attempts of the sort have already been made. We may take it, then, that she does not carry it about with her."

"Where, then?"

"Her banker or her lawyer. There is that double possibility. But I am inclined to think neither. Women are naturally secretive, and they like to do their own secreting. Why should she hand it over to anyone else? She could trust her own guardianship, but she could not tell what indirect or political influence might be brought to bear upon a business man. Besides, remember that she had resolved to use it within a few days. It must be where she can lay her hands upon it. It must be in her own house."

"But it has twice been burgled."

"Pshaw! They did not know how to look."

"But how will you look?"

"I will not look."

"What then?"

"I will get her to show me."

"But she will refuse."

"She will not be able to. But I hear the rumble of wheels. It is her carriage. Now carry out my orders to the letter."

As he spoke the gleam of the side-lights of a carriage came round the curve of the avenue. It was a smart little landau which rattled up to the door of Briony Lodge. As it pulled up, one of the loafing men at the corner dashed forward to open the door in the hope of earning a copper, but was elbowed away by another loafer, who had rushed up with the same intention. A fierce quarrel broke out, which was increased by the two guardsmen, who took sides with one of the loungers, and by the scissors-grinder, who was equally hot upon the other side. A blow was struck, and in an instant the lady, who had stepped from her carriage, was the centre of a little knot of flushed and struggling men, who struck savagely at each other with their fists and sticks. Holmes dashed into the crowd to protect the lady; but just as he reached her he gave a cry and dropped to the ground, with the blood running freely down his face. At his fall the guardsmen took to their heels in one direction and the loungers in the other, while a number of better-dressed people, who had watched the scuffle without taking part in it, crowded in to help the lady and to attend to the injured man. Irene Adler, as I will still call her, had hurried up the steps; but she stood at the top with her superb figure outlined against the lights of the hall, looking back into the street.

"Is the poor gentleman much hurt?" she asked.

"He is dead," cried several voices.

"No, no, there's life in him!" shouted another. "But he'll be gone before you can get him to hospital."

"He's a brave fellow," said a woman. "They would have had the lady's purse and watch if it hadn't been for him. They were a gang, and a rough one, too. Ah, he's breathing now."

"He can't lie in the street. May we bring him in, marm?"

"Surely. Bring him into the sitting-room. There is a comfortable sofa. This way, please!"

Slowly and solemnly he was borne into Briony Lodge and laid out in the principal room, while I still observed the proceedings from my post by the window. The lamps had been lit, but the blinds had not been drawn, so that I could see Holmes as he lay upon the couch. I do not know whether he was seized with compunction at that moment for the part he was playing, but I know that I never felt more heartily ashamed of myself in my life than when I saw the beautiful creature against whom I was conspiring, or the grace and kindliness with which she waited upon the injured man. And yet it would be the blackest treachery to Holmes to draw back now from the part which he had intrusted to me. I hardened my heart, and took the smoke-rocket from under my ulster. After all, I thought, we are not injuring her. We are but preventing her from injuring another.

Holmes had sat up upon the couch, and I saw him motion like a man who is in need of air. A maid rushed across and threw open the window. At the same instant I saw him raise his hand and at the signal I tossed my rocket into the room with a cry of "Fire!" The word was no sooner out of my mouth than the whole crowd of spectators, well dressed and ill—gentlemen, ostlers, and servant-maids—joined in a general shriek of "Fire!" Thick clouds of smoke curled through the room and out at the open window. I caught a glimpse of rushing figures, and a moment later the voice of Holmes from within assuring them that it was a false alarm. Slipping through the shouting crowd I made my way to the corner of the street, and in ten minutes was rejoiced to find my friend's arm in mine, and to get away from the scene of uproar. He walked swiftly and in silence for some few minutes until we had turned down one of the quiet streets which lead towards the Edgeware Road.

"You did it very nicely, Doctor," he remarked. "Nothing could have been better. It is all right."

"You have the photograph?"

"I know where it is."

"And how did you find out?"

"She showed me, as I told you she would."

"I am still in the dark."

"I do not wish to make a mystery," said he, laughing. "The matter was perfectly simple. You, of course, saw that everyone in the street was an accomplice. They were all engaged for the evening."

"I guessed as much."

"Then, when the row broke out, I had a little moist red paint in the palm of my hand. I rushed forward, fell down, clapped my hand to my face, and became a piteous spectacle. It is an old trick."

"That also I could fathom."

"Then they carried me in. She was bound to have me in. What else could she do? And into her sitting-room, which was the very room which I suspected. It lay between that and her bedroom, and I was determined to see which. They laid me on a couch, I motioned for air, they were compelled to open the window, and you had your chance."

"How did that help you?"

"It was all-important. When a woman thinks that her house is on fire, her instinct is at once to rush to the thing which she values most. It is a perfectly overpowering impulse, and I have more than once taken advantage of it. In the case of the Darlington substitution scandal it was of use to me, and also in the Arnsworth Castle business. A married woman grabs at her baby; an unmarried one reaches for her jewel-box. Now it was clear to me that our lady of today had nothing in the house more precious to her than what we are in quest of. She would rush to secure it. The alarm of fire was admirably done. The smoke and shouting were enough to shake nerves of steel. She responded beautifully. The photograph is in a recess behind a sliding panel just above the right bell-pull. She was there in an instant, and I caught a glimpse of it as she half-drew it out. When I cried out that it was a false alarm, she replaced it, glanced at the rocket, rushed from the room, and I have not seen her since. I rose, and, making my excuses, escaped from the house. I hesitated whether to attempt to secure the photograph at once; but the coachman had come in, and as he was watching me narrowly it seemed safer to wait. A little over-precipitance may ruin all."

"And now?" I asked.

"Our quest is practically finished. I shall call with the King tomorrow, and with you, if you care to come with us. We will be shown into the sitting-room to wait for the lady, but it is probable that when she comes she may find neither us nor the photograph. It might be a satisfaction to his Majesty to regain it with his own hands."

"And when will you call?"

"At eight in the morning. She will not be up, so that we shall have a clear field. Besides, we must be prompt, for this marriage may mean a complete change in her life and habits. I must wire to the King without delay."

We had reached Baker Street and had stopped at the door. He was searching his pockets for the key when someone passing said:

"Good-night, Mister Sherlock Holmes."

There were several people on the pavement at the time, but the greeting appeared to come from a slim youth in an ulster who had hurried by.

"I've heard that voice before," said Holmes, staring down the dimly lit street. "Now, I wonder who the deuce that could have been."

III.

I slept at Baker Street that night, and we were engaged upon our toast and coffee in the morning when the King of Bohemia rushed into the room.

"You have really got it!" he cried, grasping Sherlock Holmes by either shoulder and looking eagerly into his face.

"Not yet."

"But you have hopes?"

"I have hopes."

"Then, come. I am all impatience to be gone."

"We must have a cab."

"No, my brougham is waiting."

"Then that will simplify matters." We descended and started off once more for Briony Lodge.

"Irene Adler is married," remarked Holmes.

"Married! When?"

"Yesterday."

"But to whom?"

"To an English lawyer named Norton."

"But she could not love him."

"I am in hopes that she does."

"And why in hopes?"

"Because it would spare your Majesty all fear of future annoyance. If the lady loves her husband, she does not love your Majesty. If she does not love your Majesty, there is no reason why she should interfere with your Majesty's plan."

"It is true. And yet—Well! I wish she had been of my own station! What a queen she would have made!" He relapsed into a moody silence, which was not broken until we drew up in Serpentine Avenue.

The door of Briony Lodge was open, and an elderly woman stood upon the steps. She watched us with a sardonic eye as we stepped from the brougham.

"Mr. Sherlock Holmes, I believe?" said she.

"I am Mr. Holmes," answered my companion, looking at her with a questioning and rather startled gaze.

"Indeed! My mistress told me that you were likely to call. She left this morning with her husband by the 5:15 train from Charing Cross for the Continent."

"What!" Sherlock Holmes staggered back, white with chagrin and surprise. "Do you mean that she has left England?"

"Never to return."

"And the papers?" asked the King hoarsely. "All is lost."

"We shall see." He pushed past the servant and rushed into the drawing-room, followed by the King and myself. The furniture was scattered about in every direction, with dismantled shelves and open drawers, as if the lady had hurriedly ransacked them before her flight. Holmes rushed at the bell-pull, tore back a small sliding shutter, and, plunging in his hand, pulled out a photograph and a letter. The photograph was of Irene Adler herself in evening dress, the letter was superscribed to "Sherlock Holmes, Esq. To be left till called for." My friend tore it open and we all three read it together. It was dated at midnight of the preceding night and ran in this way:

"My Dear Mr. Sherlock Holmes,--You really did it very well. You took me in completely. Until after the alarm of fire, I had not a suspicion. But then, when I found how I had betrayed myself, I began to think. I had been warned against you months ago. I had been told that if the King employed an agent it would certainly be you. And your address had been given me. Yet, with all this, you made me reveal what you wanted to know. Even after I became suspicious, I found it hard to think evil of such a dear, kind old clergyman. But, you know, I have been trained as an actress myself. Male costume is nothing new to me. I often take advantage of the freedom which it gives. I sent John, the coachman, to watch you, ran up stairs, got into my walking-clothes, as I call them, and came down just as you departed.

"Well, I followed you to your door, and so made sure that I was really an object of interest to the celebrated Mr. Sherlock Holmes. Then I, rather imprudently, wished you good-night, and started for the Temple to see my husband.

"We both thought the best resource was flight, when pursued by so formidable an antagonist; so you will find the nest empty when you call tomorrow. As to the photograph, your client may rest in peace. I love and am loved by a better man than he. The King may do what he will without hindrance from one whom he has cruelly wronged. I keep it only to safeguard myself, and to preserve a weapon which will always secure me from any steps which he might take in the future. I leave a photograph which he might care to possess; and I remain, dear Mr. Sherlock Holmes,

"Very truly yours, "Irene Norton, Née Adler."

"What a woman—oh, what a woman!" cried the King of Bohemia, when we had all three read this epistle. "Did I not tell you how quick and resolute she was? Would she not have made an admirable queen? Is it not a pity that she was not on my level?"

"From what I have seen of the lady she seems indeed to be on a very different level to your Majesty," said Holmes coldly. "I am sorry that I have not been able to bring your Majesty's business to a more successful conclusion."

"On the contrary, my dear sir," cried the King; "nothing could be more successful. I know that her word is inviolate. The photograph is now as safe as if it were in the fire."

"I am glad to hear your Majesty say so."

"I am immensely indebted to you. Pray tell me in what way I can reward you. This ring—" He slipped an emerald snake ring from his finger and held it out upon the palm of his hand.

"Your Majesty has something which I should value even more highly," said Holmes.

"You have but to name it."

"This photograph!"

The King stared at him in amazement.

"Irene's photograph!" he cried. "Certainly, if you wish it."

"I thank your Majesty. Then there is no more to be done in the matter. I have the honour to wish you a very good-morning." He bowed, and, turning away without observing the hand which the King had stretched out to him, he set off in my company for his chambers.

And that was how a great scandal threatened to affect the kingdom of Bohemia, and how the best plans of Mr. Sherlock Holmes were beaten by a woman's wit. He used to make merry over the cleverness of women, but I have not heard him do it of late. And when he speaks of Irene Adler, or when he refers to her photograph, it is always under the honourable title of the woman.

Adventure II. The Red-Headed League

I had called upon my friend, Mr. Sherlock Holmes, one day in the autumn of last year and found him in deep conversation with a very stout, florid-faced, elderly gentleman with fiery red hair. With an apology for my intrusion, I was about to withdraw when Holmes pulled me abruptly into the room and closed the door behind me.

"You could not possibly have come at a better time, my dear Watson," he said cordially.

"I was afraid that you were engaged."

"So I am. Very much so."

"Then I can wait in the next room."

"Not at all. This gentleman, Mr. Wilson, has been my partner and helper in many of my most successful cases, and I have no doubt that he will be of the utmost use to me in yours also."

The stout gentleman half rose from his chair and gave a bob of greeting, with a quick little questioning glance from his small fat-encircled eyes.

"Try the settee," said Holmes, relapsing into his armchair and putting his fingertips together, as was his custom when in judicial moods. "I know, my dear Watson, that you share my love of all that is bizarre and outside the conventions and humdrum routine of everyday life. You have shown your relish for it by the enthusiasm which has prompted you to chronicle, and, if you will excuse my saying so, somewhat to embellish so many of my own little adventures."

"Your cases have indeed been of the greatest interest to me," I observed.

"You will remember that I remarked the other day, just before we went into the very simple problem presented by Miss Mary Sutherland, that for strange effects and extraordinary combinations we must go to life itself, which is always far more daring than any effort of the imagination."

"A proposition which I took the liberty of doubting."

"You did, Doctor, but none the less you must come round to my view, for otherwise I shall keep on piling fact upon fact on you until your reason breaks down under them and acknowledges me to be right. Now, Mr. Jabez Wilson here has been good enough to call upon me this morning, and to begin a narrative which promises to be one of the most singular which I have listened to for some time. You have heard me remark that the strangest and most unique things are very often connected not with the larger but with the smaller crimes, and occasionally, indeed, where there is room for doubt whether any positive crime has been committed. As far as I have heard it is impossible for me to say whether the present case is an instance of crime or not, but the course of events is certainly among the most singular that I have ever listened to. Perhaps, Mr. Wilson, you would have the great kindness to recommence your narrative. I ask you not merely because my friend Dr. Watson has not heard the opening part but also because the peculiar nature of the story makes me anxious to have every possible detail from your lips. As a rule, when I have heard some slight indication of the course of events, I am able to guide myself by the thousands of other similar cases which occur to my memory. In the present instance I am forced to admit that the facts are, to the best of my belief, unique."

The portly client puffed out his chest with an appearance of some little pride and pulled a dirty and wrinkled newspaper from the inside pocket of his greatcoat. As he glanced down the advertisement column, with his head thrust forward and the paper flattened out upon his knee, I took a good look at the man and endeavoured, after the fashion of my companion, to read the indications which might be presented by his dress or appearance.

I did not gain very much, however, by my inspection. Our visitor bore every mark of being an average commonplace British tradesman, obese, pompous, and slow. He wore rather baggy grey shepherd's check trousers, a not over-clean black frock-coat, unbuttoned in the front, and a drab waistcoat with a heavy brassy Albert chain, and a square pierced bit of metal dangling down as an ornament. A frayed top-hat and a faded brown overcoat with a wrinkled velvet collar lay upon a chair beside him. Altogether, look as I would, there was nothing remarkable about the man save his blazing red head, and the expression of extreme chagrin and discontent upon his features.

Sherlock Holmes' quick eye took in my occupation, and he shook his head with a smile as he noticed my questioning glances. "Beyond the obvious facts that he has at some time done manual labour, that he takes snuff, that he is a Freemason, that he has been in China, and that he has done a considerable amount of writing lately, I can deduce nothing else."

Mr. Jabez Wilson started up in his chair, with his forefinger upon the paper, but his eyes upon my companion.

"How, in the name of good-fortune, did you know all that, Mr. Holmes?" he asked. "How did you know, for example, that I did manual labour. It's as true as gospel, for I began as a ship's carpenter."

"Your hands, my dear sir. Your right hand is quite a size larger than your left. You have worked with it, and the muscles are more developed."

"Well, the snuff, then, and the Freemasonry?"

"I won't insult your intelligence by telling you how I read that, especially as, rather against the strict rules of your order, you use an arc-and-compass breastpin."

"Ah, of course, I forgot that. But the writing?"

"What else can be indicated by that right cuff so very shiny for five inches, and the left one with the smooth patch near the elbow where you rest it upon the desk?"

"Well, but China?"

"The fish that you have tattooed immediately above your right wrist could only have been done in China. I have made a small study of tattoo marks and have even contributed to the literature of the subject. That trick of staining the fishes' scales of a delicate pink is quite peculiar to China. When, in addition, I see a Chinese coin hanging from your watch-chain, the matter becomes even more simple."

Mr. Jabez Wilson laughed heavily. "Well, I never!" said he. "I thought at first that you had done something clever, but I see that there was nothing in it, after all."

"I begin to think, Watson," said Holmes, "that I make a mistake in explaining. '*Omne ignotum pro magnifico,*' you know, and my poor little reputation, such as it is, will suffer shipwreck if I am so candid. Can you not find the advertisement, Mr. Wilson?"

"Yes, I have got it now," he answered with his thick red finger planted halfway down the column. "Here it is. This is what began it all. You just read it for yourself, sir."

I took the paper from him and read as follows:

"*To The Red-Headed League*: On account of the bequest of the late Ezekiah Hopkins, of Lebanon, Pennsylvania, U. S. A., there is now another vacancy open which entitles a member of the League to a salary of 4 pounds a week for purely nominal services. All red-headed men who are sound in body and mind and above the age of twenty-one years, are eligible. Apply in person on Monday, at eleven o'clock, to Duncan Ross, at the offices of the League, 7 Pope's Court, Fleet Street."

"What on earth does this mean?" I ejaculated after I had twice read over the extraordinary announcement.

Holmes chuckled and wriggled in his chair, as was his habit when in high spirits. "It is a little off the beaten track, isn't it?" said he. "And now, Mr. Wilson, off you go at scratch and tell us all about yourself, your household, and the effect which this advertisement had upon your fortunes. You will first make a note, Doctor, of the paper and the date."

"It is The Morning Chronicle of April 27, 1890. Just two months ago."

"Very good. Now, Mr. Wilson?"

"Well, it is just as I have been telling you, Mr. Sherlock Holmes," said Jabez Wilson, mopping his forehead; "I have a small pawnbroker's business at Coburg Square, near the City. It's not a very large affair, and of late years it has not done more than just give me a living. I used to be able to keep two assistants, but now I only keep one; and I would have a job to pay him but that he is willing to come for half wages so as to learn the business."

"What is the name of this obliging youth?" asked Sherlock Holmes.

"His name is Vincent Spaulding, and he's not such a youth, either. It's hard to say his age. I should not wish a smarter assistant, Mr. Holmes; and I know very well that he could better himself and earn twice what I am able to give him. But, after all, if he is satisfied, why should I put ideas in his head?"

"Why, indeed? You seem most fortunate in having an employé who comes under the full market price. It is not a common experience among employers in this age. I don't know that your assistant is not as remarkable as your advertisement."

"Oh, he has his faults, too," said Mr. Wilson. "Never was such a fellow for photography. Snapping away with a camera when he ought to be improving his mind, and then diving down into the cellar like a rabbit into its hole to develop his pictures. That is his main fault, but on the whole he's a good worker. There's no vice in him."

"He is still with you, I presume?"

"Yes, sir. He and a girl of fourteen, who does a bit of simple cooking and keeps the place clean—that's all I have in the house, for I am a widower and never had any family. We live very quietly, sir, the three of us; and we keep a roof over our heads and pay our debts, if we do nothing more.

"The first thing that put us out was that advertisement. Spaulding, he came down into the office just this day eight weeks, with this very paper in his hand, and he says:

"'I wish to the Lord, Mr. Wilson, that I was a red-headed man.'

"'Why that?' I asks.

"'Why,' says he, 'here's another vacancy on the League of the Red-headed Men. It's worth quite a little fortune to any man who gets it, and I understand that there are more vacancies than there are men, so that the trustees are at their wits' end what to do with the money. If my hair would only change colour, here's a nice little crib all ready for me to step into.'

"'Why, what is it, then?' I asked. You see, Mr. Holmes, I am a very stay-at-home man, and as my business came to me instead of my having to go to it, I was often weeks on end without putting my foot over the door-mat. In that way I didn't know much of what was going on outside, and I was always glad of a bit of news.

"'Have you never heard of the League of the Red-headed Men?' he asked with his eyes open.

"'Never.'

"'Why, I wonder at that, for you are eligible yourself for one of the vacancies.'

"'And what are they worth?' I asked.

"'Oh, merely a couple of hundred a year, but the work is slight, and it need not interfere very much with one's other occupations.'

"Well, you can easily think that that made me prick up my ears, for the business has not been over-good for some years, and an extra couple of hundred would have been very handy.

"'Tell me all about it,' said I.

"'Well,' said he, showing me the advertisement, 'you can see for yourself that the League has a vacancy, and there is the address where you should apply for particulars. As far as I can make out, the League was founded by an American millionaire, Ezekiah Hopkins, who was very peculiar in his ways. He was himself red-headed, and he had a great sympathy for all red-headed men; so when he died it was found that he had left his enormous fortune in the hands of trustees, with instructions to apply the interest to the providing of easy berths to men whose hair is of that colour. From all I hear it is splendid pay and very little to do.'

"'But,' said I, 'there would be millions of red-headed men who would apply.'

"'Not so many as you might think,' he answered. 'You see it is really confined to Londoners, and to grown men. This American had started from London when he was young, and he wanted to do the old town a good turn. Then, again, I have heard it is no use your applying if your hair is light red, or dark red, or anything but real bright, blazing, fiery red. Now, if you cared to apply, Mr. Wilson, you would just walk in; but perhaps it would hardly be worth your while to put yourself out of the way for the sake of a few hundred pounds.'

"Now, it is a fact, gentlemen, as you may see for yourselves, that my hair is of a very full and rich tint, so that it seemed to me that if there was to be any competition in the matter I stood as good a chance as any man that I had ever met. Vincent Spaulding seemed to know so much about it that I thought he might prove useful, so I just ordered him to put up the shutters for the day and to come right away with me. He was very willing to have a holiday, so we shut the business up and started off for the address that was given us in the advertisement.

"I never hope to see such a sight as that again, Mr. Holmes. From north, south, east, and west every man who had a shade of red in his hair had tramped into the city to answer the advertisement. Fleet Street was choked with red-headed folk, and Pope's Court looked like a coster's orange barrow. I should not have thought there were so many in the whole country as were brought together by that single advertisement. Every shade of colour they were—straw, lemon, orange, brick, Irish-setter, liver, clay; but, as Spaulding said, there were not many who had the real vivid flame-coloured tint. When I saw how many were waiting, I would have given it up in despair; but Spaulding would not hear of it. How he did it I could not imagine, but he pushed and pulled and butted until he got me through the crowd, and right up to the steps which led to the office. There was a double stream upon the stair, some going up in hope, and some coming back dejected; but we wedged in as well as we could and soon found ourselves in the office."

"Your experience has been a most entertaining one," remarked Holmes as his client paused and refreshed his memory with a huge pinch of snuff. "Pray continue your very interesting statement."

"There was nothing in the office but a couple of wooden chairs and a deal table, behind which sat a small man with a head that was even redder than mine. He said a few words to each candidate as he came up, and then he always managed to find some fault in them which would disqualify them. Getting a vacancy did not seem to be such a very easy matter, after all. However, when our turn came the little man was much more favourable to me than to any of the others, and he closed the door as we entered, so that he might have a private word with us.

"'This is Mr. Jabez Wilson,' said my assistant, 'and he is willing to fill a vacancy in the League.'

"'And he is admirably suited for it,' the other answered. 'He has every requirement. I cannot recall when I have seen anything so fine.' He took a step backward, cocked his head on one side, and gazed at my hair until I felt quite bashful. Then suddenly he plunged forward, wrung my hand, and congratulated me warmly on my success.

"'It would be injustice to hesitate,' said he. 'You will, however, I am sure, excuse me for taking an obvious precaution.' With that he seized my hair in both his hands, and tugged until I yelled with the pain. 'There is water in your eyes,' said he as he released me. 'I perceive that all is as it should be. But we have to be careful, for we have twice been deceived by wigs and once by paint. I could tell you tales of cobbler's wax which would disgust you with human nature.' He stepped over to the window and shouted through it at the top of his voice that the vacancy was filled. A groan of disappointment came up from below, and the folk all trooped away in different directions until there was not a red-head to be seen except my own and that of the manager.

"'My name,' said he, 'is Mr. Duncan Ross, and I am myself one of the pensioners upon the fund left by our noble benefactor. Are you a married man, Mr. Wilson? Have you a family?'

"I answered that I had not.

"His face fell immediately.

"'Dear me!' he said gravely, 'that is very serious indeed! I am sorry to hear you say that. The fund was, of course, for the propagation and spread of the red-heads as well as for their maintenance. It is exceedingly unfortunate that you should be a bachelor.'

"My face lengthened at this, Mr. Holmes, for I thought that I was not to have the vacancy after all; but after thinking it over for a few minutes he said that it would be all right.

"'In the case of another,' said he, 'the objection might be fatal, but we must stretch a point in favour of a man with such a head of hair as yours. When shall you be able to enter upon your new duties?'

"'Well, it is a little awkward, for I have a business already,' said I.

"'Oh, never mind about that, Mr. Wilson!' said Vincent Spaulding. 'I should be able to look after that for you.'

"'What would be the hours?' I asked.

"'Ten to two.'

"Now a pawnbroker's business is mostly done of an evening, Mr. Holmes, especially Thursday and Friday evening, which is just before pay-day; so it would suit me very well to earn a little in the mornings. Besides, I knew that my assistant was a good man, and that he would see to anything that turned up.

"'That would suit me very well,' said I. 'And the pay?'

"'Is 4 pounds a week.'

"'And the work?'

"'Is purely nominal.'

"'What do you call purely nominal?'

"'Well, you have to be in the office, or at least in the building, the whole time. If you leave, you forfeit your whole position forever. The will is very clear upon that point. You don't comply with the conditions if you budge from the office during that time.'

"'It's only four hours a day, and I should not think of leaving,' said I.

"'No excuse will avail,' said Mr. Duncan Ross; 'neither sickness nor business nor anything else. There you must stay, or you lose your billet.'

"'And the work?'

"'Is to copy out the "Encyclopaedia Britannica." There is the first volume of it in that press. You must find your own ink, pens, and blotting-paper, but we provide this table and chair. Will you be ready tomorrow?'

"'Certainly,' I answered.

"'Then, good-bye, Mr. Jabez Wilson, and let me congratulate you once more on the important position which you have been fortunate enough to gain.' He bowed me out of the room and I went home with my assistant, hardly knowing what to say or do, I was so pleased at my own good fortune.

"Well, I thought over the matter all day, and by evening I was in low spirits again; for I had quite persuaded myself that the whole affair must be some great hoax or fraud, though what its object might be I could not imagine. It seemed altogether past belief that anyone could make such a will, or that they would pay such a sum for doing anything so simple as copying out the 'Encyclopaedia Britannica.' Vincent Spaulding did what he could to cheer me up, but by bedtime I had reasoned myself out of the whole thing. However, in the morning I determined to have a look at it anyhow, so I bought a penny bottle of ink, and with a quill-pen, and seven sheets of foolscap paper, I started off for Pope's Court.

"Well, to my surprise and delight, everything was as right as possible. The table was set out ready for me, and Mr. Duncan Ross was there to see that I got fairly to work. He started me off upon the letter A, and then he left me; but he would drop in from time to time to see that all was right with me. At two o'clock he bade me good-day, complimented me upon the amount that I had written, and locked the door of the office after me.

"This went on day after day, Mr. Holmes, and on Saturday the manager came in and planked down four golden sovereigns for my week's work. It was the same next week, and the same the week after. Every morning I was there at ten, and every afternoon I left at two. By degrees Mr. Duncan Ross took to coming in only once of a morning, and then, after a time, he did not come in at all. Still, of course, I never dared to leave the room for an instant, for I was not sure when he might come, and the billet was such a good one, and suited me so well, that I would not risk the loss of it.

"Eight weeks passed away like this, and I had written about Abbots and Archery and Armour and Architecture and Attica, and hoped with diligence that I might get on to the B's before very long. It cost me something in foolscap, and I had pretty nearly filled a shelf with my writings. And then suddenly the whole business came to an end."

"To an end?"

"Yes, sir. And no later than this morning. I went to my work as usual at ten o'clock, but the door was shut and locked, with a little square of cardboard hammered on to the middle of the panel with a tack. Here it is, and you can read for yourself."

He held up a piece of white cardboard about the size of a sheet of note-paper. It read in this fashion:

THE RED-HEADED LEAGUE
IS
DISSOLVED.
October 9, 1890.

Sherlock Holmes and I surveyed this curt announcement and the rueful face behind it, until the comical side of the affair so completely overtopped every other consideration that we both burst out into a roar of laughter.

"I cannot see that there is anything very funny," cried our client, flushing up to the roots of his flaming head. "If you can do nothing better than laugh at me, I can go elsewhere."

"No, no," cried Holmes, shoving him back into the chair from which he had half risen. "I really wouldn't miss your case for the world. It is most refreshingly unusual. But there is, if you will excuse my saying so, something just a little funny about it. Pray what steps did you take when you found the card upon the door?"

"I was staggered, sir. I did not know what to do. Then I called at the offices round, but none of them seemed to know anything about it. Finally, I went to the landlord, who is an accountant living on the ground-floor, and I asked him if he could tell me what had become of the Red-headed League. He said that he had never heard of any such body. Then I asked him who Mr. Duncan Ross was. He answered that the name was new to him.

"'Well,' said I, 'the gentleman at No. 4.'

"'What, the red-headed man?'

"'Yes.'

"'Oh,' said he, 'his name was William Morris. He was a solicitor and was using my room as a temporary convenience until his new premises were ready. He moved out yesterday.'

"'Where could I find him?'

"'Oh, at his new offices. He did tell me the address. Yes, 17 King Edward Street, near St. Paul's.'

"I started off, Mr. Holmes, but when I got to that address it was a manufactory of artificial knee-caps, and no one in it had ever heard of either Mr. William Morris or Mr. Duncan Ross."

"And what did you do then?" asked Holmes.

"I went home to Saxe-Coburg Square, and I took the advice of my assistant. But he could not help me in any way. He could only say that if I waited I should hear by post. But that was not quite good enough, Mr. Holmes. I did not wish to lose such a place without a struggle, so, as I had heard that you were good enough to give advice to poor folk who were in need of it, I came right away to you."

"And you did very wisely," said Holmes. "Your case is an exceedingly remarkable one, and I shall be happy to look into it. From what you have told me I think that it is possible that graver issues hang from it than might at first sight appear."

"Grave enough!" said Mr. Jabez Wilson. "Why, I have lost four pound a week."

"As far as you are personally concerned," remarked Holmes, "I do not see that you have any grievance against this extraordinary league. On the contrary, you are, as I understand, richer by some 30 pounds, to say nothing of the minute knowledge which you have gained on every subject which comes under the letter A. You have lost nothing by them."

"No, sir. But I want to find out about them, and who they are, and what their object was in playing this prank—if it was a prank—upon me. It was a pretty expensive joke for them, for it cost them two and thirty pounds."

"We shall endeavour to clear up these points for you. And, first, one or two questions, Mr. Wilson. This assistant of yours who first called your attention to the advertisement—how long had he been with you?"

"About a month then."

"How did he come?"

"In answer to an advertisement."

"Was he the only applicant?"

"No, I had a dozen."

"Why did you pick him?"

"Because he was handy and would come cheap."

"At half-wages, in fact."

"Yes."

"What is he like, this Vincent Spaulding?"

"Small, stout-built, very quick in his ways, no hair on his face, though he's not short of thirty. Has a white splash of acid upon his forehead."

Holmes sat up in his chair in considerable excitement. "I thought as much," said he. "Have you ever observed that his ears are pierced for earrings?"

"Yes, sir. He told me that a gipsy had done it for him when he was a lad."

"Hum!" said Holmes, sinking back in deep thought. "He is still with you?"

"Oh, yes, sir; I have only just left him."

"And has your business been attended to in your absence?"

"Nothing to complain of, sir. There's never very much to do of a morning."

"That will do, Mr. Wilson. I shall be happy to give you an opinion upon the subject in the course of a day or two. Today is Saturday, and I hope that by Monday we may come to a conclusion."

"Well, Watson," said Holmes when our visitor had left us, "what do you make of it all?"

"I make nothing of it," I answered frankly. "It is a most mysterious business."

"As a rule," said Holmes, "the more bizarre a thing is the less mysterious it proves to be. It is your commonplace, featureless crimes which are really puzzling, just as a commonplace face is the most difficult to identify. But I must be prompt over this matter."

"What are you going to do, then?" I asked.

"To smoke," he answered. "It is quite a three pipe problem, and I beg that you won't speak to me for fifty minutes." He curled himself up in his chair, with his thin knees drawn up to his hawk-like nose, and there he sat with his eyes closed and his black clay pipe thrusting out like the bill of some strange bird. I had come to the conclusion that he had dropped asleep, and indeed was nodding myself, when he suddenly sprang out of his chair with the gesture of a man who has made up his mind and put his pipe down upon the mantelpiece.

"Sarasate plays at the St. James's Hall this afternoon," he remarked. "What do you think, Watson? Could your patients spare you for a few hours?"

"I have nothing to do today. My practice is never very absorbing."

"Then put on your hat and come. I am going through the City first, and we can have some lunch on the way. I observe that there is a good deal of German music on the programme, which is rather more to my taste than Italian or French. It is introspective, and I want to introspect. Come along!"

We travelled by the Underground as far as Aldersgate; and a short walk took us to Saxe-Coburg Square, the scene of the singular story which we had listened to in the morning. It was a poky, little, shabby-genteel place, where four lines of dingy two-storied brick houses looked out into a small railed-in enclosure, where a lawn of weedy grass and a few clumps of faded laurel-bushes made a hard fight against a smoke-laden and uncongenial atmosphere. Three gilt balls and a brown board with "JABEZ WILSON" in white letters, upon a corner house, announced the place where our red-headed client carried on his business. Sherlock Holmes stopped in front of it with his head on one side and looked it all over, with his eyes shining brightly between puckered lids. Then he walked slowly up the street, and then down again to the corner, still looking keenly at the houses. Finally he returned to the pawnbroker's, and, having thumped vigorously upon the pavement with his stick two or three times, he went up to the door and knocked. It was instantly opened by a bright-looking, clean-shaven young fellow, who asked him to step in.

"Thank you," said Holmes, "I only wished to ask you how you would go from here to the Strand."

"Third right, fourth left," answered the assistant promptly, closing the door.

"Smart fellow, that," observed Holmes as we walked away. "He is, in my judgment, the fourth smartest man in London, and for daring I am not sure that he has not a claim to be third. I have known something of him before."

"Evidently," said I, "Mr. Wilson's assistant counts for a good deal in this mystery of the Red-headed League. I am sure that you inquired your way merely in order that you might see him."

"Not him."

"What then?"

"The knees of his trousers."

"And what did you see?"

"What I expected to see."

"Why did you beat the pavement?"

"My dear doctor, this is a time for observation, not for talk. We are spies in an enemy's country. We know something of Saxe-Coburg Square. Let us now explore the parts which lie behind it."

The road in which we found ourselves as we turned round the corner from the retired Saxe-Coburg Square presented as great a contrast to it as the front of a picture does to the back. It was one of the main arteries which conveyed the traffic of the City to the north and west. The roadway was blocked with the immense stream of commerce flowing in a double tide inward and outward, while the footpaths were black with the hurrying swarm of pedestrians. It was difficult to realise as we looked at the line of fine shops and stately business premises that they really abutted on the other side upon the faded and stagnant square which we had just quitted.

"Let me see," said Holmes, standing at the corner and glancing along the line, "I should like just to remember the order of the houses here. It is a hobby of mine to have an exact knowledge of London. There is Mortimer's, the tobacconist, the little newspaper shop, the Coburg branch of the City and Suburban Bank, the Vegetarian Restaurant, and McFarlane's carriage-building depot. That carries us right on to the other block. And now, Doctor, we've done our work, so it's time we had some play. A sandwich and a cup of coffee, and then off to violin-land, where all is sweetness and delicacy and harmony, and there are no red-headed clients to vex us with their conundrums."

My friend was an enthusiastic musician, being himself not only a very capable performer but a composer of no ordinary merit. All the afternoon he sat in the stalls wrapped in the most perfect happiness, gently waving his long, thin fingers in time to the music, while his gently smiling face and his languid, dreamy eyes were as unlike those of Holmes the sleuth-hound, Holmes the relentless, keen-witted, ready-handed criminal agent, as it was possible to conceive. In his singular character the dual nature alternately asserted itself, and his extreme exactness and astuteness represented, as I have often thought, the reaction against the poetic and contemplative mood which occasionally predominated in him. The swing of his nature took him from extreme languor to devouring energy; and, as I knew well, he was never so truly formidable as when, for days on end, he had been lounging in his armchair amid his improvisations and his black-letter editions. Then it was that the lust of the chase would suddenly come upon him, and that his brilliant reasoning power would rise to the level of intuition, until those who were unacquainted with his methods would look askance at him as on a man whose knowledge was not that of other mortals. When I saw him that afternoon so enwrapped in the music at St. James's Hall I felt that an evil time might be coming upon those whom he had set himself to hunt down.

"You want to go home, no doubt, Doctor," he remarked as we emerged.

"Yes, it would be as well."

"And I have some business to do which will take some hours. This business at Coburg Square is serious."

"Why serious?"

"A considerable crime is in contemplation. I have every reason to believe that we shall be in time to stop it. But today being Saturday rather complicates matters. I shall want your help to-night."

"At what time?"

"Ten will be early enough."

"I shall be at Baker Street at ten."

"Very well. And, I say, Doctor, there may be some little danger, so kindly put your army revolver in your pocket." He waved his hand, turned on his heel, and disappeared in an instant among the crowd.

I trust that I am not more dense than my neighbours, but I was always oppressed with a sense of my own stupidity in my dealings with Sherlock Holmes. Here I had heard what he had heard, I had seen what he had seen, and yet from his words it was evident that he saw clearly not only what had happened but what was about to happen, while to me the whole business was still confused and grotesque. As I drove home to my house in Kensington I thought over it all, from the extraordinary story of the red-headed copier of the "Encyclopaedia" down to the visit to Saxe-Coburg

Square, and the ominous words with which he had parted from me. What was this nocturnal expedition, and why should I go armed? Where were we going, and what were we to do? I had the hint from Holmes that this smooth-faced pawnbroker's assistant was a formidable man—a man who might play a deep game. I tried to puzzle it out, but gave it up in despair and set the matter aside until night should bring an explanation.

It was a quarter-past nine when I started from home and made my way across the Park, and so through Oxford Street to Baker Street. Two hansoms were standing at the door, and as I entered the passage I heard the sound of voices from above. On entering his room I found Holmes in animated conversation with two men, one of whom I recognised as Peter Jones, the official police agent, while the other was a long, thin, sad-faced man, with a very shiny hat and oppressively respectable frock-coat.

"Ha! Our party is complete," said Holmes, buttoning up his pea-jacket and taking his heavy hunting crop from the rack. "Watson, I think you know Mr. Jones, of Scotland Yard? Let me introduce you to Mr. Merryweather, who is to be our companion in to-night's adventure."

"We're hunting in couples again, Doctor, you see," said Jones in his consequential way. "Our friend here is a wonderful man for starting a chase. All he wants is an old dog to help him to do the running down."

"I hope a wild goose may not prove to be the end of our chase," observed Mr. Merryweather gloomily.

"You may place considerable confidence in Mr. Holmes, sir," said the police agent loftily. "He has his own little methods, which are, if he won't mind my saying so, just a little too theoretical and fantastic, but he has the makings of a detective in him. It is not too much to say that once or twice, as in that business of the Sholto murder and the Agra treasure, he has been more nearly correct than the official force."

"Oh, if you say so, Mr. Jones, it is all right," said the stranger with deference. "Still, I confess that I miss my rubber. It is the first Saturday night for seven-and-twenty years that I have not had my rubber."

"I think you will find," said Sherlock Holmes, "that you will play for a higher stake to-night than you have ever done yet, and that the play will be more exciting. For you, Mr. Merryweather, the stake will be some 30,000 pounds; and for you, Jones, it will be the man upon whom you wish to lay your hands."

"John Clay, the murderer, thief, smasher, and forger. He's a young man, Mr. Merryweather, but he is at the head of his profession, and I would rather have my bracelets on him than on any criminal in London. He's a remarkable man, is young John Clay. His grandfather was a royal duke, and he himself has been to Eton and Oxford. His brain is as cunning as his fingers, and though we meet signs of him at every turn, we never know where to find the man himself. He'll crack a crib in Scotland one week, and be raising money to build an orphanage in Cornwall the next. I've been on his track for years and have never set eyes on him yet."

"I hope that I may have the pleasure of introducing you to-night. I've had one or two little turns also with Mr. John Clay, and I agree with you that he is at the head of his profession. It is past ten, however, and quite time that we started. If you two will take the first hansom, Watson and I will follow in the second."

Sherlock Holmes was not very communicative during the long drive and lay back in the cab humming the tunes which he had heard in the afternoon. We rattled through an endless labyrinth of gas-lit streets until we emerged into Farrington Street.

"We are close there now," my friend remarked. "This fellow Merryweather is a bank director, and personally interested in the matter. I thought it as well to have Jones with us also. He is not a bad fellow, though an absolute imbecile in his profession. He has one positive virtue. He is as brave as a bulldog and as tenacious as a lobster if he gets his claws upon anyone. Here we are, and they are waiting for us."

We had reached the same crowded thoroughfare in which we had found ourselves in the morning. Our cabs were dismissed, and, following the guidance of Mr. Merryweather, we passed down a narrow passage and through a side door, which he opened for us. Within there was a small corridor, which ended in a very massive iron gate. This also was opened, and led down a flight of winding stone steps, which terminated at another formidable gate. Mr. Merryweather stopped to light a lantern, and then conducted us down a dark, earth-smelling passage, and so, after opening a third door, into a huge vault or cellar, which was piled all round with crates and massive boxes.

"You are not very vulnerable from above," Holmes remarked as he held up the lantern and gazed about him.

"Nor from below," said Mr. Merryweather, striking his stick upon the flags which lined the floor. "Why, dear me, it sounds quite hollow!" he remarked, looking up in surprise.

"I must really ask you to be a little more quiet!" said Holmes severely. "You have already imperilled the whole success of our expedition. Might I beg that you would have the goodness to sit down upon one of those boxes, and not to interfere?"

The solemn Mr. Merryweather perched himself upon a crate, with a very injured expression upon his face, while Holmes fell upon his knees upon the floor and, with the lantern and a magnifying lens, began to examine minutely the cracks between the stones. A few seconds sufficed to satisfy him, for he sprang to his feet again and put his glass in his pocket.

"We have at least an hour before us," he remarked, "for they can hardly take any steps until the good pawnbroker is safely in bed. Then they will not lose a minute, for the sooner they do their work the longer time they will have for their escape. We are at present, Doctor—as no doubt you have divined—in the cellar of the City branch of one of the principal London banks. Mr. Merryweather is the chairman of directors, and he will explain to you that there are reasons why the more daring criminals of London should take a considerable interest in this cellar at present."

"It is our French gold," whispered the director. "We have had several warnings that an attempt might be made upon it."

"Your French gold?"

"Yes. We had occasion some months ago to strengthen our resources and borrowed for that purpose 30,000 napoleons from the Bank of France. It has become known that we have never had occasion to unpack the money, and that it is still lying in our cellar. The crate upon which I sit contains 2,000 napoleons packed between layers of lead foil. Our reserve of bullion is much larger at present than is usually kept in a single branch office, and the directors have had misgivings upon the subject."

"Which were very well justified," observed Holmes. "And now it is time that we arranged our little plans. I expect that within an hour matters will come to a head. In the meantime Mr. Merryweather, we must put the screen over that dark lantern."

"And sit in the dark?"

"I am afraid so. I had brought a pack of cards in my pocket, and I thought that, as we were a partie carrée, you might have your rubber after all. But I see that the enemy's preparations have gone so far that we cannot risk the presence of a light. And, first of all, we must choose our positions. These are daring men, and though we shall take them at a disadvantage, they may do us some harm unless we are careful. I shall stand behind this crate, and do you conceal yourselves behind those. Then, when I flash a light upon them, close in swiftly. If they fire, Watson, have no compunction about shooting them down."

I placed my revolver, cocked, upon the top of the wooden case behind which I crouched. Holmes shot the slide across the front of his lantern and left us in pitch darkness—such an absolute darkness as I have never before experienced. The smell of hot metal remained to assure us that the light was still there, ready to flash out at a moment's notice. To me, with my nerves worked up to a pitch of expectancy, there was something depressing and subduing in the sudden gloom, and in the cold dank air of the vault.

"They have but one retreat," whispered Holmes. "That is back through the house into Saxe-Coburg Square. I hope that you have done what I asked you, Jones?"

"I have an inspector and two officers waiting at the front door."

"Then we have stopped all the holes. And now we must be silent and wait."

What a time it seemed! From comparing notes afterwards it was but an hour and a quarter, yet it appeared to me that the night must have almost gone and the dawn be breaking above us. My limbs were weary and stiff, for I feared to change my position; yet my nerves were worked up to the highest pitch of tension, and my hearing was so acute that I could not only hear the gentle breathing of my companions, but I could distinguish the deeper, heavier in-breath of the bulky Jones from the thin, sighing note of the bank director. From my position I could look over the case in the direction of the floor. Suddenly my eyes caught the glint of a light.

At first it was but a lurid spark upon the stone pavement. Then it lengthened out until it became a yellow line, and then, without any warning or sound, a gash seemed to open and a hand appeared, a white, almost womanly hand, which felt about in the centre of the little area of light. For a minute or more the hand, with its writhing fingers, protruded out of the floor. Then it was withdrawn as suddenly as it appeared, and all was dark again save the single lurid spark which marked a chink between the stones.

Its disappearance, however, was but momentary. With a rending, tearing sound, one of the broad, white stones turned over upon its side and left a square, gaping hole, through which streamed the light of a lantern. Over the edge there peeped a clean-cut, boyish face, which looked keenly about it, and then, with a hand on either side of the aperture, drew itself shoulder-high and waist-high, until one knee rested upon the edge. In another instant he stood at the side of the hole and was hauling after him a companion, lithe and small like himself, with a pale face and a shock of very red hair.

"It's all clear," he whispered. "Have you the chisel and the bags? Great Scott! Jump, Archie, jump, and I'll swing for it!"

Sherlock Holmes had sprung out and seized the intruder by the collar. The other dived down the hole, and I heard the sound of rending cloth as Jones clutched at his skirts. The light flashed upon the barrel of a revolver, but Holmes' hunting crop came down on the man's wrist, and the pistol clinked upon the stone floor.

"It's no use, John Clay," said Holmes blandly. "You have no chance at all."

"So I see," the other answered with the utmost coolness. "I fancy that my pal is all right, though I see you have got his coat-tails."

"There are three men waiting for him at the door," said Holmes.

"Oh, indeed! You seem to have done the thing very completely. I must compliment you."

"And I you," Holmes answered. "Your red-headed idea was very new and effective."

"You'll see your pal again presently," said Jones. "He's quicker at climbing down holes than I am. Just hold out while I fix the derbies."

"I beg that you will not touch me with your filthy hands," remarked our prisoner as the handcuffs clattered upon his wrists. "You may not be aware that I have royal blood in my veins. Have the goodness, also, when you address me always to say 'sir' and 'please.'"

"All right," said Jones with a stare and a snigger. "Well, would you please, sir, march upstairs, where we can get a cab to carry your Highness to the police-station?"

"That is better," said John Clay serenely. He made a sweeping bow to the three of us and walked quietly off in the custody of the detective.

"Really, Mr. Holmes," said Mr. Merryweather as we followed them from the cellar, "I do not know how the bank can thank you or repay you. There is no doubt that you have detected and defeated in the most complete manner one of the most determined attempts at bank robbery that have ever come within my experience."

"I have had one or two little scores of my own to settle with Mr. John Clay," said Holmes. "I have been at some small expense over this matter, which I shall expect the bank to refund, but beyond that I am amply repaid by having had an experience which is in many ways unique, and by hearing the very remarkable narrative of the Red-headed League."

"You see, Watson," he explained in the early hours of the morning as we sat over a glass of whisky and soda in Baker Street, "it was perfectly obvious from the first that the only possible object of this rather fantastic business of the advertisement of the League, and the copying of the 'Encyclopaedia,' must be to get this not over-bright pawnbroker out of the way for a number of hours every day. It was a curious way of managing it, but, really, it would be difficult to suggest a better. The method was no doubt suggested to Clay's ingenious mind by the colour of his accomplice's hair. The 4 pounds a week was a lure which must draw him, and what was it to them, who were playing for thousands? They put in the advertisement, one rogue has the temporary office, the other rogue incites the man to apply for it, and together they manage to secure his absence every morning in the week. From the time that I heard of the assistant having come for half wages, it was obvious to me that he had some strong motive for securing the situation."

"But how could you guess what the motive was?"

"Had there been women in the house, I should have suspected a mere vulgar intrigue. That, however, was out of the question. The man's business was a small one, and there was nothing in his house which could account for such elaborate preparations, and such an expenditure as they were at. It must, then, be something out of the house. What could it be? I thought of the assistant's fondness for photography, and his trick of vanishing into the cellar. The cellar! There was the end of this tangled clue. Then I made inquiries as to this mysterious assistant and found that I had to deal with one of the coolest and most daring criminals in London. He was doing something in the cellar—something which took many hours a day for months on end. What could it be, once more? I could think of nothing save that he was running a tunnel to some other building.

"So far I had got when we went to visit the scene of action. I surprised you by beating upon the pavement with my stick. I was ascertaining whether the cellar stretched out in front or behind. It was not in front. Then I rang the bell, and, as I hoped, the assistant answered it. We have had some skirmishes, but we had never set eyes upon each other before. I hardly looked at his face. His knees were what I wished to see. You must yourself have remarked how worn, wrinkled, and stained they were. They spoke of those hours of burrowing. The only remaining point was what they were burrowing for. I walked round the corner, saw the City and Suburban Bank abutted on our friend's premises, and felt that I had solved my problem. When you drove home after the concert I called upon Scotland Yard and upon the chairman of the bank directors, with the result that you have seen."

"And how could you tell that they would make their attempt to-night?" I asked.

"Well, when they closed their League offices that was a sign that they cared no longer about Mr. Jabez Wilson's presence—in other words, that they had completed their tunnel. But it was essential that they should use it soon, as it might be discovered, or the bullion might be removed. Saturday would suit them better than any other day, as it would give them two days for their escape. For all these reasons I expected them to come to-night."

"You reasoned it out beautifully," I exclaimed in unfeigned admiration. "It is so long a chain, and yet every link rings true."

"It saved me from ennui," he answered, yawning. "Alas! I already feel it closing in upon me. My life is spent in one long effort to escape from the commonplaces of existence. These little problems help me to do so."

"And you are a benefactor of the race," said I.

He shrugged his shoulders. "Well, perhaps, after all, it is of some little use," he remarked. "*'L'homme c'est rien—l'oeuvre c'est tout,'* as Gustave Flaubert wrote to George Sand."

Adventure III. A Case Of Identity

"My dear fellow," said Sherlock Holmes as we sat on either side of the fire in his lodgings at Baker Street, "life is infinitely stranger than anything which the mind of man could invent. We would not dare to conceive the things which are really mere commonplaces of existence. If we could fly out of that window hand in hand, hover over this great city, gently remove the roofs, and peep in at the queer things which are going on, the strange coincidences, the plannings, the cross-purposes, the wonderful chains of events, working through generations, and leading to the most outré results, it would make all fiction with its conventionalities and foreseen conclusions most stale and unprofitable."

"And yet I am not convinced of it," I answered. "The cases which come to light in the papers are, as a rule, bald enough, and vulgar enough. We have in our police reports realism pushed to its extreme limits, and yet the result is, it must be confessed, neither fascinating nor artistic."

"A certain selection and discretion must be used in producing a realistic effect," remarked Holmes. "This is wanting in the police report, where more stress is laid, perhaps, upon the platitudes of the magistrate than upon the details, which to an observer contain the vital essence of the whole matter. Depend upon it, there is nothing so unnatural as the commonplace."

I smiled and shook my head. "I can quite understand your thinking so." I said. "Of course, in your position of unofficial adviser and helper to everybody who is absolutely puzzled, throughout three continents, you are brought in contact with all that is strange and bizarre. But here"—I picked up the morning paper from the ground—"let us put it to a practical test. Here is the first heading upon which I come. 'A husband's cruelty to his wife.' There is half a column of print, but I know without reading it that it is all perfectly familiar to me. There is, of course, the other woman, the drink, the push, the blow, the bruise, the sympathetic sister or landlady. The crudest of writers could invent nothing more crude."

"Indeed, your example is an unfortunate one for your argument," said Holmes, taking the paper and glancing his eye down it. "This is the Dundas separation case, and, as it happens, I was engaged in clearing up some small points in connection with it. The husband was a teetotaler, there was no other woman, and the conduct complained of was that he had drifted into the habit of winding up every meal by taking out his false teeth and hurling them at his wife, which, you will allow, is not an action likely to occur to the imagination of the average story-teller. Take a pinch of snuff, Doctor, and acknowledge that I have scored over you in your example."

He held out his snuffbox of old gold, with a great amethyst in the centre of the lid. Its splendour was in such contrast to his homely ways and simple life that I could not help commenting upon it.

"Ah," said he, "I forgot that I had not seen you for some weeks. It is a little souvenir from the King of Bohemia in return for my assistance in the case of the Irene Adler papers."

"And the ring?" I asked, glancing at a remarkable brilliant which sparkled upon his finger.

"It was from the reigning family of Holland, though the matter in which I served them was of such delicacy that I cannot confide it even to you, who have been good enough to chronicle one or two of my little problems."

"And have you any on hand just now?" I asked with interest.

"Some ten or twelve, but none which present any feature of interest. They are important, you understand, without being interesting. Indeed, I have found that it is usually in unimportant matters that there is a field for the observation, and for the quick analysis of cause and effect which gives the charm to an investigation. The larger crimes are apt to be the simpler, for the bigger the crime the more obvious, as a rule, is the motive. In these cases, save for one rather intricate matter which has been referred to me from Marseilles, there is nothing which presents any features of interest. It is possible, however, that I may have something better before very many minutes are over, for this is one of my clients, or I am much mistaken."

He had risen from his chair and was standing between the parted blinds gazing down into the dull neutral-tinted London street. Looking over his shoulder, I saw that on the pavement opposite there stood a large woman with a heavy fur boa round her neck, and a large curling red feather in a broad-brimmed hat which was tilted in a coquettish Duchess of Devonshire fashion over her ear. From under this great panoply she peeped up in a nervous, hesitating fashion at our windows, while her body oscillated backward and forward, and her fingers fidgeted with her glove buttons. Suddenly, with a plunge, as of the swimmer who leaves the bank, she hurried across the road, and we heard the sharp clang of the bell.

"I have seen those symptoms before," said Holmes, throwing his cigarette into the fire. "Oscillation upon the pavement always means an affaire de coeur. She would like advice, but is not sure that the matter is not too delicate for communication. And yet even here we may discriminate. When a woman has been seriously wronged by a man she no longer oscillates, and the usual symptom is a broken bell wire. Here we may take it that there is a love matter, but that the maiden is not so much angry as perplexed, or grieved. But here she comes in person to resolve our doubts."

As he spoke there was a tap at the door, and the boy in buttons entered to announce Miss Mary Sutherland, while the lady herself loomed behind his small black figure like a full-sailed merchant-man behind a tiny pilot boat. Sherlock Holmes welcomed her with the easy courtesy for which he was remarkable, and, having closed the door and bowed her into an armchair, he looked her over in the minute and yet abstracted fashion which was peculiar to him.

"Do you not find," he said, "that with your short sight it is a little trying to do so much typewriting?"

"I did at first," she answered, "but now I know where the letters are without looking." Then, suddenly realising the full purport of his words, she gave a violent start and looked up, with fear and astonishment upon her broad, good-humoured face. "You've heard about me, Mr. Holmes," she cried, "else how could you know all that?"

"Never mind," said Holmes, laughing; "it is my business to know things. Perhaps I have trained myself to see what others overlook. If not, why should you come to consult me?"

"I came to you, sir, because I heard of you from Mrs. Etherege, whose husband you found so easy when the police and everyone had given him up for dead. Oh, Mr. Holmes, I wish you would do as much for me. I'm not rich, but still I have a hundred a year in my own right, besides the little that I make by the machine, and I would give it all to know what has become of Mr. Hosmer Angel."

"Why did you come away to consult me in such a hurry?" asked Sherlock Holmes, with his finger-tips together and his eyes to the ceiling.

Again a startled look came over the somewhat vacuous face of Miss Mary Sutherland. "Yes, I did bang out of the house," she said, "for it made me angry to see the easy way in which Mr. Windibank—that is, my father—took it all. He would not go to the police, and he would not go to you, and so at last, as he would do nothing and kept on saying that there was no harm done, it made me mad, and I just on with my things and came right away to you."

"Your father," said Holmes, "your stepfather, surely, since the name is different."

"Yes, my stepfather. I call him father, though it sounds funny, too, for he is only five years and two months older than myself."

"And your mother is alive?"

"Oh, yes, mother is alive and well. I wasn't best pleased, Mr. Holmes, when she married again so soon after father's death, and a man who was nearly fifteen years younger than herself. Father was a plumber in the Tottenham Court Road, and he left a tidy business behind him, which mother carried on with Mr. Hardy, the foreman; but when Mr. Windibank came he made her sell the business, for he was very superior, being a traveller in wines. They got 4700 pounds for the goodwill and interest, which wasn't near as much as father could have got if he had been alive."

I had expected to see Sherlock Holmes impatient under this rambling and inconsequential narrative, but, on the contrary, he had listened with the greatest concentration of attention.

"Your own little income," he asked, "does it come out of the business?"

"Oh, no, sir. It is quite separate and was left me by my uncle Ned in Auckland. It is in New Zealand stock, paying 4 ½ per cent. Two thousand five hundred pounds was the amount, but I can only touch the interest."

"You interest me extremely," said Holmes. "And since you draw so large a sum as a hundred a year, with what you earn into the bargain, you no doubt travel a little and indulge yourself in every way. I believe that a single lady can get on very nicely upon an income of about 60 pounds."

"I could do with much less than that, Mr. Holmes, but you understand that as long as I live at home I don't wish to be a burden to them, and so they have the use of the money just while I am staying with them. Of course, that is only just for the time. Mr. Windibank draws my interest every quarter and pays it over to mother, and I find that I can do pretty well with what I earn at typewriting. It brings me twopence a sheet, and I can often do from fifteen to twenty sheets in a day."

"You have made your position very clear to me," said Holmes. "This is my friend, Dr. Watson, before whom you can speak as freely as before myself. Kindly tell us now all about your connection with Mr. Hosmer Angel."

A flush stole over Miss Sutherland's face, and she picked nervously at the fringe of her jacket. "I met him first at the gasfitters' ball," she said. "They used to send father tickets when he was alive, and then afterwards they remembered us, and sent them to mother. Mr. Windibank did not wish us to go. He never did wish us to go anywhere. He would get quite mad if I wanted so much as to join a Sunday-school treat. But this time I was set on going, and I would go; for what right had he to prevent? He said the folk were not fit for us to know, when all father's friends were to be there. And he said that I had nothing fit to wear, when I had my purple plush that I had never so much as taken out of the drawer. At last, when nothing else would do, he went off to France upon the business of the firm, but we went, mother and I, with Mr. Hardy, who used to be our foreman, and it was there I met Mr. Hosmer Angel."

"I suppose," said Holmes, "that when Mr. Windibank came back from France he was very annoyed at your having gone to the ball."

"Oh, well, he was very good about it. He laughed, I remember, and shrugged his shoulders, and said there was no use denying anything to a woman, for she would have her way."

"I see. Then at the gasfitters' ball you met, as I understand, a gentleman called Mr. Hosmer Angel."

"Yes, sir. I met him that night, and he called next day to ask if we had got home all safe, and after that we met him—that is to say, Mr. Holmes, I met him twice for walks, but after that father came back again, and Mr. Hosmer Angel could not come to the house any more."

"No?"

"Well, you know father didn't like anything of the sort. He wouldn't have any visitors if he could help it, and he used to say that a woman should be happy in her own family circle. But then, as I used to say to mother, a woman wants her own circle to begin with, and I had not got mine yet."

"But how about Mr. Hosmer Angel? Did he make no attempt to see you?"

"Well, father was going off to France again in a week, and Hosmer wrote and said that it would be safer and better not to see each other until he had gone. We could write in the meantime, and he used to write every day. I took the letters in in the morning, so there was no need for father to know."

"Were you engaged to the gentleman at this time?"

"Oh, yes, Mr. Holmes. We were engaged after the first walk that we took. Hosmer—Mr. Angel—was a cashier in an office in Leadenhall Street—and—"

"What office?"

"That's the worst of it, Mr. Holmes, I don't know."

"Where did he live, then?"

"He slept on the premises."

"And you don't know his address?"

"No—except that it was Leadenhall Street."

"Where did you address your letters, then?"

"To the Leadenhall Street Post Office, to be left till called for. He said that if they were sent to the office he would be chaffed by all the other clerks about having letters from a lady, so I offered to typewrite them, like he did his, but he wouldn't have that, for he said that when I wrote them they seemed to come from me, but when they were typewritten he always felt that the machine had come between us. That will just show you how fond he was of me, Mr. Holmes, and the little things that he would think of."

"It was most suggestive," said Holmes. "It has long been an axiom of mine that the little things are infinitely the most important. Can you remember any other little things about Mr. Hosmer Angel?"

"He was a very shy man, Mr. Holmes. He would rather walk with me in the evening than in the daylight, for he said that he hated to be conspicuous. Very retiring and gentlemanly he was. Even his voice was gentle. He'd had the quinsy and swollen glands when he was young, he told me, and it had left him with a weak throat, and a hesitating, whispering fashion of speech. He was always well dressed, very neat and plain, but his eyes were weak, just as mine are, and he wore tinted glasses against the glare."

"Well, and what happened when Mr. Windibank, your stepfather, returned to France?"

"Mr. Hosmer Angel came to the house again and proposed that we should marry before father came back. He was in dreadful earnest and made me swear, with my hands on the Testament, that whatever happened I would always be true to him. Mother said he was quite right to make me swear, and that it was a sign of his passion. Mother was all in his favour from the first and was even fonder of him than I was. Then, when they talked of marrying within the week, I began to ask about father; but they both said never to mind about father, but just to tell him afterwards, and mother said she would make it all right with him. I didn't quite like that, Mr. Holmes. It seemed funny that I should ask his leave, as he was only a few years older than me; but I didn't want to do anything on the sly, so I wrote to father at Bordeaux, where the company has its French offices, but the letter came back to me on the very morning of the wedding."

"It missed him, then?"

"Yes, sir; for he had started to England just before it arrived."

"Ha! that was unfortunate. Your wedding was arranged, then, for the Friday. Was it to be in church?"

"Yes, sir, but very quietly. It was to be at St. Saviour's, near King's Cross, and we were to have breakfast afterwards at the St. Pancras Hotel. Hosmer came for us in a hansom, but as there were two of us he put us both into it and stepped himself into a four-wheeler, which happened to be the only other cab in the street. We got to the church first, and when the four-wheeler drove up we waited for him to step out, but he never did, and when the cabman got down from the box and looked there was no one there! The cabman said that he could not imagine what had become of him, for he had seen him get in with his own eyes. That was last Friday, Mr. Holmes, and I have never seen or heard anything since then to throw any light upon what became of him."

"It seems to me that you have been very shamefully treated," said Holmes.

"Oh, no, sir! He was too good and kind to leave me so. Why, all the morning he was saying to me that, whatever happened, I was to be true; and that even if something quite unforeseen occurred to separate us, I was always to remember that I was pledged to him, and that he would claim his pledge sooner or later. It seemed strange talk for a wedding-morning, but what has happened since gives a meaning to it."

"Most certainly it does. Your own opinion is, then, that some unforeseen catastrophe has occurred to him?"

"Yes, sir. I believe that he foresaw some danger, or else he would not have talked so. And then I think that what he foresaw happened."

"But you have no notion as to what it could have been?"

"None."

"One more question. How did your mother take the matter?"

"She was angry, and said that I was never to speak of the matter again."

"And your father? Did you tell him?"

"Yes; and he seemed to think, with me, that something had happened, and that I should hear of Hosmer again. As he said, what interest could anyone have in bringing me to the doors of the church, and then leaving me? Now, if he had borrowed my money, or if he had married me and got my money settled on him, there might be some reason, but Hosmer was very independent about money and never would look at a shilling of mine. And yet, what could have happened? And why could he not write? Oh, it drives me half-mad to think of it, and I can't sleep a wink at night." She pulled a little handkerchief out of her muff and began to sob heavily into it.

"I shall glance into the case for you," said Holmes, rising, "and I have no doubt that we shall reach some definite result. Let the weight of the matter rest upon me now, and do not let your mind dwell upon it further. Above all, try to let Mr. Hosmer Angel vanish from your memory, as he has done from your life."

"Then you don't think I'll see him again?"

"I fear not."

"Then what has happened to him?"

"You will leave that question in my hands. I should like an accurate description of him and any letters of his which you can spare."

"I advertised for him in last Saturday's Chronicle," said she. "Here is the slip and here are four letters from him."

"Thank you. And your address?"

"No. 31 Lyon Place, Camberwell."

"Mr. Angel's address you never had, I understand. Where is your father's place of business?"

"He travels for Westhouse & Marbank, the great claret importers of Fenchurch Street."

"Thank you. You have made your statement very clearly. You will leave the papers here, and remember the advice which I have given you. Let the whole incident be a sealed book, and do not allow it to affect your life."

"You are very kind, Mr. Holmes, but I cannot do that. I shall be true to Hosmer. He shall find me ready when he comes back."

For all the preposterous hat and the vacuous face, there was something noble in the simple faith of our visitor which compelled our respect. She laid her little bundle of papers upon the table and went her way, with a promise to come again whenever she might be summoned.

Sherlock Holmes sat silent for a few minutes with his fingertips still pressed together, his legs stretched out in front of him, and his gaze directed upward to the ceiling. Then he took down from the rack the old and oily clay pipe, which was to him as a counsellor, and, having lit it, he leaned back in his chair, with the thick blue cloud-wreaths spinning up from him, and a look of infinite languor in his face.

"Quite an interesting study, that maiden," he observed. "I found her more interesting than her little problem, which, by the way, is rather a trite one. You will find parallel cases, if you consult my index, in Andover in '77, and there was something of the sort at The Hague last year. Old as is the idea, however, there were one or two details which were new to me. But the maiden herself was most instructive."

"You appeared to read a good deal upon her which was quite invisible to me," I remarked.

"Not invisible but unnoticed, Watson. You did not know where to look, and so you missed all that was important. I can never bring you to realise the importance of sleeves, the suggestiveness of thumb-nails, or the great issues that may hang from a boot-lace. Now, what did you gather from that woman's appearance? Describe it."

"Well, she had a slate-coloured, broad-brimmed straw hat, with a feather of a brickish red. Her jacket was black, with black beads sewn upon it, and a fringe of little black jet ornaments. Her dress was brown, rather darker than coffee colour, with a little purple plush at the neck and sleeves. Her gloves were greyish and were worn through at the right forefinger. Her boots I didn't observe. She had small round, hanging gold earrings, and a general air of being fairly well-to-do in a vulgar, comfortable, easy-going way."

Sherlock Holmes clapped his hands softly together and chuckled.

"'Pon my word, Watson, you are coming along wonderfully. You have really done very well indeed. It is true that you have missed everything of importance, but you have hit upon the method, and you have a quick eye for colour. Never trust to general impressions, my boy, but concentrate yourself upon details. My first glance is always at a woman's sleeve. In a man it is perhaps better first to take the knee of the trouser. As you observe, this woman had plush upon her sleeves, which is a most useful material for showing traces. The double line a little above the wrist, where the typewritist presses against the table, was beautifully defined. The sewing-machine, of the hand type, leaves a similar mark, but only on the left arm, and on the side of it farthest from the thumb, instead of being right across the broadest part, as this was. I then glanced at her face, and, observing the dint of a pince-nez at either side of her nose, I ventured a remark upon short sight and typewriting, which seemed to surprise her."

"It surprised me."

"But, surely, it was obvious. I was then much surprised and interested on glancing down to observe that, though the boots which she was wearing were not unlike each other, they were really odd ones; the one having a slightly decorated toe-cap, and the other a plain one. One was buttoned only in the two lower buttons out of five, and the other at the first, third, and fifth. Now, when you see that a young lady, otherwise neatly dressed, has come away from home with odd boots, half-buttoned, it is no great deduction to say that she came away in a hurry."

"And what else?" I asked, keenly interested, as I always was, by my friend's incisive reasoning.

"I noted, in passing, that she had written a note before leaving home but after being fully dressed. You observed that her right glove was torn at the forefinger, but you did not apparently see that both glove and finger were stained with violet ink. She had written in a hurry and dipped her pen too deep. It must have been this morning, or the mark would not remain clear upon the finger. All this is amusing, though rather elementary, but I must go back to business, Watson. Would you mind reading me the advertised description of Mr. Hosmer Angel?"

I held the little printed slip to the light.

"Missing," it said, "on the morning of the fourteenth, a gentleman named Hosmer Angel. About five ft. seven in. in height; strongly built, sallow complexion, black hair, a little bald in the centre, bushy, black side-whiskers and moustache; tinted glasses, slight infirmity of speech. Was dressed, when last seen, in black frock-coat faced with silk, black waistcoat, gold Albert chain, and grey Harris tweed trousers, with brown gaiters over elastic-sided boots. Known to have been employed in an office in Leadenhall Street. Anybody bringing—"

"That will do," said Holmes. "As to the letters," he continued, glancing over them, "they are very commonplace. Absolutely no clue in them to Mr. Angel, save that he quotes Balzac once. There is one remarkable point, however, which will no doubt strike you."

"They are typewritten," I remarked.

"Not only that, but the signature is typewritten. Look at the neat little 'Hosmer Angel' at the bottom. There is a date, you see, but no superscription except Leadenhall Street, which is rather vague. The point about the signature is very suggestive—in fact, we may call it conclusive."

"Of what?"

"My dear fellow, is it possible you do not see how strongly it bears upon the case?"

"I cannot say that I do unless it were that he wished to be able to deny his signature if an action for breach of promise were instituted."

"No, that was not the point. However, I shall write two letters, which should settle the matter. One is to a firm in the City, the other is to the young lady's stepfather, Mr. Windibank, asking him whether he could meet us here at six o'clock tomorrow evening. It is just as well that we should do business with the male relatives. And now, Doctor, we can do nothing until the answers to those letters come, so we may put our little problem upon the shelf for the interim."

I had had so many reasons to believe in my friend's subtle powers of reasoning and extraordinary energy in action that I felt that he must have some solid grounds for the assured and easy demeanour with which he treated the singular mystery which he had been called upon to fathom. Once only had I known him to fail, in the case of the King of Bohemia and of the Irene Adler photograph; but when I looked back to the weird business of the Sign of Four, and the extraordinary circumstances connected with the Study in Scarlet, I felt that it would be a strange tangle indeed which he could not unravel.

I left him then, still puffing at his black clay pipe, with the conviction that when I came again on the next evening I would find that he held in his hands all the clues which would lead up to the identity of the disappearing bridegroom of Miss Mary Sutherland.

A professional case of great gravity was engaging my own attention at the time, and the whole of next day I was busy at the bedside of the sufferer. It was not until close upon six o'clock that I found myself free and was able to spring into a hansom and drive to Baker Street, half afraid that I might be too late to assist at the dénouement of the little mystery. I found Sherlock Holmes alone, however, half asleep, with his long, thin form curled up in the recesses of his armchair. A formidable array of bottles and test-tubes, with the pungent cleanly smell of hydrochloric acid, told me that he had spent his day in the chemical work which was so dear to him.

"Well, have you solved it?" I asked as I entered.

"Yes. It was the bisulphate of baryta."

"No, no, the mystery!" I cried.

"Oh, that! I thought of the salt that I have been working upon. There was never any mystery in the matter, though, as I said yesterday, some of the details are of interest. The only drawback is that there is no law, I fear, that can touch the scoundrel."

"Who was he, then, and what was his object in deserting Miss Sutherland?"

The question was hardly out of my mouth, and Holmes had not yet opened his lips to reply, when we heard a heavy footfall in the passage and a tap at the door.

"This is the girl's stepfather, Mr. James Windibank," said Holmes. "He has written to me to say that he would be here at six. Come in!"

The man who entered was a sturdy, middle-sized fellow, some thirty years of age, clean-shaven, and sallow-skinned, with a bland, insinuating manner, and a pair of wonderfully sharp and penetrating grey eyes. He shot a questioning glance at each of us, placed his shiny top-hat upon the sideboard, and with a slight bow sidled down into the nearest chair.

"Good-evening, Mr. James Windibank," said Holmes. "I think that this typewritten letter is from you, in which you made an appointment with me for six o'clock?"

"Yes, sir. I am afraid that I am a little late, but I am not quite my own master, you know. I am sorry that Miss Sutherland has troubled you about this little matter, for I think it is far better not to wash linen of the sort in public. It was quite against my wishes that she came, but she is a very excitable, impulsive girl, as you may have noticed, and she is not easily controlled when she has made up her mind on a point. Of course, I did not mind you so much, as you are not connected with the official police, but it is not pleasant to have a family misfortune like this noised abroad. Besides, it is a useless expense, for how could you possibly find this Hosmer Angel?"

"On the contrary," said Holmes quietly; "I have every reason to believe that I will succeed in discovering Mr. Hosmer Angel."

Mr. Windibank gave a violent start and dropped his gloves. "I am delighted to hear it," he said.

"It is a curious thing," remarked Holmes, "that a typewriter has really quite as much individuality as a man's handwriting. Unless they are quite new, no two of them write exactly alike. Some letters get more worn than others, and some wear only on one side. Now, you remark in this note of yours, Mr. Windibank, that in every case there is some little slurring over of the 'e,' and a slight defect in the tail of the 'r.' There are fourteen other characteristics, but those are the more obvious."

"We do all our correspondence with this machine at the office, and no doubt it is a little worn," our visitor answered, glancing keenly at Holmes with his bright little eyes.

"And now I will show you what is really a very interesting study, Mr. Windibank," Holmes continued. "I think of writing another little monograph some of these days on the typewriter and its relation to crime. It is a subject to which I have devoted some little attention. I have here four letters which purport to come from the missing man. They are all typewritten. In each case, not only are the 'e's' slurred and the 'r's' tailless, but you will observe, if you care to use my magnifying lens, that the fourteen other characteristics to which I have alluded are there as well."

Mr. Windibank sprang out of his chair and picked up his hat. "I cannot waste time over this sort of fantastic talk, Mr. Holmes," he said. "If you can catch the man, catch him, and let me know when you have done it."

"Certainly," said Holmes, stepping over and turning the key in the door. "I let you know, then, that I have caught him!"

"What! where?" shouted Mr. Windibank, turning white to his lips and glancing about him like a rat in a trap.

"Oh, it won't do—really it won't," said Holmes suavely. "There is no possible getting out of it, Mr. Windibank. It is quite too transparent, and it was a very bad compliment when you said that it was impossible for me to solve so simple a question. That's right! Sit down and let us talk it over."

Our visitor collapsed into a chair, with a ghastly face and a glitter of moisture on his brow. "It—it's not actionable," he stammered.

"I am very much afraid that it is not. But between ourselves, Windibank, it was as cruel and selfish and heartless a trick in a petty way as ever came before me. Now, let me just run over the course of events, and you will contradict me if I go wrong."

The man sat huddled up in his chair, with his head sunk upon his breast, like one who is utterly crushed. Holmes stuck his feet up on the corner of the mantelpiece and, leaning back with his hands in his pockets, began talking, rather to himself, as it seemed, than to us.

"The man married a woman very much older than himself for her money," said he, "and he enjoyed the use of the money of the daughter as long as she lived with them. It was a considerable sum, for people in their position, and the loss of it would have made a serious difference. It was worth an effort to preserve it. The daughter was of a good, amiable disposition, but affectionate and warm-hearted in her ways, so that it was evident that with her fair personal advantages, and her little income, she would not be allowed to remain single long. Now her marriage would mean, of course, the loss of a hundred a year, so what does her stepfather do to prevent it? He takes the obvious course of keeping her at home and forbidding her to seek the company of people of her own age. But soon he found that that would not answer forever. She became restive, insisted upon her rights, and finally announced her positive intention of going to a certain ball. What does her clever stepfather do then? He conceives an idea more creditable to his head than to his heart. With the connivance and assistance of his wife he disguised himself, covered those keen eyes with tinted glasses, masked the face with a moustache and a pair of bushy whiskers, sunk that clear voice into an insinuating whisper, and doubly secure on account of the girl's short sight, he appears as Mr. Hosmer Angel, and keeps off other lovers by making love himself."

"It was only a joke at first," groaned our visitor. "We never thought that she would have been so carried away."

"Very likely not. However that may be, the young lady was very decidedly carried away, and, having quite made up her mind that her stepfather was in France, the suspicion of treachery never for an instant entered her mind. She was flattered by the gentleman's attentions, and the effect was increased by the loudly expressed admiration of her mother. Then Mr. Angel began to call, for it was obvious that the matter should be pushed as far as it would go if a real effect were to be produced. There were meetings, and an engagement, which would finally secure the girl's affections from turning towards anyone else. But the deception could not be kept up forever. These pretended journeys to France were rather cumbrous. The thing to do was clearly to bring the business to an end in such a dramatic manner that it would leave a permanent impression upon the young lady's mind and prevent her from looking upon any other suitor for some time to come. Hence those vows of fidelity exacted upon a Testament, and hence also the allusions to a possibility of something happening on the very morning of the wedding. James Windibank wished Miss Sutherland to be so bound to Hosmer Angel, and so uncertain as to his fate, that for ten years to come, at any rate, she would not listen to another man. As far as the church door he brought her, and then, as he could go no farther, he conveniently vanished away by the old trick of stepping in at one door of a four-wheeler and out at the other. I think that was the chain of events, Mr. Windibank!"

Our visitor had recovered something of his assurance while Holmes had been talking, and he rose from his chair now with a cold sneer upon his pale face.

"It may be so, or it may not, Mr. Holmes," said he, "but if you are so very sharp you ought to be sharp enough to know that it is you who are breaking the law now, and not me. I have done nothing actionable from the first, but as long as you keep that door locked you lay yourself open to an action for assault and illegal constraint."

"The law cannot, as you say, touch you," said Holmes, unlocking and throwing open the door, "yet there never was a man who deserved punishment more. If the young lady has a brother or a friend, he ought to lay a whip across your shoulders. By Jove!" he continued, flushing up at the sight of the bitter sneer upon the man's face, "it is not part of my duties to my client, but here's a hunting crop handy, and I think I shall just treat myself to—" He took two swift steps to the whip, but before he could grasp it there was a wild clatter of steps upon the stairs, the heavy hall door banged, and from the window we could see Mr. James Windibank running at the top of his speed down the road.

"There's a cold-blooded scoundrel!" said Holmes, laughing, as he threw himself down into his chair once more. "That fellow will rise from crime to crime until he does something very bad, and ends on a gallows. The case has, in some respects, been not entirely devoid of interest."

"I cannot now entirely see all the steps of your reasoning," I remarked.

"Well, of course it was obvious from the first that this Mr. Hosmer Angel must have some strong object for his curious conduct, and it was equally clear that the only man who really profited by the incident, as far as we could see, was the stepfather. Then the fact that the two men were never together, but that the one always appeared when the other was away, was suggestive. So were the tinted spectacles and the curious voice, which both hinted at a disguise, as did the bushy whiskers. My suspicions were all confirmed by his peculiar action in typewriting his signature, which, of course, inferred that his handwriting was so familiar to her that she would recognise even the smallest sample of it. You see all these isolated facts, together with many minor ones, all pointed in the same direction."

"And how did you verify them?"

"Having once spotted my man, it was easy to get corroboration. I knew the firm for which this man worked. Having taken the printed description. I eliminated everything from it which could be the result of a disguise—the whiskers, the glasses, the voice, and I sent it to the firm, with a request that they would inform me whether it answered to the description of any of their travellers. I had already noticed the peculiarities of the typewriter, and I wrote to the man himself at his business address asking him if he would come here. As I expected, his reply was typewritten and revealed the same trivial but characteristic defects. The same post brought me a letter from Westhouse & Marbank, of Fenchurch Street, to say that the description tallied in every respect with that of their employé, James Windibank. Voilà tout!"

"And Miss Sutherland?"

"If I tell her she will not believe me. You may remember the old Persian saying, 'There is danger for him who taketh the tiger cub, and danger also for whoso snatches a delusion from a woman.' There is as much sense in Hafiz as in Horace, and as much knowledge of the world."

Adventure IV. The Boscombe Valley Mystery

We were seated at breakfast one morning, my wife and I, when the maid brought in a telegram. It was from Sherlock Holmes and ran in this way:

"Have you a couple of days to spare? Have just been wired for from the west of England in connection with Boscombe Valley tragedy. Shall be glad if you will come with me. Air and scenery perfect. Leave Paddington by the 11:15."

"What do you say, dear?" said my wife, looking across at me. "Will you go?"

"I really don't know what to say. I have a fairly long list at present."

"Oh, Anstruther would do your work for you. You have been looking a little pale lately. I think that the change would do you good, and you are always so interested in Mr. Sherlock Holmes' cases."

"I should be ungrateful if I were not, seeing what I gained through one of them," I answered. "But if I am to go, I must pack at once, for I have only half an hour."

My experience of camp life in Afghanistan had at least had the effect of making me a prompt and ready traveller. My wants were few and simple, so that in less than the time stated I was in a cab with my valise, rattling away to Paddington Station. Sherlock Holmes was pacing up and down the platform, his tall, gaunt figure made even gaunter and taller by his long grey travelling-cloak and close-fitting cloth cap.

"It is really very good of you to come, Watson," said he. "It makes a considerable difference to me, having someone with me on whom I can thoroughly rely. Local aid is always either worthless or else biassed. If you will keep the two corner seats I shall get the tickets."

We had the carriage to ourselves save for an immense litter of papers which Holmes had brought with him. Among these he rummaged and read, with intervals of note-taking and of meditation, until we were past Reading. Then he suddenly rolled them all into a gigantic ball and tossed them up onto the rack.

"Have you heard anything of the case?" he asked.

"Not a word. I have not seen a paper for some days."

"The London press has not had very full accounts. I have just been looking through all the recent papers in order to master the particulars. It seems, from what I gather, to be one of those simple cases which are so extremely difficult."

"That sounds a little paradoxical."

"But it is profoundly true. Singularity is almost invariably a clue. The more featureless and commonplace a crime is, the more difficult it is to bring it home. In this case, however, they have established a very serious case against the son of the murdered man."

"It is a murder, then?"

"Well, it is conjectured to be so. I shall take nothing for granted until I have the opportunity of looking personally into it. I will explain the state of things to you, as far as I have been able to understand it, in a very few words.

"Boscombe Valley is a country district not very far from Ross, in Herefordshire. The largest landed proprietor in that part is a Mr. John Turner, who made his money in Australia and returned some years ago to the old country. One of the farms which he held, that of Hatherley, was let to Mr. Charles McCarthy, who was also an ex-Australian. The men had known each other in the colonies, so that it was not unnatural that when they came to settle down they should do so as near each other as possible. Turner was apparently the richer man, so McCarthy became his tenant but still remained, it seems, upon terms of perfect equality, as they were frequently together. McCarthy had one son, a lad of eighteen, and Turner had an only daughter of the same age, but neither of them had wives living. They appear to have avoided the society of the neighbouring English families and to have led retired lives, though both the McCarthys were fond of sport and were frequently seen at the race-meetings of the neighbourhood. McCarthy kept two servants—a man and a girl. Turner had a considerable household, some half-dozen at the least. That is as much as I have been able to gather about the families. Now for the facts.

"On June 3rd, that is, on Monday last, McCarthy left his house at Hatherley about three in the afternoon and walked down to the Boscombe Pool, which is a small lake formed by the spreading out of the stream which runs down the Boscombe Valley. He had been out with his serving-man in the morning at Ross, and he had told the man that he must hurry, as he had an appointment of importance to keep at three. From that appointment he never came back alive.

"From Hatherley Farm-house to the Boscombe Pool is a quarter of a mile, and two people saw him as he passed over this ground. One was an old woman, whose name is not mentioned, and the other was William Crowder, a game-keeper in the employ of Mr. Turner. Both these witnesses depose that Mr. McCarthy was walking alone. The game-keeper adds that within a few minutes of his seeing Mr. McCarthy pass he had seen his son, Mr. James McCarthy, going the same way with a gun under his arm. To the best of his belief, the father was actually in sight at the time, and the son was following him. He thought no more of the matter until he heard in the evening of the tragedy that had occurred.

"The two McCarthys were seen after the time when William Crowder, the game-keeper, lost sight of them. The Boscombe Pool is thickly wooded round, with just a fringe of grass and of reeds round the edge. A girl of fourteen, Patience Moran, who is the daughter of the lodge-keeper of the Boscombe Valley estate, was in one of the woods picking flowers. She states that while she was there she saw, at the border of the wood and close by the lake, Mr. McCarthy and his son, and that they appeared to be having a violent quarrel. She heard Mr. McCarthy the elder using very strong language to his son, and she saw the latter raise up his hand as if to strike his father. She was so frightened by their violence that she ran away and told her mother when she reached home that she had left the two McCarthys quarrelling near Boscombe Pool, and that she was afraid that they were going to fight. She had hardly said the words when young Mr. McCarthy came running up to the lodge to say that he had found his father dead in the wood, and to ask for the help of the lodge-keeper. He was much excited, without either his gun or his hat, and his right hand and sleeve were observed to be stained with fresh blood. On following him they found the dead body stretched out upon the grass beside the pool. The head had been beaten in by repeated blows of some heavy and blunt weapon. The injuries were such as might very well have been inflicted by the butt-end of his son's gun, which was found lying on the grass within a few paces of the body. Under these circumstances the young man was instantly arrested, and a verdict of 'wilful murder' having been returned at the inquest on Tuesday, he was on Wednesday brought before the magistrates at Ross, who have referred the case to the next Assizes. Those are the main facts of the case as they came out before the coroner and the police-court."

"I could hardly imagine a more damning case," I remarked. "If ever circumstantial evidence pointed to a criminal it does so here."

"Circumstantial evidence is a very tricky thing," answered Holmes thoughtfully. "It may seem to point very straight to one thing, but if you shift your own point of view a little, you may find it pointing in an equally uncompromising manner to something entirely different. It must be confessed, however, that the case looks exceedingly grave against the young man, and it is very possible that he is indeed the culprit. There are several people in the neighbourhood, however, and among them Miss Turner, the daughter of the neighbouring landowner, who believe in his innocence, and who have retained Lestrade, whom you may recollect in connection with the Study in Scarlet, to work out the case in his interest. Lestrade, being rather puzzled, has referred the case to me, and hence it is that two middle-aged gentlemen are flying westward at fifty miles an hour instead of quietly digesting their breakfasts at home."

"I am afraid," said I, "that the facts are so obvious that you will find little credit to be gained out of this case."

"There is nothing more deceptive than an obvious fact," he answered, laughing. "Besides, we may chance to hit upon some other obvious facts which may have been by no means obvious to Mr. Lestrade. You know me too well to think that I am boasting when I say that I shall either confirm or destroy his theory by means which he is quite incapable of employing, or even of understanding. To take the first example to hand, I very clearly perceive that in your bedroom the window is upon the right-hand side, and yet I question whether Mr. Lestrade would have noted even so self-evident a thing as that."

"How on earth—"

"My dear fellow, I know you well. I know the military neatness which characterises you. You shave every morning, and in this season you shave by the sunlight; but since your shaving is less and less complete as we get farther back on the left side, until it becomes positively slovenly as we get round the angle of the jaw, it is surely very clear that that side is less illuminated than the other. I could not imagine a man of your habits looking at himself in an equal light and being satisfied with such a result. I only quote this as a trivial example of observation and inference. Therein lies my métier, and it is just possible that it may be of some service in the investigation which lies before us. There are one or two minor points which were brought out in the inquest, and which are worth considering."

"What are they?"

"It appears that his arrest did not take place at once, but after the return to Hatherley Farm. On the inspector of constabulary informing him that he was a prisoner, he remarked that he was not surprised to hear it, and that it was no more than his deserts. This observation of his had the natural effect of removing any traces of doubt which might have remained in the minds of the coroner's jury."

"It was a confession," I ejaculated.

"No, for it was followed by a protestation of innocence."

"Coming on the top of such a damning series of events, it was at least a most suspicious remark."

"On the contrary," said Holmes, "it is the brightest rift which I can at present see in the clouds. However innocent he might be, he could not be such an absolute imbecile as not to see that the circumstances were very black against him. Had he appeared surprised at his own arrest, or feigned indignation at it, I should have looked upon it as highly suspicious, because such surprise or anger would not be natural under the circumstances, and yet might appear to be the best policy to a scheming man. His frank acceptance of the situation marks him as either an innocent man, or else as a man of considerable self-restraint and firmness. As to his remark about his deserts, it was also not unnatural if you consider that he stood beside the dead body of his father, and that there is no doubt that he had that very day so far forgotten his filial duty as to bandy words with him, and even, according to the little girl whose evidence is so important, to raise his hand as if to strike him. The self-reproach and contrition which are displayed in his remark appear to me to be the signs of a healthy mind rather than of a guilty one."

I shook my head. "Many men have been hanged on far slighter evidence," I remarked.

"So they have. And many men have been wrongfully hanged."

"What is the young man's own account of the matter?"

"It is, I am afraid, not very encouraging to his supporters, though there are one or two points in it which are suggestive. You will find it here, and may read it for yourself."

He picked out from his bundle a copy of the local Herefordshire paper, and having turned down the sheet he pointed out the paragraph in which the unfortunate young man had given his own statement of what had occurred. I settled myself down in the corner of the carriage and read it very carefully. It ran in this way:

"Mr. James McCarthy, the only son of the deceased, was then called and gave evidence as follows: 'I had been away from home for three days at Bristol, and had only just returned upon the morning of last Monday, the 3rd. My father was absent from home at the time of my arrival, and I was informed by the maid that he had driven over to Ross with John Cobb, the groom. Shortly after my return I heard the wheels of his trap in the yard, and, looking out of my window, I saw him get out and walk rapidly out of the yard, though I was not aware in which direction he was going. I then took my gun and strolled out in the direction of the Boscombe Pool, with the intention of visiting the rabbit warren which is upon the other side. On my way I saw William Crowder, the game-keeper, as he had stated in his evidence; but he is mistaken in thinking that I was following my father. I had no idea that he was in front of me. When about a hundred yards from the pool I heard a cry of "Cooee!" which was a usual signal between my father and myself. I then hurried forward, and found him standing by the pool. He appeared to be much surprised at seeing me and asked me rather roughly what I was doing there. A conversation ensued which led to high words and almost to blows, for my father was a man of a very violent temper. Seeing that his passion was becoming ungovernable, I left him and returned towards Hatherley Farm. I had not gone more than 150 yards, however, when I heard a hideous outcry behind me, which caused me to run back again. I found my father expiring upon the ground, with his head terribly injured. I dropped my gun and held him in my arms, but he almost instantly expired. I knelt beside him for some minutes, and then made my way to Mr. Turner's lodge-keeper, his house being the nearest, to ask for assistance. I saw no one near my father when I returned, and I have no idea how he came by his injuries. He was not a popular man, being somewhat cold and forbidding in his manners, but he had, as far as I know, no active enemies. I know nothing further of the matter.'

"The Coroner: Did your father make any statement to you before he died?

"Witness: He mumbled a few words, but I could only catch some allusion to a rat.

"The Coroner: What did you understand by that?

"Witness: It conveyed no meaning to me. I thought that he was delirious.

"The Coroner: What was the point upon which you and your father had this final quarrel?

"Witness: I should prefer not to answer.

"The Coroner: I am afraid that I must press it.

"Witness: It is really impossible for me to tell you. I can assure you that it has nothing to do with the sad tragedy which followed.

"The Coroner: That is for the court to decide. I need not point out to you that your refusal to answer will prejudice your case considerably in any future proceedings which may arise.

"Witness: I must still refuse.

"The Coroner: I understand that the cry of 'Cooee' was a common signal between you and your father?

"Witness: It was.

"The Coroner: How was it, then, that he uttered it before he saw you, and before he even knew that you had returned from Bristol?

"Witness (with considerable confusion): I do not know.

"A Juryman: Did you see nothing which aroused your suspicions when you returned on hearing the cry and found your father fatally injured?

"Witness: Nothing definite.

"The Coroner: What do you mean?

"Witness: I was so disturbed and excited as I rushed out into the open, that I could think of nothing except of my father. Yet I have a vague impression that as I ran forward something lay upon the ground to the left of me. It seemed to me to be something grey in colour, a coat of some sort, or a plaid perhaps. When I rose from my father I looked round for it, but it was gone.

"'Do you mean that it disappeared before you went for help?'

"'Yes, it was gone.'

"'You cannot say what it was?'

"'No, I had a feeling something was there.'

"'How far from the body?'

"'A dozen yards or so.'

"'And how far from the edge of the wood?'

"'About the same.'

"'Then if it was removed it was while you were within a dozen yards of it?'

"'Yes, but with my back towards it.'

"This concluded the examination of the witness."

"I see," said I as I glanced down the column, "that the coroner in his concluding remarks was rather severe upon young McCarthy. He calls attention, and with reason, to the discrepancy about his father having signalled to him before seeing him, also to his refusal to give details of his conversation with his father, and his singular account of his father's dying words. They are all, as he remarks, very much against the son."

Holmes laughed softly to himself and stretched himself out upon the cushioned seat. "Both you and the coroner have been at some pains," said he, "to single out the very strongest points in the young man's favour. Don't you see that you alternately give him credit for having too much imagination and too little? Too little, if he could not invent a cause of quarrel which would give him the sympathy of the jury; too much, if he evolved from his own inner consciousness anything so outré as a dying reference to a rat, and the incident of the vanishing cloth. No, sir, I shall approach this case from the point of view that what this young man says is true, and we shall see whither that hypothesis will lead us. And now here is my pocket Petrarch, and not another word shall I say of this case until we are on the scene of action. We lunch at Swindon, and I see that we shall be there in twenty minutes."

It was nearly four o'clock when we at last, after passing through the beautiful Stroud Valley, and over the broad gleaming Severn, found ourselves at the pretty little country-town of Ross. A lean, ferret-like man, furtive and sly-looking, was waiting for us upon the platform. In spite of the light brown dustcoat and leather-leggings which he wore in deference to his rustic surroundings, I had no difficulty in recognising Lestrade, of Scotland Yard. With him we drove to the Hereford Arms where a room had already been engaged for us.

"I have ordered a carriage," said Lestrade as we sat over a cup of tea. "I knew your energetic nature, and that you would not be happy until you had been on the scene of the crime."

"It was very nice and complimentary of you," Holmes answered. "It is entirely a question of barometric pressure."

Lestrade looked startled. "I do not quite follow," he said.

"How is the glass? Twenty-nine, I see. No wind, and not a cloud in the sky. I have a caseful of cigarettes here which need smoking, and the sofa is very much superior to the usual country hotel abomination. I do not think that it is probable that I shall use the carriage to-night."

Lestrade laughed indulgently. "You have, no doubt, already formed your conclusions from the newspapers," he said. "The case is as plain as a pikestaff, and the more one goes into it the plainer it becomes. Still, of course, one can't refuse a lady, and such a very positive one, too. She has heard of you, and would have your opinion, though I repeatedly told her that there was nothing which you could do which I had not already done. Why, bless my soul! here is her carriage at the door."

He had hardly spoken before there rushed into the room one of the most lovely young women that I have ever seen in my life. Her violet eyes shining, her lips parted, a pink flush upon her cheeks, all thought of her natural reserve lost in her overpowering excitement and concern.

"Oh, Mr. Sherlock Holmes!" she cried, glancing from one to the other of us, and finally, with a woman's quick intuition, fastening upon my companion, "I am so glad that you have come. I have driven down to tell you so. I know that James didn't do it. I know it, and I want you to start upon your work knowing it, too. Never let yourself doubt upon that point. We have known each other since we were little children, and I know his faults as no one else does; but he is too tender-hearted to hurt a fly. Such a charge is absurd to anyone who really knows him."

"I hope we may clear him, Miss Turner," said Sherlock Holmes. "You may rely upon my doing all that I can."

"But you have read the evidence. You have formed some conclusion? Do you not see some loophole, some flaw? Do you not yourself think that he is innocent?"

"I think that it is very probable."

"There, now!" she cried, throwing back her head and looking defiantly at Lestrade. "You hear! He gives me hopes."

Lestrade shrugged his shoulders. "I am afraid that my colleague has been a little quick in forming his conclusions," he said.

"But he is right. Oh! I know that he is right. James never did it. And about his quarrel with his father, I am sure that the reason why he would not speak about it to the coroner was because I was concerned in it."

"In what way?" asked Holmes.

"It is no time for me to hide anything. James and his father had many disagreements about me. Mr. McCarthy was very anxious that there should be a marriage between us. James and I have always loved each other as brother and sister; but of course he is young and has seen very little of life yet, and—and—well, he naturally did not wish to do anything like that yet. So there were quarrels, and this, I am sure, was one of them."

"And your father?" asked Holmes. "Was he in favour of such a union?"

"No, he was averse to it also. No one but Mr. McCarthy was in favour of it." A quick blush passed over her fresh young face as Holmes shot one of his keen, questioning glances at her.

"Thank you for this information," said he. "May I see your father if I call tomorrow?"

"I am afraid the doctor won't allow it."

"The doctor?"

"Yes, have you not heard? Poor father has never been strong for years back, but this has broken him down completely. He has taken to his bed, and Dr. Willows says that he is a wreck and that his nervous system is shattered. Mr. McCarthy was the only man alive who had known dad in the old days in Victoria."

"Ha! In Victoria! That is important."

"Yes, at the mines."

"Quite so; at the gold-mines, where, as I understand, Mr. Turner made his money."

"Yes, certainly."

"Thank you, Miss Turner. You have been of material assistance to me."

"You will tell me if you have any news tomorrow. No doubt you will go to the prison to see James. Oh, if you do, Mr. Holmes, do tell him that I know him to be innocent."

"I will, Miss Turner."

"I must go home now, for dad is very ill, and he misses me so if I leave him. Good-bye, and God help you in your undertaking." She hurried from the room as impulsively as she had entered, and we heard the wheels of her carriage rattle off down the street.

"I am ashamed of you, Holmes," said Lestrade with dignity after a few minutes' silence. "Why should you raise up hopes which you are bound to disappoint? I am not over-tender of heart, but I call it cruel."

"I think that I see my way to clearing James McCarthy," said Holmes. "Have you an order to see him in prison?"

"Yes, but only for you and me."

"Then I shall reconsider my resolution about going out. We have still time to take a train to Hereford and see him to-night?"

"Ample."

"Then let us do so. Watson, I fear that you will find it very slow, but I shall only be away a couple of hours."

I walked down to the station with them, and then wandered through the streets of the little town, finally returning to the hotel, where I lay upon the sofa and tried to interest myself in a yellow-backed novel. The puny plot of the story was so thin, however, when compared to the deep mystery through which we were groping, and I found my attention wander so continually from the action to the fact, that I at last flung it across the room and gave myself up entirely to a consideration of the events of the day. Supposing that this unhappy young man's story were absolutely true, then what hellish thing, what absolutely unforeseen and extraordinary calamity could have occurred between the time when he parted from his father, and the moment when, drawn back by his screams, he rushed into the glade? It was something terrible and deadly. What could it be? Might not the nature of the injuries reveal something to my medical instincts? I rang the bell and called for the weekly county paper, which contained a verbatim account of the inquest. In the surgeon's deposition it was stated that the posterior third of the left parietal bone and the left half of the occipital bone had been shattered by a heavy blow from a blunt weapon. I marked the spot upon my own head. Clearly such a blow must have been struck from behind. That was to some extent in favour of the accused, as when seen quarrelling he was face to face with his father. Still, it did not go for very much, for the older man might have turned his back before the blow fell. Still, it might be worth while to call Holmes' attention to it. Then there was the peculiar dying reference to a rat. What could that mean? It could not be delirium. A man dying from a sudden blow does not commonly become delirious. No, it was more likely to be an attempt to explain how he met his fate. But what could it indicate? I cudgelled my brains to find some possible explanation. And then the incident of the grey cloth seen by young McCarthy. If that were true the murderer must have dropped some part of his dress, presumably his overcoat, in his flight, and must have had the hardihood to return and to carry it away at the instant when the son was kneeling with his back turned not a dozen paces off. What a tissue of mysteries and improbabilities the whole thing was! I did not wonder at Lestrade's opinion, and yet I had so much faith in Sherlock Holmes' insight that I could not lose hope as long as every fresh fact seemed to strengthen his conviction of young McCarthy's innocence.

It was late before Sherlock Holmes returned. He came back alone, for Lestrade was staying in lodgings in the town.

"The glass still keeps very high," he remarked as he sat down. "It is of importance that it should not rain before we are able to go over the ground. On the other hand, a man should be at his very best and keenest for such nice work as that, and I did not wish to do it when fagged by a long journey. I have seen young McCarthy."

"And what did you learn from him?"

"Nothing."

"Could he throw no light?"

"None at all. I was inclined to think at one time that he knew who had done it and was screening him or her, but I am convinced now that he is as puzzled as everyone else. He is not a very quick-witted youth, though comely to look at and, I should think, sound at heart."

"I cannot admire his taste," I remarked, "if it is indeed a fact that he was averse to a marriage with so charming a young lady as this Miss Turner."

"Ah, thereby hangs a rather painful tale. This fellow is madly, insanely, in love with her, but some two years ago, when he was only a lad, and before he really knew her, for she had been away five years at a boarding-school, what does the idiot do but get into the clutches of a barmaid in Bristol and marry her at a registry office? No one knows a word of the matter, but you can imagine how maddening it must be to him to be upbraided for not doing what he would give his very eyes to do, but what he knows to be absolutely impossible. It was sheer frenzy of this sort which made him throw his hands up into the air when his father, at their last interview, was goading him on to propose to Miss Turner. On the other hand, he had no means of supporting himself, and his father, who was by all accounts a very hard man, would have thrown him over utterly had he known the truth. It was with his barmaid wife that he had spent the last three days in Bristol, and his father did not know where he was. Mark that point. It is of importance. Good has come out of evil, however, for the barmaid, finding from the papers that he is in serious trouble and likely to be hanged, has thrown him over utterly and has written to him to say that she has a husband already in the Bermuda Dockyard, so that there is really no tie between them. I think that that bit of news has consoled young McCarthy for all that he has suffered."

"But if he is innocent, who has done it?"

"Ah! who? I would call your attention very particularly to two points. One is that the murdered man had an appointment with someone at the pool, and that the someone could not have been his son, for his son was away, and he did not know when he would return. The second is that the murdered man was heard to cry 'Cooee!' before he knew that his son had returned. Those are the crucial points upon which the case depends. And now let us talk about George Meredith, if you please, and we shall leave all minor matters until tomorrow."

There was no rain, as Holmes had foretold, and the morning broke bright and cloudless. At nine o'clock Lestrade called for us with the carriage, and we set off for Hatherley Farm and the Boscombe Pool.

"There is serious news this morning," Lestrade observed. "It is said that Mr. Turner, of the Hall, is so ill that his life is despaired of."

"An elderly man, I presume?" said Holmes.

"About sixty; but his constitution has been shattered by his life abroad, and he has been in failing health for some time. This business has had a very bad effect upon him. He was an old friend of McCarthy's, and, I may add, a great benefactor to him, for I have learned that he gave him Hatherley Farm rent free."

"Indeed! That is interesting," said Holmes.

"Oh, yes! In a hundred other ways he has helped him. Everybody about here speaks of his kindness to him."

"Really! Does it not strike you as a little singular that this McCarthy, who appears to have had little of his own, and to have been under such obligations to Turner, should still talk of marrying his son to Turner's daughter, who is, presumably, heiress to the estate, and that in such a very cocksure manner, as if it were merely a case of a proposal and all else would follow? It is the more strange, since we know that Turner himself was averse to the idea. The daughter told us as much. Do you not deduce something from that?"

"We have got to the deductions and the inferences," said Lestrade, winking at me. "I find it hard enough to tackle facts, Holmes, without flying away after theories and fancies."

"You are right," said Holmes demurely; "you do find it very hard to tackle the facts."

"Anyhow, I have grasped one fact which you seem to find it difficult to get hold of," replied Lestrade with some warmth.

"And that is—"

"That McCarthy senior met his death from McCarthy junior and that all theories to the contrary are the merest moonshine."

"Well, moonshine is a brighter thing than fog," said Holmes, laughing. "But I am very much mistaken if this is not Hatherley Farm upon the left."

"Yes, that is it." It was a widespread, comfortable-looking building, two-storied, slate-roofed, with great yellow blotches of lichen upon the grey walls. The drawn blinds and the smokeless chimneys, however, gave it a stricken look, as though the weight of this horror still lay heavy upon it. We called at the door, when the maid, at Holmes' request, showed us the boots which her master wore at the time of his death, and also a pair of the son's, though not the pair which he had then had. Having measured these very carefully from seven or eight different points, Holmes desired to be led to the court-yard, from which we all followed the winding track which led to Boscombe Pool.

Sherlock Holmes was transformed when he was hot upon such a scent as this. Men who had only known the quiet thinker and logician of Baker Street would have failed to recognise him. His face flushed and darkened. His brows were drawn into two hard black lines, while his eyes shone out from beneath them with a steely glitter. His face was bent downward, his shoulders bowed, his lips compressed, and the veins stood out like whipcord in his long, sinewy neck. His nostrils seemed to dilate with a purely animal lust for the chase, and his mind was so absolutely concentrated upon the matter before him that a question or remark fell unheeded upon his ears, or, at the most, only provoked a quick, impatient snarl in reply. Swiftly and silently he made his way along the track which ran through the meadows, and so by way of the woods to the Boscombe Pool. It was damp, marshy ground, as is all that district, and there were marks of many feet, both upon the path and amid the short grass which bounded it on either side. Sometimes Holmes would hurry on, sometimes stop dead, and once he made quite a little detour into the meadow. Lestrade and I walked behind him, the detective indifferent and contemptuous, while I watched my friend with the interest which sprang from the conviction that every one of his actions was directed towards a definite end.

The Boscombe Pool, which is a little reed-girt sheet of water some fifty yards across, is situated at the boundary between the Hatherley Farm and the private park of the wealthy Mr. Turner. Above the woods which lined it upon the farther side we could see the red, jutting pinnacles which marked the site of the rich landowner's dwelling. On the Hatherley side of the pool the woods grew very thick, and there was a narrow belt of sodden grass twenty paces across between the edge of the trees and the reeds which lined the lake. Lestrade showed us the exact spot at which the body had been found, and, indeed, so moist was the ground, that I could plainly see the traces which had been left by the fall of the stricken man. To Holmes, as I could see by his eager face and peering eyes, very many other things were to be read upon the trampled grass. He ran round, like a dog who is picking up a scent, and then turned upon my companion.

"What did you go into the pool for?" he asked.

"I fished about with a rake. I thought there might be some weapon or other trace. But how on earth—"

"Oh, tut, tut! I have no time! That left foot of yours with its inward twist is all over the place. A mole could trace it, and there it vanishes among the reeds. Oh, how simple it would all have been had I been here before they came like a herd of buffalo and wallowed all over it. Here is where the party with the lodge-keeper came, and they have covered all tracks for six or eight feet round the body. But here are three separate tracks of the same feet." He drew out a lens and lay down upon his waterproof to have a better view, talking all the time rather to himself than to us. "These are young McCarthy's feet. Twice he was walking, and once he ran swiftly, so that the soles are deeply marked and the heels hardly visible. That bears out his story. He ran when he saw his father on the ground. Then here are the father's feet as he paced up and down. What is this, then? It is the butt-end of the gun as the son stood listening. And this? Ha, ha! What have we here? Tiptoes! tiptoes! Square, too, quite unusual boots! They come, they go, they come again—of course that was for the cloak. Now where did they come from?" He ran up and down, sometimes losing, sometimes finding the track until we were well within the edge of the wood and under the shadow of a great beech, the largest tree in the neighbourhood. Holmes traced his way to the farther side of this and lay down once more upon his face with a little cry of satisfaction. For a long time he remained there, turning over the leaves and dried sticks, gathering up what seemed to me to be dust into an envelope and examining with his lens not only the ground but even the bark of the tree as far as he could reach. A jagged stone was lying among the moss, and this also he carefully examined and retained. Then he followed a pathway through the wood until he came to the highroad, where all traces were lost.

"It has been a case of considerable interest," he remarked, returning to his natural manner. "I fancy that this grey house on the right must be the lodge. I think that I will go in and have a word with Moran, and perhaps write a little note. Having done that, we may drive back to our luncheon. You may walk to the cab, and I shall be with you presently."

It was about ten minutes before we regained our cab and drove back into Ross, Holmes still carrying with him the stone which he had picked up in the wood.

"This may interest you, Lestrade," he remarked, holding it out. "The murder was done with it."

"I see no marks."

"There are none."

"How do you know, then?"

"The grass was growing under it. It had only lain there a few days. There was no sign of a place whence it had been taken. It corresponds with the injuries. There is no sign of any other weapon."

"And the murderer?"

"Is a tall man, left-handed, limps with the right leg, wears thick-soled shooting-boots and a grey cloak, smokes Indian cigars, uses a cigar-holder, and carries a blunt pen-knife in his pocket. There are several other indications, but these may be enough to aid us in our search."

Lestrade laughed. "I am afraid that I am still a sceptic," he said. "Theories are all very well, but we have to deal with a hard-headed British jury."

"Nous verrons," answered Holmes calmly. "You work your own method, and I shall work mine. I shall be busy this afternoon, and shall probably return to London by the evening train."

"And leave your case unfinished?"

"No, finished."

"But the mystery?"

"It is solved."

"Who was the criminal, then?"

"The gentleman I describe."

"But who is he?"

"Surely it would not be difficult to find out. This is not such a populous neighbourhood."

Lestrade shrugged his shoulders. "I am a practical man," he said, "and I really cannot undertake to go about the country looking for a left-handed gentleman with a game leg. I should become the laughing-stock of Scotland Yard."

"All right," said Holmes quietly. "I have given you the chance. Here are your lodgings. Good-bye. I shall drop you a line before I leave."

Having left Lestrade at his rooms, we drove to our hotel, where we found lunch upon the table. Holmes was silent and buried in thought with a pained expression upon his face, as one who finds himself in a perplexing position.

"Look here, Watson," he said when the cloth was cleared "just sit down in this chair and let me preach to you for a little. I don't know quite what to do, and I should value your advice. Light a cigar and let me expound."

"Pray do so."

"Well, now, in considering this case there are two points about young McCarthy's narrative which struck us both instantly, although they impressed me in his favour and you against him. One was the fact that his father should, according to his account, cry 'Cooee!' before seeing him. The other was his singular dying reference to a rat. He mumbled several words, you understand, but that was all that caught the son's ear. Now from this double point our research must commence, and we will begin it by presuming that what the lad says is absolutely true."

"What of this 'Cooee!' then?"

"Well, obviously it could not have been meant for the son. The son, as far as he knew, was in Bristol. It was mere chance that he was within earshot. The 'Cooee!' was meant to attract the attention of whoever it was that he had the appointment with. But 'Cooee' is a distinctly Australian cry, and one which is used between Australians. There is a strong presumption that the person whom McCarthy expected to meet him at Boscombe Pool was someone who had been in Australia."

"What of the rat, then?"

Sherlock Holmes took a folded paper from his pocket and flattened it out on the table. "This is a map of the Colony of Victoria," he said. "I wired to Bristol for it last night." He put his hand over part of the map. "What do you read?"

"ARAT," I read.

"And now?" He raised his hand.

"BALLARAT."

"Quite so. That was the word the man uttered, and of which his son only caught the last two syllables. He was trying to utter the name of his murderer. So and so, of Ballarat."

"It is wonderful!" I exclaimed.

"It is obvious. And now, you see, I had narrowed the field down considerably. The possession of a grey garment was a third point which, granting the son's statement to be correct, was a certainty. We have come now out of mere vagueness to the definite conception of an Australian from Ballarat with a grey cloak."

"Certainly."

"And one who was at home in the district, for the pool can only be approached by the farm or by the estate, where strangers could hardly wander."

"Quite so."

"Then comes our expedition of today. By an examination of the ground I gained the trifling details which I gave to that imbecile Lestrade, as to the personality of the criminal."

"But how did you gain them?"

"You know my method. It is founded upon the observation of trifles."

"His height I know that you might roughly judge from the length of his stride. His boots, too, might be told from their traces."

"Yes, they were peculiar boots."

"But his lameness?"

"The impression of his right foot was always less distinct than his left. He put less weight upon it. Why? Because he limped—he was lame."

"But his left-handedness."

"You were yourself struck by the nature of the injury as recorded by the surgeon at the inquest. The blow was struck from immediately behind, and yet was upon the left side. Now, how can that be unless it were by a left-handed man? He had stood behind that tree during the interview between the father and son. He had even smoked there. I found the ash of a cigar, which my special knowledge of tobacco ashes enables me to pronounce as an Indian cigar. I have, as you know, devoted some attention to this, and written a little monograph on the ashes of 140 different varieties of pipe, cigar, and cigarette tobacco. Having found the ash, I then looked round and discovered the stump among the moss where he had tossed it. It was an Indian cigar, of the variety which are rolled in Rotterdam."

"And the cigar-holder?"

"I could see that the end had not been in his mouth. Therefore he used a holder. The tip had been cut off, not bitten off, but the cut was not a clean one, so I deduced a blunt pen-knife."

"Holmes," I said, "you have drawn a net round this man from which he cannot escape, and you have saved an innocent human life as truly as if you had cut the cord which was hanging him. I see the direction in which all this points. The culprit is—"

"Mr. John Turner," cried the hotel waiter, opening the door of our sitting-room, and ushering in a visitor.

The man who entered was a strange and impressive figure. His slow, limping step and bowed shoulders gave the appearance of decrepitude, and yet his hard, deep-lined, craggy features, and his enormous limbs showed that he was possessed of unusual strength of body and of character. His tangled beard, grizzled hair, and outstanding, drooping eyebrows combined to give an air of dignity and power to his appearance, but his face was of an ashen white, while his lips and the corners of his nostrils were tinged with a shade of blue. It was clear to me at a glance that he was in the grip of some deadly and chronic disease.

"Pray sit down on the sofa," said Holmes gently. "You had my note?"

"Yes, the lodge-keeper brought it up. You said that you wished to see me here to avoid scandal."

"I thought people would talk if I went to the Hall."

"And why did you wish to see me?" He looked across at my companion with despair in his weary eyes, as though his question was already answered.

"Yes," said Holmes, answering the look rather than the words. "It is so. I know all about McCarthy."

The old man sank his face in his hands. "God help me!" he cried. "But I would not have let the young man come to harm. I give you my word that I would have spoken out if it went against him at the Assizes."

"I am glad to hear you say so," said Holmes gravely.

"I would have spoken now had it not been for my dear girl. It would break her heart—it will break her heart when she hears that I am arrested."

"It may not come to that," said Holmes.

"What?"

"I am no official agent. I understand that it was your daughter who required my presence here, and I am acting in her interests. Young McCarthy must be got off, however."

"I am a dying man," said old Turner. "I have had diabetes for years. My doctor says it is a question whether I shall live a month. Yet I would rather die under my own roof than in a gaol."

Holmes rose and sat down at the table with his pen in his hand and a bundle of paper before him. "Just tell us the truth," he said. "I shall jot down the facts. You will sign it, and Watson here can witness it. Then I could produce your confession at the last extremity to save young McCarthy. I promise you that I shall not use it unless it is absolutely needed."

"It's as well," said the old man; "it's a question whether I shall live to the Assizes, so it matters little to me, but I should wish to spare Alice the shock. And now I will make the thing clear to you; it has been a long time in the acting, but will not take me long to tell.

"You didn't know this dead man, McCarthy. He was a devil incarnate. I tell you that. God keep you out of the clutches of such a man as he. His grip has been upon me these twenty years, and he has blasted my life. I'll tell you first how I came to be in his power.

"It was in the early '60's at the diggings. I was a young chap then, hot-blooded and reckless, ready to turn my hand at anything; I got among bad companions, took to drink, had no luck with my claim, took to the bush, and in a word became what you would call over here a highway robber. There were six of us, and we had a wild, free life of it, sticking up a station from time to time, or stopping the wagons on the road to the diggings. Black Jack of Ballarat was the name I went under, and our party is still remembered in the colony as the Ballarat Gang.

"One day a gold convoy came down from Ballarat to Melbourne, and we lay in wait for it and attacked it. There were six troopers and six of us, so it was a close thing, but we emptied four of their saddles at the first volley. Three of our boys were killed, however, before we got the swag. I put my pistol to the head of the wagon-driver, who was this very man McCarthy. I wish to the Lord that I had shot him then, but I spared him, though I saw his wicked little eyes fixed on my face, as though to remember every feature. We got away with the gold, became wealthy men, and made our way over to England without being suspected. There I parted from my old pals and determined to settle down to a quiet and respectable life. I bought this estate, which chanced to be in the market, and I set myself to do a little good with my money, to make up for the way in which I had earned it. I married, too, and though my wife died young she left me my dear little Alice. Even when she was just a baby her wee hand seemed to lead me down the right path as nothing else had ever done. In a word, I turned over a new leaf and did my best to make up for the past. All was going well when McCarthy laid his grip upon me.

"I had gone up to town about an investment, and I met him in Regent Street with hardly a coat to his back or a boot to his foot.

"'Here we are, Jack,' says he, touching me on the arm; 'we'll be as good as a family to you. There's two of us, me and my son, and you can have the keeping of us. If you don't—it's a fine, law-abiding country is England, and there's always a policeman within hail.'

"Well, down they came to the west country, there was no shaking them off, and there they have lived rent free on my best land ever since. There was no rest for me, no peace, no forgetfulness; turn where I would, there was his cunning, grinning face at my elbow. It grew worse as Alice grew up, for he soon saw I was more afraid of her knowing my past than of the police. Whatever he wanted he must have, and whatever it was I gave him without question, land, money, houses, until at last he asked a thing which I could not give. He asked for Alice.

"His son, you see, had grown up, and so had my girl, and as I was known to be in weak health, it seemed a fine stroke to him that his lad should step into the whole property. But there I was firm. I would not have his cursed stock mixed with mine; not that I had any dislike to the lad, but his blood was in him, and that was enough. I stood firm. McCarthy threatened. I braved him to do his worst. We were to meet at the pool midway between our houses to talk it over.

"When I went down there I found him talking with his son, so I smoked a cigar and waited behind a tree until he should be alone. But as I listened to his talk all that was black and bitter in me seemed to come uppermost. He was urging his son to marry my daughter with as little regard for what she might think as if she were a slut from off the streets. It drove me mad to think that I and all that I held most dear should be in the power of such a man as this. Could I not snap the bond? I was already a dying and a desperate man. Though clear of mind and fairly strong of limb, I knew that my own fate was sealed. But my memory and my girl! Both could be saved if I could but silence that foul tongue. I did it, Mr. Holmes. I would do it again. Deeply as I have sinned, I have led a life of martyrdom to atone for it. But that my girl should be entangled in the same meshes which held me was more than I could suffer. I struck him down with no more compunction than if he had been some foul and venomous beast. His cry brought back his son; but I had gained the cover of the wood, though I was forced to go back to fetch the cloak which I had dropped in my flight. That is the true story, gentlemen, of all that occurred."

"Well, it is not for me to judge you," said Holmes as the old man signed the statement which had been drawn out. "I pray that we may never be exposed to such a temptation."

"I pray not, sir. And what do you intend to do?"

"In view of your health, nothing. You are yourself aware that you will soon have to answer for your deed at a higher court than the Assizes. I will keep your confession, and if McCarthy is condemned I shall be forced to use it. If not, it shall never be seen by mortal eye; and your secret, whether you be alive or dead, shall be safe with us."

"Farewell, then," said the old man solemnly. "Your own deathbeds, when they come, will be the easier for the thought of the peace which you have given to mine." Tottering and shaking in all his giant frame, he stumbled slowly from the room.

"God help us!" said Holmes after a long silence. "Why does fate play such tricks with poor, helpless worms? I never hear of such a case as this that I do not think of Baxter's words, and say, 'There, but for the grace of God, goes Sherlock Holmes.'"

James McCarthy was acquitted at the Assizes on the strength of a number of objections which had been drawn out by Holmes and submitted to the defending counsel. Old Turner lived for seven months after our interview, but he is now dead; and there is every prospect that the son and daughter may come to live happily together in ignorance of the black cloud which rests upon their past.

Adventure V. The Five Orange Pips

When I glance over my notes and records of the Sherlock Holmes cases between the years '82 and '90, I am faced by so many which present strange and interesting features that it is no easy matter to know which to choose and which to leave. Some, however, have already gained publicity through the papers, and others have not offered a field for those peculiar qualities which my friend possessed in so high a degree, and which it is the object of these papers to illustrate. Some, too, have baffled his analytical skill, and would be, as narratives, beginnings without an ending, while others have been but partially cleared up, and have their explanations founded rather upon conjecture and surmise than on that absolute logical proof which was so dear to him. There is, however, one of these last which was so remarkable in its details and so startling in its results that I am tempted to give some account of it in spite of the fact that there are points in connection with it which never have been, and probably never will be, entirely cleared up.

The year '87 furnished us with a long series of cases of greater or less interest, of which I retain the records. Among my headings under this one twelve months I find an account of the adventure of the Paradol Chamber, of the Amateur Mendicant Society, who held a luxurious club in the lower vault of a furniture warehouse, of the facts connected with the loss of the British barque "Sophy Anderson", of the singular adventures of the Grice Patersons in the island of Uffa, and finally of the Camberwell poisoning case. In the latter, as may be remembered, Sherlock Holmes was able, by winding up the dead man's watch, to prove that it had been wound up two hours before, and that therefore the deceased had gone to bed within that time—a deduction which was of the greatest importance in clearing up the case. All these I may sketch out at some future date, but none of them present such singular features as the strange train of circumstances which I have now taken up my pen to describe.

It was in the latter days of September, and the equinoctial gales had set in with exceptional violence. All day the wind had screamed and the rain had beaten against the windows, so that even here in the heart of great, hand-made London we were forced to raise our minds for the instant from the routine of life and to recognise the presence of those great elemental forces which shriek at mankind through the bars of his civilisation, like untamed beasts in a cage. As evening drew in, the storm grew higher and louder, and the wind cried and sobbed like a child in the chimney. Sherlock Holmes sat moodily at one side of the fireplace cross-indexing his records of crime, while I at the other was deep in one of Clark Russell's fine sea-stories until the howl of the gale from without seemed to blend with the text, and the splash of the rain to lengthen out into the long swash of the sea waves. My wife was on a visit to her mother's, and for a few days I was a dweller once more in my old quarters at Baker Street.

"Why," said I, glancing up at my companion, "that was surely the bell. Who could come to-night? Some friend of yours, perhaps?"

"Except yourself I have none," he answered. "I do not encourage visitors."

"A client, then?"

"If so, it is a serious case. Nothing less would bring a man out on such a day and at such an hour. But I take it that it is more likely to be some crony of the landlady's."

Sherlock Holmes was wrong in his conjecture, however, for there came a step in the passage and a tapping at the door. He stretched out his long arm to turn the lamp away from himself and towards the vacant chair upon which a newcomer must sit.

"Come in!" said he.

The man who entered was young, some two-and-twenty at the outside, well-groomed and trimly clad, with something of refinement and delicacy in his bearing. The streaming umbrella which he held in his hand, and his long shining waterproof told of the fierce weather through which he had come. He looked about him anxiously in the glare of the lamp, and I could see that his face was pale and his eyes heavy, like those of a man who is weighed down with some great anxiety.

"I owe you an apology," he said, raising his golden pince-nez to his eyes. "I trust that I am not intruding. I fear that I have brought some traces of the storm and rain into your snug chamber."

"Give me your coat and umbrella," said Holmes. "They may rest here on the hook and will be dry presently. You have come up from the south-west, I see."

"Yes, from Horsham."

"That clay and chalk mixture which I see upon your toe caps is quite distinctive."

"I have come for advice."

"That is easily got."

"And help."

"That is not always so easy."

"I have heard of you, Mr. Holmes. I heard from Major Prendergast how you saved him in the Tankerville Club scandal."

"Ah, of course. He was wrongfully accused of cheating at cards."

"He said that you could solve anything."

"He said too much."

"That you are never beaten."

"I have been beaten four times—three times by men, and once by a woman."

"But what is that compared with the number of your successes?"

"It is true that I have been generally successful."

"Then you may be so with me."

"I beg that you will draw your chair up to the fire and favour me with some details as to your case."

"It is no ordinary one."

"None of those which come to me are. I am the last court of appeal."

"And yet I question, sir, whether, in all your experience, you have ever listened to a more mysterious and inexplicable chain of events than those which have happened in my own family."

"You fill me with interest," said Holmes. "Pray give us the essential facts from the commencement, and I can afterwards question you as to those details which seem to me to be most important."

The young man pulled his chair up and pushed his wet feet out towards the blaze.

"My name," said he, "is John Openshaw, but my own affairs have, as far as I can understand, little to do with this awful business. It is a hereditary matter; so in order to give you an idea of the facts, I must go back to the commencement of the affair.

"You must know that my grandfather had two sons—my uncle Elias and my father Joseph. My father had a small factory at Coventry, which he enlarged at the time of the invention of bicycling. He was a patentee of the Openshaw unbreakable tire, and his business met with such success that he was able to sell it and to retire upon a handsome competence.

"My uncle Elias emigrated to America when he was a young man and became a planter in Florida, where he was reported to have done very well. At the time of the war he fought in Jackson's army, and afterwards under Hood, where he rose to be a colonel. When Lee laid down his arms my uncle returned to his plantation, where he remained for three or four years. About 1869 or 1870 he came back to Europe and took a small estate in Sussex, near Horsham. He had made a very considerable fortune in the States, and his reason for leaving them was his aversion to the negroes, and his dislike of the Republican policy in extending the franchise to them. He was a singular man, fierce and quick-tempered, very foul-mouthed when he was angry, and of a most retiring disposition. During all the years that he lived at Horsham, I doubt if ever he set foot in the town. He had a garden and two or three fields round his house, and there he would take his exercise, though very often for weeks on end he would never leave his room. He drank a great deal of brandy and smoked very heavily, but he would see no society and did not want any friends, not even his own brother.

"He didn't mind me; in fact, he took a fancy to me, for at the time when he saw me first I was a youngster of twelve or so. This would be in the year 1878, after he had been eight or nine years in England. He begged my father to let me live with him and he was very kind to me in his way. When he was sober he used to be fond of playing backgammon and draughts with me, and he would make me his representative both with the servants and with the tradespeople, so that by the time that I was sixteen I was quite master of the house. I kept all the keys and could go where I liked and do what I liked, so long as I did not disturb him in his privacy. There was one singular exception, however, for he had a single room, a lumber-room up among the attics, which was invariably locked, and which he would never permit either me or anyone else to enter. With a boy's curiosity I have peeped through the keyhole, but I was never able to see more than such a collection of old trunks and bundles as would be expected in such a room.

"One day—it was in March, 1883--a letter with a foreign stamp lay upon the table in front of the colonel's plate. It was not a common thing for him to receive letters, for his bills were all paid in ready money, and he had no friends of any sort. 'From India!' said he as he took it up, 'Pondicherry postmark! What can this be?' Opening it hurriedly, out there jumped five little dried orange pips, which pattered down upon his plate. I began to laugh at this, but the laugh was struck from my lips at the sight of his face. His lip had fallen, his eyes were protruding, his skin the colour of putty, and he glared at the envelope which he still held in his trembling hand, 'K. K. K.!' he shrieked, and then, 'My God, my God, my sins have overtaken me!'

"'What is it, uncle?' I cried.

"'Death,' said he, and rising from the table he retired to his room, leaving me palpitating with horror. I took up the envelope and saw scrawled in red ink upon the inner flap, just above the gum, the letter K three times repeated. There was nothing else save the five dried pips. What could be the reason of his overpowering terror? I left the breakfast-table, and as I ascended the stair I met him coming down with an old rusty key, which must have belonged to the attic, in one hand, and a small brass box, like a cashbox, in the other.

"'They may do what they like, but I'll checkmate them still,' said he with an oath. 'Tell Mary that I shall want a fire in my room today, and send down to Fordham, the Horsham lawyer.'

"I did as he ordered, and when the lawyer arrived I was asked to step up to the room. The fire was burning brightly, and in the grate there was a mass of black, fluffy ashes, as of burned paper, while the brass box stood open and empty beside it. As I glanced at the box I noticed, with a start, that upon the lid was printed the treble K which I had read in the morning upon the envelope.

"'I wish you, John,' said my uncle, 'to witness my will. I leave my estate, with all its advantages and all its disadvantages, to my brother, your father, whence it will, no doubt, descend to you. If you can enjoy it in peace, well and good! If you find you cannot, take my advice, my boy, and leave it to your deadliest enemy. I am sorry to give you such a two-edged thing, but I can't say what turn things are going to take. Kindly sign the paper where Mr. Fordham shows you.'

"I signed the paper as directed, and the lawyer took it away with him. The singular incident made, as you may think, the deepest impression upon me, and I pondered over it and turned it every way in my mind without being able to make anything of it. Yet I could not shake off the vague feeling of dread which it left behind, though the sensation grew less keen as the weeks passed and nothing happened to disturb the usual routine of our lives. I could see a change in my uncle, however. He drank more than ever, and he was less inclined for any sort of society.

Most of his time he would spend in his room, with the door locked upon the inside, but sometimes he would emerge in a sort of drunken frenzy and would burst out of the house and tear about the garden with a revolver in his hand, screaming out that he was afraid of no man, and that he was not to be cooped up, like a sheep in a pen, by man or devil. When these hot fits were over, however, he would rush tumultuously in at the door and lock and bar it behind him, like a man who can brazen it out no longer against the terror which lies at the roots of his soul. At such times I have seen his face, even on a cold day, glisten with moisture, as though it were new raised from a basin.

"Well, to come to an end of the matter, Mr. Holmes, and not to abuse your patience, there came a night when he made one of those drunken sallies from which he never came back. We found him, when we went to search for him, face downward in a little green-scummed pool, which lay at the foot of the garden. There was no sign of any violence, and the water was but two feet deep, so that the jury, having regard to his known eccentricity, brought in a verdict of 'suicide.' But I, who knew how he winced from the very thought of death, had much ado to persuade myself that he had gone out of his way to meet it. The matter passed, however, and my father entered into possession of the estate, and of some 14,000 pounds, which lay to his credit at the bank."

"One moment," Holmes interposed, "your statement is, I foresee, one of the most remarkable to which I have ever listened. Let me have the date of the reception by your uncle of the letter, and the date of his supposed suicide."

"The letter arrived on March 10, 1883. His death was seven weeks later, upon the night of May 2nd."

"Thank you. Pray proceed."

"When my father took over the Horsham property, he, at my request, made a careful examination of the attic, which had been always locked up. We found the brass box there, although its contents had been destroyed. On the inside of the cover was a paper label, with the initials of K. K. K. repeated upon it, and 'Letters, memoranda, receipts, and a register' written beneath. These, we presume, indicated the nature of the papers which had been destroyed by Colonel Openshaw. For the rest, there was nothing of much importance in the attic save a great many scattered papers and note-books bearing upon my uncle's life in America. Some of them were of the war time and showed that he had done his duty well and had borne the repute of a brave soldier. Others were of a date during the reconstruction of the Southern states, and were mostly concerned with politics, for he had evidently taken a strong part in opposing the carpet-bag politicians who had been sent down from the North.

"Well, it was the beginning of '84 when my father came to live at Horsham, and all went as well as possible with us until the January of '85. On the fourth day after the new year I heard my father give a sharp cry of surprise as we sat together at the breakfast-table. There he was, sitting with a newly opened envelope in one hand and five dried orange pips in the outstretched palm of the other one. He had always laughed at what he called my cock-and-bull story about the colonel, but he looked very scared and puzzled now that the same thing had come upon himself.

"'Why, what on earth does this mean, John?' he stammered.

"My heart had turned to lead. 'It is K. K. K.,' said I.

"He looked inside the envelope. 'So it is,' he cried. 'Here are the very letters. But what is this written above them?'

"'Put the papers on the sundial,' I read, peeping over his shoulder.

"'What papers? What sundial?' he asked.

"'The sundial in the garden. There is no other,' said I; 'but the papers must be those that are destroyed.'

"'Pooh!' said he, gripping hard at his courage. 'We are in a civilised land here, and we can't have tomfoolery of this kind. Where does the thing come from?'

"'From Dundee,' I answered, glancing at the postmark.

"'Some preposterous practical joke,' said he. 'What have I to do with sundials and papers? I shall take no notice of such nonsense.'

"'I should certainly speak to the police,' I said.

"'And be laughed at for my pains. Nothing of the sort.'

"'Then let me do so?'

"'No, I forbid you. I won't have a fuss made about such nonsense.'

"It was in vain to argue with him, for he was a very obstinate man. I went about, however, with a heart which was full of forebodings.

"On the third day after the coming of the letter my father went from home to visit an old friend of his, Major Freebody, who is in command of one of the forts upon Portsdown Hill. I was glad that he should go, for it seemed to me that he was farther from danger when he was away from home. In that, however, I was in error. Upon the second day of his absence I received a telegram from the major, imploring me to come at once. My father had fallen over one of the deep chalk-pits which abound in the neighbourhood, and was lying senseless, with a shattered skull. I hurried to him, but he passed away without having ever recovered his consciousness. He had, as it appears, been returning from Fareham in the twilight, and as the country was unknown to him, and the chalk-pit unfenced, the jury had no hesitation in bringing in a verdict of 'death from accidental causes.' Carefully as I examined every fact connected with his death, I was unable to find anything which could suggest the idea of murder. There were no signs of violence, no footmarks, no robbery, no record of strangers having been seen upon the roads. And yet I need not tell you that my mind was far from at ease, and that I was well-nigh certain that some foul plot had been woven round him.

"In this sinister way I came into my inheritance. You will ask me why I did not dispose of it? I answer, because I was well convinced that our troubles were in some way dependent upon an incident in my uncle's life, and that the danger would be as pressing in one house as in another.

"It was in January, '85, that my poor father met his end, and two years and eight months have elapsed since then. During that time I have lived happily at Horsham, and I had begun to hope that this curse had passed away from the family, and that it had ended with the last generation. I had begun to take comfort too soon, however; yesterday morning the blow fell in the very shape in which it had come upon my father."

The young man took from his waistcoat a crumpled envelope, and turning to the table he shook out upon it five little dried orange pips.

"This is the envelope," he continued. "The postmark is London—eastern division. Within are the very words which were upon my father's last message: 'K. K. K.'; and then 'Put the papers on the sundial.'"

"What have you done?" asked Holmes.

"Nothing."

"Nothing?"

"To tell the truth"—he sank his face into his thin, white hands—"I have felt helpless. I have felt like one of those poor rabbits when the snake is writhing towards it. I seem to be in the grasp of some resistless, inexorable evil, which no foresight and no precautions can guard against."

"Tut! tut!" cried Sherlock Holmes. "You must act, man, or you are lost. Nothing but energy can save you. This is no time for despair."

"I have seen the police."

"Ah!"

"But they listened to my story with a smile. I am convinced that the inspector has formed the opinion that the letters are all practical jokes, and that the deaths of my relations were really accidents, as the jury stated, and were not to be connected with the warnings."

Holmes shook his clenched hands in the air. "Incredible imbecility!" he cried.

"They have, however, allowed me a policeman, who may remain in the house with me."

"Has he come with you to-night?"

"No. His orders were to stay in the house."

Again Holmes raved in the air.

"Why did you come to me," he cried, "and, above all, why did you not come at once?"

"I did not know. It was only today that I spoke to Major Prendergast about my troubles and was advised by him to come to you."

"It is really two days since you had the letter. We should have acted before this. You have no further evidence, I suppose, than that which you have placed before us—no suggestive detail which might help us?"

"There is one thing," said John Openshaw. He rummaged in his coat pocket, and, drawing out a piece of discoloured, blue-tinted paper, he laid it out upon the table. "I have some remembrance," said he, "that on the day when my uncle burned the papers I observed that the small, unburned margins which lay amid the ashes were of this particular colour. I found this single sheet upon the floor of his room, and I am inclined to think that it may be one of the papers which has, perhaps, fluttered out from among the others, and in that way has escaped destruction. Beyond the mention of pips, I do not see that it helps us much. I think myself that it is a page from some private diary. The writing is undoubtedly my uncle's."

Holmes moved the lamp, and we both bent over the sheet of paper, which showed by its ragged edge that it had indeed been torn from a book. It was headed, "March, 1869," and beneath were the following enigmatical notices:

"4th. Hudson came. Same old platform.

"7th. Set the pips on McCauley, Paramore, and John Swain, of St. Augustine.

"9th. McCauley cleared.

"10th. John Swain cleared.

"12th. Visited Paramore. All well."

"Thank you!" said Holmes, folding up the paper and returning it to our visitor. "And now you must on no account lose another instant. We cannot spare time even to discuss what you have told me. You must get home instantly and act."

"What shall I do?"

"There is but one thing to do. It must be done at once. You must put this piece of paper which you have shown us into the brass box which you have described. You must also put in a note to say that all the other papers were burned by your uncle, and that this is the only one which remains. You must assert that in such words as will carry conviction with them. Having done this, you must at once put the box out upon the sundial, as directed. Do you understand?"

"Entirely."

"Do not think of revenge, or anything of the sort, at present. I think that we may gain that by means of the law; but we have our web to weave, while theirs is already woven. The first consideration is to remove the pressing danger which threatens you. The second is to clear up the mystery and to punish the guilty parties."

"I thank you," said the young man, rising and pulling on his overcoat. "You have given me fresh life and hope. I shall certainly do as you advise."

"Do not lose an instant. And, above all, take care of yourself in the meanwhile, for I do not think that there can be a doubt that you are threatened by a very real and imminent danger. How do you go back?"

"By train from Waterloo."

"It is not yet nine. The streets will be crowded, so I trust that you may be in safety. And yet you cannot guard yourself too closely."

"I am armed."

"That is well. Tomorrow I shall set to work upon your case."

"I shall see you at Horsham, then?"

"No, your secret lies in London. It is there that I shall seek it."

"Then I shall call upon you in a day, or in two days, with news as to the box and the papers. I shall take your advice in every particular." He shook hands with us and took his leave. Outside the wind still screamed and the rain splashed and pattered against the windows. This strange, wild story seemed to have come to us from amid the mad elements—blown in upon us like a sheet of sea-weed in a gale—and now to have been reabsorbed by them once more.

Sherlock Holmes sat for some time in silence, with his head sunk forward and his eyes bent upon the red glow of the fire. Then he lit his pipe, and leaning back in his chair he watched the blue smoke-rings as they chased each other up to the ceiling.

"I think, Watson," he remarked at last, "that of all our cases we have had none more fantastic than this."

"Save, perhaps, the Sign of Four."

"Well, yes. Save, perhaps, that. And yet this John Openshaw seems to me to be walking amid even greater perils than did the Sholtos."

"But have you," I asked, "formed any definite conception as to what these perils are?"

"There can be no question as to their nature," he answered.

"Then what are they? Who is this K. K. K., and why does he pursue this unhappy family?"

Sherlock Holmes closed his eyes and placed his elbows upon the arms of his chair, with his finger-tips together. "The ideal reasoner," he remarked, "would, when he had once been shown a single fact in all its bearings, deduce from it not only all the chain of events which led up to it but also all the results which would follow from it. As Cuvier could correctly describe a whole animal by the contemplation of a single bone, so the observer who has thoroughly understood one link in a series of incidents should be able to accurately state all the other ones, both before and after. We have not yet grasped the results which the reason alone can attain to. Problems may be solved in the study which have baffled all those who have sought a solution by the aid of their senses. To carry the art, however, to its highest pitch, it is necessary that the reasoner should be able to utilise all the facts which have come to his knowledge; and this in itself implies, as you will readily see, a possession of all knowledge, which, even in these days of free education and encyclopaedias, is a somewhat rare accomplishment. It is not so impossible, however, that a man should possess all knowledge which is likely to be useful to him in his work, and this I have endeavoured in my case to do. If I remember rightly, you on one occasion, in the early days of our friendship, defined my limits in a very precise fashion."

"Yes," I answered, laughing. "It was a singular document. Philosophy, astronomy, and politics were marked at zero, I remember. Botany variable, geology profound as regards the mud-stains from any region within fifty miles of town, chemistry eccentric, anatomy unsystematic, sensational literature and crime records unique, violin-player, boxer, swordsman, lawyer, and self-poisoner by cocaine and tobacco. Those, I think, were the main points of my analysis."

Holmes grinned at the last item. "Well," he said, "I say now, as I said then, that a man should keep his little brain-attic stocked with all the furniture that he is likely to use, and the rest he can put away in the lumber-room of his library, where he can get it if he wants it. Now, for such a case as the one which has been submitted to us to-night, we need certainly to muster all our resources. Kindly hand me down the letter K of the 'American Encyclopaedia' which stands upon the shelf beside you. Thank you. Now let us consider the situation and see what may be deduced from it. In the first place, we may start with a strong presumption that Colonel Openshaw had some very strong reason for leaving America. Men at his time of life do not change all their habits and exchange willingly the charming climate of Florida for the lonely life of an English provincial town. His extreme love of solitude in England suggests the idea that he was in fear of someone or something, so we may assume as a working hypothesis that it was fear of someone or something which drove him from America. As to what it was he feared, we can only deduce that by considering the formidable letters which were received by himself and his successors. Did you remark the postmarks of those letters?"

"The first was from Pondicherry, the second from Dundee, and the third from London."

"From East London. What do you deduce from that?"

"They are all seaports. That the writer was on board of a ship."

"Excellent. We have already a clue. There can be no doubt that the probability—the strong probability—is that the writer was on board of a ship. And now let us consider another point. In the case of Pondicherry, seven weeks elapsed between the threat and its fulfilment, in Dundee it was only some three or four days. Does that suggest anything?"

"A greater distance to travel."

"But the letter had also a greater distance to come."

"Then I do not see the point."

"There is at least a presumption that the vessel in which the man or men are is a sailing-ship. It looks as if they always send their singular warning or token before them when starting upon their mission. You see how quickly the deed followed the sign when it came from Dundee. If they had come from Pondicherry in a steamer they would have arrived almost as soon as their letter. But, as a matter of fact, seven weeks elapsed. I think that those seven weeks represented the difference between the mail-boat which brought the letter and the sailing vessel which brought the writer."

"It is possible."

"More than that. It is probable. And now you see the deadly urgency of this new case, and why I urged young Openshaw to caution. The blow has always fallen at the end of the time which it would take the senders to travel the distance. But this one comes from London, and therefore we cannot count upon delay."

"Good God!" I cried. "What can it mean, this relentless persecution?"

"The papers which Openshaw carried are obviously of vital importance to the person or persons in the sailing-ship. I think that it is quite clear that there must be more than one of them. A single man could not have carried out two deaths in such a way as to deceive a coroner's jury. There must have been several in it, and they must have been men of resource and determination. Their papers they mean to have, be the holder of them who it may. In this way you see K. K. K. ceases to be the initials of an individual and becomes the badge of a society."

"But of what society?"

"Have you never—" said Sherlock Holmes, bending forward and sinking his voice—"have you never heard of the Ku Klux Klan?"

"I never have."

Holmes turned over the leaves of the book upon his knee. "Here it is," said he presently:

"'Ku Klux Klan. A name derived from the fanciful resemblance to the sound produced by cocking a rifle. This terrible secret society was formed by some ex-Confederate soldiers in the Southern states after the Civil War, and it rapidly formed local branches in different parts of the country, notably in Tennessee, Louisiana, the Carolinas, Georgia, and Florida. Its power was used for political purposes, principally for the terrorising of the negro voters and the murdering and driving from the country of those who were opposed to its views. Its outrages were usually preceded by a warning sent to the marked man in some fantastic but generally recognised shape—a sprig of oak-leaves in some parts, melon seeds or orange pips in others. On receiving this the victim might either openly abjure his former ways, or might fly from the country. If he braved the matter out, death would unfailingly come upon him, and usually in some strange and unforeseen manner. So perfect was the organisation of the society, and so systematic its methods, that there is hardly a case upon record where any man succeeded in braving it with impunity, or in which any of its outrages were traced home to the perpetrators. For some years the organisation flourished in spite of the efforts of the United States government and of the better classes of the community in the South. Eventually, in the year 1869, the movement rather suddenly collapsed, although there have been sporadic outbreaks of the same sort since that date.'

"You will observe," said Holmes, laying down the volume, "that the sudden breaking up of the society was coincident with the disappearance of Openshaw from America with their papers. It may well have been cause and effect. It is no wonder that he and his family have some of the more implacable spirits upon their track. You can understand that this register and diary may implicate some of the first men in the South, and that there may be many who will not sleep easy at night until it is recovered."

"Then the page we have seen—"

"Is such as we might expect. It ran, if I remember right, 'sent the pips to A, B, and C'—that is, sent the society's warning to them. Then there are successive entries that A and B cleared, or left the country, and finally that C was visited, with, I fear, a sinister result for C. Well, I think, Doctor, that we may let some light into this dark place, and I believe that the only chance young Openshaw has in the meantime is to do what I have told him. There is nothing more to be said or to be done to-night, so hand me over my violin and let us try to forget for half an hour the miserable weather and the still more miserable ways of our fellow-men."

It had cleared in the morning, and the sun was shining with a subdued brightness through the dim veil which hangs over the great city. Sherlock Holmes was already at breakfast when I came down.

"You will excuse me for not waiting for you," said he; "I have, I foresee, a very busy day before me in looking into this case of young Openshaw's."

"What steps will you take?" I asked.

"It will very much depend upon the results of my first inquiries. I may have to go down to Horsham, after all."

"You will not go there first?"

"No, I shall commence with the City. Just ring the bell and the maid will bring up your coffee."

As I waited, I lifted the unopened newspaper from the table and glanced my eye over it. It rested upon a heading which sent a chill to my heart.

"Holmes," I cried, "you are too late."

"Ah!" said he, laying down his cup, "I feared as much. How was it done?" He spoke calmly, but I could see that he was deeply moved.

"My eye caught the name of Openshaw, and the heading 'Tragedy Near Waterloo Bridge.' Here is the account:

"Between nine and ten last night Police-Constable Cook, of the H Division, on duty near Waterloo Bridge, heard a cry for help and a splash in the water. The night, however, was extremely dark and stormy, so that, in spite of the help of several passers-by, it was quite impossible to effect a rescue. The alarm, however, was given, and, by the aid of the water-police, the body was eventually recovered. It proved to be that of a young gentleman whose name, as it appears from an envelope which was found in his pocket, was John Openshaw, and whose residence is near Horsham. It is conjectured that he may have been hurrying down to catch the last train from Waterloo Station, and that in his haste and the extreme darkness he missed his path and walked over the edge of one of the small landing-places for river steamboats. The body exhibited no traces of violence, and there can be no doubt that the deceased had been the victim of an unfortunate accident, which should have the effect of calling the attention of the authorities to the condition of the riverside landing-stages."

We sat in silence for some minutes, Holmes more depressed and shaken than I had ever seen him.

"That hurts my pride, Watson," he said at last. "It is a petty feeling, no doubt, but it hurts my pride. It becomes a personal matter with me now, and, if God sends me health, I shall set my hand upon this gang. That he should come to me for help, and that I should send him away to his death--!" He sprang from his chair and paced about the room in uncontrollable agitation, with a flush upon his sallow cheeks and a nervous clasping and unclasping of his long thin hands.

"They must be cunning devils," he exclaimed at last. "How could they have decoyed him down there? The Embankment is not on the direct line to the station. The bridge, no doubt, was too crowded, even on such a night, for their purpose. Well, Watson, we shall see who will win in the long run. I am going out now!"

"To the police?"

"No; I shall be my own police. When I have spun the web they may take the flies, but not before."

All day I was engaged in my professional work, and it was late in the evening before I returned to Baker Street. Sherlock Holmes had not come back yet. It was nearly ten o'clock before he entered, looking pale and worn. He walked up to the sideboard, and tearing a piece from the loaf he devoured it voraciously, washing it down with a long draught of water.

"You are hungry," I remarked.

"Starving. It had escaped my memory. I have had nothing since breakfast."

"Nothing?"

"Not a bite. I had no time to think of it."

"And how have you succeeded?"

"Well."

"You have a clue?"

"I have them in the hollow of my hand. Young Openshaw shall not long remain unavenged. Why, Watson, let us put their own devilish trade-mark upon them. It is well thought of!"

"What do you mean?"

He took an orange from the cupboard, and tearing it to pieces he squeezed out the pips upon the table. Of these he took five and thrust them into an envelope. On the inside of the flap he wrote "S. H. for J. O." Then he sealed it and addressed it to "Captain James Calhoun, Barque 'Lone Star,' Savannah, Georgia."

"That will await him when he enters port," said he, chuckling. "It may give him a sleepless night. He will find it as sure a precursor of his fate as Openshaw did before him."

"And who is this Captain Calhoun?"

"The leader of the gang. I shall have the others, but he first."

"How did you trace it, then?"

He took a large sheet of paper from his pocket, all covered with dates and names.

"I have spent the whole day," said he, "over Lloyd's registers and files of the old papers, following the future career of every vessel which touched at Pondicherry in January and February in '83. There were thirty-six ships of fair tonnage which were reported there during those months. Of these, one, the 'Lone Star,' instantly attracted my attention, since, although it was reported as having cleared from London, the name is that which is given to one of the states of the Union."

"Texas, I think."

"I was not and am not sure which; but I knew that the ship must have an American origin."

"What then?"

"I searched the Dundee records, and when I found that the barque 'Lone Star' was there in January, '85, my suspicion became a certainty. I then inquired as to the vessels which lay at present in the port of London."

"Yes?"

"The 'Lone Star' had arrived here last week. I went down to the Albert Dock and found that she had been taken down the river by the early tide this morning, homeward bound to Savannah. I wired to Gravesend and learned that she had passed some time ago, and as the wind is easterly I have no doubt that she is now past the Goodwins and not very far from the Isle of Wight."

"What will you do, then?"

"Oh, I have my hand upon him. He and the two mates, are as I learn, the only native-born Americans in the ship. The others are Finns and Germans. I know, also, that they were all three away from the ship last night. I had it from the stevedore who has been loading their cargo. By the time that their sailing-ship reaches Savannah the mail-boat will have carried this letter, and the cable will have informed the police of Savannah that these three gentlemen are badly wanted here upon a charge of murder."

There is ever a flaw, however, in the best laid of human plans, and the murderers of John Openshaw were never to receive the orange pips which would show them that another, as cunning and as resolute as themselves, was upon their track. Very long and very severe were the equinoctial gales that year. We waited long for news of the "Lone Star" of Savannah, but none ever reached us. We did at last hear that somewhere far out in the Atlantic a shattered stern-post of a boat was seen swinging in the trough of a wave, with the letters "L. S." carved upon it, and that is all which we shall ever know of the fate of the "Lone Star."

Adventure VI. The Man With The Twisted Lip

Isa Whitney, brother of the late Elias Whitney, D.D., Principal of the Theological College of St. George's, was much addicted to opium. The habit grew upon him, as I understand, from some foolish freak when he was at college; for having read De Quincey's description of his dreams and sensations, he had drenched his tobacco with laudanum in an attempt to produce the same effects. He found, as so many more have done, that the practice is easier to attain than to get rid of, and for many years he continued to be a slave to the drug, an object of mingled horror and pity to his friends and relatives. I can see him now, with yellow, pasty face, drooping lids, and pin-point pupils, all huddled in a chair, the wreck and ruin of a noble man.

One night—it was in June, '89--there came a ring to my bell, about the hour when a man gives his first yawn and glances at the clock. I sat up in my chair, and my wife laid her needle-work down in her lap and made a little face of disappointment.

"A patient!" said she. "You'll have to go out."

I groaned, for I was newly come back from a weary day.

We heard the door open, a few hurried words, and then quick steps upon the linoleum. Our own door flew open, and a lady, clad in some dark-coloured stuff, with a black veil, entered the room.

"You will excuse my calling so late," she began, and then, suddenly losing her self-control, she ran forward, threw her arms about my wife's neck, and sobbed upon her shoulder. "Oh, I'm in such trouble!" she cried; "I do so want a little help."

"Why," said my wife, pulling up her veil, "it is Kate Whitney. How you startled me, Kate! I had not an idea who you were when you came in."

"I didn't know what to do, so I came straight to you." That was always the way. Folk who were in grief came to my wife like birds to a light-house.

"It was very sweet of you to come. Now, you must have some wine and water, and sit here comfortably and tell us all about it. Or should you rather that I sent James off to bed?"

"Oh, no, no! I want the doctor's advice and help, too. It's about Isa. He has not been home for two days. I am so frightened about him!"

It was not the first time that she had spoken to us of her husband's trouble, to me as a doctor, to my wife as an old friend and school companion. We soothed and comforted her by such words as we could find. Did she know where her husband was? Was it possible that we could bring him back to her?

It seems that it was. She had the surest information that of late he had, when the fit was on him, made use of an opium den in the farthest east of the City. Hitherto his orgies had always been confined to one day, and he had come back, twitching and shattered, in the evening. But now the spell had been upon him eight-and-forty hours, and he lay there, doubtless among the dregs of the docks, breathing in the poison or sleeping off the effects. There he was to be found, she was sure of it, at the Bar of Gold, in Upper Swandam Lane. But what was she to do? How could she, a young and timid woman, make her way into such a place and pluck her husband out from among the ruffians who surrounded him?

There was the case, and of course there was but one way out of it. Might I not escort her to this place? And then, as a second thought, why should she come at all? I was Isa Whitney's medical adviser, and as such I had influence over him. I could manage it better if I were alone. I promised her on my word that I would send him home in a cab within two hours if he were indeed at the address which she had given me. And so in ten minutes I had left my armchair and cheery sitting-room behind me, and was speeding eastward in a hansom on a strange errand, as it seemed to me at the time, though the future only could show how strange it was to be.

But there was no great difficulty in the first stage of my adventure. Upper Swandam Lane is a vile alley lurking behind the high wharves which line the north side of the river to the east of London Bridge. Between a slop-shop and a gin-shop, approached by a steep flight of steps leading down to a black gap like the mouth of a cave, I found the den of which I was in search. Ordering my cab to wait, I passed down the steps, worn hollow in the centre by the ceaseless tread of drunken feet; and by the light of a flickering oil-lamp above the door I found the latch and made my way into a long, low room, thick and heavy with the brown opium smoke, and terraced with wooden berths, like the forecastle of an emigrant ship.

Through the gloom one could dimly catch a glimpse of bodies lying in strange fantastic poses, bowed shoulders, bent knees, heads thrown back, and chins pointing upward, with here and there a dark, lack-lustre eye turned upon the newcomer. Out of the black shadows there glimmered little red circles of light, now bright, now faint, as the burning poison waxed or waned in the bowls of the metal pipes. The most lay silent, but some muttered to themselves, and others talked together in a strange, low, monotonous voice, their conversation coming in gushes, and then suddenly tailing off into silence, each mumbling out his own thoughts and paying little heed to the words of his neighbour. At the farther end was a small brazier of burning charcoal, beside which on a three-legged wooden stool there sat a tall, thin old man, with his jaw resting upon his two fists, and his elbows upon his knees, staring into the fire.

As I entered, a sallow Malay attendant had hurried up with a pipe for me and a supply of the drug, beckoning me to an empty berth.

"Thank you. I have not come to stay," said I. "There is a friend of mine here, Mr. Isa Whitney, and I wish to speak with him."

There was a movement and an exclamation from my right, and peering through the gloom, I saw Whitney, pale, haggard, and unkempt, staring out at me.

"My God! It's Watson," said he. He was in a pitiable state of reaction, with every nerve in a twitter. "I say, Watson, what o'clock is it?"

"Nearly eleven."

"Of what day?"

"Of Friday, June 19th."

"Good heavens! I thought it was Wednesday. It is Wednesday. What d'you want to frighten a chap for?" He sank his face onto his arms and began to sob in a high treble key.

"I tell you that it is Friday, man. Your wife has been waiting this two days for you. You should be ashamed of yourself!"

"So I am. But you've got mixed, Watson, for I have only been here a few hours, three pipes, four pipes—I forget how many. But I'll go home with you. I wouldn't frighten Kate—poor little Kate. Give me your hand! Have you a cab?"

"Yes, I have one waiting."

"Then I shall go in it. But I must owe something. Find what I owe, Watson. I am all off colour. I can do nothing for myself."

I walked down the narrow passage between the double row of sleepers, holding my breath to keep out the vile, stupefying fumes of the drug, and looking about for the manager. As I passed the tall man who sat by the brazier I felt a sudden pluck at my skirt, and a low voice whispered, "Walk past me, and then look back at me." The words fell quite distinctly upon my ear. I glanced down. They could only have come from the old man at my side, and yet he sat now as absorbed as ever, very thin, very wrinkled, bent with age, an opium pipe dangling down from between his knees, as though it had dropped in sheer lassitude from his fingers. I took two steps forward and looked back. It took all my self-control to prevent me from breaking out into a cry of astonishment. He had turned his back so that none could see him but I. His form had filled out, his wrinkles were gone, the dull eyes had regained their fire, and there, sitting by the fire and grinning at my surprise, was none other than Sherlock Holmes. He made a slight motion to me to approach him, and instantly, as he turned his face half round to the company once more, subsided into a doddering, loose-lipped senility.

"Holmes!" I whispered, "what on earth are you doing in this den?"

"As low as you can," he answered; "I have excellent ears. If you would have the great kindness to get rid of that sottish friend of yours I should be exceedingly glad to have a little talk with you."

"I have a cab outside."

"Then pray send him home in it. You may safely trust him, for he appears to be too limp to get into any mischief. I should recommend you also to send a note by the cabman to your wife to say that you have thrown in your lot with me. If you will wait outside, I shall be with you in five minutes."

It was difficult to refuse any of Sherlock Holmes' requests, for they were always so exceedingly definite, and put forward with such a quiet air of mastery. I felt, however, that when Whitney was once confined in the cab my mission was practically accomplished; and for the rest, I could not wish anything better than to be associated with my friend in one of those singular adventures which were the normal condition of his existence. In a few minutes I had written my note, paid Whitney's bill, led him out to the cab, and seen him driven through the darkness. In a very short time a decrepit figure had emerged from the opium den, and I was walking down the street with Sherlock Holmes. For two streets he shuffled along with a bent back and an uncertain foot. Then, glancing quickly round, he straightened himself out and burst into a hearty fit of laughter.

"I suppose, Watson," said he, "that you imagine that I have added opium-smoking to cocaine injections, and all the other little weaknesses on which you have favoured me with your medical views."

"I was certainly surprised to find you there."

"But not more so than I to find you."

"I came to find a friend."

"And I to find an enemy."

"An enemy?"

"Yes; one of my natural enemies, or, shall I say, my natural prey. Briefly, Watson, I am in the midst of a very remarkable inquiry, and I have hoped to find a clue in the incoherent ramblings of these sots, as I have done before now. Had I been recognised in that den my life would not have been worth an hour's purchase; for I have used it before now for my own purposes, and the rascally Lascar who runs it has sworn to have vengeance upon me. There is a trap-door at the back of that building, near the corner of Paul's Wharf, which could tell some strange tales of what has passed through it upon the moonless nights."

"What! You do not mean bodies?"

"Ay, bodies, Watson. We should be rich men if we had 1000 pounds for every poor devil who has been done to death in that den. It is the vilest murder-trap on the whole riverside, and I fear that Neville St. Clair has entered it never to leave it more. But our trap should be here." He put his two forefingers between his teeth and whistled shrilly—a signal which was answered by a similar whistle from the distance, followed shortly by the rattle of wheels and the clink of horses' hoofs.

"Now, Watson," said Holmes, as a tall dog-cart dashed up through the gloom, throwing out two golden tunnels of yellow light from its side lanterns. "You'll come with me, won't you?"

"If I can be of use."

"Oh, a trusty comrade is always of use; and a chronicler still more so. My room at The Cedars is a double-bedded one."

"The Cedars?"

"Yes; that is Mr. St. Clair's house. I am staying there while I conduct the inquiry."

"Where is it, then?"

"Near Lee, in Kent. We have a seven-mile drive before us."

"But I am all in the dark."

"Of course you are. You'll know all about it presently. Jump up here. All right, John; we shall not need you. Here's half a crown. Look out for me tomorrow, about eleven. Give her her head. So long, then!"

He flicked the horse with his whip, and we dashed away through the endless succession of sombre and deserted streets, which widened gradually, until we were flying across a broad balustraded bridge, with the murky river flowing sluggishly beneath us. Beyond lay another dull wilderness of bricks and mortar, its silence broken only by the heavy, regular footfall of the policeman, or the songs and shouts of some belated party of revellers. A dull wrack was drifting slowly across the sky, and a star or two twinkled dimly here and there through the rifts of the clouds. Holmes drove in silence, with his head sunk upon his breast, and the air of a man who is lost in thought, while I sat beside him, curious to learn what this new quest might be which seemed to tax his powers so sorely, and yet afraid to break in upon the current of his thoughts. We had driven several miles, and were beginning to get to the fringe of the belt of suburban villas, when he shook himself, shrugged his shoulders, and lit up his pipe with the air of a man who has satisfied himself that he is acting for the best.

"You have a grand gift of silence, Watson," said he. "It makes you quite invaluable as a companion. 'Pon my word, it is a great thing for me to have someone to talk to, for my own thoughts are not over-pleasant. I was wondering what I should say to this dear little woman to-night when she meets me at the door."

"You forget that I know nothing about it."

"I shall just have time to tell you the facts of the case before we get to Lee. It seems absurdly simple, and yet, somehow I can get nothing to go upon. There's plenty of thread, no doubt, but I can't get the end of it into my hand. Now, I'll state the case clearly and concisely to you, Watson, and maybe you can see a spark where all is dark to me."

"Proceed, then."

"Some years ago—to be definite, in May, 1884--there came to Lee a gentleman, Neville St. Clair by name, who appeared to have plenty of money. He took a large villa, laid out the grounds very nicely, and lived generally in good style. By degrees he made friends in the neighbourhood, and in 1887 he married the daughter of a local brewer, by whom he now has two children. He had no occupation, but was interested in several companies and went into town as a rule in the morning, returning by the 5:14 from Cannon Street every night. Mr. St. Clair is now thirty-seven years of age, is a man of temperate habits, a good husband, a very affectionate father, and a man who is popular with all who know him. I may add that his whole debts at the present moment, as far as we have been able to ascertain, amount to 88 pounds 10s., while he has 220 pounds standing to his credit in the Capital and Counties Bank. There is no reason, therefore, to think that money troubles have been weighing upon his mind.

"Last Monday Mr. Neville St. Clair went into town rather earlier than usual, remarking before he started that he had two important commissions to perform, and that he would bring his little boy home a box of bricks. Now, by the merest chance, his wife received a telegram upon this same Monday, very shortly after his departure, to the effect that a small parcel of considerable value which she had been expecting was waiting for her at the offices of the Aberdeen Shipping Company. Now, if you are well up in your London, you will know that the office of the company is in Fresno Street, which branches out of Upper Swandam Lane, where you found me to-night. Mrs. St. Clair had her lunch, started for the City, did some shopping, proceeded to the company's office, got her packet, and found herself at exactly 4:35 walking through Swandam Lane on her way back to the station. Have you followed me so far?"

"It is very clear."

"If you remember, Monday was an exceedingly hot day, and Mrs. St. Clair walked slowly, glancing about in the hope of seeing a cab, as she did not like the neighbourhood in which she found herself. While she was walking in this way down Swandam Lane, she suddenly heard an ejaculation or cry, and was struck cold to see her husband looking down at her and, as it seemed to her, beckoning to her from a second-floor window. The window was open, and she distinctly saw his face, which she describes as being terribly agitated. He waved his hands frantically to her, and then vanished from the window so suddenly that it seemed to her that he had been plucked back by some irresistible force from behind. One singular point which struck her quick feminine eye was that although he wore some dark coat, such as he had started to town in, he had on neither collar nor necktie.

"Convinced that something was amiss with him, she rushed down the steps—for the house was none other than the opium den in which you found me to-night—and running through the front room she attempted to ascend the stairs which led to the first floor. At the foot of the stairs, however, she met this Lascar scoundrel of whom I have spoken, who thrust her back and, aided by a Dane, who acts as assistant there, pushed her out into the street. Filled with the most maddening doubts and fears, she rushed down the lane and, by rare good-fortune, met in Fresno Street a number of constables with an inspector, all on their way to their beat. The inspector and two men accompanied her back, and in spite of the continued resistance of the proprietor, they made their way to the room in which Mr. St. Clair had last been seen. There was no sign of him there. In fact, in the whole of that floor there was no one to be found save a crippled wretch of hideous aspect, who, it seems, made his home there. Both he and the Lascar stoutly swore that no one else had been in the front room during the afternoon. So determined was their denial that the inspector was staggered, and had almost come to believe that Mrs. St. Clair had been deluded when, with a cry, she sprang at a small deal box which lay upon the table and tore the lid from it. Out there fell a cascade of children's bricks. It was the toy which he had promised to bring home.

"This discovery, and the evident confusion which the cripple showed, made the inspector realise that the matter was serious. The rooms were carefully examined, and results all pointed to an abominable crime. The front room was plainly furnished as a sitting-room and led into a small bedroom, which looked out upon the back of one of the wharves. Between the wharf and the bedroom window is a narrow strip, which is dry at low tide but is covered at high tide with at least four and a half feet of water. The bedroom window was a broad one and opened from below. On examination traces of blood were to be seen upon the windowsill, and several scattered drops were visible upon the wooden floor of the bedroom. Thrust away behind a curtain in the front room were all the clothes of Mr. Neville St. Clair, with the exception of his coat. His boots, his socks, his hat, and his watch—all were there. There were no signs of violence upon any of these garments, and there were no other traces of Mr. Neville St. Clair. Out of the window he must apparently have gone for no other exit could be discovered, and the ominous bloodstains upon the sill gave little promise that he could save himself by swimming, for the tide was at its very highest at the moment of the tragedy.

"And now as to the villains who seemed to be immediately implicated in the matter. The Lascar was known to be a man of the vilest antecedents, but as, by Mrs. St. Clair's story, he was known to have been at the foot of the stair within a very few seconds of her husband's appearance at the window, he could hardly have been more than an accessory to the crime. His defence was one of absolute ignorance, and he protested that he had no knowledge as to the doings of Hugh Boone, his lodger, and that he could not account in any way for the presence of the missing gentleman's clothes.

"So much for the Lascar manager. Now for the sinister cripple who lives upon the second floor of the opium den, and who was certainly the last human being whose eyes rested upon Neville St. Clair. His name is Hugh Boone, and his hideous face is one which is familiar to every man who goes much to the City. He is a professional beggar, though in order to avoid the police regulations he pretends to a small trade in wax vestas. Some little distance down Threadneedle Street, upon the left-hand side, there is, as you may have remarked, a small angle in the wall. Here it is that this creature takes his daily seat, cross-legged with his tiny stock of matches on his lap, and as he is a piteous spectacle a small rain of charity descends into the greasy leather cap which lies upon the pavement beside him. I have watched the fellow more than once before ever I thought of making his professional acquaintance, and I have been surprised at the harvest which he has reaped in a short time. His appearance, you see, is so remarkable that no one can pass him without observing him. A shock of orange hair, a pale face disfigured by a horrible scar, which, by its contraction, has turned up the outer edge of his upper lip, a bulldog chin, and a pair of very penetrating dark eyes, which present a singular contrast to the colour of his hair, all mark him out from amid the common crowd of mendicants and so, too, does his wit, for he is ever ready with a reply to any piece of chaff which may be thrown at him by the passers-by. This is the man whom we now learn to have been the lodger at the opium den, and to have been the last man to see the gentleman of whom we are in quest."

"But a cripple!" said I. "What could he have done single-handed against a man in the prime of life?"

"He is a cripple in the sense that he walks with a limp; but in other respects he appears to be a powerful and well-nurtured man. Surely your medical experience would tell you, Watson, that weakness in one limb is often compensated for by exceptional strength in the others."

"Pray continue your narrative."

"Mrs. St. Clair had fainted at the sight of the blood upon the window, and she was escorted home in a cab by the police, as her presence could be of no help to them in their investigations. Inspector Barton, who had charge of the case, made a very careful examination of the premises, but without finding anything which threw any light upon the matter. One mistake had been made in not arresting Boone instantly, as he was allowed some few minutes during which he might have communicated with his friend the Lascar, but this fault was soon remedied, and he was seized and searched, without anything being found which could incriminate him. There were, it is true, some blood-stains upon his right shirt-sleeve, but he pointed to his ring-finger, which had been cut near the nail, and explained that the bleeding came from there, adding that he had been to the window not long before, and that the stains which had been observed there came doubtless from the same source. He denied strenuously having ever seen Mr. Neville St. Clair and swore that the presence of the clothes in his room was as much a mystery to him as to the police. As to Mrs. St. Clair's assertion that she had actually seen her husband at the window, he declared that she must have been either mad or dreaming. He was removed, loudly protesting, to the police-station, while the inspector remained upon the premises in the hope that the ebbing tide might afford some fresh clue.

"And it did, though they hardly found upon the mud-bank what they had feared to find. It was Neville St. Clair's coat, and not Neville St. Clair, which lay uncovered as the tide receded. And what do you think they found in the pockets?"

"I cannot imagine."

"No, I don't think you would guess. Every pocket stuffed with pennies and half-pennies--421 pennies and 270 half-pennies. It was no wonder that it had not been swept away by the tide. But a human body is a different matter. There is a fierce eddy between the wharf and the house. It seemed likely enough that the weighted coat had remained when the stripped body had been sucked away into the river."

"But I understand that all the other clothes were found in the room. Would the body be dressed in a coat alone?"

"No, sir, but the facts might be met speciously enough. Suppose that this man Boone had thrust Neville St. Clair through the window, there is no human eye which could have seen the deed. What would he do then? It would of course instantly strike him that he must get rid of the tell-tale garments. He would seize the coat, then, and be in the act of throwing it out, when it would occur to him that it would swim and not sink. He has little time, for he has heard the scuffle downstairs when the wife tried to force her way up, and perhaps he has already heard from his Lascar confederate that the police are hurrying up the street. There is not an instant to be lost. He rushes to some secret hoard, where he has accumulated the fruits of his beggary, and he stuffs all the coins upon which he can lay his hands into the pockets to make sure of the coat's sinking. He throws it out, and would have done the same with the other garments had not he heard the rush of steps below, and only just had time to close the window when the police appeared."

"It certainly sounds feasible."

"Well, we will take it as a working hypothesis for want of a better. Boone, as I have told you, was arrested and taken to the station, but it could not be shown that there had ever before been anything against him. He had for years been known as a professional beggar, but his life appeared to have been a very quiet and innocent one. There the matter stands at present, and the questions which have to be solved—what Neville St. Clair was doing in the opium den, what happened to him when there, where is he now, and what Hugh Boone had to do with his disappearance—are all as far from a solution as ever. I confess that I cannot recall any case within my experience which looked at the first glance so simple and yet which presented such difficulties."

While Sherlock Holmes had been detailing this singular series of events, we had been whirling through the outskirts of the great town until the last straggling houses had been left behind, and we rattled along with a country hedge upon either side of us. Just as he finished, however, we drove through two scattered villages, where a few lights still glimmered in the windows.

"We are on the outskirts of Lee," said my companion. "We have touched on three English counties in our short drive, starting in Middlesex, passing over an angle of Surrey, and ending in Kent. See that light among the trees? That is The Cedars, and beside that lamp sits a woman whose anxious ears have already, I have little doubt, caught the clink of our horse's feet."

"But why are you not conducting the case from Baker Street?" I asked.

"Because there are many inquiries which must be made out here. Mrs. St. Clair has most kindly put two rooms at my disposal, and you may rest assured that she will have nothing but a welcome for my friend and colleague. I hate to meet her, Watson, when I have no news of her husband. Here we are. Whoa, there, whoa!"

We had pulled up in front of a large villa which stood within its own grounds. A stable-boy had run out to the horse's head, and springing down, I followed Holmes up the small, winding gravel-drive which led to the house. As we approached, the door flew open, and a little blonde woman stood in the opening, clad in some sort of light mousseline de soie, with a touch of fluffy pink chiffon at her neck and wrists. She stood with her figure outlined against the flood of light, one hand upon the door, one half-raised in her eagerness, her body slightly bent, her head and face protruded, with eager eyes and parted lips, a standing question.

"Well?" she cried, "well?" And then, seeing that there were two of us, she gave a cry of hope which sank into a groan as she saw that my companion shook his head and shrugged his shoulders.

"No good news?"

"None."

"No bad?"

"No."

"Thank God for that. But come in. You must be weary, for you have had a long day."

"This is my friend, Dr. Watson. He has been of most vital use to me in several of my cases, and a lucky chance has made it possible for me to bring him out and associate him with this investigation."

"I am delighted to see you," said she, pressing my hand warmly. "You will, I am sure, forgive anything that may be wanting in our arrangements, when you consider the blow which has come so suddenly upon us."

"My dear madam," said I, "I am an old campaigner, and if I were not I can very well see that no apology is needed. If I can be of any assistance, either to you or to my friend here, I shall be indeed happy."

"Now, Mr. Sherlock Holmes," said the lady as we entered a well-lit dining-room, upon the table of which a cold supper had been laid out, "I should very much like to ask you one or two plain questions, to which I beg that you will give a plain answer."

"Certainly, madam."

"Do not trouble about my feelings. I am not hysterical, nor given to fainting. I simply wish to hear your real, real opinion."

"Upon what point?"

"In your heart of hearts, do you think that Neville is alive?"

Sherlock Holmes seemed to be embarrassed by the question. "Frankly, now!" she repeated, standing upon the rug and looking keenly down at him as he leaned back in a basket-chair.

"Frankly, then, madam, I do not."

"You think that he is dead?"

"I do."

"Murdered?"

"I don't say that. Perhaps."

"And on what day did he meet his death?"

"On Monday."

"Then perhaps, Mr. Holmes, you will be good enough to explain how it is that I have received a letter from him today."

Sherlock Holmes sprang out of his chair as if he had been galvanised.

"What!" he roared.

"Yes, today." She stood smiling, holding up a little slip of paper in the air.

"May I see it?"

"Certainly."

He snatched it from her in his eagerness, and smoothing it out upon the table he drew over the lamp and examined it intently. I had left my chair and was gazing at it over his shoulder. The envelope was a very coarse one and was stamped with the Gravesend postmark and with the date of that very day, or rather of the day before, for it was considerably after midnight.

"Coarse writing," murmured Holmes. "Surely this is not your husband's writing, madam."

"No, but the enclosure is."

"I perceive also that whoever addressed the envelope had to go and inquire as to the address."

"How can you tell that?"

"The name, you see, is in perfectly black ink, which has dried itself. The rest is of the greyish colour, which shows that blotting-paper has been used. If it had been written straight off, and then blotted, none would be of a deep black shade. This man has written the name, and there has then been a pause before he wrote the address, which can only mean that he was not familiar with it. It is, of course, a trifle, but there is nothing so important as trifles. Let us now see the letter. Ha! there has been an enclosure here!"

"Yes, there was a ring. His signet-ring."

"And you are sure that this is your husband's hand?"

"One of his hands."

"One?"

"His hand when he wrote hurriedly. It is very unlike his usual writing, and yet I know it well."

"'Dearest do not be frightened. All will come well. There is a huge error which it may take some little time to rectify. Wait in patience.—NEVILLE.' Written in pencil upon the fly-leaf of a book, octavo size, no water-mark. Hum! Posted today in Gravesend by a man with a dirty thumb. Ha! And the flap has been gummed, if I am not very much in error, by a person who had been chewing tobacco. And you have no doubt that it is your husband's hand, madam?"

"None. Neville wrote those words."

"And they were posted today at Gravesend. Well, Mrs. St. Clair, the clouds lighten, though I should not venture to say that the danger is over."

"But he must be alive, Mr. Holmes."

"Unless this is a clever forgery to put us on the wrong scent. The ring, after all, proves nothing. It may have been taken from him."

"No, no; it is, it is his very own writing!"

"Very well. It may, however, have been written on Monday and only posted today."

"That is possible."

"If so, much may have happened between."

"Oh, you must not discourage me, Mr. Holmes. I know that all is well with him. There is so keen a sympathy between us that I should know if evil came upon him. On the very day that I saw him last he cut himself in the bedroom, and yet I in the dining-room rushed upstairs instantly with the utmost certainty that something had happened. Do you think that I would respond to such a trifle and yet be ignorant of his death?"

"I have seen too much not to know that the impression of a woman may be more valuable than the conclusion of an analytical reasoner. And in this letter you certainly have a very strong piece of evidence to corroborate your view. But if your husband is alive and able to write letters, why should he remain away from you?"

"I cannot imagine. It is unthinkable."

"And on Monday he made no remarks before leaving you?"

"No."

"And you were surprised to see him in Swandam Lane?"

"Very much so."

"Was the window open?"

"Yes."

"Then he might have called to you?"

"He might."

"He only, as I understand, gave an inarticulate cry?"

"Yes."

"A call for help, you thought?"

"Yes. He waved his hands."

"But it might have been a cry of surprise. Astonishment at the unexpected sight of you might cause him to throw up his hands?"

"It is possible."

"And you thought he was pulled back?"

"He disappeared so suddenly."

"He might have leaped back. You did not see anyone else in the room?"

"No, but this horrible man confessed to having been there, and the Lascar was at the foot of the stairs."

"Quite so. Your husband, as far as you could see, had his ordinary clothes on?"

"But without his collar or tie. I distinctly saw his bare throat."

"Had he ever spoken of Swandam Lane?"

"Never."

"Had he ever showed any signs of having taken opium?"

"Never."

"Thank you, Mrs. St. Clair. Those are the principal points about which I wished to be absolutely clear. We shall now have a little supper and then retire, for we may have a very busy day tomorrow."

A large and comfortable double-bedded room had been placed at our disposal, and I was quickly between the sheets, for I was weary after my night of adventure. Sherlock Holmes was a man, however, who, when he had an unsolved problem upon his mind, would go for days, and even for a week, without rest, turning it over, rearranging his facts, looking at it from every point of view until he had either fathomed it or convinced himself that his data were insufficient. It was soon evident to me that he was now preparing for an all-night sitting. He took off his coat and waistcoat, put on a large blue dressing-gown, and then wandered about the room collecting pillows from his bed and cushions from the sofa and armchairs. With these he constructed a sort of Eastern divan, upon which he perched himself cross-legged, with an ounce of shag tobacco and a box of matches laid out in front of him. In the dim light of the lamp I saw him sitting there, an old briar pipe between his lips, his eyes fixed vacantly upon the corner of the ceiling, the blue smoke curling up from him, silent, motionless, with the light shining upon his strong-set aquiline features. So he sat as I dropped off to sleep, and so he sat when a sudden ejaculation caused me to wake up, and I found the summer sun shining into the apartment. The pipe was still between his lips, the smoke still curled upward, and the room was full of a dense tobacco haze, but nothing remained of the heap of shag which I had seen upon the previous night.

"Awake, Watson?" he asked.

"Yes."

"Game for a morning drive?"

"Certainly."

"Then dress. No one is stirring yet, but I know where the stable-boy sleeps, and we shall soon have the trap out." He chuckled to himself as he spoke, his eyes twinkled, and he seemed a different man to the sombre thinker of the previous night.

As I dressed I glanced at my watch. It was no wonder that no one was stirring. It was twenty-five minutes past four. I had hardly finished when Holmes returned with the news that the boy was putting in the horse.

"I want to test a little theory of mine," said he, pulling on his boots. "I think, Watson, that you are now standing in the presence of one of the most absolute fools in Europe. I deserve to be kicked from here to Charing Cross. But I think I have the key of the affair now."

"And where is it?" I asked, smiling.

"In the bathroom," he answered. "Oh, yes, I am not joking," he continued, seeing my look of incredulity. "I have just been there, and I have taken it out, and I have got it in this Gladstone bag. Come on, my boy, and we shall see whether it will not fit the lock."

We made our way downstairs as quietly as possible, and out into the bright morning sunshine. In the road stood our horse and trap, with the half-clad stable-boy waiting at the head. We both sprang in, and away we dashed down the London Road. A few country carts were stirring, bearing in vegetables to the metropolis, but the lines of villas on either side were as silent and lifeless as some city in a dream.

"It has been in some points a singular case," said Holmes, flicking the horse on into a gallop. "I confess that I have been as blind as a mole, but it is better to learn wisdom late than never to learn it at all."

In town the earliest risers were just beginning to look sleepily from their windows as we drove through the streets of the Surrey side. Passing down the Waterloo Bridge Road we crossed over the river, and dashing up Wellington Street wheeled sharply to the right and found ourselves in Bow Street. Sherlock Holmes was well known to the force, and the two constables at the door saluted him. One of them held the horse's head while the other led us in.

"Who is on duty?" asked Holmes.

"Inspector Bradstreet, sir."

"Ah, Bradstreet, how are you?" A tall, stout official had come down the stone-flagged passage, in a peaked cap and frogged jacket. "I wish to have a quiet word with you, Bradstreet." "Certainly, Mr. Holmes. Step into my room here." It was a small, office-like room, with a huge ledger upon the table, and a telephone projecting from the wall. The inspector sat down at his desk.

"What can I do for you, Mr. Holmes?"

"I called about that beggarman, Boone—the one who was charged with being concerned in the disappearance of Mr. Neville St. Clair, of Lee."

"Yes. He was brought up and remanded for further inquiries."

"So I heard. You have him here?"

"In the cells."

"Is he quiet?"

"Oh, he gives no trouble. But he is a dirty scoundrel."

"Dirty?"

"Yes, it is all we can do to make him wash his hands, and his face is as black as a tinker's. Well, when once his case has been settled, he will have a regular prison bath; and I think, if you saw him, you would agree with me that he needed it."

"I should like to see him very much."

"Would you? That is easily done. Come this way. You can leave your bag."

"No, I think that I'll take it."

"Very good. Come this way, if you please." He led us down a passage, opened a barred door, passed down a winding stair, and brought us to a whitewashed corridor with a line of doors on each side.

"The third on the right is his," said the inspector. "Here it is!" He quietly shot back a panel in the upper part of the door and glanced through.

"He is asleep," said he. "You can see him very well."

We both put our eyes to the grating. The prisoner lay with his face towards us, in a very deep sleep, breathing slowly and heavily. He was a middle-sized man, coarsely clad as became his calling, with a coloured shirt protruding through the rent in his tattered coat. He was, as the inspector had said, extremely dirty, but the grime which covered his face could not conceal its repulsive ugliness. A broad wheal from an old scar ran right across it from eye to chin, and by its contraction had turned up one side of the upper lip, so that three teeth were exposed in a perpetual snarl. A shock of very bright red hair grew low over his eyes and forehead.

"He's a beauty, isn't he?" said the inspector.

"He certainly needs a wash," remarked Holmes. "I had an idea that he might, and I took the liberty of bringing the tools with me." He opened the Gladstone bag as he spoke, and took out, to my astonishment, a very large bath-sponge.

"He! he! You are a funny one," chuckled the inspector.

"Now, if you will have the great goodness to open that door very quietly, we will soon make him cut a much more respectable figure."

"Well, I don't know why not," said the inspector. "He doesn't look a credit to the Bow Street cells, does he?" He slipped his key into the lock, and we all very quietly entered the cell. The sleeper half turned, and then settled down once more into a deep slumber. Holmes stooped to the water-jug, moistened his sponge, and then rubbed it twice vigorously across and down the prisoner's face.

"Let me introduce you," he shouted, "to Mr. Neville St. Clair, of Lee, in the county of Kent."

Never in my life have I seen such a sight. The man's face peeled off under the sponge like the bark from a tree. Gone was the coarse brown tint! Gone, too, was the horrid scar which had seamed it across, and the twisted lip which had given the repulsive sneer to the face! A twitch brought away the tangled red hair, and there, sitting up in his bed, was a pale, sad-faced, refined-looking man, black-haired and smooth-skinned, rubbing his eyes and staring about him with sleepy bewilderment. Then suddenly realising the exposure, he broke into a scream and threw himself down with his face to the pillow.

"Great heavens!" cried the inspector, "it is, indeed, the missing man. I know him from the photograph."

The prisoner turned with the reckless air of a man who abandons himself to his destiny. "Be it so," said he. "And pray what am I charged with?"

"With making away with Mr. Neville St.—Oh, come, you can't be charged with that unless they make a case of attempted suicide of it," said the inspector with a grin. "Well, I have been twenty-seven years in the force, but this really takes the cake."

"If I am Mr. Neville St. Clair, then it is obvious that no crime has been committed, and that, therefore, I am illegally detained."

"No crime, but a very great error has been committed," said Holmes. "You would have done better to have trusted you wife."

"It was not the wife; it was the children," groaned the prisoner. "God help me, I would not have them ashamed of their father. My God! What an exposure! What can I do?"

Sherlock Holmes sat down beside him on the couch and patted him kindly on the shoulder.

"If you leave it to a court of law to clear the matter up," said he, "of course you can hardly avoid publicity. On the other hand, if you convince the police authorities that there is no possible case against you, I do not know that there is any reason that the details should find their way into the papers. Inspector Bradstreet would, I am sure, make notes upon anything which you might tell us and submit it to the proper authorities. The case would then never go into court at all."

"God bless you!" cried the prisoner passionately. "I would have endured imprisonment, ay, even execution, rather than have left my miserable secret as a family blot to my children.

"You are the first who have ever heard my story. My father was a schoolmaster in Chesterfield, where I received an excellent education. I travelled in my youth, took to the stage, and finally became a reporter on an evening paper in London. One day my editor wished to have a series of articles upon begging in the metropolis, and I volunteered to supply them. There was the point from which all my adventures started. It was only by trying begging as an amateur that I could get the facts upon which to base my articles. When an actor I had, of course, learned all the secrets of making up, and had been famous in the green-room for my skill. I took advantage now of my attainments. I painted my face, and to make myself as pitiable as possible I made a good scar and fixed one side of my lip in a twist by the aid of a small slip of flesh-coloured plaster. Then with a red head of hair, and an appropriate dress, I took my station in the business part of the city, ostensibly as a match-seller but really as a beggar. For seven hours I plied my trade, and when I returned home in the evening I found to my surprise that I had received no less than 26s. 4d.

"I wrote my articles and thought little more of the matter until, some time later, I backed a bill for a friend and had a writ served upon me for 25 pounds. I was at my wit's end where to get the money, but a sudden idea came to me. I begged a fortnight's grace from the creditor, asked for a holiday from my employers, and spent the time in begging in the City under my disguise. In ten days I had the money and had paid the debt.

"Well, you can imagine how hard it was to settle down to arduous work at 2 pounds a week when I knew that I could earn as much in a day by smearing my face with a little paint, laying my cap on the ground, and sitting still. It was a long fight between my pride and the money, but the dollars won at last, and I threw up reporting and sat day after day in the corner which I had first chosen, inspiring pity by my ghastly face and filling my pockets with coppers. Only one man knew my secret. He was the keeper of a low den in which I used to lodge in Swandam Lane, where I could every morning emerge as a squalid beggar and in the evenings transform myself into a well-dressed man about town. This fellow, a Lascar, was well paid by me for his rooms, so that I knew that my secret was safe in his possession.

"Well, very soon I found that I was saving considerable sums of money. I do not mean that any beggar in the streets of London could earn 700 pounds a year—which is less than my average takings—but I had exceptional advantages in my power of making up, and also in a facility of repartee, which improved by practice and made me quite a recognised character in the City. All day a stream of pennies, varied by silver, poured in upon me, and it was a very bad day in which I failed to take 2 pounds.

"As I grew richer I grew more ambitious, took a house in the country, and eventually married, without anyone having a suspicion as to my real occupation. My dear wife knew that I had business in the City. She little knew what.

"Last Monday I had finished for the day and was dressing in my room above the opium den when I looked out of my window and saw, to my horror and astonishment, that my wife was standing in the street, with her eyes fixed full upon me. I gave a cry of surprise, threw up my arms to cover my face, and, rushing to my confidant, the Lascar, entreated him to prevent anyone from coming up to me. I heard her voice downstairs, but I knew that she could not ascend. Swiftly I threw off my clothes, pulled on those of a beggar, and put on my pigments and wig. Even a wife's eyes could not pierce so complete a disguise. But then it occurred to me that there might be a search in the room, and that the clothes might betray me. I threw open the window, reopening by my violence a small cut which I had inflicted upon myself in the bedroom that morning. Then I seized my coat, which was weighted by the coppers which I had just transferred to it from the leather bag in which I carried my takings. I hurled it out of the window, and it disappeared into the Thames. The other clothes would have followed, but at that moment there was a rush of constables up the stair, and a few minutes after I found, rather, I confess, to my relief, that instead of being identified as Mr. Neville St. Clair, I was arrested as his murderer.

"I do not know that there is anything else for me to explain. I was determined to preserve my disguise as long as possible, and hence my preference for a dirty face. Knowing that my wife would be terribly anxious, I slipped off my ring and confided it to the Lascar at a moment when no constable was watching me, together with a hurried scrawl, telling her that she had no cause to fear."

"That note only reached her yesterday," said Holmes.

"Good God! What a week she must have spent!"

"The police have watched this Lascar," said Inspector Bradstreet, "and I can quite understand that he might find it difficult to post a letter unobserved. Probably he handed it to some sailor customer of his, who forgot all about it for some days."

"That was it," said Holmes, nodding approvingly; "I have no doubt of it. But have you never been prosecuted for begging?"

"Many times; but what was a fine to me?"

"It must stop here, however," said Bradstreet. "If the police are to hush this thing up, there must be no more of Hugh Boone."

"I have sworn it by the most solemn oaths which a man can take."

"In that case I think that it is probable that no further steps may be taken. But if you are found again, then all must come out. I am sure, Mr. Holmes, that we are very much indebted to you for having cleared the matter up. I wish I knew how you reach your results."

"I reached this one," said my friend, "by sitting upon five pillows and consuming an ounce of shag. I think, Watson, that if we drive to Baker Street we shall just be in time for breakfast."

VII. The Adventure Of The Blue Carbuncle

I had called upon my friend Sherlock Holmes upon the second morning after Christmas, with the intention of wishing him the compliments of the season. He was lounging upon the sofa in a purple dressing-gown, a pipe-rack within his reach upon the right, and a pile of crumpled morning papers, evidently newly studied, near at hand. Beside the couch was a wooden chair, and on the angle of the back hung a very seedy and disreputable hard-felt hat, much the worse for wear, and cracked in several places. A lens and a forceps lying upon the seat of the chair suggested that the hat had been suspended in this manner for the purpose of examination.

"You are engaged," said I; "perhaps I interrupt you."

"Not at all. I am glad to have a friend with whom I can discuss my results. The matter is a perfectly trivial one"—he jerked his thumb in the direction of the old hat—"but there are points in connection with it which are not entirely devoid of interest and even of instruction."

I seated myself in his armchair and warmed my hands before his crackling fire, for a sharp frost had set in, and the windows were thick with the ice crystals. "I suppose," I remarked, "that, homely as it looks, this thing has some deadly story linked on to it—that it is the clue which will guide you in the solution of some mystery and the punishment of some crime."

"No, no. No crime," said Sherlock Holmes, laughing. "Only one of those whimsical little incidents which will happen when you have four million human beings all jostling each other within the space of a few square miles. Amid the action and reaction of so dense a swarm of humanity, every possible combination of events may be expected to take place, and many a little problem will be presented which may be striking and bizarre without being criminal. We have already had experience of such."

"So much so," I remarked, "that of the last six cases which I have added to my notes, three have been entirely free of any legal crime."

"Precisely. You allude to my attempt to recover the Irene Adler papers, to the singular case of Miss Mary Sutherland, and to the adventure of the man with the twisted lip. Well, I have no doubt that this small matter will fall into the same innocent category. You know Peterson, the commissionaire?"

"Yes."

"It is to him that this trophy belongs."

"It is his hat."

"No, no, he found it. Its owner is unknown. I beg that you will look upon it not as a battered billycock but as an intellectual problem. And, first, as to how it came here. It arrived upon Christmas morning, in company with a good fat goose, which is, I have no doubt, roasting at this moment in front of Peterson's fire. The facts are these: about four o'clock on Christmas morning, Peterson, who, as you know, is a very honest fellow, was returning from some small jollification and was making his way homeward down Tottenham Court Road. In front of him he saw, in the gaslight, a tallish man, walking with a slight stagger, and carrying a white goose slung over his shoulder. As he reached the corner of Goodge Street, a row broke out between this stranger and a little knot of roughs. One of the latter knocked off the man's hat, on which he raised his stick to defend himself and, swinging it over his head, smashed the shop window behind him. Peterson had rushed forward to protect the stranger from his assailants; but the man, shocked at having broken the window, and seeing an official-looking person in uniform rushing towards him, dropped his goose, took to his heels, and vanished amid the labyrinth of small streets which lie at the back of Tottenham Court Road. The roughs had also fled at the appearance of Peterson, so that he was left in possession of the field of battle, and also of the spoils of victory in the shape of this battered hat and a most unimpeachable Christmas goose."

"Which surely he restored to their owner?"

"My dear fellow, there lies the problem. It is true that 'For Mrs. Henry Baker' was printed upon a small card which was tied to the bird's left leg, and it is also true that the initials 'H. B.' are legible upon the lining of this hat, but as there are some thousands of Bakers, and some hundreds of Henry Bakers in this city of ours, it is not easy to restore lost property to any one of them."

"What, then, did Peterson do?"

"He brought round both hat and goose to me on Christmas morning, knowing that even the smallest problems are of interest to me. The goose we retained until this morning, when there were signs that, in spite of the slight frost, it would be well that it should be eaten without unnecessary delay. Its finder has carried it off, therefore, to fulfil the ultimate destiny of a goose, while I continue to retain the hat of the unknown gentleman who lost his Christmas dinner."

"Did he not advertise?"

"No."

"Then, what clue could you have as to his identity?"

"Only as much as we can deduce."

"From his hat?"

"Precisely."

"But you are joking. What can you gather from this old battered felt?"

"Here is my lens. You know my methods. What can you gather yourself as to the individuality of the man who has worn this article?"

I took the tattered object in my hands and turned it over rather ruefully. It was a very ordinary black hat of the usual round shape, hard and much the worse for wear. The lining had been of red silk, but was a good deal discoloured. There was no maker's name; but, as Holmes had remarked, the initials "H. B." were scrawled upon one side. It was pierced in the brim for a hat-securer, but the elastic was missing. For the rest, it was cracked, exceedingly dusty, and spotted in several places, although there seemed to have been some attempt to hide the discoloured patches by smearing them with ink.

"I can see nothing," said I, handing it back to my friend.

"On the contrary, Watson, you can see everything. You fail, however, to reason from what you see. You are too timid in drawing your inferences."

"Then, pray tell me what it is that you can infer from this hat?"

He picked it up and gazed at it in the peculiar introspective fashion which was characteristic of him. "It is perhaps less suggestive than it might have been," he remarked, "and yet there are a few inferences which are very distinct, and a few others which represent at least a strong balance of probability. That the man was highly intellectual is of course obvious upon the face of it, and also that he was fairly well-to-do within the last three years, although he has now fallen upon evil days. He had foresight, but has less now than formerly, pointing to a moral retrogression, which, when taken with the decline of his fortunes, seems to indicate some evil influence, probably drink, at work upon him. This may account also for the obvious fact that his wife has ceased to love him."

"My dear Holmes!"

"He has, however, retained some degree of self-respect," he continued, disregarding my remonstrance. "He is a man who leads a sedentary life, goes out little, is out of training entirely, is middle-aged, has grizzled hair which he has had cut within the last few days, and which he anoints with lime-cream. These are the more patent facts which are to be deduced from his hat. Also, by the way, that it is extremely improbable that he has gas laid on in his house."

"You are certainly joking, Holmes."

"Not in the least. Is it possible that even now, when I give you these results, you are unable to see how they are attained?"

"I have no doubt that I am very stupid, but I must confess that I am unable to follow you. For example, how did you deduce that this man was intellectual?"

For answer Holmes clapped the hat upon his head. It came right over the forehead and settled upon the bridge of his nose. "It is a question of cubic capacity," said he; "a man with so large a brain must have something in it."

"The decline of his fortunes, then?"

"This hat is three years old. These flat brims curled at the edge came in then. It is a hat of the very best quality. Look at the band of ribbed silk and the excellent lining. If this man could afford to buy so expensive a hat three years ago, and has had no hat since, then he has assuredly gone down in the world."

"Well, that is clear enough, certainly. But how about the foresight and the moral retrogression?"

Sherlock Holmes laughed. "Here is the foresight," said he putting his finger upon the little disc and loop of the hat-securer. "They are never sold upon hats. If this man ordered one, it is a sign of a certain amount of foresight, since he went out of his way to take this precaution against the wind. But since we see that he has broken the elastic and has not troubled to replace it, it is obvious that he has less foresight now than formerly, which is a distinct proof of a weakening nature. On the other hand, he has endeavoured to conceal some of these stains upon the felt by daubing them with ink, which is a sign that he has not entirely lost his self-respect."

"Your reasoning is certainly plausible."

"The further points, that he is middle-aged, that his hair is grizzled, that it has been recently cut, and that he uses lime-cream, are all to be gathered from a close examination of the lower part of the lining. The lens discloses a large number of hair-ends, clean cut by the scissors of the barber. They all appear to be adhesive, and there is a distinct odour of lime-cream. This dust, you will observe, is not the gritty, grey dust of the street but the fluffy brown dust of the house, showing that it has been hung up indoors most of the time, while the marks of moisture upon the inside are proof positive that the wearer perspired very freely, and could therefore, hardly be in the best of training."

"But his wife—you said that she had ceased to love him."

"This hat has not been brushed for weeks. When I see you, my dear Watson, with a week's accumulation of dust upon your hat, and when your wife allows you to go out in such a state, I shall fear that you also have been unfortunate enough to lose your wife's affection."

"But he might be a bachelor."

"Nay, he was bringing home the goose as a peace-offering to his wife. Remember the card upon the bird's leg."

"You have an answer to everything. But how on earth do you deduce that the gas is not laid on in his house?"

"One tallow stain, or even two, might come by chance; but when I see no less than five, I think that there can be little doubt that the individual must be brought into frequent contact with burning tallow—walks upstairs at night probably with his hat in one hand and a guttering candle in the other. Anyhow, he never got tallow-stains from a gas-jet. Are you satisfied?"

"Well, it is very ingenious," said I, laughing; "but since, as you said just now, there has been no crime committed, and no harm done save the loss of a goose, all this seems to be rather a waste of energy."

Sherlock Holmes had opened his mouth to reply, when the door flew open, and Peterson, the commissionaire, rushed into the apartment with flushed cheeks and the face of a man who is dazed with astonishment.

"The goose, Mr. Holmes! The goose, sir!" he gasped.

"Eh? What of it, then? Has it returned to life and flapped off through the kitchen window?" Holmes twisted himself round upon the sofa to get a fairer view of the man's excited face.

"See here, sir! See what my wife found in its crop!" He held out his hand and displayed upon the centre of the palm a brilliantly scintillating blue stone, rather smaller than a bean in size, but of such purity and radiance that it twinkled like an electric point in the dark hollow of his hand.

Sherlock Holmes sat up with a whistle. "By Jove, Peterson!" said he, "this is treasure trove indeed. I suppose you know what you have got?"

"A diamond, sir? A precious stone. It cuts into glass as though it were putty."

"It's more than a precious stone. It is the precious stone."

"Not the Countess of Morcar's blue carbuncle!" I ejaculated.

"Precisely so. I ought to know its size and shape, seeing that I have read the advertisement about it in The Times every day lately. It is absolutely unique, and its value can only be conjectured, but the reward offered of 1000 pounds is certainly not within a twentieth part of the market price."

"A thousand pounds! Great Lord of mercy!" The commissionaire plumped down into a chair and stared from one to the other of us.

"That is the reward, and I have reason to know that there are sentimental considerations in the background which would induce the Countess to part with half her fortune if she could but recover the gem."

"It was lost, if I remember aright, at the Hotel Cosmopolitan," I remarked.

"Precisely so, on December 22nd, just five days ago. John Horner, a plumber, was accused of having abstracted it from the lady's jewel-case. The evidence against him was so strong that the case has been referred to the Assizes. I have some account of the matter here, I believe." He rummaged amid his newspapers, glancing over the dates, until at last he smoothed one out, doubled it over, and read the following paragraph:

"Hotel Cosmopolitan Jewel Robbery. John Horner, 26, plumber, was brought up upon the charge of having upon the 22nd inst., abstracted from the jewel-case of the Countess of Morcar the valuable gem known as the blue carbuncle. James Ryder, upper-attendant at the hotel, gave his evidence to the effect that he had shown Horner up to the dressing-room of the Countess of Morcar upon the day of the robbery in order that he might solder the second bar of the grate, which was loose. He had remained with Horner some little time, but had finally been called away. On returning, he found that Horner had disappeared, that the bureau had been forced open, and that the small morocco casket in which, as it afterwards transpired, the

Countess was accustomed to keep her jewel, was lying empty upon the dressing-table. Ryder instantly gave the alarm, and Horner was arrested the same evening; but the stone could not be found either upon his person or in his rooms. Catherine Cusack, maid to the Countess, deposed to having heard Ryder's cry of dismay on discovering the robbery, and to having rushed into the room, where she found matters as described by the last witness. Inspector Bradstreet, B division, gave evidence as to the arrest of Horner, who struggled frantically, and protested his innocence in the strongest terms. Evidence of a previous conviction for robbery having been given against the prisoner, the magistrate refused to deal summarily with the offence, but referred it to the Assizes. Horner, who had shown signs of intense emotion during the proceedings, fainted away at the conclusion and was carried out of court."

"Hum! So much for the police-court," said Holmes thoughtfully, tossing aside the paper. "The question for us now to solve is the sequence of events leading from a rifled jewel-case at one end to the crop of a goose in Tottenham Court Road at the other. You see, Watson, our little deductions have suddenly assumed a much more important and less innocent aspect. Here is the stone; the stone came from the goose, and the goose came from Mr. Henry Baker, the gentleman with the bad hat and all the other characteristics with which I have bored you. So now we must set ourselves very seriously to finding this gentleman and ascertaining what part he has played in this little mystery. To do this, we must try the simplest means first, and these lie undoubtedly in an advertisement in all the evening papers. If this fail, I shall have recourse to other methods."

"What will you say?"

"Give me a pencil and that slip of paper. Now, then: 'Found at the corner of Goodge Street, a goose and a black felt hat. Mr. Henry Baker can have the same by applying at 6:30 this evening at 221B, Baker Street.' That is clear and concise."

"Very. But will he see it?"

"Well, he is sure to keep an eye on the papers, since, to a poor man, the loss was a heavy one. He was clearly so scared by his mischance in breaking the window and by the approach of Peterson that he thought of nothing but flight, but since then he must have bitterly regretted the impulse which caused him to drop his bird. Then, again, the introduction of his name will cause him to see it, for everyone who knows him will direct his attention to it. Here you are, Peterson, run down to the advertising agency and have this put in the evening papers."

"In which, sir?"

"Oh, in the Globe, Star, Pall Mall, St. James's, Evening News, Standard, Echo, and any others that occur to you."

"Very well, sir. And this stone?"

"Ah, yes, I shall keep the stone. Thank you. And, I say, Peterson, just buy a goose on your way back and leave it here with me, for we must have one to give to this gentleman in place of the one which your family is now devouring."

When the commissionaire had gone, Holmes took up the stone and held it against the light. "It's a bonny thing," said he. "Just see how it glints and sparkles. Of course it is a nucleus and focus of crime. Every good stone is. They are the devil's pet baits. In the larger and older jewels every facet may stand for a bloody deed. This stone is not yet twenty years old. It was found in the banks of the Amoy River in southern China and is remarkable in having every characteristic of the carbuncle, save that it is blue in shade instead of ruby red. In spite of its youth, it has already a sinister history. There have been two murders, a vitriol-throwing, a suicide, and several robberies brought about for the sake of this forty-grain weight of crystallised charcoal. Who would think that so pretty a toy would be a purveyor to the gallows and the prison? I'll lock it up in my strong box now and drop a line to the Countess to say that we have it."

"Do you think that this man Horner is innocent?"

"I cannot tell."

"Well, then, do you imagine that this other one, Henry Baker, had anything to do with the matter?"

"It is, I think, much more likely that Henry Baker is an absolutely innocent man, who had no idea that the bird which he was carrying was of considerably more value than if it were made of solid gold. That, however, I shall determine by a very simple test if we have an answer to our advertisement."

"And you can do nothing until then?"

"Nothing."

"In that case I shall continue my professional round. But I shall come back in the evening at the hour you have mentioned, for I should like to see the solution of so tangled a business."

"Very glad to see you. I dine at seven. There is a woodcock, I believe. By the way, in view of recent occurrences, perhaps I ought to ask Mrs. Hudson to examine its crop."

I had been delayed at a case, and it was a little after half-past six when I found myself in Baker Street once more. As I approached the house I saw a tall man in a Scotch bonnet with a coat which was buttoned up to his chin waiting outside in the bright semicircle which was thrown from the fanlight. Just as I arrived the door was opened, and we were shown up together to Holmes' room.

"Mr. Henry Baker, I believe," said he, rising from his armchair and greeting his visitor with the easy air of geniality which he could so readily assume. "Pray take this chair by the fire, Mr. Baker. It is a cold night, and I observe that your circulation is more adapted for summer than for winter. Ah, Watson, you have just come at the right time. Is that your hat, Mr. Baker?"

"Yes, sir, that is undoubtedly my hat."

He was a large man with rounded shoulders, a massive head, and a broad, intelligent face, sloping down to a pointed beard of grizzled brown. A touch of red in nose and cheeks, with a slight tremor of his extended hand, recalled Holmes' surmise as to his habits. His rusty black frock-coat was buttoned right up in front, with the collar turned up, and his lank wrists protruded from his sleeves without a sign of cuff or shirt. He spoke in a slow staccato fashion, choosing his words with care, and gave the impression generally of a man of learning and letters who had had ill-usage at the hands of fortune.

"We have retained these things for some days," said Holmes, "because we expected to see an advertisement from you giving your address. I am at a loss to know now why you did not advertise."

Our visitor gave a rather shamefaced laugh. "Shillings have not been so plentiful with me as they once were," he remarked. "I had no doubt that the gang of roughs who assaulted me had carried off both my hat and the bird. I did not care to spend more money in a hopeless attempt at recovering them."

"Very naturally. By the way, about the bird, we were compelled to eat it."

"To eat it!" Our visitor half rose from his chair in his excitement.

"Yes, it would have been of no use to anyone had we not done so. But I presume that this other goose upon the sideboard, which is about the same weight and perfectly fresh, will answer your purpose equally well?"

"Oh, certainly, certainly," answered Mr. Baker with a sigh of relief.

"Of course, we still have the feathers, legs, crop, and so on of your own bird, so if you wish—"

The man burst into a hearty laugh. "They might be useful to me as relics of my adventure," said he, "but beyond that I can hardly see what use the disjecta membra of my late acquaintance are going to be to me. No, sir, I think that, with your permission, I will confine my attentions to the excellent bird which I perceive upon the sideboard."

Sherlock Holmes glanced sharply across at me with a slight shrug of his shoulders.

"There is your hat, then, and there your bird," said he. "By the way, would it bore you to tell me where you got the other one from? I am somewhat of a fowl fancier, and I have seldom seen a better grown goose."

"Certainly, sir," said Baker, who had risen and tucked his newly gained property under his arm. "There are a few of us who frequent the Alpha Inn, near the Museum—we are to be found in the Museum itself during the day, you understand. This year our good host, Windigate by name, instituted a goose club, by which, on consideration of some few pence every week, we were each to receive a bird at Christmas. My pence were duly paid, and the rest is familiar to you. I am much indebted to you, sir, for a Scotch bonnet is fitted neither to my years nor my gravity." With a comical pomposity of manner he bowed solemnly to both of us and strode off upon his way.

"So much for Mr. Henry Baker," said Holmes when he had closed the door behind him. "It is quite certain that he knows nothing whatever about the matter. Are you hungry, Watson?"

"Not particularly."

"Then I suggest that we turn our dinner into a supper and follow up this clue while it is still hot."

"By all means."

It was a bitter night, so we drew on our ulsters and wrapped cravats about our throats. Outside, the stars were shining coldly in a cloudless sky, and the breath of the passers-by blew out into smoke like so many pistol shots. Our footfalls rang out crisply and loudly as we swung through the doctors' quarter, Wimpole Street, Harley Street, and so through Wigmore Street into Oxford Street. In a quarter of an hour we were in Bloomsbury at the Alpha Inn, which is a small public-house at the corner of one of the streets which runs down into Holborn. Holmes pushed open the door of the private bar and ordered two glasses of beer from the ruddy-faced, white-aproned landlord.

"Your beer should be excellent if it is as good as your geese," said he.

"My geese!" The man seemed surprised.

"Yes. I was speaking only half an hour ago to Mr. Henry Baker, who was a member of your goose club."

"Ah! yes, I see. But you see, sir, them's not our geese."

"Indeed! Whose, then?"

"Well, I got the two dozen from a salesman in Covent Garden."

"Indeed? I know some of them. Which was it?"

"Breckinridge is his name."

"Ah! I don't know him. Well, here's your good health landlord, and prosperity to your house. Good-night."

"Now for Mr. Breckinridge," he continued, buttoning up his coat as we came out into the frosty air. "Remember, Watson that though we have so homely a thing as a goose at one end of this chain, we have at the other a man who will certainly get seven years' penal servitude unless we can establish his innocence. It is possible that our inquiry may but confirm his guilt; but, in any case, we have a line of investigation which has been missed by the police, and which a singular chance has placed in our hands. Let us follow it out to the bitter end. Faces to the south, then, and quick march!"

We passed across Holborn, down Endell Street, and so through a zigzag of slums to Covent Garden Market. One of the largest stalls bore the name of Breckinridge upon it, and the proprietor a horsey-looking man, with a sharp face and trim side-whiskers was helping a boy to put up the shutters.

"Good-evening. It's a cold night," said Holmes.

The salesman nodded and shot a questioning glance at my companion.

"Sold out of geese, I see," continued Holmes, pointing at the bare slabs of marble.

"Let you have five hundred tomorrow morning."

"That's no good."

"Well, there are some on the stall with the gas-flare."

"Ah, but I was recommended to you."

"Who by?"

"The landlord of the Alpha."

"Oh, yes; I sent him a couple of dozen."

"Fine birds they were, too. Now where did you get them from?"

To my surprise the question provoked a burst of anger from the salesman.

"Now, then, mister," said he, with his head cocked and his arms akimbo, "what are you driving at? Let's have it straight, now."

"It is straight enough. I should like to know who sold you the geese which you supplied to the Alpha."

"Well then, I shan't tell you. So now!"

"Oh, it is a matter of no importance; but I don't know why you should be so warm over such a trifle."

"Warm! You'd be as warm, maybe, if you were as pestered as I am. When I pay good money for a good article there should be an end of the business; but it's 'Where are the geese?' and 'Who did you sell the geese to?' and 'What will you take for the geese?' One would think they were the only geese in the world, to hear the fuss that is made over them."

"Well, I have no connection with any other people who have been making inquiries," said Holmes carelessly. "If you won't tell us the bet is off, that is all. But I'm always ready to back my opinion on a matter of fowls, and I have a fiver on it that the bird I ate is country bred."

"Well, then, you've lost your fiver, for it's town bred," snapped the salesman.

"It's nothing of the kind."

"I say it is."

"I don't believe it."

"D'you think you know more about fowls than I, who have handled them ever since I was a nipper? I tell you, all those birds that went to the Alpha were town bred."

"You'll never persuade me to believe that."

"Will you bet, then?"

"It's merely taking your money, for I know that I am right. But I'll have a sovereign on with you, just to teach you not to be obstinate."

The salesman chuckled grimly. "Bring me the books, Bill," said he.

The small boy brought round a small thin volume and a great greasy-backed one, laying them out together beneath the hanging lamp.

"Now then, Mr. Cocksure," said the salesman, "I thought that I was out of geese, but before I finish you'll find that there is still one left in my shop. You see this little book?"

"Well?"

"That's the list of the folk from whom I buy. D'you see? Well, then, here on this page are the country folk, and the numbers after their names are where their accounts are in the big ledger. Now, then! You see this other page in red ink? Well, that is a list of my town suppliers. Now, look at that third name. Just read it out to me."

"Mrs. Oakshott, 117, Brixton Road--249," read Holmes.

"Quite so. Now turn that up in the ledger."

Holmes turned to the page indicated. "Here you are, 'Mrs. Oakshott, 117, Brixton Road, egg and poultry supplier.'"

"Now, then, what's the last entry?"

"'December 22nd. Twenty-four geese at 7s. 6d.'"

"Quite so. There you are. And underneath?"

"'Sold to Mr. Windigate of the Alpha, at 12s.'"

"What have you to say now?"

Sherlock Holmes looked deeply chagrined. He drew a sovereign from his pocket and threw it down upon the slab, turning away with the air of a man whose disgust is too deep for words. A few yards off he stopped under a lamp-post and laughed in the hearty, noiseless fashion which was peculiar to him.

"When you see a man with whiskers of that cut and the 'Pink 'un' protruding out of his pocket, you can always draw him by a bet," said he. "I daresay that if I had put 100 pounds down in front of him, that man would not have given me such complete information as was drawn from him by the idea that he was doing me on a wager. Well, Watson, we are, I fancy, nearing the end of our quest, and the only point which remains to be determined is whether we should go on to this Mrs. Oakshott to-night, or whether we should reserve it for tomorrow. It is clear from what that surly fellow said that there are others besides ourselves who are anxious about the matter, and I should—"

His remarks were suddenly cut short by a loud hubbub which broke out from the stall which we had just left. Turning round we saw a little rat-faced fellow standing in the centre of the circle of yellow light which was thrown by the swinging lamp, while Breckinridge, the salesman, framed in the door of his stall, was shaking his fists fiercely at the cringing figure.

"I've had enough of you and your geese," he shouted. "I wish you were all at the devil together. If you come pestering me any more with your silly talk I'll set the dog at you. You bring Mrs. Oakshott here and I'll answer her, but what have you to do with it? Did I buy the geese off you?"

"No; but one of them was mine all the same," whined the little man.

"Well, then, ask Mrs. Oakshott for it."

"She told me to ask you."

"Well, you can ask the King of Proosia, for all I care. I've had enough of it. Get out of this!" He rushed fiercely forward, and the inquirer flitted away into the darkness.

"Ha! this may save us a visit to Brixton Road," whispered Holmes. "Come with me, and we will see what is to be made of this fellow." Striding through the scattered knots of people who lounged round the flaring stalls, my companion speedily overtook the little man and touched him upon the shoulder. He sprang round, and I could see in the gas-light that every vestige of colour had been driven from his face.

"Who are you, then? What do you want?" he asked in a quavering voice.

"You will excuse me," said Holmes blandly, "but I could not help overhearing the questions which you put to the salesman just now. I think that I could be of assistance to you."

"You? Who are you? How could you know anything of the matter?"

"My name is Sherlock Holmes. It is my business to know what other people don't know."

"But you can know nothing of this?"

"Excuse me, I know everything of it. You are endeavouring to trace some geese which were sold by Mrs. Oakshott, of Brixton Road, to a salesman named Breckinridge, by him in turn to Mr. Windigate, of the Alpha, and by him to his club, of which Mr. Henry Baker is a member."

"Oh, sir, you are the very man whom I have longed to meet," cried the little fellow with outstretched hands and quivering fingers. "I can hardly explain to you how interested I am in this matter."

Sherlock Holmes hailed a four-wheeler which was passing. "In that case we had better discuss it in a cosy room rather than in this wind-swept market-place," said he. "But pray tell me, before we go farther, who it is that I have the pleasure of assisting."

The man hesitated for an instant. "My name is John Robinson," he answered with a sidelong glance.

"No, no; the real name," said Holmes sweetly. "It is always awkward doing business with an alias."

A flush sprang to the white cheeks of the stranger. "Well then," said he, "my real name is James Ryder."

"Precisely so. Head attendant at the Hotel Cosmopolitan. Pray step into the cab, and I shall soon be able to tell you everything which you would wish to know."

The little man stood glancing from one to the other of us with half-frightened, half-hopeful eyes, as one who is not sure whether he is on the verge of a windfall or of a catastrophe. Then he stepped into the cab, and in half an hour we were back in the sitting-room at Baker Street. Nothing had been said during our drive, but the high, thin breathing of our new companion, and the claspings and unclaspings of his hands, spoke of the nervous tension within him.

"Here we are!" said Holmes cheerily as we filed into the room. "The fire looks very seasonable in this weather. You look cold, Mr. Ryder. Pray take the basket-chair. I will just put on my slippers before we settle this little matter of yours. Now, then! You want to know what became of those geese?"

"Yes, sir."

"Or rather, I fancy, of that goose. It was one bird, I imagine in which you were interested—white, with a black bar across the tail."

Ryder quivered with emotion. "Oh, sir," he cried, "can you tell me where it went to?"

"It came here."

"Here?"

"Yes, and a most remarkable bird it proved. I don't wonder that you should take an interest in it. It laid an egg after it was dead—the bonniest, brightest little blue egg that ever was seen. I have it here in my museum."

Our visitor staggered to his feet and clutched the mantelpiece with his right hand. Holmes unlocked his strong-box and held up the blue carbuncle, which shone out like a star, with a cold, brilliant, many-pointed radiance. Ryder stood glaring with a drawn face, uncertain whether to claim or to disown it.

"The game's up, Ryder," said Holmes quietly. "Hold up, man, or you'll be into the fire! Give him an arm back into his chair, Watson. He's not got blood enough to go in for felony with impunity. Give him a dash of brandy. So! Now he looks a little more human. What a shrimp it is, to be sure!"

For a moment he had staggered and nearly fallen, but the brandy brought a tinge of colour into his cheeks, and he sat staring with frightened eyes at his accuser.

"I have almost every link in my hands, and all the proofs which I could possibly need, so there is little which you need tell me. Still, that little may as well be cleared up to make the case complete. You had heard, Ryder, of this blue stone of the Countess of Morcar's?"

"It was Catherine Cusack who told me of it," said he in a crackling voice.

"I see—her ladyship's waiting-maid. Well, the temptation of sudden wealth so easily acquired was too much for you, as it has been for better men before you; but you were not very scrupulous in the means you used. It seems to me, Ryder, that there is the making of a very pretty villain in you. You knew that this man Horner, the plumber, had been concerned in some such matter before, and that suspicion would rest the more readily upon him. What did you do, then? You made some small job in my lady's room—you and your confederate Cusack—and you managed that he should be the man sent for. Then, when he had left, you rifled the jewel-case, raised the alarm, and had this unfortunate man arrested. You then—"

Ryder threw himself down suddenly upon the rug and clutched at my companion's knees. "For God's sake, have mercy!" he shrieked. "Think of my father! Of my mother! It would break their hearts. I never went wrong before! I never will again. I swear it. I'll swear it on a Bible. Oh, don't bring it into court! For Christ's sake, don't!"

"Get back into your chair!" said Holmes sternly. "It is very well to cringe and crawl now, but you thought little enough of this poor Horner in the dock for a crime of which he knew nothing."

"I will fly, Mr. Holmes. I will leave the country, sir. Then the charge against him will break down."

"Hum! We will talk about that. And now let us hear a true account of the next act. How came the stone into the goose, and how came the goose into the open market? Tell us the truth, for there lies your only hope of safety."

Ryder passed his tongue over his parched lips. "I will tell you it just as it happened, sir," said he. "When Horner had been arrested, it seemed to me that it would be best for me to get away with the stone at once, for I did not know at what moment the police might not take it into their heads to search me and my room. There was no place about the hotel where it would be safe. I went out, as if on some commission, and I made for my sister's house. She had married a man named Oakshott, and lived in Brixton Road, where she fattened fowls for the market. All the way there every man I met seemed to me to be a policeman or a detective; and, for all that it was a cold night, the sweat was pouring down my face before I came to the Brixton Road. My sister asked me what was the matter, and why I was so pale; but I told her that I had been upset by the jewel robbery at the hotel. Then I went into the back yard and smoked a pipe and wondered what it would be best to do.

"I had a friend once called Maudsley, who went to the bad, and has just been serving his time in Pentonville. One day he had met me, and fell into talk about the ways of thieves, and how they could get rid of what they stole. I knew that he would be true to me, for I knew one or two things about him; so I made up my mind to go right on to Kilburn, where he lived, and take him into my confidence. He would show me how to turn the stone into money. But how to get to him in safety? I thought of the agonies I had gone through in coming from the hotel. I might at any moment be seized and searched, and there would be the stone in my waistcoat pocket. I was leaning against the wall at the time and looking at the geese which were waddling about round my feet, and suddenly an idea came into my head which showed me how I could beat the best detective that ever lived.

"My sister had told me some weeks before that I might have the pick of her geese for a Christmas present, and I knew that she was always as good as her word. I would take my goose now, and in it I would carry my stone to Kilburn. There was a little shed in the yard, and behind this I drove one of the birds—a fine big one, white, with a barred tail. I caught it, and prying its bill open, I thrust the stone down its throat as far as my finger could reach. The bird gave a gulp, and I felt the stone pass along its gullet and down into its crop. But the creature flapped and struggled, and out came my sister to know what was the matter. As I turned to speak to her the brute broke loose and fluttered off among the others.

"'Whatever were you doing with that bird, Jem?' says she.

"'Well,' said I, 'you said you'd give me one for Christmas, and I was feeling which was the fattest.'

"'Oh,' says she, 'we've set yours aside for you—Jem's bird, we call it. It's the big white one over yonder. There's twenty-six of them, which makes one for you, and one for us, and two dozen for the market.'

"'Thank you, Maggie,' says I; 'but if it is all the same to you, I'd rather have that one I was handling just now.'

"'The other is a good three pound heavier,' said she, 'and we fattened it expressly for you.'

"'Never mind. I'll have the other, and I'll take it now,' said I.

"'Oh, just as you like,' said she, a little huffed. 'Which is it you want, then?'

"'That white one with the barred tail, right in the middle of the flock.'

"'Oh, very well. Kill it and take it with you.'

"Well, I did what she said, Mr. Holmes, and I carried the bird all the way to Kilburn. I told my pal what I had done, for he was a man that it was easy to tell a thing like that to. He laughed until he choked, and we got a knife and opened the goose. My heart turned to water, for there was no sign of the stone, and I knew that some terrible mistake had occurred. I left the bird, rushed back to my sister's, and hurried into the back yard. There was not a bird to be seen there.

"'Where are they all, Maggie?' I cried.

"'Gone to the dealer's, Jem.'

"'Which dealer's?'

"'Breckinridge, of Covent Garden.'

"'But was there another with a barred tail?' I asked, 'the same as the one I chose?'

"'Yes, Jem; there were two barred-tailed ones, and I could never tell them apart.'

"Well, then, of course I saw it all, and I ran off as hard as my feet would carry me to this man Breckinridge; but he had sold the lot at once, and not one word would he tell me as to where they had gone. You heard him yourselves to-night. Well, he has always answered me like that. My sister thinks that I am going mad. Sometimes I think that I am myself. And now—and now I am myself a branded thief, without ever having touched the wealth for which I sold my character. God help me! God help me!" He burst into convulsive sobbing, with his face buried in his hands.

There was a long silence, broken only by his heavy breathing and by the measured tapping of Sherlock Holmes' finger-tips upon the edge of the table. Then my friend rose and threw open the door.

"Get out!" said he.

"What, sir! Oh, Heaven bless you!"

"No more words. Get out!"

And no more words were needed. There was a rush, a clatter upon the stairs, the bang of a door, and the crisp rattle of running footfalls from the street.

"After all, Watson," said Holmes, reaching up his hand for his clay pipe, "I am not retained by the police to supply their deficiencies. If Horner were in danger it would be another thing; but this fellow will not appear against him, and the case must collapse. I suppose that I am commuting a felony, but it is just possible that I am saving a soul. This fellow will not go wrong again; he is too terribly frightened. Send him to gaol now, and you make him a gaol-bird for life. Besides, it is the season of forgiveness. Chance has put in our way a most singular and whimsical problem, and its solution is its own reward. If you will have the goodness to touch the bell, Doctor, we will begin another investigation, in which, also a bird will be the chief feature."

VIII. The Adventure Of The Speckled Band

On glancing over my notes of the seventy odd cases in which I have during the last eight years studied the methods of my friend Sherlock Holmes, I find many tragic, some comic, a large number merely strange, but none commonplace; for, working as he did rather for the love of his art than for the acquirement of wealth, he refused to associate himself with any investigation which did not tend towards the unusual, and even the fantastic. Of all these varied cases, however, I cannot recall any which presented more singular features than that which was associated with the well-known Surrey family of the Roylotts of Stoke Moran. The events in question occurred in the early days of my association with Holmes, when we were sharing rooms as bachelors in Baker Street. It is possible that I might have placed them upon record before, but a promise of secrecy was made at the time, from which I have only been freed during the last month by the untimely death of the lady to whom the pledge was given. It is perhaps as well that the facts should now come to light, for I have reasons to know that there are widespread rumours as to the death of Dr. Grimesby Roylott which tend to make the matter even more terrible than the truth.

It was early in April in the year '83 that I woke one morning to find Sherlock Holmes standing, fully dressed, by the side of my bed. He was a late riser, as a rule, and as the clock on the mantelpiece showed me that it was only a quarter-past seven, I blinked up at him in some surprise, and perhaps just a little resentment, for I was myself regular in my habits.

"Very sorry to knock you up, Watson," said he, "but it's the common lot this morning. Mrs. Hudson has been knocked up, she retorted upon me, and I on you."

"What is it, then—a fire?"

"No; a client. It seems that a young lady has arrived in a considerable state of excitement, who insists upon seeing me. She is waiting now in the sitting-room. Now, when young ladies wander about the metropolis at this hour of the morning, and knock sleepy people up out of their beds, I presume that it is something very pressing which they have to communicate. Should it prove to be an interesting case, you would, I am sure, wish to follow it from the outset. I thought, at any rate, that I should call you and give you the chance."

"My dear fellow, I would not miss it for anything."

I had no keener pleasure than in following Holmes in his professional investigations, and in admiring the rapid deductions, as swift as intuitions, and yet always founded on a logical basis with which he unravelled the problems which were submitted to him. I rapidly threw on my clothes and was ready in a few minutes to accompany my friend down to the sitting-room. A lady dressed in black and heavily veiled, who had been sitting in the window, rose as we entered.

"Good-morning, madam," said Holmes cheerily. "My name is Sherlock Holmes. This is my intimate friend and associate, Dr. Watson, before whom you can speak as freely as before myself. Ha! I am glad to see that Mrs. Hudson has had the good sense to light the fire. Pray draw up to it, and I shall order you a cup of hot coffee, for I observe that you are shivering."

"It is not cold which makes me shiver," said the woman in a low voice, changing her seat as requested.

"What, then?"

"It is fear, Mr. Holmes. It is terror." She raised her veil as she spoke, and we could see that she was indeed in a pitiable state of agitation, her face all drawn and grey, with restless frightened eyes, like those of some hunted animal. Her features and figure were those of a woman of thirty, but her hair was shot with premature grey, and her expression was weary and haggard. Sherlock Holmes ran her over with one of his quick, all-comprehensive glances.

"You must not fear," said he soothingly, bending forward and patting her forearm. "We shall soon set matters right, I have no doubt. You have come in by train this morning, I see."

"You know me, then?"

"No, but I observe the second half of a return ticket in the palm of your left glove. You must have started early, and yet you had a good drive in a dog-cart, along heavy roads, before you reached the station."

The lady gave a violent start and stared in bewilderment at my companion.

"There is no mystery, my dear madam," said he, smiling. "The left arm of your jacket is spattered with mud in no less than seven places. The marks are perfectly fresh. There is no vehicle save a dog-cart which throws up mud in that way, and then only when you sit on the left-hand side of the driver."

"Whatever your reasons may be, you are perfectly correct," said she. "I started from home before six, reached Leatherhead at twenty past, and came in by the first train to Waterloo. Sir, I can stand this strain no longer; I shall go mad if it continues. I have no one to turn to—none, save only one, who cares for me, and he, poor fellow, can be of little aid. I have heard of you, Mr. Holmes; I have heard of you from Mrs. Farintosh, whom you helped in the hour of her sore need. It was from her that I had your address. Oh, sir, do you not think that you could help me, too, and at least throw a little light through the dense darkness which surrounds me? At present it is out of my power to reward you for your services, but in a month or six weeks I shall be married, with the control of my own income, and then at least you shall not find me ungrateful."

Holmes turned to his desk and, unlocking it, drew out a small case-book, which he consulted.

"Farintosh," said he. "Ah yes, I recall the case; it was concerned with an opal tiara. I think it was before your time, Watson. I can only say, madam, that I shall be happy to devote the same care to your case as I did to that of your friend. As to reward, my profession is its own reward; but you are at liberty to defray whatever expenses I may be put to, at the time which suits you best. And now I beg that you will lay before us everything that may help us in forming an opinion upon the matter."

"Alas!" replied our visitor, "the very horror of my situation lies in the fact that my fears are so vague, and my suspicions depend so entirely upon small points, which might seem trivial to another, that even he to whom of all others I have a right to look for help and advice looks upon all that I tell him about it as the fancies of a nervous woman. He does not say so, but I can read it from his soothing answers and averted eyes. But I have heard, Mr. Holmes, that you can see deeply into the manifold wickedness of the human heart. You may advise me how to walk amid the dangers which encompass me."

"I am all attention, madam."

"My name is Helen Stoner, and I am living with my stepfather, who is the last survivor of one of the oldest Saxon families in England, the Roylotts of Stoke Moran, on the western border of Surrey."

Holmes nodded his head. "The name is familiar to me," said he.

"The family was at one time among the richest in England, and the estates extended over the borders into Berkshire in the north, and Hampshire in the west. In the last century, however, four successive heirs were of a dissolute and wasteful disposition, and the family ruin was eventually completed by a gambler in the days of the Regency. Nothing was left save a few acres of ground, and the two-hundred-year-old house, which is itself crushed under a heavy mortgage. The last squire dragged out his existence there, living the horrible life of an aristocratic pauper; but his only son, my stepfather, seeing that he must adapt himself to the new conditions, obtained an advance from a relative, which enabled him to take a medical degree and went out to Calcutta, where, by his professional skill and his force of character, he established a large practice. In a fit of anger, however, caused by some robberies which had been perpetrated in the house, he beat his native butler to death and narrowly escaped a capital sentence. As it was, he suffered a long term of imprisonment and afterwards returned to England a morose and disappointed man.

"When Dr. Roylott was in India he married my mother, Mrs. Stoner, the young widow of Major-General Stoner, of the Bengal Artillery. My sister Julia and I were twins, and we were only two years old at the time of my mother's re-marriage. She had a considerable sum of money—not less than 1000 pounds a year—and this she bequeathed to Dr. Roylott entirely while we resided with him, with a provision that a certain annual sum should be allowed to each of us in the event of our marriage. Shortly after our return to England my mother died—she was killed eight years ago in a railway accident near Crewe. Dr. Roylott then abandoned his attempts to establish himself in practice in London and took us to live with him in the old ancestral house at Stoke Moran. The money which my mother had left was enough for all our wants, and there seemed to be no obstacle to our happiness.

"But a terrible change came over our stepfather about this time. Instead of making friends and exchanging visits with our neighbours, who had at first been overjoyed to see a Roylott of Stoke Moran back in the old family seat, he shut himself up in his house and seldom came out save to indulge in ferocious quarrels with whoever might cross his path. Violence of temper approaching to mania has been hereditary in the men of the family, and in my stepfather's case it had, I believe, been intensified by his long residence in the tropics. A series of disgraceful brawls took place, two of which ended in the police-court, until at last he became the terror of the village, and the folks would fly at his approach, for he is a man of immense strength, and absolutely uncontrollable in his anger.

"Last week he hurled the local blacksmith over a parapet into a stream, and it was only by paying over all the money which I could gather together that I was able to avert another public exposure. He had no friends at all save the wandering gipsies, and he would give these vagabonds leave to encamp upon the few acres of bramble-covered land which represent the family estate, and would accept in return the hospitality of their tents, wandering away with them sometimes for weeks on end. He has a passion also for Indian animals, which are sent over to him by a correspondent, and he has at this moment a cheetah and a baboon, which wander freely over his grounds and are feared by the villagers almost as much as their master.

"You can imagine from what I say that my poor sister Julia and I had no great pleasure in our lives. No servant would stay with us, and for a long time we did all the work of the house. She was but thirty at the time of her death, and yet her hair had already begun to whiten, even as mine has."

"Your sister is dead, then?"

"She died just two years ago, and it is of her death that I wish to speak to you. You can understand that, living the life which I have described, we were little likely to see anyone of our own age and position. We had, however, an aunt, my mother's maiden sister, Miss Honoria Westphail, who lives near Harrow, and we were occasionally allowed to pay short visits at this lady's house. Julia went there at Christmas two years ago, and met there a half-pay major of marines, to whom she became engaged. My stepfather learned of the engagement when my sister returned and offered no objection to the marriage; but within a fortnight of the day which had been fixed for the wedding, the terrible event occurred which has deprived me of my only companion."

Sherlock Holmes had been leaning back in his chair with his eyes closed and his head sunk in a cushion, but he half opened his lids now and glanced across at his visitor.

"Pray be precise as to details," said he.

"It is easy for me to be so, for every event of that dreadful time is seared into my memory. The manor-house is, as I have already said, very old, and only one wing is now inhabited. The bedrooms in this wing are on the ground floor, the sitting-rooms being in the central block of the buildings. Of these bedrooms the first is Dr. Roylott's, the second my sister's, and the third my own. There is no communication between them, but they all open out into the same corridor. Do I make myself plain?"

"Perfectly so."

"The windows of the three rooms open out upon the lawn. That fatal night Dr. Roylott had gone to his room early, though we knew that he had not retired to rest, for my sister was troubled by the smell of the strong Indian cigars which it was his custom to smoke. She left her room, therefore, and came into mine, where she sat for some time, chatting about her approaching wedding. At eleven o'clock she rose to leave me, but she paused at the door and looked back.

"'Tell me, Helen,' said she, 'have you ever heard anyone whistle in the dead of the night?'

"'Never,' said I.

"'I suppose that you could not possibly whistle, yourself, in your sleep?'

"'Certainly not. But why?'

"'Because during the last few nights I have always, about three in the morning, heard a low, clear whistle. I am a light sleeper, and it has awakened me. I cannot tell where it came from—perhaps from the next room, perhaps from the lawn. I thought that I would just ask you whether you had heard it.'

"'No, I have not. It must be those wretched gipsies in the plantation.'

"'Very likely. And yet if it were on the lawn, I wonder that you did not hear it also.'

"'Ah, but I sleep more heavily than you.'

"'Well, it is of no great consequence, at any rate.' She smiled back at me, closed my door, and a few moments later I heard her key turn in the lock."

"Indeed," said Holmes. "Was it your custom always to lock yourselves in at night?"

"Always."

"And why?"

"I think that I mentioned to you that the doctor kept a cheetah and a baboon. We had no feeling of security unless our doors were locked."

"Quite so. Pray proceed with your statement."

"I could not sleep that night. A vague feeling of impending misfortune impressed me. My sister and I, you will recollect, were twins, and you know how subtle are the links which bind two souls which are so closely allied. It was a wild night. The wind was howling outside, and the rain was beating and splashing against the windows. Suddenly, amid all the hubbub of the gale, there burst forth the wild scream of a terrified woman. I knew that it was my sister's voice. I sprang from my bed, wrapped a shawl round me, and rushed into the corridor. As I opened my door I seemed to hear a low whistle, such as my sister described, and a few moments later a clanging sound, as if a mass of metal had fallen. As I ran down the passage, my sister's door was unlocked, and revolved slowly upon its hinges. I stared at it horror-stricken, not knowing what was about to issue from it. By the light of the corridor-lamp I saw my sister appear at the opening, her face blanched with terror, her hands groping for help, her whole figure swaying to and fro like that of a drunkard. I ran to her and threw my arms round her, but at that moment her knees seemed to give way and she fell to the ground. She writhed as one who is in terrible pain, and her limbs were dreadfully convulsed. At first I thought that she had not recognised me, but as I bent over her she suddenly shrieked out in a voice which I shall never forget, 'Oh, my God! Helen! It was the band! The speckled band!' There was something else which she would fain have said, and she stabbed with her finger into the air in the direction of the doctor's room, but a fresh convulsion seized her and choked her words. I rushed out, calling loudly for my stepfather, and I met him hastening from his room in his dressing-gown. When he reached my sister's side she was unconscious, and though he poured brandy down her throat and sent for medical aid from the village, all efforts were in vain, for she slowly sank and died without having recovered her consciousness. Such was the dreadful end of my beloved sister."

"One moment," said Holmes, "are you sure about this whistle and metallic sound? Could you swear to it?"

"That was what the county coroner asked me at the inquiry. It is my strong impression that I heard it, and yet, among the crash of the gale and the creaking of an old house, I may possibly have been deceived."

"Was your sister dressed?"

"No, she was in her night-dress. In her right hand was found the charred stump of a match, and in her left a match-box."

"Showing that she had struck a light and looked about her when the alarm took place. That is important. And what conclusions did the coroner come to?"

"He investigated the case with great care, for Dr. Roylott's conduct had long been notorious in the county, but he was unable to find any satisfactory cause of death. My evidence showed that the door had been fastened upon the inner side, and the windows were blocked by old-fashioned shutters with broad iron bars, which were secured every night. The walls were carefully sounded, and were shown to be quite solid all round, and the flooring was also thoroughly examined, with the same result. The chimney is wide, but is barred up by four large staples. It is certain, therefore, that my sister was quite alone when she met her end. Besides, there were no marks of any violence upon her."

"How about poison?"

"The doctors examined her for it, but without success."

"What do you think that this unfortunate lady died of, then?"

"It is my belief that she died of pure fear and nervous shock, though what it was that frightened her I cannot imagine."

"Were there gipsies in the plantation at the time?"

"Yes, there are nearly always some there."

"Ah, and what did you gather from this allusion to a band—a speckled band?"

"Sometimes I have thought that it was merely the wild talk of delirium, sometimes that it may have referred to some band of people, perhaps to these very gipsies in the plantation. I do not know whether the spotted handkerchiefs which so many of them wear over their heads might have suggested the strange adjective which she used."

Holmes shook his head like a man who is far from being satisfied.

"These are very deep waters," said he; "pray go on with your narrative."

"Two years have passed since then, and my life has been until lately lonelier than ever. A month ago, however, a dear friend, whom I have known for many years, has done me the honour to ask my hand in marriage. His name is Armitage—Percy Armitage—the second son of Mr. Armitage, of Crane Water, near Reading. My stepfather has offered no opposition to the match, and we are to be married in the course of the spring. Two days ago some repairs were started in the west wing of the building, and my bedroom wall has been pierced, so that I have had to move into the chamber in which my sister died, and to sleep in the very bed in which she slept. Imagine, then, my thrill of terror when last night, as I lay awake, thinking over her terrible fate, I suddenly heard in the silence of the night the low whistle which had been the herald of her own death. I sprang up and lit the lamp, but nothing was to be seen in the room. I was too shaken to go to bed again, however, so I dressed, and as soon as it was daylight I slipped down, got a dog-cart at the Crown Inn, which is opposite, and drove to Leatherhead, from whence I have come on this morning with the one object of seeing you and asking your advice."

"You have done wisely," said my friend. "But have you told me all?"

"Yes, all."

"Miss Roylott, you have not. You are screening your stepfather."

"Why, what do you mean?"

For answer Holmes pushed back the frill of black lace which fringed the hand that lay upon our visitor's knee. Five little livid spots, the marks of four fingers and a thumb, were printed upon the white wrist.

"You have been cruelly used," said Holmes.

The lady coloured deeply and covered over her injured wrist. "He is a hard man," she said, "and perhaps he hardly knows his own strength."

There was a long silence, during which Holmes leaned his chin upon his hands and stared into the crackling fire.

"This is a very deep business," he said at last. "There are a thousand details which I should desire to know before I decide upon our course of action. Yet we have not a moment to lose. If we were to come to Stoke Moran today, would it be possible for us to see over these rooms without the knowledge of your stepfather?"

"As it happens, he spoke of coming into town today upon some most important business. It is probable that he will be away all day, and that there would be nothing to disturb you. We have a housekeeper now, but she is old and foolish, and I could easily get her out of the way."

"Excellent. You are not averse to this trip, Watson?"

"By no means."

"Then we shall both come. What are you going to do yourself?"

"I have one or two things which I would wish to do now that I am in town. But I shall return by the twelve o'clock train, so as to be there in time for your coming."

"And you may expect us early in the afternoon. I have myself some small business matters to attend to. Will you not wait and breakfast?"

"No, I must go. My heart is lightened already since I have confided my trouble to you. I shall look forward to seeing you again this afternoon." She dropped her thick black veil over her face and glided from the room.

"And what do you think of it all, Watson?" asked Sherlock Holmes, leaning back in his chair.

"It seems to me to be a most dark and sinister business."

"Dark enough and sinister enough."

"Yet if the lady is correct in saying that the flooring and walls are sound, and that the door, window, and chimney are impassable, then her sister must have been undoubtedly alone when she met her mysterious end."

"What becomes, then, of these nocturnal whistles, and what of the very peculiar words of the dying woman?"

"I cannot think."

"When you combine the ideas of whistles at night, the presence of a band of gipsies who are on intimate terms with this old doctor, the fact that we have every reason to believe that the doctor has an interest in preventing his stepdaughter's marriage, the dying allusion to a band, and, finally, the fact that Miss Helen Stoner heard a metallic clang, which might have been caused by one of those metal bars that secured the shutters falling back into its place, I think that there is good ground to think that the mystery may be cleared along those lines."

"But what, then, did the gipsies do?"

"I cannot imagine."

"I see many objections to any such theory."

"And so do I. It is precisely for that reason that we are going to Stoke Moran this day. I want to see whether the objections are fatal, or if they may be explained away. But what in the name of the devil!"

The ejaculation had been drawn from my companion by the fact that our door had been suddenly dashed open, and that a huge man had framed himself in the aperture. His costume was a peculiar mixture of the professional and of the agricultural, having a black top-hat, a long frock-coat, and a pair of high gaiters, with a hunting-crop swinging in his hand. So tall was he that his hat actually brushed the cross bar of the doorway, and his breadth seemed to span it across from side to side. A large face, seared with a thousand wrinkles, burned yellow with the sun, and marked with every evil passion, was turned from one to the other of us, while his deep-set, bile-shot eyes, and his high, thin, fleshless nose, gave him somewhat the resemblance to a fierce old bird of prey.

"Which of you is Holmes?" asked this apparition.

"My name, sir; but you have the advantage of me," said my companion quietly.

"I am Dr. Grimesby Roylott, of Stoke Moran."

"Indeed, Doctor," said Holmes blandly. "Pray take a seat."

"I will do nothing of the kind. My stepdaughter has been here. I have traced her. What has she been saying to you?"

"It is a little cold for the time of the year," said Holmes.

"What has she been saying to you?" screamed the old man furiously.

"But I have heard that the crocuses promise well," continued my companion imperturbably.

"Ha! You put me off, do you?" said our new visitor, taking a step forward and shaking his hunting-crop. "I know you, you scoundrel! I have heard of you before. You are Holmes, the meddler."

My friend smiled.

"Holmes, the busybody!"

His smile broadened.

"Holmes, the Scotland Yard Jack-in-office!"

Holmes chuckled heartily. "Your conversation is most entertaining," said he. "When you go out close the door, for there is a decided draught."

"I will go when I have said my say. Don't you dare to meddle with my affairs. I know that Miss Stoner has been here. I traced her! I am a dangerous man to fall foul of! See here." He stepped swiftly forward, seized the poker, and bent it into a curve with his huge brown hands.

"See that you keep yourself out of my grip," he snarled, and hurling the twisted poker into the fireplace he strode out of the room.

"He seems a very amiable person," said Holmes, laughing. "I am not quite so bulky, but if he had remained I might have shown him that my grip was not much more feeble than his own." As he spoke he picked up the steel poker and, with a sudden effort, straightened it out again.

"Fancy his having the insolence to confound me with the official detective force! This incident gives zest to our investigation, however, and I only trust that our little friend will not suffer from her imprudence in allowing this brute to trace her. And now, Watson, we shall order breakfast, and afterwards I shall walk down to Doctors' Commons, where I hope to get some data which may help us in this matter."

It was nearly one o'clock when Sherlock Holmes returned from his excursion. He held in his hand a sheet of blue paper, scrawled over with notes and figures.

"I have seen the will of the deceased wife," said he. "To determine its exact meaning I have been obliged to work out the present prices of the investments with which it is concerned. The total income, which at the time of the wife's death was little short of 1100 pounds, is now, through the fall in agricultural prices, not more than 750 pounds. Each daughter can claim an income of 250 pounds, in case of marriage. It is evident, therefore, that if both girls had married, this beauty would have had a mere pittance, while even one of them would cripple him to a very serious extent. My morning's work has not been wasted, since it has proved that he has the very strongest motives for standing in the way of anything of the sort. And now, Watson, this is too serious for dawdling, especially as the old man is aware that we are interesting ourselves in his affairs; so if you are ready, we shall call a cab and drive to Waterloo. I should be very much obliged if you would slip your revolver into your pocket. An Eley's No. 2 is an excellent argument with gentlemen who can twist steel pokers into knots. That and a tooth-brush are, I think, all that we need."

At Waterloo we were fortunate in catching a train for Leatherhead, where we hired a trap at the station inn and drove for four or five miles through the lovely Surrey lanes. It was a perfect day, with a bright sun and a few fleecy clouds in the heavens. The trees and wayside hedges were just throwing out their first green shoots, and the air was full of the pleasant smell of the moist earth. To me at least there was a strange contrast between the sweet promise of the spring and this sinister quest upon which we were engaged. My companion sat in the front of the trap, his arms folded, his hat pulled down over his eyes, and his chin sunk upon his breast, buried in the deepest thought. Suddenly, however, he started, tapped me on the shoulder, and pointed over the meadows.

"Look there!" said he.

A heavily timbered park stretched up in a gentle slope, thickening into a grove at the highest point. From amid the branches there jutted out the grey gables and high roof-tree of a very old mansion.

"Stoke Moran?" said he.

"Yes, sir, that be the house of Dr. Grimesby Roylott," remarked the driver.

"There is some building going on there," said Holmes; "that is where we are going."

"There's the village," said the driver, pointing to a cluster of roofs some distance to the left; "but if you want to get to the house, you'll find it shorter to get over this stile, and so by the foot-path over the fields. There it is, where the lady is walking."

"And the lady, I fancy, is Miss Stoner," observed Holmes, shading his eyes. "Yes, I think we had better do as you suggest."

We got off, paid our fare, and the trap rattled back on its way to Leatherhead.

"I thought it as well," said Holmes as we climbed the stile, "that this fellow should think we had come here as architects, or on some definite business. It may stop his gossip. Good-afternoon, Miss Stoner. You see that we have been as good as our word."

Our client of the morning had hurried forward to meet us with a face which spoke her joy. "I have been waiting so eagerly for you," she cried, shaking hands with us warmly. "All has turned out splendidly. Dr. Roylott has gone to town, and it is unlikely that he will be back before evening."

"We have had the pleasure of making the doctor's acquaintance," said Holmes, and in a few words he sketched out what had occurred. Miss Stoner turned white to the lips as she listened.

"Good heavens!" she cried, "he has followed me, then."

"So it appears."

"He is so cunning that I never know when I am safe from him. What will he say when he returns?"

"He must guard himself, for he may find that there is someone more cunning than himself upon his track. You must lock yourself up from him to-night. If he is violent, we shall take you away to your aunt's at Harrow. Now, we must make the best use of our time, so kindly take us at once to the rooms which we are to examine."

The building was of grey, lichen-blotched stone, with a high central portion and two curving wings, like the claws of a crab, thrown out on each side. In one of these wings the windows were broken and blocked with wooden boards, while the roof was partly caved in, a picture of ruin. The central portion was in little better repair, but the right-hand block was comparatively modern, and the blinds in the windows, with the blue smoke curling up from the chimneys, showed that this was where the family resided. Some scaffolding had been erected against the end wall, and the stone-work had been broken into, but there were no signs of any workmen at the moment of our visit. Holmes walked slowly up and down the ill-trimmed lawn and examined with deep attention the outsides of the windows.

"This, I take it, belongs to the room in which you used to sleep, the centre one to your sister's, and the one next to the main building to Dr. Roylott's chamber?"

"Exactly so. But I am now sleeping in the middle one."

"Pending the alterations, as I understand. By the way, there does not seem to be any very pressing need for repairs at that end wall."

"There were none. I believe that it was an excuse to move me from my room."

"Ah! that is suggestive. Now, on the other side of this narrow wing runs the corridor from which these three rooms open. There are windows in it, of course?"

"Yes, but very small ones. Too narrow for anyone to pass through."

"As you both locked your doors at night, your rooms were unapproachable from that side. Now, would you have the kindness to go into your room and bar your shutters?"

Miss Stoner did so, and Holmes, after a careful examination through the open window, endeavoured in every way to force the shutter open, but without success. There was no slit through which a knife could be passed to raise the bar. Then with his lens he tested the hinges, but they were of solid iron, built firmly into the massive masonry. "Hum!" said he, scratching his chin in some perplexity, "my theory certainly presents some difficulties. No one could pass these shutters if they were bolted. Well, we shall see if the inside throws any light upon the matter."

A small side door led into the whitewashed corridor from which the three bedrooms opened. Holmes refused to examine the third chamber, so we passed at once to the second, that in which Miss Stoner was now sleeping, and in which her sister had met with her fate. It was a homely little room, with a low ceiling and a gaping fireplace, after the fashion of old country-houses. A brown chest of drawers stood in one corner, a narrow white-counterpaned bed in another, and a dressing-table on the left-hand side of the window. These articles, with two small wicker-work chairs, made up all the furniture in the room save for a square of Wilton carpet in the centre. The boards round and the panelling of the walls were of brown, worm-eaten oak, so old and discoloured that it may have dated from the original building of the house. Holmes drew one of the chairs into a corner and sat silent, while his eyes travelled round and round and up and down, taking in every detail of the apartment.

"Where does that bell communicate with?" he asked at last pointing to a thick bell-rope which hung down beside the bed, the tassel actually lying upon the pillow.

"It goes to the housekeeper's room."

"It looks newer than the other things?"

"Yes, it was only put there a couple of years ago."

"Your sister asked for it, I suppose?"

"No, I never heard of her using it. We used always to get what we wanted for ourselves."

"Indeed, it seemed unnecessary to put so nice a bell-pull there. You will excuse me for a few minutes while I satisfy myself as to this floor." He threw himself down upon his face with his lens in his hand and crawled swiftly backward and forward, examining minutely the cracks between the boards. Then he did the same with the wood-work with which the chamber was panelled. Finally he walked over to the bed and spent some time in staring at it and in running his eye up and down the wall. Finally he took the bell-rope in his hand and gave it a brisk tug.

"Why, it's a dummy," said he.

"Won't it ring?"

"No, it is not even attached to a wire. This is very interesting. You can see now that it is fastened to a hook just above where the little opening for the ventilator is."

"How very absurd! I never noticed that before."

"Very strange!" muttered Holmes, pulling at the rope. "There are one or two very singular points about this room. For example, what a fool a builder must be to open a ventilator into another room, when, with the same trouble, he might have communicated with the outside air!"

"That is also quite modern," said the lady.

"Done about the same time as the bell-rope?" remarked Holmes.

"Yes, there were several little changes carried out about that time."

"They seem to have been of a most interesting character—dummy bell-ropes, and ventilators which do not ventilate. With your permission, Miss Stoner, we shall now carry our researches into the inner apartment."

Dr. Grimesby Roylott's chamber was larger than that of his step-daughter, but was as plainly furnished. A camp-bed, a small wooden shelf full of books, mostly of a technical character, an armchair beside the bed, a plain wooden chair against the wall, a round table, and a large iron safe were the principal things which met the eye. Holmes walked slowly round and examined each and all of them with the keenest interest.

"What's in here?" he asked, tapping the safe.

"My stepfather's business papers."

"Oh! you have seen inside, then?"

"Only once, some years ago. I remember that it was full of papers."

"There isn't a cat in it, for example?"

"No. What a strange idea!"

"Well, look at this!" He took up a small saucer of milk which stood on the top of it.

"No; we don't keep a cat. But there is a cheetah and a baboon."

"Ah, yes, of course! Well, a cheetah is just a big cat, and yet a saucer of milk does not go very far in satisfying its wants, I daresay. There is one point which I should wish to determine." He squatted down in front of the wooden chair and examined the seat of it with the greatest attention.

"Thank you. That is quite settled," said he, rising and putting his lens in his pocket. "Hullo! Here is something interesting!"

The object which had caught his eye was a small dog lash hung on one corner of the bed. The lash, however, was curled upon itself and tied so as to make a loop of whipcord.

"What do you make of that, Watson?"

"It's a common enough lash. But I don't know why it should be tied."

"That is not quite so common, is it? Ah, me! it's a wicked world, and when a clever man turns his brains to crime it is the worst of all. I think that I have seen enough now, Miss Stoner, and with your permission we shall walk out upon the lawn."

I had never seen my friend's face so grim or his brow so dark as it was when we turned from the scene of this investigation. We had walked several times up and down the lawn, neither Miss Stoner nor myself liking to break in upon his thoughts before he roused himself from his reverie.

"It is very essential, Miss Stoner," said he, "that you should absolutely follow my advice in every respect."

"I shall most certainly do so."

"The matter is too serious for any hesitation. Your life may depend upon your compliance."

"I assure you that I am in your hands."

"In the first place, both my friend and I must spend the night in your room."

Both Miss Stoner and I gazed at him in astonishment.

"Yes, it must be so. Let me explain. I believe that that is the village inn over there?"

"Yes, that is the Crown."

"Very good. Your windows would be visible from there?"

"Certainly."

"You must confine yourself to your room, on pretence of a headache, when your stepfather comes back. Then when you hear him retire for the night, you must open the shutters of your window, undo the hasp, put your lamp there as a signal to us, and then withdraw quietly with everything which you are likely to want into the room which you used to occupy. I have no doubt that, in spite of the repairs, you could manage there for one night."

"Oh, yes, easily."

"The rest you will leave in our hands."

"But what will you do?"

"We shall spend the night in your room, and we shall investigate the cause of this noise which has disturbed you."

"I believe, Mr. Holmes, that you have already made up your mind," said Miss Stoner, laying her hand upon my companion's sleeve.

"Perhaps I have."

"Then, for pity's sake, tell me what was the cause of my sister's death."

"I should prefer to have clearer proofs before I speak."

"You can at least tell me whether my own thought is correct, and if she died from some sudden fright."

"No, I do not think so. I think that there was probably some more tangible cause. And now, Miss Stoner, we must leave you for if Dr. Roylott returned and saw us our journey would be in vain. Good-bye, and be brave, for if you will do what I have told you, you may rest assured that we shall soon drive away the dangers that threaten you."

Sherlock Holmes and I had no difficulty in engaging a bedroom and sitting-room at the Crown Inn. They were on the upper floor, and from our window we could command a view of the avenue gate, and of the inhabited wing of Stoke Moran Manor House. At dusk we saw Dr. Grimesby Roylott drive past, his huge form looming up beside the little figure of the lad who drove him. The boy had some slight difficulty in undoing the heavy iron gates, and we heard the hoarse roar of the doctor's voice and saw the fury with which he shook his clinched fists at him. The trap drove on, and a few minutes later we saw a sudden light spring up among the trees as the lamp was lit in one of the sitting-rooms.

"Do you know, Watson," said Holmes as we sat together in the gathering darkness, "I have really some scruples as to taking you to-night. There is a distinct element of danger."

"Can I be of assistance?"

"Your presence might be invaluable."

"Then I shall certainly come."

"It is very kind of you."

"You speak of danger. You have evidently seen more in these rooms than was visible to me."

"No, but I fancy that I may have deduced a little more. I imagine that you saw all that I did."

"I saw nothing remarkable save the bell-rope, and what purpose that could answer I confess is more than I can imagine."

"You saw the ventilator, too?"

"Yes, but I do not think that it is such a very unusual thing to have a small opening between two rooms. It was so small that a rat could hardly pass through."

"I knew that we should find a ventilator before ever we came to Stoke Moran."

"My dear Holmes!"

"Oh, yes, I did. You remember in her statement she said that her sister could smell Dr. Roylott's cigar. Now, of course that suggested at once that there must be a communication between the two rooms. It could only be a small one, or it would have been remarked upon at the coroner's inquiry. I deduced a ventilator."

"But what harm can there be in that?"

"Well, there is at least a curious coincidence of dates. A ventilator is made, a cord is hung, and a lady who sleeps in the bed dies. Does not that strike you?"

"I cannot as yet see any connection."

"Did you observe anything very peculiar about that bed?"

"No."

"It was clamped to the floor. Did you ever see a bed fastened like that before?"

"I cannot say that I have."

"The lady could not move her bed. It must always be in the same relative position to the ventilator and to the rope—or so we may call it, since it was clearly never meant for a bell-pull."

"Holmes," I cried, "I seem to see dimly what you are hinting at. We are only just in time to prevent some subtle and horrible crime."

"Subtle enough and horrible enough. When a doctor does go wrong he is the first of criminals. He has nerve and he has knowledge. Palmer and Pritchard were among the heads of their profession. This man strikes even deeper, but I think, Watson, that we shall be able to strike deeper still. But we shall have horrors enough before the night is over; for goodness' sake let us have a quiet pipe and turn our minds for a few hours to something more cheerful."

About nine o'clock the light among the trees was extinguished, and all was dark in the direction of the Manor House. Two hours passed slowly away, and then, suddenly, just at the stroke of eleven, a single bright light shone out right in front of us.

"That is our signal," said Holmes, springing to his feet; "it comes from the middle window."

As we passed out he exchanged a few words with the landlord, explaining that we were going on a late visit to an acquaintance, and that it was possible that we might spend the night there. A moment later we were out on the dark road, a chill wind blowing in our faces, and one yellow light twinkling in front of us through the gloom to guide us on our sombre errand.

There was little difficulty in entering the grounds, for unrepaired breaches gaped in the old park wall. Making our way among the trees, we reached the lawn, crossed it, and were about to enter through the window when out from a clump of laurel bushes there darted what seemed to be a hideous and distorted child, who threw itself upon the grass with writhing limbs and then ran swiftly across the lawn into the darkness.

"My God!" I whispered; "did you see it?"

Holmes was for the moment as startled as I. His hand closed like a vice upon my wrist in his agitation. Then he broke into a low laugh and put his lips to my ear.

"It is a nice household," he murmured. "That is the baboon."

I had forgotten the strange pets which the doctor affected. There was a cheetah, too; perhaps we might find it upon our shoulders at any moment. I confess that I felt easier in my mind when, after following Holmes' example and slipping off my shoes, I found myself inside the bedroom. My companion noiselessly closed the shutters, moved the lamp onto the table, and cast his eyes round the room. All was as we had seen it in the daytime. Then creeping up to me and making a trumpet of his hand, he whispered into my ear again so gently that it was all that I could do to distinguish the words:

"The least sound would be fatal to our plans."

I nodded to show that I had heard.

"We must sit without light. He would see it through the ventilator."

I nodded again.

"Do not go asleep; your very life may depend upon it. Have your pistol ready in case we should need it. I will sit on the side of the bed, and you in that chair."

I took out my revolver and laid it on the corner of the table.

Holmes had brought up a long thin cane, and this he placed upon the bed beside him. By it he laid the box of matches and the stump of a candle. Then he turned down the lamp, and we were left in darkness.

How shall I ever forget that dreadful vigil? I could not hear a sound, not even the drawing of a breath, and yet I knew that my companion sat open-eyed, within a few feet of me, in the same state of nervous tension in which I was myself. The shutters cut off the least ray of light, and we waited in absolute darkness.

From outside came the occasional cry of a night-bird, and once at our very window a long drawn catlike whine, which told us that the cheetah was indeed at liberty. Far away we could hear the deep tones of the parish clock, which boomed out every quarter of an hour. How long they seemed, those quarters! Twelve struck, and one and two and three, and still we sat waiting silently for whatever might befall.

Suddenly there was the momentary gleam of a light up in the direction of the ventilator, which vanished immediately, but was succeeded by a strong smell of burning oil and heated metal. Someone in the next room had lit a dark-lantern. I heard a gentle sound of movement, and then all was silent once more, though the smell grew stronger. For half an hour I sat with straining ears. Then suddenly another sound became audible—a very gentle, soothing sound, like that of a small jet of steam escaping continually from a kettle. The instant that we heard it, Holmes sprang from the bed, struck a match, and lashed furiously with his cane at the bell-pull.

"You see it, Watson?" he yelled. "You see it?"

But I saw nothing. At the moment when Holmes struck the light I heard a low, clear whistle, but the sudden glare flashing into my weary eyes made it impossible for me to tell what it was at which my friend lashed so savagely. I could, however, see that his face was deadly pale and filled with horror and loathing. He had ceased to strike and was gazing up at the ventilator when suddenly there broke from the silence of the night the most horrible cry to which I have ever listened. It swelled up louder and louder, a hoarse yell of pain and fear and anger all mingled in the one dreadful shriek. They say that away down in the village, and even in the distant parsonage, that cry raised the sleepers from their beds. It struck cold to our hearts, and I stood gazing at Holmes, and he at me, until the last echoes of it had died away into the silence from which it rose.

"What can it mean?" I gasped.

"It means that it is all over," Holmes answered. "And perhaps, after all, it is for the best. Take your pistol, and we will enter Dr. Roylott's room."

With a grave face he lit the lamp and led the way down the corridor. Twice he struck at the chamber door without any reply from within. Then he turned the handle and entered, I at his heels, with the cocked pistol in my hand.

It was a singular sight which met our eyes. On the table stood a dark-lantern with the shutter half open, throwing a brilliant beam of light upon the iron safe, the door of which was ajar. Beside this table, on the wooden chair, sat Dr. Grimesby Roylott clad in a long grey dressing-gown, his bare ankles protruding beneath, and his feet thrust into red heelless Turkish slippers. Across his lap lay the short stock with the long lash which we had noticed during the day. His chin was cocked upward and his eyes were fixed in a dreadful, rigid stare at the corner of the ceiling. Round his brow he had a peculiar yellow band, with brownish speckles, which seemed to be bound tightly round his head. As we entered he made neither sound nor motion.

"The band! the speckled band!" whispered Holmes.

I took a step forward. In an instant his strange headgear began to move, and there reared itself from among his hair the squat diamond-shaped head and puffed neck of a loathsome serpent.

"It is a swamp adder!" cried Holmes; "the deadliest snake in India. He has died within ten seconds of being bitten. Violence does, in truth, recoil upon the violent, and the schemer falls into the pit which he digs for another. Let us thrust this creature back into its den, and we can then remove Miss Stoner to some place of shelter and let the county police know what has happened."

As he spoke he drew the dog-whip swiftly from the dead man's lap, and throwing the noose round the reptile's neck he drew it from its horrid perch and, carrying it at arm's length, threw it into the iron safe, which he closed upon it.

Such are the true facts of the death of Dr. Grimesby Roylott, of Stoke Moran. It is not necessary that I should prolong a narrative which has already run to too great a length by telling how we broke the sad news to the terrified girl, how we conveyed her by the morning train to the care of her good aunt at Harrow, of how the slow process of official inquiry came to the conclusion that the doctor met his fate while indiscreetly playing with a dangerous pet. The little which I had yet to learn of the case was told me by Sherlock Holmes as we travelled back next day.

"I had," said he, "come to an entirely erroneous conclusion which shows, my dear Watson, how dangerous it always is to reason from insufficient data. The presence of the gipsies, and the use of the word 'band,' which was used by the poor girl, no doubt, to explain the appearance which she had caught a hurried glimpse of by the light of her match, were sufficient to put me upon an entirely wrong scent. I can only claim the merit that I instantly reconsidered my position when, however, it became clear to me that whatever danger threatened an occupant of the room could not come either from the window or the door. My attention was speedily drawn, as I have already remarked to you, to this ventilator, and to the bell-rope which hung down to the bed. The discovery that this was a dummy, and that the bed was clamped to the floor, instantly gave rise to the suspicion that the rope was there as a bridge for something passing through the hole and coming to the bed. The idea of a snake instantly occurred to me, and when I coupled it with my knowledge that the doctor was furnished with a supply of creatures from India, I felt that I was probably on the right track. The idea of using a form of poison which could not possibly be discovered by any chemical test was just such a one as would occur to a clever and ruthless man who had had an Eastern training. The rapidity with which such a poison would take effect would also, from his point of view, be an advantage. It would be a sharp-eyed coroner, indeed, who could distinguish the two little dark punctures which would show where the poison fangs had done their work. Then I thought of the whistle. Of course he must recall the snake before the morning light revealed it to the victim. He had trained it, probably by the use of the milk which we saw, to return to him when summoned. He would put it through this ventilator at the hour that he thought best, with the certainty that it would crawl down the rope and land on the bed. It might or might not bite the occupant, perhaps she might escape every night for a week, but sooner or later she must fall a victim.

"I had come to these conclusions before ever I had entered his room. An inspection of his chair showed me that he had been in the habit of standing on it, which of course would be necessary in order that he should reach the ventilator. The sight of the safe, the saucer of milk, and the loop of whipcord were enough to finally dispel any doubts which may have remained. The metallic clang heard by Miss Stoner was obviously caused by her stepfather hastily closing the door of his safe upon its terrible occupant. Having once made up my mind, you know the steps which I took in order to put the matter to the proof. I heard the creature hiss as I have no doubt that you did also, and I instantly lit the light and attacked it."

"With the result of driving it through the ventilator."

"And also with the result of causing it to turn upon its master at the other side. Some of the blows of my cane came home and roused its snakish temper, so that it flew upon the first person it saw. In this way I am no doubt indirectly responsible for Dr. Grimesby Roylott's death, and I cannot say that it is likely to weigh very heavily upon my conscience."

IX. The Adventure Of The Engineer's Thumb

Of all the problems which have been submitted to my friend, Mr. Sherlock Holmes, for solution during the years of our intimacy, there were only two which I was the means of introducing to his notice—that of Mr. Hatherley's thumb, and that of Colonel Warburton's madness. Of these the latter may have afforded a finer field for an acute and original observer, but the other was so strange in its inception and so dramatic in its details that it may be the more worthy of being placed upon record, even if it gave my friend fewer openings for those deductive methods of reasoning by which he achieved such remarkable results. The story has, I believe, been told more than once in the newspapers, but, like all such narratives, its effect is much less striking when set forth en bloc in a single half-column of print than when the facts slowly evolve before your own eyes, and the mystery clears gradually away as each new discovery furnishes a step which leads on to the complete truth. At the time the circumstances made a deep impression upon me, and the lapse of two years has hardly served to weaken the effect.

It was in the summer of '89, not long after my marriage, that the events occurred which I am now about to summarise. I had returned to civil practice and had finally abandoned Holmes in his Baker Street rooms, although I continually visited him and occasionally even persuaded him to forgo his Bohemian habits so far as to come and visit us. My practice had steadily increased, and as I happened to live at no very great distance from Paddington Station, I got a few patients from among the officials. One of these, whom I had cured of a painful and lingering disease, was never weary of advertising my virtues and of endeavouring to send me on every sufferer over whom he might have any influence.

One morning, at a little before seven o'clock, I was awakened by the maid tapping at the door to announce that two men had come from Paddington and were waiting in the consulting-room. I dressed hurriedly, for I knew by experience that railway cases were seldom trivial, and hastened downstairs. As I descended, my old ally, the guard, came out of the room and closed the door tightly behind him.

"I've got him here," he whispered, jerking his thumb over his shoulder; "he's all right."

"What is it, then?" I asked, for his manner suggested that it was some strange creature which he had caged up in my room.

"It's a new patient," he whispered. "I thought I'd bring him round myself; then he couldn't slip away. There he is, all safe and sound. I must go now, Doctor; I have my dooties, just the same as you." And off he went, this trusty tout, without even giving me time to thank him.

I entered my consulting-room and found a gentleman seated by the table. He was quietly dressed in a suit of heather tweed with a soft cloth cap which he had laid down upon my books. Round one of his hands he had a handkerchief wrapped, which was mottled all over with bloodstains. He was young, not more than five-and-twenty, I should say, with a strong, masculine face; but he was exceedingly pale and gave me the impression of a man who was suffering from some strong agitation, which it took all his strength of mind to control.

"I am sorry to knock you up so early, Doctor," said he, "but I have had a very serious accident during the night. I came in by train this morning, and on inquiring at Paddington as to where I might find a doctor, a worthy fellow very kindly escorted me here. I gave the maid a card, but I see that she has left it upon the side-table."

I took it up and glanced at it. "Mr. Victor Hatherley, hydraulic engineer, 16A, Victoria Street (3rd floor)." That was the name, style, and abode of my morning visitor. "I regret that I have kept you waiting," said I, sitting down in my library-chair. "You are fresh from a night journey, I understand, which is in itself a monotonous occupation."

"Oh, my night could not be called monotonous," said he, and laughed. He laughed very heartily, with a high, ringing note, leaning back in his chair and shaking his sides. All my medical instincts rose up against that laugh.

"Stop it!" I cried; "pull yourself together!" and I poured out some water from a caraffe.

It was useless, however. He was off in one of those hysterical outbursts which come upon a strong nature when some great crisis is over and gone. Presently he came to himself once more, very weary and pale-looking.

"I have been making a fool of myself," he gasped.

"Not at all. Drink this." I dashed some brandy into the water, and the colour began to come back to his bloodless cheeks.

"That's better!" said he. "And now, Doctor, perhaps you would kindly attend to my thumb, or rather to the place where my thumb used to be."

He unwound the handkerchief and held out his hand. It gave even my hardened nerves a shudder to look at it. There were four protruding fingers and a horrid red, spongy surface where the thumb should have been. It had been hacked or torn right out from the roots.

"Good heavens!" I cried, "this is a terrible injury. It must have bled considerably."

"Yes, it did. I fainted when it was done, and I think that I must have been senseless for a long time. When I came to I found that it was still bleeding, so I tied one end of my handkerchief very tightly round the wrist and braced it up with a twig."

"Excellent! You should have been a surgeon."

"It is a question of hydraulics, you see, and came within my own province."

"This has been done," said I, examining the wound, "by a very heavy and sharp instrument."

"A thing like a cleaver," said he.

"An accident, I presume?"

"By no means."

"What! a murderous attack?"

"Very murderous indeed."

"You horrify me."

I sponged the wound, cleaned it, dressed it, and finally covered it over with cotton wadding and carbolised bandages. He lay back without wincing, though he bit his lip from time to time.

"How is that?" I asked when I had finished.

"Capital! Between your brandy and your bandage, I feel a new man. I was very weak, but I have had a good deal to go through."

"Perhaps you had better not speak of the matter. It is evidently trying to your nerves."

"Oh, no, not now. I shall have to tell my tale to the police; but, between ourselves, if it were not for the convincing evidence of this wound of mine, I should be surprised if they believed my statement, for it is a very extraordinary one, and I have not much in the way of proof with which to back it up; and, even if they believe me, the clues which I can give them are so vague that it is a question whether justice will be done."

"Ha!" cried I, "if it is anything in the nature of a problem which you desire to see solved, I should strongly recommend you to come to my friend, Mr. Sherlock Holmes, before you go to the official police."

"Oh, I have heard of that fellow," answered my visitor, "and I should be very glad if he would take the matter up, though of course I must use the official police as well. Would you give me an introduction to him?"

"I'll do better. I'll take you round to him myself."

"I should be immensely obliged to you."

"We'll call a cab and go together. We shall just be in time to have a little breakfast with him. Do you feel equal to it?"

"Yes; I shall not feel easy until I have told my story."

"Then my servant will call a cab, and I shall be with you in an instant." I rushed upstairs, explained the matter shortly to my wife, and in five minutes was inside a hansom, driving with my new acquaintance to Baker Street.

Sherlock Holmes was, as I expected, lounging about his sitting-room in his dressing-gown, reading the agony column of The Times and smoking his before-breakfast pipe, which was composed of all the plugs and dottles left from his smokes of the day before, all carefully dried and collected on the corner of the mantelpiece. He received us in his quietly genial fashion, ordered fresh rashers and eggs, and joined us in a hearty meal. When it was concluded he settled our new acquaintance upon the sofa, placed a pillow beneath his head, and laid a glass of brandy and water within his reach.

"It is easy to see that your experience has been no common one, Mr. Hatherley," said he. "Pray, lie down there and make yourself absolutely at home. Tell us what you can, but stop when you are tired and keep up your strength with a little stimulant."

"Thank you," said my patient. "but I have felt another man since the doctor bandaged me, and I think that your breakfast has completed the cure. I shall take up as little of your valuable time as possible, so I shall start at once upon my peculiar experiences."

Holmes sat in his big armchair with the weary, heavy-lidded expression which veiled his keen and eager nature, while I sat opposite to him, and we listened in silence to the strange story which our visitor detailed to us.

"You must know," said he, "that I am an orphan and a bachelor, residing alone in lodgings in London. By profession I am a hydraulic engineer, and I have had considerable experience of my work during the seven years that I was apprenticed to Venner & Matheson, the well-known firm, of Greenwich. Two years ago, having served my time, and having also come into a fair sum of money through my poor father's death, I determined to start in business for myself and took professional chambers in Victoria Street.

"I suppose that everyone finds his first independent start in business a dreary experience. To me it has been exceptionally so. During two years I have had three consultations and one small job, and that is absolutely all that my profession has brought me. My gross takings amount to 27 pounds 10s. Every day, from nine in the morning until four in the afternoon, I waited in my little den, until at last my heart began to sink, and I came to believe that I should never have any practice at all.

"Yesterday, however, just as I was thinking of leaving the office, my clerk entered to say there was a gentleman waiting who wished to see me upon business. He brought up a card, too, with the name of 'Colonel Lysander Stark' engraved upon it. Close at his heels came the colonel himself, a man rather over the middle size, but of an exceeding thinness. I do not think that I have ever seen so thin a man. His whole face sharpened away into nose and chin, and the skin of his cheeks was drawn quite tense over his outstanding bones. Yet this emaciation seemed to be his natural habit, and due to no disease, for his eye was bright, his step brisk, and his bearing assured. He was plainly but neatly dressed, and his age, I should judge, would be nearer forty than thirty.

"'Mr. Hatherley?' said he, with something of a German accent. 'You have been recommended to me, Mr. Hatherley, as being a man who is not only proficient in his profession but is also discreet and capable of preserving a secret.'

"I bowed, feeling as flattered as any young man would at such an address. 'May I ask who it was who gave me so good a character?'

"'Well, perhaps it is better that I should not tell you that just at this moment. I have it from the same source that you are both an orphan and a bachelor and are residing alone in London.'

"'That is quite correct,' I answered; 'but you will excuse me if I say that I cannot see how all this bears upon my professional qualifications. I understand that it was on a professional matter that you wished to speak to me?'

"'Undoubtedly so. But you will find that all I say is really to the point. I have a professional commission for you, but absolute secrecy is quite essential—absolute secrecy, you understand, and of course we may expect that more from a man who is alone than from one who lives in the bosom of his family.'

"'If I promise to keep a secret,' said I, 'you may absolutely depend upon my doing so.'

"He looked very hard at me as I spoke, and it seemed to me that I had never seen so suspicious and questioning an eye.

"'Do you promise, then?' said he at last.

"'Yes, I promise.'

"'Absolute and complete silence before, during, and after? No reference to the matter at all, either in word or writing?'

"'I have already given you my word.'

"'Very good.' He suddenly sprang up, and darting like lightning across the room he flung open the door. The passage outside was empty.

"'That's all right,' said he, coming back. 'I know that clerks are sometimes curious as to their master's affairs. Now we can talk in safety.' He drew up his chair very close to mine and began to stare at me again with the same questioning and thoughtful look.

"A feeling of repulsion, and of something akin to fear had begun to rise within me at the strange antics of this fleshless man. Even my dread of losing a client could not restrain me from showing my impatience.

"'I beg that you will state your business, sir,' said I; 'my time is of value.' Heaven forgive me for that last sentence, but the words came to my lips.

"'How would fifty guineas for a night's work suit you?' he asked.

"'Most admirably.'

"'I say a night's work, but an hour's would be nearer the mark. I simply want your opinion about a hydraulic stamping machine which has got out of gear. If you show us what is wrong we shall soon set it right ourselves. What do you think of such a commission as that?'

"'The work appears to be light and the pay munificent.'

"'Precisely so. We shall want you to come to-night by the last train.'

"'Where to?'

"'To Eyford, in Berkshire. It is a little place near the borders of Oxfordshire, and within seven miles of Reading. There is a train from Paddington which would bring you there at about 11:15.'

"'Very good.'

"'I shall come down in a carriage to meet you.'

"'There is a drive, then?'

"'Yes, our little place is quite out in the country. It is a good seven miles from Eyford Station.'

"'Then we can hardly get there before midnight. I suppose there would be no chance of a train back. I should be compelled to stop the night.'

"'Yes, we could easily give you a shake-down.'

"'That is very awkward. Could I not come at some more convenient hour?'

"'We have judged it best that you should come late. It is to recompense you for any inconvenience that we are paying to you, a young and unknown man, a fee which would buy an opinion from the very heads of your profession. Still, of course, if you would like to draw out of the business, there is plenty of time to do so.'

"I thought of the fifty guineas, and of how very useful they would be to me. 'Not at all,' said I, 'I shall be very happy to accommodate myself to your wishes. I should like, however, to understand a little more clearly what it is that you wish me to do.'

"'Quite so. It is very natural that the pledge of secrecy which we have exacted from you should have aroused your curiosity. I have no wish to commit you to anything without your having it all laid before you. I suppose that we are absolutely safe from eavesdroppers?'

"'Entirely.'

"'Then the matter stands thus. You are probably aware that fuller's-earth is a valuable product, and that it is only found in one or two places in England?'

"'I have heard so.'

"'Some little time ago I bought a small place—a very small place—within ten miles of Reading. I was fortunate enough to discover that there was a deposit of fuller's-earth in one of my fields. On examining it, however, I found that this deposit was a comparatively small one, and that it formed a link between two very much larger ones upon the right and left—both of them, however, in the grounds of my neighbours. These good people were absolutely ignorant that their land contained that which was quite as valuable as a gold-mine. Naturally, it was to my interest to buy their land before they discovered its true value, but unfortunately I had no capital by which I could do this. I took a few of my friends into the secret, however, and they suggested that we should quietly and secretly work our own little deposit and that in this way we should earn the money which would enable us to buy the neighbouring fields. This we have now been doing for some time, and in order to help us in our operations we erected a hydraulic press. This press, as I have already explained, has got out of order, and we wish your advice upon the subject. We guard our secret very jealously, however, and if it once became known that we had hydraulic engineers coming to our little house, it would soon rouse inquiry, and then, if the facts came out, it would be good-bye to any chance of getting these fields and carrying out our plans. That is why I have made you promise me that you will not tell a human being that you are going to Eyford to-night. I hope that I make it all plain?'

"'I quite follow you,' said I. 'The only point which I could not quite understand was what use you could make of a hydraulic press in excavating fuller's-earth, which, as I understand, is dug out like gravel from a pit.'

"'Ah!' said he carelessly, 'we have our own process. We compress the earth into bricks, so as to remove them without revealing what they are. But that is a mere detail. I have taken you fully into my confidence now, Mr. Hatherley, and I have shown you how I trust you.' He rose as he spoke. 'I shall expect you, then, at Eyford at 11:15.'

"'I shall certainly be there.'

"'And not a word to a soul.' He looked at me with a last long, questioning gaze, and then, pressing my hand in a cold, dank grasp, he hurried from the room.

"Well, when I came to think it all over in cool blood I was very much astonished, as you may both think, at this sudden commission which had been intrusted to me. On the one hand, of course, I was glad, for the fee was at least tenfold what I should have asked had I set a price upon my own services, and it was possible that this order might lead to other ones. On the other hand, the face and manner of my patron had made an unpleasant impression upon me, and I could not think that his explanation of the fuller's-earth was sufficient to explain the necessity for my coming at midnight, and his extreme anxiety lest I should tell anyone of my errand. However, I threw all fears to the winds, ate a hearty supper, drove to Paddington, and started off, having obeyed to the letter the injunction as to holding my tongue.

"At Reading I had to change not only my carriage but my station. However, I was in time for the last train to Eyford, and I reached the little dim-lit station after eleven o'clock. I was the only passenger who got out there, and there was no one upon the platform save a single sleepy porter with a lantern. As I passed out through the wicket gate, however, I found my acquaintance of the morning waiting in the shadow upon the other side. Without a word he grasped my arm and hurried me into a carriage, the door of which was standing open. He drew up the windows on either side, tapped on the wood-work, and away we went as fast as the horse could go."

"One horse?" interjected Holmes.

"Yes, only one."

"Did you observe the colour?"

"Yes, I saw it by the side-lights when I was stepping into the carriage. It was a chestnut."

"Tired-looking or fresh?"

"Oh, fresh and glossy."

"Thank you. I am sorry to have interrupted you. Pray continue your most interesting statement."

"Away we went then, and we drove for at least an hour. Colonel Lysander Stark had said that it was only seven miles, but I should think, from the rate that we seemed to go, and from the time that we took, that it must have been nearer twelve. He sat at my side in silence all the time, and I was aware, more than once when I glanced in his direction, that he was looking at me with great intensity. The country roads seem to be not very good in that part of the world, for we lurched and jolted terribly. I tried to look out of the windows to see something of where we were, but they were made of frosted glass, and I could make out nothing save the occasional bright blur of a passing light. Now and then I hazarded some remark to break the monotony of the journey, but the colonel answered only in monosyllables, and the conversation soon flagged. At last, however, the bumping of the road was exchanged for the crisp smoothness of a gravel-drive, and the carriage came to a stand. Colonel Lysander Stark sprang out, and, as I followed after him, pulled me swiftly into a porch which gaped in front of us. We stepped, as it were, right out of the carriage and into the hall, so that I failed to catch the most fleeting glance of the front of the house. The instant that I had crossed the threshold the door slammed heavily behind us, and I heard faintly the rattle of the wheels as the carriage drove away.

"It was pitch dark inside the house, and the colonel fumbled about looking for matches and muttering under his breath. Suddenly a door opened at the other end of the passage, and a long, golden bar of light shot out in our direction. It grew broader, and a woman appeared with a lamp in her hand, which she held above her head, pushing her face forward and peering at us. I could see that she was pretty, and from the gloss with which the light shone upon her dark dress I knew that it was a rich material. She spoke a few words in a foreign tongue in a tone as though asking a question, and when my companion answered in a gruff monosyllable she gave such a start that the lamp nearly fell from her hand. Colonel Stark went up to her, whispered something in her ear, and then, pushing her back into the room from whence she had come, he walked towards me again with the lamp in his hand.

"'Perhaps you will have the kindness to wait in this room for a few minutes,' said he, throwing open another door. It was a quiet, little, plainly furnished room, with a round table in the centre, on which several German books were scattered. Colonel Stark laid down the lamp on the top of a harmonium beside the door. 'I shall not keep you waiting an instant,' said he, and vanished into the darkness.

"I glanced at the books upon the table, and in spite of my ignorance of German I could see that two of them were treatises on science, the others being volumes of poetry. Then I walked across to the window, hoping that I might catch some glimpse of the country-side, but an oak shutter, heavily barred, was folded across it. It was a wonderfully silent house. There was an old clock ticking loudly somewhere in the passage, but otherwise everything was deadly still. A vague feeling of uneasiness began to steal over me. Who were these German people, and what were they doing living in this strange, out-of-the-way place? And where was the place? I was ten miles or so from Eyford, that was all I knew, but whether north, south, east, or west I had no idea. For that matter, Reading, and possibly other large towns, were within that radius, so the place might not be so secluded, after all. Yet it was quite certain, from the absolute stillness, that we were in the country. I paced up and down the room, humming a tune under my breath to keep up my spirits and feeling that I was thoroughly earning my fifty-guinea fee.

"Suddenly, without any preliminary sound in the midst of the utter stillness, the door of my room swung slowly open. The woman was standing in the aperture, the darkness of the hall behind her, the yellow light from my lamp beating upon her eager and beautiful face. I could see at a glance that she was sick with fear, and the sight sent a chill to my own heart. She held up one shaking finger to warn me to be silent, and she shot a few whispered words of broken English at me, her eyes glancing back, like those of a frightened horse, into the gloom behind her.

"'I would go,' said she, trying hard, as it seemed to me, to speak calmly; 'I would go. I should not stay here. There is no good for you to do.'

"'But, madam,' said I, 'I have not yet done what I came for. I cannot possibly leave until I have seen the machine.'

"'It is not worth your while to wait,' she went on. 'You can pass through the door; no one hinders.' And then, seeing that I smiled and shook my head, she suddenly threw aside her constraint and made a step forward, with her hands wrung together. 'For the love of Heaven!' she whispered, 'get away from here before it is too late!'

"But I am somewhat headstrong by nature, and the more ready to engage in an affair when there is some obstacle in the way. I thought of my fifty-guinea fee, of my wearisome journey, and of the unpleasant night which seemed to be before me. Was it all to go for nothing? Why should I slink away without having carried out my commission, and without the payment which was my due? This woman might, for all I knew, be a monomaniac. With a stout bearing, therefore, though her manner had shaken me more than I cared to confess, I still shook my head and declared my intention of remaining where I was. She was about to renew her entreaties when a door slammed overhead, and the sound of several footsteps was heard upon the stairs. She listened for an instant, threw up her hands with a despairing gesture, and vanished as suddenly and as noiselessly as she had come.

"The newcomers were Colonel Lysander Stark and a short thick man with a chinchilla beard growing out of the creases of his double chin, who was introduced to me as Mr. Ferguson.

"'This is my secretary and manager,' said the colonel. 'By the way, I was under the impression that I left this door shut just now. I fear that you have felt the draught.'

"'On the contrary,' said I, 'I opened the door myself because I felt the room to be a little close.'

"He shot one of his suspicious looks at me. 'Perhaps we had better proceed to business, then,' said he. 'Mr. Ferguson and I will take you up to see the machine.'

"'I had better put my hat on, I suppose.'

"'Oh, no, it is in the house.'

"'What, you dig fuller's-earth in the house?'

"'No, no. This is only where we compress it. But never mind that. All we wish you to do is to examine the machine and to let us know what is wrong with it.'

"We went upstairs together, the colonel first with the lamp, the fat manager and I behind him. It was a labyrinth of an old house, with corridors, passages, narrow winding staircases, and little low doors, the thresholds of which were hollowed out by the generations who had crossed them. There were no carpets and no signs of any furniture above the ground floor, while the plaster was peeling off the walls, and the damp was breaking through in green, unhealthy blotches. I tried to put on as unconcerned an air as possible, but I had not forgotten the warnings of the lady, even though I disregarded them, and I kept a keen eye upon my two companions. Ferguson appeared to be a morose and silent man, but I could see from the little that he said that he was at least a fellow-countryman.

"Colonel Lysander Stark stopped at last before a low door, which he unlocked. Within was a small, square room, in which the three of us could hardly get at one time. Ferguson remained outside, and the colonel ushered me in.

"'We are now,' said he, 'actually within the hydraulic press, and it would be a particularly unpleasant thing for us if anyone were to turn it on. The ceiling of this small chamber is really the end of the descending piston, and it comes down with the force of many tons upon this metal floor. There are small lateral columns of water outside which receive the force, and which transmit and multiply it in the manner which is familiar to you. The machine goes readily enough, but there is some stiffness in the working of it, and it has lost a little of its force. Perhaps you will have the goodness to look it over and to show us how we can set it right.'

"I took the lamp from him, and I examined the machine very thoroughly. It was indeed a gigantic one, and capable of exercising enormous pressure. When I passed outside, however, and pressed down the levers which controlled it, I knew at once by the whishing sound that there was a slight leakage, which allowed a regurgitation of water through one of the side cylinders. An examination showed that one of the india-rubber bands which was round the head of a driving-rod had shrunk so as not quite to fill the socket along which it worked. This was clearly the cause of the loss of power, and I pointed it out to my companions, who followed my remarks very carefully and asked several practical questions as to how they should proceed to set it right. When I had made it clear to them, I returned to the main chamber of the machine and took a good look at it to satisfy my own curiosity. It was obvious at a glance that the story of the fuller's-earth was the merest fabrication, for it would be absurd to suppose that so powerful an engine could be designed for so inadequate a purpose. The walls were of wood, but the floor consisted of a large iron trough, and when I came to examine it I could see a crust of metallic deposit all over it. I had stooped and was scraping at this to see exactly what it was when I heard a muttered exclamation in German and saw the cadaverous face of the colonel looking down at me.

"'What are you doing there?' he asked.

"I felt angry at having been tricked by so elaborate a story as that which he had told me. 'I was admiring your fuller's-earth,' said I; 'I think that I should be better able to advise you as to your machine if I knew what the exact purpose was for which it was used.'

"The instant that I uttered the words I regretted the rashness of my speech. His face set hard, and a baleful light sprang up in his grey eyes.

"'Very well,' said he, 'you shall know all about the machine.' He took a step backward, slammed the little door, and turned the key in the lock. I rushed towards it and pulled at the handle, but it was quite secure, and did not give in the least to my kicks and shoves. 'Hullo!' I yelled. 'Hullo! Colonel! Let me out!'

"And then suddenly in the silence I heard a sound which sent my heart into my mouth. It was the clank of the levers and the swish of the leaking cylinder. He had set the engine at work. The lamp still stood upon the floor where I had placed it when examining the trough. By its light I saw that the black ceiling was coming down upon me, slowly, jerkily, but, as none knew better than myself, with a force which must within a minute grind me to a shapeless pulp. I threw myself, screaming, against the door, and dragged with my nails at the lock. I implored the colonel to let me out, but the remorseless clanking of the levers drowned my cries. The ceiling was only a foot or two above my head, and with my hand upraised I could feel its hard, rough surface. Then it flashed through my mind that the pain of my death would depend very much upon the position in which I met it. If I lay on my face the weight would come upon my spine, and I shuddered to think of that dreadful snap. Easier the other way, perhaps; and yet, had I the nerve to lie and look up at that deadly black shadow wavering down upon me? Already I was unable to stand erect, when my eye caught something which brought a gush of hope back to my heart.

"I have said that though the floor and ceiling were of iron, the walls were of wood. As I gave a last hurried glance around, I saw a thin line of yellow light between two of the boards, which broadened and broadened as a small panel was pushed backward. For an instant I could hardly believe that here was indeed a door which led away from death. The next instant I threw myself through, and lay half-fainting upon the other side. The panel had closed again behind me, but the crash of the lamp, and a few moments afterwards the clang of the two slabs of metal, told me how narrow had been my escape.

"I was recalled to myself by a frantic plucking at my wrist, and I found myself lying upon the stone floor of a narrow corridor, while a woman bent over me and tugged at me with her left hand, while she held a candle in her right. It was the same good friend whose warning I had so foolishly rejected.

"'Come! come!' she cried breathlessly. 'They will be here in a moment. They will see that you are not there. Oh, do not waste the so-precious time, but come!'

"This time, at least, I did not scorn her advice. I staggered to my feet and ran with her along the corridor and down a winding stair. The latter led to another broad passage, and just as we reached it we heard the sound of running feet and the shouting of two voices, one answering the other from the floor on which we were and from the one beneath. My guide stopped and looked about her like one who is at her wit's end. Then she threw open a door which led into a bedroom, through the window of which the moon was shining brightly.

"'It is your only chance,' said she. 'It is high, but it may be that you can jump it.'

"As she spoke a light sprang into view at the further end of the passage, and I saw the lean figure of Colonel Lysander Stark rushing forward with a lantern in one hand and a weapon like a butcher's cleaver in the other. I rushed across the bedroom, flung open the window, and looked out. How quiet and sweet and wholesome the garden looked in the moonlight, and it could not be more than thirty feet down. I clambered out upon the sill, but I hesitated to jump until I should have heard what passed between my saviour and the ruffian who pursued me. If she were ill-used, then at any risks I was determined to go back to her assistance. The thought had hardly flashed through my mind before he was at the door, pushing his way past her; but she threw her arms round him and tried to hold him back.

"'Fritz! Fritz!' she cried in English, 'remember your promise after the last time. You said it should not be again. He will be silent! Oh, he will be silent!'

"'You are mad, Elise!' he shouted, struggling to break away from her. 'You will be the ruin of us. He has seen too much. Let me pass, I say!' He dashed her to one side, and, rushing to the window, cut at me with his heavy weapon. I had let myself go, and was hanging by the hands to the sill, when his blow fell. I was conscious of a dull pain, my grip loosened, and I fell into the garden below.

"I was shaken but not hurt by the fall; so I picked myself up and rushed off among the bushes as hard as I could run, for I understood that I was far from being out of danger yet. Suddenly, however, as I ran, a deadly dizziness and sickness came over me. I glanced down at my hand, which was throbbing painfully, and then, for the first time, saw that my thumb had been cut off and that the blood was pouring from my wound. I endeavoured to tie my handkerchief round it, but there came a sudden buzzing in my ears, and next moment I fell in a dead faint among the rose-bushes.

"How long I remained unconscious I cannot tell. It must have been a very long time, for the moon had sunk, and a bright morning was breaking when I came to myself. My clothes were all sodden with dew, and my coat-sleeve was drenched with blood from my wounded thumb. The smarting of it recalled in an instant all the particulars of my night's adventure, and I sprang to my feet with the feeling that I might hardly yet be safe from my pursuers. But to my astonishment, when I came to look round me, neither house nor garden were to be seen. I had been lying in an angle of the hedge close by the highroad, and just a little lower down was a long building, which proved, upon my approaching it, to be the very station at which I had arrived upon the previous night. Were it not for the ugly wound upon my hand, all that had passed during those dreadful hours might have been an evil dream.

"Half dazed, I went into the station and asked about the morning train. There would be one to Reading in less than an hour. The same porter was on duty, I found, as had been there when I arrived. I inquired of him whether he had ever heard of Colonel Lysander Stark. The name was strange to him. Had he observed a carriage the night before waiting for me? No, he had not. Was there a police-station anywhere near? There was one about three miles off.

"It was too far for me to go, weak and ill as I was. I determined to wait until I got back to town before telling my story to the police. It was a little past six when I arrived, so I went first to have my wound dressed, and then the doctor was kind enough to bring me along here. I put the case into your hands and shall do exactly what you advise."

We both sat in silence for some little time after listening to this extraordinary narrative. Then Sherlock Holmes pulled down from the shelf one of the ponderous commonplace books in which he placed his cuttings.

"Here is an advertisement which will interest you," said he. "It appeared in all the papers about a year ago. Listen to this: 'Lost, on the 9th inst., Mr. Jeremiah Hayling, aged twenty-six, a hydraulic engineer. Left his lodgings at ten o'clock at night, and has not been heard of since. Was dressed in,' etc., etc. Ha! That represents the last time that the colonel needed to have his machine overhauled, I fancy."

"Good heavens!" cried my patient. "Then that explains what the girl said."

"Undoubtedly. It is quite clear that the colonel was a cool and desperate man, who was absolutely determined that nothing should stand in the way of his little game, like those out-and-out pirates who will leave no survivor from a captured ship.

Well, every moment now is precious, so if you feel equal to it we shall go down to Scotland Yard at once as a preliminary to starting for Eyford."

Some three hours or so afterwards we were all in the train together, bound from Reading to the little Berkshire village. There were Sherlock Holmes, the hydraulic engineer, Inspector Bradstreet, of Scotland Yard, a plain-clothes man, and myself. Bradstreet had spread an ordnance map of the county out upon the seat and was busy with his compasses drawing a circle with Eyford for its centre.

"There you are," said he. "That circle is drawn at a radius of ten miles from the village. The place we want must be somewhere near that line. You said ten miles, I think, sir."

"It was an hour's good drive."

"And you think that they brought you back all that way when you were unconscious?"

"They must have done so. I have a confused memory, too, of having been lifted and conveyed somewhere."

"What I cannot understand," said I, "is why they should have spared you when they found you lying fainting in the garden. Perhaps the villain was softened by the woman's entreaties."

"I hardly think that likely. I never saw a more inexorable face in my life."

"Oh, we shall soon clear up all that," said Bradstreet. "Well, I have drawn my circle, and I only wish I knew at what point upon it the folk that we are in search of are to be found."

"I think I could lay my finger on it," said Holmes quietly.

"Really, now!" cried the inspector, "you have formed your opinion! Come, now, we shall see who agrees with you. I say it is south, for the country is more deserted there."

"And I say east," said my patient.

"I am for west," remarked the plain-clothes man. "There are several quiet little villages up there."

"And I am for north," said I, "because there are no hills there, and our friend says that he did not notice the carriage go up any."

"Come," cried the inspector, laughing; "it's a very pretty diversity of opinion. We have boxed the compass among us. Who do you give your casting vote to?"

"You are all wrong."

"But we can't all be."

"Oh, yes, you can. This is my point." He placed his finger in the centre of the circle. "This is where we shall find them."

"But the twelve-mile drive?" gasped Hatherley.

"Six out and six back. Nothing simpler. You say yourself that the horse was fresh and glossy when you got in. How could it be that if it had gone twelve miles over heavy roads?"

"Indeed, it is a likely ruse enough," observed Bradstreet thoughtfully. "Of course there can be no doubt as to the nature of this gang."

"None at all," said Holmes. "They are coiners on a large scale, and have used the machine to form the amalgam which has taken the place of silver."

"We have known for some time that a clever gang was at work," said the inspector. "They have been turning out half-crowns by the thousand. We even traced them as far as Reading, but could get no farther, for they had covered their traces in a way that showed that they were very old hands. But now, thanks to this lucky chance, I think that we have got them right enough."

But the inspector was mistaken, for those criminals were not destined to fall into the hands of justice. As we rolled into Eyford Station we saw a gigantic column of smoke which streamed up from behind a small clump of trees in the neighbourhood and hung like an immense ostrich feather over the landscape.

"A house on fire?" asked Bradstreet as the train steamed off again on its way.

"Yes, sir!" said the station-master.

"When did it break out?"

"I hear that it was during the night, sir, but it has got worse, and the whole place is in a blaze."

"Whose house is it?"

"Dr. Becher's."

"Tell me," broke in the engineer, "is Dr. Becher a German, very thin, with a long, sharp nose?"

The station-master laughed heartily. "No, sir, Dr. Becher is an Englishman, and there isn't a man in the parish who has a better-lined waistcoat. But he has a gentleman staying with him, a patient, as I understand, who is a foreigner, and he looks as if a little good Berkshire beef would do him no harm."

The station-master had not finished his speech before we were all hastening in the direction of the fire. The road topped a low hill, and there was a great widespread whitewashed building in front of us, spouting fire at every chink and window, while in the garden in front three fire-engines were vainly striving to keep the flames under.

"That's it!" cried Hatherley, in intense excitement. "There is the gravel-drive, and there are the rose-bushes where I lay. That second window is the one that I jumped from."

"Well, at least," said Holmes, "you have had your revenge upon them. There can be no question that it was your oil-lamp which, when it was crushed in the press, set fire to the wooden walls, though no doubt they were too excited in the chase after you to observe it at the time. Now keep your eyes open in this crowd for your friends of last night, though I very much fear that they are a good hundred miles off by now."

And Holmes' fears came to be realised, for from that day to this no word has ever been heard either of the beautiful woman, the sinister German, or the morose Englishman. Early that morning a peasant had met a cart containing several people and some very bulky boxes driving rapidly in the direction of Reading, but there all traces of the fugitives disappeared, and even Holmes' ingenuity failed ever to discover the least clue as to their whereabouts.

The firemen had been much perturbed at the strange arrangements which they had found within, and still more so by discovering a newly severed human thumb upon a window-sill of the second floor. About sunset, however, their efforts were at last successful, and they subdued the flames, but not before the roof had fallen in, and the whole place been reduced to such absolute ruin that, save some twisted cylinders and iron piping, not a trace remained of the machinery which had cost our unfortunate acquaintance so dearly. Large masses of nickel and of tin were discovered stored in an out-house, but no coins were to be found, which may have explained the presence of those bulky boxes which have been already referred to.

How our hydraulic engineer had been conveyed from the garden to the spot where he recovered his senses might have remained forever a mystery were it not for the soft mould, which told us a very plain tale. He had evidently been carried down by two persons, one of whom had remarkably small feet and the other unusually large ones. On the whole, it was most probable that the silent Englishman, being less bold or less murderous than his companion, had assisted the woman to bear the unconscious man out of the way of danger.

"Well," said our engineer ruefully as we took our seats to return once more to London, "it has been a pretty business for me! I have lost my thumb and I have lost a fifty-guinea fee, and what have I gained?"

"Experience," said Holmes, laughing. "Indirectly it may be of value, you know; you have only to put it into words to gain the reputation of being excellent company for the remainder of your existence."

X. The Adventure Of The Noble Bachelor

The Lord St. Simon marriage, and its curious termination, have long ceased to be a subject of interest in those exalted circles in which the unfortunate bridegroom moves. Fresh scandals have eclipsed it, and their more piquant details have drawn the gossips away from this four-year-old drama. As I have reason to believe, however, that the full facts have never been revealed to the general public, and as my friend Sherlock Holmes had a considerable share in clearing the matter up, I feel that no memoir of him would be complete without some little sketch of this remarkable episode.

It was a few weeks before my own marriage, during the days when I was still sharing rooms with Holmes in Baker Street, that he came home from an afternoon stroll to find a letter on the table waiting for him. I had remained indoors all day, for the weather had taken a sudden turn to rain, with high autumnal winds, and the Jezail bullet which I had brought back in one of my limbs as a relic of my Afghan campaign throbbed with dull persistence. With my body in one easy-chair and my legs upon another, I had surrounded myself with a cloud of newspapers until at last, saturated with the news of the day, I tossed them all aside and lay listless, watching the huge crest and monogram upon the envelope upon the table and wondering lazily who my friend's noble correspondent could be.

"Here is a very fashionable epistle," I remarked as he entered. "Your morning letters, if I remember right, were from a fish-monger and a tide-waiter."

"Yes, my correspondence has certainly the charm of variety," he answered, smiling, "and the humbler are usually the more interesting. This looks like one of those unwelcome social summonses which call upon a man either to be bored or to lie."

He broke the seal and glanced over the contents.

"Oh, come, it may prove to be something of interest, after all."

"Not social, then?"

"No, distinctly professional."

"And from a noble client?"

"One of the highest in England."

"My dear fellow, I congratulate you."

"I assure you, Watson, without affectation, that the status of my client is a matter of less moment to me than the interest of his case. It is just possible, however, that

that also may not be wanting in this new investigation. You have been reading the papers diligently of late, have you not?"

"It looks like it," said I ruefully, pointing to a huge bundle in the corner. "I have had nothing else to do."

"It is fortunate, for you will perhaps be able to post me up. I read nothing except the criminal news and the agony column. The latter is always instructive. But if you have followed recent events so closely you must have read about Lord St. Simon and his wedding?"

"Oh, yes, with the deepest interest."

"That is well. The letter which I hold in my hand is from Lord St. Simon. I will read it to you, and in return you must turn over these papers and let me have whatever bears upon the matter. This is what he says:

"'My Dear Mr. Sherlock Holmes:--Lord Backwater tells me that I may place implicit reliance upon your judgment and discretion. I have determined, therefore, to call upon you and to consult you in reference to the very painful event which has occurred in connection with my wedding. Mr. Lestrade, of Scotland Yard, is acting already in the matter, but he assures me that he sees no objection to your co-operation, and that he even thinks that it might be of some assistance. I will call at four o'clock in the afternoon, and, should you have any other engagement at that time, I hope that you will postpone it, as this matter is of paramount importance. Yours faithfully, ST. SIMON.'

"It is dated from Grosvenor Mansions, written with a quill pen, and the noble lord has had the misfortune to get a smear of ink upon the outer side of his right little finger," remarked Holmes as he folded up the epistle.

"He says four o'clock. It is three now. He will be here in an hour."

"Then I have just time, with your assistance, to get clear upon the subject. Turn over those papers and arrange the extracts in their order of time, while I take a glance as to who our client is." He picked a red-covered volume from a line of books of reference beside the mantelpiece. "Here he is," said he, sitting down and flattening it out upon his knee. "'Lord Robert Walsingham de Vere St. Simon, second son of the Duke of Balmoral.' Hum! 'Arms: Azure, three caltrops in chief over a fess sable. Born in 1846.' He's forty-one years of age, which is mature for marriage. Was Under-Secretary for the colonies in a late administration. The Duke, his father, was at one time Secretary for Foreign Affairs. They inherit Plantagenet blood by direct descent, and Tudor on the distaff side. Ha! Well, there is nothing very instructive in all this. I think that I must turn to you Watson, for something more solid."

"I have very little difficulty in finding what I want," said I, "for the facts are quite recent, and the matter struck me as remarkable. I feared to refer them to you, however, as I knew that you had an inquiry on hand and that you disliked the intrusion of other matters."

"Oh, you mean the little problem of the Grosvenor Square furniture van. That is quite cleared up now—though, indeed, it was obvious from the first. Pray give me the results of your newspaper selections."

"Here is the first notice which I can find. It is in the personal column of the Morning Post, and dates, as you see, some weeks back: 'A marriage has been arranged,' it says, 'and will, if rumour is correct, very shortly take place, between Lord Robert St. Simon, second son of the Duke of Balmoral, and Miss Hatty Doran, the only daughter of Aloysius Doran. Esq., of San Francisco, Cal., U.S.A.' That is all."

"Terse and to the point," remarked Holmes, stretching his long, thin legs towards the fire.

"There was a paragraph amplifying this in one of the society papers of the same week. Ah, here it is: 'There will soon be a call for protection in the marriage market, for the present free-trade principle appears to tell heavily against our home product. One by one the management of the noble houses of Great Britain is passing into the hands of our fair cousins from across the Atlantic. An important addition has been made during the last week to the list of the prizes which have been borne away by these charming invaders. Lord St. Simon, who has shown himself for over twenty years proof against the little god's arrows, has now definitely announced his approaching marriage with Miss Hatty Doran, the fascinating daughter of a California millionaire. Miss Doran, whose graceful figure and striking face attracted much attention at the Westbury House festivities, is an only child, and it is currently reported that her dowry will run to considerably over the six figures, with expectancies for the future. As it is an open secret that the Duke of Balmoral has been compelled to sell his pictures within the last few years, and as Lord St. Simon has no property of his own save the small estate of Birchmoor, it is obvious that the Californian heiress is not the only gainer by an alliance which will enable her to make the easy and common transition from a Republican lady to a British peeress.'"

"Anything else?" asked Holmes, yawning.

"Oh, yes; plenty. Then there is another note in the Morning Post to say that the marriage would be an absolutely quiet one, that it would be at St. George's, Hanover Square, that only half a dozen intimate friends would be invited, and that the party would return to the furnished house at Lancaster Gate which has been taken by Mr. Aloysius Doran. Two days later—that is, on Wednesday last—there is a curt announcement that the wedding had taken place, and that the honeymoon would be passed at Lord Backwater's place, near Petersfield. Those are all the notices which appeared before the disappearance of the bride."

"Before the what?" asked Holmes with a start.

"The vanishing of the lady."

"When did she vanish, then?"

"At the wedding breakfast."

"Indeed. This is more interesting than it promised to be; quite dramatic, in fact."

"Yes; it struck me as being a little out of the common."

"They often vanish before the ceremony, and occasionally during the honeymoon; but I cannot call to mind anything quite so prompt as this. Pray let me have the details."

"I warn you that they are very incomplete."

"Perhaps we may make them less so."

"Such as they are, they are set forth in a single article of a morning paper of yesterday, which I will read to you. It is headed, 'Singular Occurrence at a Fashionable Wedding':

"'The family of Lord Robert St. Simon has been thrown into the greatest consternation by the strange and painful episodes which have taken place in connection with his wedding. The ceremony, as shortly announced in the papers of yesterday, occurred on the previous morning; but it is only now that it has been possible to confirm the strange rumours which have been so persistently floating about. In spite of the attempts of the friends to hush the matter up, so much public attention has now been drawn to it that no good purpose can be served by affecting to disregard what is a common subject for conversation.

"'The ceremony, which was performed at St. George's, Hanover Square, was a very quiet one, no one being present save the father of the bride, Mr. Aloysius Doran, the Duchess of Balmoral, Lord Backwater, Lord Eustace and Lady Clara St. Simon (the younger brother and sister of the bridegroom), and Lady Alicia Whittington. The whole party proceeded afterwards to the house of Mr. Aloysius Doran, at Lancaster Gate, where breakfast had been prepared. It appears that some little trouble was caused by a woman, whose name has not been ascertained, who endeavoured to force her way into the house after the bridal party, alleging that she had some claim upon Lord St. Simon. It was only after a painful and prolonged scene that she was ejected by the butler and the footman. The bride, who had fortunately entered the house before this unpleasant interruption, had sat down to breakfast with the rest, when she complained of a sudden indisposition and retired to her room. Her prolonged absence having caused some comment, her father followed her, but learned from her maid that she had only come up to her chamber for an instant, caught up an ulster and bonnet, and hurried down to the passage. One of the footmen declared that he had seen a lady leave the house thus apparelled, but had refused to credit that it was his mistress, believing her to be with the company. On ascertaining that his daughter had disappeared, Mr. Aloysius Doran, in conjunction with the bridegroom, instantly put themselves in communication with the police, and very energetic inquiries are being made, which will probably result in a speedy clearing up of this very singular business. Up to a late hour last night, however, nothing had transpired as to the whereabouts of the missing lady. There are rumours of foul play in the matter, and it is said that the police have caused the arrest of the woman who had caused the original disturbance, in the belief that, from jealousy or some other motive, she may have been concerned in the strange disappearance of the bride.'"

"And is that all?"

"Only one little item in another of the morning papers, but it is a suggestive one."

"And it is—"

"That Miss Flora Millar, the lady who had caused the disturbance, has actually been arrested. It appears that she was formerly a danseuse at the Allegro, and that she has known the bridegroom for some years. There are no further particulars, and the whole case is in your hands now—so far as it has been set forth in the public press."

"And an exceedingly interesting case it appears to be. I would not have missed it for worlds. But there is a ring at the bell, Watson, and as the clock makes it a few minutes after four, I have no doubt that this will prove to be our noble client. Do not dream of going, Watson, for I very much prefer having a witness, if only as a check to my own memory."

"Lord Robert St. Simon," announced our page-boy, throwing open the door. A gentleman entered, with a pleasant, cultured face, high-nosed and pale, with something perhaps of petulance about the mouth, and with the steady, well-opened eye of a man whose pleasant lot it had ever been to command and to be obeyed. His manner was brisk, and yet his general appearance gave an undue impression of age, for he had a slight forward stoop and a little bend of the knees as he walked. His hair, too, as he swept off his very curly-brimmed hat, was grizzled round the edges and thin upon the top. As to his dress, it was careful to the verge of foppishness, with high collar, black frock-coat, white waistcoat, yellow gloves, patent-leather shoes, and light-coloured gaiters. He advanced slowly into the room, turning his head from left to right, and swinging in his right hand the cord which held his golden eyeglasses.

"Good-day, Lord St. Simon," said Holmes, rising and bowing. "Pray take the basket-chair. This is my friend and colleague, Dr. Watson. Draw up a little to the fire, and we will talk this matter over."

"A most painful matter to me, as you can most readily imagine, Mr. Holmes. I have been cut to the quick. I understand that you have already managed several delicate cases of this sort, sir, though I presume that they were hardly from the same class of society."

"No, I am descending."

"I beg pardon."

"My last client of the sort was a king."

"Oh, really! I had no idea. And which king?"

"The King of Scandinavia."

"What! Had he lost his wife?"

"You can understand," said Holmes suavely, "that I extend to the affairs of my other clients the same secrecy which I promise to you in yours."

"Of course! Very right! very right! I'm sure I beg pardon. As to my own case, I am ready to give you any information which may assist you in forming an opinion."

"Thank you. I have already learned all that is in the public prints, nothing more. I presume that I may take it as correct—this article, for example, as to the disappearance of the bride."

Lord St. Simon glanced over it. "Yes, it is correct, as far as it goes."

"But it needs a great deal of supplementing before anyone could offer an opinion. I think that I may arrive at my facts most directly by questioning you."

"Pray do so."

"When did you first meet Miss Hatty Doran?"

"In San Francisco, a year ago."

"You were travelling in the States?"

"Yes."

"Did you become engaged then?"

"No."

"But you were on a friendly footing?"

"I was amused by her society, and she could see that I was amused."

"Her father is very rich?"

"He is said to be the richest man on the Pacific slope."

"And how did he make his money?"

"In mining. He had nothing a few years ago. Then he struck gold, invested it, and came up by leaps and bounds."

"Now, what is your own impression as to the young lady's—your wife's character?"

The nobleman swung his glasses a little faster and stared down into the fire. "You see, Mr. Holmes," said he, "my wife was twenty before her father became a rich man. During that time she ran free in a mining camp and wandered through woods or mountains, so that her education has come from Nature rather than from the schoolmaster. She is what we call in England a tomboy, with a strong nature, wild and free, unfettered by any sort of traditions. She is impetuous—volcanic, I was about to say. She is swift in making up her mind and fearless in carrying out her resolutions. On the other hand, I would not have given her the name which I have the honour to bear"—he gave a little stately cough—"had not I thought her to be at bottom a noble woman. I believe that she is capable of heroic self-sacrifice and that anything dishonourable would be repugnant to her."

"Have you her photograph?"

"I brought this with me." He opened a locket and showed us the full face of a very lovely woman. It was not a photograph but an ivory miniature, and the artist had brought out the full effect of the lustrous black hair, the large dark eyes, and the exquisite mouth. Holmes gazed long and earnestly at it. Then he closed the locket and handed it back to Lord St. Simon.

"The young lady came to London, then, and you renewed your acquaintance?"

"Yes, her father brought her over for this last London season. I met her several times, became engaged to her, and have now married her."

"She brought, I understand, a considerable dowry?"

"A fair dowry. Not more than is usual in my family."

"And this, of course, remains to you, since the marriage is a fait accompli?"

"I really have made no inquiries on the subject."

"Very naturally not. Did you see Miss Doran on the day before the wedding?"

"Yes."

"Was she in good spirits?"

"Never better. She kept talking of what we should do in our future lives."

"Indeed! That is very interesting. And on the morning of the wedding?"

"She was as bright as possible—at least until after the ceremony."

"And did you observe any change in her then?"

"Well, to tell the truth, I saw then the first signs that I had ever seen that her temper was just a little sharp. The incident however, was too trivial to relate and can have no possible bearing upon the case."

"Pray let us have it, for all that."

"Oh, it is childish. She dropped her bouquet as we went towards the vestry. She was passing the front pew at the time, and it fell over into the pew. There was a moment's delay, but the gentleman in the pew handed it up to her again, and it did not appear to be the worse for the fall. Yet when I spoke to her of the matter, she answered me abruptly; and in the carriage, on our way home, she seemed absurdly agitated over this trifling cause."

"Indeed! You say that there was a gentleman in the pew. Some of the general public were present, then?"

"Oh, yes. It is impossible to exclude them when the church is open."

"This gentleman was not one of your wife's friends?"

"No, no; I call him a gentleman by courtesy, but he was quite a common-looking person. I hardly noticed his appearance. But really I think that we are wandering rather far from the point."

"Lady St. Simon, then, returned from the wedding in a less cheerful frame of mind than she had gone to it. What did she do on re-entering her father's house?"

"I saw her in conversation with her maid."

"And who is her maid?"

"Alice is her name. She is an American and came from California with her."

"A confidential servant?"

"A little too much so. It seemed to me that her mistress allowed her to take great liberties. Still, of course, in America they look upon these things in a different way."

"How long did she speak to this Alice?"

"Oh, a few minutes. I had something else to think of."

"You did not overhear what they said?"

"Lady St. Simon said something about 'jumping a claim.' She was accustomed to use slang of the kind. I have no idea what she meant."

"American slang is very expressive sometimes. And what did your wife do when she finished speaking to her maid?"

"She walked into the breakfast-room."

"On your arm?"

"No, alone. She was very independent in little matters like that. Then, after we had sat down for ten minutes or so, she rose hurriedly, muttered some words of apology, and left the room. She never came back."

"But this maid, Alice, as I understand, deposes that she went to her room, covered her bride's dress with a long ulster, put on a bonnet, and went out."

"Quite so. And she was afterwards seen walking into Hyde Park in company with Flora Millar, a woman who is now in custody, and who had already made a disturbance at Mr. Doran's house that morning."

"Ah, yes. I should like a few particulars as to this young lady, and your relations to her."

Lord St. Simon shrugged his shoulders and raised his eyebrows. "We have been on a friendly footing for some years—I may say on a very friendly footing. She used to be at the Allegro. I have not treated her ungenerously, and she had no just cause of complaint against me, but you know what women are, Mr. Holmes. Flora was a dear little thing, but exceedingly hot-headed and devotedly attached to me. She wrote me dreadful letters when she heard that I was about to be married, and, to tell the truth, the reason why I had the marriage celebrated so quietly was that I feared lest there might be a scandal in the church. She came to Mr. Doran's door just after we returned, and she endeavoured to push her way in, uttering very abusive expressions towards my wife, and even threatening her, but I had foreseen the possibility of something of the sort, and I had two police fellows there in private clothes, who soon pushed her out again. She was quiet when she saw that there was no good in making a row."

"Did your wife hear all this?"

"No, thank goodness, she did not."

"And she was seen walking with this very woman afterwards?"

"Yes. That is what Mr. Lestrade, of Scotland Yard, looks upon as so serious. It is thought that Flora decoyed my wife out and laid some terrible trap for her."

"Well, it is a possible supposition."

"You think so, too?"

"I did not say a probable one. But you do not yourself look upon this as likely?"

"I do not think Flora would hurt a fly."

"Still, jealousy is a strange transformer of characters. Pray what is your own theory as to what took place?"

"Well, really, I came to seek a theory, not to propound one. I have given you all the facts. Since you ask me, however, I may say that it has occurred to me as possible that the excitement of this affair, the consciousness that she had made so immense a social stride, had the effect of causing some little nervous disturbance in my wife."

"In short, that she had become suddenly deranged?"

"Well, really, when I consider that she has turned her back—I will not say upon me, but upon so much that many have aspired to without success—I can hardly explain it in any other fashion."

"Well, certainly that is also a conceivable hypothesis," said Holmes, smiling. "And now, Lord St. Simon, I think that I have nearly all my data. May I ask whether you were seated at the breakfast-table so that you could see out of the window?"

"We could see the other side of the road and the Park."

"Quite so. Then I do not think that I need to detain you longer. I shall communicate with you."

"Should you be fortunate enough to solve this problem," said our client, rising.

"I have solved it."

"Eh? What was that?"

"I say that I have solved it."

"Where, then, is my wife?"

"That is a detail which I shall speedily supply."

Lord St. Simon shook his head. "I am afraid that it will take wiser heads than yours or mine," he remarked, and bowing in a stately, old-fashioned manner he departed.

"It is very good of Lord St. Simon to honour my head by putting it on a level with his own," said Sherlock Holmes, laughing. "I think that I shall have a whisky and soda and a cigar after all this cross-questioning. I had formed my conclusions as to the case before our client came into the room."

"My dear Holmes!"

"I have notes of several similar cases, though none, as I remarked before, which were quite as prompt. My whole examination served to turn my conjecture into a certainty. Circumstantial evidence is occasionally very convincing, as when you find a trout in the milk, to quote Thoreau's example."

"But I have heard all that you have heard."

"Without, however, the knowledge of pre-existing cases which serves me so well. There was a parallel instance in Aberdeen some years back, and something on very much the same lines at Munich the year after the Franco-Prussian War. It is one of these cases—but, hullo, here is Lestrade! Good-afternoon, Lestrade! You will find an extra tumbler upon the sideboard, and there are cigars in the box."

The official detective was attired in a pea-jacket and cravat, which gave him a decidedly nautical appearance, and he carried a black canvas bag in his hand. With a short greeting he seated himself and lit the cigar which had been offered to him.

"What's up, then?" asked Holmes with a twinkle in his eye. "You look dissatisfied."

"And I feel dissatisfied. It is this infernal St. Simon marriage case. I can make neither head nor tail of the business."

"Really! You surprise me."

"Who ever heard of such a mixed affair? Every clue seems to slip through my fingers. I have been at work upon it all day."

"And very wet it seems to have made you," said Holmes laying his hand upon the arm of the pea-jacket.

"Yes, I have been dragging the Serpentine."

"In heaven's name, what for?"

"In search of the body of Lady St. Simon."

Sherlock Holmes leaned back in his chair and laughed heartily.

"Have you dragged the basin of Trafalgar Square fountain?" he asked.

"Why? What do you mean?"

"Because you have just as good a chance of finding this lady in the one as in the other."

Lestrade shot an angry glance at my companion. "I suppose you know all about it," he snarled.

"Well, I have only just heard the facts, but my mind is made up."

"Oh, indeed! Then you think that the Serpentine plays no part in the matter?"

"I think it very unlikely."

"Then perhaps you will kindly explain how it is that we found this in it?" He opened his bag as he spoke, and tumbled onto the floor a wedding-dress of watered silk, a pair of white satin shoes and a bride's wreath and veil, all discoloured and soaked in water. "There," said he, putting a new wedding-ring upon the top of the pile. "There is a little nut for you to crack, Master Holmes."

"Oh, indeed!" said my friend, blowing blue rings into the air. "You dragged them from the Serpentine?"

"No. They were found floating near the margin by a park-keeper. They have been identified as her clothes, and it seemed to me that if the clothes were there the body would not be far off."

"By the same brilliant reasoning, every man's body is to be found in the neighbourhood of his wardrobe. And pray what did you hope to arrive at through this?"

"At some evidence implicating Flora Millar in the disappearance."

"I am afraid that you will find it difficult."

"Are you, indeed, now?" cried Lestrade with some bitterness. "I am afraid, Holmes, that you are not very practical with your deductions and your inferences. You have made two blunders in as many minutes. This dress does implicate Miss Flora Millar."

"And how?"

"In the dress is a pocket. In the pocket is a card-case. In the card-case is a note. And here is the very note." He slapped it down upon the table in front of him. "Listen to this: 'You will see me when all is ready. Come at once. F.H.M.' Now my theory all along has been that Lady St. Simon was decoyed away by Flora Millar, and that she, with confederates, no doubt, was responsible for her disappearance. Here, signed with her initials, is the very note which was no doubt quietly slipped into her hand at the door and which lured her within their reach."

"Very good, Lestrade," said Holmes, laughing. "You really are very fine indeed. Let me see it." He took up the paper in a listless way, but his attention instantly became riveted, and he gave a little cry of satisfaction. "This is indeed important," said he.

"Ha! you find it so?"

"Extremely so. I congratulate you warmly."

Lestrade rose in his triumph and bent his head to look. "Why," he shrieked, "you're looking at the wrong side!"

"On the contrary, this is the right side."

"The right side? You're mad! Here is the note written in pencil over here."

"And over here is what appears to be the fragment of a hotel bill, which interests me deeply."

"There's nothing in it. I looked at it before," said Lestrade. "'Oct. 4th, rooms 8s., breakfast 2s. 6d., cocktail 1s., lunch 2s. 6d., glass sherry, 8d.' I see nothing in that."

"Very likely not. It is most important, all the same. As to the note, it is important also, or at least the initials are, so I congratulate you again."

"I've wasted time enough," said Lestrade, rising. "I believe in hard work and not in sitting by the fire spinning fine theories. Good-day, Mr. Holmes, and we shall see which gets to the bottom of the matter first." He gathered up the garments, thrust them into the bag, and made for the door.

"Just one hint to you, Lestrade," drawled Holmes before his rival vanished; "I will tell you the true solution of the matter. Lady St. Simon is a myth. There is not, and there never has been, any such person."

Lestrade looked sadly at my companion. Then he turned to me, tapped his forehead three times, shook his head solemnly, and hurried away.

He had hardly shut the door behind him when Holmes rose to put on his overcoat. "There is something in what the fellow says about outdoor work," he remarked, "so I think, Watson, that I must leave you to your papers for a little."

It was after five o'clock when Sherlock Holmes left me, but I had no time to be lonely, for within an hour there arrived a confectioner's man with a very large flat box. This he unpacked with the help of a youth whom he had brought with him, and presently, to my very great astonishment, a quite epicurean little cold supper began to be laid out upon our humble lodging-house mahogany. There were a couple of brace of cold woodcock, a pheasant, a pâté de foie gras pie with a group of ancient and cobwebby bottles. Having laid out all these luxuries, my two visitors vanished away, like the genii of the Arabian Nights, with no explanation save that the things had been paid for and were ordered to this address.

Just before nine o'clock Sherlock Holmes stepped briskly into the room. His features were gravely set, but there was a light in his eye which made me think that he had not been disappointed in his conclusions.

"They have laid the supper, then," he said, rubbing his hands.

"You seem to expect company. They have laid for five."

"Yes, I fancy we may have some company dropping in," said he. "I am surprised that Lord St. Simon has not already arrived. Ha! I fancy that I hear his step now upon the stairs."

It was indeed our visitor of the afternoon who came bustling in, dangling his glasses more vigorously than ever, and with a very perturbed expression upon his aristocratic features.

"My messenger reached you, then?" asked Holmes.

"Yes, and I confess that the contents startled me beyond measure. Have you good authority for what you say?"

"The best possible."

Lord St. Simon sank into a chair and passed his hand over his forehead.

"What will the Duke say," he murmured, "when he hears that one of the family has been subjected to such humiliation?"

"It is the purest accident. I cannot allow that there is any humiliation."

"Ah, you look on these things from another standpoint."

"I fail to see that anyone is to blame. I can hardly see how the lady could have acted otherwise, though her abrupt method of doing it was undoubtedly to be regretted. Having no mother, she had no one to advise her at such a crisis."

"It was a slight, sir, a public slight," said Lord St. Simon, tapping his fingers upon the table.

"You must make allowance for this poor girl, placed in so unprecedented a position."

"I will make no allowance. I am very angry indeed, and I have been shamefully used."

"I think that I heard a ring," said Holmes. "Yes, there are steps on the landing. If I cannot persuade you to take a lenient view of the matter, Lord St. Simon, I have brought an advocate here who may be more successful." He opened the door and ushered in a lady and gentleman. "Lord St. Simon," said he "allow me to introduce you to Mr. and Mrs. Francis Hay Moulton. The lady, I think, you have already met."

At the sight of these newcomers our client had sprung from his seat and stood very erect, with his eyes cast down and his hand thrust into the breast of his frock-coat, a picture of offended dignity. The lady had taken a quick step forward and had held out her hand to him, but he still refused to raise his eyes. It was as well for his resolution, perhaps, for her pleading face was one which it was hard to resist.

"You're angry, Robert," said she. "Well, I guess you have every cause to be."

"Pray make no apology to me," said Lord St. Simon bitterly.

"Oh, yes, I know that I have treated you real bad and that I should have spoken to you before I went; but I was kind of rattled, and from the time when I saw Frank here again I just didn't know what I was doing or saying. I only wonder I didn't fall down and do a faint right there before the altar."

"Perhaps, Mrs. Moulton, you would like my friend and me to leave the room while you explain this matter?"

"If I may give an opinion," remarked the strange gentleman, "we've had just a little too much secrecy over this business already. For my part, I should like all Europe and America to hear the rights of it." He was a small, wiry, sunburnt man, clean-shaven, with a sharp face and alert manner.

"Then I'll tell our story right away," said the lady. "Frank here and I met in '84, in McQuire's camp, near the Rockies, where pa was working a claim. We were engaged to each other, Frank and I; but then one day father struck a rich pocket and made a pile, while poor Frank here had a claim that petered out and came to nothing. The richer pa grew the poorer was Frank; so at last pa wouldn't hear of our engagement lasting any longer, and he took me away to 'Frisco. Frank wouldn't throw up his hand, though; so he followed me there, and he saw me without pa knowing anything about it. It would only have made him mad to know, so we just fixed it all up for ourselves. Frank said that he would go and make his pile, too, and never come back to claim me until he had as much as pa. So then I promised to wait for him to the end of time and pledged myself not to marry anyone else while he lived. 'Why shouldn't we be married right away, then,' said he, 'and then I will feel sure of you; and I won't claim to be your husband until I come back?' Well, we talked it over, and he had fixed it all up so nicely, with a clergyman all ready in waiting, that we just did it right there; and then Frank went off to seek his fortune, and I went back to pa.

"The next I heard of Frank was that he was in Montana, and then he went prospecting in Arizona, and then I heard of him from New Mexico. After that came a long newspaper story about how a miners' camp had been attacked by Apache Indians, and there was my Frank's name among the killed. I fainted dead away, and I was very sick for months after. Pa thought I had a decline and took me to half the doctors in 'Frisco. Not a word of news came for a year and more, so that I never doubted that Frank was really dead. Then Lord St. Simon came to 'Frisco, and we came to London, and a marriage was arranged, and pa was very pleased, but I felt all the time that no man on this earth would ever take the place in my heart that had been given to my poor Frank.

"Still, if I had married Lord St. Simon, of course I'd have done my duty by him. We can't command our love, but we can our actions. I went to the altar with him with the intention to make him just as good a wife as it was in me to be. But you may imagine what I felt when, just as I came to the altar rails, I glanced back and saw Frank standing and looking at me out of the first pew. I thought it was his ghost at first; but when I looked again there he was still, with a kind of question in his eyes, as if to ask me whether I were glad or sorry to see him. I wonder I didn't drop. I know that everything was turning round, and the words of the clergyman were just like the buzz of a bee in my ear. I didn't know what to do. Should I stop the service and make a scene in the church? I glanced at him again, and he seemed to know what I was thinking, for he raised his finger to his lips to tell me to be still. Then I saw him scribble on a piece of paper, and I knew that he was writing me a note. As I passed his pew on the way out I dropped my bouquet over to him, and he slipped the note into my hand when he returned me the flowers. It was only a line asking me to join him when he made the sign to me to do so. Of course I never doubted for a moment that my first duty was now to him, and I determined to do just whatever he might direct.

"When I got back I told my maid, who had known him in California, and had always been his friend. I ordered her to say nothing, but to get a few things packed and my ulster ready. I know I ought to have spoken to Lord St. Simon, but it was dreadful hard before his mother and all those great people. I just made up my mind to run away and explain afterwards. I hadn't been at the table ten minutes before I saw Frank out of the window at the other side of the road. He beckoned to me and then began walking into the Park. I slipped out, put on my things, and followed him. Some woman came talking something or other about Lord St. Simon to me—seemed to me from the little I heard as if he had a little secret of his own before marriage also—but I managed to get away from her and soon overtook Frank. We got into a cab together, and away we drove to some lodgings he had taken in Gordon Square, and that was my true wedding after all those years of waiting. Frank had been a prisoner among the Apaches, had escaped, came on to 'Frisco, found that I had given him up for dead and had gone to England, followed me there, and had come upon me at last on the very morning of my second wedding."

"I saw it in a paper," explained the American. "It gave the name and the church but not where the lady lived."

"Then we had a talk as to what we should do, and Frank was all for openness, but I was so ashamed of it all that I felt as if I should like to vanish away and never see any of them again—just sending a line to pa, perhaps, to show him that I was alive. It was awful to me to think of all those lords and ladies sitting round that breakfast-table and waiting for me to come back. So Frank took my wedding-clothes and things and made a bundle of them, so that I should not be traced, and dropped them away somewhere where no one could find them. It is likely that we should have gone on to Paris tomorrow, only that this good gentleman, Mr. Holmes, came round to us this evening, though how he found us is more than I can think, and he showed us very clearly and kindly that I was wrong and that Frank was right, and that we should be putting ourselves in the wrong if we were so secret. Then he offered to give us a chance of talking to Lord St. Simon alone, and so we came right away round to his rooms at once. Now, Robert, you have heard it all, and I am very sorry if I have given you pain, and I hope that you do not think very meanly of me."

Lord St. Simon had by no means relaxed his rigid attitude, but had listened with a frowning brow and a compressed lip to this long narrative.

"Excuse me," he said, "but it is not my custom to discuss my most intimate personal affairs in this public manner."

"Then you won't forgive me? You won't shake hands before I go?"

"Oh, certainly, if it would give you any pleasure." He put out his hand and coldly grasped that which she extended to him.

"I had hoped," suggested Holmes, "that you would have joined us in a friendly supper."

"I think that there you ask a little too much," responded his Lordship. "I may be forced to acquiesce in these recent developments, but I can hardly be expected to make merry over them. I think that with your permission I will now wish you all a very good-night." He included us all in a sweeping bow and stalked out of the room.

"Then I trust that you at least will honour me with your company," said Sherlock Holmes. "It is always a joy to meet an American, Mr. Moulton, for I am one of those who believe that the folly of a monarch and the blundering of a minister in far-gone years will not prevent our children from being some day citizens of the same world-wide country under a flag which shall be a quartering of the Union Jack with the Stars and Stripes."

"The case has been an interesting one," remarked Holmes when our visitors had left us, "because it serves to show very clearly how simple the explanation may be of an affair which at first sight seems to be almost inexplicable. Nothing could be more natural than the sequence of events as narrated by this lady, and nothing stranger than the result when viewed, for instance, by Mr. Lestrade of Scotland Yard."

"You were not yourself at fault at all, then?"

"From the first, two facts were very obvious to me, the one that the lady had been quite willing to undergo the wedding ceremony, the other that she had repented of it within a few minutes of returning home. Obviously something had occurred during the morning, then, to cause her to change her mind. What could that something be? She could not have spoken to anyone when she was out, for she had been in the company of the bridegroom. Had she seen someone, then? If she had, it must be someone from America because she had spent so short a time in this country that she could hardly have allowed anyone to acquire so deep an influence over her that the mere sight of him would induce her to change her plans so completely. You see we have already arrived, by a process of exclusion, at the idea that she might have seen an American. Then who could this American be, and why should he possess so much influence over her? It might be a lover; it might be a husband. Her young womanhood had, I knew, been spent in rough scenes and under strange conditions. So far I had got before I ever heard Lord St. Simon's narrative. When he told us of a man in a pew, of the change in the bride's manner, of so transparent a device for obtaining a note as the dropping of a bouquet, of her resort to her confidential maid, and of her very significant allusion to claim-jumping—which in miners' parlance means taking possession of that which another person has a prior claim to—the whole situation became absolutely clear. She had gone off with a man, and the man was either a lover or was a previous husband—the chances being in favour of the latter."

"And how in the world did you find them?"

"It might have been difficult, but friend Lestrade held information in his hands the value of which he did not himself know. The initials were, of course, of the highest importance, but more valuable still was it to know that within a week he had settled his bill at one of the most select London hotels."

"How did you deduce the select?"

"By the select prices. Eight shillings for a bed and eightpence for a glass of sherry pointed to one of the most expensive hotels. There are not many in London which charge at that rate. In the second one which I visited in Northumberland Avenue, I learned by an inspection of the book that Francis H. Moulton, an American gentleman, had left only the day before, and on looking over the entries against him, I came upon the very items which I had seen in the duplicate bill. His letters were to be forwarded to 226 Gordon Square; so thither I travelled, and being fortunate enough to find the loving couple at home, I ventured to give them some paternal advice and to point out to them that it would be better in every way that they should make their position a little clearer both to the general public and to Lord St. Simon in particular. I invited them to meet him here, and, as you see, I made him keep the appointment."

"But with no very good result," I remarked. "His conduct was certainly not very gracious."

"Ah, Watson," said Holmes, smiling, "perhaps you would not be very gracious either, if, after all the trouble of wooing and wedding, you found yourself deprived in an instant of wife and of fortune. I think that we may judge Lord St. Simon very mercifully and thank our stars that we are never likely to find ourselves in the same position. Draw your chair up and hand me my violin, for the only problem we have still to solve is how to while away these bleak autumnal evenings."

XI. The Adventure Of The Beryl Coronet

"Holmes," said I as I stood one morning in our bow-window looking down the street, "here is a madman coming along. It seems rather sad that his relatives should allow him to come out alone."

My friend rose lazily from his armchair and stood with his hands in the pockets of his dressing-gown, looking over my shoulder. It was a bright, crisp February morning, and the snow of the day before still lay deep upon the ground, shimmering brightly in the wintry sun. Down the centre of Baker Street it had been ploughed into a brown crumbly band by the traffic, but at either side and on the heaped-up edges of the foot-paths it still lay as white as when it fell. The grey pavement had been cleaned and scraped, but was still dangerously slippery, so that there were fewer passengers than usual. Indeed, from the direction of the Metropolitan Station no one was coming save the single gentleman whose eccentric conduct had drawn my attention.

He was a man of about fifty, tall, portly, and imposing, with a massive, strongly marked face and a commanding figure. He was dressed in a sombre yet rich style, in black frock-coat, shining hat, neat brown gaiters, and well-cut pearl-grey trousers. Yet his actions were in absurd contrast to the dignity of his dress and features, for he was running hard, with occasional little springs, such as a weary man gives who is little accustomed to set any tax upon his legs. As he ran he jerked his hands up and down, waggled his head, and writhed his face into the most extraordinary contortions.

"What on earth can be the matter with him?" I asked. "He is looking up at the numbers of the houses."

"I believe that he is coming here," said Holmes, rubbing his hands.

"Here?"

"Yes; I rather think he is coming to consult me professionally. I think that I recognise the symptoms. Ha! did I not tell you?" As he spoke, the man, puffing and blowing, rushed at our door and pulled at our bell until the whole house resounded with the clanging.

A few moments later he was in our room, still puffing, still gesticulating, but with so fixed a look of grief and despair in his eyes that our smiles were turned in an instant to horror and pity. For a while he could not get his words out, but swayed his body and plucked at his hair like one who has been driven to the extreme limits of his reason. Then, suddenly springing to his feet, he beat his head against the wall with such force that we both rushed upon him and tore him away to the centre of the room. Sherlock Holmes pushed him down into the easy-chair and, sitting beside him, patted his hand and chatted with him in the easy, soothing tones which he knew so well how to employ.

"You have come to me to tell your story, have you not?" said he. "You are fatigued with your haste. Pray wait until you have recovered yourself, and then I shall be most happy to look into any little problem which you may submit to me."

The man sat for a minute or more with a heaving chest, fighting against his emotion. Then he passed his handkerchief over his brow, set his lips tight, and turned his face towards us.

"No doubt you think me mad?" said he.

"I see that you have had some great trouble," responded Holmes.

"God knows I have!--a trouble which is enough to unseat my reason, so sudden and so terrible is it. Public disgrace I might have faced, although I am a man whose character has never yet borne a stain. Private affliction also is the lot of every man; but the two coming together, and in so frightful a form, have been enough to shake my very soul. Besides, it is not I alone. The very noblest in the land may suffer unless some way be found out of this horrible affair."

"Pray compose yourself, sir," said Holmes, "and let me have a clear account of who you are and what it is that has befallen you."

"My name," answered our visitor, "is probably familiar to your ears. I am Alexander Holder, of the banking firm of Holder & Stevenson, of Threadneedle Street."

The name was indeed well known to us as belonging to the senior partner in the second largest private banking concern in the City of London. What could have happened, then, to bring one of the foremost citizens of London to this most pitiable pass? We waited, all curiosity, until with another effort he braced himself to tell his story.

"I feel that time is of value," said he; "that is why I hastened here when the police inspector suggested that I should secure your co-operation. I came to Baker Street by the Underground and hurried from there on foot, for the cabs go slowly through this snow. That is why I was so out of breath, for I am a man who takes very little exercise. I feel better now, and I will put the facts before you as shortly and yet as clearly as I can.

"It is, of course, well known to you that in a successful banking business as much depends upon our being able to find remunerative investments for our funds as upon our increasing our connection and the number of our depositors. One of our most lucrative means of laying out money is in the shape of loans, where the security is unimpeachable. We have done a good deal in this direction during the last few years, and there are many noble families to whom we have advanced large sums upon the security of their pictures, libraries, or plate.

"Yesterday morning I was seated in my office at the bank when a card was brought in to me by one of the clerks. I started when I saw the name, for it was that of none other than—well, perhaps even to you I had better say no more than that it was a name which is a household word all over the earth—one of the highest, noblest, most exalted names in England. I was overwhelmed by the honour and attempted, when he entered, to say so, but he plunged at once into business with the air of a man who wishes to hurry quickly through a disagreeable task.

"'Mr. Holder,' said he, 'I have been informed that you are in the habit of advancing money.'

"'The firm does so when the security is good.' I answered.

"'It is absolutely essential to me,' said he, 'that I should have 50,000 pounds at once. I could, of course, borrow so trifling a sum ten times over from my friends, but I much prefer to make it a matter of business and to carry out that business myself. In my position you can readily understand that it is unwise to place one's self under obligations.'

"'For how long, may I ask, do you want this sum?' I asked.

"'Next Monday I have a large sum due to me, and I shall then most certainly repay what you advance, with whatever interest you think it right to charge. But it is very essential to me that the money should be paid at once.'

"'I should be happy to advance it without further parley from my own private purse,' said I, 'were it not that the strain would be rather more than it could bear. If, on the other hand, I am to do it in the name of the firm, then in justice to my partner I must insist that, even in your case, every businesslike precaution should be taken.'

"'I should much prefer to have it so,' said he, raising up a square, black morocco case which he had laid beside his chair. 'You have doubtless heard of the Beryl Coronet?'

"'One of the most precious public possessions of the empire,' said I.

"'Precisely.' He opened the case, and there, imbedded in soft, flesh-coloured velvet, lay the magnificent piece of jewellery which he had named. 'There are thirty-nine enormous beryls,' said he, 'and the price of the gold chasing is incalculable. The lowest estimate would put the worth of the coronet at double the sum which I have asked. I am prepared to leave it with you as my security.'

"I took the precious case into my hands and looked in some perplexity from it to my illustrious client.

"'You doubt its value?' he asked.

"'Not at all. I only doubt—'

"'The propriety of my leaving it. You may set your mind at rest about that. I should not dream of doing so were it not absolutely certain that I should be able in four days to reclaim it. It is a pure matter of form. Is the security sufficient?'

"'Ample.'

"'You understand, Mr. Holder, that I am giving you a strong proof of the confidence which I have in you, founded upon all that I have heard of you. I rely upon you not only to be discreet and to refrain from all gossip upon the matter but, above all, to preserve this coronet with every possible precaution because I need not say that a great public scandal would be caused if any harm were to befall it. Any injury to it would be almost as serious as its complete loss, for there are no beryls in the world to match these, and it would be impossible to replace them. I leave it with you, however, with every confidence, and I shall call for it in person on Monday morning.'

"Seeing that my client was anxious to leave, I said no more but, calling for my cashier, I ordered him to pay over fifty 1000 pound notes. When I was alone once more, however, with the precious case lying upon the table in front of me, I could not but think with some misgivings of the immense responsibility which it entailed upon me. There could be no doubt that, as it was a national possession, a horrible scandal would ensue if any misfortune should occur to it. I already regretted having ever consented to take charge of it. However, it was too late to alter the matter now, so I locked it up in my private safe and turned once more to my work.

"When evening came I felt that it would be an imprudence to leave so precious a thing in the office behind me. Bankers' safes had been forced before now, and why should not mine be? If so, how terrible would be the position in which I should find myself! I determined, therefore, that for the next few days I would always carry the case backward and forward with me, so that it might never be really out of my reach. With this intention, I called a cab and drove out to my house at Streatham, carrying the jewel with me. I did not breathe freely until I had taken it upstairs and locked it in the bureau of my dressing-room.

"And now a word as to my household, Mr. Holmes, for I wish you to thoroughly understand the situation. My groom and my page sleep out of the house, and may be set aside altogether. I have three maid-servants who have been with me a number of years and whose absolute reliability is quite above suspicion. Another, Lucy Parr, the second waiting-maid, has only been in my service a few months. She came with an excellent character, however, and has always given me satisfaction. She is a very pretty girl and has attracted admirers who have occasionally hung about the place. That is the only drawback which we have found to her, but we believe her to be a thoroughly good girl in every way.

"So much for the servants. My family itself is so small that it will not take me long to describe it. I am a widower and have an only son, Arthur. He has been a disappointment to me, Mr. Holmes—a grievous disappointment. I have no doubt that I am myself to blame. People tell me that I have spoiled him. Very likely I have. When my dear wife died I felt that he was all I had to love. I could not bear to see the smile fade even for a moment from his face. I have never denied him a wish. Perhaps it would have been better for both of us had I been sterner, but I meant it for the best.

"It was naturally my intention that he should succeed me in my business, but he was not of a business turn. He was wild, wayward, and, to speak the truth, I could not trust him in the handling of large sums of money. When he was young he became a member of an aristocratic club, and there, having charming manners, he was soon the intimate of a number of men with long purses and expensive habits. He learned to play heavily at cards and to squander money on the turf, until he had again and again to come to me and implore me to give him an advance upon his allowance, that he might settle his debts of honour. He tried more than once to break away from the dangerous company which he was keeping, but each time the influence of his friend, Sir George Burnwell, was enough to draw him back again.

"And, indeed, I could not wonder that such a man as Sir George Burnwell should gain an influence over him, for he has frequently brought him to my house, and I have found myself that I could hardly resist the fascination of his manner. He is older than Arthur, a man of the world to his finger-tips, one who had been everywhere, seen everything, a brilliant talker, and a man of great personal beauty. Yet when I think of him in cold blood, far away from the glamour of his presence, I am convinced from his cynical speech and the look which I have caught in his eyes that he is one who should be deeply distrusted. So I think, and so, too, thinks my little Mary, who has a woman's quick insight into character.

"And now there is only she to be described. She is my niece; but when my brother died five years ago and left her alone in the world I adopted her, and have looked upon her ever since as my daughter. She is a sunbeam in my house—sweet, loving, beautiful, a wonderful manager and housekeeper, yet as tender and quiet and gentle as a woman could be. She is my right hand. I do not know what I could do without her. In only one matter has she ever gone against my wishes. Twice my boy has asked her to marry him, for he loves her devotedly, but each time she has refused him. I think that if anyone could have drawn him into the right path it would have been she, and that his marriage might have changed his whole life; but now, alas! it is too late—forever too late!

"Now, Mr. Holmes, you know the people who live under my roof, and I shall continue with my miserable story.

"When we were taking coffee in the drawing-room that night after dinner, I told Arthur and Mary my experience, and of the precious treasure which we had under our roof, suppressing only the name of my client. Lucy Parr, who had brought in the coffee, had, I am sure, left the room; but I cannot swear that the door was closed. Mary and Arthur were much interested and wished to see the famous coronet, but I thought it better not to disturb it.

"'Where have you put it?' asked Arthur.

"'In my own bureau.'

"'Well, I hope to goodness the house won't be burgled during the night.' said he.

"'It is locked up,' I answered.

"'Oh, any old key will fit that bureau. When I was a youngster I have opened it myself with the key of the box-room cupboard.'

"He often had a wild way of talking, so that I thought little of what he said. He followed me to my room, however, that night with a very grave face.

"'Look here, dad,' said he with his eyes cast down, 'can you let me have 200 pounds?'

"'No, I cannot!' I answered sharply. 'I have been far too generous with you in money matters.'

"'You have been very kind,' said he, 'but I must have this money, or else I can never show my face inside the club again.'

"'And a very good thing, too!' I cried.

"'Yes, but you would not have me leave it a dishonoured man,' said he. 'I could not bear the disgrace. I must raise the money in some way, and if you will not let me have it, then I must try other means.'

"I was very angry, for this was the third demand during the month. 'You shall not have a farthing from me,' I cried, on which he bowed and left the room without another word.

"When he was gone I unlocked my bureau, made sure that my treasure was safe, and locked it again. Then I started to go round the house to see that all was secure—a duty which I usually leave to Mary but which I thought it well to perform myself that night. As I came down the stairs I saw Mary herself at the side window of the hall, which she closed and fastened as I approached.

"'Tell me, dad,' said she, looking, I thought, a little disturbed, 'did you give Lucy, the maid, leave to go out to-night?'

"'Certainly not.'

"'She came in just now by the back door. I have no doubt that she has only been to the side gate to see someone, but I think that it is hardly safe and should be stopped.'

"'You must speak to her in the morning, or I will if you prefer it. Are you sure that everything is fastened?'

"'Quite sure, dad.'

"'Then, good-night.' I kissed her and went up to my bedroom again, where I was soon asleep.

"I am endeavouring to tell you everything, Mr. Holmes, which may have any bearing upon the case, but I beg that you will question me upon any point which I do not make clear."

"On the contrary, your statement is singularly lucid."

"I come to a part of my story now in which I should wish to be particularly so. I am not a very heavy sleeper, and the anxiety in my mind tended, no doubt, to make me even less so than usual. About two in the morning, then, I was awakened by some sound in the house. It had ceased ere I was wide awake, but it had left an impression behind it as though a window had gently closed somewhere. I lay listening with all my ears. Suddenly, to my horror, there was a distinct sound of footsteps moving softly in the next room. I slipped out of bed, all palpitating with fear, and peeped round the corner of my dressing-room door.

"'Arthur!' I screamed, 'you villain! you thief! How dare you touch that coronet?'

"The gas was half up, as I had left it, and my unhappy boy, dressed only in his shirt and trousers, was standing beside the light, holding the coronet in his hands. He appeared to be wrenching at it, or bending it with all his strength. At my cry he dropped it from his grasp and turned as pale as death. I snatched it up and examined it. One of the gold corners, with three of the beryls in it, was missing.

"'You blackguard!' I shouted, beside myself with rage. 'You have destroyed it! You have dishonoured me forever! Where are the jewels which you have stolen?'

"'Stolen!' he cried.

"'Yes, thief!' I roared, shaking him by the shoulder.

"'There are none missing. There cannot be any missing,' said he.

"'There are three missing. And you know where they are. Must I call you a liar as well as a thief? Did I not see you trying to tear off another piece?'

"'You have called me names enough,' said he, 'I will not stand it any longer. I shall not say another word about this business, since you have chosen to insult me. I will leave your house in the morning and make my own way in the world.'

"'You shall leave it in the hands of the police!' I cried half-mad with grief and rage. 'I shall have this matter probed to the bottom.'

"'You shall learn nothing from me,' said he with a passion such as I should not have thought was in his nature. 'If you choose to call the police, let the police find what they can.'

"By this time the whole house was astir, for I had raised my voice in my anger. Mary was the first to rush into my room, and, at the sight of the coronet and of Arthur's face, she read the whole story and, with a scream, fell down senseless on the ground. I sent the house-maid for the police and put the investigation into their hands at once. When the inspector and a constable entered the house, Arthur, who had stood sullenly with his arms folded, asked me whether it was my intention to charge him with theft. I answered that it had ceased to be a private matter, but had become a public one, since the ruined coronet was national property. I was determined that the law should have its way in everything.

"'At least,' said he, 'you will not have me arrested at once. It would be to your advantage as well as mine if I might leave the house for five minutes.'

"'That you may get away, or perhaps that you may conceal what you have stolen,' said I. And then, realising the dreadful position in which I was placed, I implored him to remember that not only my honour but that of one who was far greater than I was at stake; and that he threatened to raise a scandal which would convulse the nation. He might avert it all if he would but tell me what he had done with the three missing stones.

"'You may as well face the matter,' said I; 'you have been caught in the act, and no confession could make your guilt more heinous. If you but make such reparation as is in your power, by telling us where the beryls are, all shall be forgiven and forgotten.'

"'Keep your forgiveness for those who ask for it,' he answered, turning away from me with a sneer. I saw that he was too hardened for any words of mine to influence him. There was but one way for it. I called in the inspector and gave him into custody. A search was made at once not only of his person but of his room and of every portion of the house where he could possibly have concealed the gems; but no trace of them could be found, nor would the wretched boy open his mouth for all our persuasions and our threats. This morning he was removed to a cell, and I, after going through all the police formalities, have hurried round to you to implore you to use your skill in unravelling the matter. The police have openly confessed that they can at present make nothing of it. You may go to any expense which you think necessary. I have already offered a reward of 1000 pounds. My God, what shall I do! I have lost my honour, my gems, and my son in one night. Oh, what shall I do!"

He put a hand on either side of his head and rocked himself to and fro, droning to himself like a child whose grief has got beyond words.

Sherlock Holmes sat silent for some few minutes, with his brows knitted and his eyes fixed upon the fire.

"Do you receive much company?" he asked.

"None save my partner with his family and an occasional friend of Arthur's. Sir George Burnwell has been several times lately. No one else, I think."

"Do you go out much in society?"

"Arthur does. Mary and I stay at home. We neither of us care for it."

"That is unusual in a young girl."

"She is of a quiet nature. Besides, she is not so very young. She is four-and-twenty."

"This matter, from what you say, seems to have been a shock to her also."

"Terrible! She is even more affected than I."

"You have neither of you any doubt as to your son's guilt?"

"How can we have when I saw him with my own eyes with the coronet in his hands."

"I hardly consider that a conclusive proof. Was the remainder of the coronet at all injured?"

"Yes, it was twisted."

"Do you not think, then, that he might have been trying to straighten it?"

"God bless you! You are doing what you can for him and for me. But it is too heavy a task. What was he doing there at all? If his purpose were innocent, why did he not say so?"

"Precisely. And if it were guilty, why did he not invent a lie? His silence appears to me to cut both ways. There are several singular points about the case. What did the police think of the noise which awoke you from your sleep?"

"They considered that it might be caused by Arthur's closing his bedroom door."

"A likely story! As if a man bent on felony would slam his door so as to wake a household. What did they say, then, of the disappearance of these gems?"

"They are still sounding the planking and probing the furniture in the hope of finding them."

"Have they thought of looking outside the house?"

"Yes, they have shown extraordinary energy. The whole garden has already been minutely examined."

"Now, my dear sir," said Holmes. "is it not obvious to you now that this matter really strikes very much deeper than either you or the police were at first inclined to think? It appeared to you to be a simple case; to me it seems exceedingly complex. Consider what is involved by your theory. You suppose that your son came down from his bed, went, at great risk, to your dressing-room, opened your bureau, took out your coronet, broke off by main force a small portion of it, went off to some other place, concealed three gems out of the thirty-nine, with such skill that nobody can find them, and then returned with the other thirty-six into the room in which he exposed himself to the greatest danger of being discovered. I ask you now, is such a theory tenable?"

"But what other is there?" cried the banker with a gesture of despair. "If his motives were innocent, why does he not explain them?"

"It is our task to find that out," replied Holmes; "so now, if you please, Mr. Holder, we will set off for Streatham together, and devote an hour to glancing a little more closely into details."

My friend insisted upon my accompanying them in their expedition, which I was eager enough to do, for my curiosity and sympathy were deeply stirred by the story to which we had listened. I confess that the guilt of the banker's son appeared to me to be as obvious as it did to his unhappy father, but still I had such faith in Holmes' judgment that I felt that there must be some grounds for hope as long as he was dissatisfied with the accepted explanation. He hardly spoke a word the whole way out to the southern suburb, but sat with his chin upon his breast and his hat drawn over his eyes, sunk in the deepest thought. Our client appeared to have taken fresh heart at the little glimpse of hope which had been presented to him, and he even broke into a desultory chat with me over his business affairs. A short railway journey and a shorter walk brought us to Fairbank, the modest residence of the great financier.

Fairbank was a good-sized square house of white stone, standing back a little from the road. A double carriage-sweep, with a snow-clad lawn, stretched down in front to two large iron gates which closed the entrance. On the right side was a small wooden thicket, which led into a narrow path between two neat hedges stretching from the road to the kitchen door, and forming the tradesmen's entrance. On the left ran a lane which led to the stables, and was not itself within the grounds at all, being a public, though little used, thoroughfare. Holmes left us standing at the door and walked slowly all round the house, across the front, down the tradesmen's path, and so round by the garden behind into the stable lane. So long was he that Mr. Holder and I went into the dining-room and waited by the fire until he should return. We were sitting there in silence when the door opened and a young lady came in. She was rather above the middle height, slim, with dark hair and eyes, which seemed the darker against the absolute pallor of her skin. I do not think that I have ever seen such deadly paleness in a woman's face. Her lips, too, were bloodless, but her eyes were flushed with crying. As she swept silently into the room she impressed me with a greater sense of grief than the banker had done in the morning, and it was the more striking in her as she was evidently a woman of strong character, with immense capacity for self-restraint. Disregarding my presence, she went straight to her uncle and passed her hand over his head with a sweet womanly caress.

"You have given orders that Arthur should be liberated, have you not, dad?" she asked.

"No, no, my girl, the matter must be probed to the bottom."

"But I am so sure that he is innocent. You know what woman's instincts are. I know that he has done no harm and that you will be sorry for having acted so harshly."

"Why is he silent, then, if he is innocent?"

"Who knows? Perhaps because he was so angry that you should suspect him."

"How could I help suspecting him, when I actually saw him with the coronet in his hand?"

"Oh, but he had only picked it up to look at it. Oh, do, do take my word for it that he is innocent. Let the matter drop and say no more. It is so dreadful to think of our dear Arthur in prison!"

"I shall never let it drop until the gems are found—never, Mary! Your affection for Arthur blinds you as to the awful consequences to me. Far from hushing the thing up, I have brought a gentleman down from London to inquire more deeply into it."

"This gentleman?" she asked, facing round to me.

"No, his friend. He wished us to leave him alone. He is round in the stable lane now."

"The stable lane?" She raised her dark eyebrows. "What can he hope to find there? Ah! this, I suppose, is he. I trust, sir, that you will succeed in proving, what I feel sure is the truth, that my cousin Arthur is innocent of this crime."

"I fully share your opinion, and I trust, with you, that we may prove it," returned Holmes, going back to the mat to knock the snow from his shoes. "I believe I have the honour of addressing Miss Mary Holder. Might I ask you a question or two?"

"Pray do, sir, if it may help to clear this horrible affair up."

"You heard nothing yourself last night?"

"Nothing, until my uncle here began to speak loudly. I heard that, and I came down."

"You shut up the windows and doors the night before. Did you fasten all the windows?"

"Yes."

"Were they all fastened this morning?"

"Yes."

"You have a maid who has a sweetheart? I think that you remarked to your uncle last night that she had been out to see him?"

"Yes, and she was the girl who waited in the drawing-room, and who may have heard uncle's remarks about the coronet."

"I see. You infer that she may have gone out to tell her sweetheart, and that the two may have planned the robbery."

"But what is the good of all these vague theories," cried the banker impatiently, "when I have told you that I saw Arthur with the coronet in his hands?"

"Wait a little, Mr. Holder. We must come back to that. About this girl, Miss Holder. You saw her return by the kitchen door, I presume?"

"Yes; when I went to see if the door was fastened for the night I met her slipping in. I saw the man, too, in the gloom."

"Do you know him?"

"Oh, yes! he is the green-grocer who brings our vegetables round. His name is Francis Prosper."

"He stood," said Holmes, "to the left of the door—that is to say, farther up the path than is necessary to reach the door?"

"Yes, he did."

"And he is a man with a wooden leg?"

Something like fear sprang up in the young lady's expressive black eyes. "Why, you are like a magician," said she. "How do you know that?" She smiled, but there was no answering smile in Holmes' thin, eager face.

"I should be very glad now to go upstairs," said he. "I shall probably wish to go over the outside of the house again. Perhaps I had better take a look at the lower windows before I go up."

He walked swiftly round from one to the other, pausing only at the large one which looked from the hall onto the stable lane. This he opened and made a very careful examination of the sill with his powerful magnifying lens. "Now we shall go upstairs," said he at last.

The banker's dressing-room was a plainly furnished little chamber, with a grey carpet, a large bureau, and a long mirror. Holmes went to the bureau first and looked hard at the lock.

"Which key was used to open it?" he asked.

"That which my son himself indicated—that of the cupboard of the lumber-room."

"Have you it here?"

"That is it on the dressing-table."

Sherlock Holmes took it up and opened the bureau.

"It is a noiseless lock," said he. "It is no wonder that it did not wake you. This case, I presume, contains the coronet. We must have a look at it." He opened the case, and taking out the diadem he laid it upon the table. It was a magnificent specimen of the jeweller's art, and the thirty-six stones were the finest that I have ever seen. At one side of the coronet was a cracked edge, where a corner holding three gems had been torn away.

"Now, Mr. Holder," said Holmes, "here is the corner which corresponds to that which has been so unfortunately lost. Might I beg that you will break it off."

The banker recoiled in horror. "I should not dream of trying," said he.

"Then I will." Holmes suddenly bent his strength upon it, but without result. "I feel it give a little," said he; "but, though I am exceptionally strong in the fingers, it would take me all my time to break it. An ordinary man could not do it. Now, what do you think would happen if I did break it, Mr. Holder? There would be a noise like a pistol shot. Do you tell me that all this happened within a few yards of your bed and that you heard nothing of it?"

"I do not know what to think. It is all dark to me."

"But perhaps it may grow lighter as we go. What do you think, Miss Holder?"

"I confess that I still share my uncle's perplexity."

"Your son had no shoes or slippers on when you saw him?"

"He had nothing on save only his trousers and shirt."

"Thank you. We have certainly been favoured with extraordinary luck during this inquiry, and it will be entirely our own fault if we do not succeed in clearing the matter up. With your permission, Mr. Holder, I shall now continue my investigations outside."

He went alone, at his own request, for he explained that any unnecessary footmarks might make his task more difficult. For an hour or more he was at work, returning at last with his feet heavy with snow and his features as inscrutable as ever.

"I think that I have seen now all that there is to see, Mr. Holder," said he; "I can serve you best by returning to my rooms."

"But the gems, Mr. Holmes. Where are they?"

"I cannot tell."

The banker wrung his hands. "I shall never see them again!" he cried. "And my son? You give me hopes?"

"My opinion is in no way altered."

"Then, for God's sake, what was this dark business which was acted in my house last night?"

"If you can call upon me at my Baker Street rooms tomorrow morning between nine and ten I shall be happy to do what I can to make it clearer. I understand that you give me carte blanche to act for you, provided only that I get back the gems, and that you place no limit on the sum I may draw."

"I would give my fortune to have them back."

"Very good. I shall look into the matter between this and then. Good-bye; it is just possible that I may have to come over here again before evening."

It was obvious to me that my companion's mind was now made up about the case, although what his conclusions were was more than I could even dimly imagine. Several times during our homeward journey I endeavoured to sound him upon the point, but he always glided away to some other topic, until at last I gave it over in despair. It was not yet three when we found ourselves in our rooms once more. He hurried to his chamber and was down again in a few minutes dressed as a common loafer. With his collar turned up, his shiny, seedy coat, his red cravat, and his worn boots, he was a perfect sample of the class.

"I think that this should do," said he, glancing into the glass above the fireplace. "I only wish that you could come with me, Watson, but I fear that it won't do. I may be on the trail in this matter, or I may be following a will-o'-the-wisp, but I shall soon know which it is. I hope that I may be back in a few hours." He cut a slice of beef from the joint upon the sideboard, sandwiched it between two rounds of bread, and thrusting this rude meal into his pocket he started off upon his expedition.

I had just finished my tea when he returned, evidently in excellent spirits, swinging an old elastic-sided boot in his hand. He chucked it down into a corner and helped himself to a cup of tea.

"I only looked in as I passed," said he. "I am going right on."

"Where to?"

"Oh, to the other side of the West End. It may be some time before I get back. Don't wait up for me in case I should be late."

"How are you getting on?"

"Oh, so so. Nothing to complain of. I have been out to Streatham since I saw you last, but I did not call at the house. It is a very sweet little problem, and I would not have missed it for a good deal. However, I must not sit gossiping here, but must get these disreputable clothes off and return to my highly respectable self."

I could see by his manner that he had stronger reasons for satisfaction than his words alone would imply. His eyes twinkled, and there was even a touch of colour upon his sallow cheeks. He hastened upstairs, and a few minutes later I heard the slam of the hall door, which told me that he was off once more upon his congenial hunt.

I waited until midnight, but there was no sign of his return, so I retired to my room. It was no uncommon thing for him to be away for days and nights on end when he was hot upon a scent, so that his lateness caused me no surprise. I do not know at what hour he came in, but when I came down to breakfast in the morning there he was with a cup of coffee in one hand and the paper in the other, as fresh and trim as possible.

"You will excuse my beginning without you, Watson," said he, "but you remember that our client has rather an early appointment this morning."

"Why, it is after nine now," I answered. "I should not be surprised if that were he. I thought I heard a ring."

It was, indeed, our friend the financier. I was shocked by the change which had come over him, for his face which was naturally of a broad and massive mould, was now pinched and fallen in, while his hair seemed to me at least a shade whiter. He entered with a weariness and lethargy which was even more painful than his violence of the morning before, and he dropped heavily into the armchair which I pushed forward for him.

"I do not know what I have done to be so severely tried," said he. "Only two days ago I was a happy and prosperous man, without a care in the world. Now I am left to a lonely and dishonoured age. One sorrow comes close upon the heels of another. My niece, Mary, has deserted me."

"Deserted you?"

"Yes. Her bed this morning had not been slept in, her room was empty, and a note for me lay upon the hall table. I had said to her last night, in sorrow and not in anger, that if she had married my boy all might have been well with him. Perhaps it was thoughtless of me to say so. It is to that remark that she refers in this note:

"'MY DEAREST UNCLE:--I feel that I have brought trouble upon you, and that if I had acted differently this terrible misfortune might never have occurred. I cannot, with this thought in my mind, ever again be happy under your roof, and I feel that I must leave you forever. Do not worry about my future, for that is provided for; and, above all, do not search for me, for it will be fruitless labour and an ill-service to me. In life or in death, I am ever your loving,--MARY.'

"What could she mean by that note, Mr. Holmes? Do you think it points to suicide?"

"No, no, nothing of the kind. It is perhaps the best possible solution. I trust, Mr. Holder, that you are nearing the end of your troubles."

"Ha! You say so! You have heard something, Mr. Holmes; you have learned something! Where are the gems?"

"You would not think 1000 pounds apiece an excessive sum for them?"

"I would pay ten."

"That would be unnecessary. Three thousand will cover the matter. And there is a little reward, I fancy. Have you your check-book? Here is a pen. Better make it out for 4000 pounds."

With a dazed face the banker made out the required check. Holmes walked over to his desk, took out a little triangular piece of gold with three gems in it, and threw it down upon the table.

With a shriek of joy our client clutched it up.

"You have it!" he gasped. "I am saved! I am saved!"

The reaction of joy was as passionate as his grief had been, and he hugged his recovered gems to his bosom.

"There is one other thing you owe, Mr. Holder," said Sherlock Holmes rather sternly.

"Owe!" He caught up a pen. "Name the sum, and I will pay it."

"No, the debt is not to me. You owe a very humble apology to that noble lad, your son, who has carried himself in this matter as I should be proud to see my own son do, should I ever chance to have one."

"Then it was not Arthur who took them?"

"I told you yesterday, and I repeat today, that it was not."

"You are sure of it! Then let us hurry to him at once to let him know that the truth is known."

"He knows it already. When I had cleared it all up I had an interview with him, and finding that he would not tell me the story, I told it to him, on which he had to confess that I was right and to add the very few details which were not yet quite clear to me. Your news of this morning, however, may open his lips."

"For heaven's sake, tell me, then, what is this extraordinary mystery!"

"I will do so, and I will show you the steps by which I reached it. And let me say to you, first, that which it is hardest for me to say and for you to hear: there has been an understanding between Sir George Burnwell and your niece Mary. They have now fled together."

"My Mary? Impossible!"

"It is unfortunately more than possible; it is certain. Neither you nor your son knew the true character of this man when you admitted him into your family circle. He is one of the most dangerous men in England—a ruined gambler, an absolutely desperate villain, a man without heart or conscience. Your niece knew nothing of such men. When he breathed his vows to her, as he had done to a hundred before her, she flattered herself that she alone had touched his heart. The devil knows best what he said, but at least she became his tool and was in the habit of seeing him nearly every evening."

"I cannot, and I will not, believe it!" cried the banker with an ashen face.

"I will tell you, then, what occurred in your house last night. Your niece, when you had, as she thought, gone to your room, slipped down and talked to her lover through the window which leads into the stable lane. His footmarks had pressed right through the snow, so long had he stood there. She told him of the coronet. His wicked lust for gold kindled at the news, and he bent her to his will. I have no doubt that she loved you, but there are women in whom the love of a lover extinguishes all other loves, and I think that she must have been one. She had hardly listened to his instructions when she saw you coming downstairs, on which she closed the window rapidly and told you about one of the servants' escapade with her wooden-legged lover, which was all perfectly true.

"Your boy, Arthur, went to bed after his interview with you but he slept badly on account of his uneasiness about his club debts. In the middle of the night he heard a soft tread pass his door, so he rose and, looking out, was surprised to see his cousin walking very stealthily along the passage until she disappeared into your dressing-room. Petrified with astonishment, the lad slipped on some clothes and waited there in the dark to see what would come of this strange affair. Presently she emerged from the room again, and in the light of the passage-lamp your son saw that she carried the precious coronet in her hands. She passed down the stairs, and he, thrilling with horror, ran along and slipped behind the curtain near your door, whence he could see what passed in the hall beneath. He saw her stealthily open the window, hand out the coronet to someone in the gloom, and then closing it once more hurry back to her room, passing quite close to where he stood hid behind the curtain.

"As long as she was on the scene he could not take any action without a horrible exposure of the woman whom he loved. But the instant that she was gone he realised how crushing a misfortune this would be for you, and how all-important it was to set it right. He rushed down, just as he was, in his bare feet, opened the window, sprang out into the snow, and ran down the lane, where he could see a dark figure in the moonlight. Sir George Burnwell tried to get away, but Arthur caught him, and there was a struggle between them, your lad tugging at one side of the coronet, and his opponent at the other. In the scuffle, your son struck Sir George and cut him over the eye. Then something suddenly snapped, and your son, finding that he had the coronet in his hands, rushed back, closed the window, ascended to your room, and had just observed that the coronet had been twisted in the struggle and was endeavouring to straighten it when you appeared upon the scene."

"Is it possible?" gasped the banker.

"You then roused his anger by calling him names at a moment when he felt that he had deserved your warmest thanks. He could not explain the true state of affairs without betraying one who certainly deserved little enough consideration at his hands. He took the more chivalrous view, however, and preserved her secret."

"And that was why she shrieked and fainted when she saw the coronet," cried Mr. Holder. "Oh, my God! what a blind fool I have been! And his asking to be allowed to go out for five minutes! The dear fellow wanted to see if the missing piece were at the scene of the struggle. How cruelly I have misjudged him!"

"When I arrived at the house," continued Holmes, "I at once went very carefully round it to observe if there were any traces in the snow which might help me. I knew that none had fallen since the evening before, and also that there had been a strong frost to preserve impressions. I passed along the tradesmen's path, but found it all trampled down and indistinguishable. Just beyond it, however, at the far side of the kitchen door, a woman had stood and talked with a man, whose round impressions on one side showed that he had a wooden leg. I could even tell that they had been disturbed, for the woman had run back swiftly to the door, as was shown by the deep toe and light heel marks, while Wooden-leg had waited a little, and then had gone away. I thought at the time that this might be the maid and her sweetheart, of whom you had already spoken to me, and inquiry showed it was so. I passed round the garden without seeing anything more than random tracks, which I took to be the police; but when I got into the stable lane a very long and complex story was written in the snow in front of me.

"There was a double line of tracks of a booted man, and a second double line which I saw with delight belonged to a man with naked feet. I was at once convinced from what you had told me that the latter was your son. The first had walked both ways, but the other had run swiftly, and as his tread was marked in places over the depression of the boot, it was obvious that he had passed after the other. I followed them up and found they led to the hall window, where Boots had worn all the snow away while waiting. Then I walked to the other end, which was a hundred yards or more down the lane. I saw where Boots had faced round, where the snow was cut up as though there had been a struggle, and, finally, where a few drops of blood had fallen, to show me that I was not mistaken. Boots had then run down the lane, and another little smudge of blood showed that it was he who had been hurt. When he came to the highroad at the other end, I found that the pavement had been cleared, so there was an end to that clue.

"On entering the house, however, I examined, as you remember, the sill and framework of the hall window with my lens, and I could at once see that someone had passed out. I could distinguish the outline of an instep where the wet foot had been placed in coming in. I was then beginning to be able to form an opinion as to what had occurred. A man had waited outside the window; someone had brought the gems; the deed had been overseen by your son; he had pursued the thief; had struggled with him; they had each tugged at the coronet, their united strength causing injuries which neither alone could have effected. He had returned with the prize, but had left a fragment in the grasp of his opponent. So far I was clear. The question now was, who was the man and who was it brought him the coronet?

"It is an old maxim of mine that when you have excluded the impossible, whatever remains, however improbable, must be the truth. Now, I knew that it was not you who had brought it down, so there only remained your niece and the maids. But if it were the maids, why should your son allow himself to be accused in their place? There could be no possible reason. As he loved his cousin, however, there was an excellent explanation why he should retain her secret—the more so as the secret was a disgraceful one. When I remembered that you had seen her at that window, and how she had fainted on seeing the coronet again, my conjecture became a certainty.

"And who could it be who was her confederate? A lover evidently, for who else could outweigh the love and gratitude which she must feel to you? I knew that you went out little, and that your circle of friends was a very limited one. But among them was Sir George Burnwell. I had heard of him before as being a man of evil reputation among women. It must have been he who wore those boots and retained the missing gems. Even though he knew that Arthur had discovered him, he might still flatter himself that he was safe, for the lad could not say a word without compromising his own family.

"Well, your own good sense will suggest what measures I took next. I went in the shape of a loafer to Sir George's house, managed to pick up an acquaintance with his valet, learned that his master had cut his head the night before, and, finally, at the expense of six shillings, made all sure by buying a pair of his cast-off shoes. With these I journeyed down to Streatham and saw that they exactly fitted the tracks."

"I saw an ill-dressed vagabond in the lane yesterday evening," said Mr. Holder.

"Precisely. It was I. I found that I had my man, so I came home and changed my clothes. It was a delicate part which I had to play then, for I saw that a prosecution must be avoided to avert scandal, and I knew that so astute a villain would see that our hands were tied in the matter. I went and saw him. At first, of course, he denied everything. But when I gave him every particular that had occurred, he tried to bluster and took down a life-preserver from the wall. I knew my man, however, and I clapped a pistol to his head before he could strike. Then he became a little more reasonable. I told him that we would give him a price for the stones he held--1000 pounds apiece. That brought out the first signs of grief that he had shown. 'Why, dash it all!' said he, 'I've let them go at six hundred for the three!' I soon managed to get the address of the receiver who had them, on promising him that there would be no prosecution. Off I set to him, and after much chaffering I got our stones at 1000 pounds apiece. Then I looked in upon your son, told him that all was right, and eventually got to my bed about two o'clock, after what I may call a really hard day's work."

"A day which has saved England from a great public scandal," said the banker, rising. "Sir, I cannot find words to thank you, but you shall not find me ungrateful for what you have done. Your skill has indeed exceeded all that I have heard of it. And now I must fly to my dear boy to apologise to him for the wrong which I have done him. As to what you tell me of poor Mary, it goes to my very heart. Not even your skill can inform me where she is now."

"I think that we may safely say," returned Holmes, "that she is wherever Sir George Burnwell is. It is equally certain, too, that whatever her sins are, they will soon receive a more than sufficient punishment."

XII. The Adventure Of The Copper Beeches

"To the man who loves art for its own sake," remarked Sherlock Holmes, tossing aside the advertisement sheet of the Daily Telegraph, "it is frequently in its least important and lowliest manifestations that the keenest pleasure is to be derived. It is pleasant to me to observe, Watson, that you have so far grasped this truth that in these little records of our cases which you have been good enough to draw up, and, I am bound to say, occasionally to embellish, you have given prominence not so much to the many causes célèbres and sensational trials in which I have figured but rather to those incidents which may have been trivial in themselves, but which have given room for those faculties of deduction and of logical synthesis which I have made my special province."

"And yet," said I, smiling, "I cannot quite hold myself absolved from the charge of sensationalism which has been urged against my records."

"You have erred, perhaps," he observed, taking up a glowing cinder with the tongs and lighting with it the long cherry-wood pipe which was wont to replace his clay when he was in a disputatious rather than a meditative mood—"you have erred perhaps in attempting to put colour and life into each of your statements instead of confining yourself to the task of placing upon record that severe reasoning from cause to effect which is really the only notable feature about the thing."

"It seems to me that I have done you full justice in the matter," I remarked with some coldness, for I was repelled by the egotism which I had more than once observed to be a strong factor in my friend's singular character.

"No, it is not selfishness or conceit," said he, answering, as was his wont, my thoughts rather than my words. "If I claim full justice for my art, it is because it is an impersonal thing—a thing beyond myself. Crime is common. Logic is rare. Therefore it is upon the logic rather than upon the crime that you should dwell. You have degraded what should have been a course of lectures into a series of tales."

It was a cold morning of the early spring, and we sat after breakfast on either side of a cheery fire in the old room at Baker Street. A thick fog rolled down between the lines of dun-coloured houses, and the opposing windows loomed like dark, shapeless blurs through the heavy yellow wreaths. Our gas was lit and shone on the white cloth and glimmer of china and metal, for the table had not been cleared yet. Sherlock Holmes had been silent all the morning, dipping continuously into the advertisement columns of a succession of papers until at last, having apparently given up his search, he had emerged in no very sweet temper to lecture me upon my literary shortcomings.

"At the same time," he remarked after a pause, during which he had sat puffing at his long pipe and gazing down into the fire, "you can hardly be open to a charge of sensationalism, for out of these cases which you have been so kind as to interest yourself in, a fair proportion do not treat of crime, in its legal sense, at all. The small matter in which I endeavoured to help the King of Bohemia, the singular experience of Miss Mary Sutherland, the problem connected with the man with the twisted lip, and the incident of the noble bachelor, were all matters which are outside the pale of the law. But in avoiding the sensational, I fear that you may have bordered on the trivial."

"The end may have been so," I answered, "but the methods I hold to have been novel and of interest."

"Pshaw, my dear fellow, what do the public, the great unobservant public, who could hardly tell a weaver by his tooth or a compositor by his left thumb, care about the finer shades of analysis and deduction! But, indeed, if you are trivial. I cannot blame you, for the days of the great cases are past. Man, or at least criminal man, has lost all enterprise and originality. As to my own little practice, it seems to be degenerating into an agency for recovering lost lead pencils and giving advice to young ladies from boarding-schools. I think that I have touched bottom at last, however. This note I had this morning marks my zero-point, I fancy. Read it!" He tossed a crumpled letter across to me.

It was dated from Montague Place upon the preceding evening, and ran thus:

"DEAR MR. HOLMES:--I am very anxious to consult you as to whether I should or should not accept a situation which has been offered to me as governess. I shall call at half-past ten tomorrow if I do not inconvenience you. Yours faithfully, "VIOLET HUNTER."

"Do you know the young lady?" I asked.

"Not I."

"It is half-past ten now."

"Yes, and I have no doubt that is her ring."

"It may turn out to be of more interest than you think. You remember that the affair of the blue carbuncle, which appeared to be a mere whim at first, developed into a serious investigation. It may be so in this case, also."

"Well, let us hope so. But our doubts will very soon be solved, for here, unless I am much mistaken, is the person in question."

As he spoke the door opened and a young lady entered the room. She was plainly but neatly dressed, with a bright, quick face, freckled like a plover's egg, and with the brisk manner of a woman who has had her own way to make in the world.

"You will excuse my troubling you, I am sure," said she, as my companion rose to greet her, "but I have had a very strange experience, and as I have no parents or relations of any sort from whom I could ask advice, I thought that perhaps you would be kind enough to tell me what I should do."

"Pray take a seat, Miss Hunter. I shall be happy to do anything that I can to serve you."

I could see that Holmes was favourably impressed by the manner and speech of his new client. He looked her over in his searching fashion, and then composed himself, with his lids drooping and his finger-tips together, to listen to her story.

"I have been a governess for five years," said she, "in the family of Colonel Spence Munro, but two months ago the colonel received an appointment at Halifax, in Nova Scotia, and took his children over to America with him, so that I found myself without a situation. I advertised, and I answered advertisements, but without success. At last the little money which I had saved began to run short, and I was at my wit's end as to what I should do.

"There is a well-known agency for governesses in the West End called Westaway's, and there I used to call about once a week in order to see whether anything had turned up which might suit me. Westaway was the name of the founder of the business, but it is really managed by Miss Stoper. She sits in her own little office, and the ladies who are seeking employment wait in an anteroom, and are then shown in one by one, when she consults her ledgers and sees whether she has anything which would suit them.

"Well, when I called last week I was shown into the little office as usual, but I found that Miss Stoper was not alone. A prodigiously stout man with a very smiling face and a great heavy chin which rolled down in fold upon fold over his throat sat at her elbow with a pair of glasses on his nose, looking very earnestly at the ladies who entered. As I came in he gave quite a jump in his chair and turned quickly to Miss Stoper.

"'That will do,' said he; 'I could not ask for anything better. Capital! capital!' He seemed quite enthusiastic and rubbed his hands together in the most genial fashion. He was such a comfortable-looking man that it was quite a pleasure to look at him.

"'You are looking for a situation, miss?' he asked.

"'Yes, sir.'

"'As governess?'

"'Yes, sir.'

"'And what salary do you ask?'

"'I had 4 pounds a month in my last place with Colonel Spence Munro.'

"'Oh, tut, tut! sweating—rank sweating!' he cried, throwing his fat hands out into the air like a man who is in a boiling passion. 'How could anyone offer so pitiful a sum to a lady with such attractions and accomplishments?'

"'My accomplishments, sir, may be less than you imagine,' said I. 'A little French, a little German, music, and drawing—'

"'Tut, tut!' he cried. 'This is all quite beside the question. The point is, have you or have you not the bearing and deportment of a lady? There it is in a nutshell. If you have not, you are not fitted for the rearing of a child who may some day play a considerable part in the history of the country. But if you have why, then, how could any gentleman ask you to condescend to accept anything under the three figures? Your salary with me, madam, would commence at 100 pounds a year.'

"You may imagine, Mr. Holmes, that to me, destitute as I was, such an offer seemed almost too good to be true. The gentleman, however, seeing perhaps the look of incredulity upon my face, opened a pocket-book and took out a note.

"'It is also my custom,' said he, smiling in the most pleasant fashion until his eyes were just two little shining slits amid the white creases of his face, 'to advance to my young ladies half their salary beforehand, so that they may meet any little expenses of their journey and their wardrobe.'

"It seemed to me that I had never met so fascinating and so thoughtful a man. As I was already in debt to my tradesmen, the advance was a great convenience, and yet there was something unnatural about the whole transaction which made me wish to know a little more before I quite committed myself.

"'May I ask where you live, sir?' said I.

"'Hampshire. Charming rural place. The Copper Beeches, five miles on the far side of Winchester. It is the most lovely country, my dear young lady, and the dearest old country-house.'

"'And my duties, sir? I should be glad to know what they would be.'

"'One child—one dear little romper just six years old. Oh, if you could see him killing cockroaches with a slipper! Smack! smack! smack! Three gone before you could wink!' He leaned back in his chair and laughed his eyes into his head again.

"I was a little startled at the nature of the child's amusement, but the father's laughter made me think that perhaps he was joking.

"'My sole duties, then,' I asked, 'are to take charge of a single child?'

"'No, no, not the sole, not the sole, my dear young lady,' he cried. 'Your duty would be, as I am sure your good sense would suggest, to obey any little commands my wife might give, provided always that they were such commands as a lady might with propriety obey. You see no difficulty, heh?'

"'I should be happy to make myself useful.'

"'Quite so. In dress now, for example. We are faddy people, you know—faddy but kind-hearted. If you were asked to wear any dress which we might give you, you would not object to our little whim. Heh?'

"'No,' said I, considerably astonished at his words.

"'Or to sit here, or sit there, that would not be offensive to you?'

"'Oh, no.'

"'Or to cut your hair quite short before you come to us?'

"I could hardly believe my ears. As you may observe, Mr. Holmes, my hair is somewhat luxuriant, and of a rather peculiar tint of chestnut. It has been considered artistic. I could not dream of sacrificing it in this offhand fashion.

"'I am afraid that that is quite impossible,' said I. He had been watching me eagerly out of his small eyes, and I could see a shadow pass over his face as I spoke.

"'I am afraid that it is quite essential,' said he. 'It is a little fancy of my wife's, and ladies' fancies, you know, madam, ladies' fancies must be consulted. And so you won't cut your hair?'

"'No, sir, I really could not,' I answered firmly.

"'Ah, very well; then that quite settles the matter. It is a pity, because in other respects you would really have done very nicely. In that case, Miss Stoper, I had best inspect a few more of your young ladies.'

"The manageress had sat all this while busy with her papers without a word to either of us, but she glanced at me now with so much annoyance upon her face that I could not help suspecting that she had lost a handsome commission through my refusal.

"'Do you desire your name to be kept upon the books?' she asked.

"'If you please, Miss Stoper.'

"'Well, really, it seems rather useless, since you refuse the most excellent offers in this fashion,' said she sharply. 'You can hardly expect us to exert ourselves to find another such opening for you. Good-day to you, Miss Hunter.' She struck a gong upon the table, and I was shown out by the page.

"Well, Mr. Holmes, when I got back to my lodgings and found little enough in the cupboard, and two or three bills upon the table. I began to ask myself whether I had not done a very foolish thing. After all, if these people had strange fads and expected obedience on the most extraordinary matters, they were at least ready to pay for their eccentricity. Very few governesses in England are getting 100 pounds a year. Besides, what use was my hair to me? Many people are improved by wearing it short and perhaps I should be among the number. Next day I was inclined to think that I had made a mistake, and by the day after I was sure of it. I had almost overcome my pride so far as to go back to the agency and inquire whether the place was still open when I received this letter from the gentleman himself. I have it here and I will read it to you:

"'The Copper Beeches, near Winchester. "'DEAR MISS HUNTER:--Miss Stoper has very kindly given me your address, and I write from here to ask you whether you have reconsidered your decision. My wife is very anxious that you should come, for she has been much attracted by my description of you. We are willing to give 30 pounds a quarter, or 120 pounds a year, so as to recompense you for any little inconvenience which our fads may cause you. They are not very exacting, after all. My wife is fond of a particular shade of electric blue and would like you to wear such a dress indoors in the morning. You need not, however, go to the expense of purchasing one, as we have one belonging to my dear daughter Alice (now in Philadelphia), which would, I should think, fit you very well. Then, as to sitting here or there, or amusing yourself in any manner indicated, that need cause you no inconvenience. As regards your hair, it is no doubt a pity, especially as I could not help remarking its beauty during our short interview, but I am afraid that I must remain firm upon this point, and I only hope that the increased salary may recompense you for the loss. Your duties, as far as the child is concerned, are very light. Now do try to come, and I shall meet you with the dog-cart at Winchester. Let me know your train. Yours faithfully, JEPHRO RUCASTLE.'

"That is the letter which I have just received, Mr. Holmes, and my mind is made up that I will accept it. I thought, however, that before taking the final step I should like to submit the whole matter to your consideration."

"Well, Miss Hunter, if your mind is made up, that settles the question," said Holmes, smiling.

"But you would not advise me to refuse?"

"I confess that it is not the situation which I should like to see a sister of mine apply for."

"What is the meaning of it all, Mr. Holmes?"

"Ah, I have no data. I cannot tell. Perhaps you have yourself formed some opinion?"

"Well, there seems to me to be only one possible solution. Mr. Rucastle seemed to be a very kind, good-natured man. Is it not possible that his wife is a lunatic, that he desires to keep the matter quiet for fear she should be taken to an asylum, and that he humours her fancies in every way in order to prevent an outbreak?"

"That is a possible solution—in fact, as matters stand, it is the most probable one. But in any case it does not seem to be a nice household for a young lady."

"But the money, Mr. Holmes, the money!"

"Well, yes, of course the pay is good—too good. That is what makes me uneasy. Why should they give you 120 pounds a year, when they could have their pick for 40 pounds? There must be some strong reason behind."

"I thought that if I told you the circumstances you would understand afterwards if I wanted your help. I should feel so much stronger if I felt that you were at the back of me."

"Oh, you may carry that feeling away with you. I assure you that your little problem promises to be the most interesting which has come my way for some months. There is something distinctly novel about some of the features. If you should find yourself in doubt or in danger— "

"Danger! What danger do you foresee?"

Holmes shook his head gravely. "It would cease to be a danger if we could define it," said he. "But at any time, day or night, a telegram would bring me down to your help."

"That is enough." She rose briskly from her chair with the anxiety all swept from her face. "I shall go down to Hampshire quite easy in my mind now. I shall write to Mr. Rucastle at once, sacrifice my poor hair to-night, and start for Winchester tomorrow." With a few grateful words to Holmes she bade us both good-night and bustled off upon her way.

"At least," said I as we heard her quick, firm steps descending the stairs, "she seems to be a young lady who is very well able to take care of herself."

"And she would need to be," said Holmes gravely. "I am much mistaken if we do not hear from her before many days are past."

It was not very long before my friend's prediction was fulfilled. A fortnight went by, during which I frequently found my thoughts turning in her direction and wondering what strange side-alley of human experience this lonely woman had strayed into. The unusual salary, the curious conditions, the light duties, all pointed to something abnormal, though whether a fad or a plot, or whether the man were a philanthropist or a villain, it was quite beyond my powers to determine. As to Holmes, I observed that he sat frequently for half an hour on end, with knitted brows and an abstracted air, but he swept the matter away with a wave of his hand when I mentioned it. "Data! data! data!" he cried impatiently. "I can't make bricks without clay." And yet he would always wind up by muttering that no sister of his should ever have accepted such a situation.

The telegram which we eventually received came late one night just as I was thinking of turning in and Holmes was settling down to one of those all-night chemical researches which he frequently indulged in, when I would leave him stooping over a retort and a test-tube at night and find him in the same position when I came down to breakfast in the morning. He opened the yellow envelope, and then, glancing at the message, threw it across to me.

"Just look up the trains in Bradshaw," said he, and turned back to his chemical studies.

The summons was a brief and urgent one.

"Please be at the Black Swan Hotel at Winchester at midday tomorrow," it said. "Do come! I am at my wit's end. HUNTER."

"Will you come with me?" asked Holmes, glancing up.

"I should wish to."

"Just look it up, then."

"There is a train at half-past nine," said I, glancing over my Bradshaw. "It is due at Winchester at 11:30."

"That will do very nicely. Then perhaps I had better postpone my analysis of the acetones, as we may need to be at our best in the morning."

By eleven o'clock the next day we were well upon our way to the old English capital. Holmes had been buried in the morning papers all the way down, but after we had passed the Hampshire border he threw them down and began to admire the scenery. It was an ideal spring day, a light blue sky, flecked with little fleecy white clouds drifting across from west to east. The sun was shining very brightly, and yet there was an exhilarating nip in the air, which set an edge to a man's energy. All over the countryside, away to the rolling hills around Aldershot, the little red and grey roofs of the farm-steadings peeped out from amid the light green of the new foliage.

"Are they not fresh and beautiful?" I cried with all the enthusiasm of a man fresh from the fogs of Baker Street.

But Holmes shook his head gravely.

"Do you know, Watson," said he, "that it is one of the curses of a mind with a turn like mine that I must look at everything with reference to my own special subject. You look at these scattered houses, and you are impressed by their beauty. I look at them, and the only thought which comes to me is a feeling of their isolation and of the impunity with which crime may be committed there."

"Good heavens!" I cried. "Who would associate crime with these dear old homesteads?"

"They always fill me with a certain horror. It is my belief, Watson, founded upon my experience, that the lowest and vilest alleys in London do not present a more dreadful record of sin than does the smiling and beautiful countryside."

"You horrify me!"

"But the reason is very obvious. The pressure of public opinion can do in the town what the law cannot accomplish. There is no lane so vile that the scream of a tortured child, or the thud of a drunkard's blow, does not beget sympathy and indignation among the neighbours, and then the whole machinery of justice is ever so close that a word of complaint can set it going, and there is but a step between the crime and the dock. But look at these lonely houses, each in its own fields, filled for the most part with poor ignorant folk who know little of the law. Think of the deeds of hellish cruelty, the hidden wickedness which may go on, year in, year out, in such places, and none the wiser. Had this lady who appeals to us for help gone to live in Winchester, I should never have had a fear for her. It is the five miles of country which makes the danger. Still, it is clear that she is not personally threatened."

"No. If she can come to Winchester to meet us she can get away."

"Quite so. She has her freedom."

"What *can* be the matter, then? Can you suggest no explanation?"

"I have devised seven separate explanations, each of which would cover the facts as far as we know them. But which of these is correct can only be determined by the fresh information which we shall no doubt find waiting for us. Well, there is the tower of the cathedral, and we shall soon learn all that Miss Hunter has to tell."

The Black Swan is an inn of repute in the High Street, at no distance from the station, and there we found the young lady waiting for us. She had engaged a sitting-room, and our lunch awaited us upon the table.

"I am so delighted that you have come," she said earnestly. "It is so very kind of you both; but indeed I do not know what I should do. Your advice will be altogether invaluable to me."

"Pray tell us what has happened to you."

"I will do so, and I must be quick, for I have promised Mr. Rucastle to be back before three. I got his leave to come into town this morning, though he little knew for what purpose."

"Let us have everything in its due order." Holmes thrust his long thin legs out towards the fire and composed himself to listen.

"In the first place, I may say that I have met, on the whole, with no actual ill-treatment from Mr. and Mrs. Rucastle. It is only fair to them to say that. But I cannot understand them, and I am not easy in my mind about them."

"What can you not understand?"

"Their reasons for their conduct. But you shall have it all just as it occurred. When I came down, Mr. Rucastle met me here and drove me in his dog-cart to the Copper Beeches. It is, as he said, beautifully situated, but it is not beautiful in itself, for it is a large square block of a house, whitewashed, but all stained and streaked with damp and bad weather. There are grounds round it, woods on three sides, and on the fourth a field which slopes down to the Southampton highroad, which curves past about a hundred yards from the front door. This ground in front belongs to the house, but the woods all round are part of Lord Southerton's preserves. A clump of copper beeches immediately in front of the hall door has given its name to the place.

"I was driven over by my employer, who was as amiable as ever, and was introduced by him that evening to his wife and the child. There was no truth, Mr. Holmes, in the conjecture which seemed to us to be probable in your rooms at Baker Street. Mrs. Rucastle is not mad. I found her to be a silent, pale-faced woman, much younger than her husband, not more than thirty, I should think, while he can hardly be less than forty-five. From their conversation I have gathered that they have been married about seven years, that he was a widower, and that his only child by the first wife was the daughter who has gone to Philadelphia. Mr. Rucastle told me in private that the reason why she had left them was that she had an unreasoning aversion to her stepmother. As the daughter could not have been less than twenty, I can quite imagine that her position must have been uncomfortable with her father's young wife.

"Mrs. Rucastle seemed to me to be colourless in mind as well as in feature. She impressed me neither favourably nor the reverse. She was a nonentity. It was easy to see that she was passionately devoted both to her husband and to her little son. Her light grey eyes wandered continually from one to the other, noting every little want and forestalling it if possible. He was kind to her also in his bluff, boisterous fashion, and on the whole they seemed to be a happy couple. And yet she had some secret sorrow, this woman. She would often be lost in deep thought, with the saddest look upon her face. More than once I have surprised her in tears. I have thought sometimes that it was the disposition of her child which weighed upon her mind, for I have never met so utterly spoiled and so ill-natured a little creature. He is small for his age, with a head which is quite disproportionately large. His whole life appears to be spent in an alternation between savage fits of passion and gloomy intervals of sulking. Giving pain to any creature weaker than himself seems to be his one idea of amusement, and he shows quite remarkable talent in planning the capture of mice, little birds, and insects. But I would rather not talk about the creature, Mr. Holmes, and, indeed, he has little to do with my story."

"I am glad of all details," remarked my friend, "whether they seem to you to be relevant or not."

"I shall try not to miss anything of importance. The one unpleasant thing about the house, which struck me at once, was the appearance and conduct of the servants. There are only two, a man and his wife. Toller, for that is his name, is a rough, uncouth man, with grizzled hair and whiskers, and a perpetual smell of drink. Twice since I have been with them he has been quite drunk, and yet Mr. Rucastle seemed to take no notice of it. His wife is a very tall and strong woman with a sour face, as silent as Mrs. Rucastle and much less amiable. They are a most unpleasant couple, but fortunately I spend most of my time in the nursery and my own room, which are next to each other in one corner of the building.

"For two days after my arrival at the Copper Beeches my life was very quiet; on the third, Mrs. Rucastle came down just after breakfast and whispered something to her husband.

"'Oh, yes,' said he, turning to me, 'we are very much obliged to you, Miss Hunter, for falling in with our whims so far as to cut your hair. I assure you that it has not detracted in the tiniest iota from your appearance. We shall now see how the electric-blue dress will become you. You will find it laid out upon the bed in your room, and if you would be so good as to put it on we should both be extremely obliged.'

"The dress which I found waiting for me was of a peculiar shade of blue. It was of excellent material, a sort of beige, but it bore unmistakable signs of having been worn before. It could not have been a better fit if I had been measured for it. Both Mr. and Mrs. Rucastle expressed a delight at the look of it, which seemed quite exaggerated in its vehemence. They were waiting for me in the drawing-room, which is a very large room, stretching along the entire front of the house, with three long windows reaching down to the floor. A chair had been placed close to the central window, with its back turned towards it. In this I was asked to sit, and then Mr. Rucastle, walking up and down on the other side of the room, began to tell me a series of the funniest stories that I have ever listened to. You cannot imagine how comical he was, and I laughed until I was quite weary. Mrs. Rucastle, however, who has evidently no sense of humour, never so much as smiled, but sat with her hands in her lap, and a sad, anxious look upon her face. After an hour or so, Mr. Rucastle suddenly remarked that it was time to commence the duties of the day, and that I might change my dress and go to little Edward in the nursery.

"Two days later this same performance was gone through under exactly similar circumstances. Again I changed my dress, again I sat in the window, and again I laughed very heartily at the funny stories of which my employer had an immense répertoire, and which he told inimitably. Then he handed me a yellow-backed novel, and moving my chair a little sideways, that my own shadow might not fall upon the page, he begged me to read aloud to him. I read for about ten minutes, beginning in the heart of a chapter, and then suddenly, in the middle of a sentence, he ordered me to cease and to change my dress.

"You can easily imagine, Mr. Holmes, how curious I became as to what the meaning of this extraordinary performance could possibly be. They were always very careful, I observed, to turn my face away from the window, so that I became consumed with the desire to see what was going on behind my back. At first it seemed to be impossible, but I soon devised a means. My hand-mirror had been broken, so a happy thought seized me, and I concealed a piece of the glass in my handkerchief. On the next occasion, in the midst of my laughter, I put my handkerchief up to my eyes, and was able with a little management to see all that there was behind me. I confess that I was disappointed. There was nothing. At least that was my first impression. At the second glance, however, I perceived that there was a man standing in the Southampton Road, a small bearded man in a grey suit, who seemed to be looking in my direction. The road is an important highway, and there are usually people there. This man, however, was leaning against the railings which bordered our field and was looking earnestly up. I lowered my handkerchief and glanced at Mrs. Rucastle to find her eyes fixed upon me with a most searching gaze. She said nothing, but I am convinced that she had divined that I had a mirror in my hand and had seen what was behind me. She rose at once.

"'Jephro,' said she, 'there is an impertinent fellow upon the road there who stares up at Miss Hunter.'

"'No friend of yours, Miss Hunter?' he asked.

"'No, I know no one in these parts.'

"'Dear me! How very impertinent! Kindly turn round and motion to him to go away.'

"'Surely it would be better to take no notice.'

"'No, no, we should have him loitering here always. Kindly turn round and wave him away like that.'

"I did as I was told, and at the same instant Mrs. Rucastle drew down the blind. That was a week ago, and from that time I have not sat again in the window, nor have I worn the blue dress, nor seen the man in the road."

"Pray continue," said Holmes. "Your narrative promises to be a most interesting one."

"You will find it rather disconnected, I fear, and there may prove to be little relation between the different incidents of which I speak. On the very first day that I was at the Copper Beeches, Mr. Rucastle took me to a small outhouse which stands near the kitchen door. As we approached it I heard the sharp rattling of a chain, and the sound as of a large animal moving about.

"'Look in here!' said Mr. Rucastle, showing me a slit between two planks. 'Is he not a beauty?'

"I looked through and was conscious of two glowing eyes, and of a vague figure huddled up in the darkness.

"'Don't be frightened,' said my employer, laughing at the start which I had given. 'It's only Carlo, my mastiff. I call him mine, but really old Toller, my groom, is the only man who can do anything with him. We feed him once a day, and not too much then, so that he is always as keen as mustard. Toller lets him loose every night, and God help the trespasser whom he lays his fangs upon. For goodness' sake don't you ever on any pretext set your foot over the threshold at night, for it's as much as your life is worth.'

"The warning was no idle one, for two nights later I happened to look out of my bedroom window about two o'clock in the morning. It was a beautiful moonlight night, and the lawn in front of the house was silvered over and almost as bright as day. I was standing, rapt in the peaceful beauty of the scene, when I was aware that something was moving under the shadow of the copper beeches. As it emerged into the moonshine I saw what it was. It was a giant dog, as large as a calf, tawny tinted, with hanging jowl, black muzzle, and huge projecting bones. It walked slowly across the lawn and vanished into the shadow upon the other side. That dreadful sentinel sent a chill to my heart which I do not think that any burglar could have done.

"And now I have a very strange experience to tell you. I had, as you know, cut off my hair in London, and I had placed it in a great coil at the bottom of my trunk. One evening, after the child was in bed, I began to amuse myself by examining the furniture of my room and by rearranging my own little things. There was an old chest of drawers in the room, the two upper ones empty and open, the lower one locked. I had filled the first two with my linen, and as I had still much to pack away I was naturally annoyed at not having the use of the third drawer. It struck me that it might have been fastened by a mere oversight, so I took out my bunch of keys and tried to open it. The very first key fitted to perfection, and I drew the drawer open. There was only one thing in it, but I am sure that you would never guess what it was. It was my coil of hair.

"I took it up and examined it. It was of the same peculiar tint, and the same thickness. But then the impossibility of the thing obtruded itself upon me. How could my hair have been locked in the drawer? With trembling hands I undid my trunk, turned out the contents, and drew from the bottom my own hair. I laid the two tresses together, and I assure you that they were identical. Was it not extraordinary? Puzzle as I would, I could make nothing at all of what it meant. I returned the strange hair to the drawer, and I said nothing of the matter to the Rucastles as I felt that I had put myself in the wrong by opening a drawer which they had locked.

"I am naturally observant, as you may have remarked, Mr. Holmes, and I soon had a pretty good plan of the whole house in my head. There was one wing, however, which appeared not to be inhabited at all. A door which faced that which led into the quarters of the Tollers opened into this suite, but it was invariably locked. One day, however, as I ascended the stair, I met Mr. Rucastle coming out through this door, his keys in his hand, and a look on his face which made him a very different person to the round, jovial man to whom I was accustomed. His cheeks were red, his brow was all crinkled with anger, and the veins stood out at his temples with passion. He locked the door and hurried past me without a word or a look.

"This aroused my curiosity, so when I went out for a walk in the grounds with my charge, I strolled round to the side from which I could see the windows of this part of the house. There were four of them in a row, three of which were simply dirty, while the fourth was shuttered up. They were evidently all deserted. As I strolled up and down, glancing at them occasionally, Mr. Rucastle came out to me, looking as merry and jovial as ever.

"'Ah!' said he, 'you must not think me rude if I passed you without a word, my dear young lady. I was preoccupied with business matters.'

"I assured him that I was not offended. 'By the way,' said I, 'you seem to have quite a suite of spare rooms up there, and one of them has the shutters up.'

"He looked surprised and, as it seemed to me, a little startled at my remark.

"'Photography is one of my hobbies,' said he. 'I have made my dark room up there. But, dear me! what an observant young lady we have come upon. Who would have believed it? Who would have ever believed it?' He spoke in a jesting tone, but there was no jest in his eyes as he looked at me. I read suspicion there and annoyance, but no jest.

"Well, Mr. Holmes, from the moment that I understood that there was something about that suite of rooms which I was not to know, I was all on fire to go over them. It was not mere curiosity, though I have my share of that. It was more a feeling of duty—a feeling that some good might come from my penetrating to this place. They talk of woman's instinct; perhaps it was woman's instinct which gave me that feeling. At any rate, it was there, and I was keenly on the lookout for any chance to pass the forbidden door.

"It was only yesterday that the chance came. I may tell you that, besides Mr. Rucastle, both Toller and his wife find something to do in these deserted rooms, and I once saw him carrying a large black linen bag with him through the door. Recently he has been drinking hard, and yesterday evening he was very drunk; and when I came upstairs there was the key in the door. I have no doubt at all that he had left it there. Mr. and Mrs. Rucastle were both downstairs, and the child was with them, so that I had an admirable opportunity. I turned the key gently in the lock, opened the door, and slipped through.

"There was a little passage in front of me, unpapered and uncarpeted, which turned at a right angle at the farther end. Round this corner were three doors in a line, the first and third of which were open. They each led into an empty room, dusty and cheerless, with two windows in the one and one in the other, so thick with dirt that the evening light glimmered dimly through them. The centre door was closed, and across the outside of it had been fastened one of the broad bars of an iron bed, padlocked at one end to a ring in the wall, and fastened at the other with stout cord. The door itself was locked as well, and the key was not there. This barricaded door corresponded clearly with the shuttered window outside, and yet I could see by the glimmer from beneath it that the room was not in darkness. Evidently there was a skylight which let in light from above. As I stood in the passage gazing at the sinister door and wondering what secret it might veil, I suddenly heard the sound of steps within the room and saw a shadow pass backward and forward against the little slit of dim light which shone out from under the door. A mad, unreasoning terror rose up in me at the sight, Mr. Holmes. My overstrung nerves failed me suddenly, and I turned and ran—ran as though some dreadful hand were behind me clutching at the skirt of my dress. I rushed down the passage, through the door, and straight into the arms of Mr. Rucastle, who was waiting outside.

"'So,' said he, smiling, 'it was you, then. I thought that it must be when I saw the door open.'

"'Oh, I am so frightened!' I panted.

"'My dear young lady! my dear young lady!'—you cannot think how caressing and soothing his manner was—'and what has frightened you, my dear young lady?'

"But his voice was just a little too coaxing. He overdid it. I was keenly on my guard against him.

"'I was foolish enough to go into the empty wing,' I answered. 'But it is so lonely and eerie in this dim light that I was frightened and ran out again. Oh, it is so dreadfully still in there!'

"'Only that?' said he, looking at me keenly.

"'Why, what did you think?' I asked.

"'Why do you think that I lock this door?'

"'I am sure that I do not know.'

"'It is to keep people out who have no business there. Do you see?' He was still smiling in the most amiable manner.

"'I am sure if I had known—'

"'Well, then, you know now. And if you ever put your foot over that threshold again'—here in an instant the smile hardened into a grin of rage, and he glared down at me with the face of a demon—'I'll throw you to the mastiff.'

"I was so terrified that I do not know what I did. I suppose that I must have rushed past him into my room. I remember nothing until I found myself lying on my bed trembling all over. Then I thought of you, Mr. Holmes. I could not live there longer without some advice. I was frightened of the house, of the man, of the woman, of the servants, even of the child. They were all horrible to me. If I could only bring you down all would be well. Of course I might have fled from the house, but my curiosity was almost as strong as my fears. My mind was soon made up. I would send you a wire. I put on my hat and cloak, went down to the office, which is about half a mile from the house, and then returned, feeling very much easier. A horrible doubt came into my mind as I approached the door lest the dog might be loose, but I remembered that Toller had drunk himself into a state of insensibility that evening, and I knew that he was the only one in the household who had any influence with the savage creature, or who would venture to set him free. I slipped in in safety and lay awake half the night in my joy at the thought of seeing you. I had no difficulty in getting leave to come into Winchester this morning, but I must be back before three o'clock, for Mr. and Mrs. Rucastle are going on a visit, and will be away all the evening, so that I must look after the child. Now I have told you all my adventures, Mr. Holmes, and I should be very glad if you could tell me what it all means, and, above all, what I should do."

Holmes and I had listened spellbound to this extraordinary story. My friend rose now and paced up and down the room, his hands in his pockets, and an expression of the most profound gravity upon his face.

"Is Toller still drunk?" he asked.

"Yes. I heard his wife tell Mrs. Rucastle that she could do nothing with him."

"That is well. And the Rucastles go out to-night?"

"Yes."

"Is there a cellar with a good strong lock?"

"Yes, the wine-cellar."

"You seem to me to have acted all through this matter like a very brave and sensible girl, Miss Hunter. Do you think that you could perform one more feat? I should not ask it of you if I did not think you a quite exceptional woman."

"I will try. What is it?"

"We shall be at the Copper Beeches by seven o'clock, my friend and I. The Rucastles will be gone by that time, and Toller will, we hope, be incapable. There only remains Mrs. Toller, who might give the alarm. If you could send her into the cellar on some errand, and then turn the key upon her, you would facilitate matters immensely."

"I will do it."

"Excellent! We shall then look thoroughly into the affair. Of course there is only one feasible explanation. You have been brought there to personate someone, and the real person is imprisoned in this chamber. That is obvious. As to who this prisoner is, I have no doubt that it is the daughter, Miss Alice Rucastle, if I remember right, who was said to have gone to America. You were chosen, doubtless, as resembling her in height, figure, and the colour of your hair. Hers had been cut off, very possibly in some illness through which she has passed, and so, of course, yours had to be sacrificed also. By a curious chance you came upon her tresses. The man in the road was undoubtedly some friend of hers—possibly her fiancé—and no doubt, as you wore the girl's dress and were so like her, he was convinced from your laughter, whenever he saw you, and afterwards from your gesture, that Miss Rucastle was perfectly happy, and that she no longer desired his attentions. The dog is let loose at night to prevent him from endeavouring to communicate with her. So much is fairly clear. The most serious point in the case is the disposition of the child."

"What on earth has that to do with it?" I ejaculated.

"My dear Watson, you as a medical man are continually gaining light as to the tendencies of a child by the study of the parents. Don't you see that the converse is equally valid. I have frequently gained my first real insight into the character of parents by studying their children. This child's disposition is abnormally cruel, merely for cruelty's sake, and whether he derives this from his smiling father, as I should suspect, or from his mother, it bodes evil for the poor girl who is in their power."

"I am sure that you are right, Mr. Holmes," cried our client. "A thousand things come back to me which make me certain that you have hit it. Oh, let us lose not an instant in bringing help to this poor creature."

"We must be circumspect, for we are dealing with a very cunning man. We can do nothing until seven o'clock. At that hour we shall be with you, and it will not be long before we solve the mystery."

We were as good as our word, for it was just seven when we reached the Copper Beeches, having put up our trap at a wayside public-house. The group of trees, with their dark leaves shining like burnished metal in the light of the setting sun, were sufficient to mark the house even had Miss Hunter not been standing smiling on the door-step.

"Have you managed it?" asked Holmes.

A loud thudding noise came from somewhere downstairs. "That is Mrs. Toller in the cellar," said she. "Her husband lies snoring on the kitchen rug. Here are his keys, which are the duplicates of Mr. Rucastle's."

"You have done well indeed!" cried Holmes with enthusiasm. "Now lead the way, and we shall soon see the end of this black business."

We passed up the stair, unlocked the door, followed on down a passage, and found ourselves in front of the barricade which Miss Hunter had described. Holmes cut the cord and removed the transverse bar. Then he tried the various keys in the lock, but without success. No sound came from within, and at the silence Holmes' face clouded over.

"I trust that we are not too late," said he. "I think, Miss Hunter, that we had better go in without you. Now, Watson, put your shoulder to it, and we shall see whether we cannot make our way in."

It was an old rickety door and gave at once before our united strength. Together we rushed into the room. It was empty. There was no furniture save a little pallet bed, a small table, and a basketful of linen. The skylight above was open, and the prisoner gone.

"There has been some villainy here," said Holmes; "this beauty has guessed Miss Hunter's intentions and has carried his victim off."

"But how?"

"Through the skylight. We shall soon see how he managed it." He swung himself up onto the roof. "Ah, yes," he cried, "here's the end of a long light ladder against the eaves. That is how he did it."

"But it is impossible," said Miss Hunter; "the ladder was not there when the Rucastles went away."

"He has come back and done it. I tell you that he is a clever and dangerous man. I should not be very much surprised if this were he whose step I hear now upon the stair. I think, Watson, that it would be as well for you to have your pistol ready."

The words were hardly out of his mouth before a man appeared at the door of the room, a very fat and burly man, with a heavy stick in his hand. Miss Hunter screamed and shrunk against the wall at the sight of him, but Sherlock Holmes sprang forward and confronted him.

"You villain!" said he, "where's your daughter?"

The fat man cast his eyes round, and then up at the open skylight.

"It is for me to ask you that," he shrieked, "you thieves! Spies and thieves! I have caught you, have I? You are in my power. I'll serve you!" He turned and clattered down the stairs as hard as he could go.

"He's gone for the dog!" cried Miss Hunter.

"I have my revolver," said I.

"Better close the front door," cried Holmes, and we all rushed down the stairs together. We had hardly reached the hall when we heard the baying of a hound, and then a scream of agony, with a horrible worrying sound which it was dreadful to listen to. An elderly man with a red face and shaking limbs came staggering out at a side door.

"My God!" he cried. "Someone has loosed the dog. It's not been fed for two days. Quick, quick, or it'll be too late!"

Holmes and I rushed out and round the angle of the house, with Toller hurrying behind us. There was the huge famished brute, its black muzzle buried in Rucastle's throat, while he writhed and screamed upon the ground. Running up, I blew its brains out, and it fell over with its keen white teeth still meeting in the great creases of his neck. With much labour we separated them and carried him, living but horribly mangled, into the house. We laid him upon the drawing-room sofa, and having dispatched the sobered Toller to bear the news to his wife, I did what I could to relieve his pain. We were all assembled round him when the door opened, and a tall, gaunt woman entered the room.

"Mrs. Toller!" cried Miss Hunter.

"Yes, miss. Mr. Rucastle let me out when he came back before he went up to you. Ah, miss, it is a pity you didn't let me know what you were planning, for I would have told you that your pains were wasted."

"Ha!" said Holmes, looking keenly at her. "It is clear that Mrs. Toller knows more about this matter than anyone else."

"Yes, sir, I do, and I am ready enough to tell what I know."

"Then, pray, sit down, and let us hear it for there are several points on which I must confess that I am still in the dark."

"I will soon make it clear to you," said she; "and I'd have done so before now if I could ha' got out from the cellar. If there's police-court business over this, you'll remember that I was the one that stood your friend, and that I was Miss Alice's friend too.

"She was never happy at home, Miss Alice wasn't, from the time that her father married again. She was slighted like and had no say in anything, but it never really became bad for her until after she met Mr. Fowler at a friend's house. As well as I could learn, Miss Alice had rights of her own by will, but she was so quiet and patient, she was, that she never said a word about them but just left everything in Mr. Rucastle's hands. He knew he was safe with her; but when there was a chance of a husband coming forward, who would ask for all that the law would give him, then her father thought it time to put a stop on it. He wanted her to sign a paper, so that whether she married or not, he could use her money. When she wouldn't do it, he kept on worrying her until she got brain-fever, and for six weeks was at death's door. Then she got better at last, all worn to a shadow, and with her beautiful hair cut off; but that didn't make no change in her young man, and he stuck to her as true as man could be."

"Ah," said Holmes, "I think that what you have been good enough to tell us makes the matter fairly clear, and that I can deduce all that remains. Mr. Rucastle then, I presume, took to this system of imprisonment?"

"Yes, sir."

"And brought Miss Hunter down from London in order to get rid of the disagreeable persistence of Mr. Fowler."

"That was it, sir."

"But Mr. Fowler being a persevering man, as a good seaman should be, blockaded the house, and having met you succeeded by certain arguments, metallic or otherwise, in convincing you that your interests were the same as his."

"Mr. Fowler was a very kind-spoken, free-handed gentleman," said Mrs. Toller serenely.

"And in this way he managed that your good man should have no want of drink, and that a ladder should be ready at the moment when your master had gone out."

"You have it, sir, just as it happened."

"I am sure we owe you an apology, Mrs. Toller," said Holmes, "for you have certainly cleared up everything which puzzled us. And here comes the country surgeon and Mrs. Rucastle, so I think, Watson, that we had best escort Miss Hunter back to Winchester, as it seems to me that our locus standi now is rather a questionable one."

And thus was solved the mystery of the sinister house with the copper beeches in front of the door. Mr. Rucastle survived, but was always a broken man, kept alive solely through the care of his devoted wife. They still live with their old servants, who probably know so much of Rucastle's past life that he finds it difficult to part from them. Mr. Fowler and Miss Rucastle were married, by special license, in Southampton the day after their flight, and he is now the holder of a government appointment in the island of Mauritius. As to Miss Violet Hunter, my friend Holmes, rather to my disappointment, manifested no further interest in her when once she had ceased to be the centre of one of his problems, and she is now the head of a private school at Walsall, where I believe that she has met with considerable success.

The Hound Of The Baskervilles

Chapter 1. Mr. Sherlock Holmes

Mr. Sherlock Holmes, who was usually very late in the mornings, save upon those not infrequent occasions when he was up all night, was seated at the breakfast table. I stood upon the hearth-rug and picked up the stick which our visitor had left behind him the night before. It was a fine, thick piece of wood, bulbous-headed, of the sort which is known as a "Penang lawyer." Just under the head was a broad silver band nearly an inch across. "To James Mortimer, M.R.C.S., from his friends of the C.C.H.," was engraved upon it, with the date "1884." It was just such a stick as the old-fashioned family practitioner used to carry—dignified, solid, and reassuring.

"Well, Watson, what do you make of it?"

Holmes was sitting with his back to me, and I had given him no sign of my occupation.

"How did you know what I was doing? I believe you have eyes in the back of your head."

"I have, at least, a well-polished, silver-plated coffee-pot in front of me," said he. "But, tell me, Watson, what do you make of our visitor's stick? Since we have been so unfortunate as to miss him and have no notion of his errand, this accidental souvenir becomes of importance. Let me hear you reconstruct the man by an examination of it."

"I think," said I, following as far as I could the methods of my companion, "that Dr. Mortimer is a successful, elderly medical man, well-esteemed since those who know him give him this mark of their appreciation."

"Good!" said Holmes. "Excellent!"

"I think also that the probability is in favour of his being a country practitioner who does a great deal of his visiting on foot."

"Why so?"

"Because this stick, though originally a very handsome one has been so knocked about that I can hardly imagine a town practitioner carrying it. The thick-iron ferrule is worn down, so it is evident that he has done a great amount of walking with it."

"Perfectly sound!" said Holmes.

"And then again, there is the 'friends of the C.C.H.' I should guess that to be the Something Hunt, the local hunt to whose members he has possibly given some surgical assistance, and which has made him a small presentation in return."

"Really, Watson, you excel yourself," said Holmes, pushing back his chair and lighting a cigarette. "I am bound to say that in all the accounts which you have been so good as to give of my own small achievements you have habitually underrated your own abilities. It may be that you are not yourself luminous, but you are a conductor of light. Some people without possessing genius have a remarkable power of stimulating it. I confess, my dear fellow, that I am very much in your debt."

He had never said as much before, and I must admit that his words gave me keen pleasure, for I had often been piqued by his indifference to my admiration and to the attempts which I had made to give publicity to his methods. I was proud, too, to think that I had so far mastered his system as to apply it in a way which earned his approval. He now took the stick from my hands and examined it for a few minutes with his naked eyes. Then with an expression of interest he laid down his cigarette, and carrying the cane to the window, he looked over it again with a convex lens.

"Interesting, though elementary," said he as he returned to his favourite corner of the settee. "There are certainly one or two indications upon the stick. It gives us the basis for several deductions."

"Has anything escaped me?" I asked with some self-importance. "I trust that there is nothing of consequence which I have overlooked?"

"I am afraid, my dear Watson, that most of your conclusions were erroneous. When I said that you stimulated me I meant, to be frank, that in noting your fallacies I was occasionally guided towards the truth. Not that you are entirely wrong in this instance. The man is certainly a country practitioner. And he walks a good deal."

"Then I was right."

"To that extent."

"But that was all."

"No, no, my dear Watson, not all—by no means all. I would suggest, for example, that a presentation to a doctor is more likely to come from a hospital than from a hunt, and that when the initials 'C.C.' are placed before that hospital the words 'Charing Cross' very naturally suggest themselves."

"You may be right."

"The probability lies in that direction. And if we take this as a working hypothesis we have a fresh basis from which to start our construction of this unknown visitor."

"Well, then, supposing that 'C.C.H.' does stand for 'Charing Cross Hospital,' what further inferences may we draw?"

"Do none suggest themselves? You know my methods. Apply them!"

"I can only think of the obvious conclusion that the man has practised in town before going to the country."

"I think that we might venture a little farther than this. Look at it in this light. On what occasion would it be most probable that such a presentation would be made? When would his friends unite to give him a pledge of their good will? Obviously at the moment when Dr. Mortimer withdrew from the service of the hospital in order to start a practice for himself. We know there has been a presentation. We believe there has been a change from a town hospital to a country practice. Is it, then, stretching our inference too far to say that the presentation was on the occasion of the change?"

"It certainly seems probable."

"Now, you will observe that he could not have been on the staff of the hospital, since only a man well-established in a London practice could hold such a position, and such a one would not drift into the country. What was he, then? If he was in the hospital and yet not on the staff he could only have been a house-surgeon or a house-physician—little more than a senior student. And he left five years ago—the date is on the stick. So your grave, middle-aged family practitioner vanishes into thin air, my dear Watson, and there emerges a young fellow under thirty, amiable, unambitious, absent-minded, and the possessor of a favourite dog, which I should describe roughly as being larger than a terrier and smaller than a mastiff."

I laughed incredulously as Sherlock Holmes leaned back in his settee and blew little wavering rings of smoke up to the ceiling.

"As to the latter part, I have no means of checking you," said I, "but at least it is not difficult to find out a few particulars about the man's age and professional career." From my small medical shelf I took down the Medical Directory and turned up the name. There were several Mortimers, but only one who could be our visitor. I read his record aloud.

"Mortimer, James, M.R.C.S., 1882, Grimpen, Dartmoor, Devon. House-surgeon, from 1882 to 1884, at Charing Cross Hospital. Winner of the Jackson prize for Comparative Pathology, with essay entitled 'Is Disease a Reversion?' Corresponding member of the Swedish Pathological Society. Author of 'Some Freaks of Atavism' (Lancet 1882). 'Do We Progress?' (Journal of Psychology, March, 1883). Medical Officer for the parishes of Grimpen, Thorsley, and High Barrow."

"No mention of that local hunt, Watson," said Holmes with a mischievous smile, "but a country doctor, as you very astutely observed. I think that I am fairly justified in my inferences. As to the adjectives, I said, if I remember right, amiable, unambitious, and absent-minded. It is my experience that it is only an amiable man in this world who receives testimonials, only an unambitious one who abandons a London career for the country, and only an absent-minded one who leaves his stick and not his visiting-card after waiting an hour in your room."

"And the dog?"

"Has been in the habit of carrying this stick behind his master. Being a heavy stick the dog has held it tightly by the middle, and the marks of his teeth are very plainly visible. The dog's jaw, as shown in the space between these marks, is too broad in my opinion for a terrier and not broad enough for a mastiff. It may have been—yes, by Jove, it is a curly-haired spaniel."

He had risen and paced the room as he spoke. Now he halted in the recess of the window. There was such a ring of conviction in his voice that I glanced up in surprise.

"My dear fellow, how can you possibly be so sure of that?"

"For the very simple reason that I see the dog himself on our very door-step, and there is the ring of its owner. Don't move, I beg you, Watson. He is a professional brother of yours, and your presence may be of assistance to me. Now is the dramatic moment of fate, Watson, when you hear a step upon the stair which is walking into your life, and you know not whether for good or ill. What does Dr. James Mortimer, the man of science, ask of Sherlock Holmes, the specialist in crime? Come in!"

The appearance of our visitor was a surprise to me, since I had expected a typical country practitioner. He was a very tall, thin man, with a long nose like a beak, which jutted out between two keen, gray eyes, set closely together and sparkling brightly from behind a pair of gold-rimmed glasses. He was clad in a professional but rather slovenly fashion, for his frock-coat was dingy and his trousers frayed. Though young, his long back was already bowed, and he walked with a forward thrust of his head and a general air of peering benevolence. As he entered his eyes fell upon the stick in Holmes's hand, and he ran towards it with an exclamation of joy. "I am so very glad," said he. "I was not sure whether I had left it here or in the Shipping Office. I would not lose that stick for the world."

"A presentation, I see," said Holmes.

"Yes, sir."

"From Charing Cross Hospital?"

"From one or two friends there on the occasion of my marriage."

"Dear, dear, that's bad!" said Holmes, shaking his head.

Dr. Mortimer blinked through his glasses in mild astonishment. "Why was it bad?"

"Only that you have disarranged our little deductions. Your marriage, you say?"

"Yes, sir. I married, and so left the hospital, and with it all hopes of a consulting practice. It was necessary to make a home of my own."

"Come, come, we are not so far wrong, after all," said Holmes. "And now, Dr. James Mortimer—"

"Mister, sir, Mister—a humble M.R.C.S."

"And a man of precise mind, evidently."

"A dabbler in science, Mr. Holmes, a picker up of shells on the shores of the great unknown ocean. I presume that it is Mr. Sherlock Holmes whom I am addressing and not—"

"No, this is my friend Dr. Watson."

"Glad to meet you, sir. I have heard your name mentioned in connection with that of your friend. You interest me very much, Mr. Holmes. I had hardly expected so dolichocephalic a skull or such well-marked supra-orbital development. Would you have any objection to my running my finger along your parietal fissure? A cast of your skull, sir, until the original is available, would be an ornament to any anthropological museum. It is not my intention to be fulsome, but I confess that I covet your skull."

Sherlock Holmes waved our strange visitor into a chair. "You are an enthusiast in your line of thought, I perceive, sir, as I am in mine," said he. "I observe from your forefinger that you make your own cigarettes. Have no hesitation in lighting one."

The man drew out paper and tobacco and twirled the one up in the other with surprising dexterity. He had long, quivering fingers as agile and restless as the antennae of an insect.

Holmes was silent, but his little darting glances showed me the interest which he took in our curious companion. "I presume, sir," said he at last, "that it was not merely for the purpose of examining my skull that you have done me the honour to call here last night and again today?"

"No, sir, no; though I am happy to have had the opportunity of doing that as well. I came to you, Mr. Holmes, because I recognized that I am myself an unpractical man and because I am suddenly confronted with a most serious and extraordinary problem. Recognizing, as I do, that you are the second highest expert in Europe—"

"Indeed, sir! May I inquire who has the honour to be the first?" asked Holmes with some asperity.

"To the man of precisely scientific mind the work of Monsieur Bertillon must always appeal strongly."

"Then had you not better consult him?"

"I said, sir, to the precisely scientific mind. But as a practical man of affairs it is acknowledged that you stand alone. I trust, sir, that I have not inadvertently—"

"Just a little," said Holmes. "I think, Dr. Mortimer, you would do wisely if without more ado you would kindly tell me plainly what the exact nature of the problem is in which you demand my assistance."

Chapter 2. The Curse of the Baskervilles

"I have in my pocket a manuscript," said Dr. James Mortimer.

"I observed it as you entered the room," said Holmes.

"It is an old manuscript."

"Early eighteenth century, unless it is a forgery."

"How can you say that, sir?"

"You have presented an inch or two of it to my examination all the time that you have been talking. It would be a poor expert who could not give the date of a document within a decade or so. You may possibly have read my little monograph upon the subject. I put that at 1730."

"The exact date is 1742." Dr. Mortimer drew it from his breast-pocket. "This family paper was committed to my care by Sir Charles Baskerville, whose sudden and tragic death some three months ago created so much excitement in Devonshire. I may say that I was his personal friend as well as his medical attendant. He was a strong-minded man, sir, shrewd, practical, and as unimaginative as I am myself. Yet he took this document very seriously, and his mind was prepared for just such an end as did eventually overtake him."

Holmes stretched out his hand for the manuscript and flattened it upon his knee. "You will observe, Watson, the alternative use of the long s and the short. It is one of several indications which enabled me to fix the date."

I looked over his shoulder at the yellow paper and the faded script. At the head was written: "Baskerville Hall," and below in large, scrawling figures: "1742."

"It appears to be a statement of some sort."

"Yes, it is a statement of a certain legend which runs in the Baskerville family."

"But I understand that it is something more modern and practical upon which you wish to consult me?"

"Most modern. A most practical, pressing matter, which must be decided within twenty-four hours. But the manuscript is short and is intimately connected with the affair. With your permission I will read it to you."

Holmes leaned back in his chair, placed his finger-tips together, and closed his eyes, with an air of resignation. Dr. Mortimer turned the manuscript to the light and read in a high, cracking voice the following curious, old-world narrative:

"Of the origin of the Hound of the Baskervilles there have been many statements, yet as I come in a direct line from Hugo Baskerville, and as I had the story from my father, who also had it from his, I have set it down with all belief that it occurred even as is here set forth. And I would have you believe, my sons, that the same Justice which punishes sin may also most graciously forgive it, and that no ban is so heavy but that by prayer and repentance it may be removed. Learn then from this story not to fear the fruits of the past, but rather to be circumspect in the future, that those foul passions whereby our family has suffered so grievously may not again be loosed to our undoing.

"Know then that in the time of the Great Rebellion (the history of which by the learned Lord Clarendon I most earnestly commend to your attention) this Manor of Baskerville was held by Hugo of that name, nor can it be gainsaid that he was a most wild, profane, and godless man. This, in truth, his neighbours might have pardoned, seeing that saints have never flourished in those parts, but there was in him a certain wanton and cruel humour which made his name a by-word through the West. It chanced that this Hugo came to love (if, indeed, so dark a passion may be known under so bright a name) the daughter of a yeoman who held lands near the Baskerville estate. But the young maiden, being discreet and of good repute, would ever avoid him, for she feared his evil name. So it came to pass that one Michaelmas this Hugo, with five or six of his idle and wicked companions, stole down upon the farm and carried off the maiden, her father and brothers being from home, as he well knew. When they had brought her to the Hall the maiden was placed in an upper chamber, while Hugo and his friends sat down to a long carouse, as was their nightly custom. Now, the poor lass upstairs was like to have her wits turned at the singing and shouting and terrible oaths which came up to her from below, for they say that the words used by Hugo Baskerville, when he was in wine, were such as might blast the man who said them. At last in the stress of her fear she did that which might have daunted the bravest or most active man, for by the aid of the growth of ivy which covered (and still covers) the south wall she came down from under the eaves, and so homeward across the moor, there being three leagues betwixt the Hall and her father's farm.

"It chanced that some little time later Hugo left his guests to carry food and drink—with other worse things, perchance—to his captive, and so found the cage empty and the bird escaped. Then, as it would seem, he became as one that hath a devil, for, rushing down the stairs into the dining-hall, he sprang upon the great table, flagons and trenchers flying before him, and he cried aloud before all the company that he would that very night render his body and soul to the Powers of Evil if he might but overtake the wench. And while the revellers stood aghast at the fury of the man, one more wicked or, it may be, more drunken than the rest, cried out that they should put the hounds upon her. Whereat Hugo ran from the house, crying to his grooms that they should saddle his mare and unkennel the pack, and giving the hounds a kerchief of the maid's, he swung them to the line, and so off full cry in the moonlight over the moor.

"Now, for some space the revellers stood agape, unable to understand all that had been done in such haste. But anon their bemused wits awoke to the nature of the deed which was like to be done upon the moorlands. Everything was now in an uproar, some calling for their pistols, some for their horses, and some for another flask of wine. But at length some sense came back to their crazed minds, and the whole of them, thirteen in number, took horse and started in pursuit. The moon shone clear above them, and they rode swiftly abreast, taking that course which the maid must needs have taken if she were to reach her own home.

"They had gone a mile or two when they passed one of the night shepherds upon the moorlands, and they cried to him to know if he had seen the hunt. And the man, as the story goes, was so crazed with fear that he could scarce speak, but at last he said that he had indeed seen the unhappy maiden, with the hounds upon her track. 'But I have seen more than that,' said he, 'for Hugo Baskerville passed me upon his black mare, and there ran mute behind him such a hound of hell as God forbid should ever be at my heels.' So the drunken squires cursed the shepherd and rode onward. But soon their skins turned cold, for there came a galloping across the moor, and the black mare, dabbled with white froth, went past with trailing bridle and empty saddle. Then the revellers rode close together, for a great fear was on them, but they still followed over the moor, though each, had he been alone, would have been right glad to have turned his horse's head. Riding slowly in this fashion they came at last upon the hounds. These, though known for their valour and their breed, were whimpering in a cluster at the head of a deep dip or goyal, as we call it, upon the moor, some slinking away and some, with starting hackles and staring eyes, gazing down the narrow valley before them.

"The company had come to a halt, more sober men, as you may guess, than when they started. The most of them would by no means advance, but three of them, the boldest, or it may be the most drunken, rode forward down the goyal. Now, it opened into a broad space in which stood two of those great stones, still to be seen there, which were set by certain forgotten peoples in the days of old. The moon was shining bright upon the clearing, and there in the centre lay the unhappy maid where she had fallen, dead of fear and of fatigue. But it was not the sight of her body, nor yet was it that of the body of Hugo Baskerville lying near her, which raised the hair upon the heads of these three dare-devil roysterers, but it was that, standing over Hugo, and plucking at his throat, there stood a foul thing, a great, black beast, shaped like a hound, yet larger than any hound that ever mortal eye has rested upon. And even as they looked the thing tore the throat out of Hugo Baskerville, on which, as it turned its blazing eyes and dripping jaws upon them, the three shrieked with fear and rode for dear life, still screaming, across the moor. One, it is said, died that very night of what he had seen, and the other twain were but broken men for the rest of their days.

"Such is the tale, my sons, of the coming of the hound which is said to have plagued the family so sorely ever since. If I have set it down it is because that which is clearly known hath less terror than that which is but hinted at and guessed. Nor can it be denied that many of the family have been unhappy in their deaths, which have been sudden, bloody, and mysterious. Yet may we shelter ourselves in the infinite goodness of Providence, which would not forever punish the innocent beyond that third or fourth generation which is threatened in Holy Writ. To that Providence, my sons, I hereby commend you, and I counsel you by way of caution to forbear from crossing the moor in those dark hours when the powers of evil are exalted.

"[This from Hugo Baskerville to his sons Rodger and John, with instructions that they say nothing thereof to their sister Elizabeth.]"

When Dr. Mortimer had finished reading this singular narrative he pushed his spectacles up on his forehead and stared across at Mr. Sherlock Holmes. The latter yawned and tossed the end of his cigarette into the fire.

"Well?" said he.

"Do you not find it interesting?"

"To a collector of fairy tales."

Dr. Mortimer drew a folded newspaper out of his pocket.

"Now, Mr. Holmes, we will give you something a little more recent. This is the Devon County Chronicle of May 14th of this year. It is a short account of the facts elicited at the death of Sir Charles Baskerville which occurred a few days before that date."

My friend leaned a little forward and his expression became intent. Our visitor readjusted his glasses and began:

"The recent sudden death of Sir Charles Baskerville, whose name has been mentioned as the probable Liberal candidate for Mid-Devon at the next election, has cast a gloom over the county. Though Sir Charles had resided at Baskerville Hall for a comparatively short period his amiability of character and extreme generosity had won the affection and respect of all who had been brought into contact with him. In these days of nouveaux riches it is refreshing to find a case where the scion of an old county family which has fallen upon evil days is able to make his own fortune and to bring it back with him to restore the fallen grandeur of his line. Sir Charles, as is well known, made large sums of money in South African speculation. More wise than those who go on until the wheel turns against them, he realized his gains and returned to England with them. It is only two years since he took up his residence at Baskerville Hall, and it is common talk how large were those schemes of reconstruction and improvement which have been interrupted by his death. Being himself childless, it was his openly expressed desire that the whole countryside should, within his own lifetime, profit by his good fortune, and many will have personal reasons for bewailing his untimely end. His generous donations to local and county charities have been frequently chronicled in these columns.

"The circumstances connected with the death of Sir Charles cannot be said to have been entirely cleared up by the inquest, but at least enough has been done to dispose of those rumours to which local superstition has given rise. There is no reason whatever to suspect foul play, or to imagine that death could be from any but natural causes. Sir Charles was a widower, and a man who may be said to have been in some ways of an eccentric habit of mind. In spite of his considerable wealth he was simple in his personal tastes, and his indoor servants at Baskerville Hall consisted of a married couple named Barrymore, the husband acting as butler and the wife as housekeeper. Their evidence, corroborated by that of several friends, tends to show that Sir Charles's health has for some time been impaired, and points especially to some affection of the heart, manifesting itself in changes of colour, breathlessness, and acute attacks of nervous depression. Dr. James Mortimer, the friend and medical attendant of the deceased, has given evidence to the same effect.

"The facts of the case are simple. Sir Charles Baskerville was in the habit every night before going to bed of walking down the famous yew alley of Baskerville Hall. The evidence of the Barrymores shows that this had been his custom. On the fourth of May Sir Charles had declared his intention of starting next day for London, and had ordered Barrymore to prepare his luggage. That night he went out as usual for his nocturnal walk, in the course of which he was in the habit of smoking a cigar. He never returned. At twelve o'clock Barrymore, finding the hall door still open, became alarmed, and, lighting a lantern, went in search of his master. The day had been wet, and Sir Charles's footmarks were easily traced down the alley. Halfway down this walk there is a gate which leads out on to the moor. There were indications that Sir Charles had stood for some little time here. He then proceeded down the alley, and it was at the far end of it that his body was discovered. One fact which has not been explained is the statement of Barrymore that his master's footprints altered their character from the time that he passed the moor-gate, and that he appeared from thence onward to have been walking upon his toes. One Murphy, a gipsy horse-dealer, was on the moor at no great distance at the time, but he appears by his own confession to have been the worse for drink. He declares that he heard cries but is unable to state from what direction they came. No signs of violence were to be discovered upon Sir Charles's person, and though the doctor's evidence pointed to an almost incredible facial distortion—so great that Dr. Mortimer refused at first to believe that it was indeed his friend and patient who lay before him—it was explained that that is a symptom which is not unusual in cases of dyspnoea and death from cardiac exhaustion. This explanation was borne out by the post-mortem examination, which showed long-standing organic disease, and the coroner's jury returned a verdict in accordance with the medical evidence. It is well that this is so, for it is obviously of the utmost importance that Sir Charles's heir should settle at the Hall and continue the good work which has been so sadly interrupted. Had the prosaic finding of the coroner not finally put an end to the romantic stories which have been whispered in connection with the affair, it might have been difficult to find a tenant for Baskerville Hall. It is understood that the next of kin is Mr. Henry Baskerville, if he be still alive, the son of Sir Charles Baskerville's younger brother. The young man when last heard of was in America, and inquiries are being instituted with a view to informing him of his good fortune."

Dr. Mortimer refolded his paper and replaced it in his pocket. "Those are the public facts, Mr. Holmes, in connection with the death of Sir Charles Baskerville."

"I must thank you," said Sherlock Holmes, "for calling my attention to a case which certainly presents some features of interest. I had observed some newspaper comment at the time, but I was exceedingly preoccupied by that little affair of the Vatican cameos, and in my anxiety to oblige the Pope I lost touch with several interesting English cases. This article, you say, contains all the public facts?"

"It does."

"Then let me have the private ones." He leaned back, put his finger-tips together, and assumed his most impassive and judicial expression.

"In doing so," said Dr. Mortimer, who had begun to show signs of some strong emotion, "I am telling that which I have not confided to anyone. My motive for withholding it from the coroner's inquiry is that a man of science shrinks from placing himself in the public position of seeming to indorse a popular superstition. I had the further motive that Baskerville Hall, as the paper says, would certainly remain untenanted if anything were done to increase its already rather grim reputation. For both these reasons I thought that I was justified in telling rather less than I knew, since no practical good could result from it, but with you there is no reason why I should not be perfectly frank.

"The moor is very sparsely inhabited, and those who live near each other are thrown very much together. For this reason I saw a good deal of Sir Charles Baskerville. With the exception of Mr. Frankland, of Lafter Hall, and Mr. Stapleton, the naturalist, there are no other men of education within many miles. Sir Charles was a retiring man, but the chance of his illness brought us together, and a community of interests in science kept us so. He had brought back much scientific information from South Africa, and many a charming evening we have spent together discussing the comparative anatomy of the Bushman and the Hottentot.

"Within the last few months it became increasingly plain to me that Sir Charles's nervous system was strained to the breaking point. He had taken this legend which I have read you exceedingly to heart—so much so that, although he would walk in his own grounds, nothing would induce him to go out upon the moor at night. Incredible as it may appear to you, Mr. Holmes, he was honestly convinced that a dreadful fate overhung his family, and certainly the records which he was able to give of his ancestors were not encouraging. The idea of some ghastly presence constantly haunted him, and on more than one occasion he has asked me whether I had on my medical journeys at night ever seen any strange creature or heard the baying of a hound. The latter question he put to me several times, and always with a voice which vibrated with excitement.

"I can well remember driving up to his house in the evening some three weeks before the fatal event. He chanced to be at his hall door. I had descended from my gig and was standing in front of him, when I saw his eyes fix themselves over my shoulder and stare past me with an expression of the most dreadful horror. I whisked round and had just time to catch a glimpse of something which I took to be a large black calf passing at the head of the drive. So excited and alarmed was he that I was compelled to go down to the spot where the animal had been and look around for it. It was gone, however, and the incident appeared to make the worst impression upon his mind. I stayed with him all the evening, and it was on that occasion, to explain the emotion which he had shown, that he confided to my keeping that narrative which I read to you when first I came. I mention this small episode because it assumes some importance in view of the tragedy which followed, but I was convinced at the time that the matter was entirely trivial and that his excitement had no justification.

"It was at my advice that Sir Charles was about to go to London. His heart was, I knew, affected, and the constant anxiety in which he lived, however chimerical the cause of it might be, was evidently having a serious effect upon his health. I thought that a few months among the distractions of town would send him back a new man. Mr. Stapleton, a mutual friend who was much concerned at his state of health, was of the same opinion. At the last instant came this terrible catastrophe.

"On the night of Sir Charles's death Barrymore the butler, who made the discovery, sent Perkins the groom on horseback to me, and as I was sitting up late I was able to reach Baskerville Hall within an hour of the event. I checked and corroborated all the facts which were mentioned at the inquest. I followed the footsteps down the yew alley, I saw the spot at the moor-gate where he seemed to have waited, I remarked the change in the shape of the prints after that point, I noted that there were no other footsteps save those of Barrymore on the soft gravel, and finally I carefully examined the body, which had not been touched until my arrival. Sir Charles lay on his face, his arms out, his fingers dug into the ground, and his features convulsed with some strong emotion to such an extent that I could hardly have sworn to his identity. There was certainly no physical injury of any kind. But one false statement was made by Barrymore at the inquest. He said that there were no traces upon the ground round the body. He did not observe any. But I did—some little distance off, but fresh and clear."

"Footprints?"

"Footprints."

"A man's or a woman's?"

Dr. Mortimer looked strangely at us for an instant, and his voice sank almost to a whisper as he answered.

"Mr. Holmes, they were the footprints of a gigantic hound!"

Chapter 3. The Problem

I confess at these words a shudder passed through me. There was a thrill in the doctor's voice which showed that he was himself deeply moved by that which he told us. Holmes leaned forward in his excitement and his eyes had the hard, dry glitter which shot from them when he was keenly interested.

"You saw this?"

"As clearly as I see you."

"And you said nothing?"

"What was the use?"

"How was it that no one else saw it?"

"The marks were some twenty yards from the body and no one gave them a thought. I don't suppose I should have done so had I not known this legend."

"There are many sheep-dogs on the moor?"

"No doubt, but this was no sheep-dog."

"You say it was large?"

"Enormous."

"But it had not approached the body?"

"No."

"What sort of night was it?'

"Damp and raw."

"But not actually raining?"

"No."

"What is the alley like?"

"There are two lines of old yew hedge, twelve feet high and impenetrable. The walk in the centre is about eight feet across."

"Is there anything between the hedges and the walk?"

"Yes, there is a strip of grass about six feet broad on either side."

"I understand that the yew hedge is penetrated at one point by a gate?"

"Yes, the wicket-gate which leads on to the moor."

"Is there any other opening?"

"None."

"So that to reach the yew alley one either has to come down it from the house or else to enter it by the moor-gate?"

"There is an exit through a summer-house at the far end."

"Had Sir Charles reached this?"

"No; he lay about fifty yards from it."

"Now, tell me, Dr. Mortimer—and this is important—the marks which you saw were on the path and not on the grass?"

"No marks could show on the grass."

"Were they on the same side of the path as the moor-gate?"

"Yes; they were on the edge of the path on the same side as the moor-gate."

"You interest me exceedingly. Another point. Was the wicket-gate closed?"

"Closed and padlocked."

"How high was it?"

"About four feet high."

"Then anyone could have got over it?"

"Yes."

"And what marks did you see by the wicket-gate?"

"None in particular."

"Good heaven! Did no one examine?"

"Yes, I examined, myself."

"And found nothing?"

"It was all very confused. Sir Charles had evidently stood there for five or ten minutes."

"How do you know that?"

"Because the ash had twice dropped from his cigar."

"Excellent! This is a colleague, Watson, after our own heart. But the marks?"

"He had left his own marks all over that small patch of gravel. I could discern no others."

Sherlock Holmes struck his hand against his knee with an impatient gesture.

"If I had only been there!" he cried. "It is evidently a case of extraordinary interest, and one which presented immense opportunities to the scientific expert. That gravel page upon which I might have read so much has been long ere this smudged by the rain and defaced by the clogs of curious peasants. Oh, Dr. Mortimer, Dr. Mortimer, to think that you should not have called me in! You have indeed much to answer for."

"I could not call you in, Mr. Holmes, without disclosing these facts to the world, and I have already given my reasons for not wishing to do so. Besides, besides—"

"Why do you hesitate?"

"There is a realm in which the most acute and most experienced of detectives is helpless."

"You mean that the thing is supernatural?"

"I did not positively say so."

"No, but you evidently think it."

"Since the tragedy, Mr. Holmes, there have come to my ears several incidents which are hard to reconcile with the settled order of Nature."

"For example?"

"I find that before the terrible event occurred several people had seen a creature upon the moor which corresponds with this Baskerville demon, and which could not possibly be any animal known to science. They all agreed that it was a huge creature, luminous, ghastly, and spectral. I have cross-examined these men, one of them a hard-headed countryman, one a farrier, and one a moorland farmer, who all tell the same story of this dreadful apparition, exactly corresponding to the hell-hound of the legend. I assure you that there is a reign of terror in the district, and that it is a hardy man who will cross the moor at night."

"And you, a trained man of science, believe it to be supernatural?"

"I do not know what to believe."

Holmes shrugged his shoulders. "I have hitherto confined my investigations to this world," said he. "In a modest way I have combated evil, but to take on the Father of Evil himself would, perhaps, be too ambitious a task. Yet you must admit that the footmark is material."

"The original hound was material enough to tug a man's throat out, and yet he was diabolical as well."

"I see that you have quite gone over to the supernaturalists. But now, Dr. Mortimer, tell me this. If you hold these views, why have you come to consult me at all? You tell me in the same breath that it is useless to investigate Sir Charles's death, and that you desire me to do it."

"I did not say that I desired you to do it."

"Then, how can I assist you?"

"By advising me as to what I should do with Sir Henry Baskerville, who arrives at Waterloo Station"—Dr. Mortimer looked at his watch—"in exactly one hour and a quarter."

"He being the heir?"

"Yes. On the death of Sir Charles we inquired for this young gentleman and found that he had been farming in Canada. From the accounts which have reached us he is an excellent fellow in every way. I speak now not as a medical man but as a trustee and executor of Sir Charles's will."

"There is no other claimant, I presume?"

"None. The only other kinsman whom we have been able to trace was Rodger Baskerville, the youngest of three brothers of whom poor Sir Charles was the elder. The second brother, who died young, is the father of this lad Henry. The third, Rodger, was the black sheep of the family. He came of the old masterful Baskerville strain and was the very image, they tell me, of the family picture of old Hugo. He made England too hot to hold him, fled to Central America, and died there in 1876 of yellow fever. Henry is the last of the Baskervilles. In one hour and five minutes I meet him at Waterloo Station. I have had a wire that he arrived at Southampton this morning. Now, Mr. Holmes, what would you advise me to do with him?"

"Why should he not go to the home of his fathers?"

"It seems natural, does it not? And yet, consider that every Baskerville who goes there meets with an evil fate. I feel sure that if Sir Charles could have spoken with me before his death he would have warned me against bringing this, the last of the old race, and the heir to great wealth, to that deadly place. And yet it cannot be denied that the prosperity of the whole poor, bleak countryside depends upon his presence. All the good work which has been done by Sir Charles will crash to the ground if there is no tenant of the Hall. I fear lest I should be swayed too much by my own obvious interest in the matter, and that is why I bring the case before you and ask for your advice."

Holmes considered for a little time.

"Put into plain words, the matter is this," said he. "In your opinion there is a diabolical agency which makes Dartmoor an unsafe abode for a Baskerville—that is your opinion?"

"At least I might go the length of saying that there is some evidence that this may be so."

"Exactly. But surely, if your supernatural theory be correct, it could work the young man evil in London as easily as in Devonshire. A devil with merely local powers like a parish vestry would be too inconceivable a thing."

"You put the matter more flippantly, Mr. Holmes, than you would probably do if you were brought into personal contact with these things. Your advice, then, as I understand it, is that the young man will be as safe in Devonshire as in London. He comes in fifty minutes. What would you recommend?"

"I recommend, sir, that you take a cab, call off your spaniel who is scratching at my front door, and proceed to Waterloo to meet Sir Henry Baskerville."

"And then?"

"And then you will say nothing to him at all until I have made up my mind about the matter."

"How long will it take you to make up your mind?"

"Twenty-four hours. At ten o'clock tomorrow, Dr. Mortimer, I will be much obliged to you if you will call upon me here, and it will be of help to me in my plans for the future if you will bring Sir Henry Baskerville with you."

"I will do so, Mr. Holmes." He scribbled the appointment on his shirt-cuff and hurried off in his strange, peering, absent-minded fashion. Holmes stopped him at the head of the stair.

"Only one more question, Dr. Mortimer. You say that before Sir Charles Baskerville's death several people saw this apparition upon the moor?"

"Three people did."

"Did any see it after?"

"I have not heard of any."

"Thank you. Good-morning."

Holmes returned to his seat with that quiet look of inward satisfaction which meant that he had a congenial task before him.

"Going out, Watson?"

"Unless I can help you."

"No, my dear fellow, it is at the hour of action that I turn to you for aid. But this is splendid, really unique from some points of view. When you pass Bradley's, would you ask him to send up a pound of the strongest shag tobacco? Thank you. It would be as well if you could make it convenient not to return before evening. Then I should be very glad to compare impressions as to this most interesting problem which has been submitted to us this morning."

I knew that seclusion and solitude were very necessary for my friend in those hours of intense mental concentration during which he weighed every particle of evidence, constructed alternative theories, balanced one against the other, and made up his mind as to which points were essential and which immaterial. I therefore spent the day at my club and did not return to Baker Street until evening. It was nearly nine o'clock when I found myself in the sitting-room once more.

My first impression as I opened the door was that a fire had broken out, for the room was so filled with smoke that the light of the lamp upon the table was blurred by it. As I entered, however, my fears were set at rest, for it was the acrid fumes of strong coarse tobacco which took me by the throat and set me coughing. Through the haze I had a vague vision of Holmes in his dressing-gown coiled up in an armchair with his black clay pipe between his lips. Several rolls of paper lay around him.

"Caught cold, Watson?" said he.

"No, it's this poisonous atmosphere."

"I suppose it is pretty thick, now that you mention it."

"Thick! It is intolerable."

"Open the window, then! You have been at your club all day, I perceive."

"My dear Holmes!"

"Am I right?"

"Certainly, but how?"

He laughed at my bewildered expression. "There is a delightful freshness about you, Watson, which makes it a pleasure to exercise any small powers which I possess at your expense. A gentleman goes forth on a showery and miry day. He returns immaculate in the evening with the gloss still on his hat and his boots. He has been a fixture therefore all day. He is not a man with intimate friends. Where, then, could he have been? Is it not obvious?"

"Well, it is rather obvious."

"The world is full of obvious things which nobody by any chance ever observes. Where do you think that I have been?"

"A fixture also."

"On the contrary, I have been to Devonshire."

"In spirit?"

"Exactly. My body has remained in this armchair and has, I regret to observe, consumed in my absence two large pots of coffee and an incredible amount of tobacco. After you left I sent down to Stamford's for the Ordnance map of this portion of the moor, and my spirit has hovered over it all day. I flatter myself that I could find my way about."

"A large-scale map, I presume?"

"Very large."

He unrolled one section and held it over his knee. "Here you have the particular district which concerns us. That is Baskerville Hall in the middle."

"With a wood round it?"

"Exactly. I fancy the yew alley, though not marked under that name, must stretch along this line, with the moor, as you perceive, upon the right of it. This small clump of buildings here is the hamlet of Grimpen, where our friend Dr. Mortimer has his headquarters. Within a radius of five miles there are, as you see, only a very few scattered dwellings. Here is Lafter Hall, which was mentioned in the narrative. There is a house indicated here which may be the residence of the naturalist—Stapleton, if I remember right, was his name. Here are two moorland farmhouses, High Tor and Foulmire. Then fourteen miles away the great convict prison of Princetown. Between and around these scattered points extends the desolate, lifeless moor. This, then, is the stage upon which tragedy has been played, and upon which we may help to play it again."

"It must be a wild place."

"Yes, the setting is a worthy one. If the devil did desire to have a hand in the affairs of men—"

"Then you are yourself inclining to the supernatural explanation."

"The devil's agents may be of flesh and blood, may they not? There are two questions waiting for us at the outset. The one is whether any crime has been committed at all; the second is, what is the crime and how was it committed? Of course, if Dr. Mortimer's surmise should be correct, and we are dealing with forces outside the ordinary laws of Nature, there is an end of our investigation. But we are bound to exhaust all other hypotheses before falling back upon this one. I think we'll shut that window again, if you don't mind. It is a singular thing, but I find that a concentrated atmosphere helps a concentration of thought. I have not pushed it to the length of getting into a box to think, but that is the logical outcome of my convictions. Have you turned the case over in your mind?"

"Yes, I have thought a good deal of it in the course of the day."

"What do you make of it?"

"It is very bewildering."

"It has certainly a character of its own. There are points of distinction about it. That change in the footprints, for example. What do you make of that?"

"Mortimer said that the man had walked on tiptoe down that portion of the alley."

"He only repeated what some fool had said at the inquest. Why should a man walk on tiptoe down the alley?"

"What then?"

"He was running, Watson—running desperately, running for his life, running until he burst his heart—and fell dead upon his face."

"Running from what?"

"There lies our problem. There are indications that the man was crazed with fear before ever he began to run."

"How can you say that?"

"I am presuming that the cause of his fears came to him across the moor. If that were so, and it seems most probable, only a man who had lost his wits would have run from the house instead of towards it. If the gipsy's evidence may be taken as true, he ran with cries for help in the direction where help was least likely to be. Then, again, whom was he waiting for that night, and why was he waiting for him in the yew alley rather than in his own house?"

"You think that he was waiting for someone?"

"The man was elderly and infirm. We can understand his taking an evening stroll, but the ground was damp and the night inclement. Is it natural that he should stand for five or ten minutes, as Dr. Mortimer, with more practical sense than I should have given him credit for, deduced from the cigar ash?"

"But he went out every evening."

"I think it unlikely that he waited at the moor-gate every evening. On the contrary, the evidence is that he avoided the moor. That night he waited there. It was the night before he made his departure for London. The thing takes shape, Watson. It becomes coherent. Might I ask you to hand me my violin, and we will postpone all further thought upon this business until we have had the advantage of meeting Dr. Mortimer and Sir Henry Baskerville in the morning."

Chapter 4. Sir Henry Baskerville

Our breakfast table was cleared early, and Holmes waited in his dressing-gown for the promised interview. Our clients were punctual to their appointment, for the clock had just struck ten when Dr. Mortimer was shown up, followed by the young baronet. The latter was a small, alert, dark-eyed man about thirty years of age, very sturdily built, with thick black eyebrows and a strong, pugnacious face. He wore a ruddy-tinted tweed suit and had the weather-beaten appearance of one who has spent most of his time in the open air, and yet there was something in his steady eye and the quiet assurance of his bearing which indicated the gentleman.

"This is Sir Henry Baskerville," said Dr. Mortimer.

"Why, yes," said he, "and the strange thing is, Mr. Sherlock Holmes, that if my friend here had not proposed coming round to you this morning I should have come on my own account. I understand that you think out little puzzles, and I've had one this morning which wants more thinking out than I am able to give it."

"Pray take a seat, Sir Henry. Do I understand you to say that you have yourself had some remarkable experience since you arrived in London?"

"Nothing of much importance, Mr. Holmes. Only a joke, as like as not. It was this letter, if you can call it a letter, which reached me this morning."

He laid an envelope upon the table, and we all bent over it. It was of common quality, grayish in colour. The address, "Sir Henry Baskerville, Northumberland Hotel," was printed in rough characters; the post-mark "Charing Cross," and the date of posting the preceding evening.

"Who knew that you were going to the Northumberland Hotel?" asked Holmes, glancing keenly across at our visitor.

"No one could have known. We only decided after I met Dr. Mortimer."

"But Dr. Mortimer was no doubt already stopping there?"

"No, I had been staying with a friend," said the doctor.

"There was no possible indication that we intended to go to this hotel."

"Hum! Someone seems to be very deeply interested in your movements." Out of the envelope he took a half-sheet of foolscap paper folded into four. This he opened and spread flat upon the table. Across the middle of it a single sentence had been formed by the expedient of pasting printed words upon it. It ran:

As you value your life or your reason keep away from the moor.

The word "moor" only was printed in ink.

"Now," said Sir Henry Baskerville, "perhaps you will tell me, Mr. Holmes, what in thunder is the meaning of that, and who it is that takes so much interest in my affairs?"

"What do you make of it, Dr. Mortimer? You must allow that there is nothing supernatural about this, at any rate?"

"No, sir, but it might very well come from someone who was convinced that the business is supernatural."

"What business?" asked Sir Henry sharply. "It seems to me that all you gentlemen know a great deal more than I do about my own affairs."

"You shall share our knowledge before you leave this room, Sir Henry. I promise you that," said Sherlock Holmes. "We will confine ourselves for the present with your permission to this very interesting document, which must have been put together and posted yesterday evening. Have you yesterday's Times, Watson?"

"It is here in the corner."

"Might I trouble you for it—the inside page, please, with the leading articles?" He glanced swiftly over it, running his eyes up and down the columns. "Capital article this on free trade. Permit me to give you an extract from it.

'You may be cajoled into imagining that your own special trade or your own industry will be encouraged by a protective tariff, but it stands to reason that such legislation must in the long run keep away wealth from the country, diminish the value of our imports, and lower the general conditions of life in this island.'

"What do you think of that, Watson?" cried Holmes in high glee, rubbing his hands together with satisfaction. "Don't you think that is an admirable sentiment?"

Dr. Mortimer looked at Holmes with an air of professional interest, and Sir Henry Baskerville turned a pair of puzzled dark eyes upon me.

"I don't know much about the tariff and things of that kind," said he, "but it seems to me we've got a bit off the trail so far as that note is concerned."

"On the contrary, I think we are particularly hot upon the trail, Sir Henry. Watson here knows more about my methods than you do, but I fear that even he has not quite grasped the significance of this sentence."

"No, I confess that I see no connection."

"And yet, my dear Watson, there is so very close a connection that the one is extracted out of the other. 'You,' 'your,' 'your,' 'life,' 'reason,' 'value,' 'keep away,' 'from the.' Don't you see now whence these words have been taken?"

"By thunder, you're right! Well, if that isn't smart!" cried Sir Henry.

"If any possible doubt remained it is settled by the fact that 'keep away' and 'from the' are cut out in one piece."

"Well, now—so it is!"

"Really, Mr. Holmes, this exceeds anything which I could have imagined," said Dr. Mortimer, gazing at my friend in amazement. "I could understand anyone saying that the words were from a newspaper; but that you should name which, and add that it came from the leading article, is really one of the most remarkable things which I have ever known. How did you do it?"

"I presume, Doctor, that you could tell the skull of a negro from that of an Esquimau?"

"Most certainly."

"But how?"

"Because that is my special hobby. The differences are obvious. The supra-orbital crest, the facial angle, the maxillary curve, the—"

"But this is my special hobby, and the differences are equally obvious. There is as much difference to my eyes between the leaded bourgeois type of a Times article and the slovenly print of an evening half-penny paper as there could be between your negro and your Esquimau. The detection of types is one of the most elementary branches of knowledge to the special expert in crime, though I confess that once when I was very young I confused the Leeds Mercury with the Western Morning News. But a Times leader is entirely distinctive, and these words could have been taken from nothing else. As it was done yesterday the strong probability was that we should find the words in yesterday's issue."

"So far as I can follow you, then, Mr. Holmes," said Sir Henry Baskerville, "someone cut out this message with a scissors—"

"Nail-scissors," said Holmes. "You can see that it was a very short-bladed scissors, since the cutter had to take two snips over 'keep away.'"

"That is so. Someone, then, cut out the message with a pair of short-bladed scissors, pasted it with paste—"

"Gum," said Holmes.

"With gum on to the paper. But I want to know why the word 'moor' should have been written?"

"Because he could not find it in print. The other words were all simple and might be found in any issue, but 'moor' would be less common."

"Why, of course, that would explain it. Have you read anything else in this message, Mr. Holmes?"

"There are one or two indications, and yet the utmost pains have been taken to remove all clues. The address, you observe is printed in rough characters. But the Times is a paper which is seldom found in any hands but those of the highly educated. We may take it, therefore, that the letter was composed by an educated man who wished to pose as an uneducated one, and his effort to conceal his own writing suggests that that writing might be known, or come to be known, by you. Again, you will observe that the words are not gummed on in an accurate line, but that some are much higher than others. 'Life,' for example is quite out of its proper place. That may point to carelessness or it may point to agitation and hurry upon the part of the cutter. On the whole I incline to the latter view, since the matter was evidently important, and it is unlikely that the composer of such a letter would be careless. If he were in a hurry it opens up the interesting question why he should be in a hurry, since any letter posted up to early morning would reach Sir Henry before he would leave his hotel. Did the composer fear an interruption—and from whom?"

"We are coming now rather into the region of guesswork," said Dr. Mortimer.

"Say, rather, into the region where we balance probabilities and choose the most likely. It is the scientific use of the imagination, but we have always some material basis on which to start our speculation. Now, you would call it a guess, no doubt, but I am almost certain that this address has been written in a hotel."

"How in the world can you say that?"

"If you examine it carefully you will see that both the pen and the ink have given the writer trouble. The pen has spluttered twice in a single word and has run dry three times in a short address, showing that there was very little ink in the bottle. Now, a private pen or ink-bottle is seldom allowed to be in such a state, and the combination of the two must be quite rare. But you know the hotel ink and the hotel pen, where it is rare to get anything else. Yes, I have very little hesitation in saying that could we examine the waste-paper baskets of the hotels around Charing Cross until we found the remains of the mutilated Times leader we could lay our hands straight upon the person who sent this singular message. Halloa! Halloa! What's this?"

He was carefully examining the foolscap, upon which the words were pasted, holding it only an inch or two from his eyes.

"Well?"

"Nothing," said he, throwing it down. "It is a blank half-sheet of paper, without even a water-mark upon it. I think we have drawn as much as we can from this curious letter; and now, Sir Henry, has anything else of interest happened to you since you have been in London?"

"Why, no, Mr. Holmes. I think not."

"You have not observed anyone follow or watch you?"

"I seem to have walked right into the thick of a dime novel," said our visitor. "Why in thunder should anyone follow or watch me?"

"We are coming to that. You have nothing else to report to us before we go into this matter?"

"Well, it depends upon what you think worth reporting."

"I think anything out of the ordinary routine of life well worth reporting."

Sir Henry smiled. "I don't know much of British life yet, for I have spent nearly all my time in the States and in Canada. But I hope that to lose one of your boots is not part of the ordinary routine of life over here."

"You have lost one of your boots?"

"My dear sir," cried Dr. Mortimer, "it is only mislaid. You will find it when you return to the hotel. What is the use of troubling Mr. Holmes with trifles of this kind?"

"Well, he asked me for anything outside the ordinary routine."

"Exactly," said Holmes, "however foolish the incident may seem. You have lost one of your boots, you say?"

"Well, mislaid it, anyhow. I put them both outside my door last night, and there was only one in the morning. I could get no sense out of the chap who cleans them. The worst of it is that I only bought the pair last night in the Strand, and I have never had them on."

"If you have never worn them, why did you put them out to be cleaned?"

"They were tan boots and had never been varnished. That was why I put them out."

"Then I understand that on your arrival in London yesterday you went out at once and bought a pair of boots?"

"I did a good deal of shopping. Dr. Mortimer here went round with me. You see, if I am to be squire down there I must dress the part, and it may be that I have got a little careless in my ways out West. Among other things I bought these brown boots—gave six dollars for them—and had one stolen before ever I had them on my feet."

"It seems a singularly useless thing to steal," said Sherlock Holmes. "I confess that I share Dr. Mortimer's belief that it will not be long before the missing boot is found."

"And, now, gentlemen," said the baronet with decision, "it seems to me that I have spoken quite enough about the little that I know. It is time that you kept your promise and gave me a full account of what we are all driving at."

"Your request is a very reasonable one," Holmes answered. "Dr. Mortimer, I think you could not do better than to tell your story as you told it to us."

Thus encouraged, our scientific friend drew his papers from his pocket and presented the whole case as he had done upon the morning before. Sir Henry Baskerville listened with the deepest attention and with an occasional exclamation of surprise.

"Well, I seem to have come into an inheritance with a vengeance," said he when the long narrative was finished. "Of course, I've heard of the hound ever since I was in the nursery. It's the pet story of the family, though I never thought of taking it seriously before. But as to my uncle's death—well, it all seems boiling up in my head, and I can't get it clear yet. You don't seem quite to have made up your mind whether it's a case for a policeman or a clergyman."

"Precisely."

"And now there's this affair of the letter to me at the hotel. I suppose that fits into its place."

"It seems to show that someone knows more than we do about what goes on upon the moor," said Dr. Mortimer.

"And also," said Holmes, "that someone is not ill-disposed towards you, since they warn you of danger."

"Or it may be that they wish, for their own purposes, to scare me away."

"Well, of course, that is possible also. I am very much indebted to you, Dr. Mortimer, for introducing me to a problem which presents several interesting alternatives. But the practical point which we now have to decide, Sir Henry, is whether it is or is not advisable for you to go to Baskerville Hall."

"Why should I not go?"

"There seems to be danger."

"Do you mean danger from this family fiend or do you mean danger from human beings?"

"Well, that is what we have to find out."

"Whichever it is, my answer is fixed. There is no devil in hell, Mr. Holmes, and there is no man upon earth who can prevent me from going to the home of my own people, and you may take that to be my final answer." His dark brows knitted and his face flushed to a dusky red as he spoke. It was evident that the fiery temper of the

Baskervilles was not extinct in this their last representative. "Meanwhile," said he, "I have hardly had time to think over all that you have told me. It's a big thing for a man to have to understand and to decide at one sitting. I should like to have a quiet hour by myself to make up my mind. Now, look here, Mr. Holmes, it's half-past eleven now and I am going back right away to my hotel. Suppose you and your friend, Dr. Watson, come round and lunch with us at two. I'll be able to tell you more clearly then how this thing strikes me."

"Is that convenient to you, Watson?"

"Perfectly."

"Then you may expect us. Shall I have a cab called?"

"I'd prefer to walk, for this affair has flurried me rather."

"I'll join you in a walk, with pleasure," said his companion.

"Then we meet again at two o'clock. Au revoir, and good-morning!"

We heard the steps of our visitors descend the stair and the bang of the front door. In an instant Holmes had changed from the languid dreamer to the man of action.

"Your hat and boots, Watson, quick! Not a moment to lose!" He rushed into his room in his dressing-gown and was back again in a few seconds in a frock-coat. We hurried together down the stairs and into the street. Dr. Mortimer and Baskerville were still visible about two hundred yards ahead of us in the direction of Oxford Street.

"Shall I run on and stop them?"

"Not for the world, my dear Watson. I am perfectly satisfied with your company if you will tolerate mine. Our friends are wise, for it is certainly a very fine morning for a walk."

He quickened his pace until we had decreased the distance which divided us by about half. Then, still keeping a hundred yards behind, we followed into Oxford Street and so down Regent Street. Once our friends stopped and stared into a shop window, upon which Holmes did the same. An instant afterwards he gave a little cry of satisfaction, and, following the direction of his eager eyes, I saw that a hansom cab with a man inside which had halted on the other side of the street was now proceeding slowly onward again.

"There's our man, Watson! Come along! We'll have a good look at him, if we can do no more."

At that instant I was aware of a bushy black beard and a pair of piercing eyes turned upon us through the side window of the cab. Instantly the trapdoor at the top flew up, something was screamed to the driver, and the cab flew madly off down Regent Street. Holmes looked eagerly round for another, but no empty one was in sight. Then he dashed in wild pursuit amid the stream of the traffic, but the start was too great, and already the cab was out of sight.

"There now!" said Holmes bitterly as he emerged panting and white with vexation from the tide of vehicles. "Was ever such bad luck and such bad management, too? Watson, Watson, if you are an honest man you will record this also and set it against my successes!"

"Who was the man?"

"I have not an idea."

"A spy?"

"Well, it was evident from what we have heard that Baskerville has been very closely shadowed by someone since he has been in town. How else could it be known so quickly that it was the Northumberland Hotel which he had chosen? If they had followed him the first day I argued that they would follow him also the second. You may have observed that I twice strolled over to the window while Dr. Mortimer was reading his legend."

"Yes, I remember."

"I was looking out for loiterers in the street, but I saw none. We are dealing with a clever man, Watson. This matter cuts very deep, and though I have not finally made up my mind whether it is a benevolent or a malevolent agency which is in touch with us, I am conscious always of power and design. When our friends left I at once followed them in the hopes of marking down their invisible attendant. So wily was he that he had not trusted himself upon foot, but he had availed himself of a cab so that he could loiter behind or dash past them and so escape their notice. His method had the additional advantage that if they were to take a cab he was all ready to follow them. It has, however, one obvious disadvantage."

"It puts him in the power of the cabman."

"Exactly."

"What a pity we did not get the number!"

"My dear Watson, clumsy as I have been, you surely do not seriously imagine that I neglected to get the number? No. 2704 is our man. But that is no use to us for the moment."

"I fail to see how you could have done more."

"On observing the cab I should have instantly turned and walked in the other direction. I should then at my leisure have hired a second cab and followed the first at a respectful distance, or, better still, have driven to the Northumberland Hotel and waited there. When our unknown had followed Baskerville home we should have had the opportunity of playing his own game upon himself and seeing where he made for. As it is, by an indiscreet eagerness, which was taken advantage of with extraordinary quickness and energy by our opponent, we have betrayed ourselves and lost our man."

We had been sauntering slowly down Regent Street during this conversation, and Dr. Mortimer, with his companion, had long vanished in front of us.

"There is no object in our following them," said Holmes. "The shadow has departed and will not return. We must see what further cards we have in our hands and play them with decision. Could you swear to that man's face within the cab?"

"I could swear only to the beard."

"And so could I—from which I gather that in all probability it was a false one. A clever man upon so delicate an errand has no use for a beard save to conceal his features. Come in here, Watson!"

He turned into one of the district messenger offices, where he was warmly greeted by the manager.

"Ah, Wilson, I see you have not forgotten the little case in which I had the good fortune to help you?"

"No, sir, indeed I have not. You saved my good name, and perhaps my life."

"My dear fellow, you exaggerate. I have some recollection, Wilson, that you had among your boys a lad named Cartwright, who showed some ability during the investigation."

"Yes, sir, he is still with us."

"Could you ring him up?--thank you! And I should be glad to have change of this five-pound note."

A lad of fourteen, with a bright, keen face, had obeyed the summons of the manager. He stood now gazing with great reverence at the famous detective.

"Let me have the Hotel Directory," said Holmes. "Thank you! Now, Cartwright, there are the names of twenty-three hotels here, all in the immediate neighbourhood of Charing Cross. Do you see?"

"Yes, sir."

"You will visit each of these in turn."

"Yes, sir."

"You will begin in each case by giving the outside porter one shilling. Here are twenty-three shillings."

"Yes, sir."

"You will tell him that you want to see the waste-paper of yesterday. You will say that an important telegram has miscarried and that you are looking for it. You understand?"

"Yes, sir."

"But what you are really looking for is the centre page of the Times with some holes cut in it with scissors. Here is a copy of the Times. It is this page. You could easily recognize it, could you not?"

"Yes, sir."

"In each case the outside porter will send for the hall porter, to whom also you will give a shilling. Here are twenty-three shillings. You will then learn in possibly twenty cases out of the twenty-three that the waste of the day before has been burned or removed. In the three other cases you will be shown a heap of paper and you will look for this page of the Times among it. The odds are enormously against your finding it. There are ten shillings over in case of emergencies. Let me have a report by wire at Baker Street before evening. And now, Watson, it only remains for us to find out by wire the identity of the cabman, No. 2704, and then we will drop into one of the Bond Street picture galleries and fill in the time until we are due at the hotel."

Chapter 5. Three Broken Threads

Sherlock Holmes had, in a very remarkable degree, the power of detaching his mind at will. For two hours the strange business in which we had been involved appeared to be forgotten, and he was entirely absorbed in the pictures of the modern Belgian masters. He would talk of nothing but art, of which he had the crudest ideas, from our leaving the gallery until we found ourselves at the Northumberland Hotel.

"Sir Henry Baskerville is upstairs expecting you," said the clerk. "He asked me to show you up at once when you came."

"Have you any objection to my looking at your register?" said Holmes.

"Not in the least."

The book showed that two names had been added after that of Baskerville. One was Theophilus Johnson and family, of Newcastle; the other Mrs. Oldmore and maid, of High Lodge, Alton.

"Surely that must be the same Johnson whom I used to know," said Holmes to the porter. "A lawyer, is he not, gray-headed, and walks with a limp?"

"No, sir, this is Mr. Johnson, the coal-owner, a very active gentleman, not older than yourself."

"Surely you are mistaken about his trade?"

"No, sir! he has used this hotel for many years, and he is very well known to us."

"Ah, that settles it. Mrs. Oldmore, too; I seem to remember the name. Excuse my curiosity, but often in calling upon one friend one finds another."

"She is an invalid lady, sir. Her husband was once mayor of Gloucester. She always comes to us when she is in town."

"Thank you; I am afraid I cannot claim her acquaintance. We have established a most important fact by these questions, Watson," he continued in a low voice as we went upstairs together. "We know now that the people who are so interested in our friend have not settled down in his own hotel. That means that while they are, as we have seen, very anxious to watch him, they are equally anxious that he should not see them. Now, this is a most suggestive fact."

"What does it suggest?"

"It suggests—halloa, my dear fellow, what on earth is the matter?"

As we came round the top of the stairs we had run up against Sir Henry Baskerville himself. His face was flushed with anger, and he held an old and dusty boot in one of his hands. So furious was he that he was hardly articulate, and when he did speak it was in a much broader and more Western dialect than any which we had heard from him in the morning.

"Seems to me they are playing me for a sucker in this hotel," he cried. "They'll find they've started in to monkey with the wrong man unless they are careful. By thunder, if that chap can't find my missing boot there will be trouble. I can take a joke with the best, Mr. Holmes, but they've got a bit over the mark this time."

"Still looking for your boot?"

"Yes, sir, and mean to find it."

"But, surely, you said that it was a new brown boot?"

"So it was, sir. And now it's an old black one."

"What! you don't mean to say--?"

"That's just what I do mean to say. I only had three pairs in the world—the new brown, the old black, and the patent leathers, which I am wearing. Last night they took one of my brown ones, and today they have sneaked one of the black. Well, have you got it? Speak out, man, and don't stand staring!"

An agitated German waiter had appeared upon the scene.

"No, sir; I have made inquiry all over the hotel, but I can hear no word of it."

"Well, either that boot comes back before sundown or I'll see the manager and tell him that I go right straight out of this hotel."

"It shall be found, sir—I promise you that if you will have a little patience it will be found."

"Mind it is, for it's the last thing of mine that I'll lose in this den of thieves. Well, well, Mr. Holmes, you'll excuse my troubling you about such a trifle—"

"I think it's well worth troubling about."

"Why, you look very serious over it."

"How do you explain it?"

"I just don't attempt to explain it. It seems the very maddest, queerest thing that ever happened to me."

"The queerest perhaps—" said Holmes thoughtfully.

"What do you make of it yourself?"

"Well, I don't profess to understand it yet. This case of yours is very complex, Sir Henry. When taken in conjunction with your uncle's death I am not sure that of all the five hundred cases of capital importance which I have handled there is one which cuts so deep. But we hold several threads in our hands, and the odds are that one or other of them guides us to the truth. We may waste time in following the wrong one, but sooner or later we must come upon the right."

We had a pleasant luncheon in which little was said of the business which had brought us together. It was in the private sitting-room to which we afterwards repaired that Holmes asked Baskerville what were his intentions.

"To go to Baskerville Hall."

"And when?"

"At the end of the week."

"On the whole," said Holmes, "I think that your decision is a wise one. I have ample evidence that you are being dogged in London, and amid the millions of this great city it is difficult to discover who these people are or what their object can be. If their intentions are evil they might do you a mischief, and we should be powerless to prevent it. You did not know, Dr. Mortimer, that you were followed this morning from my house?"

Dr. Mortimer started violently. "Followed! By whom?"

"That, unfortunately, is what I cannot tell you. Have you among your neighbours or acquaintances on Dartmoor any man with a black, full beard?"

"No—or, let me see—why, yes. Barrymore, Sir Charles's butler, is a man with a full, black beard."

"Ha! Where is Barrymore?"

"He is in charge of the Hall."

"We had best ascertain if he is really there, or if by any possibility he might be in London."

"How can you do that?"

"Give me a telegraph form. 'Is all ready for Sir Henry?' That will do. Address to Mr. Barrymore, Baskerville Hall. What is the nearest telegraph-office? Grimpen. Very good, we will send a second wire to the postmaster, Grimpen: 'Telegram to Mr. Barrymore to be delivered into his own hand. If absent, please return wire to Sir Henry Baskerville, Northumberland Hotel.' That should let us know before evening whether Barrymore is at his post in Devonshire or not."

"That's so," said Baskerville. "By the way, Dr. Mortimer, who is this Barrymore, anyhow?"

"He is the son of the old caretaker, who is dead. They have looked after the Hall for four generations now. So far as I know, he and his wife are as respectable a couple as any in the county."

"At the same time," said Baskerville, "it's clear enough that so long as there are none of the family at the Hall these people have a mighty fine home and nothing to do."

"That is true."

"Did Barrymore profit at all by Sir Charles's will?" asked Holmes.

"He and his wife had five hundred pounds each."

"Ha! Did they know that they would receive this?"

"Yes; Sir Charles was very fond of talking about the provisions of his will."

"That is very interesting."

"I hope," said Dr. Mortimer, "that you do not look with suspicious eyes upon everyone who received a legacy from Sir Charles, for I also had a thousand pounds left to me."

"Indeed! And anyone else?"

"There were many insignificant sums to individuals, and a large number of public charities. The residue all went to Sir Henry."

"And how much was the residue?"

"Seven hundred and forty thousand pounds."

Holmes raised his eyebrows in surprise. "I had no idea that so gigantic a sum was involved," said he.

"Sir Charles had the reputation of being rich, but we did not know how very rich he was until we came to examine his securities. The total value of the estate was close on to a million."

"Dear me! It is a stake for which a man might well play a desperate game. And one more question, Dr. Mortimer. Supposing that anything happened to our young friend here—you will forgive the unpleasant hypothesis!--who would inherit the estate?"

"Since Rodger Baskerville, Sir Charles's younger brother died unmarried, the estate would descend to the Desmonds, who are distant cousins. James Desmond is an elderly clergyman in Westmoreland."

"Thank you. These details are all of great interest. Have you met Mr. James Desmond?"

"Yes; he once came down to visit Sir Charles. He is a man of venerable appearance and of saintly life. I remember that he refused to accept any settlement from Sir Charles, though he pressed it upon him."

"And this man of simple tastes would be the heir to Sir Charles's thousands."

"He would be the heir to the estate because that is entailed. He would also be the heir to the money unless it were willed otherwise by the present owner, who can, of course, do what he likes with it."

"And have you made your will, Sir Henry?"

"No, Mr. Holmes, I have not. I've had no time, for it was only yesterday that I learned how matters stood. But in any case I feel that the money should go with the title and estate. That was my poor uncle's idea. How is the owner going to restore the glories of the Baskervilles if he has not money enough to keep up the property? House, land, and dollars must go together."

"Quite so. Well, Sir Henry, I am of one mind with you as to the advisability of your going down to Devonshire without delay. There is only one provision which I must make. You certainly must not go alone."

"Dr. Mortimer returns with me."

"But Dr. Mortimer has his practice to attend to, and his house is miles away from yours. With all the goodwill in the world he may be unable to help you. No, Sir Henry, you must take with you someone, a trusty man, who will be always by your side."

"Is it possible that you could come yourself, Mr. Holmes?"

"If matters came to a crisis I should endeavour to be present in person; but you can understand that, with my extensive consulting practice and with the constant appeals which reach me from many quarters, it is impossible for me to be absent from London for an indefinite time. At the present instant one of the most revered names in England is being besmirched by a blackmailer, and only I can stop a disastrous scandal. You will see how impossible it is for me to go to Dartmoor."

"Whom would you recommend, then?"

Holmes laid his hand upon my arm. "If my friend would undertake it there is no man who is better worth having at your side when you are in a tight place. No one can say so more confidently than I."

The proposition took me completely by surprise, but before I had time to answer, Baskerville seized me by the hand and wrung it heartily.

"Well, now, that is real kind of you, Dr. Watson," said he. "You see how it is with me, and you know just as much about the matter as I do. If you will come down to Baskerville Hall and see me through I'll never forget it."

The promise of adventure had always a fascination for me, and I was complimented by the words of Holmes and by the eagerness with which the baronet hailed me as a companion.

"I will come, with pleasure," said I. "I do not know how I could employ my time better."

"And you will report very carefully to me," said Holmes. "When a crisis comes, as it will do, I will direct how you shall act. I suppose that by Saturday all might be ready?"

"Would that suit Dr. Watson?"

"Perfectly."

"Then on Saturday, unless you hear to the contrary, we shall meet at the ten-thirty train from Paddington."

We had risen to depart when Baskerville gave a cry, of triumph, and diving into one of the corners of the room he drew a brown boot from under a cabinet.

"My missing boot!" he cried.

"May all our difficulties vanish as easily!" said Sherlock Holmes.

"But it is a very singular thing," Dr. Mortimer remarked. "I searched this room carefully before lunch."

"And so did I," said Baskerville. "Every inch of it."

"There was certainly no boot in it then."

"In that case the waiter must have placed it there while we were lunching."

The German was sent for but professed to know nothing of the matter, nor could any inquiry clear it up. Another item had been added to that constant and apparently purposeless series of small mysteries which had succeeded each other so rapidly. Setting aside the whole grim story of Sir Charles's death, we had a line of inexplicable incidents all within the limits of two days, which included the receipt of the printed letter, the black-bearded spy in the hansom, the loss of the new brown boot, the loss of the old black boot, and now the return of the new brown boot. Holmes sat in silence in the cab as we drove back to Baker Street, and I knew from his drawn brows and keen face that his mind, like my own, was busy in endeavouring to frame some scheme into which all these strange and apparently disconnected episodes could be fitted. All afternoon and late into the evening he sat lost in tobacco and thought.

Just before dinner two telegrams were handed in. The first ran:

Have just heard that Barrymore is at the Hall. BASKERVILLE.

The second:

Visited twenty-three hotels as directed, but sorry, to report unable to trace cut sheet of Times. CARTWRIGHT.

"There go two of my threads, Watson. There is nothing more stimulating than a case where everything goes against you. We must cast round for another scent."

"We have still the cabman who drove the spy."

"Exactly. I have wired to get his name and address from the Official Registry. I should not be surprised if this were an answer to my question."

The ring at the bell proved to be something even more satisfactory than an answer, however, for the door opened and a rough-looking fellow entered who was evidently the man himself.

"I got a message from the head office that a gent at this address had been inquiring for No. 2704," said he. "I've driven my cab this seven years and never a word of complaint. I came here straight from the Yard to ask you to your face what you had against me."

"I have nothing in the world against you, my good man," said Holmes. "On the contrary, I have half a sovereign for you if you will give me a clear answer to my questions."

"Well, I've had a good day and no mistake," said the cabman with a grin. "What was it you wanted to ask, sir?"

"First of all your name and address, in case I want you again."

"John Clayton, 3 Turpey Street, the Borough. My cab is out of Shipley's Yard, near Waterloo Station."

Sherlock Holmes made a note of it.

"Now, Clayton, tell me all about the fare who came and watched this house at ten o'clock this morning and afterwards followed the two gentlemen down Regent Street."

The man looked surprised and a little embarrassed. "Why, there's no good my telling you things, for you seem to know as much as I do already," said he. "The truth is that the gentleman told me that he was a detective and that I was to say nothing about him to anyone."

"My good fellow; this is a very serious business, and you may find yourself in a pretty bad position if you try to hide anything from me. You say that your fare told you that he was a detective?"

"Yes, he did."

"When did he say this?"

"When he left me."

"Did he say anything more?"

"He mentioned his name."

Holmes cast a swift glance of triumph at me. "Oh, he mentioned his name, did he? That was imprudent. What was the name that he mentioned?"

"His name," said the cabman, "was Mr. Sherlock Holmes."

Never have I seen my friend more completely taken aback than by the cabman's reply. For an instant he sat in silent amazement. Then he burst into a hearty laugh.

"A touch, Watson—an undeniable touch!" said he. "I feel a foil as quick and supple as my own. He got home upon me very prettily that time. So his name was Sherlock Holmes, was it?"

"Yes, sir, that was the gentleman's name."

"Excellent! Tell me where you picked him up and all that occurred."

"He hailed me at half-past nine in Trafalgar Square. He said that he was a detective, and he offered me two guineas if I would do exactly what he wanted all day and ask no questions. I was glad enough to agree. First we drove down to the Northumberland Hotel and waited there until two gentlemen came out and took a cab from the rank. We followed their cab until it pulled up somewhere near here."

"This very door," said Holmes.

"Well, I couldn't be sure of that, but I dare say my fare knew all about it. We pulled up halfway down the street and waited an hour and a half. Then the two gentlemen passed us, walking, and we followed down Baker Street and along—"

"I know," said Holmes.

"Until we got three-quarters down Regent Street. Then my gentleman threw up the trap, and he cried that I should drive right away to Waterloo Station as hard as I could go. I whipped up the mare and we were there under the ten minutes. Then he paid up his two guineas, like a good one, and away he went into the station. Only just as he was leaving he turned round and he said: 'It might interest you to know that you have been driving Mr. Sherlock Holmes.' That's how I come to know the name."

"I see. And you saw no more of him?"

"Not after he went into the station."

"And how would you describe Mr. Sherlock Holmes?"

The cabman scratched his head. "Well, he wasn't altogether such an easy gentleman to describe. I'd put him at forty years of age, and he was of a middle height, two or three inches shorter than you, sir. He was dressed like a toff, and he had a black beard, cut square at the end, and a pale face. I don't know as I could say more than that."

"Colour of his eyes?"

"No, I can't say that."

"Nothing more that you can remember?"

"No, sir; nothing."

"Well, then, here is your half-sovereign. There's another one waiting for you if you can bring any more information. Good-night!"

"Good-night, sir, and thank you!"

John Clayton departed chuckling, and Holmes turned to me with a shrug of his shoulders and a rueful smile.

"Snap goes our third thread, and we end where we began," said he. "The cunning rascal! He knew our number, knew that Sir Henry Baskerville had consulted me, spotted who I was in Regent Street, conjectured that I had got the number of the cab and would lay my hands on the driver, and so sent back this audacious message. I tell you, Watson, this time we have got a foeman who is worthy of our steel. I've been checkmated in London. I can only wish you better luck in Devonshire. But I'm not easy in my mind about it."

"About what?"

"About sending you. It's an ugly business, Watson, an ugly dangerous business, and the more I see of it the less I like it. Yes, my dear fellow, you may laugh, but I give you my word that I shall be very glad to have you back safe and sound in Baker Street once more."

Chapter 6. Baskerville Hall

Sir Henry Baskerville and Dr. Mortimer were ready upon the appointed day, and we started as arranged for Devonshire. Mr. Sherlock Holmes drove with me to the station and gave me his last parting injunctions and advice.

"I will not bias your mind by suggesting theories or suspicions, Watson," said he; "I wish you simply to report facts in the fullest possible manner to me, and you can leave me to do the theorizing."

"What sort of facts?" I asked.

"Anything which may seem to have a bearing however indirect upon the case, and especially the relations between young Baskerville and his neighbours or any fresh particulars concerning the death of Sir Charles. I have made some inquiries myself in the last few days, but the results have, I fear, been negative. One thing only appears to be certain, and that is that Mr. James Desmond, who is the next heir, is an elderly gentleman of a very amiable disposition, so that this persecution does not arise from him. I really think that we may eliminate him entirely from our calculations. There remain the people who will actually surround Sir Henry Baskerville upon the moor."

"Would it not be well in the first place to get rid of this Barrymore couple?"

"By no means. You could not make a greater mistake. If they are innocent it would be a cruel injustice, and if they are guilty we should be giving up all chance of bringing it home to them. No, no, we will preserve them upon our list of suspects. Then there is a groom at the Hall, if I remember right. There are two moorland farmers. There is our friend Dr. Mortimer, whom I believe to be entirely honest, and there is his wife, of whom we know nothing. There is this naturalist, Stapleton, and there is his sister, who is said to be a young lady of attractions. There is Mr. Frankland, of Lafter Hall, who is also an unknown factor, and there are one or two other neighbours. These are the folk who must be your very special study."

"I will do my best."

"You have arms, I suppose?"

"Yes, I thought it as well to take them."

"Most certainly. Keep your revolver near you night and day, and never relax your precautions."

Our friends had already secured a first-class carriage and were waiting for us upon the platform.

"No, we have no news of any kind," said Dr. Mortimer in answer to my friend's questions. "I can swear to one thing, and that is that we have not been shadowed during the last two days. We have never gone out without keeping a sharp watch, and no one could have escaped our notice."

"You have always kept together, I presume?"

"Except yesterday afternoon. I usually give up one day to pure amusement when I come to town, so I spent it at the Museum of the College of Surgeons."

"And I went to look at the folk in the park," said Baskerville.

"But we had no trouble of any kind."

"It was imprudent, all the same," said Holmes, shaking his head and looking very grave. "I beg, Sir Henry, that you will not go about alone. Some great misfortune will befall you if you do. Did you get your other boot?"

"No, sir, it is gone forever."

"Indeed. That is very interesting. Well, good-bye," he added as the train began to glide down the platform. "Bear in mind, Sir Henry, one of the phrases in that queer old legend which Dr. Mortimer has read to us, and avoid the moor in those hours of darkness when the powers of evil are exalted."

I looked back at the platform when we had left it far behind and saw the tall, austere figure of Holmes standing motionless and gazing after us.

The journey was a swift and pleasant one, and I spent it in making the more intimate acquaintance of my two companions and in playing with Dr. Mortimer's spaniel. In a very few hours the brown earth had become ruddy, the brick had changed to granite, and red cows grazed in well-hedged fields where the lush grasses and more luxuriant vegetation spoke of a richer, if a damper, climate. Young Baskerville stared eagerly out of the window and cried aloud with delight as he recognized the familiar features of the Devon scenery.

"I've been over a good part of the world since I left it, Dr. Watson," said he; "but I have never seen a place to compare with it."

"I never saw a Devonshire man who did not swear by his county," I remarked.

"It depends upon the breed of men quite as much as on the county," said Dr. Mortimer. "A glance at our friend here reveals the rounded head of the Celt, which carries inside it the Celtic enthusiasm and power of attachment. Poor Sir Charles's head was of a very rare type, half Gaelic, half Ivernian in its characteristics. But you were very young when you last saw Baskerville Hall, were you not?"

"I was a boy in my teens at the time of my father's death and had never seen the Hall, for he lived in a little cottage on the South Coast. Thence I went straight to a friend in America. I tell you it is all as new to me as it is to Dr. Watson, and I'm as keen as possible to see the moor."

"Are you? Then your wish is easily granted, for there is your first sight of the moor," said Dr. Mortimer, pointing out of the carriage window.

Over the green squares of the fields and the low curve of a wood there rose in the distance a gray, melancholy hill, with a strange jagged summit, dim and vague in the distance, like some fantastic landscape in a dream. Baskerville sat for a long time, his eyes fixed upon it, and I read upon his eager face how much it meant to him, this first sight of that strange spot where the men of his blood had held sway so long and left their mark so deep. There he sat, with his tweed suit and his American accent, in the corner of a prosaic railway-carriage, and yet as I looked at his dark and expressive face I felt more than ever how true a descendant he was of that long line of high-blooded, fiery, and masterful men. There were pride, valour, and strength in his thick brows, his sensitive nostrils, and his large hazel eyes. If on that forbidding moor a difficult and dangerous quest should lie before us, this was at least a comrade for whom one might venture to take a risk with the certainty that he would bravely share it.

The train pulled up at a small wayside station and we all descended. Outside, beyond the low, white fence, a wagonette with a pair of cobs was waiting. Our coming was evidently a great event, for station-master and porters clustered round us to carry out our luggage. It was a sweet, simple country spot, but I was surprised to observe that by the gate there stood two soldierly men in dark uniforms who leaned upon their short rifles and glanced keenly at us as we passed. The coachman, a hard-faced, gnarled little fellow, saluted Sir Henry Baskerville, and in a few minutes we were flying swiftly down the broad, white road. Rolling pasture lands curved upward on either side of us, and old gabled houses peeped out from amid the thick green foliage, but behind the peaceful and sunlit countryside there rose ever, dark against the evening sky, the long, gloomy curve of the moor, broken by the jagged and sinister hills.

The wagonette swung round into a side road, and we curved upward through deep lanes worn by centuries of wheels, high banks on either side, heavy with dripping moss and fleshy hart's-tongue ferns. Bronzing bracken and mottled bramble gleamed in the light of the sinking sun. Still steadily rising, we passed over a narrow granite bridge and skirted a noisy stream which gushed swiftly down, foaming and roaring amid the gray boulders. Both road and stream wound up through a valley dense with scrub oak and fir. At every turn Baskerville gave an exclamation of delight, looking eagerly about him and asking countless questions. To his eyes all seemed beautiful, but to me a tinge of melancholy lay upon the countryside, which bore so clearly the mark of the waning year. Yellow leaves carpeted the lanes and fluttered down upon us as we passed. The rattle of our wheels died away as we drove through drifts of rotting vegetation—sad gifts, as it seemed to me, for Nature to throw before the carriage of the returning heir of the Baskervilles.

"Halloa!" cried Dr. Mortimer, "what is this?"

A steep curve of heath-clad land, an outlying spur of the moor, lay in front of us. On the summit, hard and clear like an equestrian statue upon its pedestal, was a mounted soldier, dark and stern, his rifle poised ready over his forearm. He was watching the road along which we travelled.

"What is this, Perkins?" asked Dr. Mortimer.

Our driver half turned in his seat. "There's a convict escaped from Princetown, sir. He's been out three days now, and the warders watch every road and every station, but they've had no sight of him yet. The farmers about here don't like it, sir, and that's a fact."

"Well, I understand that they get five pounds if they can give information."

"Yes, sir, but the chance of five pounds is but a poor thing compared to the chance of having your throat cut. You see, it isn't like any ordinary convict. This is a man that would stick at nothing."

"Who is he, then?"

"It is Selden, the Notting Hill murderer."

I remembered the case well, for it was one in which Holmes had taken an interest on account of the peculiar ferocity of the crime and the wanton brutality which had marked all the actions of the assassin. The commutation of his death sentence had been due to some doubts as to his complete sanity, so atrocious was his conduct. Our wagonette had topped a rise and in front of us rose the huge expanse of the moor, mottled with gnarled and craggy cairns and tors. A cold wind swept down from it and set us shivering. Somewhere there, on that desolate plain, was lurking this fiendish man, hiding in a burrow like a wild beast, his heart full of malignancy against the whole race which had cast him out. It needed but this to complete the grim suggestiveness of the barren waste, the chilling wind, and the darkling sky. Even Baskerville fell silent and pulled his overcoat more closely around him.

We had left the fertile country behind and beneath us. We looked back on it now, the slanting rays of a low sun turning the streams to threads of gold and glowing on the red earth new turned by the plough and the broad tangle of the woodlands. The road in front of us grew bleaker and wilder over huge russet and olive slopes, sprinkled with giant boulders. Now and then we passed a moorland cottage, walled and roofed with stone, with no creeper to break its harsh outline. Suddenly we looked down into a cuplike depression, patched with stunted oaks and firs which had been twisted and bent by the fury of years of storm. Two high, narrow towers rose over the trees. The driver pointed with his whip.

"Baskerville Hall," said he.

Its master had risen and was staring with flushed cheeks and shining eyes. A few minutes later we had reached the lodge-gates, a maze of fantastic tracery in wrought iron, with weather-bitten pillars on either side, blotched with lichens, and surmounted by the boars' heads of the Baskervilles. The lodge was a ruin of black granite and bared ribs of rafters, but facing it was a new building, half constructed, the first fruit of Sir Charles's South African gold.

Through the gateway we passed into the avenue, where the wheels were again hushed amid the leaves, and the old trees shot their branches in a sombre tunnel over our heads. Baskerville shuddered as he looked up the long, dark drive to where the house glimmered like a ghost at the farther end.

"Was it here?" he asked in a low voice.

"No, no, the yew alley is on the other side."

The young heir glanced round with a gloomy face.

"It's no wonder my uncle felt as if trouble were coming on him in such a place as this," said he. "It's enough to scare any man. I'll have a row of electric lamps up here inside of six months, and you won't know it again, with a thousand candle-power Swan and Edison right here in front of the hall door."

The avenue opened into a broad expanse of turf, and the house lay before us. In the fading light I could see that the centre was a heavy block of building from which a porch projected. The whole front was draped in ivy, with a patch clipped bare here and there where a window or a coat of arms broke through the dark veil. From this central block rose the twin towers, ancient, crenelated, and pierced with many loopholes. To right and left of the turrets were more modern wings of black granite. A dull light shone through heavy mullioned windows, and from the high chimneys which rose from the steep, high-angled roof there sprang a single black column of smoke.

"Welcome, Sir Henry! Welcome to Baskerville Hall!"

A tall man had stepped from the shadow of the porch to open the door of the wagonette. The figure of a woman was silhouetted against the yellow light of the hall. She came out and helped the man to hand down our bags.

"You don't mind my driving straight home, Sir Henry?" said Dr. Mortimer. "My wife is expecting me."

"Surely you will stay and have some dinner?"

"No, I must go. I shall probably find some work awaiting me. I would stay to show you over the house, but Barrymore will be a better guide than I. Good-bye, and never hesitate night or day to send for me if I can be of service."

The wheels died away down the drive while Sir Henry and I turned into the hall, and the door clanged heavily behind us. It was a fine apartment in which we found ourselves, large, lofty, and heavily raftered with huge baulks of age-blackened oak. In the great old-fashioned fireplace behind the high iron dogs a log-fire crackled and snapped. Sir Henry and I held out our hands to it, for we were numb from our long drive. Then we gazed round us at the high, thin window of old stained glass, the oak panelling, the stags' heads, the coats of arms upon the walls, all dim and sombre in the subdued light of the central lamp.

"It's just as I imagined it," said Sir Henry. "Is it not the very picture of an old family home? To think that this should be the same hall in which for five hundred years my people have lived. It strikes me solemn to think of it."

I saw his dark face lit up with a boyish enthusiasm as he gazed about him. The light beat upon him where he stood, but long shadows trailed down the walls and hung like a black canopy above him. Barrymore had returned from taking our luggage to our rooms. He stood in front of us now with the subdued manner of a well-trained servant. He was a remarkable-looking man, tall, handsome, with a square black beard and pale, distinguished features.

"Would you wish dinner to be served at once, sir?"

"Is it ready?"

"In a very few minutes, sir. You will find hot water in your rooms. My wife and I will be happy, Sir Henry, to stay with you until you have made your fresh arrangements, but you will understand that under the new conditions this house will require a considerable staff."

"What new conditions?"

"I only meant, sir, that Sir Charles led a very retired life, and we were able to look after his wants. You would, naturally, wish to have more company, and so you will need changes in your household."

"Do you mean that your wife and you wish to leave?"

"Only when it is quite convenient to you, sir."

"But your family have been with us for several generations, have they not? I should be sorry to begin my life here by breaking an old family connection."

I seemed to discern some signs of emotion upon the butler's white face.

"I feel that also, sir, and so does my wife. But to tell the truth, sir, we were both very much attached to Sir Charles, and his death gave us a shock and made these surroundings very painful to us. I fear that we shall never again be easy in our minds at Baskerville Hall."

"But what do you intend to do?"

"I have no doubt, sir, that we shall succeed in establishing ourselves in some business. Sir Charles's generosity has given us the means to do so. And now, sir, perhaps I had best show you to your rooms."

A square balustraded gallery ran round the top of the old hall, approached by a double stair. From this central point two long corridors extended the whole length of the building, from which all the bedrooms opened. My own was in the same wing as Baskerville's and almost next door to it. These rooms appeared to be much more modern than the central part of the house, and the bright paper and numerous candles did something to remove the sombre impression which our arrival had left upon my mind.

But the dining-room which opened out of the hall was a place of shadow and gloom. It was a long chamber with a step separating the dais where the family sat from the lower portion reserved for their dependents. At one end a minstrel's gallery overlooked it. Black beams shot across above our heads, with a smoke-darkened ceiling beyond them. With rows of flaring torches to light it up, and the colour and rude hilarity of an old-time banquet, it might have softened; but now, when two black-clothed gentlemen sat in the little circle of light thrown by a shaded lamp, one's voice became hushed and one's spirit subdued. A dim line of ancestors, in every variety of dress, from the Elizabethan knight to the buck of the Regency, stared down upon us and daunted us by their silent company. We talked little, and I for one was glad when the meal was over and we were able to retire into the modern billiard-room and smoke a cigarette.

"My word, it isn't a very cheerful place," said Sir Henry. "I suppose one can tone down to it, but I feel a bit out of the picture at present. I don't wonder that my uncle got a little jumpy if he lived all alone in such a house as this. However, if it suits you, we will retire early tonight, and perhaps things may seem more cheerful in the morning."

I drew aside my curtains before I went to bed and looked out from my window. It opened upon the grassy space which lay in front of the hall door. Beyond, two copses of trees moaned and swung in a rising wind. A half moon broke through the rifts of racing clouds. In its cold light I saw beyond the trees a broken fringe of rocks, and the long, low curve of the melancholy moor. I closed the curtain, feeling that my last impression was in keeping with the rest.

And yet it was not quite the last. I found myself weary and yet wakeful, tossing restlessly from side to side, seeking for the sleep which would not come. Far away a chiming clock struck out the quarters of the hours, but otherwise a deathly silence lay upon the old house. And then suddenly, in the very dead of the night, there came a sound to my ears, clear, resonant, and unmistakable. It was the sob of a woman, the muffled, strangling gasp of one who is torn by an uncontrollable sorrow. I sat up in bed and listened intently. The noise could not have been far away and was certainly in the house. For half an hour I waited with every nerve on the alert, but there came no other sound save the chiming clock and the rustle of the ivy on the wall.

Chapter 7. The Stapletons of Merripit House

The fresh beauty of the following morning did something to efface from our minds the grim and gray impression which had been left upon both of us by our first experience of Baskerville Hall. As Sir Henry and I sat at breakfast the sunlight flooded in through the high mullioned windows, throwing watery patches of colour from the coats of arms which covered them. The dark panelling glowed like bronze in the golden rays, and it was hard to realize that this was indeed the chamber which had struck such a gloom into our souls upon the evening before.

"I guess it is ourselves and not the house that we have to blame!" said the baronet. "We were tired with our journey and chilled by our drive, so we took a gray view of the place. Now we are fresh and well, so it is all cheerful once more."

"And yet it was not entirely a question of imagination," I answered. "Did you, for example, happen to hear someone, a woman I think, sobbing in the night?"

"That is curious, for I did when I was half asleep fancy that I heard something of the sort. I waited quite a time, but there was no more of it, so I concluded that it was all a dream."

"I heard it distinctly, and I am sure that it was really the sob of a woman."

"We must ask about this right away." He rang the bell and asked Barrymore whether he could account for our experience. It seemed to me that the pallid features of the butler turned a shade paler still as he listened to his master's question.

"There are only two women in the house, Sir Henry," he answered. "One is the scullery-maid, who sleeps in the other wing. The other is my wife, and I can answer for it that the sound could not have come from her."

And yet he lied as he said it, for it chanced that after breakfast I met Mrs. Barrymore in the long corridor with the sun full upon her face. She was a large, impassive, heavy-featured woman with a stern set expression of mouth. But her telltale eyes were red and glanced at me from between swollen lids. It was she, then, who wept in the night, and if she did so her husband must know it. Yet he had taken the obvious risk of discovery in declaring that it was not so. Why had he done this? And why did she weep so bitterly? Already round this pale-faced, handsome, black-bearded man there was gathering an atmosphere of mystery and of gloom. It was he who had been the first to discover the body of Sir Charles, and we had only his word for all the circumstances which led up to the old man's death. Was it possible that it was Barrymore, after all, whom we had seen in the cab in Regent Street? The beard might well have been the same. The cabman had described a somewhat shorter man, but such an impression might easily have been erroneous. How could I settle the point forever? Obviously the first thing to do was to see the Grimpen postmaster and find whether the test telegram had really been placed in Barrymore's own hands. Be the answer what it might, I should at least have something to report to Sherlock Holmes.

Sir Henry had numerous papers to examine after breakfast, so that the time was propitious for my excursion. It was a pleasant walk of four miles along the edge of the moor, leading me at last to a small gray hamlet, in which two larger buildings, which proved to be the inn and the house of Dr. Mortimer, stood high above the rest. The postmaster, who was also the village grocer, had a clear recollection of the telegram.

"Certainly, sir," said he, "I had the telegram delivered to Mr. Barrymore exactly as directed."

"Who delivered it?"

"My boy here. James, you delivered that telegram to Mr. Barrymore at the Hall last week, did you not?"

"Yes, father, I delivered it."

"Into his own hands?" I asked.

"Well, he was up in the loft at the time, so that I could not put it into his own hands, but I gave it into Mrs. Barrymore's hands, and she promised to deliver it at once."

"Did you see Mr. Barrymore?"

"No, sir; I tell you he was in the loft."

"If you didn't see him, how do you know he was in the loft?"

"Well, surely his own wife ought to know where he is," said the postmaster testily. "Didn't he get the telegram? If there is any mistake it is for Mr. Barrymore himself to complain."

It seemed hopeless to pursue the inquiry any farther, but it was clear that in spite of Holmes's ruse we had no proof that Barrymore had not been in London all the time. Suppose that it were so—suppose that the same man had been the last who had seen Sir Charles alive, and the first to dog the new heir when he returned to England. What then? Was he the agent of others or had he some sinister design of his own? What interest could he have in persecuting the Baskerville family? I thought of the strange warning clipped out of the leading article of the Times. Was that his work or was it possibly the doing of someone who was bent upon counteracting his schemes? The only conceivable motive was that which had been suggested by Sir Henry, that if the family could be scared away a comfortable and permanent home would be secured for the Barrymores. But surely such an explanation as that would be quite inadequate to account for the deep and subtle scheming which seemed to be weaving an invisible net round the young baronet. Holmes himself had said that no more complex case had come to him in all the long series of his sensational investigations. I prayed, as I walked back along the gray, lonely road, that my friend might soon be freed from his preoccupations and able to come down to take this heavy burden of responsibility from my shoulders.

Suddenly my thoughts were interrupted by the sound of running feet behind me and by a voice which called me by name. I turned, expecting to see Dr. Mortimer, but to my surprise it was a stranger who was pursuing me. He was a small, slim, clean-shaven, prim-faced man, flaxen-haired and leanjawed, between thirty and forty years of age, dressed in a gray suit and wearing a straw hat. A tin box for botanical specimens hung over his shoulder and he carried a green butterfly-net in one of his hands.

"You will, I am sure, excuse my presumption, Dr. Watson," said he as he came panting up to where I stood. "Here on the moor we are homely folk and do not wait for formal introductions. You may possibly have heard my name from our mutual friend, Mortimer. I am Stapleton, of Merripit House."

"Your net and box would have told me as much," said I, "for I knew that Mr. Stapleton was a naturalist. But how did you know me?"

"I have been calling on Mortimer, and he pointed you out to me from the window of his surgery as you passed. As our road lay the same way I thought that I would overtake you and introduce myself. I trust that Sir Henry is none the worse for his journey?"

"He is very well, thank you."

"We were all rather afraid that after the sad death of Sir Charles the new baronet might refuse to live here. It is asking much of a wealthy man to come down and bury himself in a place of this kind, but I need not tell you that it means a very great deal to the countryside. Sir Henry has, I suppose, no superstitious fears in the matter?"

"I do not think that it is likely."

"Of course you know the legend of the fiend dog which haunts the family?"

"I have heard it."

"It is extraordinary how credulous the peasants are about here! Any number of them are ready to swear that they have seen such a creature upon the moor." He spoke with a smile, but I seemed to read in his eyes that he took the matter more seriously. "The story took a great hold upon the imagination of Sir Charles, and I have no doubt that it led to his tragic end."

"But how?"

"His nerves were so worked up that the appearance of any dog might have had a fatal effect upon his diseased heart. I fancy that he really did see something of the kind upon that last night in the yew alley. I feared that some disaster might occur, for I was very fond of the old man, and I knew that his heart was weak."

"How did you know that?"

"My friend Mortimer told me."

"You think, then, that some dog pursued Sir Charles, and that he died of fright in consequence?"

"Have you any better explanation?"

"I have not come to any conclusion."

"Has Mr. Sherlock Holmes?"

The words took away my breath for an instant but a glance at the placid face and steadfast eyes of my companion showed that no surprise was intended.

"It is useless for us to pretend that we do not know you, Dr. Watson," said he. "The records of your detective have reached us here, and you could not celebrate him without being known yourself. When Mortimer told me your name he could not deny your identity. If you are here, then it follows that Mr. Sherlock Holmes is interesting himself in the matter, and I am naturally curious to know what view he may take."

"I am afraid that I cannot answer that question."

"May I ask if he is going to honour us with a visit himself?"

"He cannot leave town at present. He has other cases which engage his attention."

"What a pity! He might throw some light on that which is so dark to us. But as to your own researches, if there is any possible way in which I can be of service to you I trust that you will command me. If I had any indication of the nature of your suspicions or how you propose to investigate the case, I might perhaps even now give you some aid or advice."

"I assure you that I am simply here upon a visit to my friend, Sir Henry, and that I need no help of any kind."

"Excellent!" said Stapleton. "You are perfectly right to be wary and discreet. I am justly reproved for what I feel was an unjustifiable intrusion, and I promise you that I will not mention the matter again."

We had come to a point where a narrow grassy path struck off from the road and wound away across the moor. A steep, boulder-sprinkled hill lay upon the right which had in bygone days been cut into a granite quarry. The face which was turned towards us formed a dark cliff, with ferns and brambles growing in its niches. From over a distant rise there floated a gray plume of smoke.

"A moderate walk along this moor-path brings us to Merripit House," said he. "Perhaps you will spare an hour that I may have the pleasure of introducing you to my sister."

My first thought was that I should be by Sir Henry's side. But then I remembered the pile of papers and bills with which his study table was littered. It was certain that I could not help with those. And Holmes had expressly said that I should study the neighbours upon the moor. I accepted Stapleton's invitation, and we turned together down the path.

"It is a wonderful place, the moor," said he, looking round over the undulating downs, long green rollers, with crests of jagged granite foaming up into fantastic surges. "You never tire of the moor. You cannot think the wonderful secrets which it contains. It is so vast, and so barren, and so mysterious."

"You know it well, then?"

"I have only been here two years. The residents would call me a newcomer. We came shortly after Sir Charles settled. But my tastes led me to explore every part of the country round, and I should think that there are few men who know it better than I do."

"Is it hard to know?"

"Very hard. You see, for example, this great plain to the north here with the queer hills breaking out of it. Do you observe anything remarkable about that?"

"It would be a rare place for a gallop."

"You would naturally think so and the thought has cost several their lives before now. You notice those bright green spots scattered thickly over it?"

"Yes, they seem more fertile than the rest."

Stapleton laughed. "That is the great Grimpen Mire," said he. "A false step yonder means death to man or beast. Only yesterday I saw one of the moor ponies wander into it. He never came out. I saw his head for quite a long time craning out of the bog-hole, but it sucked him down at last. Even in dry seasons it is a danger to cross it, but after these autumn rains it is an awful place. And yet I can find my way to the very heart of it and return alive. By George, there is another of those miserable ponies!"

Something brown was rolling and tossing among the green sedges. Then a long, agonized, writhing neck shot upward and a dreadful cry echoed over the moor. It turned me cold with horror, but my companion's nerves seemed to be stronger than mine.

"It's gone!" said he. "The mire has him. Two in two days, and many more, perhaps, for they get in the way of going there in the dry weather and never know the difference until the mire has them in its clutches. It's a bad place, the great Grimpen Mire."

"And you say you can penetrate it?"

"Yes, there are one or two paths which a very active man can take. I have found them out."

"But why should you wish to go into so horrible a place?"

"Well, you see the hills beyond? They are really islands cut off on all sides by the impassable mire, which has crawled round them in the course of years. That is where the rare plants and the butterflies are, if you have the wit to reach them."

"I shall try my luck some day."

He looked at me with a surprised face. "For God's sake put such an idea out of your mind," said he. "Your blood would be upon my head. I assure you that there would not be the least chance of your coming back alive. It is only by remembering certain complex landmarks that I am able to do it."

"Halloa!" I cried. "What is that?"

A long, low moan, indescribably sad, swept over the moor. It filled the whole air, and yet it was impossible to say whence it came. From a dull murmur it swelled into a deep roar, and then sank back into a melancholy, throbbing murmur once again. Stapleton looked at me with a curious expression in his face.

"Queer place, the moor!" said he.

"But what is it?"

"The peasants say it is the Hound of the Baskervilles calling for its prey. I've heard it once or twice before, but never quite so loud."

I looked round, with a chill of fear in my heart, at the huge swelling plain, mottled with the green patches of rushes. Nothing stirred over the vast expanse save a pair of ravens, which croaked loudly from a tor behind us.

"You are an educated man. You don't believe such nonsense as that?" said I. "What do you think is the cause of so strange a sound?"

"Bogs make queer noises sometimes. It's the mud settling, or the water rising, or something."

"No, no, that was a living voice."

"Well, perhaps it was. Did you ever hear a bittern booming?"

"No, I never did."

"It's a very rare bird—practically extinct—in England now, but all things are possible upon the moor. Yes, I should not be surprised to learn that what we have heard is the cry of the last of the bitterns."

"It's the weirdest, strangest thing that ever I heard in my life."

"Yes, it's rather an uncanny place altogether. Look at the hillside yonder. What do you make of those?"

The whole steep slope was covered with gray circular rings of stone, a score of them at least.

"What are they? Sheep-pens?"

"No, they are the homes of our worthy ancestors. Prehistoric man lived thickly on the moor, and as no one in particular has lived there since, we find all his little arrangements exactly as he left them. These are his wigwams with the roofs off. You can even see his hearth and his couch if you have the curiosity to go inside.

"But it is quite a town. When was it inhabited?"

"Neolithic man—no date."

"What did he do?"

"He grazed his cattle on these slopes, and he learned to dig for tin when the bronze sword began to supersede the stone axe. Look at the great trench in the opposite hill. That is his mark. Yes, you will find some very singular points about the moor, Dr. Watson. Oh, excuse me an instant! It is surely Cyclopides."

A small fly or moth had fluttered across our path, and in an instant Stapleton was rushing with extraordinary energy and speed in pursuit of it. To my dismay the creature flew straight for the great mire, and my acquaintance never paused for an instant, bounding from tuft to tuft behind it, his green net waving in the air. His gray clothes and jerky, zigzag, irregular progress made him not unlike some huge moth himself. I was standing watching his pursuit with a mixture of admiration for his extraordinary activity and fear lest he should lose his footing in the treacherous mire, when I heard the sound of steps and, turning round, found a woman near me upon the path. She had come from the direction in which the plume of smoke indicated the position of Merripit House, but the dip of the moor had hid her until she was quite close.

I could not doubt that this was the Miss Stapleton of whom I had been told, since ladies of any sort must be few upon the moor, and I remembered that I had heard someone describe her as being a beauty. The woman who approached me was certainly that, and of a most uncommon type. There could not have been a greater contrast between brother and sister, for Stapleton was neutral tinted, with light hair and gray eyes, while she was darker than any brunette whom I have seen in England—slim, elegant, and tall. She had a proud, finely cut face, so regular that it might have seemed impassive were it not for the sensitive mouth and the beautiful dark, eager eyes. With her perfect figure and elegant dress she was, indeed, a strange apparition upon a lonely moorland path. Her eyes were on her brother as I turned, and then she quickened her pace towards me. I had raised my hat and was about to make some explanatory remark when her own words turned all my thoughts into a new channel.

"Go back!" she said. "Go straight back to London, instantly."

I could only stare at her in stupid surprise. Her eyes blazed at me, and she tapped the ground impatiently with her foot.

"Why should I go back?" I asked.

"I cannot explain." She spoke in a low, eager voice, with a curious lisp in her utterance. "But for God's sake do what I ask you. Go back and never set foot upon the moor again."

"But I have only just come."

"Man, man!" she cried. "Can you not tell when a warning is for your own good? Go back to London! Start tonight! Get away from this place at all costs! Hush, my brother is coming! Not a word of what I have said. Would you mind getting that orchid for me among the mare's-tails yonder? We are very rich in orchids on the moor, though, of course, you are rather late to see the beauties of the place."

Stapleton had abandoned the chase and came back to us breathing hard and flushed with his exertions.

"Halloa, Beryl!" said he, and it seemed to me that the tone of his greeting was not altogether a cordial one.

"Well, Jack, you are very hot."

"Yes, I was chasing a Cyclopides. He is very rare and seldom found in the late autumn. What a pity that I should have missed him!" He spoke unconcernedly, but his small light eyes glanced incessantly from the girl to me.

"You have introduced yourselves, I can see."

"Yes. I was telling Sir Henry that it was rather late for him to see the true beauties of the moor."

"Why, who do you think this is?"

"I imagine that it must be Sir Henry Baskerville."

"No, no," said I. "Only a humble commoner, but his friend. My name is Dr. Watson."

A flush of vexation passed over her expressive face. "We have been talking at cross purposes," said she.

"Why, you had not very much time for talk," her brother remarked with the same questioning eyes.

"I talked as if Dr. Watson were a resident instead of being merely a visitor," said she. "It cannot much matter to him whether it is early or late for the orchids. But you will come on, will you not, and see Merripit House?"

A short walk brought us to it, a bleak moorland house, once the farm of some grazier in the old prosperous days, but now put into repair and turned into a modern dwelling. An orchard surrounded it, but the trees, as is usual upon the moor, were stunted and nipped, and the effect of the whole place was mean and melancholy. We were admitted by a strange, wizened, rusty-coated old manservant, who seemed in keeping with the house. Inside, however, there were large rooms furnished with an elegance in which I seemed to recognize the taste of the lady. As I looked from their windows at the interminable granite-flecked moor rolling unbroken to the farthest horizon I could not but marvel at what could have brought this highly educated man and this beautiful woman to live in such a place.

"Queer spot to choose, is it not?" said he as if in answer to my thought. "And yet we manage to make ourselves fairly happy, do we not, Beryl?"

"Quite happy," said she, but there was no ring of conviction in her words.

"I had a school," said Stapleton. "It was in the north country. The work to a man of my temperament was mechanical and uninteresting, but the privilege of living with youth, of helping to mould those young minds, and of impressing them with one's own character and ideals was very dear to me. However, the fates were against us. A serious epidemic broke out in the school and three of the boys died. It never recovered from the blow, and much of my capital was irretrievably swallowed up. And yet, if it were not for the loss of the charming companionship of the boys, I could rejoice over my own misfortune, for, with my strong tastes for botany and zoology, I find an unlimited field of work here, and my sister is as devoted to Nature as I am. All this, Dr. Watson, has been brought upon your head by your expression as you surveyed the moor out of our window."

"It certainly did cross my mind that it might be a little dull—less for you, perhaps, than for your sister."

"No, no, I am never dull," said she quickly.

"We have books, we have our studies, and we have interesting neighbours. Dr. Mortimer is a most learned man in his own line. Poor Sir Charles was also an admirable companion. We knew him well and miss him more than I can tell. Do you think that I should intrude if I were to call this afternoon and make the acquaintance of Sir Henry?"

"I am sure that he would be delighted."

"Then perhaps you would mention that I propose to do so. We may in our humble way do something to make things more easy for him until he becomes accustomed to his new surroundings. Will you come upstairs, Dr. Watson, and inspect my collection of Lepidoptera? I think it is the most complete one in the south-west of England. By the time that you have looked through them lunch will be almost ready."

But I was eager to get back to my charge. The melancholy of the moor, the death of the unfortunate pony, the weird sound which had been associated with the grim legend of the Baskervilles, all these things tinged my thoughts with sadness. Then on the top of these more or less vague impressions there had come the definite and distinct warning of Miss Stapleton, delivered with such intense earnestness that I could not doubt that some grave and deep reason lay behind it. I resisted all pressure to stay for lunch, and I set off at once upon my return journey, taking the grass-grown path by which we had come.

It seems, however, that there must have been some short cut for those who knew it, for before I had reached the road I was astounded to see Miss Stapleton sitting upon a rock by the side of the track. Her face was beautifully flushed with her exertions and she held her hand to her side.

"I have run all the way in order to cut you off, Dr. Watson," said she. "I had not even time to put on my hat. I must not stop, or my brother may miss me. I wanted to say to you how sorry I am about the stupid mistake I made in thinking that you were Sir Henry. Please forget the words I said, which have no application whatever to you."

"But I can't forget them, Miss Stapleton," said I. "I am Sir Henry's friend, and his welfare is a very close concern of mine. Tell me why it was that you were so eager that Sir Henry should return to London."

"A woman's whim, Dr. Watson. When you know me better you will understand that I cannot always give reasons for what I say or do."

"No, no. I remember the thrill in your voice. I remember the look in your eyes. Please, please, be frank with me, Miss Stapleton, for ever since I have been here I have been conscious of shadows all round me. Life has become like that great Grimpen Mire, with little green patches everywhere into which one may sink and with no guide to point the track. Tell me then what it was that you meant, and I will promise to convey your warning to Sir Henry."

An expression of irresolution passed for an instant over her face, but her eyes had hardened again when she answered me.

"You make too much of it, Dr. Watson," said she. "My brother and I were very much shocked by the death of Sir Charles. We knew him very intimately, for his favourite walk was over the moor to our house. He was deeply impressed with the curse which hung over the family, and when this tragedy came I naturally felt that there must be some grounds for the fears which he had expressed. I was distressed therefore when another member of the family came down to live here, and I felt that he should be warned of the danger which he will run. That was all which I intended to convey.

"But what is the danger?"

"You know the story of the hound?"

"I do not believe in such nonsense."

"But I do. If you have any influence with Sir Henry, take him away from a place which has always been fatal to his family. The world is wide. Why should he wish to live at the place of danger?"

"Because it is the place of danger. That is Sir Henry's nature. I fear that unless you can give me some more definite information than this it would be impossible to get him to move."

"I cannot say anything definite, for I do not know anything definite."

"I would ask you one more question, Miss Stapleton. If you meant no more than this when you first spoke to me, why should you not wish your brother to overhear what you said? There is nothing to which he, or anyone else, could object."

"My brother is very anxious to have the Hall inhabited, for he thinks it is for the good of the poor folk upon the moor. He would be very angry if he knew that I have said anything which might induce Sir Henry to go away. But I have done my duty now and I will say no more. I must go back, or he will miss me and suspect that I have seen you. Good-bye!" She turned and had disappeared in a few minutes among the scattered boulders, while I, with my soul full of vague fears, pursued my way to Baskerville Hall.

Chapter 8. First Report of Dr. Watson

From this point onward I will follow the course of events by transcribing my own letters to Mr. Sherlock Holmes which lie before me on the table. One page is missing, but otherwise they are exactly as written and show my feelings and suspicions of the moment more accurately than my memory, clear as it is upon these tragic events, can possibly do.

Baskerville Hall, October 13th. MY DEAR HOLMES: My previous letters and telegrams have kept you pretty well up to date as to all that has occurred in this most God-forsaken corner of the world. The longer one stays here the more does the spirit of the moor sink into one's soul, its vastness, and also its grim charm. When you are once out upon its bosom you have left all traces of modern England behind you, but, on the other hand, you are conscious everywhere of the homes and the work of the prehistoric people. On all sides of you as you walk are the houses of these forgotten folk, with their graves and the huge monoliths which are supposed to have marked their temples. As you look at their gray stone huts against the scarred hillsides you leave your own age behind you, and if you were to see a skin-clad, hairy man crawl out from the low door fitting a flint-tipped arrow on to the string of his bow, you would feel that his presence there was more natural than your own. The strange thing is that they should have lived so thickly on what must always have been most unfruitful soil. I am no antiquarian, but I could imagine that they were some unwarlike and harried race who were forced to accept that which none other would occupy.

All this, however, is foreign to the mission on which you sent me and will probably be very uninteresting to your severely practical mind. I can still remember your complete indifference as to whether the sun moved round the earth or the earth round the sun. Let me, therefore, return to the facts concerning Sir Henry Baskerville.

If you have not had any report within the last few days it is because up to today there was nothing of importance to relate. Then a very surprising circumstance occurred, which I shall tell you in due course. But, first of all, I must keep you in touch with some of the other factors in the situation.

One of these, concerning which I have said little, is the escaped convict upon the moor. There is strong reason now to believe that he has got right away, which is a considerable relief to the lonely householders of this district. A fortnight has passed since his flight, during which he has not been seen and nothing has been heard of him. It is surely inconceivable that he could have held out upon the moor during all that time. Of course, so far as his concealment goes there is no difficulty at all. Any one of these stone huts would give him a hiding-place. But there is nothing to eat unless he were to catch and slaughter one of the moor sheep. We think, therefore, that he has gone, and the outlying farmers sleep the better in consequence.

We are four able-bodied men in this household, so that we could take good care of ourselves, but I confess that I have had uneasy moments when I have thought of the Stapletons. They live miles from any help. There are one maid, an old manservant, the sister, and the brother, the latter not a very strong man. They would be helpless in the hands of a desperate fellow like this Notting Hill criminal if he could once effect an entrance. Both Sir Henry and I were concerned at their situation, and it was suggested that Perkins the groom should go over to sleep there, but Stapleton would not hear of it.

The fact is that our friend, the baronet, begins to display a considerable interest in our fair neighbour. It is not to be wondered at, for time hangs heavily in this lonely spot to an active man like him, and she is a very fascinating and beautiful woman. There is something tropical and exotic about her which forms a singular contrast to her cool and unemotional brother. Yet he also gives the idea of hidden fires. He has certainly a very marked influence over her, for I have seen her continually glance at him as she talked as if seeking approbation for what she said. I trust that he is kind to her. There is a dry glitter in his eyes and a firm set of his thin lips, which goes with a positive and possibly a harsh nature. You would find him an interesting study.

He came over to call upon Baskerville on that first day, and the very next morning he took us both to show us the spot where the legend of the wicked Hugo is supposed to have had its origin. It was an excursion of some miles across the moor to a place which is so dismal that it might have suggested the story. We found a short valley between rugged tors which led to an open, grassy space flecked over with the white cotton grass. In the middle of it rose two great stones, worn and sharpened at the upper end until they looked like the huge corroding fangs of some monstrous beast. In every way it corresponded with the scene of the old tragedy. Sir Henry was much interested and asked Stapleton more than once whether he did really believe in the possibility of the interference of the supernatural in the affairs of men. He spoke lightly, but it was evident that he was very much in earnest. Stapleton was guarded in his replies, but it was easy to see that he said less than he might, and that he would not express his whole opinion out of consideration for the feelings of the baronet. He told us of similar cases, where families had suffered from some evil influence, and he left us with the impression that he shared the popular view upon the matter.

On our way back we stayed for lunch at Merripit House, and it was there that Sir Henry made the acquaintance of Miss Stapleton. From the first moment that he saw her he appeared to be strongly attracted by her, and I am much mistaken if the feeling was not mutual. He referred to her again and again on our walk home, and since then hardly a day has passed that we have not seen something of the brother and sister. They dine here tonight, and there is some talk of our going to them next week. One would imagine that such a match would be very welcome to Stapleton, and yet I have more than once caught a look of the strongest disapprobation in his face when Sir

Henry has been paying some attention to his sister. He is much attached to her, no doubt, and would lead a lonely life without her, but it would seem the height of selfishness if he were to stand in the way of her making so brilliant a marriage. Yet I am certain that he does not wish their intimacy to ripen into love, and I have several times observed that he has taken pains to prevent them from being tete-a-tete. By the way, your instructions to me never to allow Sir Henry to go out alone will become very much more onerous if a love affair were to be added to our other difficulties. My popularity would soon suffer if I were to carry out your orders to the letter.

The other day—Thursday, to be more exact—Dr. Mortimer lunched with us. He has been excavating a barrow at Long Down and has got a prehistoric skull which fills him with great joy. Never was there such a single-minded enthusiast as he! The Stapletons came in afterwards, and the good doctor took us all to the yew alley at Sir Henry's request to show us exactly how everything occurred upon that fatal night. It is a long, dismal walk, the yew alley, between two high walls of clipped hedge, with a narrow band of grass upon either side. At the far end is an old tumble-down summer-house. Halfway down is the moor-gate, where the old gentleman left his cigar-ash. It is a white wooden gate with a latch. Beyond it lies the wide moor. I remembered your theory of the affair and tried to picture all that had occurred. As the old man stood there he saw something coming across the moor, something which terrified him so that he lost his wits and ran and ran until he died of sheer horror and exhaustion. There was the long, gloomy tunnel down which he fled. And from what? A sheep-dog of the moor? Or a spectral hound, black, silent, and monstrous? Was there a human agency in the matter? Did the pale, watchful Barrymore know more than he cared to say? It was all dim and vague, but always there is the dark shadow of crime behind it.

One other neighbour I have met since I wrote last. This is Mr. Frankland, of Lafter Hall, who lives some four miles to the south of us. He is an elderly man, red-faced, white-haired, and choleric. His passion is for the British law, and he has spent a large fortune in litigation. He fights for the mere pleasure of fighting and is equally ready to take up either side of a question, so that it is no wonder that he has found it a costly amusement. Sometimes he will shut up a right of way and defy the parish to make him open it. At others he will with his own hands tear down some other man's gate and declare that a path has existed there from time immemorial, defying the owner to prosecute him for trespass. He is learned in old manorial and communal rights, and he applies his knowledge sometimes in favour of the villagers of Fernworthy and sometimes against them, so that he is periodically either carried in triumph down the village street or else burned in effigy, according to his latest exploit. He is said to have about seven lawsuits upon his hands at present, which will probably swallow up the remainder of his fortune and so draw his sting and leave him harmless for the future. Apart from the law he seems a kindly, good-natured person, and I only mention him because you were particular that I should send some description of the people who surround us. He is curiously employed at present, for, being an amateur astronomer, he has an excellent telescope, with which he lies upon the roof of his own house and sweeps the moor all day in the hope of catching a glimpse of the escaped convict. If he would confine his energies to this all would be well, but there are rumours that he intends to prosecute Dr. Mortimer for opening a grave without the consent of the next of kin because he dug up the Neolithic skull in the barrow on Long Down. He helps to keep our lives from being monotonous and gives a little comic relief where it is badly needed.

And now, having brought you up to date in the escaped convict, the Stapletons, Dr. Mortimer, and Frankland, of Lafter Hall, let me end on that which is most important and tell you more about the Barrymores, and especially about the surprising development of last night.

First of all about the test telegram, which you sent from London in order to make sure that Barrymore was really here. I have already explained that the testimony of the postmaster shows that the test was worthless and that we have no proof one way or the other. I told Sir Henry how the matter stood, and he at once, in his downright fashion, had Barrymore up and asked him whether he had received the telegram himself. Barrymore said that he had.

"Did the boy deliver it into your own hands?" asked Sir Henry.

Barrymore looked surprised, and considered for a little time.

"No," said he, "I was in the box-room at the time, and my wife brought it up to me."

"Did you answer it yourself?"

"No; I told my wife what to answer and she went down to write it."

In the evening he recurred to the subject of his own accord.

"I could not quite understand the object of your questions this morning, Sir Henry," said he. "I trust that they do not mean that I have done anything to forfeit your confidence?"

Sir Henry had to assure him that it was not so and pacify him by giving him a considerable part of his old wardrobe, the London outfit having now all arrived.

Mrs. Barrymore is of interest to me. She is a heavy, solid person, very limited, intensely respectable, and inclined to be puritanical. You could hardly conceive a less emotional subject. Yet I have told you how, on the first night here, I heard her sobbing bitterly, and since then I have more than once observed traces of tears upon her face. Some deep sorrow gnaws ever at her heart. Sometimes I wonder if she has a guilty memory which haunts her, and sometimes I suspect Barrymore of being a domestic tyrant. I have always felt that there was something singular and questionable in this man's character, but the adventure of last night brings all my suspicions to a head.

And yet it may seem a small matter in itself. You are aware that I am not a very sound sleeper, and since I have been on guard in this house my slumbers have been lighter than ever. Last night, about two in the morning, I was aroused by a stealthy step passing my room. I rose, opened my door, and peeped out. A long black shadow was trailing down the corridor. It was thrown by a man who walked softly down the passage with a candle held in his hand. He was in shirt and trousers, with no covering to his feet. I could merely see the outline, but his height told me that it was Barrymore. He walked very slowly and circumspectly, and there was something indescribably guilty and furtive in his whole appearance.

I have told you that the corridor is broken by the balcony which runs round the hall, but that it is resumed upon the farther side. I waited until he had passed out of sight and then I followed him. When I came round the balcony he had reached the end of the farther corridor, and I could see from the glimmer of light through an open door that he had entered one of the rooms. Now, all these rooms are unfurnished and unoccupied so that his expedition became more mysterious than ever. The light shone steadily as if he were standing motionless. I crept down the passage as noiselessly as I could and peeped round the corner of the door.

Barrymore was crouching at the window with the candle held against the glass. His profile was half turned towards me, and his face seemed to be rigid with expectation as he stared out into the blackness of the moor. For some minutes he stood watching intently. Then he gave a deep groan and with an impatient gesture he put out the light. Instantly I made my way back to my room, and very shortly came the stealthy steps passing once more upon their return journey. Long afterwards when I had fallen into a light sleep I heard a key turn somewhere in a lock, but I could not tell whence the sound came. What it all means I cannot guess, but there is some secret business going on in this house of gloom which sooner or later we shall get to the bottom of. I do not trouble you with my theories, for you asked me to furnish you only with facts. I have had a long talk with Sir Henry this morning, and we have made a plan of campaign founded upon my observations of last night. I will not speak about it just now, but it should make my next report interesting reading.

Chapter 9. The Light upon the Moor [Second Report of Dr. Watson]

Baskerville Hall, Oct. 15th. MY DEAR HOLMES: If I was compelled to leave you without much news during the early days of my mission you must acknowledge that I am making up for lost time, and that events are now crowding thick and fast upon us. In my last report I ended upon my top note with Barrymore at the window, and now I have quite a budget already which will, unless I am much mistaken, considerably surprise you. Things have taken a turn which I could not have anticipated. In some ways they have within the last forty-eight hours become much clearer and in some ways they have become more complicated. But I will tell you all and you shall judge for yourself.

Before breakfast on the morning following my adventure I went down the corridor and examined the room in which Barrymore had been on the night before. The western window through which he had stared so intently has, I noticed, one peculiarity above all other windows in the house—it commands the nearest outlook on to the moor. There is an opening between two trees which enables one from this point of view to look right down upon it, while from all the other windows it is only a distant glimpse which can be obtained. It follows, therefore, that Barrymore, since only this window would serve the purpose, must have been looking out for something or somebody upon the moor. The night was very dark, so that I can hardly imagine how he could have hoped to see anyone. It had struck me that it was possible that some love intrigue was on foot. That would have accounted for his stealthy movements and also for the uneasiness of his wife. The man is a striking-looking fellow, very well equipped to steal the heart of a country girl, so that this theory seemed to have something to support it. That opening of the door which I had heard after I had returned to my room might mean that he had gone out to keep some clandestine appointment. So I reasoned with myself in the morning, and I tell you the direction of my suspicions, however much the result may have shown that they were unfounded.

But whatever the true explanation of Barrymore's movements might be, I felt that the responsibility of keeping them to myself until I could explain them was more than I could bear. I had an interview with the baronet in his study after breakfast, and I told him all that I had seen. He was less surprised than I had expected.

"I knew that Barrymore walked about nights, and I had a mind to speak to him about it," said he. "Two or three times I have heard his steps in the passage, coming and going, just about the hour you name."

"Perhaps then he pays a visit every night to that particular window," I suggested.

"Perhaps he does. If so, we should be able to shadow him and see what it is that he is after. I wonder what your friend Holmes would do if he were here."

"I believe that he would do exactly what you now suggest," said I. "He would follow Barrymore and see what he did."

"Then we shall do it together."

"But surely he would hear us."

"The man is rather deaf, and in any case we must take our chance of that. We'll sit up in my room tonight and wait until he passes." Sir Henry rubbed his hands with pleasure, and it was evident that he hailed the adventure as a relief to his somewhat quiet life upon the moor.

The baronet has been in communication with the architect who prepared the plans for Sir Charles, and with a contractor from London, so that we may expect great changes to begin here soon. There have been decorators and furnishers up from Plymouth, and it is evident that our friend has large ideas and means to spare no pains or expense to restore the grandeur of his family. When the house is renovated and refurnished, all that he will need will be a wife to make it complete. Between ourselves there are pretty clear signs that this will not be wanting if the lady is willing, for I have seldom seen a man more infatuated with a woman than he is with our beautiful neighbour, Miss Stapleton. And yet the course of true love does not run quite as smoothly as one would under the circumstances expect. Today, for example, its surface was broken by a very unexpected ripple, which has caused our friend considerable perplexity and annoyance.

After the conversation which I have quoted about Barrymore, Sir Henry put on his hat and prepared to go out. As a matter of course I did the same.

"What, are you coming, Watson?" he asked, looking at me in a curious way.

"That depends on whether you are going on the moor," said I.

"Yes, I am."

"Well, you know what my instructions are. I am sorry to intrude, but you heard how earnestly Holmes insisted that I should not leave you, and especially that you should not go alone upon the moor."

Sir Henry put his hand upon my shoulder with a pleasant smile.

"My dear fellow," said he, "Holmes, with all his wisdom, did not foresee some things which have happened since I have been on the moor. You understand me? I am sure that you are the last man in the world who would wish to be a spoil-sport. I must go out alone."

It put me in a most awkward position. I was at a loss what to say or what to do, and before I had made up my mind he picked up his cane and was gone.

But when I came to think the matter over my conscience reproached me bitterly for having on any pretext allowed him to go out of my sight. I imagined what my feelings would be if I had to return to you and to confess that some misfortune had occurred through my disregard for your instructions. I assure you my cheeks flushed at the very thought. It might not even now be too late to overtake him, so I set off at once in the direction of Merripit House.

I hurried along the road at the top of my speed without seeing anything of Sir Henry, until I came to the point where the moor path branches off. There, fearing that perhaps I had come in the wrong direction after all, I mounted a hill from which I could command a view—the same hill which is cut into the dark quarry. Thence I saw him at once. He was on the moor path about a quarter of a mile off, and a lady was by his side who could only be Miss Stapleton. It was clear that there was already an understanding between them and that they had met by appointment. They were walking slowly along in deep conversation, and I saw her making quick little movements of her hands as if she were very earnest in what she was saying, while he listened intently, and once or twice shook his head in strong dissent. I stood among the rocks watching them, very much puzzled as to what I should do next. To follow them and break into their intimate conversation seemed to be an outrage, and yet my clear duty was never for an instant to let him out of my sight. To act the spy upon a friend was a hateful task. Still, I could see no better course than to observe him from the hill, and to clear my conscience by confessing to him afterwards what I had done. It is true that if any sudden danger had threatened him I was too far away to be of use, and yet I am sure that you will agree with me that the position was very difficult, and that there was nothing more which I could do.

Our friend, Sir Henry, and the lady had halted on the path and were standing deeply absorbed in their conversation, when I was suddenly aware that I was not the only witness of their interview. A wisp of green floating in the air caught my eye, and another glance showed me that it was carried on a stick by a man who was moving among the broken ground. It was Stapleton with his butterfly-net. He was very much closer to the pair than I was, and he appeared to be moving in their direction. At this instant Sir Henry suddenly drew Miss Stapleton to his side. His arm was round her, but it seemed to me that she was straining away from him with her face averted. He stooped his head to hers, and she raised one hand as if in protest. Next moment I saw them spring apart and turn hurriedly round. Stapleton was the cause of the interruption. He was running wildly towards them, his absurd net dangling behind him. He gesticulated and almost danced with excitement in front of the lovers. What the scene meant I could not imagine, but it seemed to me that Stapleton was abusing Sir Henry, who offered explanations, which became more angry as the other refused to accept them. The lady stood by in haughty silence. Finally Stapleton turned upon his heel and beckoned in a peremptory way to his sister, who, after an irresolute glance at Sir Henry, walked off by the side of her brother. The naturalist's angry gestures showed that the lady was included in his displeasure. The baronet stood for a minute looking after them, and then he walked slowly back the way that he had come, his head hanging, the very picture of dejection.

What all this meant I could not imagine, but I was deeply ashamed to have witnessed so intimate a scene without my friend's knowledge. I ran down the hill therefore and met the baronet at the bottom. His face was flushed with anger and his brows were wrinkled, like one who is at his wit's ends what to do.

"Halloa, Watson! Where have you dropped from?" said he. "You don't mean to say that you came after me in spite of all?"

I explained everything to him: how I had found it impossible to remain behind, how I had followed him, and how I had witnessed all that had occurred. For an instant his eyes blazed at me, but my frankness disarmed his anger, and he broke at last into a rather rueful laugh.

"You would have thought the middle of that prairie a fairly safe place for a man to be private," said he, "but, by thunder, the whole countryside seems to have been out to see me do my wooing—and a mighty poor wooing at that! Where had you engaged a seat?"

"I was on that hill."

"Quite in the back row, eh? But her brother was well up to the front. Did you see him come out on us?"

"Yes, I did."

"Did he ever strike you as being crazy—this brother of hers?"

"I can't say that he ever did."

"I dare say not. I always thought him sane enough until today, but you can take it from me that either he or I ought to be in a straitjacket. What's the matter with me, anyhow? You've lived near me for some weeks, Watson. Tell me straight, now! Is there anything that would prevent me from making a good husband to a woman that I loved?"

"I should say not."

"He can't object to my worldly position, so it must be myself that he has this down on. What has he against me? I never hurt man or woman in my life that I know of. And yet he would not so much as let me touch the tips of her fingers."

"Did he say so?"

"That, and a deal more. I tell you, Watson, I've only known her these few weeks, but from the first I just felt that she was made for me, and she, too—she was happy when she was with me, and that I'll swear. There's a light in a woman's eyes that speaks louder than words. But he has never let us get together and it was only today for the first time that I saw a chance of having a few words with her alone. She was glad to meet me, but when she did it was not love that she would talk about, and she wouldn't have let me talk about it either if she could have stopped it. She kept coming back to it that this was a place of danger, and that she would never be happy until I had left it. I told her that since I had seen her I was in no hurry to leave it, and that if she really wanted me to go, the only way to work it was for her to arrange to go with me. With that I offered in as many words to marry her, but before she could answer, down came this brother of hers, running at us with a face on him like a madman. He was just white with rage, and those light eyes of his were blazing with fury. What was I doing with the lady? How dared I offer her attentions which were distasteful to her? Did I think that because I was a baronet I could do what I liked? If he had not been her brother I should have known better how to answer him. As it was I told him that my feelings towards his sister were such as I was not ashamed of, and that I hoped that she might honour me by becoming my wife. That seemed to make the matter no better, so then I lost my temper too, and I answered him rather more hotly than I should perhaps, considering that she was standing by. So it ended by his going off with her, as you saw, and here am I as badly puzzled a man as any in this county. Just tell me what it all means, Watson, and I'll owe you more than ever I can hope to pay."

I tried one or two explanations, but, indeed, I was completely puzzled myself. Our friend's title, his fortune, his age, his character, and his appearance are all in his favour, and I know nothing against him unless it be this dark fate which runs in his family. That his advances should be rejected so brusquely without any reference to the lady's own wishes and that the lady should accept the situation without protest is very amazing. However, our conjectures were set at rest by a visit from Stapleton himself that very afternoon. He had come to offer apologies for his rudeness of the morning, and after a long private interview with Sir Henry in his study the upshot of their conversation was that the breach is quite healed, and that we are to dine at Merripit House next Friday as a sign of it.

"I don't say now that he isn't a crazy man," said Sir Henry; "I can't forget the look in his eyes when he ran at me this morning, but I must allow that no man could make a more handsome apology than he has done."

"Did he give any explanation of his conduct?"

"His sister is everything in his life, he says. That is natural enough, and I am glad that he should understand her value. They have always been together, and according to his account he has been a very lonely man with only her as a companion, so that the thought of losing her was really terrible to him. He had not understood, he said, that I was becoming attached to her, but when he saw with his own eyes that it was really so, and that she might be taken away from him, it gave him such a shock that for a time he was not responsible for what he said or did. He was very sorry for all that had passed, and he recognized how foolish and how selfish it was that he should imagine that he could hold a beautiful woman like his sister to himself for her whole life. If she had to leave him he had rather it was to a neighbour like myself than to anyone else. But in any case it was a blow to him and it would take him some time before he could prepare himself to meet it. He would withdraw all opposition upon his part if I would promise for three months to let the matter rest and to be content with cultivating the lady's friendship during that time without claiming her love. This I promised, and so the matter rests."

So there is one of our small mysteries cleared up. It is something to have touched bottom anywhere in this bog in which we are floundering. We know now why Stapleton looked with disfavour upon his sister's suitor—even when that suitor was so eligible a one as Sir Henry. And now I pass on to another thread which I have extricated out of the tangled skein, the mystery of the sobs in the night, of the tear-stained face of Mrs. Barrymore, of the secret journey of the butler to the western lattice window. Congratulate me, my dear Holmes, and tell me that I have not disappointed you as an agent—that you do not regret the confidence which you showed in me when you sent me down. All these things have by one night's work been thoroughly cleared.

I have said "by one night's work," but, in truth, it was by two nights' work, for on the first we drew entirely blank. I sat up with Sir Henry in his rooms until nearly three o'clock in the morning, but no sound of any sort did we hear except the chiming clock upon the stairs. It was a most melancholy vigil and ended by each of us falling asleep in our chairs. Fortunately we were not discouraged, and we determined to try again. The next night we lowered the lamp and sat smoking cigarettes without making the least sound. It was incredible how slowly the hours crawled by, and yet we were helped through it by the same sort of patient interest which the hunter must feel as he watches the trap into which he hopes the game may wander. One struck, and two, and we had almost for the second time given it up in despair when in an instant we both sat bolt upright in our chairs with all our weary senses keenly on the alert once more. We had heard the creak of a step in the passage.

Very stealthily we heard it pass along until it died away in the distance. Then the baronet gently opened his door and we set out in pursuit. Already our man had gone round the gallery and the corridor was all in darkness. Softly we stole along until we had come into the other wing. We were just in time to catch a glimpse of the tall, black-bearded figure, his shoulders rounded as he tiptoed down the passage. Then he passed through the same door as before, and the light of the candle framed it in the darkness and shot one single yellow beam across the gloom of the corridor. We shuffled cautiously towards it, trying every plank before we dared to put our whole weight upon it. We had taken the precaution of leaving our boots behind us, but, even so, the old boards snapped and creaked beneath our tread. Sometimes it seemed impossible that he should fail to hear our approach. However, the man is fortunately rather deaf, and he was entirely preoccupied in that which he was doing. When at last we reached the door and peeped through we found him crouching at the window, candle in hand, his white, intent face pressed against the pane, exactly as I had seen him two nights before.

We had arranged no plan of campaign, but the baronet is a man to whom the most direct way is always the most natural. He walked into the room, and as he did so Barrymore sprang up from the window with a sharp hiss of his breath and stood, livid and trembling, before us. His dark eyes, glaring out of the white mask of his face, were full of horror and astonishment as he gazed from Sir Henry to me.

"What are you doing here, Barrymore?"

"Nothing, sir." His agitation was so great that he could hardly speak, and the shadows sprang up and down from the shaking of his candle. "It was the window, sir. I go round at night to see that they are fastened."

"On the second floor?"

"Yes, sir, all the windows."

"Look here, Barrymore," said Sir Henry sternly, "we have made up our minds to have the truth out of you, so it will save you trouble to tell it sooner rather than later. Come, now! No lies! What were you doing at that window?"

The fellow looked at us in a helpless way, and he wrung his hands together like one who is in the last extremity of doubt and misery.

"I was doing no harm, sir. I was holding a candle to the window."

"And why were you holding a candle to the window?"

"Don't ask me, Sir Henry—don't ask me! I give you my word, sir, that it is not my secret, and that I cannot tell it. If it concerned no one but myself I would not try to keep it from you."

A sudden idea occurred to me, and I took the candle from the trembling hand of the butler.

"He must have been holding it as a signal," said I. "Let us see if there is any answer." I held it as he had done, and stared out into the darkness of the night. Vaguely I could discern the black bank of the trees and the lighter expanse of the moor, for the moon was behind the clouds. And then I gave a cry of exultation, for a tiny pinpoint of yellow light had suddenly transfixed the dark veil, and glowed steadily in the centre of the black square framed by the window.

"There it is!" I cried.

"No, no, sir, it is nothing—nothing at all!" the butler broke in; "I assure you, sir—"

"Move your light across the window, Watson!" cried the baronet. "See, the other moves also! Now, you rascal, do you deny that it is a signal? Come, speak up! Who is your confederate out yonder, and what is this conspiracy that is going on?"

The man's face became openly defiant. "It is my business, and not yours. I will not tell."

"Then you leave my employment right away."

"Very good, sir. If I must I must."

"And you go in disgrace. By thunder, you may well be ashamed of yourself. Your family has lived with mine for over a hundred years under this roof, and here I find you deep in some dark plot against me."

"No, no, sir; no, not against you!" It was a woman's voice, and Mrs. Barrymore, paler and more horror-struck than her husband, was standing at the door. Her bulky figure in a shawl and skirt might have been comic were it not for the intensity of feeling upon her face.

"We have to go, Eliza. This is the end of it. You can pack our things," said the butler.

"Oh, John, John, have I brought you to this? It is my doing, Sir Henry—all mine. He has done nothing except for my sake and because I asked him."

"Speak out, then! What does it mean?"

"My unhappy brother is starving on the moor. We cannot let him perish at our very gates. The light is a signal to him that food is ready for him, and his light out yonder is to show the spot to which to bring it."

"Then your brother is—"

"The escaped convict, sir—Selden, the criminal."

"That's the truth, sir," said Barrymore. "I said that it was not my secret and that I could not tell it to you. But now you have heard it, and you will see that if there was a plot it was not against you."

This, then, was the explanation of the stealthy expeditions at night and the light at the window. Sir Henry and I both stared at the woman in amazement. Was it possible that this stolidly respectable person was of the same blood as one of the most notorious criminals in the country?

"Yes, sir, my name was Selden, and he is my younger brother. We humoured him too much when he was a lad and gave him his own way in everything until he came to think that the world was made for his pleasure, and that he could do what he liked in it. Then as he grew older he met wicked companions, and the devil entered into him until he broke my mother's heart and dragged our name in the dirt. From crime to crime he sank lower and lower until it is only the mercy of God which has snatched him from the scaffold; but to me, sir, he was always the little curly-headed boy that I had nursed and played with as an elder sister would. That was why he broke prison, sir. He knew that I was here and that we could not refuse to help him. When he dragged himself here one night, weary and starving, with the warders hard at his heels, what could we do? We took him in and fed him and cared for him. Then you returned, sir, and my brother thought he would be safer on the moor than anywhere else until the hue and cry was over, so he lay in hiding there. But every second night we made sure if he was still there by putting a light in the window, and if there was an answer my husband took out some bread and meat to him. Every day we hoped that he was gone, but as long as he was there we could not desert him. That is the whole truth, as I am an honest Christian woman and you will see that if there is blame in the matter it does not lie with my husband but with me, for whose sake he has done all that he has."

The woman's words came with an intense earnestness which carried conviction with them.

"Is this true, Barrymore?"

"Yes, Sir Henry. Every word of it."

"Well, I cannot blame you for standing by your own wife. Forget what I have said. Go to your room, you two, and we shall talk further about this matter in the morning."

When they were gone we looked out of the window again. Sir Henry had flung it open, and the cold night wind beat in upon our faces. Far away in the black distance there still glowed that one tiny point of yellow light.

"I wonder he dares," said Sir Henry.

"It may be so placed as to be only visible from here."

"Very likely. How far do you think it is?"

"Out by the Cleft Tor, I think."

"Not more than a mile or two off."

"Hardly that."

"Well, it cannot be far if Barrymore had to carry out the food to it. And he is waiting, this villain, beside that candle. By thunder, Watson, I am going out to take that man!"

The same thought had crossed my own mind. It was not as if the Barrymores had taken us into their confidence. Their secret had been forced from them. The man was a danger to the community, an unmitigated scoundrel for whom there was neither pity nor excuse. We were only doing our duty in taking this chance of putting him back where he could do no harm. With his brutal and violent nature, others would have to pay the price if we held our hands. Any night, for example, our neighbours the Stapletons might be attacked by him, and it may have been the thought of this which made Sir Henry so keen upon the adventure.

"I will come," said I.

"Then get your revolver and put on your boots. The sooner we start the better, as the fellow may put out his light and be off."

In five minutes we were outside the door, starting upon our expedition. We hurried through the dark shrubbery, amid the dull moaning of the autumn wind and the rustle of the falling leaves. The night air was heavy with the smell of damp and decay. Now and again the moon peeped out for an instant, but clouds were driving over the face of the sky, and just as we came out on the moor a thin rain began to fall. The light still burned steadily in front.

"Are you armed?" I asked.

"I have a hunting-crop."

"We must close in on him rapidly, for he is said to be a desperate fellow. We shall take him by surprise and have him at our mercy before he can resist."

"I say, Watson," said the baronet, "what would Holmes say to this? How about that hour of darkness in which the power of evil is exalted?"

As if in answer to his words there rose suddenly out of the vast gloom of the moor that strange cry which I had already heard upon the borders of the great Grimpen Mire. It came with the wind through the silence of the night, a long, deep mutter, then a rising howl, and then the sad moan in which it died away. Again and again it sounded, the whole air throbbing with it, strident, wild, and menacing. The baronet caught my sleeve and his face glimmered white through the darkness.

"My God, what's that, Watson?"

"I don't know. It's a sound they have on the moor. I heard it once before."

It died away, and an absolute silence closed in upon us. We stood straining our ears, but nothing came.

"Watson," said the baronet, "it was the cry of a hound."

My blood ran cold in my veins, for there was a break in his voice which told of the sudden horror which had seized him.

"What do they call this sound?" he asked.

"Who?"

"The folk on the countryside."

"Oh, they are ignorant people. Why should you mind what they call it?"

"Tell me, Watson. What do they say of it?"

I hesitated but could not escape the question.

"They say it is the cry of the Hound of the Baskervilles."

He groaned and was silent for a few moments.

"A hound it was," he said at last, "but it seemed to come from miles away, over yonder, I think."

"It was hard to say whence it came."

"It rose and fell with the wind. Isn't that the direction of the great Grimpen Mire?"

"Yes, it is."

"Well, it was up there. Come now, Watson, didn't you think yourself that it was the cry of a hound? I am not a child. You need not fear to speak the truth."

"Stapleton was with me when I heard it last. He said that it might be the calling of a strange bird."

"No, no, it was a hound. My God, can there be some truth in all these stories? Is it possible that I am really in danger from so dark a cause? You don't believe it, do you, Watson?"

"No, no."

"And yet it was one thing to laugh about it in London, and it is another to stand out here in the darkness of the moor and to hear such a cry as that. And my uncle! There was the footprint of the hound beside him as he lay. It all fits together. I don't think that I am a coward, Watson, but that sound seemed to freeze my very blood. Feel my hand!"

It was as cold as a block of marble.

"You'll be all right tomorrow."

"I don't think I'll get that cry out of my head. What do you advise that we do now?"

"Shall we turn back?"

"No, by thunder; we have come out to get our man, and we will do it. We after the convict, and a hell-hound, as likely as not, after us. Come on! We'll see it through if all the fiends of the pit were loose upon the moor."

We stumbled slowly along in the darkness, with the black loom of the craggy hills around us, and the yellow speck of light burning steadily in front. There is nothing so deceptive as the distance of a light upon a pitch-dark night, and sometimes the glimmer seemed to be far away upon the horizon and sometimes it might have been within a few yards of us. But at last we could see whence it came, and then we knew that we were indeed very close. A guttering candle was stuck in a crevice of the rocks which flanked it on each side so as to keep the wind from it and also to prevent it from being visible, save in the direction of Baskerville Hall. A boulder of granite concealed our approach, and crouching behind it we gazed over it at the signal light. It was strange to see this single candle burning there in the middle of the moor, with no sign of life near it—just the one straight yellow flame and the gleam of the rock on each side of it.

"What shall we do now?" whispered Sir Henry.

"Wait here. He must be near his light. Let us see if we can get a glimpse of him."

The words were hardly out of my mouth when we both saw him. Over the rocks, in the crevice of which the candle burned, there was thrust out an evil yellow face, a terrible animal face, all seamed and scored with vile passions. Foul with mire, with a bristling beard, and hung with matted hair, it might well have belonged to one of those old savages who dwelt in the burrows on the hillsides. The light beneath him was reflected in his small, cunning eyes which peered fiercely to right and left through the darkness like a crafty and savage animal who has heard the steps of the hunters.

Something had evidently aroused his suspicions. It may have been that Barrymore had some private signal which we had neglected to give, or the fellow may have had some other reason for thinking that all was not well, but I could read his fears upon his wicked face. Any instant he might dash out the light and vanish in the darkness. I sprang forward therefore, and Sir Henry did the same. At the same moment the convict screamed out a curse at us and hurled a rock which splintered up against the boulder which had sheltered us. I caught one glimpse of his short, squat, strongly built figure as he sprang to his feet and turned to run. At the same moment by a lucky chance the moon broke through the clouds. We rushed over the brow of the hill, and there was our man running with great speed down the other side, springing over the stones in his way with the activity of a mountain goat. A lucky long shot of my revolver might have crippled him, but I had brought it only to defend myself if attacked and not to shoot an unarmed man who was running away.

We were both swift runners and in fairly good training, but we soon found that we had no chance of overtaking him. We saw him for a long time in the moonlight until he was only a small speck moving swiftly among the boulders upon the side of a distant hill. We ran and ran until we were completely blown, but the space between us grew ever wider. Finally we stopped and sat panting on two rocks, while we watched him disappearing in the distance.

And it was at this moment that there occurred a most strange and unexpected thing. We had risen from our rocks and were turning to go home, having abandoned the hopeless chase. The moon was low upon the right, and the jagged pinnacle of a granite tor stood up against the lower curve of its silver disc. There, outlined as black as an ebony statue on that shining background, I saw the figure of a man upon the tor. Do not think that it was a delusion, Holmes. I assure you that I have never in my life seen anything more clearly. As far as I could judge, the figure was that of a tall, thin man. He stood with his legs a little separated, his arms folded, his head bowed, as if he were brooding over that enormous wilderness of peat and granite which lay before him. He might have been the very spirit of that terrible place. It was not the convict. This man was far from the place where the latter had disappeared. Besides, he was a much taller man. With a cry of surprise I pointed him out to the baronet, but in the instant during which I had turned to grasp his arm the man was gone. There was the sharp pinnacle of granite still cutting the lower edge of the moon, but its peak bore no trace of that silent and motionless figure.

I wished to go in that direction and to search the tor, but it was some distance away. The baronet's nerves were still quivering from that cry, which recalled the dark story of his family, and he was not in the mood for fresh adventures. He had not seen this lonely man upon the tor and could not feel the thrill which his strange presence and his commanding attitude had given to me. "A warder, no doubt," said he. "The moor has been thick with them since this fellow escaped." Well, perhaps his explanation may be the right one, but I should like to have some further proof of it. Today we mean to communicate to the Princetown people where they should look for their missing man, but it is hard lines that we have not actually had the triumph of bringing him back as our own prisoner. Such are the adventures of last night, and you must acknowledge, my dear Holmes, that I have done you very well in the matter of a report. Much of what I tell you is no doubt quite irrelevant, but still I feel that it is best that I should let you have all the facts and leave you to select for yourself those which will be of most service to you in helping you to your conclusions. We are certainly making some progress. So far as the Barrymores go we have found the motive of their actions, and that has cleared up the situation very much. But the moor with its mysteries and its strange inhabitants remains as inscrutable as ever. Perhaps in my next I may be able to throw some light upon this also. Best of all would it be if you could come down to us. In any case you will hear from me again in the course of the next few days.

Chapter 10. Extract from the Diary of Dr. Watson

So far I have been able to quote from the reports which I have forwarded during these early days to Sherlock Holmes. Now, however, I have arrived at a point in my narrative where I am compelled to abandon this method and to trust once more to my recollections, aided by the diary which I kept at the time. A few extracts from the latter will carry me on to those scenes which are indelibly fixed in every detail upon my memory. I proceed, then, from the morning which followed our abortive chase of the convict and our other strange experiences upon the moor.

October 16th. A dull and foggy day with a drizzle of rain. The house is banked in with rolling clouds, which rise now and then to show the dreary curves of the moor, with thin, silver veins upon the sides of the hills, and the distant boulders gleaming where the light strikes upon their wet faces. It is melancholy outside and in. The baronet is in a black reaction after the excitements of the night. I am conscious myself of a weight at my heart and a feeling of impending danger—ever present danger, which is the more terrible because I am unable to define it.

And have I not cause for such a feeling? Consider the long sequence of incidents which have all pointed to some sinister influence which is at work around us. There is the death of the last occupant of the Hall, fulfilling so exactly the conditions of the family legend, and there are the repeated reports from peasants of the appearance of a strange creature upon the moor. Twice I have with my own ears heard the sound which resembled the distant baying of a hound. It is incredible, impossible, that it should really be outside the ordinary laws of nature. A spectral hound which leaves material footmarks and fills the air with its howling is surely not to be thought of. Stapleton may fall in with such a superstition, and Mortimer also, but if I have one quality upon earth it is common sense, and nothing will persuade me to believe in such a thing. To do so would be to descend to the level of these poor peasants, who are not content with a mere fiend dog but must needs describe him with hell-fire shooting from his mouth and eyes. Holmes would not listen to such fancies, and I am his agent. But facts are facts, and I have twice heard this crying upon the moor. Suppose that there were really some huge hound loose upon it; that would go far to explain everything. But where could such a hound lie concealed, where did it get its food, where did it come from, how was it that no one saw it by day? It must be confessed that the natural explanation offers almost as many difficulties as the other.

And always, apart from the hound, there is the fact of the human agency in London, the man in the cab, and the letter which warned Sir Henry against the moor. This at least was real, but it might have been the work of a protecting friend as easily as of an enemy. Where is that friend or enemy now? Has he remained in London, or has he followed us down here? Could he—could he be the stranger whom I saw upon the tor?

It is true that I have had only the one glance at him, and yet there are some things to which I am ready to swear. He is no one whom I have seen down here, and I have now met all the neighbours. The figure was far taller than that of Stapleton, far thinner than that of Frankland. Barrymore it might possibly have been, but we had left him behind us, and I am certain that he could not have followed us. A stranger then is still dogging us, just as a stranger dogged us in London. We have never shaken him off. If I could lay my hands upon that man, then at last we might find ourselves at the end of all our difficulties. To this one purpose I must now devote all my energies.

My first impulse was to tell Sir Henry all my plans. My second and wisest one is to play my own game and speak as little as possible to anyone. He is silent and distrait. His nerves have been strangely shaken by that sound upon the moor. I will say nothing to add to his anxieties, but I will take my own steps to attain my own end.

We had a small scene this morning after breakfast. Barrymore asked leave to speak with Sir Henry, and they were closeted in his study some little time. Sitting in the billiard-room I more than once heard the sound of voices raised, and I had a pretty good idea what the point was which was under discussion. After a time the baronet opened his door and called for me. "Barrymore considers that he has a grievance," he said. "He thinks that it was unfair on our part to hunt his brother-in-law down when he, of his own free will, had told us the secret."

The butler was standing very pale but very collected before us.

"I may have spoken too warmly, sir," said he, "and if I have, I am sure that I beg your pardon. At the same time, I was very much surprised when I heard you two gentlemen come back this morning and learned that you had been chasing Selden. The poor fellow has enough to fight against without my putting more upon his track."

"If you had told us of your own free will it would have been a different thing," said the baronet, "you only told us, or rather your wife only told us, when it was forced from you and you could not help yourself."

"I didn't think you would have taken advantage of it, Sir Henry—indeed I didn't."

"The man is a public danger. There are lonely houses scattered over the moor, and he is a fellow who would stick at nothing. You only want to get a glimpse of his face to see that. Look at Mr. Stapleton's house, for example, with no one but himself to defend it. There's no safety for anyone until he is under lock and key."

"He'll break into no house, sir. I give you my solemn word upon that. But he will never trouble anyone in this country again. I assure you, Sir Henry, that in a very few days the necessary arrangements will have been made and he will be on his way to South America. For God's sake, sir, I beg of you not to let the police know that he is still on the moor. They have given up the chase there, and he can lie quiet until the ship is ready for him. You can't tell on him without getting my wife and me into trouble. I beg you, sir, to say nothing to the police."

"What do you say, Watson?"

I shrugged my shoulders. "If he were safely out of the country it would relieve the tax-payer of a burden."

"But how about the chance of his holding someone up before he goes?"

"He would not do anything so mad, sir. We have provided him with all that he can want. To commit a crime would be to show where he was hiding."

"That is true," said Sir Henry. "Well, Barrymore—"

"God bless you, sir, and thank you from my heart! It would have killed my poor wife had he been taken again."

"I guess we are aiding and abetting a felony, Watson? But, after what we have heard I don't feel as if I could give the man up, so there is an end of it. All right, Barrymore, you can go."

With a few broken words of gratitude the man turned, but he hesitated and then came back.

"You've been so kind to us, sir, that I should like to do the best I can for you in return. I know something, Sir Henry, and perhaps I should have said it before, but it was long after the inquest that I found it out. I've never breathed a word about it yet to mortal man. It's about poor Sir Charles's death."

The baronet and I were both upon our feet. "Do you know how he died?"

"No, sir, I don't know that."

"What then?"

"I know why he was at the gate at that hour. It was to meet a woman."

"To meet a woman! He?"

"Yes, sir."

"And the woman's name?"

"I can't give you the name, sir, but I can give you the initials. Her initials were L. L."

"How do you know this, Barrymore?"

"Well, Sir Henry, your uncle had a letter that morning. He had usually a great many letters, for he was a public man and well known for his kind heart, so that everyone who was in trouble was glad to turn to him. But that morning, as it chanced, there was only this one letter, so I took the more notice of it. It was from Coombe Tracey, and it was addressed in a woman's hand."

"Well?"

"Well, sir, I thought no more of the matter, and never would have done had it not been for my wife. Only a few weeks ago she was cleaning out Sir Charles's study—it had never been touched since his death—and she found the ashes of a burned letter in the back of the grate. The greater part of it was charred to pieces, but one little slip, the end of a page, hung together, and the writing could still be read, though it was gray on a black ground. It seemed to us to be a postscript at the end of the letter and it said: 'Please, please, as you are a gentleman, burn this letter, and be at the gate by ten o clock. Beneath it were signed the initials L. L."

"Have you got that slip?"

"No, sir, it crumbled all to bits after we moved it."

"Had Sir Charles received any other letters in the same writing?"

"Well, sir, I took no particular notice of his letters. I should not have noticed this one, only it happened to come alone."

"And you have no idea who L. L. is?"

"No, sir. No more than you have. But I expect if we could lay our hands upon that lady we should know more about Sir Charles's death."

"I cannot understand, Barrymore, how you came to conceal this important information."

"Well, sir, it was immediately after that our own trouble came to us. And then again, sir, we were both of us very fond of Sir Charles, as we well might be considering all that he has done for us. To rake this up couldn't help our poor master, and it's well to go carefully when there's a lady in the case. Even the best of us—"

"You thought it might injure his reputation?"

"Well, sir, I thought no good could come of it. But now you have been kind to us, and I feel as if it would be treating you unfairly not to tell you all that I know about the matter."

"Very good, Barrymore; you can go." When the butler had left us Sir Henry turned to me. "Well, Watson, what do you think of this new light?"

"It seems to leave the darkness rather blacker than before."

"So I think. But if we can only trace L. L. it should clear up the whole business. We have gained that much. We know that there is someone who has the facts if we can only find her. What do you think we should do?"

"Let Holmes know all about it at once. It will give him the clue for which he has been seeking. I am much mistaken if it does not bring him down."

I went at once to my room and drew up my report of the morning's conversation for Holmes. It was evident to me that he had been very busy of late, for the notes which I had from Baker Street were few and short, with no comments upon the information which I had supplied and hardly any reference to my mission. No doubt his blackmailing case is absorbing all his faculties. And yet this new factor must surely arrest his attention and renew his interest. I wish that he were here.

October 17th. All day today the rain poured down, rustling on the ivy and dripping from the eaves. I thought of the convict out upon the bleak, cold, shelterless moor. Poor devil! Whatever his crimes, he has suffered something to atone for them. And then I thought of that other one—the face in the cab, the figure against the moon. Was he also out in that deluged—the unseen watcher, the man of darkness? In the evening I put on my waterproof and I walked far upon the sodden moor, full of dark imaginings, the rain beating upon my face and the wind whistling about my ears. God help those who wander into the great mire now, for even the firm uplands are becoming a morass. I found the black tor upon which I had seen the solitary watcher, and from its craggy summit I looked out myself across the melancholy downs. Rain squalls drifted across their russet face, and the heavy, slate-coloured clouds hung low over the landscape, trailing in gray wreaths down the sides of the fantastic hills. In the distant hollow on the left, half hidden by the mist, the two thin towers of Baskerville Hall rose above the trees. They were the only signs of human life which I could see, save only those prehistoric huts which lay thickly upon the slopes of the hills. Nowhere was there any trace of that lonely man whom I had seen on the same spot two nights before.

As I walked back I was overtaken by Dr. Mortimer driving in his dog-cart over a rough moorland track which led from the outlying farmhouse of Foulmire. He has been very attentive to us, and hardly a day has passed that he has not called at the Hall to see how we were getting on. He insisted upon my climbing into his dog-cart, and he gave me a lift homeward. I found him much troubled over the disappearance of his little spaniel. It had wandered on to the moor and had never come back. I gave him such consolation as I might, but I thought of the pony on the Grimpen Mire, and I do not fancy that he will see his little dog again.

"By the way, Mortimer," said I as we jolted along the rough road, "I suppose there are few people living within driving distance of this whom you do not know?"

"Hardly any, I think."

"Can you, then, tell me the name of any woman whose initials are L. L.?"

He thought for a few minutes.

"No," said he. "There are a few gipsies and labouring folk for whom I can't answer, but among the farmers or gentry there is no one whose initials are those. Wait a bit though," he added after a pause. "There is Laura Lyons—her initials are L. L.—but she lives in Coombe Tracey."

"Who is she?" I asked.

"She is Frankland's daughter."

"What! Old Frankland the crank?"

"Exactly. She married an artist named Lyons, who came sketching on the moor. He proved to be a blackguard and deserted her. The fault from what I hear may not have been entirely on one side. Her father refused to have anything to do with her because she had married without his consent and perhaps for one or two other reasons as well. So, between the old sinner and the young one the girl has had a pretty bad time."

"How does she live?"

"I fancy old Frankland allows her a pittance, but it cannot be more, for his own affairs are considerably involved. Whatever she may have deserved one could not allow her to go hopelessly to the bad. Her story got about, and several of the people here did something to enable her to earn an honest living. Stapleton did for one, and Sir Charles for another. I gave a trifle myself. It was to set her up in a typewriting business."

He wanted to know the object of my inquiries, but I managed to satisfy his curiosity without telling him too much, for there is no reason why we should take anyone into our confidence. Tomorrow morning I shall find my way to Coombe Tracey, and if I can see this Mrs. Laura Lyons, of equivocal reputation, a long step will have been made towards clearing one incident in this chain of mysteries. I am certainly developing the wisdom of the serpent, for when Mortimer pressed his questions to an inconvenient extent I asked him casually to what type Frankland's skull belonged, and so heard nothing but craniology for the rest of our drive. I have not lived for years with Sherlock Holmes for nothing.

I have only one other incident to record upon this tempestuous and melancholy day. This was my conversation with Barrymore just now, which gives me one more strong card which I can play in due time.

Mortimer had stayed to dinner, and he and the baronet played ecarte afterwards. The butler brought me my coffee into the library, and I took the chance to ask him a few questions.

"Well," said I, "has this precious relation of yours departed, or is he still lurking out yonder?"

"I don't know, sir. I hope to heaven that he has gone, for he has brought nothing but trouble here! I've not heard of him since I left out food for him last, and that was three days ago."

"Did you see him then?"

"No, sir, but the food was gone when next I went that way."

"Then he was certainly there?"

"So you would think, sir, unless it was the other man who took it."

I sat with my coffee-cup halfway to my lips and stared at Barrymore.

"You know that there is another man then?"

"Yes, sir; there is another man upon the moor."

"Have you seen him?"

"No, sir."

"How do you know of him then?"

"Selden told me of him, sir, a week ago or more. He's in hiding, too, but he's not a convict as far as I can make out. I don't like it, Dr. Watson—I tell you straight, sir, that I don't like it." He spoke with a sudden passion of earnestness.

"Now, listen to me, Barrymore! I have no interest in this matter but that of your master. I have come here with no object except to help him. Tell me, frankly, what it is that you don't like."

Barrymore hesitated for a moment, as if he regretted his outburst or found it difficult to express his own feelings in words.

"It's all these goings-on, sir," he cried at last, waving his hand towards the rain-lashed window which faced the moor. "There's foul play somewhere, and there's black villainy brewing, to that I'll swear! Very glad I should be, sir, to see Sir Henry on his way back to London again!"

"But what is it that alarms you?"

"Look at Sir Charles's death! That was bad enough, for all that the coroner said. Look at the noises on the moor at night. There's not a man would cross it after sundown if he was paid for it. Look at this stranger hiding out yonder, and watching and waiting! What's he waiting for? What does it mean? It means no good to anyone of the name of Baskerville, and very glad I shall be to be quit of it all on the day that Sir Henry's new servants are ready to take over the Hall."

"But about this stranger," said I. "Can you tell me anything about him? What did Selden say? Did he find out where he hid, or what he was doing?"

"He saw him once or twice, but he is a deep one and gives nothing away. At first he thought that he was the police, but soon he found that he had some lay of his own. A kind of gentleman he was, as far as he could see, but what he was doing he could not make out."

"And where did he say that he lived?"

"Among the old houses on the hillside—the stone huts where the old folk used to live."

"But how about his food?"

"Selden found out that he has got a lad who works for him and brings all he needs. I dare say he goes to Coombe Tracey for what he wants."

"Very good, Barrymore. We may talk further of this some other time." When the butler had gone I walked over to the black window, and I looked through a blurred pane at the driving clouds and at the tossing outline of the wind-swept trees. It is a wild night indoors, and what must it be in a stone hut upon the moor. What passion of hatred can it be which leads a man to lurk in such a place at such a time! And what deep and earnest purpose can he have which calls for such a trial! There, in that hut upon the moor, seems to lie the very centre of that problem which has vexed me so sorely. I swear that another day shall not have passed before I have done all that man can do to reach the heart of the mystery.

Chapter 11. The Man on the Tor

The extract from my private diary which forms the last chapter has brought my narrative up to the eighteenth of October, a time when these strange events began to move swiftly towards their terrible conclusion. The incidents of the next few days are indelibly graven upon my recollection, and I can tell them without reference to the notes made at the time. I start them from the day which succeeded that upon which I had established two facts of great importance, the one that Mrs. Laura Lyons of Coombe Tracey had written to Sir Charles Baskerville and made an appointment with him at the very place and hour that he met his death, the other that the lurking man upon the moor was to be found among the stone huts upon the hillside. With these two facts in my possession I felt that either my intelligence or my courage must be deficient if I could not throw some further light upon these dark places.

I had no opportunity to tell the baronet what I had learned about Mrs. Lyons upon the evening before, for Dr. Mortimer remained with him at cards until it was very late. At breakfast, however, I informed him about my discovery and asked him whether he would care to accompany me to Coombe Tracey. At first he was very eager to come, but on second thoughts it seemed to both of us that if I went alone the results might be better. The more formal we made the visit the less information we might obtain. I left Sir Henry behind, therefore, not without some prickings of conscience, and drove off upon my new quest.

When I reached Coombe Tracey I told Perkins to put up the horses, and I made inquiries for the lady whom I had come to interrogate. I had no difficulty in finding her rooms, which were central and well appointed. A maid showed me in without ceremony, and as I entered the sitting-room a lady, who was sitting before a Remington typewriter, sprang up with a pleasant smile of welcome. Her face fell, however, when she saw that I was a stranger, and she sat down again and asked me the object of my visit.

The first impression left by Mrs. Lyons was one of extreme beauty. Her eyes and hair were of the same rich hazel colour, and her cheeks, though considerably freckled, were flushed with the exquisite bloom of the brunette, the dainty pink which lurks at the heart of the sulphur rose. Admiration was, I repeat, the first impression. But the second was criticism. There was something subtly wrong with the face, some coarseness of expression, some hardness, perhaps, of eye, some looseness of lip which marred its perfect beauty. But these, of course, are afterthoughts. At the moment I was simply conscious that I was in the presence of a very handsome woman, and that she was asking me the reasons for my visit. I had not quite understood until that instant how delicate my mission was.

"I have the pleasure," said I, "of knowing your father."

It was a clumsy introduction, and the lady made me feel it. "There is nothing in common between my father and me," she said. "I owe him nothing, and his friends are not mine. If it were not for the late Sir Charles Baskerville and some other kind hearts I might have starved for all that my father cared."

"It was about the late Sir Charles Baskerville that I have come here to see you."

The freckles started out on the lady's face.

"What can I tell you about him?" she asked, and her fingers played nervously over the stops of her typewriter.

"You knew him, did you not?"

"I have already said that I owe a great deal to his kindness. If I am able to support myself it is largely due to the interest which he took in my unhappy situation."

"Did you correspond with him?"

The lady looked quickly up with an angry gleam in her hazel eyes.

"What is the object of these questions?" she asked sharply.

"The object is to avoid a public scandal. It is better that I should ask them here than that the matter should pass outside our control."

She was silent and her face was still very pale. At last she looked up with something reckless and defiant in her manner.

"Well, I'll answer," she said. "What are your questions?"

"Did you correspond with Sir Charles?"

"I certainly wrote to him once or twice to acknowledge his delicacy and his generosity."

"Have you the dates of those letters?"

"No."

"Have you ever met him?"

"Yes, once or twice, when he came into Coombe Tracey. He was a very retiring man, and he preferred to do good by stealth."

"But if you saw him so seldom and wrote so seldom, how did he know enough about your affairs to be able to help you, as you say that he has done?"

She met my difficulty with the utmost readiness.

"There were several gentlemen who knew my sad history and united to help me. One was Mr. Stapleton, a neighbour and intimate friend of Sir Charles's. He was exceedingly kind, and it was through him that Sir Charles learned about my affairs."

I knew already that Sir Charles Baskerville had made Stapleton his almoner upon several occasions, so the lady's statement bore the impress of truth upon it.

"Did you ever write to Sir Charles asking him to meet you?" I continued.

Mrs. Lyons flushed with anger again. "Really, sir, this is a very extraordinary question."

"I am sorry, madam, but I must repeat it."

"Then I answer, certainly not."

"Not on the very day of Sir Charles's death?"

The flush had faded in an instant, and a deathly face was before me. Her dry lips could not speak the "No" which I saw rather than heard.

"Surely your memory deceives you," said I. "I could even quote a passage of your letter. It ran 'Please, please, as you are a gentleman, burn this letter, and be at the gate by ten o'clock.'"

I thought that she had fainted, but she recovered herself by a supreme effort.

"Is there no such thing as a gentleman?" she gasped.

"You do Sir Charles an injustice. He did burn the letter. But sometimes a letter may be legible even when burned. You acknowledge now that you wrote it?"

"Yes, I did write it," she cried, pouring out her soul in a torrent of words. "I did write it. Why should I deny it? I have no reason to be ashamed of it. I wished him to help me. I believed that if I had an interview I could gain his help, so I asked him to meet me."

"But why at such an hour?"

"Because I had only just learned that he was going to London next day and might be away for months. There were reasons why I could not get there earlier."

"But why a rendezvous in the garden instead of a visit to the house?"

"Do you think a woman could go alone at that hour to a bachelor's house?"

"Well, what happened when you did get there?"

"I never went."

"Mrs. Lyons!"

"No, I swear it to you on all I hold sacred. I never went. Something intervened to prevent my going."

"What was that?"

"That is a private matter. I cannot tell it."

"You acknowledge then that you made an appointment with Sir Charles at the very hour and place at which he met his death, but you deny that you kept the appointment."

"That is the truth."

Again and again I cross-questioned her, but I could never get past that point.

"Mrs. Lyons," said I as I rose from this long and inconclusive interview, "you are taking a very great responsibility and putting yourself in a very false position by not making an absolutely clean breast of all that you know. If I have to call in the aid of the police you will find how seriously you are compromised. If your position is innocent, why did you in the first instance deny having written to Sir Charles upon that date?"

"Because I feared that some false conclusion might be drawn from it and that I might find myself involved in a scandal."

"And why were you so pressing that Sir Charles should destroy your letter?"

"If you have read the letter you will know."

"I did not say that I had read all the letter."

"You quoted some of it."

"I quoted the postscript. The letter had, as I said, been burned and it was not all legible. I ask you once again why it was that you were so pressing that Sir Charles should destroy this letter which he received on the day of his death."

"The matter is a very private one."

"The more reason why you should avoid a public investigation."

"I will tell you, then. If you have heard anything of my unhappy history you will know that I made a rash marriage and had reason to regret it."

"I have heard so much."

"My life has been one incessant persecution from a husband whom I abhor. The law is upon his side, and every day I am faced by the possibility that he may force me to live with him. At the time that I wrote this letter to Sir Charles I had learned that there was a prospect of my regaining my freedom if certain expenses could be met. It meant everything to me—peace of mind, happiness, self-respect—everything. I knew Sir Charles's generosity, and I thought that if he heard the story from my own lips he would help me."

"Then how is it that you did not go?"

"Because I received help in the interval from another source."

"Why then, did you not write to Sir Charles and explain this?"

"So I should have done had I not seen his death in the paper next morning."

The woman's story hung coherently together, and all my questions were unable to shake it. I could only check it by finding if she had, indeed, instituted divorce proceedings against her husband at or about the time of the tragedy.

It was unlikely that she would dare to say that she had not been to Baskerville Hall if she really had been, for a trap would be necessary to take her there, and could not have returned to Coombe Tracey until the early hours of the morning. Such an excursion could not be kept secret. The probability was, therefore, that she was telling the truth, or, at least, a part of the truth. I came away baffled and disheartened. Once again I had reached that dead wall which seemed to be built across every path by which I tried to get at the object of my mission. And yet the more I thought of the lady's face and of her manner the more I felt that something was being held back from me. Why should she turn so pale? Why should she fight against every admission until it was forced from her? Why should she have been so reticent at the time of the tragedy? Surely the explanation of all this could not be as innocent as she would have me believe. For the moment I could proceed no farther in that direction, but must turn back to that other clue which was to be sought for among the stone huts upon the moor.

And that was a most vague direction. I realized it as I drove back and noted how hill after hill showed traces of the ancient people. Barrymore's only indication had been that the stranger lived in one of these abandoned huts, and many hundreds of them are scattered throughout the length and breadth of the moor. But I had my own experience for a guide since it had shown me the man himself standing upon the summit of the Black Tor. That, then, should be the centre of my search. From there I should explore every hut upon the moor until I lighted upon the right one. If this man were inside it I should find out from his own lips, at the point of my revolver if necessary, who he was and why he had dogged us so long. He might slip away from us in the crowd of Regent Street, but it would puzzle him to do so upon the lonely moor. On the other hand, if I should find the hut and its tenant should not be within it I must remain there, however long the vigil, until he returned. Holmes had missed him in London. It would indeed be a triumph for me if I could run him to earth where my master had failed.

Luck had been against us again and again in this inquiry, but now at last it came to my aid. And the messenger of good fortune was none other than Mr. Frankland, who was standing, gray-whiskered and red-faced, outside the gate of his garden, which opened on to the highroad along which I travelled.

"Good-day, Dr. Watson," cried he with unwonted good humour, "you must really give your horses a rest and come in to have a glass of wine and to congratulate me."

My feelings towards him were very far from being friendly after what I had heard of his treatment of his daughter, but I was anxious to send Perkins and the wagonette home, and the opportunity was a good one. I alighted and sent a message to Sir Henry that I should walk over in time for dinner. Then I followed Frankland into his dining-room.

"It is a great day for me, sir—one of the red-letter days of my life," he cried with many chuckles. "I have brought off a double event. I mean to teach them in these parts that law is law, and that there is a man here who does not fear to invoke it. I have established a right of way through the centre of old Middleton's park, slap across it, sir, within a hundred yards of his own front door. What do you think of that? We'll teach these magnates that they cannot ride roughshod over the rights of the commoners, confound them! And I've closed the wood where the Fernworthy folk used to picnic. These infernal people seem to think that there are no rights of property, and that they can swarm where they like with their papers and their bottles.

Both cases decided, Dr. Watson, and both in my favour. I haven't had such a day since I had Sir John Morland for trespass because he shot in his own warren."

"How on earth did you do that?"

"Look it up in the books, sir. It will repay reading—Frankland v. Morland, Court of Queen's Bench. It cost me 200 pounds, but I got my verdict."

"Did it do you any good?"

"None, sir, none. I am proud to say that I had no interest in the matter. I act entirely from a sense of public duty. I have no doubt, for example, that the Fernworthy people will burn me in effigy tonight. I told the police last time they did it that they should stop these disgraceful exhibitions. The County Constabulary is in a scandalous state, sir, and it has not afforded me the protection to which I am entitled. The case of Frankland v. Regina will bring the matter before the attention of the public. I told them that they would have occasion to regret their treatment of me, and already my words have come true."

"How so?" I asked.

The old man put on a very knowing expression. "Because I could tell them what they are dying to know; but nothing would induce me to help the rascals in any way."

I had been casting round for some excuse by which I could get away from his gossip, but now I began to wish to hear more of it. I had seen enough of the contrary nature of the old sinner to understand that any strong sign of interest would be the surest way to stop his confidences.

"Some poaching case, no doubt?" said I with an indifferent manner.

"Ha, ha, my boy, a very much more important matter than that! What about the convict on the moor?"

I stared. "You don't mean that you know where he is?" said I.

"I may not know exactly where he is, but I am quite sure that I could help the police to lay their hands on him. Has it never struck you that the way to catch that man was to find out where he got his food and so trace it to him?"

He certainly seemed to be getting uncomfortably near the truth. "No doubt," said I; "but how do you know that he is anywhere upon the moor?"

"I know it because I have seen with my own eyes the messenger who takes him his food."

My heart sank for Barrymore. It was a serious thing to be in the power of this spiteful old busybody. But his next remark took a weight from my mind.

"You'll be surprised to hear that his food is taken to him by a child. I see him every day through my telescope upon the roof. He passes along the same path at the same hour, and to whom should he be going except to the convict?"

Here was luck indeed! And yet I suppressed all appearance of interest. A child! Barrymore had said that our unknown was supplied by a boy. It was on his track, and not upon the convict's, that Frankland had stumbled. If I could get his knowledge it might save me a long and weary hunt. But incredulity and indifference were evidently my strongest cards.

"I should say that it was much more likely that it was the son of one of the moorland shepherds taking out his father's dinner."

The least appearance of opposition struck fire out of the old autocrat. His eyes looked malignantly at me, and his gray whiskers bristled like those of an angry cat.

"Indeed, sir!" said he, pointing out over the wide-stretching moor. "Do you see that Black Tor over yonder? Well, do you see the low hill beyond with the thornbush upon it? It is the stoniest part of the whole moor. Is that a place where a shepherd would be likely to take his station? Your suggestion, sir, is a most absurd one."

I meekly answered that I had spoken without knowing all the facts. My submission pleased him and led him to further confidences.

"You may be sure, sir, that I have very good grounds before I come to an opinion. I have seen the boy again and again with his bundle. Every day, and sometimes twice a day, I have been able—but wait a moment, Dr. Watson. Do my eyes deceive me, or is there at the present moment something moving upon that hillside?"

It was several miles off, but I could distinctly see a small dark dot against the dull green and gray.

"Come, sir, come!" cried Frankland, rushing upstairs. "You will see with your own eyes and judge for yourself."

The telescope, a formidable instrument mounted upon a tripod, stood upon the flat leads of the house. Frankland clapped his eye to it and gave a cry of satisfaction.

"Quick, Dr. Watson, quick, before he passes over the hill!"

There he was, sure enough, a small urchin with a little bundle upon his shoulder, toiling slowly up the hill. When he reached the crest I saw the ragged uncouth figure outlined for an instant against the cold blue sky. He looked round him with a furtive and stealthy air, as one who dreads pursuit. Then he vanished over the hill.

"Well! Am I right?"

"Certainly, there is a boy who seems to have some secret errand."

"And what the errand is even a county constable could guess. But not one word shall they have from me, and I bind you to secrecy also, Dr. Watson. Not a word! You understand!"

"Just as you wish."

"They have treated me shamefully—shamefully. When the facts come out in Frankland v. Regina I venture to think that a thrill of indignation will run through the country. Nothing would induce me to help the police in any way. For all they cared it might have been me, instead of my effigy, which these rascals burned at the stake. Surely you are not going! You will help me to empty the decanter in honour of this great occasion!"

But I resisted all his solicitations and succeeded in dissuading him from his announced intention of walking home with me. I kept the road as long as his eye was on me, and then I struck off across the moor and made for the stony hill over which the boy had disappeared. Everything was working in my favour, and I swore that it should not be through lack of energy or perseverance that I should miss the chance which fortune had thrown in my way.

The sun was already sinking when I reached the summit of the hill, and the long slopes beneath me were all golden-green on one side and gray shadow on the other. A haze lay low upon the farthest sky-line, out of which jutted the fantastic shapes of Belliver and Vixen Tor. Over the wide expanse there was no sound and no movement. One great gray bird, a gull or curlew, soared aloft in the blue heaven. He and I seemed to be the only living things between the huge arch of the sky and the desert beneath it. The barren scene, the sense of loneliness, and the mystery and urgency of my task all struck a chill into my heart. The boy was nowhere to be seen. But down beneath me in a cleft of the hills there was a circle of the old stone huts, and in the middle of them there was one which retained sufficient roof to act as a screen against the weather. My heart leaped within me as I saw it. This must be the burrow where the stranger lurked. At last my foot was on the threshold of his hiding place—his secret was within my grasp.

As I approached the hut, walking as warily as Stapleton would do when with poised net he drew near the settled butterfly, I satisfied myself that the place had indeed been used as a habitation. A vague pathway among the boulders led to the dilapidated opening which served as a door. All was silent within. The unknown might be lurking there, or he might be prowling on the moor. My nerves tingled with the sense of adventure. Throwing aside my cigarette, I closed my hand upon the butt of my revolver and, walking swiftly up to the door, I looked in. The place was empty.

But there were ample signs that I had not come upon a false scent. This was certainly where the man lived. Some blankets rolled in a waterproof lay upon that very stone slab upon which Neolithic man had once slumbered. The ashes of a fire were heaped in a rude grate. Beside it lay some cooking utensils and a bucket half-full of water. A litter of empty tins showed that the place had been occupied for some time, and I saw, as my eyes became accustomed to the checkered light, a pannikin and a half-full bottle of spirits standing in the corner. In the middle of the hut a flat stone served the purpose of a table, and upon this stood a small cloth bundle—the same, no doubt, which I had seen through the telescope upon the shoulder of the boy. It contained a loaf of bread, a tinned tongue, and two tins of preserved peaches. As I set it down again, after having examined it, my heart leaped to see that beneath it there lay a sheet of paper with writing upon it. I raised it, and this was what I read, roughly scrawled in pencil: "Dr. Watson has gone to Coombe Tracey."

For a minute I stood there with the paper in my hands thinking out the meaning of this curt message. It was I, then, and not Sir Henry, who was being dogged by this secret man. He had not followed me himself, but he had set an agent—the boy, perhaps—upon my track, and this was his report. Possibly I had taken no step since I had been upon the moor which had not been observed and reported. Always there was this feeling of an unseen force, a fine net drawn round us with infinite skill and delicacy, holding us so lightly that it was only at some supreme moment that one realized that one was indeed entangled in its meshes.

If there was one report there might be others, so I looked round the hut in search of them. There was no trace, however, of anything of the kind, nor could I discover any sign which might indicate the character or intentions of the man who lived in this singular place, save that he must be of Spartan habits and cared little for the comforts of life. When I thought of the heavy rains and looked at the gaping roof I understood how strong and immutable must be the purpose which had kept him in that inhospitable abode. Was he our malignant enemy, or was he by chance our guardian angel? I swore that I would not leave the hut until I knew.

Outside the sun was sinking low and the west was blazing with scarlet and gold. Its reflection was shot back in ruddy patches by the distant pools which lay amid the great Grimpen Mire. There were the two towers of Baskerville Hall, and there a distant blur of smoke which marked the village of Grimpen. Between the two, behind the hill, was the house of the Stapletons. All was sweet and mellow and peaceful in the golden evening light, and yet as I looked at them my soul shared none of the peace of Nature but quivered at the vagueness and the terror of that interview which every instant was bringing nearer. With tingling nerves but a fixed purpose, I sat in the dark recess of the hut and waited with sombre patience for the coming of its tenant.

And then at last I heard him. Far away came the sharp clink of a boot striking upon a stone. Then another and yet another, coming nearer and nearer. I shrank back into the darkest corner and cocked the pistol in my pocket, determined not to discover myself until I had an opportunity of seeing something of the stranger. There was a long pause which showed that he had stopped. Then once more the footsteps approached and a shadow fell across the opening of the hut.

"It is a lovely evening, my dear Watson," said a well-known voice. "I really think that you will be more comfortable outside than in."

Chapter 12. Death on the Moor

For a moment or two I sat breathless, hardly able to believe my ears. Then my senses and my voice came back to me, while a crushing weight of responsibility seemed in an instant to be lifted from my soul. That cold, incisive, ironical voice could belong to but one man in all the world.

"Holmes!" I cried—"Holmes!"

"Come out," said he, "and please be careful with the revolver."

I stooped under the rude lintel, and there he sat upon a stone outside, his gray eyes dancing with amusement as they fell upon my astonished features. He was thin and worn, but clear and alert, his keen face bronzed by the sun and roughened by the wind. In his tweed suit and cloth cap he looked like any other tourist upon the moor, and he had contrived, with that catlike love of personal cleanliness which was one of his characteristics, that his chin should be as smooth and his linen as perfect as if he were in Baker Street.

"I never was more glad to see anyone in my life," said I as I wrung him by the hand.

"Or more astonished, eh?"

"Well, I must confess to it."

"The surprise was not all on one side, I assure you. I had no idea that you had found my occasional retreat, still less that you were inside it, until I was within twenty paces of the door."

"My footprint, I presume?"

"No, Watson, I fear that I could not undertake to recognize your footprint amid all the footprints of the world. If you seriously desire to deceive me you must change your tobacconist; for when I see the stub of a cigarette marked Bradley, Oxford Street, I know that my friend Watson is in the neighbourhood. You will see it there beside the path. You threw it down, no doubt, at that supreme moment when you charged into the empty hut."

"Exactly."

"I thought as much—and knowing your admirable tenacity I was convinced that you were sitting in ambush, a weapon within reach, waiting for the tenant to return. So you actually thought that I was the criminal?"

"I did not know who you were, but I was determined to find out."

"Excellent, Watson! And how did you localize me? You saw me, perhaps, on the night of the convict hunt, when I was so imprudent as to allow the moon to rise behind me?"

"Yes, I saw you then."

"And have no doubt searched all the huts until you came to this one?"

"No, your boy had been observed, and that gave me a guide where to look."

"The old gentleman with the telescope, no doubt. I could not make it out when first I saw the light flashing upon the lens." He rose and peeped into the hut. "Ha, I see that Cartwright has brought up some supplies. What's this paper? So you have been to Coombe Tracey, have you?"

"Yes."

"To see Mrs. Laura Lyons?"

"Exactly."

"Well done! Our researches have evidently been running on parallel lines, and when we unite our results I expect we shall have a fairly full knowledge of the case."

"Well, I am glad from my heart that you are here, for indeed the responsibility and the mystery were both becoming too much for my nerves. But how in the name of wonder did you come here, and what have you been doing? I thought that you were in Baker Street working out that case of blackmailing."

"That was what I wished you to think."

"Then you use me, and yet do not trust me!" I cried with some bitterness. "I think that I have deserved better at your hands, Holmes."

"My dear fellow, you have been invaluable to me in this as in many other cases, and I beg that you will forgive me if I have seemed to play a trick upon you. In truth, it was partly for your own sake that I did it, and it was my appreciation of the danger which you ran which led me to come down and examine the matter for myself. Had I been with Sir Henry and you it is confident that my point of view would have been the same as yours, and my presence would have warned our very formidable opponents to be on their guard. As it is, I have been able to get about as I could not possibly have done had I been living in the Hall, and I remain an unknown factor in the business, ready to throw in all my weight at a critical moment."

"But why keep me in the dark?"

"For you to know could not have helped us and might possibly have led to my discovery. You would have wished to tell me something, or in your kindness you would have brought me out some comfort or other, and so an unnecessary risk would be run. I brought Cartwright down with me—you remember the little chap at the express office—and he has seen after my simple wants: a loaf of bread and a clean collar. What does man want more? He has given me an extra pair of eyes upon a very active pair of feet, and both have been invaluable."

"Then my reports have all been wasted!"—My voice trembled as I recalled the pains and the pride with which I had composed them.

Holmes took a bundle of papers from his pocket.

"Here are your reports, my dear fellow, and very well thumbed, I assure you. I made excellent arrangements, and they are only delayed one day upon their way. I must compliment you exceedingly upon the zeal and the intelligence which you have shown over an extraordinarily difficult case."

I was still rather raw over the deception which had been practised upon me, but the warmth of Holmes's praise drove my anger from my mind. I felt also in my heart that he was right in what he said and that it was really best for our purpose that I should not have known that he was upon the moor.

"That's better," said he, seeing the shadow rise from my face. "And now tell me the result of your visit to Mrs. Laura Lyons—it was not difficult for me to guess that it was to see her that you had gone, for I am already aware that she is the one person in Coombe Tracey who might be of service to us in the matter. In fact, if you had not gone today it is exceedingly probable that I should have gone tomorrow."

The sun had set and dusk was settling over the moor. The air had turned chill and we withdrew into the hut for warmth. There, sitting together in the twilight, I told Holmes of my conversation with the lady. So interested was he that I had to repeat some of it twice before he was satisfied.

"This is most important," said he when I had concluded. "It fills up a gap which I had been unable to bridge in this most complex affair. You are aware, perhaps, that a close intimacy exists between this lady and the man Stapleton?"

"I did not know of a close intimacy."

"There can be no doubt about the matter. They meet, they write, there is a complete understanding between them. Now, this puts a very powerful weapon into our hands. If I could only use it to detach his wife—"

"His wife?"

"I am giving you some information now, in return for all that you have given me. The lady who has passed here as Miss Stapleton is in reality his wife."

"Good heavens, Holmes! Are you sure of what you say? How could he have permitted Sir Henry to fall in love with her?"

"Sir Henry's falling in love could do no harm to anyone except Sir Henry. He took particular care that Sir Henry did not make love to her, as you have yourself observed. I repeat that the lady is his wife and not his sister."

"But why this elaborate deception?"

"Because he foresaw that she would be very much more useful to him in the character of a free woman."

All my unspoken instincts, my vague suspicions, suddenly took shape and centred upon the naturalist. In that impassive colourless man, with his straw hat and his butterfly-net, I seemed to see something terrible—a creature of infinite patience and craft, with a smiling face and a murderous heart.

"It is he, then, who is our enemy—it is he who dogged us in London?"

"So I read the riddle."

"And the warning—it must have come from her!"

"Exactly."

The shape of some monstrous villainy, half seen, half guessed, loomed through the darkness which had girt me so long.

"But are you sure of this, Holmes? How do you know that the woman is his wife?"

"Because he so far forgot himself as to tell you a true piece of autobiography upon the occasion when he first met you, and I dare say he has many a time regretted it since. He was once a schoolmaster in the north of England. Now, there is no one more easy to trace than a schoolmaster. There are scholastic agencies by which one may identify any man who has been in the profession. A little investigation showed me that a school had come to grief under atrocious circumstances, and that the man who had owned it—the name was different—had disappeared with his wife. The descriptions agreed. When I learned that the missing man was devoted to entomology the identification was complete."

The darkness was rising, but much was still hidden by the shadows.

"If this woman is in truth his wife, where does Mrs. Laura Lyons come in?" I asked.

"That is one of the points upon which your own researches have shed a light. Your interview with the lady has cleared the situation very much. I did not know about a projected divorce between herself and her husband. In that case, regarding Stapleton as an unmarried man, she counted no doubt upon becoming his wife."

"And when she is undeceived?"

"Why, then we may find the lady of service. It must be our first duty to see her—both of us—tomorrow. Don't you think, Watson, that you are away from your charge rather long? Your place should be at Baskerville Hall."

The last red streaks had faded away in the west and night had settled upon the moor. A few faint stars were gleaming in a violet sky.

"One last question, Holmes," I said as I rose. "Surely there is no need of secrecy between you and me. What is the meaning of it all? What is he after?"

Holmes's voice sank as he answered:

"It is murder, Watson—refined, cold-blooded, deliberate murder. Do not ask me for particulars. My nets are closing upon him, even as his are upon Sir Henry, and with your help he is already almost at my mercy. There is but one danger which can threaten us. It is that he should strike before we are ready to do so. Another day—two at the most—and I have my case complete, but until then guard your charge as closely as ever a fond mother watched her ailing child. Your mission today has justified itself, and yet I could almost wish that you had not left his side. Hark!"

A terrible scream—a prolonged yell of horror and anguish—burst out of the silence of the moor. That frightful cry turned the blood to ice in my veins.

"Oh, my God!" I gasped. "What is it? What does it mean?"

Holmes had sprung to his feet, and I saw his dark, athletic outline at the door of the hut, his shoulders stooping, his head thrust forward, his face peering into the darkness.

"Hush!" he whispered. "Hush!"

The cry had been loud on account of its vehemence, but it had pealed out from somewhere far off on the shadowy plain. Now it burst upon our ears, nearer, louder, more urgent than before.

"Where is it?" Holmes whispered; and I knew from the thrill of his voice that he, the man of iron, was shaken to the soul. "Where is it, Watson?"

"There, I think." I pointed into the darkness.

"No, there!"

Again the agonized cry swept through the silent night, louder and much nearer than ever. And a new sound mingled with it, a deep, muttered rumble, musical and yet menacing, rising and falling like the low, constant murmur of the sea.

"The hound!" cried Holmes. "Come, Watson, come! Great heavens, if we are too late!"

He had started running swiftly over the moor, and I had followed at his heels. But now from somewhere among the broken ground immediately in front of us there came one last despairing yell, and then a dull, heavy thud. We halted and listened. Not another sound broke the heavy silence of the windless night.

I saw Holmes put his hand to his forehead like a man distracted. He stamped his feet upon the ground.

"He has beaten us, Watson. We are too late."

"No, no, surely not!"

"Fool that I was to hold my hand. And you, Watson, see what comes of abandoning your charge! But, by Heaven, if the worst has happened we'll avenge him!"

Blindly we ran through the gloom, blundering against boulders, forcing our way through gorse bushes, panting up hills and rushing down slopes, heading always in the direction whence those dreadful sounds had come. At every rise Holmes looked eagerly round him, but the shadows were thick upon the moor, and nothing moved upon its dreary face.

"Can you see anything?"

"Nothing."

"But, hark, what is that?"

A low moan had fallen upon our ears. There it was again upon our left! On that side a ridge of rocks ended in a sheer cliff which overlooked a stone-strewn slope. On its jagged face was spread-eagled some dark, irregular object. As we ran towards it the vague outline hardened into a definite shape. It was a prostrate man face downward upon the ground, the head doubled under him at a horrible angle, the shoulders rounded and the body hunched together as if in the act of throwing a somersault. So grotesque was the attitude that I could not for the instant realize that that moan had been the passing of his soul. Not a whisper, not a rustle, rose now from the dark figure over which we stooped. Holmes laid his hand upon him and held it up again with an exclamation of horror. The gleam of the match which he struck shone upon his clotted fingers and upon the ghastly pool which widened slowly from the crushed skull of the victim. And it shone upon something else which turned our hearts sick and faint within us—the body of Sir Henry Baskerville!

There was no chance of either of us forgetting that peculiar ruddy tweed suit—the very one which he had worn on the first morning that we had seen him in Baker Street. We caught the one clear glimpse of it, and then the match flickered and went out, even as the hope had gone out of our souls. Holmes groaned, and his face glimmered white through the darkness.

"The brute! The brute!" I cried with clenched hands. "Oh Holmes, I shall never forgive myself for having left him to his fate."

"I am more to blame than you, Watson. In order to have my case well rounded and complete, I have thrown away the life of my client. It is the greatest blow which has befallen me in my career. But how could I know—how could I know—that he would risk his life alone upon the moor in the face of all my warnings?"

"That we should have heard his screams—my God, those screams!--and yet have been unable to save him! Where is this brute of a hound which drove him to his death? It may be lurking among these rocks at this instant. And Stapleton, where is he? He shall answer for this deed."

"He shall. I will see to that. Uncle and nephew have been murdered—the one frightened to death by the very sight of a beast which he thought to be supernatural, the other driven to his end in his wild flight to escape from it. But now we have to prove the connection between the man and the beast. Save from what we heard, we cannot even swear to the existence of the latter, since Sir Henry has evidently died from the fall. But, by heavens, cunning as he is, the fellow shall be in my power before another day is past!"

We stood with bitter hearts on either side of the mangled body, overwhelmed by this sudden and irrevocable disaster which had brought all our long and weary labours to so piteous an end. Then as the moon rose we climbed to the top of the rocks over which our poor friend had fallen, and from the summit we gazed out over the shadowy moor, half silver and half gloom. Far away, miles off, in the direction of

Grimpen, a single steady yellow light was shining. It could only come from the lonely abode of the Stapletons. With a bitter curse I shook my fist at it as I gazed.

"Why should we not seize him at once?"

"Our case is not complete. The fellow is wary and cunning to the last degree. It is not what we know, but what we can prove. If we make one false move the villain may escape us yet."

"What can we do?"

"There will be plenty for us to do tomorrow. Tonight we can only perform the last offices to our poor friend."

Together we made our way down the precipitous slope and approached the body, black and clear against the silvered stones. The agony of those contorted limbs struck me with a spasm of pain and blurred my eyes with tears.

"We must send for help, Holmes! We cannot carry him all the way to the Hall. Good heavens, are you mad?"

He had uttered a cry and bent over the body. Now he was dancing and laughing and wringing my hand. Could this be my stern, self-contained friend? These were hidden fires, indeed!

"A beard! A beard! The man has a beard!"

"A beard?"

"It is not the baronet—it is—why, it is my neighbour, the convict!"

With feverish haste we had turned the body over, and that dripping beard was pointing up to the cold, clear moon. There could be no doubt about the beetling forehead, the sunken animal eyes. It was indeed the same face which had glared upon me in the light of the candle from over the rock—the face of Selden, the criminal.

Then in an instant it was all clear to me. I remembered how the baronet had told me that he had handed his old wardrobe to Barrymore. Barrymore had passed it on in order to help Selden in his escape. Boots, shirt, cap—it was all Sir Henry's. The tragedy was still black enough, but this man had at least deserved death by the laws of his country. I told Holmes how the matter stood, my heart bubbling over with thankfulness and joy.

"Then the clothes have been the poor devil's death," said he. "It is clear enough that the hound has been laid on from some article of Sir Henry's—the boot which was abstracted in the hotel, in all probability—and so ran this man down. There is one very singular thing, however: How came Selden, in the darkness, to know that the hound was on his trail?"

"He heard him."

"To hear a hound upon the moor would not work a hard man like this convict into such a paroxysm of terror that he would risk recapture by screaming wildly for help. By his cries he must have run a long way after he knew the animal was on his track. How did he know?"

"A greater mystery to me is why this hound, presuming that all our conjectures are correct—"

"I presume nothing."

"Well, then, why this hound should be loose tonight. I suppose that it does not always run loose upon the moor. Stapleton would not let it go unless he had reason to think that Sir Henry would be there."

"My difficulty is the more formidable of the two, for I think that we shall very shortly get an explanation of yours, while mine may remain forever a mystery. The question now is, what shall we do with this poor wretch's body? We cannot leave it here to the foxes and the ravens."

"I suggest that we put it in one of the huts until we can communicate with the police."

"Exactly. I have no doubt that you and I could carry it so far. Halloa, Watson, what's this? It's the man himself, by all that's wonderful and audacious! Not a word to show your suspicions—not a word, or my plans crumble to the ground."

A figure was approaching us over the moor, and I saw the dull red glow of a cigar. The moon shone upon him, and I could distinguish the dapper shape and jaunty walk of the naturalist. He stopped when he saw us, and then came on again.

"Why, Dr. Watson, that's not you, is it? You are the last man that I should have expected to see out on the moor at this time of night. But, dear me, what's this? Somebody hurt? Not—don't tell me that it is our friend Sir Henry!" He hurried past me and stooped over the dead man. I heard a sharp intake of his breath and the cigar fell from his fingers.

"Who—who's this?" he stammered.

"It is Selden, the man who escaped from Princetown."

Stapleton turned a ghastly face upon us, but by a supreme effort he had overcome his amazement and his disappointment. He looked sharply from Holmes to me. "Dear me! What a very shocking affair! How did he die?"

"He appears to have broken his neck by falling over these rocks. My friend and I were strolling on the moor when we heard a cry."

"I heard a cry also. That was what brought me out. I was uneasy about Sir Henry."

"Why about Sir Henry in particular?" I could not help asking.

"Because I had suggested that he should come over. When he did not come I was surprised, and I naturally became alarmed for his safety when I heard cries upon the moor. By the way"—his eyes darted again from my face to Holmes's—"did you hear anything else besides a cry?"

"No," said Holmes; "did you?"

"No."

"What do you mean, then?"

"Oh, you know the stories that the peasants tell about a phantom hound, and so on. It is said to be heard at night upon the moor. I was wondering if there were any evidence of such a sound tonight."

"We heard nothing of the kind," said I.

"And what is your theory of this poor fellow's death?"

"I have no doubt that anxiety and exposure have driven him off his head. He has rushed about the moor in a crazy state and eventually fallen over here and broken his neck."

"That seems the most reasonable theory," said Stapleton, and he gave a sigh which I took to indicate his relief. "What do you think about it, Mr. Sherlock Holmes?"

My friend bowed his compliments. "You are quick at identification," said he.

"We have been expecting you in these parts since Dr. Watson came down. You are in time to see a tragedy."

"Yes, indeed. I have no doubt that my friend's explanation will cover the facts. I will take an unpleasant remembrance back to London with me tomorrow."

"Oh, you return tomorrow?"

"That is my intention."

"I hope your visit has cast some light upon those occurrences which have puzzled us?"

Holmes shrugged his shoulders.

"One cannot always have the success for which one hopes. An investigator needs facts and not legends or rumours. It has not been a satisfactory case."

My friend spoke in his frankest and most unconcerned manner. Stapleton still looked hard at him. Then he turned to me.

"I would suggest carrying this poor fellow to my house, but it would give my sister such a fright that I do not feel justified in doing it. I think that if we put something over his face he will be safe until morning."

And so it was arranged. Resisting Stapleton's offer of hospitality, Holmes and I set off to Baskerville Hall, leaving the naturalist to return alone. Looking back we saw the figure moving slowly away over the broad moor, and behind him that one black smudge on the silvered slope which showed where the man was lying who had come so horribly to his end.

Chapter 13. Fixing the Nets

"We're at close grips at last," said Holmes as we walked together across the moor. "What a nerve the fellow has! How he pulled himself together in the face of what must have been a paralyzing shock when he found that the wrong man had fallen a victim to his plot. I told you in London, Watson, and I tell you now again, that we have never had a foeman more worthy of our steel."

"I am sorry that he has seen you."

"And so was I at first. But there was no getting out of it."

"What effect do you think it will have upon his plans now that he knows you are here?"

"It may cause him to be more cautious, or it may drive him to desperate measures at once. Like most clever criminals, he may be too confident in his own cleverness and imagine that he has completely deceived us."

"Why should we not arrest him at once?"

"My dear Watson, you were born to be a man of action. Your instinct is always to do something energetic. But supposing, for argument's sake, that we had him arrested tonight, what on earth the better off should we be for that? We could prove nothing against him. There's the devilish cunning of it! If he were acting through a human agent we could get some evidence, but if we were to drag this great dog to the light of day it would not help us in putting a rope round the neck of its master."

"Surely we have a case."

"Not a shadow of one—only surmise and conjecture. We should be laughed out of court if we came with such a story and such evidence."

"There is Sir Charles's death."

"Found dead without a mark upon him. You and I know that he died of sheer fright, and we know also what frightened him, but how are we to get twelve stolid jurymen to know it? What signs are there of a hound? Where are the marks of its fangs? Of course we know that a hound does not bite a dead body and that Sir Charles was dead before ever the brute overtook him. But we have to prove all this, and we are not in a position to do it."

"Well, then, tonight?"

"We are not much better off tonight. Again, there was no direct connection between the hound and the man's death. We never saw the hound. We heard it, but we could not prove that it was running upon this man's trail. There is a complete absence of motive. No, my dear fellow; we must reconcile ourselves to the fact that we have no case at present, and that it is worth our while to run any risk in order to establish one."

"And how do you propose to do so?"

"I have great hopes of what Mrs. Laura Lyons may do for us when the position of affairs is made clear to her. And I have my own plan as well. Sufficient for tomorrow is the evil thereof; but I hope before the day is past to have the upper hand at last."

I could draw nothing further from him, and he walked, lost in thought, as far as the Baskerville gates.

"Are you coming up?"

"Yes; I see no reason for further concealment. But one last word, Watson. Say nothing of the hound to Sir Henry. Let him think that Selden's death was as Stapleton would have us believe. He will have a better nerve for the ordeal which he will have to undergo tomorrow, when he is engaged, if I remember your report aright, to dine with these people."

"And so am I."

"Then you must excuse yourself and he must go alone. That will be easily arranged. And now, if we are too late for dinner, I think that we are both ready for our suppers."

Sir Henry was more pleased than surprised to see Sherlock Holmes, for he had for some days been expecting that recent events would bring him down from London. He did raise his eyebrows, however, when he found that my friend had neither any luggage nor any explanations for its absence. Between us we soon supplied his wants, and then over a belated supper we explained to the baronet as much of our experience as it seemed desirable that he should know. But first I had the unpleasant duty of breaking the news to Barrymore and his wife. To him it may have been an unmitigated relief, but she wept bitterly in her apron. To all the world he was the man of violence, half animal and half demon; but to her he always remained the little wilful boy of her own girlhood, the child who had clung to her hand. Evil indeed is the man who has not one woman to mourn him.

"I've been moping in the house all day since Watson went off in the morning," said the baronet. "I guess I should have some credit, for I have kept my promise. If I hadn't sworn not to go about alone I might have had a more lively evening, for I had a message from Stapleton asking me over there."

"I have no doubt that you would have had a more lively evening," said Holmes drily. "By the way, I don't suppose you appreciate that we have been mourning over you as having broken your neck?"

Sir Henry opened his eyes. "How was that?"

"This poor wretch was dressed in your clothes. I fear your servant who gave them to him may get into trouble with the police."

"That is unlikely. There was no mark on any of them, as far as I know."

"That's lucky for him—in fact, it's lucky for all of you, since you are all on the wrong side of the law in this matter. I am not sure that as a conscientious detective my first duty is not to arrest the whole household. Watson's reports are most incriminating documents."

"But how about the case?" asked the baronet. "Have you made anything out of the tangle? I don't know that Watson and I are much the wiser since we came down."

"I think that I shall be in a position to make the situation rather more clear to you before long. It has been an exceedingly difficult and most complicated business. There are several points upon which we still want light—but it is coming all the same."

"We've had one experience, as Watson has no doubt told you. We heard the hound on the moor, so I can swear that it is not all empty superstition. I had something to do with dogs when I was out West, and I know one when I hear one. If you can muzzle that one and put him on a chain I'll be ready to swear you are the greatest detective of all time."

"I think I will muzzle him and chain him all right if you will give me your help."

"Whatever you tell me to do I will do."

"Very good; and I will ask you also to do it blindly, without always asking the reason."

"Just as you like."

"If you will do this I think the chances are that our little problem will soon be solved. I have no doubt—"

He stopped suddenly and stared fixedly up over my head into the air. The lamp beat upon his face, and so intent was it and so still that it might have been that of a clear-cut classical statue, a personification of alertness and expectation.

"What is it?" we both cried.

I could see as he looked down that he was repressing some internal emotion. His features were still composed, but his eyes shone with amused exultation.

"Excuse the admiration of a connoisseur," said he as he waved his hand towards the line of portraits which covered the opposite wall. "Watson won't allow that I know anything of art but that is mere jealousy because our views upon the subject differ. Now, these are a really very fine series of portraits."

"Well, I'm glad to hear you say so," said Sir Henry, glancing with some surprise at my friend. "I don't pretend to know much about these things, and I'd be a better judge of a horse or a steer than of a picture. I didn't know that you found time for such things."

"I know what is good when I see it, and I see it now. That's a Kneller, I'll swear, that lady in the blue silk over yonder, and the stout gentleman with the wig ought to be a Reynolds. They are all family portraits, I presume?"

"Every one."

"Do you know the names?"

"Barrymore has been coaching me in them, and I think I can say my lessons fairly well."

"Who is the gentleman with the telescope?"

"That is Rear-Admiral Baskerville, who served under Rodney in the West Indies. The man with the blue coat and the roll of paper is Sir William Baskerville, who was Chairman of Committees of the House of Commons under Pitt."

"And this Cavalier opposite to me—the one with the black velvet and the lace?"

"Ah, you have a right to know about him. That is the cause of all the mischief, the wicked Hugo, who started the Hound of the Baskervilles. We're not likely to forget him."

I gazed with interest and some surprise upon the portrait.

"Dear me!" said Holmes, "he seems a quiet, meek-mannered man enough, but I dare say that there was a lurking devil in his eyes. I had pictured him as a more robust and ruffianly person."

"There's no doubt about the authenticity, for the name and the date, 1647, are on the back of the canvas."

Holmes said little more, but the picture of the old roysterer seemed to have a fascination for him, and his eyes were continually fixed upon it during supper. It was not until later, when Sir Henry had gone to his room, that I was able to follow the trend of his thoughts. He led me back into the banqueting-hall, his bedroom candle in his hand, and he held it up against the time-stained portrait on the wall.

"Do you see anything there?"

I looked at the broad plumed hat, the curling love-locks, the white lace collar, and the straight, severe face which was framed between them. It was not a brutal countenance, but it was prim, hard, and stern, with a firm-set, thin-lipped mouth, and a coldly intolerant eye.

"Is it like anyone you know?"

"There is something of Sir Henry about the jaw."

"Just a suggestion, perhaps. But wait an instant!" He stood upon a chair, and, holding up the light in his left hand, he curved his right arm over the broad hat and round the long ringlets.

"Good heavens!" I cried in amazement.

The face of Stapleton had sprung out of the canvas.

"Ha, you see it now. My eyes have been trained to examine faces and not their trimmings. It is the first quality of a criminal investigator that he should see through a disguise."

"But this is marvellous. It might be his portrait."

"Yes, it is an interesting instance of a throwback, which appears to be both physical and spiritual. A study of family portraits is enough to convert a man to the doctrine of reincarnation. The fellow is a Baskerville—that is evident."

"With designs upon the succession."

"Exactly. This chance of the picture has supplied us with one of our most obvious missing links. We have him, Watson, we have him, and I dare swear that before tomorrow night he will be fluttering in our net as helpless as one of his own butterflies. A pin, a cork, and a card, and we add him to the Baker Street collection!" He burst into one of his rare fits of laughter as he turned away from the picture. I have not heard him laugh often, and it has always boded ill to somebody.

I was up betimes in the morning, but Holmes was afoot earlier still, for I saw him as I dressed, coming up the drive.

"Yes, we should have a full day today," he remarked, and he rubbed his hands with the joy of action. "The nets are all in place, and the drag is about to begin. We'll know before the day is out whether we have caught our big, leanjawed pike, or whether he has got through the meshes."

"Have you been on the moor already?"

"I have sent a report from Grimpen to Princetown as to the death of Selden. I think I can promise that none of you will be troubled in the matter. And I have also communicated with my faithful Cartwright, who would certainly have pined away at the door of my hut, as a dog does at his master's grave, if I had not set his mind at rest about my safety."

"What is the next move?"

"To see Sir Henry. Ah, here he is!"

"Good-morning, Holmes," said the baronet. "You look like a general who is planning a battle with his chief of the staff."

"That is the exact situation. Watson was asking for orders."

"And so do I."

"Very good. You are engaged, as I understand, to dine with our friends the Stapletons tonight."

"I hope that you will come also. They are very hospitable people, and I am sure that they would be very glad to see you."

"I fear that Watson and I must go to London."

"To London?"

"Yes, I think that we should be more useful there at the present juncture."

The baronet's face perceptibly lengthened.

"I hoped that you were going to see me through this business. The Hall and the moor are not very pleasant places when one is alone."

"My dear fellow, you must trust me implicitly and do exactly what I tell you. You can tell your friends that we should have been happy to have come with you, but that urgent business required us to be in town. We hope very soon to return to Devonshire. Will you remember to give them that message?"

"If you insist upon it."

"There is no alternative, I assure you."

I saw by the baronet's clouded brow that he was deeply hurt by what he regarded as our desertion.

"When do you desire to go?" he asked coldly.

"Immediately after breakfast. We will drive in to Coombe Tracey, but Watson will leave his things as a pledge that he will come back to you. Watson, you will send a note to Stapleton to tell him that you regret that you cannot come."

"I have a good mind to go to London with you," said the baronet. "Why should I stay here alone?"

"Because it is your post of duty. Because you gave me your word that you would do as you were told, and I tell you to stay."

"All right, then, I'll stay."

"One more direction! I wish you to drive to Merripit House. Send back your trap, however, and let them know that you intend to walk home."

"To walk across the moor?"

"Yes."

"But that is the very thing which you have so often cautioned me not to do."

"This time you may do it with safety. If I had not every confidence in your nerve and courage I would not suggest it, but it is essential that you should do it."

"Then I will do it."

"And as you value your life do not go across the moor in any direction save along the straight path which leads from Merripit House to the Grimpen Road, and is your natural way home."

"I will do just what you say."

"Very good. I should be glad to get away as soon after breakfast as possible, so as to reach London in the afternoon."

I was much astounded by this programme, though I remembered that Holmes had said to Stapleton on the night before that his visit would terminate next day. It had not crossed my mind however, that he would wish me to go with him, nor could

I understand how we could both be absent at a moment which he himself declared to be critical. There was nothing for it, however, but implicit obedience; so we bade good-bye to our rueful friend, and a couple of hours afterwards we were at the station of Coombe Tracey and had dispatched the trap upon its return journey. A small boy was waiting upon the platform.

"Any orders, sir?"

"You will take this train to town, Cartwright. The moment you arrive you will send a wire to Sir Henry Baskerville, in my name, to say that if he finds the pocketbook which I have dropped he is to send it by registered post to Baker Street."

"Yes, sir."

"And ask at the station office if there is a message for me."

The boy returned with a telegram, which Holmes handed to me. It ran:

Wire received. Coming down with unsigned warrant. Arrive five-forty. Lestrade.

"That is in answer to mine of this morning. He is the best of the professionals, I think, and we may need his assistance. Now, Watson, I think that we cannot employ our time better than by calling upon your acquaintance, Mrs. Laura Lyons."

His plan of campaign was beginning to be evident. He would use the baronet in order to convince the Stapletons that we were really gone, while we should actually return at the instant when we were likely to be needed. That telegram from London, if mentioned by Sir Henry to the Stapletons, must remove the last suspicions from their minds. Already I seemed to see our nets drawing closer around that leanjawed pike.

Mrs. Laura Lyons was in her office, and Sherlock Holmes opened his interview with a frankness and directness which considerably amazed her.

"I am investigating the circumstances which attended the death of the late Sir Charles Baskerville," said he. "My friend here, Dr. Watson, has informed me of what you have communicated, and also of what you have withheld in connection with that matter."

"What have I withheld?" she asked defiantly.

"You have confessed that you asked Sir Charles to be at the gate at ten o'clock. We know that that was the place and hour of his death. You have withheld what the connection is between these events."

"There is no connection."

"In that case the coincidence must indeed be an extraordinary one. But I think that we shall succeed in establishing a connection, after all. I wish to be perfectly frank with you, Mrs. Lyons. We regard this case as one of murder, and the evidence may implicate not only your friend Mr. Stapleton but his wife as well."

The lady sprang from her chair.

"His wife!" she cried.

"The fact is no longer a secret. The person who has passed for his sister is really his wife."

Mrs. Lyons had resumed her seat. Her hands were grasping the arms of her chair, and I saw that the pink nails had turned white with the pressure of her grip.

"His wife!" she said again. "His wife! He is not a married man."

Sherlock Holmes shrugged his shoulders.

"Prove it to me! Prove it to me! And if you can do so--!"

The fierce flash of her eyes said more than any words.

"I have come prepared to do so," said Holmes, drawing several papers from his pocket. "Here is a photograph of the couple taken in York four years ago. It is indorsed 'Mr. and Mrs. Vandeleur,' but you will have no difficulty in recognizing him, and her also, if you know her by sight. Here are three written descriptions by trustworthy witnesses of Mr. and Mrs. Vandeleur, who at that time kept St. Oliver's private school. Read them and see if you can doubt the identity of these people."

She glanced at them, and then looked up at us with the set, rigid face of a desperate woman.

"Mr. Holmes," she said, "this man had offered me marriage on condition that I could get a divorce from my husband. He has lied to me, the villain, in every conceivable way. Not one word of truth has he ever told me. And why—why? I imagined that all was for my own sake. But now I see that I was never anything but a tool in his hands. Why should I preserve faith with him who never kept any with me? Why should I try to shield him from the consequences of his own wicked acts? Ask me what you like, and there is nothing which I shall hold back. One thing I swear to you, and that is that when I wrote the letter I never dreamed of any harm to the old gentleman, who had been my kindest friend."

"I entirely believe you, madam," said Sherlock Holmes. "The recital of these events must be very painful to you, and perhaps it will make it easier if I tell you what occurred, and you can check me if I make any material mistake. The sending of this letter was suggested to you by Stapleton?"

"He dictated it."

"I presume that the reason he gave was that you would receive help from Sir Charles for the legal expenses connected with your divorce?"

"Exactly."

"And then after you had sent the letter he dissuaded you from keeping the appointment?"

"He told me that it would hurt his self-respect that any other man should find the money for such an object, and that though he was a poor man himself he would devote his last penny to removing the obstacles which divided us."

"He appears to be a very consistent character. And then you heard nothing until you read the reports of the death in the paper?"

"No."

"And he made you swear to say nothing about your appointment with Sir Charles?"

"He did. He said that the death was a very mysterious one, and that I should certainly be suspected if the facts came out. He frightened me into remaining silent."

"Quite so. But you had your suspicions?"

She hesitated and looked down.

"I knew him," she said. "But if he had kept faith with me I should always have done so with him."

"I think that on the whole you have had a fortunate escape," said Sherlock Holmes. "You have had him in your power and he knew it, and yet you are alive. You have been walking for some months very near to the edge of a precipice. We must wish you good-morning now, Mrs. Lyons, and it is probable that you will very shortly hear from us again."

"Our case becomes rounded off, and difficulty after difficulty thins away in front of us," said Holmes as we stood waiting for the arrival of the express from town. "I shall soon be in the position of being able to put into a single connected narrative one of the most singular and sensational crimes of modern times. Students of criminology will remember the analogous incidents in Godno, in Little Russia, in the year '66, and of course there are the Anderson murders in North Carolina, but this case possesses some features which are entirely its own. Even now we have no clear case against this very wily man. But I shall be very much surprised if it is not clear enough before we go to bed this night."

The London express came roaring into the station, and a small, wiry bulldog of a man had sprung from a first-class carriage. We all three shook hands, and I saw at once from the reverential way in which Lestrade gazed at my companion that he had learned a good deal since the days when they had first worked together. I could well remember the scorn which the theories of the reasoner used then to excite in the practical man.

"Anything good?" he asked.

"The biggest thing for years," said Holmes. "We have two hours before we need think of starting. I think we might employ it in getting some dinner and then, Lestrade, we will take the London fog out of your throat by giving you a breath of the pure night air of Dartmoor. Never been there? Ah, well, I don't suppose you will forget your first visit."

Chapter 14. The Hound of the Baskervilles

One of Sherlock Holmes's defects—if, indeed, one may call it a defect—was that he was exceedingly loath to communicate his full plans to any other person until the instant of their fulfilment. Partly it came no doubt from his own masterful nature, which loved to dominate and surprise those who were around him. Partly also from his professional caution, which urged him never to take any chances. The result, however, was very trying for those who were acting as his agents and assistants. I had often suffered under it, but never more so than during that long drive in the darkness. The great ordeal was in front of us; at last we were about to make our final effort, and yet Holmes had said nothing, and I could only surmise what his course of action would be. My nerves thrilled with anticipation when at last the cold wind upon our faces and the dark, void spaces on either side of the narrow road told me that we were back upon the moor once again. Every stride of the horses and every turn of the wheels was taking us nearer to our supreme adventure.

Our conversation was hampered by the presence of the driver of the hired wagonette, so that we were forced to talk of trivial matters when our nerves were tense with emotion and anticipation. It was a relief to me, after that unnatural restraint, when we at last passed Frankland's house and knew that we were drawing near to the Hall and to the scene of action. We did not drive up to the door but got down near the gate of the avenue. The wagonette was paid off and ordered to return to Coombe Tracey forthwith, while we started to walk to Merripit House.

"Are you armed, Lestrade?"

The little detective smiled. "As long as I have my trousers I have a hip-pocket, and as long as I have my hip-pocket I have something in it."

"Good! My friend and I are also ready for emergencies."

"You're mighty close about this affair, Mr. Holmes. What's the game now?"

"A waiting game."

"My word, it does not seem a very cheerful place," said the detective with a shiver, glancing round him at the gloomy slopes of the hill and at the huge lake of fog which lay over the Grimpen Mire. "I see the lights of a house ahead of us."

"That is Merripit House and the end of our journey. I must request you to walk on tiptoe and not to talk above a whisper."

We moved cautiously along the track as if we were bound for the house, but Holmes halted us when we were about two hundred yards from it.

"This will do," said he. "These rocks upon the right make an admirable screen."

"We are to wait here?"

"Yes, we shall make our little ambush here. Get into this hollow, Lestrade. You have been inside the house, have you not, Watson? Can you tell the position of the rooms? What are those latticed windows at this end?"

"I think they are the kitchen windows."

"And the one beyond, which shines so brightly?"

"That is certainly the dining-room."

"The blinds are up. You know the lie of the land best. Creep forward quietly and see what they are doing—but for heaven's sake don't let them know that they are watched!"

I tiptoed down the path and stooped behind the low wall which surrounded the stunted orchard. Creeping in its shadow I reached a point whence I could look straight through the uncurtained window.

There were only two men in the room, Sir Henry and Stapleton. They sat with their profiles towards me on either side of the round table. Both of them were smoking cigars, and coffee and wine were in front of them. Stapleton was talking with animation, but the baronet looked pale and distrait. Perhaps the thought of that lonely walk across the ill-omened moor was weighing heavily upon his mind.

As I watched them Stapleton rose and left the room, while Sir Henry filled his glass again and leaned back in his chair, puffing at his cigar. I heard the creak of a door and the crisp sound of boots upon gravel. The steps passed along the path on the other side of the wall under which I crouched. Looking over, I saw the naturalist pause at the door of an out-house in the corner of the orchard. A key turned in a lock, and as he passed in there was a curious scuffling noise from within. He was only a minute or so inside, and then I heard the key turn once more and he passed me and reentered the house. I saw him rejoin his guest, and I crept quietly back to where my companions were waiting to tell them what I had seen.

"You say, Watson, that the lady is not there?" Holmes asked when I had finished my report.

"No."

"Where can she be, then, since there is no light in any other room except the kitchen?"

"I cannot think where she is."

I have said that over the great Grimpen Mire there hung a dense, white fog. It was drifting slowly in our direction and banked itself up like a wall on that side of us, low but thick and well defined. The moon shone on it, and it looked like a great shimmering ice-field, with the heads of the distant tors as rocks borne upon its surface. Holmes's face was turned towards it, and he muttered impatiently as he watched its sluggish drift.

"It's moving towards us, Watson."

"Is that serious?"

"Very serious, indeed—the one thing upon earth which could have disarranged my plans. He can't be very long, now. It is already ten o'clock. Our success and even his life may depend upon his coming out before the fog is over the path."

The night was clear and fine above us. The stars shone cold and bright, while a half-moon bathed the whole scene in a soft, uncertain light. Before us lay the dark bulk of the house, its serrated roof and bristling chimneys hard outlined against the silver-spangled sky. Broad bars of golden light from the lower windows stretched across the orchard and the moor. One of them was suddenly shut off. The servants had left the kitchen. There only remained the lamp in the dining-room where the two men, the murderous host and the unconscious guest, still chatted over their cigars.

Every minute that white woolly plain which covered one-half of the moor was drifting closer and closer to the house. Already the first thin wisps of it were curling across the golden square of the lighted window. The farther wall of the orchard was already invisible, and the trees were standing out of a swirl of white vapour. As we watched it the fog-wreaths came crawling round both corners of the house and rolled slowly into one dense bank on which the upper floor and the roof floated like a strange ship upon a shadowy sea. Holmes struck his hand passionately upon the rock in front of us and stamped his feet in his impatience.

"If he isn't out in a quarter of an hour the path will be covered. In half an hour we won't be able to see our hands in front of us."

"Shall we move farther back upon higher ground?"

"Yes, I think it would be as well."

So as the fog-bank flowed onward we fell back before it until we were half a mile from the house, and still that dense white sea, with the moon silvering its upper edge, swept slowly and inexorably on.

"We are going too far," said Holmes. "We dare not take the chance of his being overtaken before he can reach us. At all costs we must hold our ground where we are." He dropped on his knees and clapped his ear to the ground. "Thank God, I think that I hear him coming."

A sound of quick steps broke the silence of the moor. Crouching among the stones we stared intently at the silver-tipped bank in front of us. The steps grew louder, and through the fog, as through a curtain, there stepped the man whom we were awaiting. He looked round him in surprise as he emerged into the clear, starlit night. Then he came swiftly along the path, passed close to where we lay, and went on up the long slope behind us. As he walked he glanced continually over either shoulder, like a man who is ill at ease.

"Hist!" cried Holmes, and I heard the sharp click of a cocking pistol. "Look out! It's coming!"

There was a thin, crisp, continuous patter from somewhere in the heart of that crawling bank. The cloud was within fifty yards of where we lay, and we glared at it, all three, uncertain what horror was about to break from the heart of it. I was at Holmes's elbow, and I glanced for an instant at his face. It was pale and exultant, his eyes shining brightly in the moonlight. But suddenly they started forward in a rigid, fixed stare, and his lips parted in amazement. At the same instant Lestrade gave a yell of terror and threw himself face downward upon the ground. I sprang to my feet, my inert hand grasping my pistol, my mind paralyzed by the dreadful shape which had sprung out upon us from the shadows of the fog. A hound it was, an enormous coal-black hound, but not such a hound as mortal eyes have ever seen. Fire burst from its open mouth, its eyes glowed with a smouldering glare, its muzzle and hackles and dewlap were outlined in flickering flame. Never in the delirious dream of a disordered brain could anything more savage, more appalling, more hellish be conceived than that dark form and savage face which broke upon us out of the wall of fog.

With long bounds the huge black creature was leaping down the track, following hard upon the footsteps of our friend. So paralyzed were we by the apparition that we allowed him to pass before we had recovered our nerve. Then Holmes and I both fired together, and the creature gave a hideous howl, which showed that one at least had hit him. He did not pause, however, but bounded onward. Far away on the path we saw Sir Henry looking back, his face white in the moonlight, his hands raised in horror, glaring helplessly at the frightful thing which was hunting him down. But that cry of pain from the hound had blown all our fears to the winds. If he was vulnerable he was mortal, and if we could wound him we could kill him. Never have I seen a man run as Holmes ran that night. I am reckoned fleet of foot, but he outpaced me as much as I outpaced the little professional. In front of us as we flew up the track we heard scream after scream from Sir Henry and the deep roar of the hound. I was in time to see the beast spring upon its victim, hurl him to the ground, and worry at his throat. But the next instant Holmes had emptied five barrels of his revolver into the creature's flank. With a last howl of agony and a vicious snap in the air, it rolled upon its back, four feet pawing furiously, and then fell limp upon its side. I stooped, panting, and pressed my pistol to the dreadful, shimmering head, but it was useless to press the trigger. The giant hound was dead.

Sir Henry lay insensible where he had fallen. We tore away his collar, and Holmes breathed a prayer of gratitude when we saw that there was no sign of a wound and that the rescue had been in time. Already our friend's eyelids shivered and he made a feeble effort to move. Lestrade thrust his brandy-flask between the baronet's teeth, and two frightened eyes were looking up at us.

"My God!" he whispered. "What was it? What, in heaven's name, was it?"

"It's dead, whatever it is," said Holmes. "We've laid the family ghost once and forever."

In mere size and strength it was a terrible creature which was lying stretched before us. It was not a pure bloodhound and it was not a pure mastiff; but it appeared to be a combination of the two—gaunt, savage, and as large as a small lioness. Even now in the stillness of death, the huge jaws seemed to be dripping with a bluish flame and the small, deep-set, cruel eyes were ringed with fire. I placed my hand upon the glowing muzzle, and as I held them up my own fingers smouldered and gleamed in the darkness.

"Phosphorus," I said.

"A cunning preparation of it," said Holmes, sniffing at the dead animal. "There is no smell which might have interfered with his power of scent. We owe you a deep apology, Sir Henry, for having exposed you to this fright. I was prepared for a hound, but not for such a creature as this. And the fog gave us little time to receive him."

"You have saved my life."

"Having first endangered it. Are you strong enough to stand?"

"Give me another mouthful of that brandy and I shall be ready for anything. So! Now, if you will help me up. What do you propose to do?"

"To leave you here. You are not fit for further adventures tonight. If you will wait, one or other of us will go back with you to the Hall."

He tried to stagger to his feet; but he was still ghastly pale and trembling in every limb. We helped him to a rock, where he sat shivering with his face buried in his hands.

"We must leave you now," said Holmes. "The rest of our work must be done, and every moment is of importance. We have our case, and now we only want our man.

"It's a thousand to one against our finding him at the house," he continued as we retraced our steps swiftly down the path. "Those shots must have told him that the game was up."

"We were some distance off, and this fog may have deadened them."

"He followed the hound to call him off—of that you may be certain. No, no, he's gone by this time! But we'll search the house and make sure."

The front door was open, so we rushed in and hurried from room to room to the amazement of a doddering old manservant, who met us in the passage. There was no light save in the dining-room, but Holmes caught up the lamp and left no corner of the house unexplored. No sign could we see of the man whom we were chasing. On the upper floor, however, one of the bedroom doors was locked.

"There's someone in here," cried Lestrade. "I can hear a movement. Open this door!"

A faint moaning and rustling came from within. Holmes struck the door just over the lock with the flat of his foot and it flew open. Pistol in hand, we all three rushed into the room.

But there was no sign within it of that desperate and defiant villain whom we expected to see. Instead we were faced by an object so strange and so unexpected that we stood for a moment staring at it in amazement.

The room had been fashioned into a small museum, and the walls were lined by a number of glass-topped cases full of that collection of butterflies and moths the formation of which had been the relaxation of this complex and dangerous man. In the centre of this room there was an upright beam, which had been placed at some period as a support for the old worm-eaten baulk of timber which spanned the roof. To this post a figure was tied, so swathed and muffled in the sheets which had been used to secure it that one could not for the moment tell whether it was that of a man or a woman. One towel passed round the throat and was secured at the back of the pillar. Another covered the lower part of the face, and over it two dark eyes—eyes full of grief and shame and a dreadful questioning—stared back at us. In a minute we had torn off the gag, unswathed the bonds, and Mrs. Stapleton sank upon the floor in front of us. As her beautiful head fell upon her chest I saw the clear red weal of a whiplash across her neck.

"The brute!" cried Holmes. "Here, Lestrade, your brandy-bottle! Put her in the chair! She has fainted from ill-usage and exhaustion."

She opened her eyes again.

"Is he safe?" she asked. "Has he escaped?"

"He cannot escape us, madam."

"No, no, I did not mean my husband. Sir Henry? Is he safe?"

"Yes."

"And the hound?"

"It is dead."

She gave a long sigh of satisfaction.

"Thank God! Thank God! Oh, this villain! See how he has treated me!" She shot her arms out from her sleeves, and we saw with horror that they were all mottled with bruises. "But this is nothing—nothing! It is my mind and soul that he has tortured and defiled. I could endure it all, ill-usage, solitude, a life of deception, everything, as long as I could still cling to the hope that I had his love, but now I know that in this also I have been his dupe and his tool." She broke into passionate sobbing as she spoke.

"You bear him no good will, madam," said Holmes. "Tell us then where we shall find him. If you have ever aided him in evil, help us now and so atone."

"There is but one place where he can have fled," she answered. "There is an old tin mine on an island in the heart of the mire. It was there that he kept his hound and there also he had made preparations so that he might have a refuge. That is where he would fly."

The fog-bank lay like white wool against the window. Holmes held the lamp towards it.

"See," said he. "No one could find his way into the Grimpen Mire tonight."

She laughed and clapped her hands. Her eyes and teeth gleamed with fierce merriment.

"He may find his way in, but never out," she cried. "How can he see the guiding wands tonight? We planted them together, he and I, to mark the pathway through the mire. Oh, if I could only have plucked them out today. Then indeed you would have had him at your mercy!"

It was evident to us that all pursuit was in vain until the fog had lifted. Meanwhile we left Lestrade in possession of the house while Holmes and I went back with the baronet to Baskerville Hall. The story of the Stapletons could no longer be withheld from him, but he took the blow bravely when he learned the truth about the woman whom he had loved. But the shock of the night's adventures had shattered his nerves, and before morning he lay delirious in a high fever under the care of Dr. Mortimer. The two of them were destined to travel together round the world before Sir Henry had become once more the hale, hearty man that he had been before he became master of that ill-omened estate.

And now I come rapidly to the conclusion of this singular narrative, in which I have tried to make the reader share those dark fears and vague surmises which clouded our lives so long and ended in so tragic a manner. On the morning after the death of the hound the fog had lifted and we were guided by Mrs. Stapleton to the point where they had found a pathway through the bog. It helped us to realize the horror of this woman's life when we saw the eagerness and joy with which she laid us on her husband's track. We left her standing upon the thin peninsula of firm, peaty soil which tapered out into the widespread bog. From the end of it a small wand planted here and there showed where the path zigzagged from tuft to tuft of rushes among those green-scummed pits and foul quagmires which barred the way to the stranger. Rank reeds and lush, slimy water-plants sent an odour of decay and a heavy miasmatic vapour onto our faces, while a false step plunged us more than once thigh-deep into the dark, quivering mire, which shook for yards in soft undulations around our feet. Its tenacious grip plucked at our heels as we walked, and when we sank into it it was as if some malignant hand was tugging us down into those obscene depths, so grim and purposeful was the clutch in which it held us. Once only we saw a trace that someone had passed that perilous way before us. From amid a tuft of cotton grass which bore it up out of the slime some dark thing was projecting. Holmes sank to his waist as he stepped from the path to seize it, and had we not been there to drag him out he could never have set his foot upon firm land again. He held an old black boot in the air. "Meyers, Toronto," was printed on the leather inside.

"It is worth a mud bath," said he. "It is our friend Sir Henry's missing boot."

"Thrown there by Stapleton in his flight."

"Exactly. He retained it in his hand after using it to set the hound upon the track. He fled when he knew the game was up, still clutching it. And he hurled it away at this point of his flight. We know at least that he came so far in safety."

But more than that we were never destined to know, though there was much which we might surmise. There was no chance of finding footsteps in the mire, for the rising mud oozed swiftly in upon them, but as we at last reached firmer ground beyond the morass we all looked eagerly for them. But no slightest sign of them ever met our eyes. If the earth told a true story, then Stapleton never reached that island of refuge towards which he struggled through the fog upon that last night. Somewhere in the heart of the great Grimpen Mire, down in the foul slime of the huge morass which had sucked him in, this cold and cruel-hearted man is forever buried.

Many traces we found of him in the bog-girt island where he had hid his savage ally. A huge driving-wheel and a shaft half-filled with rubbish showed the position of an abandoned mine. Beside it were the crumbling remains of the cottages of the miners, driven away no doubt by the foul reek of the surrounding swamp. In one of these a staple and chain with a quantity of gnawed bones showed where the animal had been confined. A skeleton with a tangle of brown hair adhering to it lay among the debris.

"A dog!" said Holmes. "By Jove, a curly-haired spaniel. Poor Mortimer will never see his pet again. Well, I do not know that this place contains any secret which we have not already fathomed. He could hide his hound, but he could not hush its voice, and hence came those cries which even in daylight were not pleasant to hear. On an emergency he could keep the hound in the out-house at Merripit, but it was always a risk, and it was only on the supreme day, which he regarded as the end of all his efforts, that he dared do it. This paste in the tin is no doubt the luminous mixture with which the creature was daubed. It was suggested, of course, by the story of the family hell-hound, and by the desire to frighten old Sir Charles to death. No wonder the poor devil of a convict ran and screamed, even as our friend did, and as we ourselves might have done, when he saw such a creature bounding through the darkness of the moor upon his track. It was a cunning device, for, apart from the chance of driving your victim to his death, what peasant would venture to inquire too closely into such a creature should he get sight of it, as many have done, upon the moor? I said it in London, Watson, and I say it again now, that never yet have we helped to hunt down a more dangerous man than he who is lying yonder"—he swept his long arm towards the huge mottled expanse of green-splotched bog which stretched away until it merged into the russet slopes of the moor.

Chapter 15. A Retrospection

It was the end of November, and Holmes and I sat, upon a raw and foggy night, on either side of a blazing fire in our sitting-room in Baker Street. Since the tragic upshot of our visit to Devonshire he had been engaged in two affairs of the utmost importance, in the first of which he had exposed the atrocious conduct of Colonel Upwood in connection with the famous card scandal of the Nonpareil Club, while in the second he had defended the unfortunate Mme. Montpensier from the charge of murder which hung over her in connection with the death of her step-daughter, Mlle. Carere, the young lady who, as it will be remembered, was found six months later alive and married in New York. My friend was in excellent spirits over the success which had attended a succession of difficult and important cases, so that I was able to induce him to discuss the details of the Baskerville mystery. I had waited patiently for the opportunity for I was aware that he would never permit cases to overlap, and that his clear and logical mind would not be drawn from its present work to dwell upon memories of the past. Sir Henry and Dr. Mortimer were, however, in London, on their way to that long voyage which had been recommended for the restoration of his shattered nerves. They had called upon us that very afternoon, so that it was natural that the subject should come up for discussion.

"The whole course of events," said Holmes, "from the point of view of the man who called himself Stapleton was simple and direct, although to us, who had no means in the beginning of knowing the motives of his actions and could only learn part of the facts, it all appeared exceedingly complex. I have had the advantage of two conversations with Mrs. Stapleton, and the case has now been so entirely cleared up that I am not aware that there is anything which has remained a secret to us. You will find a few notes upon the matter under the heading B in my indexed list of cases."

"Perhaps you would kindly give me a sketch of the course of events from memory."

"Certainly, though I cannot guarantee that I carry all the facts in my mind. Intense mental concentration has a curious way of blotting out what has passed. The barrister who has his case at his fingers' ends and is able to argue with an expert upon his own subject finds that a week or two of the courts will drive it all out of his head once more. So each of my cases displaces the last, and Mlle. Carere has blurred my recollection of Baskerville Hall. Tomorrow some other little problem may be submitted to my notice which will in turn dispossess the fair French lady and the infamous Upwood. So far as the case of the hound goes, however, I will give you the course of events as nearly as I can, and you will suggest anything which I may have forgotten.

"My inquiries show beyond all question that the family portrait did not lie, and that this fellow was indeed a Baskerville. He was a son of that Rodger Baskerville, the younger brother of Sir Charles, who fled with a sinister reputation to South America, where he was said to have died unmarried. He did, as a matter of fact, marry, and had one child, this fellow, whose real name is the same as his father's. He married Beryl Garcia, one of the beauties of Costa Rica, and, having purloined a considerable sum of public money, he changed his name to Vandeleur and fled to England, where he established a school in the east of Yorkshire. His reason for attempting this special line of business was that he had struck up an acquaintance with a consumptive tutor upon the voyage home, and that he had used this man's ability to make the undertaking a success. Fraser, the tutor, died however, and the school which had begun well sank from disrepute into infamy. The Vandeleurs found it convenient to change their name to Stapleton, and he brought the remains of his fortune, his schemes for the future, and his taste for entomology to the south of England. I learned at the British Museum that he was a recognized authority upon the subject, and that the name of Vandeleur has been permanently attached to a certain moth which he had, in his Yorkshire days, been the first to describe.

"We now come to that portion of his life which has proved to be of such intense interest to us. The fellow had evidently made inquiry and found that only two lives intervened between him and a valuable estate. When he went to Devonshire his plans were, I believe, exceedingly hazy, but that he meant mischief from the first is evident from the way in which he took his wife with him in the character of his sister. The idea of using her as a decoy was clearly already in his mind, though he may not have been certain how the details of his plot were to be arranged. He meant in the end to have the estate, and he was ready to use any tool or run any risk for that end. His first act was to establish himself as near to his ancestral home as he could, and his second was to cultivate a friendship with Sir Charles Baskerville and with the neighbours.

"The baronet himself told him about the family hound, and so prepared the way for his own death. Stapleton, as I will continue to call him, knew that the old man's heart was weak and that a shock would kill him. So much he had learned from Dr. Mortimer. He had heard also that Sir Charles was superstitious and had taken this grim legend very seriously. His ingenious mind instantly suggested a way by which the baronet could be done to death, and yet it would be hardly possible to bring home the guilt to the real murderer.

"Having conceived the idea he proceeded to carry it out with considerable finesse. An ordinary schemer would have been content to work with a savage hound. The use of artificial means to make the creature diabolical was a flash of genius upon his part. The dog he bought in London from Ross and Mangles, the dealers in Fulham Road. It was the strongest and most savage in their possession. He brought it down by the North Devon line and walked a great distance over the moor so as to get it home without exciting any remarks. He had already on his insect hunts learned to penetrate the Grimpen Mire, and so had found a safe hiding-place for the creature. Here he kennelled it and waited his chance.

"But it was some time coming. The old gentleman could not be decoyed outside of his grounds at night. Several times Stapleton lurked about with his hound, but without avail. It was during these fruitless quests that he, or rather his ally, was seen by peasants, and that the legend of the demon dog received a new confirmation. He had hoped that his wife might lure Sir Charles to his ruin, but here she proved unexpectedly independent. She would not endeavour to entangle the old gentleman in a sentimental attachment which might deliver him over to his enemy. Threats and even, I am sorry to say, blows refused to move her. She would have nothing to do with it, and for a time Stapleton was at a deadlock.

"He found a way out of his difficulties through the chance that Sir Charles, who had conceived a friendship for him, made him the minister of his charity in the case of this unfortunate woman, Mrs. Laura Lyons. By representing himself as a single man he acquired complete influence over her, and he gave her to understand that in the event of her obtaining a divorce from her husband he would marry her. His plans were suddenly brought to a head by his knowledge that Sir Charles was about to leave the Hall on the advice of Dr. Mortimer, with whose opinion he himself pretended to coincide. He must act at once, or his victim might get beyond his power. He therefore put pressure upon Mrs. Lyons to write this letter, imploring the old man to give her an interview on the evening before his departure for London. He then, by a specious argument, prevented her from going, and so had the chance for which he had waited.

"Driving back in the evening from Coombe Tracey he was in time to get his hound, to treat it with his infernal paint, and to bring the beast round to the gate at which he had reason to expect that he would find the old gentleman waiting. The dog, incited by its master, sprang over the wicket-gate and pursued the unfortunate baronet, who fled screaming down the yew alley. In that gloomy tunnel it must indeed have been a dreadful sight to see that huge black creature, with its flaming jaws and blazing eyes, bounding after its victim. He fell dead at the end of the alley from heart disease and terror. The hound had kept upon the grassy border while the baronet had run down the path, so that no track but the man's was visible. On seeing him lying still the creature had probably approached to sniff at him, but finding him dead had turned away again. It was then that it left the print which was actually observed by Dr. Mortimer. The hound was called off and hurried away to its lair in the Grimpen Mire, and a mystery was left which puzzled the authorities, alarmed the countryside, and finally brought the case within the scope of our observation.

"So much for the death of Sir Charles Baskerville. You perceive the devilish cunning of it, for really it would be almost impossible to make a case against the real murderer. His only accomplice was one who could never give him away, and the grotesque, inconceivable nature of the device only served to make it more effective. Both of the women concerned in the case, Mrs. Stapleton and Mrs. Laura Lyons, were left with a strong suspicion against Stapleton. Mrs. Stapleton knew that he had designs upon the old man, and also of the existence of the hound. Mrs. Lyons knew neither of these things, but had been impressed by the death occurring at the time of an uncancelled appointment which was only known to him. However, both of them were under his influence, and he had nothing to fear from them. The first half of his task was successfully accomplished but the more difficult still remained.

"It is possible that Stapleton did not know of the existence of an heir in Canada. In any case he would very soon learn it from his friend Dr. Mortimer, and he was told by the latter all details about the arrival of Henry Baskerville. Stapleton's first idea was that this young stranger from Canada might possibly be done to death in London without coming down to Devonshire at all. He distrusted his wife ever since she had refused to help him in laying a trap for the old man, and he dared not leave her long out of his sight for fear he should lose his influence over her. It was for this reason that he took her to London with him. They lodged, I find, at the Mexborough Private Hotel, in Craven Street, which was actually one of those called upon by my agent in search of evidence. Here he kept his wife imprisoned in her room while he, disguised in a beard, followed Dr. Mortimer to Baker Street and afterwards to the station and to the Northumberland Hotel. His wife had some inkling of his plans; but she had such a fear of her husband—a fear founded upon brutal ill-treatment—that she dare not write to warn the man whom she knew to be in danger. If the letter should fall into Stapleton's hands her own life would not be safe. Eventually, as we know, she adopted the expedient of cutting out the words which would form the message, and addressing the letter in a disguised hand. It reached the baronet, and gave him the first warning of his danger.

"It was very essential for Stapleton to get some article of Sir Henry's attire so that, in case he was driven to use the dog, he might always have the means of setting him upon his track. With characteristic promptness and audacity he set about this at once, and we cannot doubt that the boots or chamber-maid of the hotel was well bribed to help him in his design. By chance, however, the first boot which was procured for him was a new one and, therefore, useless for his purpose. He then had it returned and obtained another—a most instructive incident, since it proved conclusively to my mind that we were dealing with a real hound, as no other supposition could explain this anxiety to obtain an old boot and this indifference to a new one. The more outre and grotesque an incident is the more carefully it deserves to be examined, and the very point which appears to complicate a case is, when duly considered and scientifically handled, the one which is most likely to elucidate it.

"Then we had the visit from our friends next morning, shadowed always by Stapleton in the cab. From his knowledge of our rooms and of my appearance, as well as from his general conduct, I am inclined to think that Stapleton's career of crime has been by no means limited to this single Baskerville affair. It is suggestive that during the last three years there have been four considerable burglaries in the west country, for none of which was any criminal ever arrested. The last of these, at Folkestone Court, in May, was remarkable for the cold-blooded pistolling of the page, who surprised the masked and solitary burglar. I cannot doubt that Stapleton recruited his waning resources in this fashion, and that for years he has been a desperate and dangerous man.

"We had an example of his readiness of resource that morning when he got away from us so successfully, and also of his audacity in sending back my own name to me through the cabman. From that moment he understood that I had taken over the case in London, and that therefore there was no chance for him there. He returned to Dartmoor and awaited the arrival of the baronet."

"One moment!" said I. "You have, no doubt, described the sequence of events correctly, but there is one point which you have left unexplained. What became of the hound when its master was in London?"

"I have given some attention to this matter and it is undoubtedly of importance. There can be no question that Stapleton had a confidant, though it is unlikely that he ever placed himself in his power by sharing all his plans with him. There was an old manservant at Merripit House, whose name was Anthony. His connection with the Stapletons can be traced for several years, as far back as the school-mastering days, so that he must have been aware that his master and mistress were really husband and wife. This man has disappeared and has escaped from the country. It is suggestive that Anthony is not a common name in England, while Antonio is so in all Spanish or Spanish-American countries. The man, like Mrs. Stapleton herself, spoke good English, but with a curious lisping accent. I have myself seen this old man cross the Grimpen Mire by the path which Stapleton had marked out. It is very probable, therefore, that in the absence of his master it was he who cared for the hound, though he may never have known the purpose for which the beast was used.

"The Stapletons then went down to Devonshire, whither they were soon followed by Sir Henry and you. One word now as to how I stood myself at that time. It may possibly recur to your memory that when I examined the paper upon which the printed words were fastened I made a close inspection for the water-mark. In doing so I held it within a few inches of my eyes, and was conscious of a faint smell of the scent known as white jessamine. There are seventy-five perfumes, which it is very necessary that a criminal expert should be able to distinguish from each other, and cases have more than once within my own experience depended upon their prompt recognition. The scent suggested the presence of a lady, and already my thoughts began to turn towards the Stapletons. Thus I had made certain of the hound, and had guessed at the criminal before ever we went to the west country.

"It was my game to watch Stapleton. It was evident, however, that I could not do this if I were with you, since he would be keenly on his guard. I deceived everybody, therefore, yourself included, and I came down secretly when I was supposed to be in London. My hardships were not so great as you imagined, though such trifling details must never interfere with the investigation of a case. I stayed for the most part at Coombe Tracey, and only used the hut upon the moor when it was necessary to be near the scene of action. Cartwright had come down with me, and in his disguise as a country boy he was of great assistance to me. I was dependent upon him for food and clean linen. When I was watching Stapleton, Cartwright was frequently watching you, so that I was able to keep my hand upon all the strings.

"I have already told you that your reports reached me rapidly, being forwarded instantly from Baker Street to Coombe Tracey. They were of great service to me, and especially that one incidentally truthful piece of biography of Stapleton's. I was able to establish the identity of the man and the woman and knew at last exactly how I stood. The case had been considerably complicated through the incident of the escaped convict and the relations between him and the Barrymores. This also you cleared up in a very effective way, though I had already come to the same conclusions from my own observations.

"By the time that you discovered me upon the moor I had a complete knowledge of the whole business, but I had not a case which could go to a jury. Even Stapleton's attempt upon Sir Henry that night which ended in the death of the unfortunate convict did not help us much in proving murder against our man. There seemed to be no alternative but to catch him red-handed, and to do so we had to use Sir Henry, alone and apparently unprotected, as a bait. We did so, and at the cost of a severe shock to our client we succeeded in completing our case and driving Stapleton to his destruction. That Sir Henry should have been exposed to this is, I must confess, a reproach to my management of the case, but we had no means of foreseeing the terrible and paralyzing spectacle which the beast presented, nor could we predict the fog which enabled him to burst upon us at such short notice. We succeeded in our object at a cost which both the specialist and Dr. Mortimer assure me will be a temporary one. A long journey may enable our friend to recover not only from his shattered nerves but also from his wounded feelings. His love for the lady was deep and sincere, and to him the saddest part of all this black business was that he should have been deceived by her.

"It only remains to indicate the part which she had played throughout. There can be no doubt that Stapleton exercised an influence over her which may have been love or may have been fear, or very possibly both, since they are by no means incompatible emotions. It was, at least, absolutely effective. At his command she consented to pass as his sister, though he found the limits of his power over her when he endeavoured to make her the direct accessory to murder. She was ready to warn Sir Henry so far as she could without implicating her husband, and again and again she tried to do so. Stapleton himself seems to have been capable of jealousy, and when he saw the baronet paying court to the lady, even though it was part of his own plan, still he could not help interrupting with a passionate outburst which revealed the fiery soul which his self-contained manner so cleverly concealed. By encouraging the intimacy he made it certain that Sir Henry would frequently come to Merripit House and that he would sooner or later get the opportunity which he desired. On the day of the crisis, however, his wife turned suddenly against him. She had learned something of the death of the convict, and she knew that the hound was being kept in the outhouse on the evening that Sir Henry was coming to dinner. She taxed her husband with his intended crime, and a furious scene followed in which he showed her for the first time that she had a rival in his love. Her fidelity turned in an instant to bitter hatred, and he saw that she would betray him. He tied her up, therefore, that she might have no chance of warning Sir Henry, and he hoped, no doubt, that when the whole countryside put down the baronet's death to the curse of his family, as they certainly would do, he could win his wife back to accept an accomplished fact and to keep silent upon what she knew. In this I fancy that in any case he made a miscalculation, and that, if we had not been there, his doom would none the less have been sealed. A woman of Spanish blood does not condone such an injury so lightly. And now, my dear Watson, without referring to my notes, I cannot give you a more detailed account of this curious case. I do not know that anything essential has been left unexplained."

"He could not hope to frighten Sir Henry to death as he had done the old uncle with his bogie hound."

"The beast was savage and half-starved. If its appearance did not frighten its victim to death, at least it would paralyze the resistance which might be offered."

"No doubt. There only remains one difficulty. If Stapleton came into the succession, how could he explain the fact that he, the heir, had been living unannounced under another name so close to the property? How could he claim it without causing suspicion and inquiry?"

"It is a formidable difficulty, and I fear that you ask too much when you expect me to solve it. The past and the present are within the field of my inquiry, but what a man may do in the future is a hard question to answer. Mrs. Stapleton has heard her husband discuss the problem on several occasions. There were three possible courses. He might claim the property from South America, establish his identity before the British authorities there and so obtain the fortune without ever coming to England at all, or he might adopt an elaborate disguise during the short time that he need be in London; or, again, he might furnish an accomplice with the proofs and papers, putting him in as heir, and retaining a claim upon some proportion of his income. We cannot doubt from what we know of him that he would have found some way out of the difficulty. And now, my dear Watson, we have had some weeks of severe work, and for one evening, I think, we may turn our thoughts into more pleasant channels. I have a box for 'Les Huguenots.' Have you heard the De Reszkes? Might I trouble you then to be ready in half an hour, and we can stop at Marcini's for a little dinner on the way?"

The Lost World

I have wrought my simple plan
If I give one hour of joy
To the boy who's half a man,
Or the man who's half a boy.

Sir Arthur Conan Doyle

Foreword

Mr. E. D. Malone desires to state that both the injunction for restraint and the libel action have been withdrawn unreservedly by Professor G. E. Challenger, who, being satisfied that no criticism or comment in this book is meant in an offensive spirit, has guaranteed that he will place no impediment to its publication and circulation.

Chapter I; "There Are Heroisms All Round Us"

Mr. Hungerton, her father, really was the most tactless person upon earth, a fluffy, feathery, untidy cockatoo of a man, perfectly good-natured, but absolutely centered upon his own silly self. If anything could have driven me from Gladys, it would have been the thought of such a father-in-law. I am convinced that he really believed in his heart that I came round to the Chestnuts three days a week for the pleasure of his company, and very especially to hear his views upon bimetallism, a subject upon which he was by way of being an authority.

For an hour or more that evening I listened to his monotonous chirrup about bad money driving out good, the token value of silver, the depreciation of the rupee, and the true standards of exchange.

"Suppose," he cried with feeble violence, "that all the debts in the world were called up simultaneously, and immediate payment insisted upon,--what under our present conditions would happen then?"

I gave the self-evident answer that I should be a ruined man, upon which he jumped from his chair, reproved me for my habitual levity, which made it impossible for him to discuss any reasonable subject in my presence, and bounced off out of the room to dress for a Masonic meeting.

At last I was alone with Gladys, and the moment of Fate had come! All that evening I had felt like the soldier who awaits the signal which will send him on a forlorn hope; hope of victory and fear of repulse alternating in his mind.

She sat with that proud, delicate profile of hers outlined against the red curtain. How beautiful she was! And yet how aloof! We had been friends, quite good friends; but never could I get beyond the same comradeship which I might have established with one of my fellow-reporters upon the Gazette, perfectly frank, perfectly kindly, and perfectly unsexual. My instincts are all against a woman being too frank and at her ease with me. It is no compliment to a man. Where the real sex feeling begins, timidity and distrust are its companions, heritage from old wicked days when love and violence went often hand in hand. The bent head, the averted eye, the faltering voice, the wincing figure—these, and not the unshrinking gaze and frank reply, are the true signals of passion. Even in my short life I had learned as much as that—or had inherited it in that race memory which we call instinct.

Gladys was full of every womanly quality. Some judged her to be cold and hard; but such a thought was treason. That delicately bronzed skin, almost oriental in its coloring, that raven hair, the large liquid eyes, the full but exquisite lips,--all the stigmata of passion were there. But I was sadly conscious that up to now I had never found the secret of drawing it forth. However, come what might, I should have done with suspense and bring matters to a head to-night. She could but refuse me, and better be a repulsed lover than an accepted brother.

So far my thoughts had carried me, and I was about to break the long and uneasy silence, when two critical, dark eyes looked round at me, and the proud head was shaken in smiling reproof. "I have a presentiment that you are going to propose, Ned. I do wish you wouldn't; for things are so much nicer as they are."

I drew my chair a little nearer. "Now, how did you know that I was going to propose?" I asked in genuine wonder.

"Don't women always know? Do you suppose any woman in the world was ever taken unawares? But—oh, Ned, our friendship has been so good and so pleasant! What a pity to spoil it! Don't you feel how splendid it is that a young man and a young woman should be able to talk face to face as we have talked?"

"I don't know, Gladys. You see, I can talk face to face with—with the station-master." I can't imagine how that official came into the matter; but in he trotted, and set us both laughing. "That does not satisfy me in the least. I want my arms round you, and your head on my breast, and—oh, Gladys, I want--"

She had sprung from her chair, as she saw signs that I proposed to demonstrate some of my wants. "You've spoiled everything, Ned," she said. "It's all so beautiful and natural until this kind of thing comes in! It is such a pity! Why can't you control yourself?"

"I didn't invent it," I pleaded. "It's nature. It's love."

"Well, perhaps if both love, it may be different. I have never felt it."

"But you must—you, with your beauty, with your soul! Oh, Gladys, you were made for love! You must love!"

"One must wait till it comes."

"But why can't you love me, Gladys? Is it my appearance, or what?"

She did unbend a little. She put forward a hand—such a gracious, stooping attitude it was—and she pressed back my head. Then she looked into my upturned face with a very wistful smile.

"No it isn't that," she said at last. "You're not a conceited boy by nature, and so I can safely tell you it is not that. It's deeper."

"My character?"

She nodded severely.

"What can I do to mend it? Do sit down and talk it over. No, really, I won't if you'll only sit down!"

She looked at me with a wondering distrust which was much more to my mind than her whole-hearted confidence. How primitive and bestial it looks when you put it down in black and white!--and perhaps after all it is only a feeling peculiar to myself. Anyhow, she sat down.

"Now tell me what's amiss with me?"

"I'm in love with somebody else," said she.

It was my turn to jump out of my chair.

"It's nobody in particular," she explained, laughing at the expression of my face: "only an ideal. I've never met the kind of man I mean."

"Tell me about him. What does he look like?"

"Oh, he might look very much like you."

"How dear of you to say that! Well, what is it that he does that I don't do? Just say the word,--teetotal, vegetarian, aeronaut, theosophist, superman. I'll have a try at it, Gladys, if you will only give me an idea what would please you."

She laughed at the elasticity of my character. "Well, in the first place, I don't think my ideal would speak like that," said she. "He would be a harder, sterner man, not so ready to adapt himself to a silly girl's whim. But, above all, he must be a man who could do, who could act, who could look Death in the face and have no fear of him, a man of great deeds and strange experiences. It is never a man that I should love, but always the glories he had won; for they would be reflected upon me. Think of Richard Burton! When I read his wife's life of him I could so understand her love! And Lady Stanley! Did you ever read the wonderful last chapter of that book about her husband? These are the sort of men that a woman could worship with all her soul, and yet be the greater, not the less, on account of her love, honored by all the world as the inspirer of noble deeds."

She looked so beautiful in her enthusiasm that I nearly brought down the whole level of the interview. I gripped myself hard, and went on with the argument.

"We can't all be Stanleys and Burtons," said I; "besides, we don't get the chance,--at least, I never had the chance. If I did, I should try to take it."

"But chances are all around you. It is the mark of the kind of man I mean that he makes his own chances. You can't hold him back. I've never met him, and yet I seem to know him so well. There are heroisms all round us waiting to be done. It's for men to do them, and for women to reserve their love as a reward for such men. Look at that young Frenchman who went up last week in a balloon. It was blowing a gale of wind; but because he was announced to go he insisted on starting. The wind blew him fifteen hundred miles in twenty-four hours, and he fell in the middle of Russia. That was the kind of man I mean. Think of the woman he loved, and how other women must have envied her! That's what I should like to be,--envied for my man."

"I'd have done it to please you."

"But you shouldn't do it merely to please me. You should do it because you can't help yourself, because it's natural to you, because the man in you is crying out for heroic expression. Now, when you described the Wigan coal explosion last month, could you not have gone down and helped those people, in spite of the choke-damp?"

"I did."

"You never said so."

"There was nothing worth bucking about."

"I didn't know." She looked at me with rather more interest. "That was brave of you."

"I had to. If you want to write good copy, you must be where the things are."

"What a prosaic motive! It seems to take all the romance out of it. But, still, whatever your motive, I am glad that you went down that mine." She gave me her hand; but with such sweetness and dignity that I could only stoop and kiss it. "I dare say I am merely a foolish woman with a young girl's fancies. And yet it is so real with me, so entirely part of my very self, that I cannot help acting upon it. If I marry, I do want to marry a famous man!"

"Why should you not?" I cried. "It is women like you who brace men up. Give me a chance, and see if I will take it! Besides, as you say, men ought to *make* their own chances, and not wait until they are given. Look at Clive—just a clerk, and he conquered India! By George! I'll do something in the world yet!"

She laughed at my sudden Irish effervescence. "Why not?" she said. "You have everything a man could have,--youth, health, strength, education, energy. I was sorry you spoke. And now I am glad—so glad—if it wakens these thoughts in you!"

"And if I do—"

Her dear hand rested like warm velvet upon my lips. "Not another word, Sir! You should have been at the office for evening duty half an hour ago; only I hadn't the heart to remind you. Some day, perhaps, when you have won your place in the world, we shall talk it over again."

And so it was that I found myself that foggy November evening pursuing the Camberwell tram with my heart glowing within me, and with the eager determination that not another day should elapse before I should find some deed which was worthy of my lady. But who—who in all this wide world could ever have imagined the incredible shape which that deed was to take, or the strange steps by which I was led to the doing of it?

And, after all, this opening chapter will seem to the reader to have nothing to do with my narrative; and yet there would have been no narrative without it, for it is only when a man goes out into the world with the thought that there are heroisms all round him, and with the desire all alive in his heart to follow any which may come within sight of him, that he breaks away as I did from the life he knows, and ventures forth into the wonderful mystic twilight land where lie the great adventures and the great rewards. Behold me, then, at the office of the Daily Gazette, on the staff of which I was a most insignificant unit, with the settled determination that very night, if possible, to find the quest which should be worthy of my Gladys! Was it hardness, was it selfishness, that she should ask me to risk my life for her own glorification. Such thoughts may come to middle age; but never to ardent three-and-twenty in the fever of his first love.

Chapter II; "Try Your Luck with Professor Challenger"

I always liked McArdle, the crabbed, old, round-backed, red-headed news editor, and I rather hoped that he liked me. Of course, Beaumont was the real boss; but he lived in the rarefied atmosphere of some Olympian height from which he could distinguish nothing smaller than an international crisis or a split in the Cabinet. Sometimes we saw him passing in lonely majesty to his inner sanctum, with his eyes staring vaguely and his mind hovering over the Balkans or the Persian Gulf. He was above and beyond us. But McArdle was his first lieutenant, and it was he that we knew. The old man nodded as I entered the room, and he pushed his spectacles far up on his bald forehead.

"Well, Mr. Malone, from all I hear, you seem to be doing very well," said he in his kindly Scotch accent.

I thanked him.

"The colliery explosion was excellent. So was the Southwark fire. You have the true descreeptive touch. What did you want to see me about?"

"To ask a favor."

He looked alarmed, and his eyes shunned mine. "Tut, tut! What is it?"

"Do you think, Sir, that you could possibly send me on some mission for the paper? I would do my best to put it through and get you some good copy."

"What sort of meesion had you in your mind, Mr. Malone?"

"Well, Sir, anything that had adventure and danger in it. I really would do my very best. The more difficult it was, the better it would suit me."

"You seem very anxious to lose your life."

"To justify my life, Sir."

"Dear me, Mr. Malone, this is very—very exalted. I'm afraid the day for this sort of thing is rather past. The expense of the 'special meesion' business hardly justifies the result, and, of course, in any case it would only be an experienced man with a name that would command public confidence who would get such an order. The big blank spaces in the map are all being filled in, and there's no room for romance anywhere. Wait a bit, though!" he added, with a sudden smile upon his face. "Talking of the blank spaces of the map gives me an idea. What about exposing a fraud—a modern Munchausen—and making him rideeculous? You could show him up as the liar that he is! Eh, man, it would be fine. How does it appeal to you?"

"Anything—anywhere—I care nothing."

McArdle was plunged in thought for some minutes.

"I wonder whether you could get on friendly—or at least on talking terms with the fellow," he said, at last. "You seem to have a sort of genius for establishing relations with people—seempathy, I suppose, or animal magnetism, or youthful vitality, or something. I am conscious of it myself."

"You are very good, sir."

"So why should you not try your luck with Professor Challenger, of Enmore Park?"

I dare say I looked a little startled.

llenger!" I cried. "Professor Challenger, the famous zoologist! Wasn't he the broke the skull of Blundell, of the Telegraph?"

news editor smiled grimly.

you mind? Didn't you say it was adventures you were after?"

"It is all in the way of business, sir," I answered.

"Exactly. I don't suppose he can always be so violent as that. I'm thinking that Blundell got him at the wrong moment, maybe, or in the wrong fashion. You may have better luck, or more tact in handling him. There's something in your line there, I am sure, and the Gazette should work it."

"I really know nothing about him," said I. "I only remember his name in connection with the police-court proceedings, for striking Blundell."

"I have a few notes for your guidance, Mr. Malone. I've had my eye on the Professor for some little time." He took a paper from a drawer. "Here is a summary of his record. I give it you briefly:--

"'Challenger, George Edward. Born: Largs, N. B., 1863. Educ.: Largs Academy; Edinburgh University. British Museum Assistant, 1892. Assistant-Keeper of Comparative Anthropology Department, 1893. Resigned after acrimonious correspondence same year. Winner of Crayston Medal for Zoological Research. Foreign Member of'—well, quite a lot of things, about two inches of small type—'Societe Belge, American Academy of Sciences, La Plata, etc., etc. Ex-President Palaeontological Society. Section H, British Association'—so on, so on!--'Publications: "Some Observations Upon a Series of Kalmuck Skulls"; "Outlines of Vertebrate Evolution"; and numerous papers, including "The underlying fallacy of Weissmannism," which caused heated discussion at the Zoological Congress of Vienna. Recreations: Walking, Alpine climbing. Address: Enmore Park, Kensington, W.'

"There, take it with you. I've nothing more for you to-night."

I pocketed the slip of paper.

"One moment, sir," I said, as I realized that it was a pink bald head, and not a red face, which was fronting me. "I am not very clear yet why I am to interview this gentleman. What has he done?"

The face flashed back again.

"Went to South America on a solitary expedeetion two years ago. Came back last year. Had undoubtedly been to South America, but refused to say exactly where. Began to tell his adventures in a vague way, but somebody started to pick holes, and he just shut up like an oyster. Something wonderful happened—or the man's a champion liar, which is the more probable supposeetion. Had some damaged photographs, said to be fakes. Got so touchy that he assaults anyone who asks questions, and heaves reporters down the stairs. In my opinion he's just a homicidal megalomaniac with a turn for science. That's your man, Mr. Malone. Now, off you run, and see what you can make of him. You're big enough to look after yourself. Anyway, you are all safe. Employers' Liability Act, you know."

A grinning red face turned once more into a pink oval, fringed with gingery fluff; the interview was at an end.

I walked across to the Savage Club, but instead of turning into it I leaned upon the railings of Adelphi Terrace and gazed thoughtfully for a long time at the brown, oily river. I can always think most sanely and clearly in the open air. I took out the list of Professor Challenger's exploits, and I read it over under the electric lamp. Then I had what I can only regard as an inspiration. As a Pressman, I felt sure from what I had been told that I could never hope to get into touch with this cantank Professor. But these recriminations, twice mentioned in his skeleton biography, cou only mean that he was a fanatic in science. Was there not an exposed margin there upon which he might be accessible? I would try.

I entered the club. It was just after eleven, and the big room was fairly full, though the rush had not yet set in. I noticed a tall, thin, angular man seated in an arm-chair by the fire. He turned as I drew my chair up to him. It was the man of all others whom I should have chosen—Tarp Henry, of the staff of Nature, a thin, dry, leathery creature, who was full, to those who knew him, of kindly humanity. I plunged instantly into my subject.

"What do you know of Professor Challenger?"

"Challenger?" He gathered his brows in scientific disapproval. "Challenger was the man who came with some cock-and-bull story from South America."

"What story?"

"Oh, it was rank nonsense about some queer animals he had discovered. I believe he has retracted since. Anyhow, he has suppressed it all. He gave an interview to Reuter's, and there was such a howl that he saw it wouldn't do. It was a discreditable business. There were one or two folk who were inclined to take him seriously, but he soon choked them off."

"How?"

"Well, by his insufferable rudeness and impossible behavior. There was poor old Wadley, of the Zoological Institute. Wadley sent a message: 'The President of the Zoological Institute presents his compliments to Professor Challenger, and would take it as a personal favor if he would do them the honor to come to their next meeting.' The answer was unprintable."

"You don't say?"

"Well, a bowdlerized version of it would run: 'Professor Challenger presents his compliments to the President of the Zoological Institute, and would take it as a personal favor if he would go to the devil.'"

"Good Lord!"

"Yes, I expect that's what old Wadley said. I remember his wail at the meeting, which began: 'In fifty years experience of scientific intercourse----' It quite broke the old man up."

"Anything more about Challenger?"

"Well, I'm a bacteriologist, you know. I live in a nine-hundred-diameter microscope. I can hardly claim to take serious notice of anything that I can see with my naked eye. I'm a frontiersman from the extreme edge of the Knowable, and I feel quite out of place when I leave my study and come into touch with all you great, rough, hulking creatures. I'm too detached to talk scandal, and yet at scientific conversaziones I *have* heard something of Challenger, for he is one of those men whom nobody can ignore. He's as clever as they make 'em—a full-charged battery of force and vitality, but a quarrelsome, ill-conditioned faddist, and unscrupulous at that. He had gone the length of faking some photographs over the South American business."

"You say he is a faddist. What is his particular fad?"

"He has a thousand, but the latest is something about Weissmann and Evolution. He had a fearful row about it in Vienna, I believe."

"Can't you tell me the point?"

he moment, but a translation of the proceedings exists. We have it filed Would you care to come?"

t what I want. I have to interview the fellow, and I need some lead up to lly awfully good of you to give me a lift. I'll go with you now, if it is not

Half an hour later I was seated in the newspaper office with a huge tome in front of me, which had been opened at the article "Weissmann versus Darwin," with the sub heading, "Spirited Protest at Vienna. Lively Proceedings." My scientific education having been somewhat neglected, I was unable to follow the whole argument, but it was evident that the English Professor had handled his subject in a very aggressive fashion, and had thoroughly annoyed his Continental colleagues. "Protests," "Uproar," and "General appeal to the Chairman" were three of the first brackets which caught my eye. Most of the matter might have been written in Chinese for any definite meaning that it conveyed to my brain.

"I wish you could translate it into English for me," I said, pathetically, to my help-mate.

"Well, it is a translation."

"Then I'd better try my luck with the original."

"It is certainly rather deep for a layman."

"If I could only get a single good, meaty sentence which seemed to convey some sort of definite human idea, it would serve my turn. Ah, yes, this one will do. I seem in a vague way almost to understand it. I'll copy it out. This shall be my link with the terrible Professor."

"Nothing else I can do?"

"Well, yes; I propose to write to him. If I could frame the letter here, and use your address it would give atmosphere."

"We'll have the fellow round here making a row and breaking the furniture."

"No, no; you'll see the letter—nothing contentious, I assure you."

"Well, that's my chair and desk. You'll find paper there. I'd like to censor it before it goes."

It took some doing, but I flatter myself that it wasn't such a bad job when it was finished. I read it aloud to the critical bacteriologist with some pride in my handiwork.

"Dear Professor Challenger," it said, "As a humble student of Nature, I have always taken the most profound interest in your speculations as to the differences between Darwin and Weissmann. I have recently had occasion to refresh my memory by re-reading—"

"You infernal liar!" murmured Tarp Henry.

"by re-reading your masterly address at Vienna. That lucid and admirable statement seems to be the last word in the matter. There is one sentence in it, however—namely: 'I protest strongly against the insufferable and entirely dogmatic assertion that each separate id is a microcosm possessed of an historical architecture elaborated slowly through the series of generations.' Have you no desire, in view of later research, to modify this statement? Do you not think that it is over-accentuated? With your permission, I would ask the favor of an interview, as I feel strongly upon the subject, and have certain suggestions which I could only elaborate in a personal conversation. With your consent, I trust to have the honor of calling at eleven o'clock the day after tomorrow (Wednesday) morning.

"I remain, Sir, with assurances of profound respect, yours very truly,

Edward D. Malone."

"How's that?" I asked, triumphantly.

"Well if your conscience can stand it----"

"It has never failed me yet."

"But what do you mean to do?"

"To get there. Once I am in his room I may see some opening. I may even go the length of open confession. If he is a sportsman he will be tickled."

"Tickled, indeed! He's much more likely to do the tickling. Chain mail, or an American football suit—that's what you'll want. Well, good-bye. I'll have the answer for you here on Wednesday morning—if he ever deigns to answer you. He is a violent, dangerous, cantankerous character, hated by everyone who comes across him, and the butt of the students, so far as they dare take a liberty with him. Perhaps it would be best for you if you never heard from the fellow at all."

Chapter III; "He is a Perfectly Impossible Person"

My friend's fear or hope was not destined to be realized. When I called on Wednesday there was a letter with the West Kensington postmark upon it, and my name scrawled across the envelope in a handwriting which looked like a barbed-wire railing. The contents were as follows:

"Enmore Park, W.

"Sir, I have duly received your note, in which you claim to endorse my views, although I am not aware that they are dependent upon endorsement either from you or anyone else. You have ventured to use the word 'speculation' with regard to my statement upon the subject of Darwinism, and I would call your attention to the fact that such a word in such a connection is offensive to a degree. The context convinces me, however, that you have sinned rather through ignorance and tactlessness than through malice, so I am content to pass the matter by. You quote an isolated sentence from my lecture, and appear to have some difficulty in understanding it. I should have thought that only a sub-human intelligence could have failed to grasp the point, but if it really needs amplification I shall consent to see you at the hour named, though visits and visitors of every sort are exceeding distasteful to me. As to your suggestion that I may modify my opinion, I would have you know that it is not my habit to do so after a deliberate expression of my mature views. You will kindly show the envelope of this letter to my man, Austin, when you call, as he has to take every precaution to shield me from the intrusive rascals who call themselves 'journalists.'

"Yours faithfully,

"George Edward Challenger."

This was the letter that I read aloud to Tarp Henry, who had come down early to hear the result of my venture. His only remark was, "There's some new stuff, cuticura or something, which is better than arnica." Some people have such extraordinary notions of humor.

It was nearly half-past ten before I had received my message, but a taxicab took me round in good time for my appointment. It was an imposing porticoed house at which we stopped, and the heavily-curtained windows gave every indication of wealth upon the part of this formidable Professor. The door was opened by an odd, swarthy, dried-up person of uncertain age, with a dark pilot jacket and brown leather gaiters. I found afterwards that he was the chauffeur, who filled the gaps left by a succession of fugitive butlers. He looked me up and down with a searching light blue eye.

"Expected?" he asked.

"An appointment."

"Got your letter?"

I produced the envelope.

"Right!" He seemed to be a person of few words. Following him down the passage I was suddenly interrupted by a small woman, who stepped out from what proved to be the dining-room door. She was a bright, vivacious, dark-eyed lady, more French than English in her type.

"One moment," she said. "You can wait, Austin. Step in here, sir. May I ask if you have met my husband before?"

"No, madam, I have not had the honor."

"Then I apologize to you in advance. I must tell you that he is a perfectly impossible person—absolutely impossible. If you are forewarned you will be the more ready to make allowances."

"It is most considerate of you, madam."

"Get quickly out of the room if he seems inclined to be violent. Don't wait to argue with him. Several people have been injured through doing that. Afterwards there is a public scandal and it reflects upon me and all of us. I suppose it wasn't about South America you wanted to see him?"

I could not lie to a lady.

"Dear me! That is his most dangerous subject. You won't believe a word he says—I'm sure I don't wonder. But don't tell him so, for it makes him very violent. Pretend to believe him, and you may get through all right. Remember he believes it himself. Of that you may be assured. A more honest man never lived. Don't wait any longer or he may suspect. If you find him dangerous—really dangerous—ring the bell and hold him off until I come. Even at his worst I can usually control him."

With these encouraging words the lady handed me over to the taciturn Austin, who had waited like a bronze statue of discretion during our short interview, and I was conducted to the end of the passage. There was a tap at a door, a bull's bellow from within, and I was face to face with the Professor.

He sat in a rotating chair behind a broad table, which was covered with books, maps, and diagrams. As I entered, his seat spun round to face me. His appearance made me gasp. I was prepared for something strange, but not for so overpowering a personality as this. It was his size which took one's breath away—his size and his imposing presence. His head was enormous, the largest I have ever seen upon a human being. I am sure that his top-hat, had I ever ventured to don it, would have slipped over me entirely and rested on my shoulders. He had the face and beard which I associate with an Assyrian bull; the former florid, the latter so black as almost to have a suspicion of blue, spade-shaped and rippling down over his chest. The hair was peculiar, plastered down in front in a long, curving wisp over his massive forehead. The eyes were blue-gray under great black tufts, very clear, very critical, and very masterful. A huge spread of shoulders and a chest like a barrel were the other parts of him which appeared above the table, save for two enormous hands covered with long black hair. This and a bellowing, roaring, rumbling voice made up my first impression of the notorious Professor Challenger.

"Well?" said he, with a most insolent stare. "What now?"

I must keep up my deception for at least a little time longer, otherwise here was evidently an end of the interview.

"You were good enough to give me an appointment, sir," said I, humbly, producing his envelope.

He took my letter from his desk and laid it out before him.

"Oh, you are the young person who cannot understand plain English, are you? My general conclusions you are good enough to approve, as I understand?"

"Entirely, sir—entirely!" I was very emphatic.

"Dear me! That strengthens my position very much, does it not? Your age and appearance make your support doubly valuable. Well, at least you are better than that herd of swine in Vienna, whose gregarious grunt is, however, not more offensive than the isolated effort of the British hog." He glared at me as the present representative of the beast.

"They seem to have behaved abominably," said I.

"I assure you that I can fight my own battles, and that I have no possible need of your sympathy. Put me alone, sir, and with my back to the wall. G. E. C. is happiest then. Well, sir, let us do what we can to curtail this visit, which can hardly be agreeable to you, and is inexpressibly irksome to me. You had, as I have been led to believe, some comments to make upon the proposition which I advanced in my thesis."

There was a brutal directness about his methods which made evasion difficult. I must still make play and wait for a better opening. It had seemed simple enough at a distance. Oh, my Irish wits, could they not help me now, when I needed help so sorely? He transfixed me with two sharp, steely eyes. "Come, come!" he rumbled.

"I am, of course, a mere student," said I, with a fatuous smile, "hardly more, I might say, than an earnest inquirer. At the same time, it seemed to me that you were a little severe upon Weissmann in this matter. Has not the general evidence since that date tended to—well, to strengthen his position?"

"What evidence?" He spoke with a menacing calm.

"Well, of course, I am aware that there is not any what you might call *definite* evidence. I alluded merely to the trend of modern thought and the general scientific point of view, if I might so express it."

He leaned forward with great earnestness.

"I suppose you are aware," said he, checking off points upon his fingers, "that the cranial index is a constant factor?"

"Naturally," said I.

"And that telegony is still sub judice?"

"Undoubtedly."

"And that the germ plasm is different from the parthenogenetic egg?"

"Why, surely!" I cried, and gloried in my own audacity.

"But what does that prove?" he asked, in a gentle, persuasive voice.

"Ah, what indeed?" I murmured. "What does it prove?"

"Shall I tell you?" he cooed.

"Pray do."

"It proves," he roared, with a sudden blast of fury, "that you are the damnedest imposter in London—a vile, crawling journalist, who has no more science than he has decency in his composition!"

He had sprung to his feet with a mad rage in his eyes. Even at that moment of tension I found time for amazement at the discovery that he was quite a short man, his head not higher than my shoulder—a stunted Hercules whose tremendous vitality had all run to depth, breadth, and brain.

"Gibberish!" he cried, leaning forward, with his fingers on the table and his face projecting. "That's what I have been talking to you, sir—scientific gibberish! Did you think you could match cunning with me—you with your walnut of a brain? You think you are omnipotent, you infernal scribblers, don't you? That your praise can make a man and your blame can break him? We must all bow to you, and try to get a favorable word, must we? This man shall have a leg up, and this man shall have a dressing down! Creeping vermin, I know you! You've got out of your station. Time was when your ears were clipped. You've lost your sense of proportion. Swollen gas-bags! I'll keep you in your proper place. Yes, sir, you haven't got over G. E. C. There's one man who is still your master. He warned you off, but if you *will* come, by the Lord you do it at your own risk. Forfeit, my good Mr. Malone, I claim forfeit! You have played a rather dangerous game, and it strikes me that you have lost it."

"Look here, sir," said I, backing to the door and opening it; "you can be as abusive as you like. But there is a limit. You shall not assault me."

"Shall I not?" He was slowly advancing in a peculiarly menacing way, but he stopped now and put his big hands into the side-pockets of a rather boyish short jacket which he wore. "I have thrown several of you out of the house. You will be the fourth or fifth. Three pound fifteen each—that is how it averaged. Expensive, but very necessary. Now, sir, why should you not follow your brethren? I rather think you must." He resumed his unpleasant and stealthy advance, pointing his toes as he walked, like a dancing master.

I could have bolted for the hall door, but it would have been too ignominious. Besides, a little glow of righteous anger was springing up within me. I had been hopelessly in the wrong before, but this man's menaces were putting me in the right.

"I'll trouble you to keep your hands off, sir. I'll not stand it."

"Dear me!" His black moustache lifted and a white fang twinkled in a sneer. "You won't stand it, eh?"

"Don't be such a fool, Professor!" I cried. "What can you hope for? I'm fifteen stone, as hard as nails, and play center three-quarter every Saturday for the London Irish. I'm not the man----"

It was at that moment that he rushed me. It was lucky that I had opened the door, or we should have gone through it. We did a Catharine-wheel together down the passage. Somehow we gathered up a chair upon our way, and bounded on with it towards the street. My mouth was full of his beard, our arms were locked, our bodies intertwined, and that infernal chair radiated its legs all round us. The watchful Austin had thrown open the hall door. We went with a back somersault down the front steps. I have seen the two Macs attempt something of the kind at the halls, but it appears to take some practise to do it without hurting oneself. The chair went to matchwood at the bottom, and we rolled apart into the gutter. He sprang to his feet, waving his fists and wheezing like an asthmatic.

"Had enough?" he panted.

"You infernal bully!" I cried, as I gathered myself together.

Then and there we should have tried the thing out, for he was effervescing with fight, but fortunately I was rescued from an odious situation. A policeman was beside us, his notebook in his hand.

"What's all this? You ought to be ashamed" said the policeman. It was the most rational remark which I had heard in Enmore Park. "Well," he insisted, turning to me, "what is it, then?"

"This man attacked me," said I.

"Did you attack him?" asked the policeman.

The Professor breathed hard and said nothing.

"It's not the first time, either," said the policeman, severely, shaking his head. "You were in trouble last month for the same thing. You've blackened this young man's eye. Do you give him in charge, sir?"

I relented.

"No," said I, "I do not."

"What's that?" said the policeman.

"I was to blame myself. I intruded upon him. He gave me fair warning."

The policeman snapped up his notebook.

"Don't let us have any more such goings-on," said he. "Now, then! Move on, there, move on!" This to a butcher's boy, a maid, and one or two loafers who had collected. He clumped heavily down the street, driving this little flock before him. The Professor looked at me, and there was something humorous at the back of his eyes.

"Come in!" said he. "I've not done with you yet."

The speech had a sinister sound, but I followed him none the less into the house. The man-servant, Austin, like a wooden image, closed the door behind us.

Chapter IV; "It's Just the very Biggest Thing in the World"

Hardly was it shut when Mrs. Challenger darted out from the dining-room. The small woman was in a furious temper. She barred her husband's way like an enraged chicken in front of a bulldog. It was evident that she had seen my exit, but had not observed my return.

"You brute, George!" she screamed. "You've hurt that nice young man."

He jerked backwards with his thumb.

"Here he is, safe and sound behind me."

She was confused, but not unduly so.

"I am so sorry, I didn't see you."

"I assure you, madam, that it is all right."

"He has marked your poor face! Oh, George, what a brute you are! Nothing but scandals from one end of the week to the other. Everyone hating and making fun of you. You've finished my patience. This ends it."

"Dirty linen," he rumbled.

"It's not a secret," she cried. "Do you suppose that the whole street—the whole of London, for that matter---- Get away, Austin, we don't want you here. Do you suppose they don't all talk about you? Where is your dignity? You, a man who should have been Regius Professor at a great University with a thousand students all revering you. Where is your dignity, George?"

"How about yours, my dear?"

"You try me too much. A ruffian—a common brawling ruffian—that's what you have become."

"Be good, Jessie."

"A roaring, raging bully!"

"That's done it! Stool of penance!" said he.

To my amazement he stooped, picked her up, and placed her sitting upon a high pedestal of black marble in the angle of the hall. It was at least seven feet high, and so thin that she could hardly balance upon it. A more absurd object than she presented cocked up there with her face convulsed with anger, her feet dangling, and her body rigid for fear of an upset, I could not imagine.

"Let me down!" she wailed.

"Say 'please.'"

"You brute, George! Let me down this instant!"

"Come into the study, Mr. Malone."

"Really, sir!" said I, looking at the lady.

"Here's Mr. Malone pleading for you, Jessie. Say 'please,' and down you come."

"Oh, you brute! Please! Please!"

He took her down as if she had been a canary.

"You must behave yourself, dear. Mr. Malone is a Pressman. He will have it all in his rag tomorrow, and sell an extra dozen among our neighbors. 'Strange story of high life'—you felt fairly high on that pedestal, did you not? Then a sub-title, 'Glimpse of a singular menage.' He's a foul feeder, is Mr. Malone, a carrion eater, like all of his kind—*porcus ex grege diaboli*—a swine from the devil's herd. That's it, Malone—what?"

"You are really intolerable!" said I, hotly.

He bellowed with laughter.

"We shall have a coalition presently," he boomed, looking from his wife to me and puffing out his enormous chest. Then, suddenly altering his tone, "Excuse this frivolous family badinage, Mr. Malone. I called you back for some more serious purpose than to mix you up with our little domestic pleasantries. Run away, little woman, and don't fret." He placed a huge hand upon each of her shoulders. "All that you say is perfectly true. I should be a better man if I did what you advise, but I shouldn't be quite George Edward Challenger. There are plenty of better men, my dear, but only one G. E. C. So make the best of him." He suddenly gave her a resounding kiss, which embarrassed me even more than his violence had done. "Now, Mr. Malone," he continued, with a great accession of dignity, "this way, if YOU please."

We re-entered the room which we had left so tumultuously ten minutes before. The Professor closed the door carefully behind us, motioned me into an arm-chair, and pushed a cigar-box under my nose.

"Real San Juan Colorado," he said. "Excitable people like you are the better for narcotics. Heavens! don't bite it! Cut—and cut with reverence! Now lean back, and listen attentively to whatever I may care to say to you. If any remark should occur to you, you can reserve it for some more opportune time.

"First of all, as to your return to my house after your most justifiable expulsion"—he protruded his beard, and stared at me as one who challenges and invites contradiction—"after, as I say, your well-merited expulsion. The reason lay in your answer to that most officious policeman, in which I seemed to discern some glimmering of good feeling upon your part—more, at any rate, than I am accustomed to associate with your profession. In admitting that the fault of the incident lay with you, you gave some evidence of a certain mental detachment and breadth of view which attracted my favorable notice. The sub-species of the human race to which you unfortunately belong has always been below my mental horizon. Your words brought you suddenly above it. You swam up into my serious notice. For this reason I asked you to return with me, as I was minded to make your further acquaintance.

You will kindly deposit your ash in the small Japanese tray on the ban. which stands at your left elbow."

All this he boomed forth like a professor addressing his class. He had round his revolving chair so as to face me, and he sat all puffed out like an enor. bull-frog, his head laid back and his eyes half-covered by supercilious lids. Now he suddenly turned himself sideways, and all I could see of him was tangled hair with a red, protruding ear. He was scratching about among the litter of papers upon his desk. He faced me presently with what looked like a very tattered sketch-book in his hand.

"I am going to talk to you about South America," said he. "No comments if you please. First of all, I wish you to understand that nothing I tell you now is to be repeated in any public way unless you have my express permission. That permission will, in all human probability, never be given. Is that clear?"

"It is very hard," said I. "Surely a judicious account----"

He replaced the notebook upon the table.

"That ends it," said he. "I wish you a very good morning."

"No, no!" I cried. "I submit to any conditions. So far as I can see, I have no choice."

"None in the world," said he.

"Well, then, I promise."

"Word of honor?"

"Word of honor."

He looked at me with doubt in his insolent eyes.

"After all, what do I know about your honor?" said he.

"Upon my word, sir," I cried, angrily, "you take very great liberties! I have never been so insulted in my life."

He seemed more interested than annoyed at my outbreak.

"Round-headed," he muttered. "Brachycephalic, gray-eyed, black-haired, with suggestion of the negroid. Celtic, I presume?"

"I am an Irishman, sir."

"Irish Irish?"

"Yes, sir."

"That, of course, explains it. Let me see; you have given me your promise that my confidence will be respected? That confidence, I may say, will be far from complete. But I am prepared to give you a few indications which will be of interest. In the first place, you are probably aware that two years ago I made a journey to South America—one which will be classical in the scientific history of the world? The object of my journey was to verify some conclusions of Wallace and of Bates, which could only be done by observing their reported facts under the same conditions in which they had themselves noted them. If my expedition had no other results it would still have been noteworthy, but a curious incident occurred to me while there which opened up an entirely fresh line of inquiry.

"You are aware—or probably, in this half-educated age, you are not aware—that the country round some parts of the Amazon is still only partially explored, and that a great number of tributaries, some of them entirely uncharted, run into the main river. It was my business to visit this little-known back-country and to examine its fauna, which furnished me with the materials for several chapters for that great and monumental work upon zoology which will be my life's justification. I was returning, my work accomplished, when I had occasion to spend a night at a small Indian village at a point where a certain tributary—the name and position of which I withhold—opens into the main river. The natives were Cucama Indians, an amiable but degraded race, with mental powers hardly superior to the average Londoner. I had effected some cures among them upon my way up the river, and had impressed them considerably with my personality, so that I was not surprised to find myself eagerly awaited upon my return. I gathered from their signs that someone had urgent need of my medical services, and I followed the chief to one of his huts. When I entered I found that the sufferer to whose aid I had been summoned had that instant expired. He was, to my surprise, no Indian, but a white man; indeed, I may say a very white man, for he was flaxen-haired and had some characteristics of an albino. He was clad in rags, was very emaciated, and bore every trace of prolonged hardship. So far as I could understand the account of the natives, he was a complete stranger to them, and had come upon their village through the woods alone and in the last stage of exhaustion.

"The man's knapsack lay beside the couch, and I examined the contents. His name was written upon a tab within it—Maple White, Lake Avenue, Detroit, Michigan. It is a name to which I am prepared always to lift my hat. It is not too much to say that it will rank level with my own when the final credit of this business comes to be apportioned.

"From the contents of the knapsack it was evident that this man had been an artist and poet in search of effects. There were scraps of verse. I do not profess to be a judge of such things, but they appeared to me to be singularly wanting in merit. There were also some rather commonplace pictures of river scenery, a paint-box, a box of colored chalks, some brushes, that curved bone which lies upon my inkstand, a volume of Baxter's 'Moths and Butterflies,' a cheap revolver, and a few cartridges. Of personal equipment he either had none or he had lost it in his journey. Such were the total effects of this strange American Bohemian.

"I was turning away from him when I observed that something projected from the front of his ragged jacket. It was this sketch-book, which was as dilapidated then as you see it now. Indeed, I can assure you that a first folio of Shakespeare could not be treated with greater reverence than this relic has been since it came into my possession. I hand it to you now, and I ask you to take it page by page and to examine the contents."

He helped himself to a cigar and leaned back with a fiercely critical pair of eyes, taking note of the effect which this document would produce.

I had opened the volume with some expectation of a revelation, though of what nature I could not imagine. The first page was disappointing, however, as it contained nothing but the picture of a very fat man in a pea-jacket, with the legend, "Jimmy Colver on the Mail-boat," written beneath it. There followed several pages which were filled with small sketches of Indians and their ways. Then came a picture of a cheerful and corpulent ecclesiastic in a shovel hat, sitting opposite a very thin European, and the inscription: "Lunch with Fra Cristofero at Rosario." Studies of women and babies accounted for several more pages, and then there was an unbroken series of animal drawings with such explanations as "Manatee upon Sandbank," "Turtles and Their Eggs," "Black Ajouti under a Miriti Palm"—the matter disclosing some sort of pig-like animal; and finally came a double page of studies of long-snouted and very unpleasant saurians. I could make nothing of it, and said so to the Professor.

"Surely these are only crocodiles?"

"Alligators! Alligators! There is hardly such a thing as a true crocodile America. The distinction between them----"

"I meant that I could see nothing unusual—nothing to justify what yo said."

He smiled serenely.

"Try the next page," said he.

I was still unable to sympathize. It was a full-page sketch of a landscape roughly tinted in color—the kind of painting which an open-air artist takes as a guide to a future more elaborate effort. There was a pale-green foreground of feathery vegetation, which sloped upwards and ended in a line of cliffs dark red in color, and curiously ribbed like some basaltic formations which I have seen. They extended in an unbroken wall right across the background. At one point was an isolated pyramidal rock, crowned by a great tree, which appeared to be separated by a cleft from the main crag. Behind it all, a blue tropical sky. A thin green line of vegetation fringed the summit of the ruddy cliff.

"Well?" he asked.

"It is no doubt a curious formation," said I "but I am not geologist enough to say that it is wonderful."

"Wonderful!" he repeated. "It is unique. It is incredible. No one on earth has ever dreamed of such a possibility. Now the next."

I turned it over, and gave an exclamation of surprise. There was a full-page picture of the most extraordinary creature that I had ever seen. It was the wild dream of an opium smoker, a vision of delirium. The head was like that of a fowl, the body that of a bloated lizard, the trailing tail was furnished with upward-turned spikes, and the curved back was edged with a high serrated fringe, which looked like a dozen cocks' wattles placed behind each other. In front of this creature was an absurd mannikin, or dwarf, in human form, who stood staring at it.

"Well, what do you think of that?" cried the Professor, rubbing his hands with an air of triumph.

"It is monstrous—grotesque."

"But what made him draw such an animal?"

"Trade gin, I should think."

"Oh, that's the best explanation you can give, is it?"

"Well, sir, what is yours?"

"The obvious one that the creature exists. That is actually sketched from the life."

I should have laughed only that I had a vision of our doing another Catharine-wheel down the passage.

"No doubt," said I, "no doubt," as one humors an imbecile. "I confess, however," I added, "that this tiny human figure puzzles me. If it were an Indian we could set it down as evidence of some pigmy race in America, but it appears to be a European in a sun-hat."

The Professor snorted like an angry buffalo. "You really touch the limit," said he. "You enlarge my view of the possible. Cerebral paresis! Mental inertia! Wonderful!"

He was too absurd to make me angry. Indeed, it was a waste of energy, for if you were going to be angry with this man you would be angry all the time. I contented myself with smiling wearily. "It struck me that the man was small," said I.

"Look here!" he cried, leaning forward and dabbing a great hairy sausage of a finger on to the picture. "You see that plant behind the animal; I suppose you thought it was a dandelion or a Brussels sprout—what? Well, it is a vegetable ivory palm, and

I predict they will go on an adventure together.

they run to about fifty or sixty feet. Don't you see that the man is put in for a purpose? He couldn't really have stood in front of that brute and lived to draw it. He sketched himself in to give a scale of heights. He was, we will say, over five feet high. The tree is ten times bigger, which is what one would expect."

"Good heavens!" I cried. "Then you think the beast was---- Why, Charing Cross station would hardly make a kennel for such a brute!"

"Apart from exaggeration, he is certainly a well-grown specimen," said the Professor, complacently.

"But," I cried, "surely the whole experience of the human race is not to be set aside on account of a single sketch"—I had turned over the leaves and ascertained that there was nothing more in the book—"a single sketch by a wandering American artist who may have done it under hashish, or in the delirium of fever, or simply in order to gratify a freakish imagination. You can't, as a man of science, defend such a position as that."

For answer the Professor took a book down from a shelf.

"This is an excellent monograph by my gifted friend, Ray Lankester!" said he. "There is an illustration here which would interest you. Ah, yes, here it is! The inscription beneath it runs: 'Probable appearance in life of the Jurassic Dinosaur Stegosaurus. The hind leg alone is twice as tall as a full-grown man.' Well, what do you make of that?"

He handed me the open book. I started as I looked at the picture. In this reconstructed animal of a dead world there was certainly a very great resemblance to the sketch of the unknown artist.

"That is certainly remarkable," said I.

"But you won't admit that it is final?"

"Surely it might be a coincidence, or this American may have seen a picture of the kind and carried it in his memory. It would be likely to recur to a man in a delirium."

"Very good," said the Professor, indulgently; "we leave it at that. I will now ask you to look at this bone." He handed over the one which he had already described as part of the dead man's possessions. It was about six inches long, and thicker than my thumb, with some indications of dried cartilage at one end of it.

"To what known creature does that bone belong?" asked the Professor.

I examined it with care and tried to recall some half-forgotten knowledge.

"It might be a very thick human collar-bone," I said.

My companion waved his hand in contemptuous deprecation.

"The human collar-bone is curved. This is straight. There is a groove upon its surface showing that a great tendon played across it, which could not be the case with a clavicle."

"Then I must confess that I don't know what it is."

"You need not be ashamed to expose your ignorance, for I don't suppose the whole South Kensington staff could give a name to it." He took a little bone the size of a bean out of a pill-box. "So far as I am a judge this human bone is the analogue of the one which you hold in your hand. That will give you some idea of the size of the creature. You will observe from the cartilage that this is no fossil specimen, but recent. What do you say to that?"

"Surely in an elephant----"

He winced as if in pain.

"Don't! Don't talk of elephants in South America. Even in these days of Boar schools----"

"Well," I interrupted, "any large South American animal—a tapir, for example."

"You may take it, young man, that I am versed in the elements of my business. This is not a conceivable bone either of a tapir or of any other creature known to zoology. It belongs to a very large, a very strong, and, by all analogy, a very fierce animal which exists upon the face of the earth, but has not yet come under the notice of science. You are still unconvinced?"

"I am at least deeply interested."

"Then your case is not hopeless. I feel that there is reason lurking in you somewhere, so we will patiently grope round for it. We will now leave the dead American and proceed with my narrative. You can imagine that I could hardly come away from the Amazon without probing deeper into the matter. There were indications as to the direction from which the dead traveler had come. Indian legends would alone have been my guide, for I found that rumors of a strange land were common among all the riverine tribes. You have heard, no doubt, of Curupuri?"

"Never."

"Curupuri is the spirit of the woods, something terrible, something malevolent, something to be avoided. None can describe its shape or nature, but it is a word of terror along the Amazon. Now all tribes agree as to the direction in which Curupuri lives. It was the same direction from which the American had come. Something terrible lay that way. It was my business to find out what it was."

"What did you do?" My flippancy was all gone. This massive man compelled one's attention and respect.

"I overcame the extreme reluctance of the natives—a reluctance which extends even to talk upon the subject—and by judicious persuasion and gifts, aided, I will admit, by some threats of coercion, I got two of them to act as guides. After many adventures which I need not describe, and after traveling a distance which I will not mention, in a direction which I withhold, we came at last to a tract of country which has never been described, nor, indeed, visited save by my unfortunate predecessor. Would you kindly look at this?"

He handed me a photograph—half-plate size.

"The unsatisfactory appearance of it is due to the fact," said he, "that on descending the river the boat was upset and the case which contained the undeveloped films was broken, with disastrous results. Nearly all of them were totally ruined—an irreparable loss. This is one of the few which partially escaped. This explanation of deficiencies or abnormalities you will kindly accept. There was talk of faking. I am not in a mood to argue such a point."

The photograph was certainly very off-colored. An unkind critic might easily have misinterpreted that dim surface. It was a dull gray landscape, and as I gradually deciphered the details of it I realized that it represented a long and enormously high line of cliffs exactly like an immense cataract seen in the distance, with a sloping, tree-clad plain in the foreground.

"I believe it is the same place as the painted picture," said I.

"It is the same place," the Professor answered. "I found traces of the fellow's camp. Now look at this."

It was a nearer view of the same scene, though the photograph was extremely defective. I could distinctly see the isolated, tree-crowned pinnacle of rock which was detached from the crag.

no doubt of it at all," said I.

ı, that is something gained," said he. "We progress, do we not? Now, will ase look at the top of that rocky pinnacle? Do you observe something there?"

An enormous tree."

"But on the tree?"

"A large bird," said I.

He handed me a lens.

"Yes," I said, peering through it, "a large bird stands on the tree. It appears to have a considerable beak. I should say it was a pelican."

"I cannot congratulate you upon your eyesight," said the Professor. "It is not a pelican, nor, indeed, is it a bird. It may interest you to know that I succeeded in shooting that particular specimen. It was the only absolute proof of my experiences which I was able to bring away with me."

"You have it, then?" Here at last was tangible corroboration.

"I had it. It was unfortunately lost with so much else in the same boat accident which ruined my photographs. I clutched at it as it disappeared in the swirl of the rapids, and part of its wing was left in my hand. I was insensible when washed ashore, but the miserable remnant of my superb specimen was still intact; I now lay it before you."

From a drawer he produced what seemed to me to be the upper portion of the wing of a large bat. It was at least two feet in length, a curved bone, with a membranous veil beneath it.

"A monstrous bat!" I suggested.

"Nothing of the sort," said the Professor, severely. "Living, as I do, in an educated and scientific atmosphere, I could not have conceived that the first principles of zoology were so little known. Is it possible that you do not know the elementary fact in comparative anatomy, that the wing of a bird is really the forearm, while the wing of a bat consists of three elongated fingers with membranes between? Now, in this case, the bone is certainly not the forearm, and you can see for yourself that this is a single membrane hanging upon a single bone, and therefore that it cannot belong to a bat. But if it is neither bird nor bat, what is it?"

My small stock of knowledge was exhausted.

"I really do not know," said I.

He opened the standard work to which he had already referred me.

"Here," said he, pointing to the picture of an extraordinary flying monster, "is an excellent reproduction of the dimorphodon, or pterodactyl, a flying reptile of the Jurassic period. On the next page is a diagram of the mechanism of its wing. Kindly compare it with the specimen in your hand."

A wave of amazement passed over me as I looked. I was convinced. There could be no getting away from it. The cumulative proof was overwhelming. The sketch, the photographs, the narrative, and now the actual specimen—the evidence was complete. I said so—I said so warmly, for I felt that the Professor was an ill-used man. He leaned back in his chair with drooping eyelids and a tolerant smile, basking in this sudden gleam of sunshine.

"It's just the very biggest thing that I ever heard of!" said I, though it was my journalistic rather than my scientific enthusiasm that was roused. "It is colossal. You are a Columbus of science who has discovered a lost world. I'm awfully sorry if I seemed to doubt you. It was all so unthinkable. But I understand evidence when I see it, and this should be good enough for anyone."

The Professor purred with satisfaction.

"And then, sir, what did you do next?"

"It was the wet season, Mr. Malone, and my stores were exhausted. I explored some portion of this huge cliff, but I was unable to find any way to scale it. The pyramidal rock upon which I saw and shot the pterodactyl was more accessible. Being something of a cragsman, I did manage to get half way to the top of that. From that height I had a better idea of the plateau upon the top of the crags. It appeared to be very large; neither to east nor to west could I see any end to the vista of green-capped cliffs. Below, it is a swampy, jungly region, full of snakes, insects, and fever. It is a natural protection to this singular country."

"Did you see any other trace of life?"

"No, sir, I did not; but during the week that we lay encamped at the base of the cliff we heard some very strange noises from above."

"But the creature that the American drew? How do you account for that?"

"We can only suppose that he must have made his way to the summit and seen it there. We know, therefore, that there is a way up. We know equally that it must be a very difficult one, otherwise the creatures would have come down and overrun the surrounding country. Surely that is clear?"

"But how did they come to be there?"

"I do not think that the problem is a very obscure one," said the Professor; "there can only be one explanation. South America is, as you may have heard, a granite continent. At this single point in the interior there has been, in some far distant age, a great, sudden volcanic upheaval. These cliffs, I may remark, are basaltic, and therefore plutonic. An area, as large perhaps as Sussex, has been lifted up en bloc with all its living contents, and cut off by perpendicular precipices of a hardness which defies erosion from all the rest of the continent. What is the result? Why, the ordinary laws of Nature are suspended. The various checks which influence the struggle for existence in the world at large are all neutralized or altered. Creatures survive which would otherwise disappear. You will observe that both the pterodactyl and the stegosaurus are Jurassic, and therefore of a great age in the order of life. They have been artificially conserved by those strange accidental conditions."

"But surely your evidence is conclusive. You have only to lay it before the proper authorities."

"So in my simplicity, I had imagined," said the Professor, bitterly. "I can only tell you that it was not so, that I was met at every turn by incredulity, born partly of stupidity and partly of jealousy. It is not my nature, sir, to cringe to any man, or to seek to prove a fact if my word has been doubted. After the first I have not condescended to show such corroborative proofs as I possess. The subject became hateful to me—I would not speak of it. When men like yourself, who represent the foolish curiosity of the public, came to disturb my privacy I was unable to meet them with dignified reserve. By nature I am, I admit, somewhat fiery, and under provocation I am inclined to be violent. I fear you may have remarked it."

I nursed my eye and was silent.

"My wife has frequently remonstrated with me upon the subject, and yet I fancy that any man of honor would feel the same. To-night, however, I propose to give an extreme example of the control of the will over the emotions. I invite you to be present at the exhibition." He handed me a card from his desk. "You will perceive that Mr. Percival Waldron, a naturalist of some popular repute, is announced to lecture at eight-thirty at the Zoological Institute's Hall upon 'The Record of the Ages.'

I have been specially invited to be present upon the platform, and to move a vote of thanks to the lecturer. While doing so, I shall make it my business, with infinite tact and delicacy, to throw out a few remarks which may arouse the interest of the audience and cause some of them to desire to go more deeply into the matter. Nothing contentious, you understand, but only an indication that there are greater deeps beyond. I shall hold myself strongly in leash, and see whether by this self-restraint I attain a more favorable result."

"And I may come?" I asked eagerly.

"Why, surely," he answered, cordially. He had an enormously massive genial manner, which was almost as overpowering as his violence. His smile of benevolence was a wonderful thing, when his cheeks would suddenly bunch into two red apples, between his half-closed eyes and his great black beard. "By all means, come. It will be a comfort to me to know that I have one ally in the hall, however inefficient and ignorant of the subject he may be. I fancy there will be a large audience, for Waldron, though an absolute charlatan, has a considerable popular following. Now, Mr. Malone, I have given you rather more of my time than I had intended. The individual must not monopolize what is meant for the world. I shall be pleased to see you at the lecture to-night. In the meantime, you will understand that no public use is to be made of any of the material that I have given you."

"But Mr. McArdle—my news editor, you know—will want to know what I have done."

"Tell him what you like. You can say, among other things, that if he sends anyone else to intrude upon me I shall call upon him with a riding-whip. But I leave it to you that nothing of all this appears in print. Very good. Then the Zoological Institute's Hall at eight-thirty to-night." I had a last impression of red cheeks, blue rippling beard, and intolerant eyes, as he waved me out of the room.

Chapter V; "Question!"

What with the physical shocks incidental to my first interview with Professor Challenger and the mental ones which accompanied the second, I was a somewhat demoralized journalist by the time I found myself in Enmore Park once more. In my aching head the one thought was throbbing that there really was truth in this man's story, that it was of tremendous consequence, and that it would work up into inconceivable copy for the Gazette when I could obtain permission to use it. A taxicab was waiting at the end of the road, so I sprang into it and drove down to the office. McArdle was at his post as usual.

"Well," he cried, expectantly, "what may it run to? I'm thinking, young man, you have been in the wars. Don't tell me that he assaulted you."

"We had a little difference at first."

"What a man it is! What did you do?"

"Well, he became more reasonable and we had a chat. But I got nothing out of him—nothing for publication."

"I'm not so sure about that. You got a black eye out of him, and that's for publication. We can't have this reign of terror, Mr. Malone. We must bring the man to his bearings. I'll have a leaderette on him tomorrow that will raise a blister. Just give me the material and I will engage to brand the fellow for ever. Professor Munchausen—how's that for an inset headline? Sir John Mandeville redivivus—

Cagliostro—all the imposters and bullies in history. I'll show him up for the fraud he is."

"I wouldn't do that, sir."

"Why not?"

"Because he is not a fraud at all."

"What!" roared McArdle. "You don't mean to say you really believe this stuff of his about mammoths and mastodons and great sea sairpents?"

"Well, I don't know about that. I don't think he makes any claims of that kind. But I do believe he has got something new."

"Then for Heaven's sake, man, write it up!"

"I'm longing to, but all I know he gave me in confidence and on condition that I didn't." I condensed into a few sentences the Professor's narrative. "That's how it stands."

McArdle looked deeply incredulous.

"Well, Mr. Malone," he said at last, "about this scientific meeting to-night; there can be no privacy about that, anyhow. I don't suppose any paper will want to report it, for Waldron has been reported already a dozen times, and no one is aware that Challenger will speak. We may get a scoop, if we are lucky. You'll be there in any case, so you'll just give us a pretty full report. I'll keep space up to midnight."

My day was a busy one, and I had an early dinner at the Savage Club with Tarp Henry, to whom I gave some account of my adventures. He listened with a sceptical smile on his gaunt face, and roared with laughter on hearing that the Professor had convinced me.

"My dear chap, things don't happen like that in real life. People don't stumble upon enormous discoveries and then lose their evidence. Leave that to the novelists. The fellow is as full of tricks as the monkey-house at the Zoo. It's all bosh."

"But the American poet?"

"He never existed."

"I saw his sketch-book."

"Challenger's sketch-book."

"You think he drew that animal?"

"Of course he did. Who else?"

"Well, then, the photographs?"

"There was nothing in the photographs. By your own admission you only saw a bird."

"A pterodactyl."

"That's what *he* says. He put the pterodactyl into your head."

"Well, then, the bones?"

"First one out of an Irish stew. Second one vamped up for the occasion. If you are clever and know your business you can fake a bone as easily as you can a photograph."

I began to feel uneasy. Perhaps, after all, I had been premature in my acquiescence. Then I had a sudden happy thought.

"Will you come to the meeting?" I asked.

Tarp Henry looked thoughtful.

"He is not a popular person, the genial Challenger," said he. "A lot of people have accounts to settle with him. I should say he is about the best-hated man in London. If the medical students turn out there will be no end of a rag. I don't want to get into a bear-garden."

"You might at least do him the justice to hear him state his own case."

"Well, perhaps it's only fair. All right. I'm your man for the evening."

When we arrived at the hall we found a much greater concourse than I had expected. A line of electric broughams discharged their little cargoes of white-bearded professors, while the dark stream of humbler pedestrians, who crowded through the arched door-way, showed that the audience would be popular as well as scientific. Indeed, it became evident to us as soon as we had taken our seats that a youthful and even boyish spirit was abroad in the gallery and the back portions of the hall. Looking behind me, I could see rows of faces of the familiar medical student type. Apparently the great hospitals had each sent down their contingent. The behavior of the audience at present was good-humored, but mischievous. Scraps of popular songs were chorused with an enthusiasm which was a strange prelude to a scientific lecture, and there was already a tendency to personal chaff which promised a jovial evening to others, however embarrassing it might be to the recipients of these dubious honors.

Thus, when old Doctor Meldrum, with his well-known curly-brimmed opera-hat, appeared upon the platform, there was such a universal query of "Where *did* you get that tile?" that he hurriedly removed it, and concealed it furtively under his chair. When gouty Professor Wadley limped down to his seat there were general affectionate inquiries from all parts of the hall as to the exact state of his poor toe, which caused him obvious embarrassment. The greatest demonstration of all, however, was at the entrance of my new acquaintance, Professor Challenger, when he passed down to take his place at the extreme end of the front row of the platform. Such a yell of welcome broke forth when his black beard first protruded round the corner that I began to suspect Tarp Henry was right in his surmise, and that this assemblage was there not merely for the sake of the lecture, but because it had got rumored abroad that the famous Professor would take part in the proceedings.

There was some sympathetic laughter on his entrance among the front benches of well-dressed spectators, as though the demonstration of the students in this instance was not unwelcome to them. That greeting was, indeed, a frightful outburst of sound, the uproar of the carnivora cage when the step of the bucket-bearing keeper is heard in the distance. There was an offensive tone in it, perhaps, and yet in the main it struck me as mere riotous outcry, the noisy reception of one who amused and interested them, rather than of one they disliked or despised. Challenger smiled with weary and tolerant contempt, as a kindly man would meet the yapping of a litter of puppies. He sat slowly down, blew out his chest, passed his hand caressingly down his beard, and looked with drooping eyelids and supercilious eyes at the crowded hall before him. The uproar of his advent had not yet died away when Professor Ronald Murray, the chairman, and Mr. Waldron, the lecturer, threaded their way to the front, and the proceedings began.

Professor Murray will, I am sure, excuse me if I say that he has the common fault of most Englishmen of being inaudible. Why on earth people who have something to say which is worth hearing should not take the slight trouble to learn how to make it heard is one of the strange mysteries of modern life. Their methods are as reasonable as to try to pour some precious stuff from the spring to the reservoir through a non-conducting pipe, which could by the least effort be opened. Professor Murray made several profound remarks to his white tie and to the water-carafe upon the table, with a humorous, twinkling aside to the silver candlestick upon his right. Then he sat down, and Mr. Waldron, the famous popular lecturer, rose amid a general murmur of applause. He was a stern, gaunt man, with a harsh voice, and an aggressive manner, but he had the merit of knowing how to assimilate the ideas of other men, and to pass them on in a way which was intelligible and even interesting to the lay public, with a happy knack of being funny about the most unlikely objects, so that the precession of the Equinox or the formation of a vertebrate became a highly humorous process as treated by him.

It was a bird's-eye view of creation, as interpreted by science, which, in language always clear and sometimes picturesque, he unfolded before us. He told us of the globe, a huge mass of flaming gas, flaring through the heavens. Then he pictured the solidification, the cooling, the wrinkling which formed the mountains, the steam which turned to water, the slow preparation of the stage upon which was to be played the inexplicable drama of life. On the origin of life itself he was discreetly vague. That the germs of it could hardly have survived the original roasting was, he declared, fairly certain. Therefore it had come later. Had it built itself out of the cooling, inorganic elements of the globe? Very likely. Had the germs of it arrived from outside upon a meteor? It was hardly conceivable. On the whole, the wisest man was the least dogmatic upon the point. We could not—or at least we had not succeeded up to date in making organic life in our laboratories out of inorganic materials. The gulf between the dead and the living was something which our chemistry could not as yet bridge. But there was a higher and subtler chemistry of Nature, which, working with great forces over long epochs, might well produce results which were impossible for us. There the matter must be left.

This brought the lecturer to the great ladder of animal life, beginning low down in molluscs and feeble sea creatures, then up rung by rung through reptiles and fishes, till at last we came to a kangaroo-rat, a creature which brought forth its young alive, the direct ancestor of all mammals, and presumably, therefore, of everyone in the audience. ("No, no," from a sceptical student in the back row.) If the young gentleman in the red tie who cried "No, no," and who presumably claimed to have been hatched out of an egg, would wait upon him after the lecture, he would be glad to see such a curiosity. (Laughter.) It was strange to think that the climax of all the age-long process of Nature had been the creation of that gentleman in the red tie. But had the process stopped? Was this gentleman to be taken as the final type—the be-all and end-all of development? He hoped that he would not hurt the feelings of the gentleman in the red tie if he maintained that, whatever virtues that gentleman might possess in private life, still the vast processes of the universe were not fully justified if they were to end entirely in his production. Evolution was not a spent force, but one still working, and even greater achievements were in store.

Having thus, amid a general titter, played very prettily with his interrupter, the lecturer went back to his picture of the past, the drying of the seas, the emergence of the sand-bank, the sluggish, viscous life which lay upon their margins, the overcrowded lagoons, the tendency of the sea creatures to take refuge upon the mud-flats, the abundance of food awaiting them, their consequent enormous growth. "Hence, ladies and gentlemen," he added, "that frightful brood of saurians which still affright our eyes when seen in the Wealden or in the Solenhofen slates, but which were fortunately extinct long before the first appearance of mankind upon this planet."

"Question!" boomed a voice from the platform.

Mr. Waldron was a strict disciplinarian with a gift of acid humor, as exemplified upon the gentleman with the red tie, which made it perilous to interrupt him. But this interjection appeared to him so absurd that he was at a loss how to deal with it. So looks the Shakespearean who is confronted by a rancid Baconian, or the astronomer who is assailed by a flat-earth fanatic. He paused for a moment, and then, raising his voice, repeated slowly the words: "Which were extinct before the coming of man."

"Question!" boomed the voice once more.

Waldron looked with amazement along the line of professors upon the platform until his eyes fell upon the figure of Challenger, who leaned back in his chair with closed eyes and an amused expression, as if he were smiling in his sleep.

"I see!" said Waldron, with a shrug. "It is my friend Professor Challenger," and amid laughter he renewed his lecture as if this was a final explanation and no more need be said.

But the incident was far from being closed. Whatever path the lecturer took amid the wilds of the past seemed invariably to lead him to some assertion as to extinct or prehistoric life which instantly brought the same bulls' bellow from the Professor. The audience began to anticipate it and to roar with delight when it came. The packed benches of students joined in, and every time Challenger's beard opened, before any sound could come forth, there was a yell of "Question!" from a hundred voices, and an answering counter cry of "Order!" and "Shame!" from as many more. Waldron, though a hardened lecturer and a strong man, became rattled. He hesitated, stammered, repeated himself, got snarled in a long sentence, and finally turned furiously upon the cause of his troubles.

"This is really intolerable!" he cried, glaring across the platform. "I must ask you, Professor Challenger, to cease these ignorant and unmannerly interruptions."

There was a hush over the hall, the students rigid with delight at seeing the high gods on Olympus quarrelling among themselves. Challenger levered his bulky figure slowly out of his chair.

"I must in turn ask you, Mr. Waldron," he said, "to cease to make assertions which are not in strict accordance with scientific fact."

The words unloosed a tempest. "Shame! Shame!" "Give him a hearing!" "Put him out!" "Shove him off the platform!" "Fair play!" emerged from a general roar of amusement or execration. The chairman was on his feet flapping both his hands and bleating excitedly. "Professor Challenger—personal—views—later," were the solid peaks above his clouds of inaudible mutter. The interrupter bowed, smiled, stroked his beard, and relapsed into his chair. Waldron, very flushed and warlike, continued his observations. Now and then, as he made an assertion, he shot a venomous glance at his opponent, who seemed to be slumbering deeply, with the same broad, happy smile upon his face.

At last the lecture came to an end—I am inclined to think that it was a premature one, as the peroration was hurried and disconnected. The thread of the argument had been rudely broken, and the audience was restless and expectant. Waldron sat down, and, after a chirrup from the chairman, Professor Challenger rose and advanced to the edge of the platform. In the interests of my paper I took down his speech verbatim.

"Ladies and Gentlemen," he began, amid a sustained interruption from the back. "I beg pardon—Ladies, Gentlemen, and Children—I must apologize, I had inadvertently omitted a considerable section of this audience" (tumult, during which the Professor stood with one hand raised and his enormous head nodding sympathetically, as if he were bestowing a pontifical blessing upon the crowd), "I have been selected to move a vote of thanks to Mr. Waldron for the very picturesque and imaginative address to which we have just listened. There are points in it with which I disagree, and it has been my duty to indicate them as they arose, but, none the less, Mr. Waldron has accomplished his object well, that object being to give a simple and interesting account of what he conceives to have been the history of our planet. Popular lectures are the easiest to listen to, but Mr. Waldron" (here he beamed and blinked at the lecturer) "will excuse me when I say that they are necessarily both superficial and misleading, since they have to be graded to the comprehension of an ignorant audience." (Ironical cheering.) "Popular lecturers are in their nature parasitic." (Angry gesture of protest from Mr. Waldron.) "They exploit for fame or cash the work which has been done by their indigent and unknown brethren. One smallest new fact obtained in the laboratory, one brick built into the temple of science, far outweighs any second-hand exposition which passes an idle hour, but can leave no useful result behind it. I put forward this obvious reflection, not out of any desire to disparage Mr. Waldron in particular, but that you may not lose your sense of proportion and mistake the acolyte for the high priest." (At this point Mr. Waldron whispered to the chairman, who half rose and said something severely to his water-carafe.) "But enough of this!" (Loud and prolonged cheers.) "Let me pass to some subject of wider interest. What is the particular point upon which I, as an original investigator, have challenged our lecturer's accuracy? It is upon the permanence of certain types of animal life upon the earth. I do not speak upon this subject as an amateur, nor, I may add, as a popular lecturer, but I speak as one whose scientific conscience compels him to adhere closely to facts, when I say that Mr. Waldron is very wrong in supposing that because he has never himself seen a so-called prehistoric animal, therefore these creatures no longer exist. They are indeed, as he has said, our ancestors, but they are, if I may use the expression, our contemporary ancestors, who can still be found with all their hideous and formidable characteristics if one has but the energy and hardihood to seek their haunts. Creatures which were supposed to be Jurassic, monsters who would hunt down and devour our largest and fiercest mammals, still exist." (Cries of "Bosh!" "Prove it!" "How do *you* know?" "Question!") "How do I know, you ask me? I know because I have visited their secret haunts. I know because I have seen some of them." (Applause, uproar, and a voice, "Liar!") "Am I a liar?" (General hearty and noisy assent.) "Did I hear someone say that I was a liar? Will the person who called me a liar kindly stand up that I may know him?" (A voice, "Here he is, sir!" and an inoffensive little person in spectacles, struggling violently, was held up among a group of students.) "Did you venture to call me a liar?" ("No, sir, no!" shouted the accused, and disappeared like a jack-in-the-box.) "If any person in this hall dares to doubt my veracity, I shall be glad to have a few words with him after the lecture." ("Liar!") "Who said that?" (Again the inoffensive one plunging desperately, was elevated high into the air.) "If I come down among you--" (General chorus of "Come, love, come!" which interrupted the proceedings for some moments, while the chairman, standing up and waving both his arms, seemed to be conducting the music. The Professor, with his face flushed, his nostrils dilated, and his beard bristling, was now in a proper Berserk mood.) "Every great discoverer has been met with the same incredulity—the sure brand of a generation of fools. When great facts are laid before you, you have not the intuition, the imagination which would help you to understand them. You can only throw mud at the men who have risked their lives to open new fields to science. You persecute the prophets! Galileo! Darwin, and I----" (Prolonged cheering and complete interruption.)

All this is from my hurried notes taken at the time, which give little notion of the absolute chaos to which the assembly had by this time been reduced. So terrific was the uproar that several ladies had already beaten a hurried retreat. Grave and reverend seniors seemed to have caught the prevailing spirit as badly as the students, and I saw white-bearded men rising and shaking their fists at the obdurate Professor. The whole great audience seethed and simmered like a boiling pot. The Professor took a step forward and raised both his hands. There was something so big and arresting and virile in the man that the clatter and shouting died gradually away before his commanding gesture and his masterful eyes. He seemed to have a definite message. They hushed to hear it.

"I will not detain you," he said. "It is not worth it. Truth is truth, and the noise of a number of foolish young men—and, I fear I must add, of their equally foolish seniors—cannot affect the matter. I claim that I have opened a new field of science. You dispute it." (Cheers.) "Then I put you to the test. Will you accredit one or more of your own number to go out as your representatives and test my statement in your name?"

Mr. Summerlee, the veteran Professor of Comparative Anatomy, rose among the audience, a tall, thin, bitter man, with the withered aspect of a theologian. He wished, he said, to ask Professor Challenger whether the results to which he had alluded in his remarks had been obtained during a journey to the headwaters of the Amazon made by him two years before.

Professor Challenger answered that they had.

Mr. Summerlee desired to know how it was that Professor Challenger claimed to have made discoveries in those regions which had been overlooked by Wallace, Bates, and other previous explorers of established scientific repute.

Professor Challenger answered that Mr. Summerlee appeared to be confusing the Amazon with the Thames; that it was in reality a somewhat larger river; that Mr. Summerlee might be interested to know that with the Orinoco, which communicated with it, some fifty thousand miles of country were opened up, and that in so vast a space it was not impossible for one person to find what another had missed.

Mr. Summerlee declared, with an acid smile, that he fully appreciated the difference between the Thames and the Amazon, which lay in the fact that any assertion about the former could be tested, while about the latter it could not. He would be obliged if Professor Challenger would give the latitude and the longitude of the country in which prehistoric animals were to be found.

Professor Challenger replied that he reserved such information for good reasons of his own, but would be prepared to give it with proper precautions to a committee chosen from the audience. Would Mr. Summerlee serve on such a committee and test his story in person?

Mr. Summerlee: "Yes, I will." (Great cheering.)

Professor Challenger: "Then I guarantee that I will place in your hands such material as will enable you to find your way. It is only right, however, since Mr. Summerlee goes to check my statement that I should have one or more with him who may check his. I will not disguise from you that there are difficulties and dangers. Mr. Summerlee will need a younger colleague. May I ask for volunteers?"

It is thus that the great crisis of a man's life springs out at him. Could I have imagined when I entered that hall that I was about to pledge myself to a wilder adventure than had ever come to me in my dreams? But Gladys—was it not the very opportunity of which she spoke? Gladys would have told me to go. I had sprung to my feet. I was speaking, and yet I had prepared no words. Tarp Henry, my companion, was plucking at my skirts and I heard him whispering, "Sit down, Malone! Don't make a public ass of yourself." At the same time I was aware that a tall, thin man, with dark gingery hair, a few seats in front of me, was also upon his feet. He glared back at me with hard angry eyes, but I refused to give way.

"I will go, Mr. Chairman," I kept repeating over and over again.

"Name! Name!" cried the audience.

"My name is Edward Dunn Malone. I am the reporter of the Daily Gazette. I claim to be an absolutely unprejudiced witness."

"What is *your* name, sir?" the chairman asked of my tall rival.

"I am Lord John Roxton. I have already been up the Amazon, I know all the ground, and have special qualifications for this investigation."

"Lord John Roxton's reputation as a sportsman and a traveler is, of course, world-famous," said the chairman; "at the same time it would certainly be as well to have a member of the Press upon such an expedition."

"Then I move," said Professor Challenger, "that both these gentlemen be elected, as representatives of this meeting, to accompany Professor Summerlee upon his journey to investigate and to report upon the truth of my statements."

And so, amid shouting and cheering, our fate was decided, and I found myself borne away in the human current which swirled towards the door, with my mind half stunned by the vast new project which had risen so suddenly before it. As I emerged from the hall I was conscious for a moment of a rush of laughing students—down the pavement, and of an arm wielding a heavy umbrella, which rose and fell in the midst of them. Then, amid a mixture of groans and cheers, Professor Challenger's electric brougham slid from the curb, and I found myself walking under the silvery lights of Regent Street, full of thoughts of Gladys and of wonder as to my future.

Suddenly there was a touch at my elbow. I turned, and found myself looking into the humorous, masterful eyes of the tall, thin man who had volunteered to be my companion on this strange quest.

"Mr. Malone, I understand," said he. "We are to be companions—what? My rooms are just over the road, in the Albany. Perhaps you would have the kindness to spare me half an hour, for there are one or two things that I badly want to say to you."

Chapter VI; "I was the Flail of the Lord"

Lord John Roxton and I turned down Vigo Street together and through the dingy portals of the famous aristocratic rookery. At the end of a long drab passage my new acquaintance pushed open a door and turned on an electric switch. A number of lamps shining through tinted shades bathed the whole great room before us in a ruddy radiance. Standing in the doorway and glancing round me, I had a general impression of extraordinary comfort and elegance combined with an atmosphere of masculine virility. Everywhere there were mingled the luxury of the wealthy man of taste and the careless untidiness of the bachelor. Rich furs and strange iridescent mats from some Oriental bazaar were scattered upon the floor. Pictures and prints which even my unpractised eyes could recognize as being of great price and rarity hung thick upon the walls. Sketches of boxers, of ballet-girls, and of racehorses alternated with a sensuous Fragonard, a martial Girardet, and a dreamy Turner. But amid these varied ornaments there were scattered the trophies which brought back strongly to my recollection the fact that Lord John Roxton was one of the great all-round sportsmen and athletes of his day. A dark-blue oar crossed with a cherry-pink one above his mantel-piece spoke of the old Oxonian and Leander man, while the foils and boxing-gloves above and below them were the tools of a man who had won supremacy with each. Like a dado round the room was the jutting line of splendid heavy game-heads, the best of their sort from every quarter of the world, with the rare white rhinoceros of the Lado Enclave drooping its supercilious lip above them all.

In the center of the rich red carpet was a black and gold Louis Quinze table, a lovely antique, now sacrilegiously desecrated with marks of glasses and the scars of cigar-stumps. On it stood a silver tray of smokables and a burnished spirit-stand, from which and an adjacent siphon my silent host proceeded to charge two high glasses. Having indicated an arm-chair to me and placed my refreshment near it, he handed me a long, smooth Havana. Then, seating himself opposite to me, he looked at me long and fixedly with his strange, twinkling, reckless eyes—eyes of a cold light blue, the color of a glacier lake.

Through the thin haze of my cigar-smoke I noted the details of a face which was already familiar to me from many photographs—the strongly-curved nose, the hollow, worn cheeks, the dark, ruddy hair, thin at the top, the crisp, virile moustaches, the small, aggressive tuft upon his projecting chin. Something there was of Napoleon III., something of Don Quixote, and yet again something which was the essence of the English country gentleman, the keen, alert, open-air lover of dogs and of horses. His skin was of a rich flower-pot red from sun and wind. His eyebrows were tufted and overhanging, which gave those naturally cold eyes an almost ferocious aspect, an impression which was increased by his strong and furrowed brow. In figure he was spare, but very strongly built—indeed, he had often proved that there were few men in England capable of such sustained exertions. His height was a little over six feet, but he seemed shorter on account of a peculiar rounding of the shoulders. Such was the famous Lord John Roxton as he sat opposite to me, biting hard upon his cigar and watching me steadily in a long and embarrassing silence.

"Well," said he, at last, "we've gone and done it, young fellah my lad." (This curious phrase he pronounced as if it were all one word—"young-fellah-me-lad.") "Yes, we've taken a jump, you an' me. I suppose, now, when you went into that room there was no such notion in your head—what?"

"No thought of it."

"The same here. No thought of it. And here we are, up to our necks in the tureen. Why, I've only been back three weeks from Uganda, and taken a place in Scotland, and signed the lease and all. Pretty goin's on—what? How does it hit you?"

"Well, it is all in the main line of my business. I am a journalist on the Gazette."

"Of course—you said so when you took it on. By the way, I've got a small job for you, if you'll help me."

"With pleasure."

"Don't mind takin' a risk, do you?"

"What is the risk?"

"Well, it's Ballinger—he's the risk. You've heard of him?"

"No."

"Why, young fellah, where *have* you lived? Sir John Ballinger is the best gentleman jock in the north country. I could hold him on the flat at my best, but over jumps he's my master. Well, it's an open secret that when he's out of trainin' he drinks hard—strikin' an average, he calls it. He got delirium on Toosday, and has been ragin' like a devil ever since. His room is above this. The doctors say that it is all up with the old dear unless some food is got into him, but as he lies in bed with a revolver on his coverlet, and swears he will put six of the best through anyone that comes near him, there's been a bit of a strike among the serving-men. He's a hard nail, is Jack, and a dead shot, too, but you can't leave a Grand National winner to die like that—what?"

"What do you mean to do, then?" I asked.

"Well, my idea was that you and I could rush him. He may be dozin', and at the worst he can only wing one of us, and the other should have him. If we can get his bolster-cover round his arms and then 'phone up a stomach-pump, we'll give the old dear the supper of his life."

It was a rather desperate business to come suddenly into one's day's work. I don't think that I am a particularly brave man. I have an Irish imagination which makes the unknown and the untried more terrible than they are. On the other hand, I was brought up with a horror of cowardice and with a terror of such a stigma. I dare say that I could throw myself over a precipice, like the Hun in the history books, if my courage to do it were questioned, and yet it would surely be pride and fear, rather than courage, which would be my inspiration. Therefore, although every nerve in my body shrank from the whisky-maddened figure which I pictured in the room above, I still answered, in as careless a voice as I could command, that I was ready to go. Some further remark of Lord Roxton's about the danger only made me irritable.

"Talking won't make it any better," said I. "Come on."

I rose from my chair and he from his. Then with a little confidential chuckle of laughter, he patted me two or three times on the chest, finally pushing me back into my chair.

"All right, sonny my lad—you'll do," said he. I looked up in surprise.

"I saw after Jack Ballinger myself this mornin'. He blew a hole in the skirt of my kimono, bless his shaky old hand, but we got a jacket on him, and he's to be all right in a week. I say, young fellah, I hope you don't mind—what? You see, between you an' me close-tiled, I look on this South American business as a mighty serious thing, and if I have a pal with me I want a man I can bank on. So I sized you down, and I'm bound to say that you came well out of it. You see, it's all up to you and me, for this old Summerlee man will want dry-nursin' from the first. By the way, are you by any chance the Malone who is expected to get his Rugby cap for Ireland?"

"A reserve, perhaps."

"I thought I remembered your face. Why, I was there when you got that try against Richmond—as fine a swervin' run as I saw the whole season. I never miss a Rugby match if I can help it, for it is the manliest game we have left. Well, I didn't ask you in here just to talk sport. We've got to fix our business. Here are the sailin's, on the first page of the Times. There's a Booth boat for Para next Wednesday week, and if the Professor and you can work it, I think we should take it—what? Very good, I'll fix it with him. What about your outfit?"

"My paper will see to that."

"Can you shoot?"

"About average Territorial standard."

"Good Lord! as bad as that? It's the last thing you young fellahs think of learnin'. You're all bees without stings, so far as lookin' after the hive goes. You'll look silly, some o' these days, when someone comes along an' sneaks the honey. But you'll need to hold your gun straight in South America, for, unless our friend the Professor is a madman or a liar, we may see some queer things before we get back. What gun have you?"

He crossed to an oaken cupboard, and as he threw it open I caught a glimpse of glistening rows of parallel barrels, like the pipes of an organ.

"I'll see what I can spare you out of my own battery," said he.

One by one he took out a succession of beautiful rifles, opening and shutting them with a snap and a clang, and then patting them as he put them back into the rack as tenderly as a mother would fondle her children.

"This is a Bland's .577 axite express," said he. "I got that big fellow with it." He glanced up at the white rhinoceros. "Ten more yards, and he'd would have added me to *his* collection.

'On that conical bullet his one chance hangs, 'Tis the weak one's advantage fair.'

Hope you know your Gordon, for he's the poet of the horse and the gun and the man that handles both. Now, here's a useful tool--.470, telescopic sight, double ejector, point-blank up to three-fifty. That's the rifle I used against the Peruvian slave-drivers three years ago. I was the flail of the Lord up in those parts, I may tell you, though you won't find it in any Blue-book. There are times, young fellah, when every one of us must make a stand for human right and justice, or you never feel clean again. That's why I made a little war on my own. Declared it myself, waged it myself, ended it myself. Each of those nicks is for a slave murderer—a good row of them—what? That big one is for Pedro Lopez, the king of them all, that I killed in a backwater of the Putomayo River. Now, here's something that would do for you." He took out a beautiful brown-and-silver rifle. "Well rubbered at the stock, sharply sighted, five cartridges to the clip. You can trust your life to that." He handed it to me and closed the door of his oak cabinet.

"By the way," he continued, coming back to his chair, "what do you know of this Professor Challenger?"

"I never saw him till today."

"Well, neither did I. It's funny we should both sail under sealed orders from a man we don't know. He seemed an uppish old bird. His brothers of science don't seem too fond of him, either. How came you to take an interest in the affair?"

I told him shortly my experiences of the morning, and he listened intently. Then he drew out a map of South America and laid it on the table.

"I believe every single word he said to you was the truth," said he, earnestly, "and, mind you, I have something to go on when I speak like that. South America is a place I love, and I think, if you take it right through from Darien to Fuego, it's the grandest, richest, most wonderful bit of earth upon this planet. People don't know it yet, and don't realize what it may become. I've been up an' down it from end to end, and had two dry seasons in those very parts, as I told you when I spoke of the war I made on the slave-dealers. Well, when I was up there I heard some yarns of the same kind—traditions of Indians and the like, but with somethin' behind them, no doubt. The more you knew of that country, young fellah, the more you would understand that anythin' was possible—*anythin'*! There are just some narrow water-lanes along which folk travel, and outside that it is all darkness. Now, down here in the Matto Grande"—he swept his cigar over a part of the map—"or up in this corner where three countries meet, nothin' would surprise me. As that chap said to-night, there are fifty-thousand miles of water-way runnin' through a forest that is very near the size of Europe. You and I could be as far away from each other as Scotland is from Constantinople, and yet each of us be in the same great Brazilian forest. Man has just made a track here and a scrape there in the maze. Why, the river rises and falls the best part of forty feet, and half the country is a morass that you can't pass over. Why shouldn't somethin' new and wonderful lie in such a country? And why shouldn't we be the men to find it out? Besides," he added, his queer, gaunt face shining with delight, "there's a sportin' risk in every mile of it. I'm like an old golf-ball—I've had all the white paint knocked off me long ago. Life can whack me about now, and it can't leave a mark. But a sportin' risk, young fellah, that's the salt of existence. Then it's worth livin' again. We're all gettin' a deal too soft and dull and comfy. Give me the great waste lands and the wide spaces, with a gun in my fist and somethin' to look for that's worth findin'. I've tried war and steeplechasin' and aeroplanes, but this huntin' of beasts that look like a lobster-supper dream is a brand-new sensation." He chuckled with glee at the prospect.

Perhaps I have dwelt too long upon this new acquaintance, but he is to be my comrade for many a day, and so I have tried to set him down as I first saw him, with his quaint personality and his queer little tricks of speech and of thought. It was only the need of getting in the account of my meeting which drew me at last from his company. I left him seated amid his pink radiance, oiling the lock of his favorite rifle, while he still chuckled to himself at the thought of the adventures which awaited us. It was very clear to me that if dangers lay before us I could not in all England have found a cooler head or a braver spirit with which to share them.

That night, wearied as I was after the wonderful happenings of the day, I sat late with McArdle, the news editor, explaining to him the whole situation, which he thought important enough to bring next morning before the notice of Sir George Beaumont, the chief. It was agreed that I should write home full accounts of my adventures in the shape of successive letters to McArdle, and that these should either be edited for the Gazette as they arrived, or held back to be published later, according to the wishes of Professor Challenger, since we could not yet know what conditions he might attach to those directions which should guide us to the unknown land. In response to a telephone inquiry, we received nothing more definite than a fulmination against the Press, ending up with the remark that if we would notify our boat he would hand us any directions which he might think it proper to give us at the moment of starting. A second question from us failed to elicit any answer at all, save a plaintive bleat from his wife to the effect that her husband was in a very violent temper already, and that she hoped we would do nothing to make it worse. A third attempt, later in the day, provoked a terrific crash, and a subsequent message from the Central Exchange that Professor Challenger's receiver had been shattered. After that we abandoned all attempt at communication.

And now my patient readers, I can address you directly no longer. From now onwards (if, indeed, any continuation of this narrative should ever reach you) it can only be through the paper which I represent. In the hands of the editor I leave this account of the events which have led up to one of the most remarkable expeditions of all time, so that if I never return to England there shall be some record as to how the affair came about. I am writing these last lines in the saloon of the Booth liner Francisca, and they will go back by the pilot to the keeping of Mr. McArdle. Let me draw one last picture before I close the notebook—a picture which is the last memory of the old country which I bear away with me. It is a wet, foggy morning in the late spring; a thin, cold rain is falling. Three shining mackintoshed figures are walking down the quay, making for the gang-plank of the great liner from which the blue-peter is flying. In front of them a porter pushes a trolley piled high with trunks, wraps, and gun-cases. Professor Summerlee, a long, melancholy figure, walks with dragging steps and drooping head, as one who is already profoundly sorry for himself. Lord John Roxton steps briskly, and his thin, eager face beams forth between his hunting-cap and his muffler. As for myself, I am glad to have got the bustling days of preparation and the pangs of leave-taking behind me, and I have no doubt that I show it in my bearing. Suddenly, just as we reach the vessel, there is a shout behind us. It is Professor Challenger, who had promised to see us off. He runs after us, a puffing, red-faced, irascible figure.

"No thank you," says he; "I should much prefer not to go aboard. I have only a few words to say to you, and they can very well be said where we are. I beg you not to imagine that I am in any way indebted to you for making this journey. I would have you to understand that it is a matter of perfect indifference to me, and I refuse to entertain the most remote sense of personal obligation. Truth is truth, and nothing which you can report can affect it in any way, though it may excite the emotions and allay the curiosity of a number of very ineffectual people. My directions for your instruction and guidance are in this sealed envelope. You will open it when you reach a town upon the Amazon which is called Manaos, but not until the date and hour which is marked upon the outside. Have I made myself clear? I leave the strict observance of my conditions entirely to your honor. No, Mr. Malone, I will place no restriction upon your correspondence, since the ventilation of the facts is the object of your journey; but I demand that you shall give no particulars as to your exact destination, and that nothing be actually published until your return. Good-bye, sir. You have done something to mitigate my feelings for the loathsome profession to which you unhappily belong. Good-bye, Lord John. Science is, as I understand, a sealed book to you; but you may congratulate yourself upon the hunting-field which awaits you. You will, no doubt, have the opportunity of describing in the Field how you brought down the rocketing dimorphodon. And good-bye to you also, Professor Summerlee. If you are still capable of self-improvement, of which I am frankly unconvinced, you will surely return to London a wiser man."

So he turned upon his heel, and a minute later from the deck I could see his short, squat figure bobbing about in the distance as he made his way back to his train. Well, we are well down Channel now. There's the last bell for letters, and it's good-bye to the pilot. We'll be "down, hull-down, on the old trail" from now on. God bless all we leave behind us, and send us safely back.

Chapter VII; "Tomorrow we Disappear into the Unknown"

I will not bore those whom this narrative may reach by an account of our luxurious voyage upon the Booth liner, nor will I tell of our week's stay at Para (save that I should wish to acknowledge the great kindness of the Pereira da Pinta Company in helping us to get together our equipment). I will also allude very briefly to our river journey, up a wide, slow-moving, clay-tinted stream, in a steamer which was little smaller than that which had carried us across the Atlantic. Eventually we found ourselves through the narrows of Obidos and reached the town of Manaos. Here we were rescued from the limited attractions of the local inn by Mr. Shortman, the representative of the British and Brazilian Trading Company. In his hospital Fazenda we spent our time until the day when we were empowered to open the letter of instructions given to us by Professor Challenger. Before I reach the surprising events of that date I would desire to give a clearer sketch of my comrades in this enterprise, and of the associates whom we had already gathered together in South America. I speak freely, and I leave the use of my material to your own discretion, Mr. McArdle, since it is through your hands that this report must pass before it reaches the world.

The scientific attainments of Professor Summerlee are too well known for me to trouble to recapitulate them. He is better equipped for a rough expedition of this sort than one would imagine at first sight. His tall, gaunt, stringy figure is insensible to fatigue, and his dry, half-sarcastic, and often wholly unsympathetic manner is uninfluenced by any change in his surroundings. Though in his sixty-sixth year, I have never heard him express any dissatisfaction at the occasional hardships which we have had to encounter. I had regarded his presence as an encumbrance to the expedition, but, as a matter of fact, I am now well convinced that his power of endurance is as great as my own. In temper he is naturally acid and sceptical. From the beginning he has never concealed his belief that Professor Challenger is an absolute fraud, that we are all embarked upon an absurd wild-goose chase and that we are likely to reap nothing but disappointment and danger in South America, and corresponding ridicule in England. Such are the views which, with much passionate distortion of his thin features and wagging of his thin, goat-like beard, he poured into our ears all the way from Southampton to Manaos. Since landing from the boat he has obtained some consolation from the beauty and variety of the insect and bird life around him, for he is absolutely whole-hearted in his devotion to science. He spends his days flitting through the woods with his shot-gun and his butterfly-net, and his evenings in mounting the many specimens he has acquired. Among his minor peculiarities are that he is careless as to his attire, unclean in his person, exceedingly absent-minded in his habits, and addicted to smoking a short briar pipe, which is seldom out of his mouth. He has been upon several scientific expeditions in his youth (he was with Robertson in Papua), and the life of the camp and the canoe is nothing fresh to him.

Lord John Roxton has some points in common with Professor Summerlee, and others in which they are the very antithesis to each other. He is twenty years younger, but has something of the same spare, scraggy physique. As to his appearance, I have, as I recollect, described it in that portion of my narrative which I have left behind me in London. He is exceedingly neat and prim in his ways, dresses always with great care in white drill suits and high brown mosquito-boots, and shaves at least once a day. Like most men of action, he is laconic in speech, and sinks readily into his own thoughts, but he is always quick to answer a question or join in a conversation, talking in a queer, jerky, half-humorous fashion. His knowledge of the world, and very especially of South America, is surprising, and he has a whole-hearted belief in the possibilities of our journey which is not to be dashed by the sneers of Professor Summerlee. He has a gentle voice and a quiet manner, but behind his twinkling blue eyes there lurks a capacity for furious wrath and implacable resolution, the more dangerous because they are held in leash. He spoke little of his own exploits in Brazil and Peru, but it was a revelation to me to find the excitement which was caused by his presence among the riverine natives, who looked upon him as their champion and protector. The exploits of the Red Chief, as they called him, had become legends among them, but the real facts, as far as I could learn them, were amazing enough.

These were that Lord John had found himself some years before in that no-man's-land which is formed by the half-defined frontiers between Peru, Brazil, and Columbia. In this great district the wild rubber tree flourishes, and has become, as in the Congo, a curse to the natives which can only be compared to their forced labor under the Spaniards upon the old silver mines of Darien. A handful of villainous half-breeds dominated the country, armed such Indians as would support them, and turned the rest into slaves, terrorizing them with the most inhuman tortures in order to force them to gather the india-rubber, which was then floated down the river to Para. Lord John Roxton expostulated on behalf of the wretched victims, and received nothing but threats and insults for his pains. He then formally declared war against Pedro Lopez, the leader of the slave-drivers, enrolled a band of runaway slaves in his service, armed them, and conducted a campaign, which ended by his killing with his own hands the notorious half-breed and breaking down the system which he represented.

No wonder that the ginger-headed man with the silky voice and the free and easy manners was now looked upon with deep interest upon the banks of the great South American river, though the feelings he inspired were naturally mixed, since the gratitude of the natives was equaled by the resentment of those who desired to exploit them. One useful result of his former experiences was that he could talk fluently in the Lingoa Geral, which is the peculiar talk, one-third Portuguese and two-thirds Indian, which is current all over Brazil.

I have said before that Lord John Roxton was a South Americomaniac. He could not speak of that great country without ardor, and this ardor was infectious, for, ignorant as I was, he fixed my attention and stimulated my curiosity. How I wish I could reproduce the glamour of his discourses, the peculiar mixture of accurate knowledge and of racy imagination which gave them their fascination, until even the Professor's cynical and sceptical smile would gradually vanish from his thin face as he listened. He would tell the history of the mighty river so rapidly explored (for some of the first conquerors of Peru actually crossed the entire continent upon its waters), and yet so unknown in regard to all that lay behind its ever-changing banks.

"What is there?" he would cry, pointing to the north. "Wood and marsh and unpenetrated jungle. Who knows what it may shelter? And there to the south? A wilderness of swampy forest, where no white man has ever been. The unknown is up against us on every side. Outside the narrow lines of the rivers what does anyone know? Who will say what is possible in such a country? Why should old man Challenger not be right?" At which direct defiance the stubborn sneer would reappear upon Professor Summerlee's face, and he would sit, shaking his sardonic head in unsympathetic silence, behind the cloud of his briar-root pipe.

So much, for the moment, for my two white companions, whose characters and limitations will be further exposed, as surely as my own, as this narrative proceeds. But already we have enrolled certain retainers who may play no small part in what is to come. The first is a gigantic negro named Zambo, who is a black Hercules, as willing as any horse, and about as intelligent. Him we enlisted at Para, on the recommendation of the steamship company, on whose vessels he had learned to speak a halting English.

It was at Para also that we engaged Gomez and Manuel, two half-breeds from up the river, just come down with a cargo of redwood. They were swarthy fellows, bearded and fierce, as active and wiry as panthers. Both of them had spent their lives in those upper waters of the Amazon which we were about to explore, and it was this recommendation which had caused Lord John to engage them. One of them, Gomez, had the further advantage that he could speak excellent English. These men were willing to act as our personal servants, to cook, to row, or to make themselves useful in any way at a payment of fifteen dollars a month. Besides these, we had engaged three Mojo Indians from Bolivia, who are the most skilful at fishing and boat work of all the river tribes. The chief of these we called Mojo, after his tribe, and the others are known as Jose and Fernando. Three white men, then, two half-breeds, one negro, and three Indians made up the personnel of the little expedition which lay waiting for its instructions at Manaos before starting upon its singular quest.

At last, after a weary week, the day had come and the hour. I ask you to picture the shaded sitting-room of the Fazenda St. Ignatio, two miles inland from the town of Manaos. Outside lay the yellow, brassy glare of the sunshine, with the shadows of the palm trees as black and definite as the trees themselves. The air was calm, full of the eternal hum of insects, a tropical chorus of many octaves, from the deep drone of the bee to the high, keen pipe of the mosquito. Beyond the veranda was a small cleared garden, bounded with cactus hedges and adorned with clumps of flowering shrubs, round which the great blue butterflies and the tiny humming-birds fluttered and darted in crescents of sparkling light. Within we were seated round the cane table, on which lay a sealed envelope. Inscribed upon it, in the jagged handwriting of Professor Challenger, were the words:--

"Instructions to Lord John Roxton and party. To be opened at Manaos upon July 15th, at 12 o'clock precisely."

Lord John had placed his watch upon the table beside him.

"We have seven more minutes," said he. "The old dear is very precise."

Professor Summerlee gave an acid smile as he picked up the envelope in his gaunt hand.

"What can it possibly matter whether we open it now or in seven minutes?" said he. "It is all part and parcel of the same system of quackery and nonsense, for which I regret to say that the writer is notorious."

"Oh, come, we must play the game accordin' to rules," said Lord John. "It's old man Challenger's show and we are here by his good will, so it would be rotten bad form if we didn't follow his instructions to the letter."

"A pretty business it is!" cried the Professor, bitterly. "It struck me as preposterous in London, but I'm bound to say that it seems even more so upon closer acquaintance. I don't know what is inside this envelope, but, unless it is something pretty definite, I shall be much tempted to take the next down-river boat and catch the Bolivia at Para. After all, I have some more responsible work in the world than to run about disproving the assertions of a lunatic. Now, Roxton, surely it is time."

"Time it is," said Lord John. "You can blow the whistle." He took up the envelope and cut it with his penknife. From it he drew a folded sheet of paper. This he carefully opened out and flattened on the table. It was a blank sheet. He turned it over. Again it was blank. We looked at each other in a bewildered silence, which was broken by a discordant burst of derisive laughter from Professor Summerlee.

"It is an open admission," he cried. "What more do you want? The fellow is a self-confessed humbug. We have only to return home and report him as the brazen imposter that he is."

"Invisible ink!" I suggested.

"I don't think!" said Lord Roxton, holding the paper to the light. "No, young fellah my lad, there is no use deceiving yourself. I'll go bail for it that nothing has ever been written upon this paper."

"May I come in?" boomed a voice from the veranda.

The shadow of a squat figure had stolen across the patch of sunlight. That voice! That monstrous breadth of shoulder! We sprang to our feet with a gasp of astonishment as Challenger, in a round, boyish straw-hat with a colored ribbon—Challenger, with his hands in his jacket-pockets and his canvas shoes daintily pointing as he walked—appeared in the open space before us. He threw back his head, and there he stood in the golden glow with all his old Assyrian luxuriance of beard, all his native insolence of drooping eyelids and intolerant eyes.

"I fear," said he, taking out his watch, "that I am a few minutes too late. When I gave you this envelope I must confess that I had never intended that you should open it, for it had been my fixed intention to be with you before the hour. The unfortunate delay can be apportioned between a blundering pilot and an intrusive sandbank. I fear that it has given my colleague, Professor Summerlee, occasion to blaspheme."

"I am bound to say, sir," said Lord John, with some sternness of voice, "that your turning up is a considerable relief to us, for our mission seemed to have come to a premature end. Even now I can't for the life of me understand why you should have worked it in so extraordinary a manner."

Instead of answering, Professor Challenger entered, shook hands with myself and Lord John, bowed with ponderous insolence to Professor Summerlee, and sank back into a basket-chair, which creaked and swayed beneath his weight.

"Is all ready for your journey?" he asked.

"We can start tomorrow."

"Then so you shall. You need no chart of directions now, since you will have the inestimable advantage of my own guidance. From the first I had determined that I would myself preside over your investigation. The most elaborate charts would, as you will readily admit, be a poor substitute for my own intelligence and advice. As to the small ruse which I played upon you in the matter of the envelope, it is clear that, had I told you all my intentions, I should have been forced to resist unwelcome pressure to travel out with you."

"Not from me, sir!" exclaimed Professor Summerlee, heartily. "So long as there was another ship upon the Atlantic."

Challenger waved him away with his great hairy hand.

"Your common sense will, I am sure, sustain my objection and realize that it was better that I should direct my own movements and appear only at the exact moment when my presence was needed. That moment has now arrived. You are in safe hands. You will not now fail to reach your destination. From henceforth I take command of this expedition, and I must ask you to complete your preparations to-night, so that we may be able to make an early start in the morning. My time is of value, and the same thing may be said, no doubt, in a lesser degree of your own. I propose, therefore, that we push on as rapidly as possible, until I have demonstrated what you have come to see."

Lord John Roxton has chartered a large steam launch, the Esmeralda, which was to carry us up the river. So far as climate goes, it was immaterial what time we chose for our expedition, as the temperature ranges from seventy-five to ninety degrees both summer and winter, with no appreciable difference in heat. In moisture, however, it is otherwise; from December to May is the period of the rains, and during this time the river slowly rises until it attains a height of nearly forty feet above its low-water mark. It floods the banks, extends in great lagoons over a monstrous waste of country, and forms a huge district, called locally the Gapo, which is for the most part too marshy for foot-travel and too shallow for boating. About June the waters begin to fall, and are at their lowest at October or November. Thus our expedition was at the time of the dry season, when the great river and its tributaries were more or less in a normal condition.

The current of the river is a slight one, the drop being not greater than eight inches in a mile. No stream could be more convenient for navigation, since the prevailing wind is south-east, and sailing boats may make a continuous progress to the Peruvian frontier, dropping down again with the current. In our own case the excellent engines of the Esmeralda could disregard the sluggish flow of the stream, and we made as rapid progress as if we were navigating a stagnant lake. For three days we steamed north-westwards up a stream which even here, a thousand miles from its mouth, was still so enormous that from its center the two banks were mere shadows upon the distant skyline. On the fourth day after leaving Manaos we turned into a tributary which at its mouth was little smaller than the main stream. It narrowed rapidly, however, and after two more days' steaming we reached an Indian village, where the Professor insisted that we should land, and that the Esmeralda should be sent back to Manaos. We should soon come upon rapids, he explained, which would make its further use impossible. He added privately that we were now approaching the door of the unknown country, and that the fewer whom we took into our confidence the better it would be. To this end also he made each of us give our word of honor that we would publish or say nothing which would give any exact clue as to the whereabouts of our travels, while the servants were all solemnly sworn to the same effect. It is for this reason that I am compelled to be vague in my narrative, and I would warn my readers that in any map or diagram which I may give the relation of places to each other may be correct, but the points of the compass are carefully confused, so that in no way can it be taken as an actual guide to the country. Professor Challenger's reasons for secrecy may be valid or not, but we had no choice but to adopt them, for he was prepared to abandon the whole expedition rather than modify the conditions upon which he would guide us.

It was August 2nd when we snapped our last link with the outer world by bidding farewell to the Esmeralda. Since then four days have passed, during which we have engaged two large canoes from the Indians, made of so light a material (skins over a bamboo framework) that we should be able to carry them round any obstacle. These we have loaded with all our effects, and have engaged two additional Indians to help us in the navigation. I understand that they are the very two—Ataca and Ipetu by name—who accompanied Professor Challenger upon his previous journey. They appeared to be terrified at the prospect of repeating it, but the chief has patriarchal powers in these countries, and if the bargain is good in his eyes the clansman has little choice in the matter.

So tomorrow we disappear into the unknown. This account I am transmitting down the river by canoe, and it may be our last word to those who are interested in our fate. I have, according to our arrangement, addressed it to you, my dear Mr. McArdle, and I leave it to your discretion to delete, alter, or do what you like with it. From the assurance of Professor Challenger's manner—and in spite of the continued scepticism of Professor Summerlee—I have no doubt that our leader will make good his statement, and that we are really on the eve of some most remarkable experiences.

Chapter VIII; "The Outlying Pickets of the New World"

Our friends at home may well rejoice with us, for we are at our goal, and up to a point, at least, we have shown that the statement of Professor Challenger can be verified. We have not, it is true, ascended the plateau, but it lies before us, and even Professor Summerlee is in a more chastened mood. Not that he will for an instant admit that his rival could be right, but he is less persistent in his incessant objections, and has sunk for the most part into an observant silence. I must hark back, however, and continue my narrative from where I dropped it. We are sending home one of our local Indians who is injured, and I am committing this letter to his charge, with considerable doubts in my mind as to whether it will ever come to hand.

When I wrote last we were about to leave the Indian village where we had been deposited by the Esmeralda. I have to begin my report by bad news, for the first serious personal trouble (I pass over the incessant bickerings between the Professors) occurred this evening, and might have had a tragic ending. I have spoken of our English-speaking half-breed, Gomez—a fine worker and a willing fellow, but afflicted, I fancy, with the vice of curiosity, which is common enough among such men. On the last evening he seems to have hid himself near the hut in which we were discussing our plans, and, being observed by our huge negro Zambo, who is as faithful as a dog and has the hatred which all his race bear to the half-breeds, he was dragged out and carried into our presence. Gomez whipped out his knife, however, and but for the huge strength of his captor, which enabled him to disarm him with one hand, he would certainly have stabbed him. The matter has ended in reprimands, the opponents have been compelled to shake hands, and there is every hope that all will be well. As to the feuds of the two learned men, they are continuous and bitter. It must be admitted that Challenger is provocative in the last degree, but Summerlee has an acid tongue, which makes matters worse. Last night Challenger said that he never cared to walk on the Thames Embankment and look up the river, as it was always sad to see one's own eventual goal. He is convinced, of course, that he is destined for Westminster Abbey. Summerlee rejoined, however, with a sour smile, by saying that he understood that Millbank Prison had been pulled down. Challenger's conceit is too colossal to allow him to be really annoyed. He only smiled in his beard and repeated "Really! Really!" in the pitying tone one would use to a child. Indeed, they are children both—the one wizened and cantankerous, the other formidable and overbearing, yet each with a brain which has put him in the front rank of his scientific age. Brain, character, soul—only as one sees more of life does one understand how distinct is each.

The very next day we did actually make our start upon this remarkable expedition. We found that all our possessions fitted very easily into the two canoes, and we divided our personnel, six in each, taking the obvious precaution in the interests of peace of putting one Professor into each canoe. Personally, I was with Challenger, who was in a beatific humor, moving about as one in a silent ecstasy and beaming benevolence from every feature. I have had some experience of him in other moods, however, and shall be the less surprised when the thunderstorms suddenly come up amidst the sunshine. If it is impossible to be at your ease, it is equally impossible to be dull in his company, for one is always in a state of half-tremulous doubt as to what sudden turn his formidable temper may take.

For two days we made our way up a good-sized river some hundreds of yards broad, and dark in color, but transparent, so that one could usually see the bottom. The affluents of the Amazon are, half of them, of this nature, while the other half are whitish and opaque, the difference depending upon the class of country through which they have flowed. The dark indicate vegetable decay, while the others point to clayey soil. Twice we came across rapids, and in each case made a portage of half a mile or so to avoid them. The woods on either side were primeval, which are more easily penetrated than woods of the second growth, and we had no great difficulty in carrying our canoes through them. How shall I ever forget the solemn mystery of it? The height of the trees and the thickness of the boles exceeded anything which I in my town-bred life could have imagined, shooting upwards in magnificent columns until, at an enormous distance above our heads, we could dimly discern the spot where they threw out their side-branches into Gothic upward curves which coalesced to form one great matted roof of verdure, through which only an occasional golden ray of sunshine shot downwards to trace a thin dazzling line of light amidst the majestic obscurity. As we walked noiselessly amid the thick, soft carpet of decaying vegetation the hush fell upon our souls which comes upon us in the twilight of the Abbey, and even Professor Challenger's full-chested notes sank into a whisper. Alone, I should have been ignorant of the names of these giant growths, but our men of science pointed out the cedars, the great silk cotton trees, and the redwood trees, with all that profusion of various plants which has made this continent the chief supplier to the human race of those gifts of Nature which depend upon the vegetable world, while it is the most backward in those products which come from animal life. Vivid orchids and wonderful colored lichens smoldered upon the swarthy tree-trunks and where a wandering shaft of light fell full upon the golden allamanda, the scarlet star-clusters of the tacsonia, or the rich deep blue of ipomaea, the effect was as a dream of fairyland. In these great wastes of forest, life, which abhors darkness, struggles ever upwards to the light. Every plant, even the smaller ones, curls and writhes to the green surface, twining itself round its stronger and taller brethren in the effort. Climbing plants are monstrous and luxuriant, but others which have never been known to climb elsewhere learn the art as an escape from that somber shadow, so that the common nettle, the jasmine, and even the jacitara palm tree can be seen circling the stems of the cedars and striving to reach their crowns. Of animal life there was no movement amid the majestic vaulted aisles which stretched from us as we walked, but a constant movement far above our heads told of that multitudinous world of snake and monkey, bird and sloth, which lived in the sunshine, and looked down in wonder at our tiny, dark, stumbling figures in the obscure depths immeasurably below them. At dawn and at sunset the howler monkeys screamed together and the parrakeets broke into shrill chatter, but during the hot hours of the day only the full drone of insects, like the beat of a distant surf, filled the ear, while nothing moved amid the solemn vistas of stupendous trunks, fading away into the darkness which held us in. Once some bandy-legged, lurching creature, an ant-eater or a bear, scuttled clumsily amid the shadows. It was the only sign of earth life which I saw in this great Amazonian forest.

And yet there were indications that even human life itself was not far from us in those mysterious recesses. On the third day out we were aware of a singular deep throbbing in the air, rhythmic and solemn, coming and going fitfully throughout the morning. The two boats were paddling within a few yards of each other when first

tribes?

we heard it, and our Indians remained motionless, as if they had been turned to bronze, listening intently with expressions of terror upon their faces.

"What is it, then?" I asked.

"Drums," said Lord John, carelessly; "war drums. I have heard them before."

"Yes, sir, war drums," said Gomez, the half-breed. "Wild Indians, bravos, not mansos; they watch us every mile of the way; kill us if they can."

"How can they watch us?" I asked, gazing into the dark, motionless void.

The half-breed shrugged his broad shoulders.

"The Indians know. They have their own way. They watch us. They talk the drum talk to each other. Kill us if they can."

By the afternoon of that day—my pocket diary shows me that it was Tuesday, August 18th—at least six or seven drums were throbbing from various points. Sometimes they beat quickly, sometimes slowly, sometimes in obvious question and answer, one far to the east breaking out in a high staccato rattle, and being followed after a pause by a deep roll from the north. There was something indescribably nerve-shaking and menacing in that constant mutter, which seemed to shape itself into the very syllables of the half-breed, endlessly repeated, "We will kill you if we can. We will kill you if we can." No one ever moved in the silent woods. All the peace and soothing of quiet Nature lay in that dark curtain of vegetation, but away from behind there came ever the one message from our fellow-man. "We will kill you if we can," said the men in the east. "We will kill you if we can," said the men in the north.

All day the drums rumbled and whispered, while their menace reflected itself in the faces of our colored companions. Even the hardy, swaggering half-breed seemed cowed. I learned, however, that day once for all that both Summerlee and Challenger possessed that highest type of bravery, the bravery of the scientific mind. Theirs was the spirit which upheld Darwin among the gauchos of the Argentine or Wallace among the head-hunters of Malaya. It is decreed by a merciful Nature that the human brain cannot think of two things simultaneously, so that if it be steeped in curiosity as to science it has no room for merely personal considerations. All day amid that incessant and mysterious menace our two Professors watched every bird upon the wing, and every shrub upon the bank, with many a sharp wordy contention, when the snarl of Summerlee came quick upon the deep growl of Challenger, but with no more sense of danger and no more reference to drum-beating Indians than if they were seated together in the smoking-room of the Royal Society's Club in St. James's Street. Once only did they condescend to discuss them.

"Miranha or Amajuaca cannibals," said Challenger, jerking his thumb towards the reverberating wood.

"No doubt, sir," Summerlee answered. "Like all such tribes, I shall expect to find them of poly-synthetic speech and of Mongolian type."

"Polysynthetic certainly," said Challenger, indulgently. "I am not aware that any other type of language exists in this continent, and I have notes of more than a hundred. The Mongolian theory I regard with deep suspicion."

"I should have thought that even a limited knowledge of comparative anatomy would have helped to verify it," said Summerlee, bitterly.

Challenger thrust out his aggressive chin until he was all beard and hat-rim. "No doubt, sir, a limited knowledge would have that effect. When one's knowledge is exhaustive, one comes to other conclusions." They glared at each other in mutual defiance, while all round rose the distant whisper, "We will kill you—we will kill you if we can."

um?

why would they kill them?

That night we moored our canoes with heavy stones for anchors in the center of the stream, and made every preparation for a possible attack. Nothing came, however, and with the dawn we pushed upon our way, the drum-beating dying out behind us. About three o'clock in the afternoon we came to a very steep rapid, more than a mile long—the very one in which Professor Challenger had suffered disaster upon his first journey. I confess that the sight of it consoled me, for it was really the first direct corroboration, slight as it was, of the truth of his story. The Indians carried first our canoes and then our stores through the brushwood, which is very thick at this point, while we four whites, our rifles on our shoulders, walked between them and any danger coming from the woods. Before evening we had successfully passed the rapids, and made our way some ten miles above them, where we anchored for the night. At this point I reckoned that we had come not less than a hundred miles up the tributary from the main stream.

It was in the early forenoon of the next day that we made the great departure. Since dawn Professor Challenger had been acutely uneasy, continually scanning each bank of the river. Suddenly he gave an exclamation of satisfaction and pointed to a single tree, which projected at a peculiar angle over the side of the stream.

"What do you make of that?" he asked.

"It is surely an Assai palm," said Summerlee.

"Exactly. It was an Assai palm which I took for my landmark. The secret opening is half a mile onwards upon the other side of the river. There is no break in the trees. That is the wonder and the mystery of it. There where you see light-green rushes instead of dark-green undergrowth, there between the great cotton woods, that is my private gate into the unknown. Push through, and you will understand."

It was indeed a wonderful place. Having reached the spot marked by a line of light-green rushes, we poled out two canoes through them for some hundreds of yards, and eventually emerged into a placid and shallow stream, running clear and transparent over a sandy bottom. It may have been twenty yards across, and was banked in on each side by most luxuriant vegetation. No one who had not observed that for a short distance reeds had taken the place of shrubs, could possibly have guessed the existence of such a stream or dreamed of the fairyland beyond.

For a fairyland it was—the most wonderful that the imagination of man could conceive. The thick vegetation met overhead, interlacing into a natural pergola, and through this tunnel of verdure in a golden twilight flowed the green, pellucid river, beautiful in itself, but marvelous from the strange tints thrown by the vivid light from above filtered and tempered in its fall. Clear as crystal, motionless as a sheet of glass, green as the edge of an iceberg, it stretched in front of us under its leafy archway, every stroke of our paddles sending a thousand ripples across its shining surface. It was a fitting avenue to a land of wonders. All sign of the Indians had passed away, but animal life was more frequent, and the tameness of the creatures showed that they knew nothing of the hunter. Fuzzy little black-velvet monkeys, with snow-white teeth and gleaming, mocking eyes, chattered at us as we passed. With a dull, heavy splash an occasional cayman plunged in from the bank. Once a dark, clumsy tapir stared at us from a gap in the bushes, and then lumbered away through the forest; once, too, the yellow, sinuous form of a great puma whisked amid the brushwood, and its green, baleful eyes glared hatred at us over its tawny shoulder. Bird life was abundant, especially the wading birds, stork, heron, and ibis gathering in little groups, blue, scarlet, and white, upon every log which jutted from the bank, while beneath us the crystal water was alive with fish of every shape and color.

So is this like a seperate forrest? No one goes to?

For three days we made our way up this tunnel of hazy green sunshine. On the longer stretches one could hardly tell as one looked ahead where the distant green water ended and the distant green archway began. The deep peace of this strange waterway was unbroken by any sign of man.

"No Indian here. Too much afraid. Curupuri," said Gomez.

"Curupuri is the spirit of the woods," Lord John explained. "It's a name for any kind of devil. The poor beggars think that there is something fearsome in this direction, and therefore they avoid it."

On the third day it became evident that our journey in the canoes could not last much longer, for the stream was rapidly growing more shallow. Twice in as many hours we stuck upon the bottom. Finally we pulled the boats up among the brushwood and spent the night on the bank of the river. In the morning Lord John and I made our way for a couple of miles through the forest, keeping parallel with the stream; but as it grew ever shallower we returned and reported, what Professor Challenger had already suspected, that we had reached the highest point to which the canoes could be brought. We drew them up, therefore, and concealed them among the bushes, blazing a tree with our axes, so that we should find them again. Then we distributed the various burdens among us—guns, ammunition, food, a tent, blankets, and the rest—and, shouldering our packages, we set forth upon the more laborious stage of our journey.

An unfortunate quarrel between our pepper-pots marked the outset of our new stage. Challenger had from the moment of joining us issued directions to the whole party, much to the evident discontent of Summerlee. Now, upon his assigning some duty to his fellow-Professor (it was only the carrying of an aneroid barometer), the matter suddenly came to a head.

"May I ask, sir," said Summerlee, with vicious calm, "in what capacity you take it upon yourself to issue these orders?"

Challenger glared and bristled.

"I do it, Professor Summerlee, as leader of this expedition."

"I am compelled to tell you, sir, that I do not recognize you in that capacity."

"Indeed!" Challenger bowed with unwieldy sarcasm. "Perhaps you would define my exact position."

"Yes, sir. You are a man whose veracity is upon trial, and this committee is here to try it. You walk, sir, with your judges."

"Dear me!" said Challenger, seating himself on the side of one of the canoes. "In that case you will, of course, go on your way, and I will follow at my leisure. If I am not the leader you cannot expect me to lead."

Thank heaven that there were two sane men—Lord John Roxton and myself—to prevent the petulance and folly of our learned Professors from sending us back empty-handed to London. Such arguing and pleading and explaining before we could get them mollified! Then at last Summerlee, with his sneer and his pipe, would move forwards, and Challenger would come rolling and grumbling after. By some good fortune we discovered about this time that both our savants had the very poorest opinion of Dr. Illingworth of Edinburgh. Thenceforward that was our one safety, and every strained situation was relieved by our introducing the name of the Scotch zoologist, when both our Professors would form a temporary alliance and friendship in their detestation and abuse of this common rival.

Advancing in single file along the bank of the stream, we soon found that it narrowed down to a mere brook, and finally that it lost itself in a great green morass of sponge-like mosses, into which we sank up to our knees. The place was horribly haunted by clouds of mosquitoes and every form of flying pest, so we were glad to find solid ground again and to make a circuit among the trees, which enabled us to outflank this pestilent morass, which droned like an organ in the distance, so loud was it with insect life.

On the second day after leaving our canoes we found that the whole character of the country changed. Our road was persistently upwards, and as we ascended the woods became thinner and lost their tropical luxuriance. The huge trees of the alluvial Amazonian plain gave place to the Phoenix and coco palms, growing in scattered clumps, with thick brushwood between. In the damper hollows the Mauritia palms threw out their graceful drooping fronds. We traveled entirely by compass, and once or twice there were differences of opinion between Challenger and the two Indians, when, to quote the Professor's indignant words, the whole party agreed to "trust the fallacious instincts of undeveloped savages rather than the highest product of modern European culture." That we were justified in doing so was shown upon the third day, when Challenger admitted that he recognized several landmarks of his former journey, and in one spot we actually came upon four fire-blackened stones, which must have marked a camping-place.

The road still ascended, and we crossed a rock-studded slope which took two days to traverse. The vegetation had again changed, and only the vegetable ivory tree remained, with a great profusion of wonderful orchids, among which I learned to recognize the rare Nuttonia Vexillaria and the glorious pink and scarlet blossoms of Cattleya and odontoglossum. Occasional brooks with pebbly bottoms and fern-draped banks gurgled down the shallow gorges in the hill, and offered good camping-grounds every evening on the banks of some rock-studded pool, where swarms of little blue-backed fish, about the size and shape of English trout, gave us a delicious supper.

On the ninth day after leaving the canoes, having done, as I reckon, about a hundred and twenty miles, we began to emerge from the trees, which had grown smaller until they were mere shrubs. Their place was taken by an immense wilderness of bamboo, which grew so thickly that we could only penetrate it by cutting a pathway with the machetes and billhooks of the Indians. It took us a long day, traveling from seven in the morning till eight at night, with only two breaks of one hour each, to get through this obstacle. Anything more monotonous and wearying could not be imagined, for, even at the most open places, I could not see more than ten or twelve yards, while usually my vision was limited to the back of Lord John's cotton jacket in front of me, and to the yellow wall within a foot of me on either side. From above came one thin knife-edge of sunshine, and fifteen feet over our heads one saw the tops of the reeds swaying against the deep blue sky. I do not know what kind of creatures inhabit such a thicket, but several times we heard the plunging of large, heavy animals quite close to us. From their sounds Lord John judged them to be some form of wild cattle. Just as night fell we cleared the belt of bamboos, and at once formed our camp, exhausted by the interminable day.

Early next morning we were again afoot, and found that the character of the country had changed once again. Behind us was the wall of bamboo, as definite as if it marked the course of a river. In front was an open plain, sloping slightly upwards and dotted with clumps of tree-ferns, the whole curving before us until it ended in a long, whale-backed ridge. This we reached about midday, only to find a shallow valley beyond, rising once again into a gentle incline which led to a low, rounded

where do ~~we~~ they sleep

sky-line. It was here, while we crossed the first of these hills, that an incident occurred which may or may not have been important.

Professor Challenger, who with the two local Indians was in the van of the party, stopped suddenly and pointed excitedly to the right. As he did so we saw, at the distance of a mile or so, something which appeared to be a huge gray bird flap slowly up from the ground and skim smoothly off, flying very low and straight, until it was lost among the tree-ferns.

"Did you see it?" cried Challenger, in exultation. "Summerlee, did you see it?"

His colleague was staring at the spot where the creature had disappeared.

"What do you claim that it was?" he asked.

"To the best of my belief, a pterodactyl."

Summerlee burst into derisive laughter "A pter-fiddlestick!" said he. "It was a stork, if ever I saw one."

Challenger was too furious to speak. He simply swung his pack upon his back and continued upon his march. Lord John came abreast of me, however, and his face was more grave than was his wont. He had his Zeiss glasses in his hand.

"I focused it before it got over the trees," said he. "I won't undertake to say what it was, but I'll risk my reputation as a sportsman that it wasn't any bird that ever I clapped eyes on in my life."

So there the matter stands. Are we really just at the edge of the unknown, encountering the outlying pickets of this lost world of which our leader speaks? I give you the incident as it occurred and you will know as much as I do. It stands alone, for we saw nothing more which could be called remarkable.

And now, my readers, if ever I have any, I have brought you up the broad river, and through the screen of rushes, and down the green tunnel, and up the long slope of palm trees, and through the bamboo brake, and across the plain of tree-ferns. At last our destination lay in full sight of us. When we had crossed the second ridge we saw before us an irregular, palm-studded plain, and then the line of high red cliffs which I have seen in the picture. There it lies, even as I write, and there can be no question that it is the same. At the nearest point it is about seven miles from our present camp, and it curves away, stretching as far as I can see. Challenger struts about like a prize peacock, and Summerlee is silent, but still sceptical. Another day should bring some of our doubts to an end. Meanwhile, as Jose, whose arm was pierced by a broken bamboo, insists upon returning, I send this letter back in his charge, and only hope that it may eventually come to hand. I will write again as the occasion serves. I have enclosed with this a rough chart of our journey, which may have the effect of making the account rather easier to understand.

Chapter IX; "Who could have Foreseen it?"

A dreadful thing has happened to us. Who could have foreseen it? I cannot foresee any end to our troubles. It may be that we are condemned to spend our whole lives in this strange, inaccessible place. I am still so confused that I can hardly think clearly of the facts of the present or of the chances of the future. To my astounded senses the one seems most terrible and the other as black as night.

What?

No men have ever found themselves in a worse position; nor is there any use in disclosing to you our exact geographical situation and asking our friends for a relief party. Even if they could send one, our fate will in all human probability be decided long before it could arrive in South America.

We are, in truth, as far from any human aid as if we were in the moon. If we ... to win through, it is only our own qualities which can save us. I have as companions three remarkable men, men of great brain-power and of unshaken courage. There lies our one and only hope. It is only when I look upon the untroubled faces of my comrades that I see some glimmer through the darkness. Outwardly I trust that I appear as unconcerned as they. Inwardly I am filled with apprehension.

Let me give you, with as much detail as I can, the sequence of events which have led us to this catastrophe.

When I finished my last letter I stated that we were within seven miles from an enormous line of ruddy cliffs, which encircled, beyond all doubt, the plateau of which Professor Challenger spoke. Their height, as we approached them, seemed to me in some places to be greater than he had stated—running up in parts to at least a thousand feet—and they were curiously striated, in a manner which is, I believe, characteristic of basaltic upheavals. Something of the sort is to be seen in Salisbury Crags at Edinburgh. The summit showed every sign of a luxuriant vegetation, with bushes near the edge, and farther back many high trees. There was no indication of any life that we could see.

That night we pitched our camp immediately under the cliff—a most wild and desolate spot. The crags above us were not merely perpendicular, but curved outwards at the top, so that ascent was out of the question. Close to us was the high thin pinnacle of rock which I believe I mentioned earlier in this narrative. It is like a broad red church spire, the top of it being level with the plateau, but a great chasm gaping between. On the summit of it there grew one high tree. Both pinnacle and cliff were comparatively low—some five or six hundred feet, I should think.

"It was on that," said Professor Challenger, pointing to this tree, "that the pterodactyl was perched. I climbed half-way up the rock before I shot him. I am inclined to think that a good mountaineer like myself could ascend the rock to the top, though he would, of course, be no nearer to the plateau when he had done so."

As Challenger spoke of his pterodactyl I glanced at Professor Summerlee, and for the first time I seemed to see some signs of a dawning credulity and repentance. There was no sneer upon his thin lips, but, on the contrary, a gray, drawn look of excitement and amazement. Challenger saw it, too, and reveled in the first taste of victory.

"Of course," said he, with his clumsy and ponderous sarcasm, "Professor Summerlee will understand that when I speak of a pterodactyl I mean a stork—only it is the kind of stork which has no feathers, a leathery skin, membranous wings, and teeth in its jaws." He grinned and blinked and bowed until his colleague turned and walked away.

In the morning, after a frugal breakfast of coffee and manioc—we had to be economical of our stores—we held a council of war as to the best method of ascending to the plateau above us.

Challenger presided with a solemnity as if he were the Lord Chief Justice on the Bench. Picture him seated upon a rock, his absurd boyish straw hat tilted on the back of his head, his supercilious eyes dominating us from under his drooping lids, his great black beard wagging as he slowly defined our present situation and our future movements.

Beneath him you might have seen the three of us—myself, sunburnt, young, and vigorous after our open-air tramp; Summerlee, solemn but still critical, behind his eternal pipe; Lord John, as keen as a razor-edge, with his supple, alert figure leaning ifle, and his eager eyes fixed eagerly upon the speaker. Behind us were ne two swarthy half-breeds and the little knot of Indians, while in front and towered those huge, ruddy ribs of rocks which kept us from our goal.

eed not say," said our leader, "that on the occasion of my last visit I exhausted every means of climbing the cliff, and where I failed I do not think that anyone else is likely to succeed, for I am something of a mountaineer. I had none of the appliances of a rock-climber with me, but I have taken the precaution to bring them now. With their aid I am positive I could climb that detached pinnacle to the summit; but so long as the main cliff overhangs, it is vain to attempt ascending that. I was hurried upon my last visit by the approach of the rainy season and by the exhaustion of my supplies. These considerations limited my time, and I can only claim that I have surveyed about six miles of the cliff to the east of us, finding no possible way up. What, then, shall we now do?"

"There seems to be only one reasonable course," said Professor Summerlee. "If you have explored the east, we should travel along the base of the cliff to the west, and seek for a practicable point for our ascent."

"That's it," said Lord John. "The odds are that this plateau is of no great size, and we shall travel round it until we either find an easy way up it, or come back to the point from which we started."

"I have already explained to our young friend here," said Challenger (he has a way of alluding to me as if I were a school child ten years old), "that it is quite impossible that there should be an easy way up anywhere, for the simple reason that if there were the summit would not be isolated, and those conditions would not obtain which have effected so singular an interference with the general laws of survival. Yet I admit that there may very well be places where an expert human climber may reach the summit, and yet a cumbrous and heavy animal be unable to descend. It is certain that there is a point where an ascent is possible."

"How do you know that, sir?" asked Summerlee, sharply.

"Because my predecessor, the American Maple White, actually made such an ascent. How otherwise could he have seen the monster which he sketched in his notebook?"

"There you reason somewhat ahead of the proved facts," said the stubborn Summerlee. "I admit your plateau, because I have seen it; but I have not as yet satisfied myself that it contains any form of life whatever."

"What you admit, sir, or what you do not admit, is really of inconceivably small importance. I am glad to perceive that the plateau itself has actually obtruded itself upon your intelligence." He glanced up at it, and then, to our amazement, he sprang from his rock, and, seizing Summerlee by the neck, he tilted his face into the air. "Now sir!" he shouted, hoarse with excitement. "Do I help you to realize that the plateau contains some animal life?"

I have said that a thick fringe of green overhung the edge of the cliff. Out of this there had emerged a black, glistening object. As it came slowly forth and overhung the chasm, we saw that it was a very large snake with a peculiar flat, spade-like head. It wavered and quivered above us for a minute, the morning sun gleaming upon its sleek, sinuous coils. Then it slowly drew inwards and disappeared.

Summerlee had been so interested that he had stood unresisting while Challenger tilted his head into the air. Now he shook his colleague off and came back to his dignity.

"I should be glad, Professor Challenger," said he, "if you could see your way to make any remarks which may occur to you without seizing me by the chin. Even the appearance of a very ordinary rock python does not appear to justify such a liberty."

"But there is life upon the plateau all the same," his colleague replied in triumph. "And now, having demonstrated this important conclusion so that it is clear to anyone, however prejudiced or obtuse, I am of opinion that we cannot do better than break up our camp and travel to westward until we find some means of ascent."

The ground at the foot of the cliff was rocky and broken so that the going was slow and difficult. Suddenly we came, however, upon something which cheered our hearts. It was the site of an old encampment, with several empty Chicago meat tins, a bottle labeled "Brandy," a broken tin-opener, and a quantity of other travelers' debris. A crumpled, disintegrated newspaper revealed itself as the Chicago *Democrat*, though the date had been obliterated.

"Not mine," said Challenger. "It must be Maple White's."

Lord John had been gazing curiously at a great tree-fern which overshadowed the encampment. "I say, look at this," said he. "I believe it is meant for a sign-post."

A slip of hard wood had been nailed to the tree in such a way as to point to the westward.

"Most certainly a sign-post," said Challenger. "What else? Finding himself upon a dangerous errand, our pioneer has left this sign so that any party which follows him may know the way he has taken. Perhaps we shall come upon some other indications as we proceed."

We did indeed, but they were of a terrible and most unexpected nature. Immediately beneath the cliff there grew a considerable patch of high bamboo, like that which we had traversed in our journey. Many of these stems were twenty feet high, with sharp, strong tops, so that even as they stood they made formidable spears. We were passing along the edge of this cover when my eye was caught by the gleam of something white within it. Thrusting in my head between the stems, I found myself gazing at a fleshless skull. The whole skeleton was there, but the skull had detached itself and lay some feet nearer to the open.

With a few blows from the machetes of our Indians we cleared the spot and were able to study the details of this old tragedy. Only a few shreds of clothes could still be distinguished, but there were the remains of boots upon the bony feet, and it was very clear that the dead man was a European. A gold watch by Hudson, of New York, and a chain which held a stylographic pen, lay among the bones. There was also a silver cigarette-case, with "J. C., from A. E. S.," upon the lid. The state of the metal seemed to show that the catastrophe had occurred no great time before. what did it?

"Who can he be?" asked Lord John. "Poor devil! every bone in his body seems to be broken."

"And the bamboo grows through his smashed ribs," said Summerlee. "It is a fast-growing plant, but it is surely inconceivable that this body could have been here while the canes grew to be twenty feet in length."

"As to the man's identity," said Professor Challenger, "I have no doubt whatever upon that point. As I made my way up the river before I reached you at the fazenda I instituted very particular inquiries about Maple White. At Para they knew nothing. Fortunately, I had a definite clew, for there was a particular picture in his sketch-book which showed him taking lunch with a certain ecclesiastic at Rosario. This priest I was able to find, and though he proved a very argumentative fellow, who took it absurdly amiss that I should point out to him the corrosive effect which modern science must have upon his beliefs, he none the less gave me some positive information. Maple White passed Rosario four years ago, or two years before I saw his dead body. He was not alone at the time, but there was a friend, an American named James Colver, who remained in the boat and did not meet this ecclesiastic. I think, therefore, that there can be no doubt that we are now looking upon the remains of this James Colver."

"Nor," said Lord John, "is there much doubt as to how he met his death. He has fallen or been chucked from the top, and so been impaled. How else could he come by his broken bones, and how could he have been stuck through by these canes with their points so high above our heads?"

A hush came over us as we stood round these shattered remains and realized the truth of Lord John Roxton's words. The beetling head of the cliff projected over the cane-brake. Undoubtedly he had fallen from above. But had he fallen? Had it been an accident? Or—already ominous and terrible possibilities began to form round that unknown land.

We moved off in silence, and continued to coast round the line of cliffs, which were as even and unbroken as some of those monstrous Antarctic ice-fields which I have seen depicted as stretching from horizon to horizon and towering high above the mast-heads of the exploring vessel.

In five miles we saw no rift or break. And then suddenly we perceived something which filled us with new hope. In a hollow of the rock, protected from rain, there was drawn a rough arrow in chalk, pointing still to the westwards.

"Maple White again," said Professor Challenger. "He had some presentiment that worthy footsteps would follow close behind him."

"He had chalk, then?"

"A box of colored chalks was among the effects I found in his knapsack. I remember that the white one was worn to a stump."

"That is certainly good evidence," said Summerlee. "We can only accept his guidance and follow on to the westward."

We had proceeded some five more miles when again we saw a white arrow upon the rocks. It was at a point where the face of the cliff was for the first time split into a narrow cleft. Inside the cleft was a second guidance mark, which pointed right up it with the tip somewhat elevated, as if the spot indicated were above the level of the ground.

It was a solemn place, for the walls were so gigantic and the slit of blue sky so narrow and so obscured by a double fringe of verdure, that only a dim and shadowy light penetrated to the bottom. We had had no food for many hours, and were very weary with the stony and irregular journey, but our nerves were too strung to allow us to halt. We ordered the camp to be pitched, however, and, leaving the Indians to arrange it, we four, with the two half-breeds, proceeded up the narrow gorge.

It was not more than forty feet across at the mouth, but it rapidly closed until it ended in an acute angle, too straight and smooth for an ascent. Certainly it was not this which our pioneer had attempted to indicate. We made our way back—the whole gorge was not more than a quarter of a mile deep—and then suddenly the quick eyes of Lord John fell upon what we were seeking. High up above our heads, amid the dark shadows, there was one circle of deeper gloom. Surely it could only be the opening of a cave.

The base of the cliff was heaped with loose stones at the spot, and it was not difficult to clamber up. When we reached it, all doubt was removed. Not only was it an opening into the rock, but on the side of it there was marked once again the sign of the arrow. Here was the point, and this the means by which Maple White and his ill-fated comrade had made their ascent.

We were too excited to return to the camp, but must make our first exploration at once. Lord John had an electric torch in his knapsack, and this had to serve us as light. He advanced, throwing his little clear circlet of yellow radiance before him, while in single file we followed at his heels.

The cave had evidently been water-worn, the sides being smooth and the floor covered with rounded stones. It was of such a size that a single man could just fit through by stooping. For fifty yards it ran almost straight into the rock, and then it ascended at an angle of forty-five. Presently this incline became even steeper, and we found ourselves climbing upon hands and knees among loose rubble which slid from beneath us. Suddenly an exclamation broke from Lord Roxton.

"It's blocked!" said he.

Clustering behind him we saw in the yellow field of light a wall of broken basalt which extended to the ceiling.

"The roof has fallen in!"

In vain we dragged out some of the pieces. The only effect was that the larger ones became detached and threatened to roll down the gradient and crush us. It was evident that the obstacle was far beyond any efforts which we could make to remove it. The road by which Maple White had ascended was no longer available.

Too much cast down to speak, we stumbled down the dark tunnel and made our way back to the camp.

One incident occurred, however, before we left the gorge, which is of importance in view of what came afterwards.

We had gathered in a little group at the bottom of the chasm, some forty feet beneath the mouth of the cave, when a huge rock rolled suddenly downwards—and shot past us with tremendous force. It was the narrowest escape for one or all of us. We could not ourselves see whence the rock had come, but our half-breed servants, who were still at the opening of the cave, said that it had flown past them, and must therefore have fallen from the summit. Looking upwards, we could see no sign of movement above us amidst the green jungle which topped the cliff. There could be little doubt, however, that the stone was aimed at us, so the incident surely pointed to humanity—and malevolent humanity—upon the plateau.

We withdrew hurriedly from the chasm, our minds full of this new development and its bearing upon our plans. The situation was difficult enough before, but if the obstructions of Nature were increased by the deliberate opposition of man, then our case was indeed a hopeless one. And yet, as we looked up at that beautiful fringe of verdure only a few hundreds of feet above our heads, there was not one of us who could conceive the idea of returning to London until we had explored it to its depths.

On discussing the situation, we determined that our best course was to continue to coast round the plateau in the hope of finding some other means of reaching the top. The line of cliffs, which had decreased considerably in height, had already begun to trend from west to north, and if we could take this as representing the arc of a circle, the whole circumference could not be very great. At the worst, then, we should be back in a few days at our starting-point.

We made a march that day which totaled some two-and-twenty miles, without any change in our prospects. I may mention that our aneroid shows us that in the continual incline which we have ascended since we abandoned our canoes we have risen to no less than three thousand feet above sea-level. Hence there is a considerable change both in the temperature and in the vegetation. We have shaken off some of that horrible insect life which is the bane of tropical travel. A few palms still survive, and many tree-ferns, but the Amazonian trees have been all left behind. It was pleasant to see the convolvulus, the passion-flower, and the begonia, all reminding me of home, here among these inhospitable rocks. There was a red begonia just the same color as one that is kept in a pot in the window of a certain villa in Streatham—but I am drifting into private reminiscence.

That night—I am still speaking of the first day of our circumnavigation of the plateau—a great experience awaited us, and one which for ever set at rest any doubt which we could have had as to the wonders so near us.

You will realize as you read it, my dear Mr. McArdle, and possibly for the first time that the paper has not sent me on a wild-goose chase, and that there is inconceivably fine copy waiting for the world whenever we have the Professor's leave to make use of it. I shall not dare to publish these articles unless I can bring back my proofs to England, or I shall be hailed as the journalistic Munchausen of all time. I have no doubt that you feel the same way yourself, and that you would not care to stake the whole credit of the Gazette upon this adventure until we can meet the chorus of criticism and scepticism which such articles must of necessity elicit. So this wonderful incident, which would make such a headline for the old paper, must still wait its turn in the editorial drawer.

And yet it was all over in a flash, and there was no sequel to it, save in our own convictions.

What occurred was this. Lord John had shot an ajouti—which is a small, pig-like animal—and, half of it having been given to the Indians, we were cooking the other half upon our fire. There is a chill in the air after dark, and we had all drawn close to the blaze. The night was moonless, but there were some stars, and one could see for a little distance across the plain. Well, suddenly out of the darkness, out of the night, there swooped something with a swish like an aeroplane. The whole group of us were covered for an instant by a canopy of leathery wings, and I had a momentary vision of a long, snake-like neck, a fierce, red, greedy eye, and a great snapping beak, filled, to my amazement, with little, gleaming teeth. The next instant it was gone—and so was our dinner. A huge black shadow, twenty feet across, skimmed up into the air; for an instant the monster wings blotted out the stars, and then it vanished over the brow of the cliff above us. We all sat in amazed silence round the fire, like the heroes of Virgil when the Harpies came down upon them. It was Summerlee who was the first to speak.

"Professor Challenger," said he, in a solemn voice, which quavered with emotion, "I owe you an apology. Sir, I am very much in the wrong, and I beg that you will forget what is past."

It was handsomely said, and the two men for the first time shook hands. So much we have gained by this clear vision of our first pterodactyl. It was worth a stolen supper to bring two such men together.

But if prehistoric life existed upon the plateau it was not superabundant, for we had no further glimpse of it during the next three days. During this time we traversed a barren and forbidding country, which alternated between stony desert and desolate marshes full of many wild-fowl, upon the north and east of the cliffs. From that direction the place is really inaccessible, and, were it not for a hardish ledge which runs at the very base of the precipice, we should have had to turn back. Many times we were up to our waists in the slime and blubber of an old, semi-tropical swamp. To make matters worse, the place seemed to be a favorite breeding-place of the Jaracaca snake, the most venomous and aggressive in South America. Again and again these horrible creatures came writhing and springing towards us across the surface of this putrid bog, and it was only by keeping our shot-guns for ever ready that we could feel safe from them. One funnel-shaped depression in the morass, of a livid green in color from some lichen which festered in it, will always remain as a nightmare memory in my mind. It seems to have been a special nest of these vermins, and the slopes were alive with them, all writhing in our direction, for it is a peculiarity of the Jaracaca that he will always attack man at first sight. There were too many for us to shoot, so we fairly took to our heels and ran until we were exhausted. I shall always remember as we looked back how far behind we could see the heads and necks of our horrible pursuers rising and falling amid the reeds. Jaracaca Swamp we named it in the map which we are constructing.

The cliffs upon the farther side had lost their ruddy tint, being chocolate-brown in color; the vegetation was more scattered along the top of them, and they had sunk to three or four hundred feet in height, but in no place did we find any point where they could be ascended. If anything, they were more impossible than at the first point where we had met them. Their absolute steepness is indicated in the photograph which I took over the stony desert.

"Surely," said I, as we discussed the situation, "the rain must find its way down somehow. There are bound to be water-channels in the rocks."

"Our young friend has glimpses of lucidity," said Professor Challenger, patting me upon the shoulder.

"The rain must go somewhere," I repeated.

"He keeps a firm grip upon actuality. The only drawback is that we have conclusively proved by ocular demonstration that there are no water channels down the rocks."

"Where, then, does it go?" I persisted.

"I think it may be fairly assumed that if it does not come outwards it must run inwards."

"Then there is a lake in the center."

"So I should suppose."

"It is more than likely that the lake may be an old crater," said Summerlee. "The whole formation is, of course, highly volcanic. But, however that may be, I should expect to find the surface of the plateau slope inwards with a considerable sheet of water in the center, which may drain off, by some subterranean channel, into the marshes of the Jaracaca Swamp."

"Or evaporation might preserve an equilibrium," remarked Challenger, and the two learned men wandered off into one of their usual scientific arguments, which were as comprehensible as Chinese to the layman.

On the sixth day we completed our first circuit of the cliffs, and found ourselves back at the first camp, beside the isolated pinnacle of rock. We were a disconsolate party, for nothing could have been more minute than our investigation, and it was absolutely certain that there was no single point where the most active human being could possibly hope to scale the cliff. The place which Maple White's chalk-marks had indicated as his own means of access was now entirely impassable.

What were we to do now? Our stores of provisions, supplemented by our guns, were holding out well, but the day must come when they would need replenishment.

In a couple of months the rains might be expected, and we should be washed out of our camp. The rock was harder than marble, and any attempt at cutting a path for so great a height was more than our time or resources would admit. No wonder that we looked gloomily at each other that night, and sought our blankets with hardly a word exchanged. I remember that as I dropped off to sleep my last recollection was that Challenger was squatting, like a monstrous bull-frog, by the fire, his huge head in his hands, sunk apparently in the deepest thought, and entirely oblivious to the good-night which I wished him.

But it was a very different Challenger who greeted us in the morning—a Challenger with contentment and self-congratulation shining from his whole person. He faced us as we assembled for breakfast with a deprecating false modesty in his eyes, as who should say, "I know that I deserve all that you can say, but I pray you to spare my blushes by not saying it." His beard bristled exultantly, his chest was thrown out, and his hand was thrust into the front of his jacket. So, in his fancy, may he see himself sometimes, gracing the vacant pedestal in Trafalgar Square, and adding one more to the horrors of the London streets.

"Eureka!" he cried, his teeth shining through his beard. "Gentlemen, you may congratulate me and we may congratulate each other. The problem is solved."

"You have found a way up?"

"I venture to think so."

"And where?"

For answer he pointed to the spire-like pinnacle upon our right.

Our faces—or mine, at least—fell as we surveyed it. That it could be climbed we had our companion's assurance. But a horrible abyss lay between it and the plateau.

"We can never get across," I gasped.

"We can at least all reach the summit," said he. "When we are up I may be able to show you that the resources of an inventive mind are not yet exhausted."

After breakfast we unpacked the bundle in which our leader had brought his climbing accessories. From it he took a coil of the strongest and lightest rope, a hundred and fifty feet in length, with climbing irons, clamps, and other devices. Lord John was an experienced mountaineer, and Summerlee had done some rough climbing at various times, so that I was really the novice at rock-work of the party; but my strength and activity may have made up for my want of experience.

It was not in reality a very stiff task, though there were moments which made my hair bristle upon my head. The first half was perfectly easy, but from there upwards it became continually steeper until, for the last fifty feet, we were literally clinging with our fingers and toes to tiny ledges and crevices in the rock. I could not have accomplished it, nor could Summerlee, if Challenger had not gained the summit (it was extraordinary to see such activity in so unwieldy a creature) and there fixed the rope round the trunk of the considerable tree which grew there. With this as our support, we were soon able to scramble up the jagged wall until we found ourselves upon the small grassy platform, some twenty-five feet each way, which formed the summit.

The first impression which I received when I had recovered my breath was of the extraordinary view over the country which we had traversed. The whole Brazilian plain seemed to lie beneath us, extending away and away until it ended in dim blue mists upon the farthest sky-line. In the foreground was the long slope, strewn with rocks and dotted with tree-ferns; farther off in the middle distance, looking over the saddle-back hill, I could just see the yellow and green mass of bamboos through which we had passed; and then, gradually, the vegetation increased until it formed the huge forest which extended as far as the eyes could reach, and for a good two thousand miles beyond.

I was still drinking in this wonderful panorama when the heavy hand of the Professor fell upon my shoulder.

"This way, my young friend," said he; "vestigia nulla retrorsum. Never look rearwards, but always to our glorious goal."

The level of the plateau, when I turned, was exactly that on which we stood, and the green bank of bushes, with occasional trees, was so near that it was difficult to realize how inaccessible it remained. At a rough guess the gulf was forty feet across, but, so far as I could see, it might as well have been forty miles. I placed one arm round the trunk of the tree and leaned over the abyss. Far down were the small dark figures of our servants, looking up at us. The wall was absolutely precipitous, as was that which faced me.

"This is indeed curious," said the creaking voice of Professor Summerlee.

I turned, and found that he was examining with great interest the tree to which I clung. That smooth bark and those small, ribbed leaves seemed familiar to my eyes. "Why," I cried, "it's a beech!"

"Exactly," said Summerlee. "A fellow-countryman in a far land."

"Not only a fellow-countryman, my good sir," said Challenger, "but also, if I may be allowed to enlarge your simile, an ally of the first value. This beech tree will be our saviour."

"By George!" cried Lord John, "a bridge!"

"Exactly, my friends, a bridge! It is not for nothing that I expended an hour last night in focusing my mind upon the situation. I have some recollection of once remarking to our young friend here that G. E. C. is at his best when his back is to the wall. Last night you will admit that all our backs were to the wall. But where will-power and intellect go together, there is always a way out. A drawbridge had to be found which could be dropped across the abyss. Behold it!"

It was certainly a brilliant idea. The tree was a good sixty feet in height, and if it only fell the right way it would easily cross the chasm. Challenger had slung the camp axe over his shoulder when he ascended. Now he handed it to me.

"Our young friend has the thews and sinews," said he. "I think he will be the most useful at this task. I must beg, however, that you will kindly refrain from thinking for yourself, and that you will do exactly what you are told."

Under his direction I cut such gashes in the sides of the trees as would ensure that it should fall as we desired. It had already a strong, natural tilt in the direction of the plateau, so that the matter was not difficult. Finally I set to work in earnest upon the trunk, taking turn and turn with Lord John. In a little over an hour there was a loud crack, the tree swayed forward, and then crashed over, burying its branches among the bushes on the farther side. The severed trunk rolled to the very edge of our platform, and for one terrible second we all thought it was over. It balanced itself, however, a few inches from the edge, and there was our bridge to the unknown.

All of us, without a word, shook hands with Professor Challenger, who raised his straw hat and bowed deeply to each in turn.

"I claim the honor," said he, "to be the first to cross to the unknown land—a fitting subject, no doubt, for some future historical painting."

He had approached the bridge when Lord John laid his hand upon his coat.

"My dear chap," said he, "I really cannot allow it."

"Cannot allow it, sir!" The head went back and the beard forward.

"When it is a matter of science, don't you know, I follow your lead because you are by way of bein' a man of science. But it's up to you to follow me when you come into my department."

"Your department, sir?"

"We all have our professions, and soldierin' is mine. We are, accordin' to my ideas, invadin' a new country, which may or may not be chock-full of enemies of sorts. To barge blindly into it for want of a little common sense and patience isn't my notion of management."

The remonstrance was too reasonable to be disregarded. Challenger tossed his head and shrugged his heavy shoulders.

"Well, sir, what do you propose?"

"For all I know there may be a tribe of cannibals waitin' for lunch-time among those very bushes," said Lord John, looking across the bridge. "It's better to learn wisdom before you get into a cookin'-pot; so we will content ourselves with hopin' that there is no trouble waitin' for us, and at the same time we will act as if there were. Malone and I will go down again, therefore, and we will fetch up the four rifles, together with Gomez and the other. One man can then go across and the rest will cover him with guns, until he sees that it is safe for the whole crowd to come along."

Challenger sat down upon the cut stump and groaned his impatience; but Summerlee and I were of one mind that Lord John was our leader when such practical details were in question. The climb was a more simple thing now that the rope dangled down the face of the worst part of the ascent. Within an hour we had brought up the rifles and a shot-gun. The half-breeds had ascended also, and under Lord John's orders they had carried up a bale of provisions in case our first exploration should be a long one. We had each bandoliers of cartridges.

"Now, Challenger, if you really insist upon being the first man in," said Lord John, when every preparation was complete.

"I am much indebted to you for your gracious permission," said the angry Professor; for never was a man so intolerant of every form of authority. "Since you are good enough to allow it, I shall most certainly take it upon myself to act as pioneer upon this occasion."

Seating himself with a leg overhanging the abyss on each side, and his hatchet slung upon his back, Challenger hopped his way across the trunk and was soon at the other side. He clambered up and waved his arms in the air.

"At last!" he cried; "at last!"

I gazed anxiously at him, with a vague expectation that some terrible fate would dart at him from the curtain of green behind him. But all was quiet, save that a strange, many-colored bird flew up from under his feet and vanished among the trees.

Summerlee was the second. His wiry energy is wonderful in so frail a frame. He insisted upon having two rifles slung upon his back, so that both Professors were armed when he had made his transit. I came next, and tried hard not to look down into the horrible gulf over which I was passing. Summerlee held out the butt-end of his rifle, and an instant later I was able to grasp his hand. As to Lord John, he walked across—actually walked without support! He must have nerves of iron.

And there we were, the four of us, upon the dreamland, the lost world, of Maple White. To all of us it seemed the moment of our supreme triumph. Who could have guessed that it was the prelude to our supreme disaster? Let me say in a few words how the crushing blow fell upon us.

We had turned away from the edge, and had penetrated about fifty yards of close brushwood, when there came a frightful rending crash from behind us. With one impulse we rushed back the way that we had come. The bridge was gone!

Far down at the base of the cliff I saw, as I looked over, a tangled mass of branches and splintered trunk. It was our beech tree. Had the edge of the platform crumbled and let it through? For a moment this explanation was in all our minds. The next, from the farther side of the rocky pinnacle before us a swarthy face, the face of Gomez the half-breed, was slowly protruded. Yes, it was Gomez, but no longer the Gomez of the demure smile and the mask-like expression. Here was a face with flashing eyes and distorted features, a face convulsed with hatred and with the mad joy of gratified revenge.

"Lord Roxton!" he shouted. "Lord John Roxton!"

"Well," said our companion, "here I am."

A shriek of laughter came across the abyss.

"Yes, there you are, you English dog, and there you will remain! I have waited and waited, and now has come my chance. You found it hard to get up; you will find it harder to get down. You cursed fools, you are trapped, every one of you!"

Why do they care to keep them?

We were too astounded to speak. We could only stand there staring in amazement. A great broken bough upon the grass showed whence he had gained his leverage to tilt over our bridge. The face had vanished, but presently it was up again, more frantic than before.

"We nearly killed you with a stone at the cave," he cried; "but this is better. It is slower and more terrible. Your bones will whiten up there, and none will know where you lie or come to cover them. As you lie dying, think of Lopez, whom you shot five years ago on the Putomayo River. I am his brother, and, come what will I will die happy now, for his memory has been avenged." A furious hand was shaken at us, and then all was quiet.

Had the half-breed simply wrought his vengeance and then escaped, all might have been well with him. It was that foolish, irresistible Latin impulse to be dramatic which brought his own downfall. Roxton, the man who had earned himself the name of the Flail of the Lord through three countries, was not one who could be safely taunted. The half-breed was descending on the farther side of the pinnacle; but before he could reach the ground Lord John had run along the edge of the plateau and gained a point from which he could see his man. There was a single crack of his rifle, and, though we saw nothing, we heard the scream and then the distant thud of the falling body. Roxton came back to us with a face of granite.

"I have been a blind simpleton," said he, bitterly, "It's my folly that has brought you all into this trouble. I should have remembered that these people have long memories for blood-feuds, and have been more upon my guard."

"What about the other one? It took two of them to lever that tree over the edge."

"I could have shot him, but I let him go. He may have had no part in it. Perhaps it would have been better if I had killed him, for he must, as you say, have lent a hand."

Now that we had the clue to his action, each of us could cast back and remember some sinister act upon the part of the half-breed—his constant desire to know our plans, his arrest outside our tent when he was over-hearing them, the furtive looks of hatred which from time to time one or other of us had surprised. We were still discussing it, endeavoring to adjust our minds to these new conditions, when a singular scene in the plain below arrested our attention.

A man in white clothes, who could only be the surviving half-breed, was running as one does run when Death is the pacemaker. Behind him, only a few yards in his rear, bounded the huge ebony figure of Zambo, our devoted negro. Even as we looked, he sprang upon the back of the fugitive and flung his arms round his neck. They rolled on the ground together. An instant afterwards Zambo rose, looked at the prostrate man, and then, waving his hand joyously to us, came running in our direction. The white figure lay motionless in the middle of the great plain.

Our two traitors had been destroyed, but the mischief that they had done lived after them. By no possible means could we get back to the pinnacle. We had been natives of the world; now we were natives of the plateau. The two things were separate and apart. There was the plain which led to the canoes. Yonder, beyond the violet, hazy horizon, was the stream which led back to civilization. But the link between was missing. No human ingenuity could suggest a means of bridging the chasm which yawned between ourselves and our past lives. One instant had altered the whole conditions of our existence.

It was at such a moment that I learned the stuff of which my three comrades were composed. They were grave, it is true, and thoughtful, but of an invincible serenity. For the moment we could only sit among the bushes in patience and wait the coming of Zambo. Presently his honest black face topped the rocks and his Herculean figure emerged upon the top of the pinnacle.

"What I do now?" he cried. "You tell me and I do it."

It was a question which it was easier to ask than to answer. One thing only was clear. He was our one trusty link with the outside world. On no account must he leave us.

"No no!" he cried. "I not leave you. Whatever come, you always find me here. But no able to keep Indians. Already they say too much Curupuri live on this place, and they go home. Now you leave them me no able to keep them."

It was a fact that our Indians had shown in many ways of late that they were weary of their journey and anxious to return. We realized that Zambo spoke the truth, and that it would be impossible for him to keep them.

"Make them wait till tomorrow, Zambo," I shouted; "then I can send letter back by them."

"Very good, sarr! I promise they wait till tomorrow," said the negro. "But what I do for you now?"

There was plenty for him to do, and admirably the faithful fellow did it. First of all, under our directions, he undid the rope from the tree-stump and threw one end of it across to us. It was not thicker than a clothes-line, but it was of great strength, and though we could not make a bridge of it, we might well find it invaluable if we had any climbing to do. He then fastened his end of the rope to the package of supplies which had been carried up, and we were able to drag it across. This gave us the means of life for at least a week, even if we found nothing else. Finally he descended and carried up two other packets of mixed goods—a box of ammunition and a number of other things, all of which we got across by throwing our rope to him and hauling it back. It was evening when he at last climbed down, with a final assurance that he would keep the Indians till next morning.

And so it is that I have spent nearly the whole of this our first night upon the plateau writing up our experiences by the light of a single candle-lantern.

We supped and camped at the very edge of the cliff, quenching our thirst with two bottles of Apollinaris which were in one of the cases. It is vital to us to find water, but I think even Lord John himself had had adventures enough for one day, and none of us felt inclined to make the first push into the unknown. We forbore to light a fire or to make any unnecessary sound.

Tomorrow (or today, rather, for it is already dawn as I write) we shall make our first venture into this strange land. When I shall be able to write again—or if I ever shall write again—I know not. Meanwhile, I can see that the Indians are still in their place, and I am sure that the faithful Zambo will be here presently to get my letter. I only trust that it will come to hand.

P.S.—The more I think the more desperate does our position seem. I see no possible hope of our return. If there were a high tree near the edge of the plateau we might drop a return bridge across, but there is none within fifty yards. Our united strength could not carry a trunk which would serve our purpose. The rope, of course, is far too short that we could descend by it. No, our position is hopeless—hopeless!

they left them up there with no way down

Chapter X; "The most Wonderful Things have Happened"

The most wonderful things have happened and are continually happening to us. All the paper that I possess consists of five old note-books and a lot of scraps, and I have only the one stylographic pencil; but so long as I can move my hand I will continue to set down our experiences and impressions, for, since we are the only men of the whole human race to see such things, it is of enormous importance that I should record them whilst they are fresh in my memory and before that fate which seems to be constantly impending does actually overtake us. Whether Zambo can at last take these letters to the river, or whether I shall myself in some miraculous way carry them back with me, or, finally, whether some daring explorer, coming upon our tracks with the advantage, perhaps, of a perfected monoplane, should find this bundle of manuscript, in any case I can see that what I am writing is destined to immortality as a classic of true adventure.

Gomez = bad

On the morning after our being trapped upon the plateau by the villainous Gomez we began a new stage in our experiences. The first incident in it was not such as to give me a very favorable opinion of the place to which we had wandered. As I roused myself from a short nap after day had dawned, my eyes fell upon a most singular appearance upon my own leg. My trouser had slipped up, exposing a few inches of my skin above my sock. On this there rested a large, purplish grape. Astonished at the sight, I leaned forward to pick it off, when, to my horror, it burst between my finger and thumb, squirting blood in every direction. My cry of disgust had brought the two professors to my side.

"Most interesting," said Summerlee, bending over my shin. "An enormous blood-tick, as yet, I believe, unclassified."

"The first-fruits of our labors," said Challenger in his booming, pedantic fashion. "We cannot do less than call it Ixodes Maloni. The very small inconvenience of being bitten, my young friend, cannot, I am sure, weigh with you as against the glorious privilege of having your name inscribed in the deathless roll of zoology. Unhappily you have crushed this fine specimen at the moment of satiation."

"Filthy vermin!" I cried.

Professor Challenger raised his great eyebrows in protest, and placed a soothing paw upon my shoulder.

"You should cultivate the scientific eye and the detached scientific mind," said he. "To a man of philosophic temperament like myself the blood-tick, with its lancet-like proboscis and its distending stomach, is as beautiful a work of Nature as the peacock or, for that matter, the aurora borealis. It pains me to hear you speak of it in so unappreciative a fashion. No doubt, with due diligence, we can secure some other specimen."

"There can be no doubt of that," said Summerlee, grimly, "for one has just disappeared behind your shirt-collar."

Challenger sprang into the air bellowing like a bull, and tore frantically at his coat and shirt to get them off. Summerlee and I laughed so that we could hardly help him. At last we exposed that monstrous torso (fifty-four inches, by the tailor's tape). His body was all matted with black hair, out of which jungle we picked the wandering tick before it had bitten him. But the bushes round were full of the horrible pests, and it was clear that we must shift our camp.

But first of all it was necessary to make our arrangements with the faithful negro, who appeared presently on the pinnacle with a number of tins of cocoa and biscuits, which he tossed over to us. Of the stores which remained below he was ordered to retain as much as would keep him for two months. The Indians were to have the remainder as a reward for their services and as payment for taking our letters back to the Amazon. Some hours later we saw them in single file far out upon the plain, each with a bundle on his head, making their way back along the path we had come. Zambo occupied our little tent at the base of the pinnacle, and there he remained, our one link with the world below.

And now we had to decide upon our immediate movements. We shifted our position from among the tick-laden bushes until we came to a small clearing thickly surrounded by trees upon all sides. There were some flat slabs of rock in the center, with an excellent well close by, and there we sat in cleanly comfort while we made our first plans for the invasion of this new country. Birds were calling among the foliage—especially one with a peculiar whooping cry which was new to us—but beyond these sounds there were no signs of life.

Our first care was to make some sort of list of our own stores, so that we might know what we had to rely upon. What with the things we had ourselves brought up and those which Zambo had sent across on the rope, we were fairly well supplied. Most important of all, in view of the dangers which might surround us, we had our four rifles and one thousand three hundred rounds, also a shot-gun, but not more than a hundred and fifty medium pellet cartridges. In the matter of provisions we had enough to last for several weeks, with a sufficiency of tobacco and a few scientific implements, including a large telescope and a good field-glass. All these things we collected together in the clearing, and as a first precaution, we cut down with our hatchet and knives a number of thorny bushes, which we piled round in a circle some fifteen yards in diameter. This was to be our headquarters for the time—our place of refuge against sudden danger and the guard-house for our stores. Fort Challenger, we called it.

It was midday before we had made ourselves secure, but the heat was not oppressive, and the general character of the plateau, both in its temperature and in its vegetation, was almost temperate. The beech, the oak, and even the birch were to be found among the tangle of trees which girt us in. One huge gingko tree, topping all the others, shot its great limbs and maidenhair foliage over the fort which we had constructed. In its shade we continued our discussion, while Lord John, who had quickly taken command in the hour of action, gave us his views.

"So long as neither man nor beast has seen or heard us, we are safe," said he. "From the time they know we are here our troubles begin. There are no signs that they have found us out as yet. So our game surely is to lie low for a time and spy out the land. We want to have a good look at our neighbors before we get on visitin' terms."

"But we must advance," I ventured to remark.

"By all means, sonny my boy! We will advance. But with common sense. We must never go so far that we can't get back to our base. Above all, we must never, unless it is life or death, fire off our guns."

"But YOU fired yesterday," said Summerlee.

"Well, it couldn't be helped. However, the wind was strong and blew outwards. It is not likely that the sound could have traveled far into the plateau. By the way, what shall we call this place? I suppose it is up to us to give it a name?"

There were several suggestions, more or less happy, but Challenger's was final.

"It can only have one name," said he. "It is called after the pioneer who discovered it. It is Maple White Land."

Maple White Land it became, and so it is named in that chart which has become my special task. So it will, I trust, appear in the atlas of the future.

The peaceful penetration of Maple White Land was the pressing subject before us. We had the evidence of our own eyes that the place was inhabited by some unknown creatures, and there was that of Maple White's sketch-book to show that more dreadful and more dangerous monsters might still appear. That there might also prove to be human occupants and that they were of a malevolent character was suggested by the skeleton impaled upon the bamboos, which could not have got there had it not been dropped from above. Our situation, stranded without possibility of escape in such a land, was clearly full of danger, and our reasons endorsed every measure of caution which Lord John's experience could suggest. Yet it was surely impossible that we should halt on the edge of this world of mystery when our very souls were tingling with impatience to push forward and to pluck the heart from it.

We therefore blocked the entrance to our zareba by filling it up with several thorny bushes, and left our camp with the stores entirely surrounded by this protecting hedge. We then slowly and cautiously set forth into the unknown, following the course of the little stream which flowed from our spring, as it should always serve us as a guide on our return.

Hardly had we started when we came across signs that there were indeed wonders awaiting us. After a few hundred yards of thick forest, containing many trees which were quite unknown to me, but which Summerlee, who was the botanist of the party, recognized as forms of conifera and of cycadaceous plants which have long passed away in the world below, we entered a region where the stream widened out and formed a considerable bog. High reeds of a peculiar type grew thickly before us, which were pronounced to be equisetacea, or mare's-tails, with tree-ferns scattered amongst them, all of them swaying in a brisk wind. Suddenly Lord John, who was walking first, halted with uplifted hand.

"Look at this!" said he. "By George, this must be the trail of the father of all birds!"

enormous three-toed track was imprinted in the soft mud before us. The whatever it was, had crossed the swamp and had passed on into the forest. opped to examine that monstrous spoor. If it were indeed a bird—and what animal could leave such a mark?--its foot was so much larger than an ostrich's that its height upon the same scale must be enormous. Lord John looked eagerly round him and slipped two cartridges into his elephant-gun.

"I'll stake my good name as a shikarree," said he, "that the track is a fresh one. The creature has not passed ten minutes. Look how the water is still oozing into that deeper print! By Jove! See, here is the mark of a little one!"

Sure enough, smaller tracks of the same general form were running parallel to the large ones.

"But what do you make of this?" cried Professor Summerlee, triumphantly, pointing to what looked like the huge print of a five-fingered human hand appearing among the three-toed marks.

"Wealden!" cried Challenger, in an ecstasy. "I've seen them in the Wealden clay. It is a creature walking erect upon three-toed feet, and occasionally putting one of its five-fingered forepaws upon the ground. Not a bird, my dear Roxton—not a bird."

"A beast?"

"No; a reptile—a dinosaur. Nothing else could have left such a track. They puzzled a worthy Sussex doctor some ninety years ago; but who in the world could have hoped—hoped—to have seen a sight like that?"

His words died away into a whisper, and we all stood in motionless amazement. Following the tracks, we had left the morass and passed through a screen of brushwood and trees. Beyond was an open glade, and in this were five of the most extraordinary creatures that I have ever seen. Crouching down among the bushes, we observed them at our leisure.

There were, as I say, five of them, two being adults and three young ones. In size they were enormous. Even the babies were as big as elephants, while the two large ones were far beyond all creatures I have ever seen. They had slate-colored skin, which was scaled like a lizard's and shimmered where the sun shone upon it. All five were sitting up, balancing themselves upon their broad, powerful tails and their huge three-toed hind-feet, while with their small five-fingered front-feet they pulled down the branches upon which they browsed. I do not know that I can bring their appearance home to you better than by saying that they looked like monstrous kangaroos, twenty feet in length, and with skins like black crocodiles.

I do not know how long we stayed motionless gazing at this marvelous spectacle. A strong wind blew towards us and we were well concealed, so there was no chance of discovery. From time to time the little ones played round their parents in unwieldy gambols, the great beasts bounding into the air and falling with dull thuds upon the earth. The strength of the parents seemed to be limitless, for one of them, having some difficulty in reaching a bunch of foliage which grew upon a considerable-sized tree, put his fore-legs round the trunk and tore it down as if it had been a sapling. The action seemed, as I thought, to show not only the great development of its muscles, but also the small one of its brain, for the whole weight came crashing down upon the top of it, and it uttered a series of shrill yelps to show that, big as it was, there was a limit to what it could endure. The incident made it think, apparently, that the neighborhood was dangerous, for it slowly lurched off through the wood, followed by its mate and its three enormous infants. We saw the shimmering slaty gleam of their skins between the tree-trunks, and their heads undulating high above the brush-wood. Then they vanished from our sight.

I looked at my comrades. Lord John was standing at gaze with his finger on the trigger of his elephant-gun, his eager hunter's soul shining from his fierce eyes. What would he not give for one such head to place between the two crossed oars above the mantelpiece in his snuggery at the Albany! And yet his reason held him in, for all our exploration of the wonders of this unknown land depended upon our presence being concealed from its inhabitants. The two professors were in silent ecstasy. In their excitement they had unconsciously seized each other by the hand, and stood like two little children in the presence of a marvel, Challenger's cheeks bunched up into a seraphic smile, and Summerlee's sardonic face softening for the moment into wonder and reverence.

"Nunc dimittis!" he cried at last. "What will they say in England of this?"

"My dear Summerlee, I will tell you with great confidence exactly what they will say in England," said Challenger. "They will say that you are an infernal liar and a scientific charlatan, exactly as you and others said of me."

"In the face of photographs?"

"Faked, Summerlee! Clumsily faked!"

"In the face of specimens?"

"Ah, there we may have them! Malone and his filthy Fleet Street crew may be all yelping our praises yet. August the twenty-eighth—the day we saw five live iguanodons in a glade of Maple White Land. Put it down in your diary, my young friend, and send it to your rag."

"And be ready to get the toe-end of the editorial boot in return," said Lord John. "Things look a bit different from the latitude of London, young fellah my lad. There's many a man who never tells his adventures, for he can't hope to be believed. Who's to blame them? For this will seem a bit of a dream to ourselves in a month or two. WHAT did you say they were?"

"Iguanodons," said Summerlee. "You'll find their footmarks all over the Hastings sands, in Kent, and in Sussex. The South of England was alive with them when there was plenty of good lush green-stuff to keep them going. Conditions have changed, and the beasts died. Here it seems that the conditions have not changed, and the beasts have lived."

"If ever we get out of this alive, I must have a head with me," said Lord John. "Lord, how some of that Somaliland-Uganda crowd would turn a beautiful pea-green if they saw it! I don't know what you chaps think, but it strikes me that we are on mighty thin ice all this time."

I had the same feeling of mystery and danger around us. In the gloom of the trees there seemed a constant menace and as we looked up into their shadowy foliage vague terrors crept into one's heart. It is true that these monstrous creatures which we had seen were lumbering, inoffensive brutes which were unlikely to hurt anyone, but in this world of wonders what other survivals might there not be—what fierce, active horrors ready to pounce upon us from their lair among the rocks or brushwood? I knew little of prehistoric life, but I had a clear remembrance of one book which I had read in which it spoke of creatures who would live upon our lions and tigers as a cat lives upon mice. What if these also were to be found in the woods of Maple White Land!

It was destined that on this very morning—our first in the new country—we were to find out what strange hazards lay around us. It was a loathsome adventure, and one of which I hate to think. If, as Lord John said, the glade of the iguanodons will remain with us as a dream, then surely the swamp of the pterodactyls will forever be our nightmare. Let me set down exactly what occurred.

We passed very slowly through the woods, partly because Lord Roxton acted as scout before he would let us advance, and partly because at every second step one or other of our professors would fall, with a cry of wonder, before some flower or insect which presented him with a new type. We may have traveled two or three miles in all, keeping to the right of the line of the stream, when we came upon a considerable opening in the trees. A belt of brushwood led up to a tangle of rocks—the whole plateau was strewn with boulders. We were walking slowly towards these rocks, among bushes which reached over our waists, when we became aware of a strange low gabbling and whistling sound, which filled the air with a constant clamor and appeared to come from some spot immediately before us. Lord John held up his hand as a signal for us to stop, and he made his way swiftly, stooping and running, to the line of rocks. We saw him peep over them and give a gesture of amazement. Then he stood staring as if forgetting us, so utterly entranced was he by what he saw. Finally he waved us to come on, holding up his hand as a signal for caution. His whole bearing made me feel that something wonderful but dangerous lay before us.

Creeping to his side, we looked over the rocks. The place into which we gazed was a pit, and may, in the early days, have been one of the smaller volcanic blow-holes of the plateau. It was bowl-shaped and at the bottom, some hundreds of yards from where we lay, were pools of green-scummed, stagnant water, fringed with bullrushes. It was a weird place in itself, but its occupants made it seem like a scene from the Seven Circles of Dante. The place was a rookery of pterodactyls. There were hundreds of them congregated within view. All the bottom area round the water-edge was alive with their young ones, and with hideous mothers brooding upon their leathery, yellowish eggs. From this crawling flapping mass of obscene reptilian life came the shocking clamor which filled the air and the mephitic, horrible, musty odor which turned us sick. But above, perched each upon its own stone, tall, gray, and withered, more like dead and dried specimens than actual living creatures, sat the horrible males, absolutely motionless save for the rolling of their red eyes or an occasional snap of their rat-trap beaks as a dragon-fly went past them. Their huge, membranous wings were closed by folding their fore-arms, so that they sat like gigantic old women, wrapped in hideous web-colored shawls, and with their ferocious heads protruding above them. Large and small, not less than a thousand of these filthy creatures lay in the hollow before us.

Our professors would gladly have stayed there all day, so entranced were they by this opportunity of studying the life of a prehistoric age. They pointed out the fish and dead birds lying about among the rocks as proving the nature of the food of these creatures, and I heard them congratulating each other on having cleared up the point why the bones of this flying dragon are found in such great numbers in certain well-defined areas, as in the Cambridge Green-sand, since it was now seen that, like penguins, they lived in gregarious fashion.

Finally, however, Challenger, bent upon proving some point which Summerlee had contested, thrust his head over the rock and nearly brought destruction upon us all. In an instant the nearest male gave a shrill, whistling cry, and flapped its twenty-foot span of leathery wings as it soared up into the air. The females and young ones huddled together beside the water, while the whole circle of sentinels rose one after the other and sailed off into the sky. It was a wonderful sight to see at least a hundred creatures of such enormous size and hideous appearance all swooping like swallows with swift, shearing wing-strokes above us; but soon we realized that it was not one on which we could afford to linger. At first the great brutes flew round in a huge ring, as if to make sure what the exact extent of the danger might be. Then, the flight grew lower and the circle narrower, until they were whizzing round and round us, the dry, rustling flap of their huge slate-colored wings filling the air with a volume of sound that made me think of Hendon aerodrome upon a race day.

"Make for the wood and keep together," cried Lord John, clubbing his rifle. "The brutes mean mischief."

The moment we attempted to retreat the circle closed in upon us, until the tips of the wings of those nearest to us nearly touched our faces. We beat at them with the stocks of our guns, but there was nothing solid or vulnerable to strike. Then suddenly out of the whizzing, slate-colored circle a long neck shot out, and a fierce beak made a thrust at us. Another and another followed. Summerlee gave a cry and put his hand to his face, from which the blood was streaming. I felt a prod at the back of my neck, and turned dizzy with the shock. Challenger fell, and as I stooped to pick him up I was again struck from behind and dropped on the top of him. At the same instant I heard the crash of Lord John's elephant-gun, and, looking up, saw one of the creatures with a broken wing struggling upon the ground, spitting and gurgling at us with a wide-opened beak and blood-shot, goggled eyes, like some devil in a medieval picture. Its comrades had flown higher at the sudden sound, and were circling above our heads.

"Now," cried Lord John, "now for our lives!"

We staggered through the brushwood, and even as we reached the trees the harpies were on us again. Summerlee was knocked down, but we tore him up and rushed among the trunks. Once there we were safe, for those huge wings had no space for their sweep beneath the branches. As we limped homewards, sadly mauled and discomfited, we saw them for a long time flying at a great height against the deep blue sky above our heads, soaring round and round, no bigger than wood-pigeons, with their eyes no doubt still following our progress. At last, however, as we reached the thicker woods they gave up the chase, and we saw them no more.

"A most interesting and convincing experience," said Challenger, as we halted beside the brook and he bathed a swollen knee. "We are exceptionally well informed, Summerlee, as to the habits of the enraged pterodactyl."

Summerlee was wiping the blood from a cut in his forehead, while I was tying up a nasty stab in the muscle of the neck. Lord John had the shoulder of his coat torn away, but the creature's teeth had only grazed the flesh.

"It is worth noting," Challenger continued, "that our young friend has received an undoubted stab, while Lord John's coat could only have been torn by a bite. In my own case, I was beaten about the head by their wings, so we have had a remarkable exhibition of their various methods of offence."

"It has been touch and go for our lives," said Lord John, gravely, "and I could not think of a more rotten sort of death than to be outed by such filthy vermin. I was sorry to fire my rifle, but, by Jove! there was no great choice."

"We should not be here if you hadn't," said I, with conviction.

"It may do no harm," said he. "Among these woods there must be many loud cracks from splitting or falling trees which would be just like the sound of a gun. But now, if you are of my opinion, we have had thrills enough for one day, and had best get back to the surgical box at the camp for some carbolic. Who knows what venom these beasts may have in their hideous jaws?"

But surely no men ever had just such a day since the world began. Some fresh surprise was ever in store for us. When, following the course of our brook, we at last reached our glade and saw the thorny barricade of our camp, we thought that our adventures were at an end. But we had something more to think of before we could rest. The gate of Fort Challenger had been untouched, the walls were unbroken, and yet it had been visited by some strange and powerful creature in our absence. No foot-mark showed a trace of its nature, and only the overhanging branch of the enormous ginko tree suggested how it might have come and gone; but of its malevolent strength there was ample evidence in the condition of our stores. They were strewn at random all over the ground, and one tin of meat had been crushed into pieces so as to extract the contents. A case of cartridges had been shattered into matchwood, and one of the brass shells lay shredded into pieces beside it. Again the feeling of vague horror came upon our souls, and we gazed round with frightened eyes at the dark shadows which lay around us, in all of which some fearsome shape might be lurking. How good it was when we were hailed by the voice of Zambo, and, going to the edge of the plateau, saw him sitting grinning at us upon the top of the opposite pinnacle.

"All well, Massa Challenger, all well!" he cried. "Me stay here. No fear. You always find me when you want."

His honest black face, and the immense view before us, which carried us half-way back to the affluent of the Amazon, helped us to remember that we really were upon this earth in the twentieth century, and had not by some magic been conveyed to some raw planet in its earliest and wildest state. How difficult it was to realize that the violet line upon the far horizon was well advanced to that great river upon which huge steamers ran, and folk talked of the small affairs of life, while we, marooned among the creatures of a bygone age, could but gaze towards it and yearn for all that it meant!

One other memory remains with me of this wonderful day, and with it I will close this letter. The two professors, their tempers aggravated no doubt by their injuries, had fallen out as to whether our assailants were of the genus pterodactylus or dimorphodon, and high words had ensued. To avoid their wrangling I moved some little way apart, and was seated smoking upon the trunk of a fallen tree, when Lord John strolled over in my direction.

"I say, Malone," said he, "do you remember that place where those beasts were?"

"Very clearly."

"A sort of volcanic pit, was it not?"

"Exactly," said I.

"Did you notice the soil?"

"Rocks."

"But round the water—where the reeds were?"

"It was a bluish soil. It looked like clay."

"Exactly. A volcanic tube full of blue clay."

"What of that?" I asked.

"Oh, nothing, nothing," said he, and strolled back to where the voices of the contending men of science rose in a prolonged duet, the high, strident note of Summerlee rising and falling to the sonorous bass of Challenger. I should have thought no more of Lord John's remark were it not that once again that night I heard him mutter to himself: "Blue clay—clay in a volcanic tube!" They were the last words I heard before I dropped into an exhausted sleep.

Chapter XI; "For once I was the Hero"

Lord John Roxton was right when he thought that some specially toxic quality might lie in the bite of the horrible creatures which had attacked us. On the morning after our first adventure upon the plateau, both Summerlee and I were in great pain and fever, while Challenger's knee was so bruised that he could hardly limp. We kept to our camp all day, therefore, Lord John busying himself, with such help as we could give him, in raising the height and thickness of the thorny walls which were our only defense. I remember that during the whole long day I was haunted by the feeling that we were closely observed, though by whom or whence I could give no guess.

So strong was the impression that I told Professor Challenger of it, who put it down to the cerebral excitement caused by my fever. Again and again I glanced round swiftly, with the conviction that I was about to see something, but only to meet the dark tangle of our hedge or the solemn and cavernous gloom of the great trees which arched above our heads. And yet the feeling grew ever stronger in my own mind that something observant and something malevolent was at our very elbow. I thought of the Indian superstition of the Curupuri—the dreadful, lurking spirit of the woods—and I could have imagined that his terrible presence haunted those who had invaded his most remote and sacred retreat.

That night (our third in Maple White Land) we had an experience which left a fearful impression upon our minds, and made us thankful that Lord John had worked so hard in making our retreat impregnable. We were all sleeping round our dying fire when we were aroused—or, rather, I should say, shot out of our slumbers—by a succession of the most frightful cries and screams to which I have ever listened. I know no sound to which I could compare this amazing tumult, which seemed to come from some spot within a few hundred yards of our camp. It was as ear-splitting as any whistle of a railway-engine; but whereas the whistle is a clear, mechanical, sharp-edged sound, this was far deeper in volume and vibrant with the uttermost strain of agony and horror. We clapped our hands to our ears to shut out that nerve-shaking appeal. A cold sweat broke out over my body, and my heart turned sick at the misery of it. All the woes of tortured life, all its stupendous indictment of high heaven, its innumerable sorrows, seemed to be centered and condensed into that one dreadful, agonized cry. And then, under this high-pitched, ringing sound there was another, more intermittent, a low, deep-chested laugh, a growling, throaty gurgle of merriment which formed a grotesque accompaniment to the shriek with which it was blended. For three or four minutes on end the fearsome duet continued, while all the foliage rustled with the rising of startled birds. Then it shut off as suddenly as it began. For a long time we sat in horrified silence. Then Lord John threw a bundle of twigs upon the fire, and their red glare lit up the intent faces of my companions and flickered over the great boughs above our heads.

"What was it?" I whispered.

"We shall know in the morning," said Lord John. "It was close to us—not farther than the glade."

"We have been privileged to overhear a prehistoric tragedy, the sort of drama which occurred among the reeds upon the border of some Jurassic lagoon, when the greater dragon pinned the lesser among the slime," said Challenger, with more solemnity than I had ever heard in his voice. "It was surely well for man that he came late in the order of creation. There were powers abroad in earlier days which no courage and no mechanism of his could have met. What could his sling, his throwing-stick, or his arrow avail him against such forces as have been loose to-night? Even with a modern rifle it would be all odds on the monster."

"I think I should back my little friend," said Lord John, caressing his Express. "But the beast would certainly have a good sporting chance."

Summerlee raised his hand.

"Hush!" he cried. "Surely I hear something?"

From the utter silence there emerged a deep, regular pat-pat. It was the tread of some animal—the rhythm of soft but heavy pads placed cautiously upon the ground. It stole slowly round the camp, and then halted near our gateway. There was a low, sibilant rise and fall—the breathing of the creature. Only our feeble hedge separated us from this horror of the night. Each of us had seized his rifle, and Lord John had pulled out a small bush to make an embrasure in the hedge.

"By George!" he whispered. "I think I can see it!"

I stooped and peered over his shoulder through the gap. Yes, I could see it, too. In the deep shadow of the tree there was a deeper shadow yet, black, inchoate, vague—a crouching form full of savage vigor and menace. It was no higher than a horse, but the dim outline suggested vast bulk and strength. That hissing pant, as regular and full-volumed as the exhaust of an engine, spoke of a monstrous organism. Once, as it moved, I thought I saw the glint of two terrible, greenish eyes. There was an uneasy rustling, as if it were crawling slowly forward.

"I believe it is going to spring!" said I, cocking my rifle.

"Don't fire! Don't fire!" whispered Lord John. "The crash of a gun in this silent night would be heard for miles. Keep it as a last card."

"If it gets over the hedge we're done," said Summerlee, and his voice crackled into a nervous laugh as he spoke.

"No, it must not get over," cried Lord John; "but hold your fire to the last. Perhaps I can make something of the fellow. I'll chance it, anyhow."

It was as brave an act as ever I saw a man do. He stooped to the fire, picked up a blazing branch, and slipped in an instant through a sallyport which he had made in our gateway. The thing moved forward with a dreadful snarl. Lord John never hesitated, but, running towards it with a quick, light step, he dashed the flaming wood into the brute's face. For one moment I had a vision of a horrible mask like a giant toad's, of a warty, leprous skin, and of a loose mouth all beslobbered with fresh blood. The next, there was a crash in the underwood and our dreadful visitor was gone.

"I thought he wouldn't face the fire," said Lord John, laughing, as he came back and threw his branch among the faggots.

"You should not have taken such a risk!" we all cried.

"There was nothin' else to be done. If he had got among us we should have shot each other in tryin' to down him. On the other hand, if we had fired through the hedge and wounded him he would soon have been on the top of us—to say nothin' of giving ourselves away. On the whole, I think that we are jolly well out of it. What was he, then?"

Our learned men looked at each other with some hesitation.

"Personally, I am unable to classify the creature with any certainty," said Summerlee, lighting his pipe from the fire.

"In refusing to commit yourself you are but showing a proper scientific reserve," said Challenger, with massive condescension. "I am not myself prepared to go farther than to say in general terms that we have almost certainly been in contact to-night with some form of carnivorous dinosaur. I have already expressed my anticipation that something of the sort might exist upon this plateau."

"We have to bear in mind," remarked Summerlee, "that there are many prehistoric forms which have never come down to us. It would be rash to suppose that we can give a name to all that we are likely to meet."

"Exactly. A rough classification may be the best that we can attempt. Tomorrow some further evidence may help us to an identification. Meantime we can only renew our interrupted slumbers."

"But not without a sentinel," said Lord John, with decision. "We can't afford to take chances in a country like this. Two-hour spells in the future, for each of us."

"Then I'll just finish my pipe in starting the first one," said Professor Summerlee; and from that time onwards we never trusted ourselves again without a watchman.

In the morning it was not long before we discovered the source of the hideous uproar which had aroused us in the night. The iguanodon glade was the scene of a horrible butchery. From the pools of blood and the enormous lumps of flesh scattered in every direction over the green sward we imagined at first that a number of animals had been killed, but on examining the remains more closely we discovered that all this carnage came from one of these unwieldy monsters, which had been literally torn to pieces by some creature not larger, perhaps, but far more ferocious, than itself.

Our two professors sat in absorbed argument, examining piece after piece, which showed the marks of savage teeth and of enormous claws.

"Our judgment must still be in abeyance," said Professor Challenger, with a huge slab of whitish-colored flesh across his knee. "The indications would be consistent with the presence of a saber-toothed tiger, such as are still found among the breccia of our caverns; but the creature actually seen was undoubtedly of a larger and more reptilian character. Personally, I should pronounce for allosaurus."

"Or megalosaurus," said Summerlee.

"Exactly. Any one of the larger carnivorous dinosaurs would meet the case. Among them are to be found all the most terrible types of animal life that have ever cursed the earth or blessed a museum." He laughed sonorously at his own conceit, for, though he had little sense of humor, the crudest pleasantry from his own lips moved him always to roars of appreciation.

"The less noise the better," said Lord Roxton, curtly. "We don't know who or what may be near us. If this fellah comes back for his breakfast and catches us here we won't have so much to laugh at. By the way, what is this mark upon the iguanodon's hide?"

On the dull, scaly, slate-colored skin somewhere above the shoulder, there was a singular black circle of some substance which looked like asphalt. None of us could suggest what it meant, though Summerlee was of opinion that he had seen something similar upon one of the young ones two days before. Challenger said nothing, but looked pompous and puffy, as if he could if he would, so that finally Lord John asked his opinion direct.

"If your lordship will graciously permit me to open my mouth, I shall be happy to express my sentiments," said he, with elaborate sarcasm. "I am not in the habit of being taken to task in the fashion which seems to be customary with your lordship. I was not aware that it was necessary to ask your permission before smiling at a harmless pleasantry."

It was not until he had received his apology that our touchy friend would suffer himself to be appeased. When at last his ruffled feelings were at ease, he addressed us at some length from his seat upon a fallen tree, speaking, as his habit was, as if he were imparting most precious information to a class of a thousand.

"With regard to the marking," said he, "I am inclined to agree with my friend and colleague, Professor Summerlee, that the stains are from asphalt. As this plateau is, in its very nature, highly volcanic, and as asphalt is a substance which one associates with Plutonic forces, I cannot doubt that it exists in the free liquid state, and that the creatures may have come in contact with it. A much more important problem is the question as to the existence of the carnivorous monster which has left its traces in this glade. We know roughly that this plateau is not larger than an average English county. Within this confined space a certain number of creatures, mostly types which have passed away in the world below, have lived together for innumerable years. Now, it is very clear to me that in so long a period one would have expected that the carnivorous creatures, multiplying unchecked, would have exhausted their food supply and have been compelled to either modify their flesh-eating habits or die of hunger. This we see has not been so. We can only imagine, therefore, that the balance of Nature is preserved by some check which limits the numbers of these ferocious creatures. One of the many interesting problems, therefore, which await our solution is to discover what that check may be and how it operates. I venture to trust that we may have some future opportunity for the closer study of the carnivorous dinosaurs."

"And I venture to trust we may not," I observed.

The Professor only raised his great eyebrows, as the schoolmaster meets the irrelevant observation of the naughty boy.

"Perhaps Professor Summerlee may have an observation to make," he said, and the two savants ascended together into some rarefied scientific atmosphere, where the possibilities of a modification of the birth-rate were weighed against the decline of the food supply as a check in the struggle for existence.

That morning we mapped out a small portion of the plateau, avoiding the swamp of the pterodactyls, and keeping to the east of our brook instead of to the west. In that direction the country was still thickly wooded, with so much undergrowth that our progress was very slow.

I have dwelt up to now upon the terrors of Maple White Land; but there was another side to the subject, for all that morning we wandered among lovely flowers—mostly, as I observed, white or yellow in color, these being, as our professors explained, the primitive flower-shades. In many places the ground was absolutely covered with them, and as we walked ankle-deep on that wonderful yielding carpet, the scent was almost intoxicating in its sweetness and intensity. The homely English bee buzzed everywhere around us. Many of the trees under which we passed had their branches bowed down with fruit, some of which were of familiar sorts, while other varieties were new. By observing which of them were pecked by the birds we avoided all danger of poison and added a delicious variety to our food reserve. In the jungle which we traversed were numerous hard-trodden paths made by the wild beasts, and in the more marshy places we saw a profusion of strange footmarks, including many of the iguanodon. Once in a grove we observed several of these great creatures grazing, and Lord John, with his glass, was able to report that they also were spotted with asphalt, though in a different place to the one which we examined in the morning. What this phenomenon meant we could not imagine.

We saw many small animals, such as porcupines, a scaly ant-eater, and a pig, piebald in color and with long curved tusks. Once, through a break in the trees, we saw a clear shoulder of green hill some distance away, and across this a large dun-colored animal was traveling at a considerable pace. It passed so swiftly that we were unable to say what it was; but if it were a deer, as was claimed by Lord John, it must have been as large as those monstrous Irish elk which are still dug up from time to time in the bogs of my native land.

Ever since the mysterious visit which had been paid to our camp we always returned to it with some misgivings. However, on this occasion we found everything in order.

That evening we had a grand discussion upon our present situation and future plans, which I must describe at some length, as it led to a new departure by which we were enabled to gain a more complete knowledge of Maple White Land than might have come in many weeks of exploring. It was Summerlee who opened the debate. All day he had been querulous in manner, and now some remark of Lord John's as to what we should do on the morrow brought all his bitterness to a head.

"What we ought to be doing today, tomorrow, and all the time," said he, "is finding some way out of the trap into which we have fallen. You are all turning your brains towards getting into this country. I say that we should be scheming how to get out of it."

"I am surprised, sir," boomed Challenger, stroking his majestic beard, "that any man of science should commit himself to so ignoble a sentiment. You are in a land which offers such an inducement to the ambitious naturalist as none ever has since the world began, and you suggest leaving it before we have acquired more than the most superficial knowledge of it or of its contents. I expected better things of you, Professor Summerlee."

"You must remember," said Summerlee, sourly, "that I have a large class in London who are at present at the mercy of an extremely inefficient locum tenens. This makes my situation different from yours, Professor Challenger, since, so far as I know, you have never been entrusted with any responsible educational work."

"Quite so," said Challenger. "I have felt it to be a sacrilege to divert a brain which is capable of the highest original research to any lesser object. That is why I have sternly set my face against any proffered scholastic appointment."

"For example?" asked Summerlee, with a sneer; but Lord John hastened to change the conversation.

"I must say," said he, "that I think it would be a mighty poor thing to go back to London before I know a great deal more of this place than I do at present."

"I could never dare to walk into the back office of my paper and face old McArdle," said I. (You will excuse the frankness of this report, will you not, sir?) "He'd never forgive me for leaving such unexhausted copy behind me. Besides, so far as I can see it is not worth discussing, since we can't get down, even if we wanted."

"Our young friend makes up for many obvious mental lacunae by some measure of primitive common sense," remarked Challenger. "The interests of his deplorable profession are immaterial to us; but, as he observes, we cannot get down in any case, so it is a waste of energy to discuss it."

"It is a waste of energy to do anything else," growled Summerlee from behind his pipe. "Let me remind you that we came here upon a perfectly definite mission, entrusted to us at the meeting of the Zoological Institute in London. That mission was to test the truth of Professor Challenger's statements. Those statements, as I am bound to admit, we are now in a position to endorse. Our ostensible work is therefore done. As to the detail which remains to be worked out upon this plateau, it is so enormous that only a large expedition, with a very special equipment, could hope to cope with it. Should we attempt to do so ourselves, the only possible result must be that we shall never return with the important contribution to science which we have already gained. Professor Challenger has devised means for getting us on to this plateau when it appeared to be inaccessible; I think that we should now call upon him to use the same ingenuity in getting us back to the world from which we came."

I confess that as Summerlee stated his view it struck me as altogether reasonable. Even Challenger was affected by the consideration that his enemies would never stand confuted if the confirmation of his statements should never reach those who had doubted them.

"The problem of the descent is at first sight a formidable one," said he, "and yet I cannot doubt that the intellect can solve it. I am prepared to agree with our colleague that a protracted stay in Maple White Land is at present inadvisable, and that the question of our return will soon have to be faced. I absolutely refuse to leave, however, until we have made at least a superficial examination of this country, and are able to take back with us something in the nature of a chart."

Professor Summerlee gave a snort of impatience.

"We have spent two long days in exploration," said he, "and we are no wiser as to the actual geography of the place than when we started. It is clear that it is all thickly wooded, and it would take months to penetrate it and to learn the relations of one part to another. If there were some central peak it would be different, but it all slopes downwards, so far as we can see. The farther we go the less likely it is that we will get any general view."

It was at that moment that I had my inspiration. My eyes chanced to light upon the enormous gnarled trunk of the gingko tree which cast its huge branches over us. Surely, if its bole exceeded that of all others, its height must do the same. If the rim of the plateau was indeed the highest point, then why should this mighty tree not prove to be a watchtower which commanded the whole country? Now, ever since I ran wild as a lad in Ireland I have been a bold and skilled tree-climber. My comrades might be my masters on the rocks, but I knew that I would be supreme among those branches. Could I only get my legs on to the lowest of the giant off-shoots, then it would be strange indeed if I could not make my way to the top. My comrades were delighted at my idea.

"Our young friend," said Challenger, bunching up the red apples of his cheeks, "is capable of acrobatic exertions which would be impossible to a man of a more solid, though possibly of a more commanding, appearance. I applaud his resolution."

"By George, young fellah, you've put your hand on it!" said Lord John, clapping me on the back. "How we never came to think of it before I can't imagine! There's not more than an hour of daylight left, but if you take your notebook you may be able to get some rough sketch of the place. If we put these three ammunition cases under the branch, I will soon hoist you on to it."

He stood on the boxes while I faced the trunk, and was gently raising me when Challenger sprang forward and gave me such a thrust with his huge hand that he fairly shot me into the tree. With both arms clasping the branch, I scrambled hard with my feet until I had worked, first my body, and then my knees, onto it. There were three excellent off-shoots, like huge rungs of a ladder, above my head, and a tangle of convenient branches beyond, so that I clambered onwards with such speed that I soon lost sight of the ground and had nothing but foliage beneath me. Now and then I encountered a check, and once I had to shin up a creeper for eight or ten feet, but I made excellent progress, and the booming of Challenger's voice seemed to be a great distance beneath me. The tree was, however, enormous, and, looking upwards, I could see no thinning of the leaves above my head. There was some thick, bush-like clump which seemed to be a parasite upon a branch up which I was swarming. I leaned my head round it in order to see what was beyond, and I nearly fell out of the tree in my surprise and horror at what I saw.

A face was gazing into mine—at the distance of only a foot or two. The creature that owned it had been crouching behind the parasite, and had looked round it at the same instant that I did. It was a human face—or at least it was far more human than any monkey's that I have ever seen. It was long, whitish, and blotched with pimples, the nose flattened, and the lower jaw projecting, with a bristle of coarse whiskers round the chin. The eyes, which were under thick and heavy brows, were bestial and ferocious, and as it opened its mouth to snarl what sounded like a curse at me I observed that it had curved, sharp canine teeth. For an instant I read hatred and menace in the evil eyes. Then, as quick as a flash, came an expression of overpowering fear. There was a crash of broken boughs as it dived wildly down into the tangle of green. I caught a glimpse of a hairy body like that of a reddish pig, and then it was gone amid a swirl of leaves and branches.

"What's the matter?" shouted Roxton from below. "Anything wrong with you?"

"Did you see it?" I cried, with my arms round the branch and all my nerves tingling.

"We heard a row, as if your foot had slipped. What was it?"

I was so shocked at the sudden and strange appearance of this ape-man that I hesitated whether I should not climb down again and tell my experience to my companions. But I was already so far up the great tree that it seemed a humiliation to return without having carried out my mission.

After a long pause, therefore, to recover my breath and my courage, I continued my ascent. Once I put my weight upon a rotten branch and swung for a few seconds by my hands, but in the main it was all easy climbing. Gradually the leaves thinned around me, and I was aware, from the wind upon my face, that I had topped all the trees of the forest. I was determined, however, not to look about me before I had reached the very highest point, so I scrambled on until I had got so far that the topmost branch was bending beneath my weight. There I settled into a convenient fork, and, balancing myself securely, I found myself looking down at a most wonderful panorama of this strange country in which we found ourselves.

The sun was just above the western sky-line, and the evening was a particularly bright and clear one, so that the whole extent of the plateau was visible beneath me. It was, as seen from this height, of an oval contour, with a breadth of about thirty miles and a width of twenty. Its general shape was that of a shallow funnel, all the sides sloping down to a considerable lake in the center. This lake may have been ten miles in circumference, and lay very green and beautiful in the evening light, with a thick fringe of reeds at its edges, and with its surface broken by several yellow sandbanks, which gleamed golden in the mellow sunshine. A number of long dark objects, which were too large for alligators and too long for canoes, lay upon the edges of these patches of sand. With my glass I could clearly see that they were alive, but what their nature might be I could not imagine.

From the side of the plateau on which we were, slopes of woodland, with occasional glades, stretched down for five or six miles to the central lake. I could see at my very feet the glade of the iguanodons, and farther off was a round opening in the trees which marked the swamp of the pterodactyls. On the side facing me, however, the plateau presented a very different aspect. There the basalt cliffs of the outside were reproduced upon the inside, forming an escarpment about two hundred feet high, with a woody slope beneath it. Along the base of these red cliffs, some distance above the ground, I could see a number of dark holes through the glass, which I conjectured to be the mouths of caves. At the opening of one of these something white was shimmering, but I was unable to make out what it was. I sat charting the country until the sun had set and it was so dark that I could no longer distinguish details. Then I climbed down to my companions waiting for me so eagerly at the bottom of the great tree. For once I was the hero of the expedition. Alone I had thought of it, and alone I had done it; and here was the chart which would save us a month's blind groping among unknown dangers. Each of them shook me solemnly by the hand.

But before they discussed the details of my map I had to tell them of my encounter with the ape-man among the branches.

"He has been there all the time," said I.

"How do you know that?" asked Lord John.

"Because I have never been without that feeling that something malevolent was watching us. I mentioned it to you, Professor Challenger."

"Our young friend certainly said something of the kind. He is also the one among us who is endowed with that Celtic temperament which would make him sensitive to such impressions."

"The whole theory of telepathy----" began Summerlee, filling his pipe.

"Is too vast to be now discussed," said Challenger, with decision. "Tell me, now," he added, with the air of a bishop addressing a Sunday-school, "did you happen to observe whether the creature could cross its thumb over its palm?"

"No, indeed."

"Had it a tail?"

"No."

"Was the foot prehensile?"

"I do not think it could have made off so fast among the branches if it could not get a grip with its feet."

"In South America there are, if my memory serves me—you will check the observation, Professor Summerlee—some thirty-six species of monkeys, but the anthropoid ape is unknown. It is clear, however, that he exists in this country, and that he is not the hairy, gorilla-like variety, which is never seen out of Africa or the East." (I was inclined to interpolate, as I looked at him, that I had seen his first cousin in Kensington.) "This is a whiskered and colorless type, the latter characteristic pointing to the fact that he spends his days in arboreal seclusion. The question which we have to face is whether he approaches more closely to the ape or the man. In the latter case, he may well approximate to what the vulgar have called the 'missing link.' The solution of this problem is our immediate duty."

"It is nothing of the sort," said Summerlee, abruptly. "Now that, through the intelligence and activity of Mr. Malone" (I cannot help quoting the words), "we have got our chart, our one and only immediate duty is to get ourselves safe and sound out of this awful place."

"The flesh-pots of civilization," groaned Challenger.

"The ink-pots of civilization, sir. It is our task to put on record what we have seen, and to leave the further exploration to others. You all agreed as much before Mr. Malone got us the chart."

"Well," said Challenger, "I admit that my mind will be more at ease when I am assured that the result of our expedition has been conveyed to our friends. How we are to get down from this place I have not as yet an idea. I have never yet encountered any problem, however, which my inventive brain was unable to solve, and I promise you that tomorrow I will turn my attention to the question of our descent." And so the matter was allowed to rest.

But that evening, by the light of the fire and of a single candle, the first map of the lost world was elaborated. Every detail which I had roughly noted from my watch-tower was drawn out in its relative place. Challenger's pencil hovered over the great blank which marked the lake.

"What shall we call it?" he asked.

"Why should you not take the chance of perpetuating your own name?" said Summerlee, with his usual touch of acidity.

"I trust, sir, that my name will have other and more personal claims upon posterity," said Challenger, severely. "Any ignoramus can hand down his worthless memory by imposing it upon a mountain or a river. I need no such monument."

Summerlee, with a twisted smile, was about to make some fresh assault when Lord John hastened to intervene.

"It's up to you, young fellah, to name the lake," said he. "You saw it first, and, by George, if you choose to put 'Lake Malone' on it, no one has a better right."

"By all means. Let our young friend give it a name," said Challenger.

"Then," said I, blushing, I dare say, as I said it, "let it be named Lake Gladys."

"Don't you think the Central Lake would be more descriptive?" remarked Summerlee.

"I should prefer Lake Gladys."

Challenger looked at me sympathetically, and shook his great head in mock disapproval. "Boys will be boys," said he. "Lake Gladys let it be."

Chapter XII; "It was Dreadful in the Forest"

I have said—or perhaps I have not said, for my memory plays me sad tricks these days—that I glowed with pride when three such men as my comrades thanked me for having saved, or at least greatly helped, the situation. As the youngster of the party, not merely in years, but in experience, character, knowledge, and all that goes to make a man, I had been overshadowed from the first. And now I was coming into my own. I warmed at the thought. Alas! for the pride which goes before a fall! That little glow of self-satisfaction, that added measure of self-confidence, were to lead me on that very night to the most dreadful experience of my life, ending with a shock which turns my heart sick when I think of it.

It came about in this way. I had been unduly excited by the adventure of the tree, and sleep seemed to be impossible. Summerlee was on guard, sitting hunched over our small fire, a quaint, angular figure, his rifle across his knees and his pointed, goat-like beard wagging with each weary nod of his head. Lord John lay silent, wrapped in the South American poncho which he wore, while Challenger snored with a roll and rattle which reverberated through the woods. The full moon was shining brightly, and the air was crisply cold. What a night for a walk! And then suddenly came the thought, "Why not?" Suppose I stole softly away, suppose I made my way down to the central lake, suppose I was back at breakfast with some record of the place—would I not in that case be thought an even more worthy associate? Then, if Summerlee carried the day and some means of escape were found, we should return to London with first-hand knowledge of the central mystery of the plateau, to which I alone, of all men, would have penetrated. I thought of Gladys, with her "There are heroisms all round us." I seemed to hear her voice as she said it. I thought also of McArdle. What a three column article for the paper! What a foundation for a career! A correspondentship in the next great war might be within my reach. I clutched at a gun—my pockets were full of cartridges—and, parting the thorn bushes at the gate of our zareba, quickly slipped out. My last glance showed me the unconscious Summerlee, most futile of sentinels, still nodding away like a queer mechanical toy in front of the smouldering fire.

I had not gone a hundred yards before I deeply repented my rashness. I may have said somewhere in this chronicle that I am too imaginative to be a really courageous man, but that I have an overpowering fear of seeming afraid. This was the power which now carried me onwards. I simply could not slink back with nothing done. Even if my comrades should not have missed me, and should never know of my weakness, there would still remain some intolerable self-shame in my own soul. And yet I shuddered at the position in which I found myself, and would have given all I possessed at that moment to have been honorably free of the whole business.

It was dreadful in the forest. The trees grew so thickly and their foliage spread so widely that I could see nothing of the moon-light save that here and there the high branches made a tangled filigree against the starry sky. As the eyes became more used to the obscurity one learned that there were different degrees of darkness among the trees—that some were dimly visible, while between and among them there were coal-black shadowed patches, like the mouths of caves, from which I shrank in horror as I passed. I thought of the despairing yell of the tortured iguanodon—that dreadful cry which had echoed through the woods. I thought, too, of the glimpse I had in the light of Lord John's torch of that bloated, warty, blood-slavering muzzle. Even now I was on its hunting-ground. At any instant it might spring upon me from the shadows—this nameless and horrible monster. I stopped, and, picking a cartridge from my pocket, I opened the breech of my gun. As I touched the lever my heart leaped within me. It was the shot-gun, not the rifle, which I had taken!

Again the impulse to return swept over me. Here, surely, was a most excellent reason for my failure—one for which no one would think the less of me. But again the foolish pride fought against that very word. I could not—must not—fail. After all, my rifle would probably have been as useless as a shot-gun against such dangers as I might meet. If I were to go back to camp to change my weapon I could hardly expect to enter and to leave again without being seen. In that case there would be explanations, and my attempt would no longer be all my own. After a little hesitation, then, I screwed up my courage and continued upon my way, my useless gun under my arm.

The darkness of the forest had been alarming, but even worse was the white, still flood of moonlight in the open glade of the iguanodons. Hid among the bushes, I looked out at it. None of the great brutes were in sight. Perhaps the tragedy which had befallen one of them had driven them from their feeding-ground. In the misty, silvery night I could see no sign of any living thing. Taking courage, therefore, I slipped rapidly across it, and among the jungle on the farther side I picked up once again the brook which was my guide. It was a cheery companion, gurgling and chuckling as it ran, like the dear old trout-stream in the West Country where I have fished at night in my boyhood. So long as I followed it down I must come to the lake, and so long as I followed it back I must come to the camp. Often I had to lose sight of it on account of the tangled brush-wood, but I was always within earshot of its tinkle and splash.

As one descended the slope the woods became thinner, and bushes, with occasional high trees, took the place of the forest. I could make good progress, therefore, and I could see without being seen. I passed close to the pterodactyl swamp, and as I did so, with a dry, crisp, leathery rattle of wings, one of these great creatures—it was twenty feet at least from tip to tip—rose up from somewhere near me and soared into the air. As it passed across the face of the moon the light shone clearly through the membranous wings, and it looked like a flying skeleton against the white, tropical radiance. I crouched low among the bushes, for I knew from past experience that with a single cry the creature could bring a hundred of its loathsome mates about my ears. It was not until it had settled again that I dared to steal onwards upon my journey.

The night had been exceedingly still, but as I advanced I became conscious of a low, rumbling sound, a continuous murmur, somewhere in front of me. This grew louder as I proceeded, until at last it was clearly quite close to me. When I stood still the sound was constant, so that it seemed to come from some stationary cause. It was like a boiling kettle or the bubbling of some great pot. Soon I came upon the source of it, for in the center of a small clearing I found a lake—or a pool, rather, for it was not larger than the basin of the Trafalgar Square fountain—of some black, pitch-like stuff, the surface of which rose and fell in great blisters of bursting gas. The air above it was shimmering with heat, and the ground round was so hot that I could hardly bear to lay my hand on it. It was clear that the great volcanic outburst which had raised this strange plateau so many years ago had not yet entirely spent its forces. Blackened rocks and mounds of lava I had already seen everywhere peeping out from amid the luxuriant vegetation which draped them, but this asphalt pool in the jungle was the first sign that we had of actual existing activity on the slopes of the ancient crater. I had no time to examine it further for I had need to hurry if I were to be back in camp in the morning.

It was a fearsome walk, and one which will be with me so long as memory holds. In the great moonlight clearings I slunk along among the shadows on the margin. In the jungle I crept forward, stopping with a beating heart whenever I heard, as I often did, the crash of breaking branches as some wild beast went past. Now and then great shadows loomed up for an instant and were gone—great, silent shadows which seemed to prowl upon padded feet. How often I stopped with the intention of returning, and yet every time my pride conquered my fear, and sent me on again until my object should be attained.

At last (my watch showed that it was one in the morning) I saw the gleam of water amid the openings of the jungle, and ten minutes later I was among the reeds upon the borders of the central lake. I was exceedingly dry, so I lay down and took a long draught of its waters, which were fresh and cold. There was a broad pathway with many tracks upon it at the spot which I had found, so that it was clearly one of the drinking-places of the animals. Close to the water's edge there was a huge isolated block of lava. Up this I climbed, and, lying on the top, I had an excellent view in every direction.

The first thing which I saw filled me with amazement. When I described the view from the summit of the great tree, I said that on the farther cliff I could see a number of dark spots, which appeared to be the mouths of caves. Now, as I looked up at the same cliffs, I saw discs of light in every direction, ruddy, clearly-defined patches, like the port-holes of a liner in the darkness. For a moment I thought it was the lava-glow from some volcanic action; but this could not be so. Any volcanic action would surely be down in the hollow and not high among the rocks. What, then, was the alternative? It was wonderful, and yet it must surely be. These ruddy spots must be the reflection of fires within the caves—fires which could only be lit by the hand of man. There were human beings, then, upon the plateau. How gloriously my expedition was justified! Here was news indeed for us to bear back with us to London!

For a long time I lay and watched these red, quivering blotches of light. I suppose they were ten miles off from me, yet even at that distance one could observe how, from time to time, they twinkled or were obscured as someone passed before them. What would I not have given to be able to crawl up to them, to peep in, and to take back some word to my comrades as to the appearance and character of the race who lived in so strange a place! It was out of the question for the moment, and yet surely we could not leave the plateau until we had some definite knowledge upon the point.

Lake Gladys—my own lake—lay like a sheet of quicksilver before me, with a reflected moon shining brightly in the center of it. It was shallow, for in many places I saw low sandbanks protruding above the water. Everywhere upon the still surface I could see signs of life, sometimes mere rings and ripples in the water, sometimes the gleam of a great silver-sided fish in the air, sometimes the arched, slate-colored back of some passing monster. Once upon a yellow sandbank I saw a creature like a huge swan, with a clumsy body and a high, flexible neck, shuffling about upon the margin. Presently it plunged in, and for some time I could see the arched neck and darting head undulating over the water. Then it dived, and I saw it no more.

My attention was soon drawn away from these distant sights and brought back to what was going on at my very feet. Two creatures like large armadillos had come down to the drinking-place, and were squatting at the edge of the water, their long, flexible tongues like red ribbons shooting in and out as they lapped. A huge deer, with branching horns, a magnificent creature which carried itself like a king, came down with its doe and two fawns and drank beside the armadillos. No such deer exist anywhere else upon earth, for the moose or elks which I have seen would hardly have reached its shoulders. Presently it gave a warning snort, and was off with its family among the reeds, while the armadillos also scuttled for shelter. A new-comer, a most monstrous animal, was coming down the path.

For a moment I wondered where I could have seen that ungainly shape, that arched back with triangular fringes along it, that strange bird-like head held close to the ground. Then it came back, to me. It was the stegosaurus—the very creature which Maple White had preserved in his sketch-book, and which had been the first object which arrested the attention of Challenger! There he was—perhaps the very specimen which the American artist had encountered. The ground shook beneath his tremendous weight, and his gulpings of water resounded through the still night. For five minutes he was so close to my rock that by stretching out my hand I could have touched the hideous waving hackles upon his back. Then he lumbered away and was lost among the boulders.

Looking at my watch, I saw that it was half-past two o'clock, and high time, therefore, that I started upon my homeward journey. There was no difficulty about the direction in which I should return for all along I had kept the little brook upon my left, and it opened into the central lake within a stone's-throw of the boulder upon which I had been lying. I set off, therefore, in high spirits, for I felt that I had done good work and was bringing back a fine budget of news for my companions. Foremost of all, of course, were the sight of the fiery caves and the certainty that some troglodytic race inhabited them. But besides that I could speak from experience of the central lake. I could testify that it was full of strange creatures, and I had seen several land forms of primeval life which we had not before encountered. I reflected as I walked that few men in the world could have spent a stranger night or added more to human knowledge in the course of it.

I was plodding up the slope, turning these thoughts over in my mind, and had reached a point which may have been half-way to home, when my mind was brought back to my own position by a strange noise behind me. It was something between a snore and a growl, low, deep, and exceedingly menacing. Some strange creature was evidently near me, but nothing could be seen, so I hastened more rapidly upon my way. I had traversed half a mile or so when suddenly the sound was repeated, still behind me, but louder and more menacing than before. My heart stood still within me as it flashed across me that the beast, whatever it was, must surely be after ME. My skin grew cold and my hair rose at the thought. That these monsters should tear each other to pieces was a part of the strange struggle for existence, but that they should turn upon modern man, that they should deliberately track and hunt down the predominant human, was a staggering and fearsome thought. I remembered again the blood-beslobbered face which we had seen in the glare of Lord John's torch, like some horrible vision from the deepest circle of Dante's hell. With my knees shaking beneath me, I stood and glared with starting eyes down the moonlit path which lay behind me. All was quiet as in a dream landscape. Silver clearings and the black patches of the bushes—nothing else could I see. Then from out of the silence, imminent and threatening, there came once more that low, throaty croaking, far louder and closer than before. There could no longer be a doubt. Something was on my trail, and was closing in upon me every minute.

I stood like a man paralyzed, still staring at the ground which I had traversed. Then suddenly I saw it. There was movement among the bushes at the far end of the clearing which I had just traversed. A great dark shadow disengaged itself and hopped out into the clear moonlight. I say "hopped" advisedly, for the beast moved like a kangaroo, springing along in an erect position upon its powerful hind legs, while its front ones were held bent in front of it. It was of enormous size and power, like an erect elephant, but its movements, in spite of its bulk, were exceedingly alert. For a moment, as I saw its shape, I hoped that it was an iguanodon, which I knew to be harmless, but, ignorant as I was, I soon saw that this was a very different creature. Instead of the gentle, deer-shaped head of the great three-toed leaf-eater, this beast had a broad, squat, toad-like face like that which had alarmed us in our camp. His ferocious cry and the horrible energy of his pursuit both assured me that this was surely one of the great flesh-eating dinosaurs, the most terrible beasts which have ever walked this earth. As the huge brute loped along it dropped forward upon its fore-paws and brought its nose to the ground every twenty yards or so. It was smelling out my trail. Sometimes, for an instant, it was at fault. Then it would catch it up again and come bounding swiftly along the path I had taken.

Even now when I think of that nightmare the sweat breaks out upon my brow. What could I do? My useless fowling-piece was in my hand. What help could I get from that? I looked desperately round for some rock or tree, but I was in a bushy jungle with nothing higher than a sapling within sight, while I knew that the creature behind me could tear down an ordinary tree as though it were a reed. My only possible chance lay in flight. I could not move swiftly over the rough, broken ground, but as I looked round me in despair I saw a well-marked, hard-beaten path which ran across in front of me. We had seen several of the sort, the runs of various wild beasts, during our expeditions. Along this I could perhaps hold my own, for I was a fast runner, and in excellent condition. Flinging away my useless gun, I set myself to do such a half-mile as I have never done before or since. My limbs ached, my chest heaved, I felt that my throat would burst for want of air, and yet with that horror behind me I ran and I ran and ran. At last I paused, hardly able to move. For a moment I thought that I had thrown him off. The path lay still behind me. And then suddenly, with a crashing and a rending, a thudding of giant feet and a panting of monster lungs the beast was upon me once more. He was at my very heels. I was lost.

Madman that I was to linger so long before I fled! Up to then he had hunted by scent, and his movement was slow. But he had actually seen me as I started to run. From then onwards he had hunted by sight, for the path showed him where I had gone. Now, as he came round the curve, he was springing in great bounds. The moonlight shone upon his huge projecting eyes, the row of enormous teeth in his open mouth, and the gleaming fringe of claws upon his short, powerful forearms. With a scream of terror I turned and rushed wildly down the path. Behind me the thick, gasping breathing of the creature sounded louder and louder. His heavy footfall was beside me. Every instant I expected to feel his grip upon my back. And then suddenly there came a crash—I was falling through space, and everything beyond was darkness and rest.

As I emerged from my unconsciousness—which could not, I think, have lasted more than a few minutes—I was aware of a most dreadful and penetrating smell. Putting out my hand in the darkness I came upon something which felt like a huge lump of meat, while my other hand closed upon a large bone. Up above me there was a circle of starlit sky, which showed me that I was lying at the bottom of a deep pit. Slowly I staggered to my feet and felt myself all over. I was stiff and sore from head to foot, but there was no limb which would not move, no joint which would not bend. As the circumstances of my fall came back into my confused brain, I looked up in terror, expecting to see that dreadful head silhouetted against the paling sky. There was no sign of the monster, however, nor could I hear any sound from above. I began to walk slowly round, therefore, feeling in every direction to find out what this strange place could be into which I had been so opportunely precipitated.

It was, as I have said, a pit, with sharply-sloping walls and a level bottom about twenty feet across. This bottom was littered with great gobbets of flesh, most of which was in the last state of putridity. The atmosphere was poisonous and horrible. After tripping and stumbling over these lumps of decay, I came suddenly against something hard, and I found that an upright post was firmly fixed in the center of the hollow. It was so high that I could not reach the top of it with my hand, and it appeared to be covered with grease.

Suddenly I remembered that I had a tin box of wax-vestas in my pocket. Striking one of them, I was able at last to form some opinion of this place into which I had fallen. There could be no question as to its nature. It was a trap—made by the hand of man. The post in the center, some nine feet long, was sharpened at the upper end, and was black with the stale blood of the creatures who had been impaled upon it. The remains scattered about were fragments of the victims, which had been cut away in order to clear the stake for the next who might blunder in. I remembered that Challenger had declared that man could not exist upon the plateau, since with his feeble weapons he could not hold his own against the monsters who roamed over it. But now it was clear enough how it could be done. In their narrow-mouthed caves the natives, whoever they might be, had refuges into which the huge saurians could not penetrate, while with their developed brains they were capable of setting such traps, covered with branches, across the paths which marked the run of the animals as would destroy them in spite of all their strength and activity. Man was always the master.

The sloping wall of the pit was not difficult for an active man to climb, but I hesitated long before I trusted myself within reach of the dreadful creature which had so nearly destroyed me. How did I know that he was not lurking in the nearest clump of bushes, waiting for my reappearance? I took heart, however, as I recalled a conversation between Challenger and Summerlee upon the habits of the great saurians. Both were agreed that the monsters were practically brainless, that there was no room for reason in their tiny cranial cavities, and that if they have disappeared from the rest of the world it was assuredly on account of their own stupidity, which made it impossible for them to adapt themselves to changing conditions.

To lie in wait for me now would mean that the creature had appreciated what had happened to me, and this in turn would argue some power connecting cause and effect. Surely it was more likely that a brainless creature, acting solely by vague predatory instinct, would give up the chase when I disappeared, and, after a pause of astonishment, would wander away in search of some other prey? I clambered to the edge of the pit and looked over. The stars were fading, the sky was whitening, and the cold wind of morning blew pleasantly upon my face. I could see or hear nothing of my enemy. Slowly I climbed out and sat for a while upon the ground, ready to spring back into my refuge if any danger should appear. Then, reassured by the absolute stillness and by the growing light, I took my courage in both hands and stole back along the path which I had come. Some distance down it I picked up my gun, and shortly afterwards struck the brook which was my guide. So, with many a frightened backward glance, I made for home.

And suddenly there came something to remind me of my absent companions. In the clear, still morning air there sounded far away the sharp, hard note of a single rifle-shot. I paused and listened, but there was nothing more. For a moment I was shocked at the thought that some sudden danger might have befallen them. But then a simpler and more natural explanation came to my mind. It was now broad daylight. No doubt my absence had been noticed. They had imagined, that I was lost in the woods, and had fired this shot to guide me home. It is true that we had made a strict resolution against firing, but if it seemed to them that I might be in danger they would not hesitate. It was for me now to hurry on as fast as possible, and so to reassure them.

I was weary and spent, so my progress was not so fast as I wished; but at last I came into regions which I knew. There was the swamp of the pterodactyls upon my left; there in front of me was the glade of the iguanodons. Now I was in the last belt of trees which separated me from Fort Challenger. I raised my voice in a cheery shout to allay their fears. No answering greeting came back to me. My heart sank at that ominous stillness. I quickened my pace into a run. The zareba rose before me, even as I had left it, but the gate was open. I rushed in. In the cold, morning light it was a fearful sight which met my eyes. Our effects were scattered in wild confusion over the ground; my comrades had disappeared, and close to the smouldering ashes of our fire the grass was stained crimson with a hideous pool of blood.

I was so stunned by this sudden shock that for a time I must have nearly lost my reason. I have a vague recollection, as one remembers a bad dream, of rushing about through the woods all round the empty camp, calling wildly for my companions. No answer came back from the silent shadows. The horrible thought that I might never see them again, that I might find myself abandoned all alone in that dreadful place, with no possible way of descending into the world below, that I might live and die in that nightmare country, drove me to desperation. I could have torn my hair and beaten my head in my despair. Only now did I realize how I had learned to lean upon my companions, upon the serene self-confidence of Challenger, and upon the masterful, humorous coolness of Lord John Roxton. Without them I was like a child in the dark, helpless and powerless. I did not know which way to turn or what I should do first.

After a period, during which I sat in bewilderment, I set myself to try and discover what sudden misfortune could have befallen my companions. The whole disordered appearance of the camp showed that there had been some sort of attack, and the rifle-shot no doubt marked the time when it had occurred. That there should have been only one shot showed that it had been all over in an instant. The rifles still lay upon the ground, and one of them—Lord John's—had the empty cartridge in the breech. The blankets of Challenger and of Summerlee beside the fire suggested that they had been asleep at the time. The cases of ammunition and of food were scattered about in a wild litter, together with our unfortunate cameras and plate-carriers, but none of them were missing. On the other hand, all the exposed provisions—and I remembered that there were a considerable quantity of them—were gone. They were animals, then, and not natives, who had made the inroad, for surely the latter would have left nothing behind.

But if animals, or some single terrible animal, then what had become of my comrades? A ferocious beast would surely have destroyed them and left their remains. It is true that there was that one hideous pool of blood, which told of violence. Such a monster as had pursued me during the night could have carried away a victim as easily as a cat would a mouse. In that case the others would have followed in pursuit. But then they would assuredly have taken their rifles with them. The more I tried to think it out with my confused and weary brain the less could I find any plausible explanation. I searched round in the forest, but could see no tracks which could help me to a conclusion. Once I lost myself, and it was only by good luck, and after an hour of wandering, that I found the camp once more.

Suddenly a thought came to me and brought some little comfort to my heart. I was not absolutely alone in the world. Down at the bottom of the cliff, and within call of me, was waiting the faithful Zambo. I went to the edge of the plateau and looked over. Sure enough, he was squatting among his blankets beside his fire in his little camp. But, to my amazement, a second man was seated in front of him. For an instant my heart leaped for joy, as I thought that one of my comrades had made his way safely down. But a second glance dispelled the hope. The rising sun shone red upon the man's skin. He was an Indian. I shouted loudly and waved my handkerchief. Presently Zambo looked up, waved his hand, and turned to ascend the pinnacle. In a short time he was standing close to me and listening with deep distress to the story which I told him.

"Devil got them for sure, Massa Malone," said he. "You got into the devil's country, sah, and he take you all to himself. You take advice, Massa Malone, and come down quick, else he get you as well."

"How can I come down, Zambo?"

"You get creepers from trees, Massa Malone. Throw them over here. I make fast to this stump, and so you have bridge."

"We have thought of that. There are no creepers here which could bear us."

"Send for ropes, Massa Malone."

"Who can I send, and where?"

"Send to Indian villages, sah. Plenty hide rope in Indian village. Indian down below; send him."

"Who is he?

"One of our Indians. Other ones beat him and take away his pay. He come back to us. Ready now to take letter, bring rope,--anything."

To take a letter! Why not? Perhaps he might bring help; but in any case he would ensure that our lives were not spent for nothing, and that news of all that we had won for Science should reach our friends at home. I had two completed letters already waiting. I would spend the day in writing a third, which would bring my experiences absolutely up to date. The Indian could bear this back to the world. I ordered Zambo, therefore, to come again in the evening, and I spent my miserable and lonely day in recording my own adventures of the night before. I also drew up a note, to be given to any white merchant or captain of a steam-boat whom the Indian could find, imploring them to see that ropes were sent to us, since our lives must depend upon it. These documents I threw to Zambo in the evening, and also my purse, which contained three English sovereigns. These were to be given to the Indian, and he was promised twice as much if he returned with the ropes.

So now you will understand, my dear Mr. McArdle, how this communication reaches you, and you will also know the truth, in case you never hear again from your unfortunate correspondent. To-night I am too weary and too depressed to make my plans. Tomorrow I must think out some way by which I shall keep in touch with this camp, and yet search round for any traces of my unhappy friends.

Chapter XIII; "A Sight which I shall Never Forget"

Just as the sun was setting upon that melancholy night I saw the lonely figure of the Indian upon the vast plain beneath me, and I watched him, our one faint hope of salvation, until he disappeared in the rising mists of evening which lay, rose-tinted from the setting sun, between the far-off river and me.

It was quite dark when I at last turned back to our stricken camp, and my last vision as I went was the red gleam of Zambo's fire, the one point of light in the wide world below, as was his faithful presence in my own shadowed soul. And yet I felt happier than I had done since this crushing blow had fallen upon me, for it was good to think that the world should know what we had done, so that at the worst our names should not perish with our bodies, but should go down to posterity associated with the result of our labors.

It was an awesome thing to sleep in that ill-fated camp; and yet it was even more unnerving to do so in the jungle. One or the other it must be. Prudence, on the one hand, warned me that I should remain on guard, but exhausted Nature, on the other, declared that I should do nothing of the kind. I climbed up on to a limb of the great gingko tree, but there was no secure perch on its rounded surface, and I should certainly have fallen off and broken my neck the moment I began to doze. I got down, therefore, and pondered over what I should do. Finally, I closed the door of the zareba, lit three separate fires in a triangle, and having eaten a hearty supper dropped off into a profound sleep, from which I had a strange and most welcome awakening. In the early morning, just as day was breaking, a hand was laid upon my arm, and starting up, with all my nerves in a tingle and my hand feeling for a rifle, I gave a cry of joy as in the cold gray light I saw Lord John Roxton kneeling beside me.

It was he—and yet it was not he. I had left him calm in his bearing, correct in his person, prim in his dress. Now he was pale and wild-eyed, gasping as he breathed like one who has run far and fast. His gaunt face was scratched and bloody, his clothes were hanging in rags, and his hat was gone. I stared in amazement, but he gave me no chance for questions. He was grabbing at our stores all the time he spoke.

"Quick, young fellah! Quick!" he cried. "Every moment counts. Get the rifles, both of them. I have the other two. Now, all the cartridges you can gather. Fill up your pockets. Now, some food. Half a dozen tins will do. That's all right! Don't wait to talk or think. Get a move on, or we are done!"

Still half-awake, and unable to imagine what it all might mean, I found myself hurrying madly after him through the wood, a rifle under each arm and a pile of various stores in my hands. He dodged in and out through the thickest of the scrub until he came to a dense clump of brush-wood. Into this he rushed, regardless of thorns, and threw himself into the heart of it, pulling me down by his side.

"There!" he panted. "I think we are safe here. They'll make for the camp as sure as fate. It will be their first idea. But this should puzzle 'em."

"What is it all?" I asked, when I had got my breath. "Where are the professors? And who is it that is after us?"

"The ape-men," he cried. "My God, what brutes! Don't raise your voice, for they have long ears—sharp eyes, too, but no power of scent, so far as I could judge, so I don't think they can sniff us out. Where have you been, young fellah? You were well out of it."

In a few sentences I whispered what I had done.

"Pretty bad," said he, when he had heard of the dinosaur and the pit. "It isn't quite the place for a rest cure. What? But I had no idea what its possibilities were until those devils got hold of us. The man-eatin' Papuans had me once, but they are Chesterfields compared to this crowd."

"How did it happen?" I asked.

"It was in the early mornin'. Our learned friends were just stirrin'. Hadn't even begun to argue yet. Suddenly it rained apes. They came down as thick as apples out of a tree. They had been assemblin' in the dark, I suppose, until that great tree over our heads was heavy with them. I shot one of them through the belly, but before we knew where we were they had us spread-eagled on our backs. I call them apes, but they carried sticks and stones in their hands and jabbered talk to each other, and ended up by tyin' our hands with creepers, so they are ahead of any beast that I have seen in my wanderin's. Ape-men—that's what they are—Missin' Links, and I wish they had stayed missin'. They carried off their wounded comrade—he was bleedin' like a pig—and then they sat around us, and if ever I saw frozen murder it was in their faces. They were big fellows, as big as a man and a deal stronger. Curious glassy gray eyes they have, under red tufts, and they just sat and gloated and gloated. Challenger is no chicken, but even he was cowed. He managed to struggle to his feet, and yelled out at them to have done with it and get it over. I think he had gone a bit off his head at the suddenness of it, for he raged and cursed at them like a lunatic. If they had been a row of his favorite Pressmen he could not have slanged them worse."

"Well, what did they do?" I was enthralled by the strange story which my companion was whispering into my ear, while all the time his keen eyes were shooting in every direction and his hand grasping his cocked rifle.

"I thought it was the end of us, but instead of that it started them on a new line. They all jabbered and chattered together. Then one of them stood out beside Challenger. You'll smile, young fellah, but 'pon my word they might have been kinsmen. I couldn't have believed it if I hadn't seen it with my own eyes. This old ape-man—he was their chief—was a sort of red Challenger, with every one of our friend's beauty points, only just a trifle more so. He had the short body, the big shoulders, the round chest, no neck, a great ruddy frill of a beard, the tufted eyebrows, the 'What do you want, damn you!' look about the eyes, and the whole catalogue. When the ape-man stood by Challenger and put his paw on his shoulder, the thing was complete. Summerlee was a bit hysterical, and he laughed till he cried. The ape-men laughed too—or at least they put up the devil of a cacklin'—and they set to work to drag us off through the forest. They wouldn't touch the guns and things—thought them dangerous, I expect—but they carried away all our loose food. Summerlee and I got some rough handlin' on the way—there's my skin and my clothes to prove it—for they took us a bee-line through the brambles, and their own hides are like leather. But Challenger was all right. Four of them carried him shoulder high, and he went like a Roman emperor. What's that?"

It was a strange clicking noise in the distance not unlike castanets.

"There they go!" said my companion, slipping cartridges into the second double barrelled "Express." "Load them all up, young fellah my lad, for we're not going to be taken alive, and don't you think it! That's the row they make when they are excited. By George! they'll have something to excite them if they put us up. The 'Last Stand of the Grays' won't be in it. 'With their rifles grasped in their stiffened hands, mid a ring of the dead and dyin',' as some fathead sings. Can you hear them now?"

"Very far away."

"That little lot will do no good, but I expect their search parties are all over the wood. Well, I was telling you my tale of woe. They got us soon to this town of theirs—about a thousand huts of branches and leaves in a great grove of trees near the edge of the cliff. It's three or four miles from here. The filthy beasts fingered me all over, and I feel as if I should never be clean again. They tied us up—the fellow who handled me could tie like a bosun—and there we lay with our toes up, beneath a tree, while a great brute stood guard over us with a club in his hand. When I say 'we' I mean Summerlee and myself. Old Challenger was up a tree, eatin' pines and havin' the time of his life. I'm bound to say that he managed to get some fruit to us, and with his own hands he loosened our bonds. If you'd seen him sitting up in that tree hobnobbin' with his twin brother—and singin' in that rollin' bass of his, 'Ring out, wild bells,' cause music of any kind seemed to put 'em in a good humor, you'd have smiled; but we weren't in much mood for laughin', as you can guess. They were inclined, within limits, to let him do what he liked, but they drew the line pretty sharply at us. It was a mighty consolation to us all to know that you were runnin' loose and had the archives in your keepin'.

"Well, now, young fellah, I'll tell you what will surprise you. You say you saw signs of men, and fires, traps, and the like. Well, we have seen the natives themselves. Poor devils they were, down-faced little chaps, and had enough to make them so. It seems that the humans hold one side of this plateau—over yonder, where you saw the caves—and the ape-men hold this side, and there is bloody war between them all the time. That's the situation, so far as I could follow it. Well, yesterday the ape-men got hold of a dozen of the humans and brought them in as prisoners. You never heard such a jabberin' and shriekin' in your life. The men were little red fellows, and had been bitten and clawed so that they could hardly walk. The ape-men put two of them to death there and then—fairly pulled the arm off one of them—it was perfectly beastly. Plucky little chaps they are, and hardly gave a squeak. But it turned us absolutely sick. Summerlee fainted, and even Challenger had as much as he could stand. I think they have cleared, don't you?"

We listened intently, but nothing save the calling of the birds broke the deep peace of the forest. Lord Roxton went on with his story.

"I think you have had the escape of your life, young fellah my lad. It was catchin' those Indians that put you clean out of their heads, else they would have been back to the camp for you as sure as fate and gathered you in. Of course, as you said, they have been watchin' us from the beginnin' out of that tree, and they knew perfectly well that we were one short. However, they could think only of this new haul; so it was I, and not a bunch of apes, that dropped in on you in the morning. Well, we had a horrid business afterwards. My God! what a nightmare the whole thing is! You remember the great bristle of sharp canes down below where we found the skeleton of the American? Well, that is just under ape-town, and that's the jumpin'-off place of their prisoners. I expect there's heaps of skeletons there, if we looked for 'em. They have a sort of clear parade-ground on the top, and they make a proper ceremony about it. One by one the poor devils have to jump, and the game is to see whether they are merely dashed to pieces or whether they get skewered on the canes. They took us out to see it, and the whole tribe lined up on the edge. Four of the Indians jumped, and the canes went through 'em like knittin' needles through a pat of butter. No wonder we found that poor Yankee's skeleton with the canes growin' between his ribs. It was horrible—but it was doocedly interestin' too. We were all fascinated to see them take the dive, even when we thought it would be our turn next on the spring-board.

"Well, it wasn't. They kept six of the Indians up for today—that's how I understood it—but I fancy we were to be the star performers in the show. Challenger might get off, but Summerlee and I were in the bill. Their language is more than half signs, and it was not hard to follow them. So I thought it was time we made a break for it. I had been plottin' it out a bit, and had one or two things clear in my mind. It was all on me, for Summerlee was useless and Challenger not much better. The only time they got together they got slangin' because they couldn't agree upon the scientific classification of these red-headed devils that had got hold of us. One said it was the dryopithecus of Java, the other said it was pithecanthropus. Madness, I call it—Loonies, both. But, as I say, I had thought out one or two points that were helpful. One was that these brutes could not run as fast as a man in the open. They have short, bandy legs, you see, and heavy bodies. Even Challenger could give a few yards in a hundred to the best of them, and you or I would be a perfect Shrubb. Another point was that they knew nothin' about guns. I don't believe they ever understood how the fellow I shot came by his hurt. If we could get at our guns there was no sayin' what we could do.

"So I broke away early this mornin', gave my guard a kick in the tummy that laid him out, and sprinted for the camp. There I got you and the guns, and here we are."

"But the professors!" I cried, in consternation.

"Well, we must just go back and fetch 'em. I couldn't bring 'em with me. Challenger was up the tree, and Summerlee was not fit for the effort. The only chance was to get the guns and try a rescue. Of course they may scupper them at once in revenge. I don't think they would touch Challenger, but I wouldn't answer for Summerlee. But they would have had him in any case. Of that I am certain. So I haven't made matters any worse by boltin'. But we are honor bound to go back and have them out or see it through with them. So you can make up your soul, young fellah my lad, for it will be one way or the other before evenin'."

I have tried to imitate here Lord Roxton's jerky talk, his short, strong sentences, the half-humorous, half-reckless tone that ran through it all. But he was a born leader. As danger thickened his jaunty manner would increase, his speech become more racy, his cold eyes glitter into ardent life, and his Don Quixote moustache bristle with joyous excitement. His love of danger, his intense appreciation of the drama of an adventure—all the more intense for being held tightly in—his consistent view that every peril in life is a form of sport, a fierce game betwixt you and Fate, with Death as a forfeit, made him a wonderful companion at such hours. If it were not for our fears as to the fate of our companions, it would have been a positive joy to throw myself with such a man into such an affair. We were rising from our brushwood hiding-place when suddenly I felt his grip upon my arm.

"By George!" he whispered, "here they come!"

From where we lay we could look down a brown aisle, arched with green, formed by the trunks and branches. Along this a party of the ape-men were passing. They went in single file, with bent legs and rounded backs, their hands occasionally touching the ground, their heads turning to left and right as they trotted along. Their crouching gait took away from their height, but I should put them at five feet or so, with long arms and enormous chests. Many of them carried sticks, and at the distance they looked like a line of very hairy and deformed human beings. For a moment I caught this clear glimpse of them. Then they were lost among the bushes.

"Not this time," said Lord John, who had caught up his rifle. "Our best chance is to lie quiet until they have given up the search. Then we shall see whether we can't get back to their town and hit 'em where it hurts most. Give 'em an hour and we'll march."

We filled in the time by opening one of our food tins and making sure of our breakfast. Lord Roxton had had nothing but some fruit since the morning before and ate like a starving man. Then, at last, our pockets bulging with cartridges and a rifle in each hand, we started off upon our mission of rescue. Before leaving it we carefully marked our little hiding-place among the brush-wood and its bearing to Fort Challenger, that we might find it again if we needed it. We slunk through the bushes in silence until we came to the very edge of the cliff, close to the old camp. There we halted, and Lord John gave me some idea of his plans.

"So long as we are among the thick trees these swine are our masters," said he. "They can see us and we cannot see them. But in the open it is different. There we can move faster than they. So we must stick to the open all we can. The edge of the plateau has fewer large trees than further inland. So that's our line of advance. Go slowly, keep your eyes open and your rifle ready. Above all, never let them get you prisoner while there is a cartridge left—that's my last word to you, young fellah."

When we reached the edge of the cliff I looked over and saw our good old black Zambo sitting smoking on a rock below us. I would have given a great deal to have hailed him and told him how we were placed, but it was too dangerous, lest we should be heard. The woods seemed to be full of the ape-men; again and again we heard their curious clicking chatter. At such times we plunged into the nearest clump of bushes and lay still until the sound had passed away. Our advance, therefore, was very slow, and two hours at least must have passed before I saw by Lord John's cautious movements that we must be close to our destination. He motioned to me to lie still, and he crawled forward himself. In a minute he was back again, his face quivering with eagerness.

"Come!" said he. "Come quick! I hope to the Lord we are not too late already!"

I found myself shaking with nervous excitement as I scrambled forward and lay down beside him, looking out through the bushes at a clearing which stretched before us.

It was a sight which I shall never forget until my dying day—so weird, so impossible, that I do not know how I am to make you realize it, or how in a few years I shall bring myself to believe in it if I live to sit once more on a lounge in the Savage Club and look out on the drab solidity of the Embankment. I know that it will seem then to be some wild nightmare, some delirium of fever. Yet I will set it down now, while it is still fresh in my memory, and one at least, the man who lay in the damp grasses by my side, will know if I have lied.

A wide, open space lay before us—some hundreds of yards across—all green turf and low bracken growing to the very edge of the cliff. Round this clearing there was a semi-circle of trees with curious huts built of foliage piled one above the other among the branches. A rookery, with every nest a little house, would best convey the idea. The openings of these huts and the branches of the trees were thronged with a dense mob of ape-people, whom from their size I took to be the females and infants of the tribe. They formed the background of the picture, and were all looking out with eager interest at the same scene which fascinated and bewildered us.

In the open, and near the edge of the cliff, there had assembled a crowd of some hundred of these shaggy, red-haired creatures, many of them of immense size, and all of them horrible to look upon. There was a certain discipline among them, for none of them attempted to break the line which had been formed. In front there stood a small group of Indians—little, clean-limbed, red fellows, whose skins glowed like polished bronze in the strong sunlight. A tall, thin white man was standing beside them, his head bowed, his arms folded, his whole attitude expressive of his horror and dejection. There was no mistaking the angular form of Professor Summerlee.

In front of and around this dejected group of prisoners were several ape-men, who watched them closely and made all escape impossible. Then, right out from all the others and close to the edge of the cliff, were two figures, so strange, and under other circumstances so ludicrous, that they absorbed my attention. The one was our comrade, Professor Challenger. The remains of his coat still hung in strips from his shoulders, but his shirt had been all torn out, and his great beard merged itself in the black tangle which covered his mighty chest. He had lost his hat, and his hair, which had grown long in our wanderings, was flying in wild disorder. A single day seemed to have changed him from the highest product of modern civilization to the most desperate savage in South America. Beside him stood his master, the king of the ape-men. In all things he was, as Lord John had said, the very image of our Professor, save that his coloring was red instead of black. The same short, broad figure, the same heavy shoulders, the same forward hang of the arms, the same bristling beard merging itself in the hairy chest. Only above the eyebrows, where the sloping forehead and low, curved skull of the ape-man were in sharp contrast to the broad brow and magnificent cranium of the European, could one see any marked difference. At every other point the king was an absurd parody of the Professor.

All this, which takes me so long to describe, impressed itself upon me in a few seconds. Then we had very different things to think of, for an active drama was in progress. Two of the ape-men had seized one of the Indians out of the group and dragged him forward to the edge of the cliff. The king raised his hand as a signal. They caught the man by his leg and arm, and swung him three times backwards and forwards with tremendous violence. Then, with a frightful heave they shot the poor wretch over the precipice. With such force did they throw him that he curved high in the air before beginning to drop. As he vanished from sight, the whole assembly, except the guards, rushed forward to the edge of the precipice, and there was a long pause of absolute silence, broken by a mad yell of delight. They sprang about, tossing their long, hairy arms in the air and howling with exultation. Then they fell back from the edge, formed themselves again into line, and waited for the next victim.

This time it was Summerlee. Two of his guards caught him by the wrists and pulled him brutally to the front. His thin figure and long limbs struggled and fluttered like a chicken being dragged from a coop. Challenger had turned to the king and waved his hands frantically before him. He was begging, pleading, imploring for his comrade's life. The ape-man pushed him roughly aside and shook his head. It was the last conscious movement he was to make upon earth. Lord John's rifle cracked, and the king sank down, a tangled red sprawling thing, upon the ground.

"Shoot into the thick of them! Shoot! sonny, shoot!" cried my companion. who?

There are strange red depths in the soul of the most commonplace man. I am tenderhearted by nature, and have found my eyes moist many a time over the scream of a wounded hare. Yet the blood lust was on me now. I found myself on my feet emptying one magazine, then the other, clicking open the breech to re-load, snapping it to again, while cheering and yelling with pure ferocity and joy of slaughter as I did so. With our four guns the two of us made a horrible havoc. Both the guards who held Summerlee were down, and he was staggering about like a drunken man in his amazement, unable to realize that he was a free man. The dense mob of ape-men ran about in bewilderment, marveling whence this storm of death was coming or what it might mean. They waved, gesticulated, screamed, and tripped up over those who had fallen. Then, with a sudden impulse, they all rushed in a howling crowd to the trees for shelter, leaving the ground behind them spotted with their stricken comrades. The prisoners were left for the moment standing alone in the middle of the clearing.

where'd they get guns?

Challenger's quick brain had grasped the situation. He seized the bewildered Summerlee by the arm, and they both ran towards us. Two of their guards bounded after them and fell to two bullets from Lord John. We ran forward into the open to meet our friends, and pressed a loaded rifle into the hands of each. But Summerlee was at the end of his strength. He could hardly totter. Already the ape-men were recovering from their panic. They were coming through the brushwood and threatening to cut us off. Challenger and I ran Summerlee along, one at each of his elbows, while Lord John covered our retreat, firing again and again as savage heads snarled at us out of the bushes. For a mile or more the chattering brutes were at our very heels. Then the pursuit slackened, for they learned our power and would no longer face that unerring rifle. When we had at last reached the camp, we looked back and found ourselves alone.

So it seemed to us; and yet we were mistaken. We had hardly closed the thornbush door of our zareba, clasped each other's hands, and thrown ourselves panting upon the ground beside our spring, when we heard a patter of feet and then a gentle, plaintive crying from outside our entrance. Lord Roxton rushed forward, rifle in hand, and threw it open. There, prostrate upon their faces, lay the little red figures of the four surviving Indians, trembling with fear of us and yet imploring our protection. With an expressive sweep of his hands one of them pointed to the woods around them, and indicated that they were full of danger. Then, darting forward, he threw his arms round Lord John's legs, and rested his face upon them.

"By George!" cried our peer, pulling at his moustache in great perplexity, "I say—what the deuce are we to do with these people? Get up, little chappie, and take your face off my boots."

Summerlee was sitting up and stuffing some tobacco into his old briar.

"We've got to see them safe," said he. "You've pulled us all out of the jaws of death. My word! it was a good bit of work!"

"Admirable!" cried Challenger. "Admirable! Not only we as individuals, but European science collectively, owe you a deep debt of gratitude for what you have done. I do not hesitate to say that the disappearance of Professor Summerlee and myself would have left an appreciable gap in modern zoological history. Our young friend here and you have done most excellently well."

He beamed at us with the old paternal smile, but European science would have been somewhat amazed could they have seen their chosen child, the hope of the future, with his tangled, unkempt head, his bare chest, and his tattered clothes. He had one of the meat-tins between his knees, and sat with a large piece of cold Australian mutton between his fingers. The Indian looked up at him, and then, with a little yelp, cringed to the ground and clung to Lord John's leg.

"Don't you be scared, my bonnie boy," said Lord John, patting the matted head in front of him. "He can't stick your appearance, Challenger; and, by George! I don't wonder. All right, little chap, he's only a human, just the same as the rest of us."

"Really, sir!" cried the Professor.

"Well, it's lucky for you, Challenger, that you ARE a little out of the ordinary. If you hadn't been so like the king----"

"Upon my word, Lord John, you allow yourself great latitude."

"Well, it's a fact."

"I beg, sir, that you will change the subject. Your remarks are irrelevant and unintelligible. The question before us is what are we to do with these Indians? The obvious thing is to escort them home, if we knew where their home was."

"There is no difficulty about that," said I. "They live in the caves on the other side of the central lake."

"Our young friend here knows where they live. I gather that it is some distance."

"A good twenty miles," said I.

Summerlee gave a groan.

"I, for one, could never get there. Surely I hear those brutes still howling upon our track."

As he spoke, from the dark recesses of the woods we heard far away the jabbering cry of the ape-men. The Indians once more set up a feeble wail of fear.

"We must move, and move quick!" said Lord John. "You help Summerlee, young fellah. These Indians will carry stores. Now, then, come along before they can see us."

In less than half-an-hour we had reached our brushwood retreat and concealed ourselves. All day we heard the excited calling of the ape-men in the direction of our old camp, but none of them came our way, and the tired fugitives, red and white, had a long, deep sleep. I was dozing myself in the evening when someone plucked my sleeve, and I found Challenger kneeling beside me.

"You keep a diary of these events, and you expect eventually to publish it, Mr. Malone," said he, with solemnity.

"I am only here as a Press reporter," I answered.

"Exactly. You may have heard some rather fatuous remarks of Lord John Roxton's which seemed to imply that there was some—some resemblance----"

"Yes, I heard them."

"I need not say that any publicity given to such an idea—any levity in your narrative of what occurred—would be exceedingly offensive to me."

"I will keep well within the truth."

"Lord John's observations are frequently exceedingly fanciful, and he is capable of attributing the most absurd reasons to the respect which is always shown by the most undeveloped races to dignity and character. You follow my meaning?"

"Entirely."

"I leave the matter to your discretion." Then, after a long pause, he added: "The king of the ape-men was really a creature of great distinction—a most remarkably handsome and intelligent personality. Did it not strike you?"

"A most remarkable creature," said I.

And the Professor, much eased in his mind, settled down to his slumber once more.

Chapter XIV; "Those Were the Real Conquests"

We had imagined that our pursuers, the ape-men, knew nothing of our brushwood hiding-place, but we were soon to find out our mistake. There was no sound in the woods—not a leaf moved upon the trees, and all was peace around us—but we should have been warned by our first experience how cunningly and how patiently these creatures can watch and wait until their chance comes. Whatever fate may be mine through life, I am very sure that I shall never be nearer death than I was that morning. But I will tell you the thing in its due order.

We all awoke exhausted after the terrific emotions and scanty food of yesterday. Summerlee was still so weak that it was an effort for him to stand; but the old man was full of a sort of surly courage which would never admit defeat. A council was held, and it was agreed that we should wait quietly for an hour or two where we were, have our much-needed breakfast, and then make our way across the plateau and round the central lake to the caves where my observations had shown that the Indians lived. We relied upon the fact that we could count upon the good word of whom we had rescued to ensure a warm welcome from their fellows. Then, our mission accomplished and possessing a fuller knowledge of the secrets of ɔle White Land, we should turn our whole thoughts to the vital problem of our escape and return. Even Challenger was ready to admit that we should then have done all for which we had come, and that our first duty from that time onwards was to carry back to civilization the amazing discoveries we had made.

We were able now to take a more leisurely view of the Indians whom we had rescued. They were small men, wiry, active, and well-built, with lank black hair tied up in a bunch behind their heads with a leathern thong, and leathern also were their loin-clothes. Their faces were hairless, well formed, and good-humored. The lobes of their ears, hanging ragged and bloody, showed that they had been pierced for some ornaments which their captors had torn out. Their speech, though unintelligible to us, was fluent among themselves, and as they pointed to each other and uttered the word "Accala" many times over, we gathered that this was the name of the nation. Occasionally, with faces which were convulsed with fear and hatred, they shook their clenched hands at the woods round and cried: "Doda! Doda!" which was surely their term for their enemies.

"What do you make of them, Challenger?" asked Lord John. "One thing is very clear to me, and that is that the little chap with the front of his head shaved is a chief among them."

It was indeed evident that this man stood apart from the others, and that they never ventured to address him without every sign of deep respect. He seemed to be the youngest of them all, and yet, so proud and high was his spirit that, upon Challenger laying his great hand upon his head, he started like a spurred horse and, with a quick flash of his dark eyes, moved further away from the Professor. Then, placing his hand upon his breast and holding himself with great dignity, he uttered the word "Maretas" several times. The Professor, unabashed, seized the nearest Indian by the shoulder and proceeded to lecture upon him as if he were a potted specimen in a class-room.

"The type of these people," said he in his sonorous fashion, "whether judged by cranial capacity, facial angle, or any other test, cannot be regarded as a low one; on the contrary, we must place it as considerably higher in the scale than many South American tribes which I can mention. On no possible supposition can we explain the evolution of such a race in this place. For that matter, so great a gap separates these ape-men from the primitive animals which have survived upon this plateau, that it is inadmissible to think that they could have developed where we find them."

"Then where the dooce did they drop from?" asked Lord John.

"A question which will, no doubt, be eagerly discussed in every scientific society in Europe and America," the Professor answered. "My own reading of the situation for what it is worth—" he inflated his chest enormously and looked insolently around him at the words—"is that evolution has advanced under the peculiar conditions of this country up to the vertebrate stage, the old types surviving and living on in company with the newer ones. Thus we find such modern creatures as the tapir—an animal with quite a respectable length of pedigree—the great deer, and the ant-eater in the companionship of reptilian forms of jurassic type. So much is clear. And now come the ape-men and the Indian. What is the scientific mind to think of their presence? I can only account for it by an invasion from outside. It is probable that there existed an anthropoid ape in South America, who in past ages found his way to this place, and that he developed into the creatures we have seen, some of which"—

here he looked hard at me—"were of an appearance and shape which, if it had been accompanied by corresponding intelligence, would, I do not hesitate to say, have reflected credit upon any living race. As to the Indians I cannot doubt that they are more recent immigrants from below. Under the stress of famine or of conquest they have made their way up here. Faced by ferocious creatures which they had never before seen, they took refuge in the caves which our young friend has described, but they have no doubt had a bitter fight to hold their own against wild beasts, and especially against the ape-men who would regard them as intruders, and wage a merciless war upon them with a cunning which the larger beasts would lack. Hence the fact that their numbers appear to be limited. Well, gentlemen, have I read you the riddle aright, or is there any point which you would query?"

Professor Summerlee for once was too depressed to argue, though he shook his head violently as a token of general disagreement. Lord John merely scratched his scanty locks with the remark that he couldn't put up a fight as he wasn't in the same weight or class. For my own part I performed my usual role of bringing things down to a strictly prosaic and practical level by the remark that one of the Indians was missing.

"He has gone to fetch some water," said Lord Roxton. "We fitted him up with an empty beef tin and he is off."

"To the old camp?" I asked.

"No, to the brook. It's among the trees there. It can't be more than a couple of hundred yards. But the beggar is certainly taking his time."

"I'll go and look after him," said I. I picked up my rifle and strolled in the direction of the brook, leaving my friends to lay out the scanty breakfast. It may seem to you rash that even for so short a distance I should quit the shelter of our friendly thicket, but you will remember that we were many miles from Ape-town, that so far as we knew the creatures had not discovered our retreat, and that in any case with a rifle in my hands I had no fear of them. I had not yet learned their cunning or their strength.

I could hear the murmur of our brook somewhere ahead of me, but there was a tangle of trees and brushwood between me and it. I was making my way through this at a point which was just out of sight of my companions, when, under one of the trees, I noticed something red huddled among the bushes. As I approached it, I was shocked to see that it was the dead body of the missing Indian. He lay upon his side, his limbs drawn up, and his head screwed round at a most unnatural angle, so that he seemed to be looking straight over his own shoulder. I gave a cry to warn my friends that something was amiss, and running forwards I stooped over the body. Surely my guardian angel was very near me then, for some instinct of fear, or it may have been some faint rustle of leaves, made me glance upwards. Out of the thick green foliage which hung low over my head, two long muscular arms covered with reddish hair were slowly descending. Another instant and the great stealthy hands would have been round my throat. I sprang backwards, but quick as I was, those hands were quicker still. Through my sudden spring they missed a fatal grip, but one of them caught the back of my neck and the other one my face. I threw my hands up to protect my throat, and the next moment the huge paw had slid down my face and closed over them. I was lifted lightly from the ground, and I felt an intolerable pressure forcing my head back and back until the strain upon the cervical spine was more than I could bear. My senses swam, but I still tore at the hand and forced it out from my chin. Looking up I saw a frightful face with cold inexorable light blue eyes looking down into mine. There was something hypnotic in those terrible eyes. I could struggle no longer. As the creature felt me grow limp in his grasp, two white canines gleamed for a moment at each side of the vile mouth, and the grip tightened still more upon my chin, forcing it always upwards and back. A thin, oval-tinted mist formed before my eyes and little silvery bells tinkled in my ears. Dully and far off I heard the crack of a rifle and was feebly aware of the shock as I was dropped to the earth, where I lay without sense or motion.

I awoke to find myself on my back upon the grass in our lair within the thicket. Someone had brought the water from the brook, and Lord John was sprinkling my head with it, while Challenger and Summerlee were propping me up, with concern in their faces. For a moment I had a glimpse of the human spirits behind their scientific masks. It was really shock, rather than any injury, which had prostrated me, and in half-an-hour, in spite of aching head and stiff neck, I was sitting up and ready for anything.

"But you've had the escape of your life, young fellah my lad," said Lord Roxton. "When I heard your cry and ran forward, and saw your head twisted half-off and your stohwassers kickin' in the air, I thought we were one short. I missed the beast in my flurry, but he dropped you all right and was off like a streak. By George! I wish I had fifty men with rifles. I'd clear out the whole infernal gang of them and leave this country a bit cleaner than we found it."

It was clear now that the ape-men had in some way marked us down, and that we were watched on every side. We had not so much to fear from them during the day, but they would be very likely to rush us by night; so the sooner we got away from their neighborhood the better. On three sides of us was absolute forest, and there we might find ourselves in an ambush. But on the fourth side—that which sloped down in the direction of the lake—there was only low scrub, with scattered trees and occasional open glades. It was, in fact, the route which I had myself taken in my solitary journey, and it led us straight for the Indian caves. This then must for every reason be our road.

One great regret we had, and that was to leave our old camp behind us, not only for the sake of the stores which remained there, but even more because we were losing touch with Zambo, our link with the outside world. However, we had a fair supply of cartridges and all our guns, so, for a time at least, we could look after ourselves, and we hoped soon to have a chance of returning and restoring our communications with our negro. He had faithfully promised to stay where he was, and we had not a doubt that he would be as good as his word.

It was in the early afternoon that we started upon our journey. The young chief walked at our head as our guide, but refused indignantly to carry any burden. Behind him came the two surviving Indians with our scanty possessions upon their backs. We four white men walked in the rear with rifles loaded and ready. As we started there broke from the thick silent woods behind us a sudden great ululation of the ape-men, which may have been a cheer of triumph at our departure or a jeer of contempt at our flight. Looking back we saw only the dense screen of trees, but that long-drawn yell told us how many of our enemies lurked among them. We saw no sign of pursuit, however, and soon we had got into more open country and beyond their power.

As I tramped along, the rearmost of the four, I could not help smiling at the appearance of my three companions in front. Was this the luxurious Lord John Roxton who had sat that evening in the Albany amidst his Persian rugs and his pictures in the pink radiance of the tinted lights? And was this the imposing Professor who had swelled behind the great desk in his massive study at Enmore Park? And, finally, could this be the austere and prim figure which had risen before the meeting at the Zoological Institute? No three tramps that one could have met in a Surrey lane could have looked more hopeless and bedraggled. We had, it is true, been only a week or so upon the top of the plateau, but all our spare clothing was in our camp below, and the one week had been a severe one upon us all, though least to me who had not to endure the handling of the ape-men. My three friends had all lost their hats, and had now bound handkerchiefs round their heads, their clothes hung in ribbons about them, and their unshaven grimy faces were hardly to be recognized. Both Summerlee and Challenger were limping heavily, while I still dragged my feet from weakness after the shock of the morning, and my neck was as stiff as a board from the murderous grip that held it. We were indeed a sorry crew, and I did not wonder to see our Indian companions glance back at us occasionally with horror and amazement on their faces.

In the late afternoon we reached the margin of the lake, and as we emerged from the bush and saw the sheet of water stretching before us our native friends set up a shrill cry of joy and pointed eagerly in front of them. It was indeed a wonderful sight which lay before us. Sweeping over the glassy surface was a great flotilla of canoes coming straight for the shore upon which we stood. They were some miles out when we first saw them, but they shot forward with great swiftness, and were soon so near that the rowers could distinguish our persons. Instantly a thunderous shout of delight burst from them, and we saw them rise from their seats, waving their paddles and spears madly in the air. Then bending to their work once more, they flew across the intervening water, beached their boats upon the sloping sand, and rushed up to us, prostrating themselves with loud cries of greeting before the young chief. Finally one of them, an elderly man, with a necklace and bracelet of great lustrous glass beads and the skin of some beautiful mottled amber-colored animal slung over his shoulders, ran forward and embraced most tenderly the youth whom we had saved. He then looked at us and asked some questions, after which he stepped up with much dignity and embraced us also each in turn. Then, at his order, the whole tribe lay down upon the ground before us in homage. Personally I felt shy and uncomfortable at this obsequious adoration, and I read the same feeling in the faces of Roxton and Summerlee, but Challenger expanded like a flower in the sun.

"They may be undeveloped types," said he, stroking his beard and looking round at them, "but their deportment in the presence of their superiors might be a lesson to some of our more advanced Europeans. Strange how correct are the instincts of the natural man!"

It was clear that the natives had come out upon the war-path, for every man carried his spear—a long bamboo tipped with bone—his bow and arrows, and some sort of club or stone battle-axe slung at his side. Their dark, angry glances at the woods from which we had come, and the frequent repetition of the word "Doda," made it clear enough that this was a rescue party who had set forth to save or revenge the old chief's son, for such we gathered that the youth must be. A council was now held by the whole tribe squatting in a circle, whilst we sat near on a slab of basalt and watched their proceedings. Two or three warriors spoke, and finally our young friend made a spirited harangue with such eloquent features and gestures that we could understand it all as clearly as if we had known his language.

"What is the use of returning?" he said. "Sooner or later the thing must be done. Your comrades have been murdered. What if I have returned safe? These others have been done to death. There is no safety for any of us. We are assembled now and ready." Then he pointed to us. "These strange men are our friends. They are great fighters, and they hate the ape-men even as we do. They command," here he pointed up to heaven, "the thunder and the lightning. When shall we have such a chance again? Let us go forward, and either die now or live for the future in safety. How else shall we go back unashamed to our women?"

The little red warriors hung upon the words of the speaker, and when he had finished they burst into a roar of applause, waving their rude weapons in the air. The old chief stepped forward to us, and asked us some questions, pointing at the same time to the woods. Lord John made a sign to him that he should wait for an answer and then he turned to us.

"Well, it's up to you to say what you will do," said he; "for my part I have a score to settle with these monkey-folk, and if it ends by wiping them off the face of the earth I don't see that the earth need fret about it. I'm goin' with our little red pals and I mean to see them through the scrap. What do you say, young fellah?"

"Of course I will come."

"And you, Challenger?"

"I will assuredly co-operate."

"And you, Summerlee?"

"We seem to be drifting very far from the object of this expedition, Lord John. I assure you that I little thought when I left my professional chair in London that it was for the purpose of heading a raid of savages upon a colony of anthropoid apes."

"To such base uses do we come," said Lord John, smiling. "But we are up against it, so what's the decision?"

"It seems a most questionable step," said Summerlee, argumentative to the last, "but if you are all going, I hardly see how I can remain behind."

"Then it is settled," said Lord John, and turning to the chief he nodded and slapped his rifle.

The old fellow clasped our hands, each in turn, while his men cheered louder than ever. It was too late to advance that night, so the Indians settled down into a rude bivouac. On all sides their fires began to glimmer and smoke. Some of them who had disappeared into the jungle came back presently driving a young iguanodon before them. Like the others, it had a daub of asphalt upon its shoulder, and it was only when we saw one of the natives step forward with the air of an owner and give his consent to the beast's slaughter that we understood at last that these great creatures were as much private property as a herd of cattle, and that these symbols which had so perplexed us were nothing more than the marks of the owner. Helpless, torpid, and vegetarian, with great limbs but a minute brain, they could be rounded up and driven by a child. In a few minutes the huge beast had been cut up and slabs of him were hanging over a dozen camp fires, together with great scaly ganoid fish which had been speared in the lake.

Summerlee had lain down and slept upon the sand, but we others roamed round the edge of the water, seeking to learn something more of this strange country. Twice we found pits of blue clay, such as we had already seen in the swamp of the pterodactyls. These were old volcanic vents, and for some reason excited the greatest interest in Lord John. What attracted Challenger, on the other hand, was a bubbling, gurgling mud geyser, where some strange gas formed great bursting bubbles upon the surface. He thrust a hollow reed into it and cried out with delight like a schoolboy then he was able, on touching it with a lighted match, to cause a sharp explosion and a blue flame at the far end of the tube. Still more pleased was he when, inverting a leathern pouch over the end of the reed, and so filling it with the gas, he was able to send it soaring up into the air.

"An inflammable gas, and one markedly lighter than the atmosphere. I should say beyond doubt that it contained a considerable proportion of free hydrogen. The resources of G. E. C. are not yet exhausted, my young friend. I may yet show you how a great mind molds all Nature to its use." He swelled with some secret purpose, but would say no more.

There was nothing which we could see upon the shore which seemed to me so wonderful as the great sheet of water before us. Our numbers and our noise had frightened all living creatures away, and save for a few pterodactyls, which soared round high above our heads while they waited for the carrion, all was still around the camp. But it was different out upon the rose-tinted waters of the central lake. It boiled and heaved with strange life. Great slate-colored backs and high serrated dorsal fins shot up with a fringe of silver, and then rolled down into the depths again. The sand-banks far out were spotted with uncouth crawling forms, huge turtles, strange saurians, and one great flat creature like a writhing, palpitating mat of black greasy leather, which flopped its way slowly to the lake. Here and there high serpent heads projected out of the water, cutting swiftly through it with a little collar of foam in front, and a long swirling wake behind, rising and falling in graceful, swan-like undulations as they went. It was not until one of these creatures wriggled on to a sand-bank within a few hundred yards of us, and exposed a barrel-shaped body and huge flippers behind the long serpent neck, that Challenger, and Summerlee, who had joined us, broke out into their duet of wonder and admiration.

"Plesiosaurus! A fresh-water plesiosaurus!" cried Summerlee. "That I should have lived to see such a sight! We are blessed, my dear Challenger, above all zoologists since the world began!"

It was not until the night had fallen, and the fires of our savage allies glowed red in the shadows, that our two men of science could be dragged away from the fascinations of that primeval lake. Even in the darkness as we lay upon the strand, we heard from time to time the snort and plunge of the huge creatures who lived therein.

At earliest dawn our camp was astir and an hour later we had started upon our memorable expedition. Often in my dreams have I thought that I might live to be a war correspondent. In what wildest one could I have conceived the nature of the campaign which it should be my lot to report! Here then is my first despatch from a field of battle:

Our numbers had been reinforced during the night by a fresh batch of natives from the caves, and we may have been four or five hundred strong when we made our advance. A fringe of scouts was thrown out in front, and behind them the whole force in a solid column made their way up the long slope of the bush country until we were near the edge of the forest. Here they spread out into a long straggling line of spearmen and bowmen. Roxton and Summerlee took their position upon the right flank, while Challenger and I were on the left. It was a host of the stone age that we were accompanying to battle—we with the last word of the gunsmith's art from St. James' Street and the Strand.

We had not long to wait for our enemy. A wild shrill clamor rose from the edge of the wood and suddenly a body of ape-men rushed out with clubs and stones, and made for the center of the Indian line. It was a valiant move but a foolish one, for the great bandy-legged creatures were slow of foot, while their opponents were as active as cats. It was horrible to see the fierce brutes with foaming mouths and glaring eyes, rushing and grasping, but forever missing their elusive enemies, while arrow after arrow buried itself in their hides. One great fellow ran past me roaring with pain, with a dozen darts sticking from his chest and ribs. In mercy I put a bullet through his skull, and he fell sprawling among the aloes. But this was the only shot fired, for the attack had been on the center of the line, and the Indians there had needed no help of ours in repulsing it. Of all the ape-men who had rushed out into the open, I do not think that one got back to cover.

But the matter was more deadly when we came among the trees. For an hour or more after we entered the wood, there was a desperate struggle in which for a time we hardly held our own. Springing out from among the scrub the ape-men with huge clubs broke in upon the Indians and often felled three or four of them before they could be speared. Their frightful blows shattered everything upon which they fell. One of them knocked Summerlee's rifle to matchwood and the next would have crushed his skull had an Indian not stabbed the beast to the heart. Other ape-men in the trees above us hurled down stones and logs of wood, occasionally dropping bodily on to our ranks and fighting furiously until they were felled. Once our allies broke under the pressure, and had it not been for the execution done by our rifles they would certainly have taken to their heels. But they were gallantly rallied by their old chief and came on with such a rush that the ape-men began in turn to give way. Summerlee was weaponless, but I was emptying my magazine as quick as I could fire, and on the further flank we heard the continuous cracking of our companion's rifles.

Then in a moment came the panic and the collapse. Screaming and howling, the great creatures rushed away in all directions through the brushwood, while our allies yelled in their savage delight, following swiftly after their flying enemies. All the feuds of countless generations, all the hatreds and cruelties of their narrow history, all the memories of ill-usage and persecution were to be purged that day. At last man was to be supreme and the man-beast to find forever his allotted place. Fly as they would the fugitives were too slow to escape from the active savages, and from every side in the tangled woods we heard the exultant yells, the twanging of bows, and the crash and thud as ape-men were brought down from their hiding-places in the trees.

I was following the others, when I found that Lord John and Challenger had come across to join us.

"It's over," said Lord John. "I think we can leave the tidying up to them. Perhaps the less we see of it the better we shall sleep."

Challenger's eyes were shining with the lust of slaughter.

"We have been privileged," he cried, strutting about like a gamecock, "to be present at one of the typical decisive battles of history—the battles which have determined the fate of the world. What, my friends, is the conquest of one nation by another? It is meaningless. Each produces the same result. But those fierce fights, when in the dawn of the ages the cave-dwellers held their own against the tiger folk, or the elephants first found that they had a master, those were the real conquests—the victories that count. By this strange turn of fate we have seen and helped to decide even such a contest. Now upon this plateau the future must ever be for man."

It needed a robust faith in the end to justify such tragic means. As we advanced together through the woods we found the ape-men lying thick, transfixed with spears or arrows. Here and there a little group of shattered Indians marked where one of the anthropoids had turned to bay, and sold his life dearly. Always in front of us we heard the yelling and roaring which showed the direction of the pursuit. The ape-men had been driven back to their city, they had made a last stand there, once again they had been broken, and now we were in time to see the final fearful scene of all. Some eighty or a hundred males, the last survivors, had been driven across that same little clearing which led to the edge of the cliff, the scene of our own exploit two days before. As we arrived the Indians, a semicircle of spearmen, had closed in on them, and in a minute it was over, Thirty or forty died where they stood. The others, screaming and clawing, were thrust over the precipice, and went hurtling down, as their prisoners had of old, on to the sharp bamboos six hundred feet below. It was as Challenger had said, and the reign of man was assured forever in Maple White Land. The males were exterminated, Ape Town was destroyed, the females and young were driven away to live in bondage, and the long rivalry of untold centuries had reached its bloody end.

For us the victory brought much advantage. Once again we were able to visit our camp and get at our stores. Once more also we were able to communicate with Zambo, who had been terrified by the spectacle from afar of an avalanche of apes falling from the edge of the cliff.

"Come away, Massas, come away!" he cried, his eyes starting from his head. "The debbil get you sure if you stay up there."

"It is the voice of sanity!" said Summerlee with conviction. "We have had adventures enough and they are neither suitable to our character or our position. I hold you to your word, Challenger. From now onwards you devote your energies to getting us out of this horrible country and back once more to civilization."

Chapter XV; "Our Eyes have seen Great Wonders"

I write this from day to day, but I trust that before I come to the end of it, I may be able to say that the light shines, at last, through our clouds. We are held here with no clear means of making our escape, and bitterly we chafe against it. Yet, I can well imagine that the day may come when we may be glad that we were kept, against our will, to see something more of the wonders of this singular place, and of the creatures who inhabit it.

The victory of the Indians and the annihilation of the ape-men, marked the turning point of our fortunes. From then onwards, we were in truth masters of the plateau, for the natives looked upon us with a mixture of fear and gratitude, since by our strange powers we had aided them to destroy their hereditary foe. For their own sakes they would, perhaps, be glad to see the departure of such formidable and incalculable people, but they have not themselves suggested any way by which we may reach the plains below. There had been, so far as we could follow their signs, a tunnel by which the place could be approached, the lower exit of which we had seen from below. By this, no doubt, both ape-men and Indians had at different epochs reached the top, and Maple White with his companion had taken the same way. Only the year before, however, there had been a terrific earthquake, and the upper end of the tunnel had fallen in and completely disappeared. The Indians now could only shake their heads and shrug their shoulders when we expressed by signs our desire to descend. It may be that they cannot, but it may also be that they will not, help us to get away.

At the end of the victorious campaign the surviving ape-folk were driven across the plateau (their wailings were horrible) and established in the neighborhood of the Indian caves, where they would, from now onwards, be a servile race under the eyes of their masters. It was a rude, raw, primeval version of the Jews in Babylon or the Israelites in Egypt. At night we could hear from amid the trees the long-drawn cry, as some primitive Ezekiel mourned for fallen greatness and recalled the departed glories of Ape Town. Hewers of wood and drawers of water, such were they from now onwards.

We had returned across the plateau with our allies two days after the battle, and made our camp at the foot of their cliffs. They would have had us share their caves with them, but Lord John would by no means consent to it considering that to do so would put us in their power if they were treacherously disposed. We kept our independence, therefore, and had our weapons ready for any emergency, while preserving the most friendly relations. We also continually visited their caves, which were most remarkable places, though whether made by man or by Nature we have never been able to determine. They were all on the one stratum, hollowed out of some soft rock which lay between the volcanic basalt forming the ruddy cliffs above them, and the hard granite which formed their base.

The openings were about eighty feet above the ground, and were led up to by long stone stairs, so narrow and steep that no large animal could mount them. Inside they were warm and dry, running in straight passages of varying length into the side of the hill, with smooth gray walls decorated with many excellent pictures done with charred sticks and representing the various animals of the plateau. If every living thing were swept from the country the future explorer would find upon the walls of these caves ample evidence of the strange fauna—the dinosaurs, iguanodons, and fish lizards—which had lived so recently upon earth.

Since we had learned that the huge iguanodons were kept as tame herds by their owners, and were simply walking meat-stores, we had conceived that man, even with his primitive weapons, had established his ascendancy upon the plateau. We were soon to discover that it was not so, and that he was still there upon tolerance.

It was on the third day after our forming our camp near the Indian caves that the tragedy occurred. Challenger and Summerlee had gone off together that day to the lake where some of the natives, under their direction, were engaged in harpooning specimens of the great lizards. Lord John and I had remained in our camp, while a number of the Indians were scattered about upon the grassy slope in front of the caves engaged in different ways. Suddenly there was a shrill cry of alarm, with the word "Stoa" resounding from a hundred tongues. From every side men, women, and children were rushing wildly for shelter, swarming up the staircases and into the caves in a mad stampede.

Looking up, we could see them waving their arms from the rocks above and beckoning to us to join them in their refuge. We had both seized our magazine rifles and ran out to see what the danger could be. Suddenly from the near belt of trees there broke forth a group of twelve or fifteen Indians, running for their lives, and at their very heels two of those frightful monsters which had disturbed our camp and pursued me upon my solitary journey. In shape they were like horrible toads, and moved in a succession of springs, but in size they were of an incredible bulk, larger than the largest elephant. We had never before seen them save at night, and indeed they are nocturnal animals save when disturbed in their lairs, as these had been. We now stood amazed at the sight, for their blotched and warty skins were of a curious fish-like iridescence, and the sunlight struck them with an ever-varying rainbow bloom as they moved.

We had little time to watch them, however, for in an instant they had overtaken the fugitives and were making a dire slaughter among them. Their method was to fall forward with their full weight upon each in turn, leaving him crushed and mangled, to bound on after the others. The wretched Indians screamed with terror, but were helpless, run as they would, before the relentless purpose and horrible activity of these monstrous creatures. One after another they went down, and there were not half-a-dozen surviving by the time my companion and I could come to their help. But our aid was of little avail and only involved us in the same peril. At the range of a couple of hundred yards we emptied our magazines, firing bullet after bullet into the beasts, but with no more effect than if we were pelting them with pellets of paper. Their slow reptilian natures cared nothing for wounds, and the springs of their lives, with no special brain center but scattered throughout their spinal cords, could not be tapped by any modern weapons. The most that we could do was to check their progress by distracting their attention with the flash and roar of our guns, and so to give both the natives and ourselves time to reach the steps which led to safety. But where the conical explosive bullets of the twentieth century were of no avail, the poisoned arrows of the natives, dipped in the juice of strophanthus and steeped afterwards in decayed carrion, could succeed. Such arrows were of little avail to the hunter who attacked the beast, because their action in that torpid circulation was slow, and before its powers failed it could certainly overtake and slay its assailant. But now, as the two monsters hounded us to the very foot of the stairs, a drift of darts came whistling from every chink in the cliff above them. In a minute they were feathered with them, and yet with no sign of pain they clawed and slobbered with impotent rage at the steps which would lead them to their victims, mounting clumsily up for a few yards and then sliding down again to the ground. But at last the poison worked. One of them gave a deep rumbling groan and dropped his huge squat head on to the earth. The other bounded round in an eccentric circle with shrill, wailing cries, and then lying down writhed in agony for some minutes before it also stiffened and lay still. With yells of triumph the Indians came flocking down from their caves and danced a frenzied dance of victory round the dead bodies, in mad joy that two more of the most dangerous of all their enemies had been slain. That night they cut up and removed the bodies, not to eat—for the poison was still active—but lest they should breed a pestilence. The great reptilian hearts, however, each as large as a cushion, still lay there, beating slowly and steadily, with a gentle rise and fall, in horrible independent life. It was only upon the third day that the ganglia ran down and the dreadful things were still.

Some day, when I have a better desk than a meat-tin and more helpful tools than a worn stub of pencil and a last, tattered note-book, I will write some fuller account of the Accala Indians—of our life amongst them, and of the glimpses which we had of the strange conditions of wondrous Maple White Land. Memory, at least, will never fail me, for so long as the breath of life is in me, every hour and every action of that period will stand out as hard and clear as do the first strange happenings of our childhood. No new impressions could efface those which are so deeply cut. When the time comes I will describe that wondrous moonlit night upon the great lake when a young ichthyosaurus—a strange creature, half seal, half fish, to look at, with bone-covered eyes on each side of his snout, and a third eye fixed upon the top of his head—was entangled in an Indian net, and nearly upset our canoe before we towed it ashore; the same night that a green water-snake shot out from the rushes and carried off in its coils the steersman of Challenger's canoe. I will tell, too, of the great nocturnal white thing—to this day we do not know whether it was beast or reptile—which lived in a vile swamp to the east of the lake, and flitted about with a faint phosphorescent glimmer in the darkness. The Indians were so terrified at it that they would not go near the place, and, though we twice made expeditions and saw it each time, we could not make our way through the deep marsh in which it lived. I can only say that it seemed to be larger than a cow and had the strangest musky odor. I will tell also of the huge bird which chased Challenger to the shelter of the rocks one day—a great running bird, far taller than an ostrich, with a vulture-like neck and cruel head which made it a walking death. As Challenger climbed to safety one dart of that savage curving beak shore off the heel of his boot as if it had been cut with a chisel. This time at least modern weapons prevailed and the great creature, twelve feet from head to foot—phororachus its name, according to our panting but exultant Professor—went down before Lord Roxton's rifle in a flurry of waving feathers and kicking limbs, with two remorseless yellow eyes glaring up from the midst of it. May I live to see that flattened vicious skull in its own niche amid the trophies of the Albany. Finally, I will assuredly give some account of the toxodon, the giant ten-foot guinea pig, with projecting chisel teeth, which we killed as it drank in the gray of the morning by the side of the lake.

All this I shall some day write at fuller length, and amidst these more stirring days I would tenderly sketch in these lovely summer evenings, when with the deep blue sky above us we lay in good comradeship among the long grasses by the wood and marveled at the strange fowl that swept over us and the quaint new creatures which crept from their burrows to watch us, while above us the boughs of the bushes were heavy with luscious fruit, and below us strange and lovely flowers peeped at us from among the herbage; or those long moonlit nights when we lay out upon the shimmering surface of the great lake and watched with wonder and awe the huge circles rippling out from the sudden splash of some fantastic monster; or the greenish gleam, far down in the deep water, of some strange creature upon the confines of darkness. These are the scenes which my mind and my pen will dwell upon in every detail at some future day.

But, you will ask, why these experiences and why this delay, when you and your comrades should have been occupied day and night in the devising of some means by which you could return to the outer world? My answer is, that there was not one of us who was not working for this end, but that our work had been in vain. One fact we had very speedily discovered: The Indians would do nothing to help us. In every other way they were our friends—one might almost say our devoted slaves—but when it was suggested that they should help us to make and carry a plank which would bridge the chasm, or when we wished to get from them thongs of leather or liana to weave ropes which might help us, we were met by a good-humored, but an invincible, refusal. They would smile, twinkle their eyes, shake their heads, and there was the end of it. Even the old chief met us with the same obstinate denial, and it was only Maretas, the youngster whom we had saved, who looked wistfully at us and told us by his gestures that he was grieved for our thwarted wishes. Ever since their crowning triumph with the ape-men they looked upon us as supermen, who bore victory in the tubes of strange weapons, and they believed that so long as we remained with them good fortune would be theirs. A little red-skinned wife and a cave of our own were freely offered to each of us if we would but forget our own people and dwell forever upon the plateau. So far all had been kindly, however far apart our desires might be; but we felt well assured that our actual plans of a descent must be kept secret, for we had reason to fear that at the last they might try to hold us by force.

In spite of the danger from dinosaurs (which is not great save at night, for, as I may have said before, they are mostly nocturnal in their habits) I have twice in the last three weeks been over to our old camp in order to see our negro who still kept watch and ward below the cliff. My eyes strained eagerly across the great plain in the hope of seeing afar off the help for which we had prayed. But the long cactus-strewn levels still stretched away, empty and bare, to the distant line of the cane-brake.

"They will soon come now, Massa Malone. Before another week pass Indian come back and bring rope and fetch you down." Such was the cheery cry of our excellent Zambo.

I had one strange experience as I came from this second visit which had involved my being away for a night from my companions. I was returning along the well-remembered route, and had reached a spot within a mile or so of the marsh of the pterodactyls, when I saw an extraordinary object approaching me. It was a man who walked inside a framework made of bent canes so that he was enclosed on all sides in a bell-shaped cage. As I drew nearer I was more amazed still to see that it was Lord John Roxton. When he saw me he slipped from under his curious protection and came towards me laughing, and yet, as I thought, with some confusion in his manner.

"Well, young fellah," said he, "who would have thought of meetin' you up here?"

"What in the world are you doing?" I asked.

"Visitin' my friends, the pterodactyls," said he.

"But why?"

"Interestin' beasts, don't you think? But unsociable! Nasty rude ways with strangers, as you may remember. So I rigged this framework which keeps them from bein' too pressin' in their attentions."

"But what do you want in the swamp?"

He looked at me with a very questioning eye, and I read hesitation in his face.

"Don't you think other people besides Professors can want to know things?" he said at last. "I'm studyin' the pretty dears. That's enough for you."

"No offense," said I.

His good-humor returned and he laughed.

"No offense, young fellah. I'm goin' to get a young devil chick for Challenger. That's one of my jobs. No, I don't want your company. I'm safe in this cage, and you are not. So long, and I'll be back in camp by night-fall."

He turned away and I left him wandering on through the wood with his extraordinary cage around him.

If Lord John's behavior at this time was strange, that of Challenger was more so. I may say that he seemed to possess an extraordinary fascination for the Indian women, and that he always carried a large spreading palm branch with which he beat them off as if they were flies, when their attentions became too pressing. To see him walking like a comic opera Sultan, with this badge of authority in his hand, his black beard bristling in front of him, his toes pointing at each step, and a train of wide-eyed Indian girls behind him, clad in their slender drapery of bark cloth, is one of the most grotesque of all the pictures which I will carry back with me. As to Summerlee, he was absorbed in the insect and bird life of the plateau, and spent his whole time (save that considerable portion which was devoted to abusing Challenger for not getting us out of our difficulties) in cleaning and mounting his specimens.

Challenger had been in the habit of walking off by himself every morning and returning from time to time with looks of portentous solemnity, as one who bears the full weight of a great enterprise upon his shoulders. One day, palm branch in hand, and his crowd of adoring devotees behind him, he led us down to his hidden workshop and took us into the secret of his plans.

The place was a small clearing in the center of a palm grove. In this was one of those boiling mud geysers which I have already described. Around its edge were scattered a number of leathern thongs cut from iguanodon hide, and a large collapsed membrane which proved to be the dried and scraped stomach of one of the great fish lizards from the lake. This huge sack had been sewn up at one end and only a small orifice left at the other. Into this opening several bamboo canes had been inserted and the other ends of these canes were in contact with conical clay funnels which collected the gas bubbling up through the mud of the geyser. Soon the flaccid organ began to slowly expand and show such a tendency to upward movements that Challenger fastened the cords which held it to the trunks of the surrounding trees. In half an hour a good-sized gas-bag had been formed, and the jerking and straining upon the thongs showed that it was capable of considerable lift. Challenger, like a glad father in the presence of his first-born, stood smiling and stroking his beard, in silent, self-satisfied content as he gazed at the creation of his brain. It was Summerlee who first broke the silence.

"You don't mean us to go up in that thing, Challenger?" said he, in an acid voice.

"I mean, my dear Summerlee, to give you such a demonstration of its powers that after seeing it you will, I am sure, have no hesitation in trusting yourself to it."

"You can put it right out of your head now, at once," said Summerlee with decision, "nothing on earth would induce me to commit such a folly. Lord John, I trust that you will not countenance such madness?"

"Dooced ingenious, I call it," said our peer. "I'd like to see how it works."

"So you shall," said Challenger. "For some days I have exerted my whole brain force upon the problem of how we shall descend from these cliffs. We have satisfied ourselves that we cannot climb down and that there is no tunnel. We are also unable to construct any kind of bridge which may take us back to the pinnacle from which we came. How then shall I find a means to convey us? Some little time ago I had remarked to our young friend here that free hydrogen was evolved from the geyser. The idea of a balloon naturally followed. I was, I will admit, somewhat baffled by the difficulty of discovering an envelope to contain the gas, but the contemplation of the immense entrails of these reptiles supplied me with a solution to the problem. Behold the result!"

He put one hand in the front of his ragged jacket and pointed proudly with the other.

By this time the gas-bag had swollen to a goodly rotundity and was jerking strongly upon its lashings.

"Midsummer madness!" snorted Summerlee.

Lord John was delighted with the whole idea. "Clever old dear, ain't he?" he whispered to me, and then louder to Challenger. "What about a car?"

"The car will be my next care. I have already planned how it is to be made and attached. Meanwhile I will simply show you how capable my apparatus is of supporting the weight of each of us."

"All of us, surely?"

"No, it is part of my plan that each in turn shall descend as in a parachute, and the balloon be drawn back by means which I shall have no difficulty in perfecting. If it will support the weight of one and let him gently down, it will have done all that is required of it. I will now show you its capacity in that direction."

He brought out a lump of basalt of a considerable size, constructed in the middle so that a cord could be easily attached to it. This cord was the one which we had brought with us on to the plateau after we had used it for climbing the pinnacle. It was over a hundred feet long, and though it was thin it was very strong. He had prepared a sort of collar of leather with many straps depending from it. This collar was placed over the dome of the balloon, and the hanging thongs were gathered together below, so that the pressure of any weight would be diffused over a considerable surface. Then the lump of basalt was fastened to the thongs, and the rope was allowed to hang from the end of it, being passed three times round the Professor's arm.

"I will now," said Challenger, with a smile of pleased anticipation, "demonstrate the carrying power of my balloon." As he said so he cut with a knife the various lashings that held it.

Never was our expedition in more imminent danger of complete annihilation. The inflated membrane shot up with frightful velocity into the air. In an instant Challenger was pulled off his feet and dragged after it. I had just time to throw my arms round his ascending waist when I was myself whipped up into the air. Lord John had me with a rat-trap grip round the legs, but I felt that he also was coming off the ground. For a moment I had a vision of four adventurers floating like a string of sausages over the land that they had explored. But, happily, there were limits to the strain which the rope would stand, though none apparently to the lifting powers of this infernal machine. There was a sharp crack, and we were in a heap upon the ground with coils of rope all over us. When we were able to stagger to our feet we saw far off in the deep blue sky one dark spot where the lump of basalt was speeding upon its way.

"Splendid!" cried the undaunted Challenger, rubbing his injured arm. "A most thorough and satisfactory demonstration! I could not have anticipated such a success. Within a week, gentlemen, I promise that a second balloon will be prepared, and that you can count upon taking in safety and comfort the first stage of our homeward journey." So far I have written each of the foregoing events as it occurred. Now I am rounding off my narrative from the old camp, where Zambo has waited so long, with all our difficulties and dangers left like a dream behind us upon the summit of those vast ruddy crags which tower above our heads. We have descended in safety, though in a most unexpected fashion, and all is well with us. In six weeks or two months we shall be in London, and it is possible that this letter may not reach you much earlier than we do ourselves. Already our hearts yearn and our spirits fly towards the great mother city which holds so much that is dear to us.

It was on the very evening of our perilous adventure with Challenger's home-made balloon that the change came in our fortunes. I have said that the one person from whom we had had some sign of sympathy in our attempts to get away was the young chief whom we had rescued. He alone had no desire to hold us against our will in a strange land. He had told us as much by his expressive language of signs. That evening, after dusk, he came down to our little camp, handed me (for some reason he had always shown his attentions to me, perhaps because I was the one who was nearest his age) a small roll of the bark of a tree, and then pointing solemnly up at the row of caves above him, he had put his finger to his lips as a sign of secrecy and had stolen back again to his people.

I took the slip of bark to the firelight and we examined it together. It was about a foot square, and on the inner side there was a singular arrangement of lines, which I here reproduce:

They were neatly done in charcoal upon the white surface, and looked to me at first sight like some sort of rough musical score.

"Whatever it is, I can swear that it is of importance to us," said I. "I could read that on his face as he gave it."

"Unless we have come upon a primitive practical joker," Summerlee suggested, "which I should think would be one of the most elementary developments of man."

"It is clearly some sort of script," said Challenger.

"Looks like a guinea puzzle competition," remarked Lord John, craning his neck to have a look at it. Then suddenly he stretched out his hand and seized the puzzle.

"By George!" he cried, "I believe I've got it. The boy guessed right the very first time. See here! How many marks are on that paper? Eighteen. Well, if you come to think of it there are eighteen cave openings on the hill-side above us."

"He pointed up to the caves when he gave it to me," said I.

"Well, that settles it. This is a chart of the caves. What! Eighteen of them all in a row, some short, some deep, some branching, same as we saw them. It's a map, and here's a cross on it. What's the cross for? It is placed to mark one that is much deeper than the others."

"One that goes through," I cried.

"I believe our young friend has read the riddle," said Challenger. "If the cave does not go through I do not understand why this person, who has every reason to mean us well, should have drawn our attention to it. But if it does go through and comes out at the corresponding point on the other side, we should not have more than a hundred feet to descend."

"A hundred feet!" grumbled Summerlee.

"Well, our rope is still more than a hundred feet long," I cried. "Surely we could get down."

"How about the Indians in the cave?" Summerlee objected.

"There are no Indians in any of the caves above our heads," said I. "They are all used as barns and store-houses. Why should we not go up now at once and spy out the land?"

There is a dry bituminous wood upon the plateau—a species of araucaria, according to our botanist—which is always used by the Indians for torches. Each of us picked up a faggot of this, and we made our way up weed-covered steps to the particular cave which was marked in the drawing. It was, as I had said, empty, save for a great number of enormous bats, which flapped round our heads as we advanced into it. As we had no desire to draw the attention of the Indians to our proceedings, we stumbled along in the dark until we had gone round several curves and penetrated a considerable distance into the cavern. Then, at last, we lit our torches. It was a beautiful dry tunnel with smooth gray walls covered with native symbols, a curved roof which arched over our heads, and white glistening sand beneath our feet. We hurried eagerly along it until, with a deep groan of bitter disappointment, we were brought to a halt. A sheer wall of rock had appeared before us, with no chink through which a mouse could have slipped. There was no escape for us there.

We stood with bitter hearts staring at this unexpected obstacle. It was not the result of any convulsion, as in the case of the ascending tunnel. The end wall was exactly like the side ones. It was, and had always been, a cul-de-sac.

"Never mind, my friends," said the indomitable Challenger. "You have still my firm promise of a balloon."

Summerlee groaned.

"Can we be in the wrong cave?" I suggested.

"No use, young fellah," said Lord John, with his finger on the chart. "Seventeen from the right and second from the left. This is the cave sure enough."

I looked at the mark to which his finger pointed, and I gave a sudden cry of joy.

"I believe I have it! Follow me! Follow me!"

I hurried back along the way we had come, my torch in my hand. "Here," said I, pointing to some matches upon the ground, "is where we lit up."

"Exactly."

"Well, it is marked as a forked cave, and in the darkness we passed the fork before the torches were lit. On the right side as we go out we should find the longer arm."

It was as I had said. We had not gone thirty yards before a great black opening loomed in the wall. We turned into it to find that we were in a much larger passage than before. Along it we hurried in breathless impatience for many hundreds of yards. Then, suddenly, in the black darkness of the arch in front of us we saw a gleam of dark red light. We stared in amazement. A sheet of steady flame seemed to cross the passage and to bar our way. We hastened towards it. No sound, no heat, no movement came from it, but still the great luminous curtain glowed before us, silvering all the cave and turning the sand to powdered jewels, until as we drew closer it discovered a circular edge.

"The moon, by George!" cried Lord John. "We are through, boys! We are through!"

It was indeed the full moon which shone straight down the aperture which opened upon the cliffs. It was a small rift, not larger than a window, but it was enough for all our purposes. As we craned our necks through it we could see that the descent was not a very difficult one, and that the level ground was no very great way below us. It was no wonder that from below we had not observed the place, as the cliffs curved overhead and an ascent at the spot would have seemed so impossible as to discourage close inspection. We satisfied ourselves that with the help of our rope we could find our way down, and then returned, rejoicing, to our camp to make our preparations for the next evening.

What we did we had to do quickly and secretly, since even at this last hour the Indians might hold us back. Our stores we would leave behind us, save only our guns and cartridges. But Challenger had some unwieldy stuff which he ardently desired to take with him, and one particular package, of which I may not speak, which gave us more labor than any. Slowly the day passed, but when the darkness fell we were ready for our departure. With much labor we got our things up the steps, and then, looking back, took one last long survey of that strange land, soon I fear to be vulgarized, the prey of hunter and prospector, but to each of us a dreamland of glamour and romance, a land where we had dared much, suffered much, and learned much—*our* land, as we shall ever fondly call it. Along upon our left the neighboring caves each threw out its ruddy cheery firelight into the gloom. From the slope below us rose the voices of the Indians as they laughed and sang. Beyond was the long sweep of the woods, and in the center, shimmering vaguely through the gloom, was the great lake, the mother of strange monsters. Even as we looked a high whickering cry, the call of some weird animal, rang clear out of the darkness. It was the very voice of Maple White Land bidding us good-bye. We turned and plunged into the cave which led to home.

Two hours later, we, our packages, and all we owned, were at the foot of the cliff. Save for Challenger's luggage we had never a difficulty. Leaving it all where we descended, we started at once for Zambo's camp. In the early morning we approached it, but only to find, to our amazement, not one fire but a dozen upon the plain. The rescue party had arrived. There were twenty Indians from the river, with stakes, ropes, and all that could be useful for bridging the chasm. At least we shall have no difficulty now in carrying our packages, when tomorrow we begin to make our way back to the Amazon.

And so, in humble and thankful mood, I close this account. Our eyes have seen great wonders and our souls are chastened by what we have endured. Each is in his own way a better and deeper man. It may be that when we reach Para we shall stop to refit. If we do, this letter will be a mail ahead. If not, it will reach London on the very day that I do. In either case, my dear Mr. McArdle, I hope very soon to shake you by the hand.

Chapter XVI; "A Procession! A Procession!"

I should wish to place upon record here our gratitude to all our friends upon the Amazon for the very great kindness and hospitality which was shown to us upon our return journey. Very particularly would I thank Senhor Penalosa and other officials of the Brazilian Government for the special arrangements by which we were helped upon our way, and Senhor Pereira of Para, to whose forethought we owe the complete outfit for a decent appearance in the civilized world which we found ready for us at that town. It seemed a poor return for all the courtesy which we encountered that we should deceive our hosts and benefactors, but under the circumstances we had really no alternative, and I hereby tell them that they will only waste their time and their money if they attempt to follow upon our traces. Even the names have been altered in our accounts, and I am very sure that no one, from the most careful study of them, could come within a thousand miles of our unknown land.

The excitement which had been caused through those parts of South America which we had to traverse was imagined by us to be purely local, and I can assure our friends in England that we had no notion of the uproar which the mere rumor of our experiences had caused through Europe. It was not until the Ivernia was within five hundred miles of Southampton that the wireless messages from paper after paper and agency after agency, offering huge prices for a short return message as to our actual results, showed us how strained was the attention not only of the scientific world but of the general public. It was agreed among us, however, that no definite statement should be given to the Press until we had met the members of the Zoological Institute, since as delegates it was our clear duty to give our first report to the body from which we had received our commission of investigation. Thus, although we found Southampton full of Pressmen, we absolutely refused to give any information, which had the natural effect of focussing public attention upon the meeting which was advertised for the evening of November 7th. For this gathering, the Zoological Hall which had been the scene of the inception of our task was found to be far too small, and it was only in the Queen's Hall in Regent Street that accommodation could be found. It is now common knowledge the promoters might have ventured upon the Albert Hall and still found their space too scanty.

It was for the second evening after our arrival that the great meeting had been fixed. For the first, we had each, no doubt, our own pressing personal affairs to absorb us. Of mine I cannot yet speak. It may be that as it stands further from me I may think of it, and even speak of it, with less emotion. I have shown the reader in the beginning of this narrative where lay the springs of my action. It is but right, perhaps, that I should carry on the tale and show also the results. And yet the day may come when I would not have it otherwise. At least I have been driven forth to take part in a wondrous adventure, and I cannot but be thankful to the force that drove me.

And now I turn to the last supreme eventful moment of our adventure. As I was racking my brain as to how I should best describe it, my eyes fell upon the issue of my own Journal for the morning of the 8th of November with the full and excellent account of my friend and fellow-reporter Macdona. What can I do better than transcribe his narrative—head-lines and all? I admit that the paper was exuberant in the matter, out of compliment to its own enterprise in sending a correspondent, but the other great dailies were hardly less full in their account. Thus, then, friend Mac in his report:

The New World

Great Meeting At The Queen's Hall

Scenes Of Uproar

Extraordinary Incident

What Was It?

Nocturnal Riot In Regent Street

(Special)

"The much-discussed meeting of the Zoological Institute, convened to hear the report of the Committee of Investigation sent out last year to South America to test the assertions made by Professor Challenger as to the continued existence of prehistoric life upon that Continent, was held last night in the greater Queen's Hall, and it is safe to say that it is likely to be a red letter date in the history of Science, for the proceedings were of so remarkable and sensational a character that no one present is ever likely to forget them." (Oh, brother scribe Macdona, what a monstrous opening sentence!) "The tickets were theoretically confined to members and their friends, but the latter is an elastic term, and long before eight o'clock, the hour fixed for the commencement of the proceedings, all parts of the Great Hall were tightly packed. The general public, however, which most unreasonably entertained a grievance at having been excluded, stormed the doors at a quarter to eight, after a prolonged melee in which several people were injured, including Inspector Scoble of H. Division, whose leg was unfortunately broken. After this unwarrantable invasion, which not only filled every passage, but even intruded upon the space set apart for the Press, it is estimated that nearly five thousand people awaited the arrival of the travelers. When they eventually appeared, they took their places in the front of a platform which already contained all the leading scientific men, not only of this country, but of France and of Germany. Sweden was also represented, in the person of Professor Sergius, the famous Zoologist of the University of Upsala. The entrance of the four heroes of the occasion was the signal for a remarkable demonstration of welcome, the whole audience rising and cheering for some minutes. An acute observer might, however, have detected some signs of dissent amid the applause, and gathered that the proceedings were likely to become more lively than harmonious. It may safely be prophesied, however, that no one could have foreseen the extraordinary turn which they were actually to take.

"Of the appearance of the four wanderers little need be said, since their photographs have for some time been appearing in all the papers. They bear few traces of the hardships which they are said to have undergone. Professor Challenger's beard may be more shaggy, Professor Summerlee's features more ascetic, Lord John Roxton's figure more gaunt, and all three may be burned to a darker tint than when they left our shores, but each appeared to be in most excellent health. As to our own representative, the well-known athlete and international Rugby football player, E. D. Malone, he looks trained to a hair, and as he surveyed the crowd a smile of good-humored contentment pervaded his honest but homely face." (All right, Mac, wait till I get you alone!)

"When quiet had been restored and the audience resumed their seats after the ovation which they had given to the travelers, the chairman, the Duke of Durham, addressed the meeting. 'He would not,' he said, 'stand for more than a moment between that vast assembly and the treat which lay before them. It was not for him to anticipate what Professor Summerlee, who was the spokesman of the committee, had to say to them, but it was common rumor that their expedition had been crowned by extraordinary success.' (Applause.) 'Apparently the age of romance was not dead, and there was common ground upon which the wildest imaginings of the novelist could meet the actual scientific investigations of the searcher for truth. He would only add, before he sat down, that he rejoiced—and all of them would rejoice—that these gentlemen had returned safe and sound from their difficult and dangerous task, for it cannot be denied that any disaster to such an expedition would have inflicted a well-nigh irreparable loss to the cause of Zoological science.' (Great applause, in which Professor Challenger was observed to join.)

"Professor Summerlee's rising was the signal for another extraordinary outbreak of enthusiasm, which broke out again at intervals throughout his address. That address will not be given in extenso in these columns, for the reason that a full account of the whole adventures of the expedition is being published as a supplement from the pen of our own special correspondent. Some general indications will therefore suffice. Having described the genesis of their journey, and paid a handsome tribute to his friend Professor Challenger, coupled with an apology for the incredulity with which his assertions, now fully vindicated, had been received, he gave the actual course of their journey, carefully withholding such information as would aid the public in any attempt to locate this remarkable plateau. Having described, in general terms, their course from the main river up to the time that they actually reached the base of the cliffs, he enthralled his hearers by his account of the difficulties encountered by the expedition in their repeated attempts to mount them, and finally described how they succeeded in their desperate endeavors, which cost the lives of their two devoted half-breed servants." (This amazing reading of the affair was the result of Summerlee's endeavors to avoid raising any questionable matter at the meeting.)

"Having conducted his audience in fancy to the summit, and marooned them there by reason of the fall of their bridge, the Professor proceeded to describe both the horrors and the attractions of that remarkable land. Of personal adventures he said little, but laid stress upon the rich harvest reaped by Science in the observations of the wonderful beast, bird, insect, and plant life of the plateau. Peculiarly rich in the coleoptera and in the lepidoptera, forty-six new species of the one and ninety-four of the other had been secured in the course of a few weeks. It was, however, in the larger animals, and especially in the larger animals supposed to have been long extinct, that the interest of the public was naturally centered. Of these he was able to give a goodly list, but had little doubt that it would be largely extended when the place had been more thoroughly investigated. He and his companions had seen at least a dozen creatures, most of them at a distance, which corresponded with nothing at present known to Science. These would in time be duly classified and examined. He instanced a snake, the cast skin of which, deep purple in color, was fifty-one feet in length, and mentioned a white creature, supposed to be mammalian, which gave forth well-marked phosphorescence in the darkness; also a large black moth, the bite of which was supposed by the Indians to be highly poisonous. Setting aside these entirely new forms of life, the plateau was very rich in known prehistoric forms, dating back in some cases to early Jurassic times. Among these he mentioned the gigantic and grotesque stegosaurus, seen once by Mr. Malone at a drinking-place by the lake, and drawn in the sketch-book of that adventurous American who had first penetrated this unknown world. He described also the iguanodon and the pterodactyl—two of the first of the wonders which they had encountered. He then thrilled the assembly by some account of the terrible carnivorous dinosaurs, which had on more than one occasion pursued members of the party, and which were the most formidable of all the creatures which they had encountered. Thence he passed to the huge and ferocious bird, the phororachus, and to the great elk which still roams upon this upland. It was not, however, until he sketched the mysteries of the central lake that the full interest and enthusiasm of the audience were aroused. One had to pinch oneself to be sure that one was awake as one heard this sane and practical Professor in cold measured tones describing the monstrous three-eyed fish-lizards and the huge water-snakes which inhabit this enchanted sheet of water. Next he touched upon the Indians, and upon the extraordinary colony of anthropoid apes, which might be looked upon as an advance upon the pithecanthropus of Java, and as coming therefore nearer than any known form to that hypothetical creation, the missing link. Finally he described, amongst some merriment, the ingenious but highly dangerous aeronautic invention of Professor Challenger, and wound up a most memorable address by an account of the methods by which the committee did at last find their way back to civilization.

"It had been hoped that the proceedings would end there, and that a vote of thanks and congratulation, moved by Professor Sergius, of Upsala University, would be duly seconded and carried; but it was soon evident that the course of events was not destined to flow so smoothly. Symptoms of opposition had been evident from time to time during the evening, and now Dr. James Illingworth, of Edinburgh, rose in the center of the hall. Dr. Illingworth asked whether an amendment should not be taken before a resolution.

"The Chairman: 'Yes, sir, if there must be an amendment.'

"Dr. Illingworth: 'Your Grace, there must be an amendment.'

"The Chairman: 'Then let us take it at once.'

"Professor Summerlee (springing to his feet): 'Might I explain, your Grace, that this man is my personal enemy ever since our controversy in the Quarterly Journal of Science as to the true nature of Bathybius?'

"The Chairman: 'I fear I cannot go into personal matters. Proceed.'

"Dr. Illingworth was imperfectly heard in part of his remarks on account of the strenuous opposition of the friends of the explorers. Some attempts were also made to pull him down. Being a man of enormous physique, however, and possessed of a very powerful voice, he dominated the tumult and succeeded in finishing his speech. It was clear, from the moment of his rising, that he had a number of friends and sympathizers in the hall, though they formed a minority in the audience. The attitude of the greater part of the public might be described as one of attentive neutrality.

"Dr. Illingworth began his remarks by expressing his high appreciation of the scientific work both of Professor Challenger and of Professor Summerlee. He much regretted that any personal bias should have been read into his remarks, which were entirely dictated by his desire for scientific truth. His position, in fact, was substantially the same as that taken up by Professor Summerlee at the last meeting. At that last meeting Professor Challenger had made certain assertions which had been queried by his colleague. Now this colleague came forward himself with the same assertions and expected them to remain unquestioned. Was this reasonable? ('Yes,' 'No,' and prolonged interruption, during which Professor Challenger was heard from the Press box to ask leave from the chairman to put Dr. Illingworth into the street.) A year ago one man said certain things. Now four men said other and more startling ones. Was this to constitute a final proof where the matters in question were of the most revolutionary and incredible character? There had been recent examples of travelers arriving from the unknown with certain tales which had been too readily accepted. Was the London Zoological Institute to place itself in this position? He admitted that the members of the committee were men of character. But human nature was very complex. Even Professors might be misled by the desire for notoriety. Like moths, we all love best to flutter in the light. Heavy-game shots liked to be in a position to cap the tales of their rivals, and journalists were not averse from sensational coups, even when imagination had to aid fact in the process. Each member of the committee had his own motive for making the most of his results. ('Shame! shame!') He had no desire to be offensive. ('You are!' and interruption.) The corroboration of these wondrous tales was really of the most slender description. What did it amount to? Some photographs. {Was it possible that in this age of ingenious manipulation photographs could be accepted as evidence?} What more? We have a story of a flight and a descent by ropes which precluded the production of larger specimens. It was ingenious, but not convincing. It was understood that Lord John Roxton claimed to have the skull of a phororachus. He could only say that he would like to see that skull.

"Lord John Roxton: 'Is this fellow calling me a liar?' (Uproar.)

"The Chairman: 'Order! order! Dr. Illingworth, I must direct you to bring your remarks to a conclusion and to move your amendment.'

"Dr. Illingworth: 'Your Grace, I have more to say, but I bow to your ruling. I move, then, that, while Professor Summerlee be thanked for his interesting address, the whole matter shall be regarded as 'non-proven,' and shall be referred back to a larger, and possibly more reliable Committee of Investigation.'

"It is difficult to describe the confusion caused by this amendment. A large section of the audience expressed their indignation at such a slur upon the travelers by noisy shouts of dissent and cries of, 'Don't put it!' 'Withdraw!' 'Turn him out!' On the other hand, the malcontents—and it cannot be denied that they were fairly numerous—cheered for the amendment, with cries of 'Order!' 'Chair!' and 'Fair play!' A scuffle broke out in the back benches, and blows were freely exchanged among the medical students who crowded that part of the hall. It was only the moderating influence of the presence of large numbers of ladies which prevented an absolute riot. Suddenly, however, there was a pause, a hush, and then complete silence. Professor Challenger was on his feet. His appearance and manner are peculiarly arresting, and as he raised his hand for order the whole audience settled down expectantly to give him a hearing.

"'It will be within the recollection of many present,' said Professor Challenger, 'that similar foolish and unmannerly scenes marked the last meeting at which I have been able to address them. On that occasion Professor Summerlee was the chief offender, and though he is now chastened and contrite, the matter could not be entirely forgotten. I have heard to-night similar, but even more offensive, sentiments from the person who has just sat down, and though it is a conscious effort of self-effacement to come down to that person's mental level, I will endeavor to do so, in order to allay any reasonable doubt which could possibly exist in the minds of anyone.' (Laughter and interruption.) 'I need not remind this audience that, though Professor Summerlee, as the head of the Committee of Investigation, has been put up to speak to-night, still it is I who am the real prime mover in this business, and that it is mainly to me that any successful result must be ascribed. I have safely conducted these three gentlemen to the spot mentioned, and I have, as you have heard, convinced them of the accuracy of my previous account. We had hoped that we should find upon our return that no one was so dense as to dispute our joint conclusions. Warned, however, by my previous experience, I have not come without such proofs as may convince a reasonable man. As explained by Professor Summerlee, our cameras have been tampered with by the ape-men when they ransacked our camp, and most of our negatives ruined.' (Jeers, laughter, and 'Tell us another!' from the back.) 'I have mentioned the ape-men, and I cannot forbear from saying that some of the sounds which now meet my ears bring back most vividly to my recollection my experiences with those interesting creatures.' (Laughter.) 'In spite of the destruction of so many invaluable negatives, there still remains in our collection a certain number of corroborative photographs showing the conditions of life upon the plateau. Did they accuse them of having forged these photographs?' (A voice, 'Yes,' and considerable interruption which ended in several men being put out of the hall.) 'The negatives were open to the inspection of experts. But what other evidence had they? Under the conditions of their escape it was naturally impossible to bring a large amount of baggage, but they had rescued Professor Summerlee's collections of butterflies and beetles, containing many new species. Was this not evidence?' (Several voices, 'No.') 'Who said no?'

"Dr. Illingworth (rising): 'Our point is that such a collection might have been made in other places than a prehistoric plateau.' (Applause.)

"Professor Challenger: 'No doubt, sir, we have to bow to your scientific authority, although I must admit that the name is unfamiliar. Passing, then, both the photographs and the entomological collection, I come to the varied and accurate information which we bring with us upon points which have never before been elucidated. For example, upon the domestic habits of the pterodactyl—'(A voice: 'Bosh,' and uproar)--'I say, that upon the domestic habits of the pterodactyl we can throw a flood of light. I can exhibit to you from my portfolio a picture of that creature taken from life which would convince you--'

"Dr. Illingworth: 'No picture could convince us of anything.'

"Professor Challenger: 'You would require to see the thing itself?'

"Dr. Illingworth: 'Undoubtedly.'

"Professor Challenger: 'And you would accept that?'

"Dr. Illingworth (laughing): 'Beyond a doubt.'

"It was at this point that the sensation of the evening arose—a sensation so dramatic that it can never have been paralleled in the history of scientific gatherings. Professor Challenger raised his hand in the air as a signal, and at once our colleague, Mr. E. D. Malone, was observed to rise and to make his way to the back of the platform. An instant later he re-appeared in company of a gigantic negro, the two of them bearing between them a large square packing-case. It was evidently of great weight, and was slowly carried forward and placed in front of the Professor's chair. All sound had hushed in the audience and everyone was absorbed in the spectacle before them. Professor Challenger drew off the top of the case, which formed a sliding lid. Peering down into the box he snapped his fingers several times and was heard from the Press seat to say, 'Come, then, pretty, pretty!' in a coaxing voice. An instant later, with a scratching, rattling sound, a most horrible and loathsome creature appeared from below and perched itself upon the side of the case. Even the unexpected fall of the Duke of Durham into the orchestra, which occurred at this moment, could not distract the petrified attention of the vast audience. The face of the creature was like the wildest gargoyle that the imagination of a mad medieval builder could have conceived. It was malicious, horrible, with two small red eyes as bright as points of burning coal. Its long, savage mouth, which was held half-open, was full of a double row of shark-like teeth. Its shoulders were humped, and round them were draped what appeared to be a faded gray shawl. It was the devil of our childhood in person. There was a turmoil in the audience—someone screamed, two ladies in the front row fell senseless from their chairs, and there was a general movement upon the platform to follow their chairman into the orchestra. For a moment there was danger of a general panic. Professor Challenger threw up his hands to still the commotion, but the movement alarmed the creature beside him. Its strange shawl suddenly unfurled, spread, and fluttered as a pair of leathery wings. Its owner grabbed at its legs, but too late to hold it. It had sprung from the perch and was circling slowly round the Queen's Hall with a dry, leathery flapping of its ten-foot wings, while a putrid and insidious odor pervaded the room. The cries of the people in the galleries, who were alarmed at the near approach of those glowing eyes and that murderous beak, excited the creature to a frenzy. Faster and faster it flew, beating against walls and chandeliers in a blind frenzy of alarm. 'The window! For heaven's sake shut that window!' roared the Professor from the platform, dancing and wringing his hands in an agony of apprehension. Alas, his warning was too late! In a moment the creature, beating and bumping along the wall like a huge moth within a gas-shade, came upon the opening, squeezed its hideous bulk through it, and was gone. Professor Challenger fell back into his chair with his face buried in his hands, while the audience gave one long, deep sigh of relief as they realized that the incident was over.

"Then—oh! how shall one describe what took place then—when the full exuberance of the majority and the full reaction of the minority united to make one great wave of enthusiasm, which rolled from the back of the hall, gathering volume as it came, swept over the orchestra, submerged the platform, and carried the four heroes away upon its crest?" (Good for you, Mac!) "If the audience had done less than justice, surely it made ample amends. Every one was on his feet. Every one was moving, shouting, gesticulating. A dense crowd of cheering men were round the four travelers. 'Up with them! up with them!' cried a hundred voices. In a moment four figures shot up above the crowd. In vain they strove to break loose. They were held in their lofty places of honor. It would have been hard to let them down if it had been wished, so dense was the crowd around them. 'Regent Street! Regent Street!' sounded the voices. There was a swirl in the packed multitude, and a slow current, bearing the four upon their shoulders, made for the door. Out in the street the scene was extraordinary. An assemblage of not less than a hundred thousand people was waiting. The close-packed throng extended from the other side of the Langham Hotel to Oxford Circus. A roar of acclamation greeted the four adventurers as they appeared, high above the heads of the people, under the vivid electric lamps outside the hall. 'A procession! A procession!' was the cry. In a dense phalanx, blocking the streets from side to side, the crowd set forth, taking the route of Regent Street, Pall Mall, St. James's Street, and Piccadilly. The whole central traffic of London was held up, and many collisions were reported between the demonstrators upon the one side and the police and taxi-cabmen upon the other. Finally, it was not until after midnight that the four travelers were released at the entrance to Lord John Roxton's chambers in the Albany, and that the exuberant crowd, having sung 'They are Jolly Good Fellows' in chorus, concluded their program with 'God Save the King.' So ended one of the most remarkable evenings that London has seen for a considerable time."

So far my friend Macdona; and it may be taken as a fairly accurate, if florid, account of the proceedings. As to the main incident, it was a bewildering surprise to the audience, but not, I need hardly say, to us. The reader will remember how I met Lord John Roxton upon the very occasion when, in his protective crinoline, he had gone to bring the "Devil's chick" as he called it, for Professor Challenger. I have hinted also at the trouble which the Professor's baggage gave us when we left the plateau, and had I described our voyage I might have said a good deal of the worry we had to coax with putrid fish the appetite of our filthy companion. If I have not said much about it before, it was, of course, that the Professor's earnest desire was that no possible rumor of the unanswerable argument which we carried should be allowed to leak out until the moment came when his enemies were to be confuted.

One word as to the fate of the London pterodactyl. Nothing can be said to be certain upon this point. There is the evidence of two frightened women that it perched upon the roof of the Queen's Hall and remained there like a diabolical statue for some hours. The next day it came out in the evening papers that Private Miles, of the Coldstream Guards, on duty outside Marlborough House, had deserted his post without leave, and was therefore courtmartialed. Private Miles' account, that he dropped his rifle and took to his heels down the Mall because on looking up he had suddenly seen the devil between him and the moon, was not accepted by the Court, and yet it may have a direct bearing upon the point at issue. The only other evidence which I can adduce is from the log of the SS. *Friesland*, a Dutch-American liner, which asserts that at nine next morning, Start Point being at the time ten miles upon their starboard quarter, they were passed by something between a flying goat and a monstrous bat, which was heading at a prodigious pace south and west. If its homing instinct led it upon the right line, there can be no doubt that somewhere out in the wastes of the Atlantic the last European pterodactyl found its end.

And Gladys—oh, my Gladys!--Gladys of the mystic lake, now to be re-named the Central, for never shall she have immortality through me. Did I not always see some hard fiber in her nature? Did I not, even at the time when I was proud to obey her behest, feel that it was surely a poor love which could drive a lover to his death or the danger of it? Did I not, in my truest thoughts, always recurring and always dismissed, see past the beauty of the face, and, peering into the soul, discern the twin shadows of selfishness and of fickleness glooming at the back of it? Did she love the heroic and the spectacular for its own noble sake, or was it for the glory which might, without effort or sacrifice, be reflected upon herself? Or are these thoughts the vain wisdom which comes after the event? It was the shock of my life. For a moment it had turned me to a cynic. But already, as I write, a week has passed, and we have had our momentous interview with Lord John Roxton and—well, perhaps things might be worse.

Let me tell it in a few words. No letter or telegram had come to me at Southampton, and I reached the little villa at Streatham about ten o'clock that night in a fever of alarm. Was she dead or alive? Where were all my nightly dreams of the open arms, the smiling face, the words of praise for her man who had risked his life to humor her whim? Already I was down from the high peaks and standing flat-footed upon earth. Yet some good reasons given might still lift me to the clouds once more. I rushed down the garden path, hammered at the door, heard the voice of Gladys within, pushed past the staring maid, and strode into the sitting-room. She was seated in a low settee under the shaded standard lamp by the piano. In three steps I was across the room and had both her hands in mine.

"Gladys!" I cried, "Gladys!"

She looked up with amazement in her face. She was altered in some subtle way. The expression of her eyes, the hard upward stare, the set of the lips, was new to me. She drew back her hands.

"What do you mean?" she said.

"Gladys!" I cried. "What is the matter? You are my Gladys, are you not—little Gladys Hungerton?"

"No," said she, "I am Gladys Potts. Let me introduce you to my husband."

How absurd life is! I found myself mechanically bowing and shaking hands with a little ginger-haired man who was coiled up in the deep arm-chair which had once been sacred to my own use. We bobbed and grinned in front of each other.

"Father lets us stay here. We are getting our house ready," said Gladys.

"Oh, yes," said I.

"You didn't get my letter at Para, then?"

"No, I got no letter."

"Oh, what a pity! It would have made all clear."

"It is quite clear," said I.

"I've told William all about you," said she. "We have no secrets. I am so sorry about it. But it couldn't have been so very deep, could it, if you could go off to the other end of the world and leave me here alone. You're not crabby, are you?"

"No, no, not at all. I think I'll go."

"Have some refreshment," said the little man, and he added, in a confidential way, "It's always like this, ain't it? And must be unless you had polygamy, only the other way round; you understand." He laughed like an idiot, while I made for the door.

I was through it, when a sudden fantastic impulse came upon me, and I went back to my successful rival, who looked nervously at the electric push.

"Will you answer a question?" I asked.

"Well, within reason," said he.

"How did you do it? Have you searched for hidden treasure, or discovered a pole, or done time on a pirate, or flown the Channel, or what? Where is the glamour of romance? How did you get it?"

He stared at me with a hopeless expression upon his vacuous, good-natured, scrubby little face.

"Don't you think all this is a little too personal?" he said.

"Well, just one question," I cried. "What are you? What is your profession?"

"I am a solicitor's clerk," said he. "Second man at Johnson and Merivale's, 41 Chancery Lane."

"Good-night!" said I, and vanished, like all disconsolate and broken-hearted heroes, into the darkness, with grief and rage and laughter all simmering within me like a boiling pot.

One more little scene, and I have done. Last night we all supped at Lord John Roxton's rooms, and sitting together afterwards we smoked in good comradeship and talked our adventures over. It was strange under these altered surroundings to see the old, well-known faces and figures. There was Challenger, with his smile of condescension, his drooping eyelids, his intolerant eyes, his aggressive beard, his huge chest, swelling and puffing as he laid down the law to Summerlee. And Summerlee, too, there he was with his short briar between his thin moustache and his gray goat's-beard, his worn face protruded in eager debate as he queried all Challenger's propositions. Finally, there was our host, with his rugged, eagle face, and his cold, blue, glacier eyes with always a shimmer of devilment and of humor down in the depths of them. Such is the last picture of them that I have carried away.

It was after supper, in his own sanctum—the room of the pink radiance and the innumerable trophies—that Lord John Roxton had something to say to us. From a cupboard he had brought an old cigar-box, and this he laid before him on the table.

"There's one thing," said he, "that maybe I should have spoken about before this, but I wanted to know a little more clearly where I was. No use to raise hopes and let them down again. But it's facts, not hopes, with us now. You may remember that day we found the pterodactyl rookery in the swamp—what? Well, somethin' in the lie of the land took my notice. Perhaps it has escaped you, so I will tell you. It was a volcanic vent full of blue clay." The Professors nodded.

"Well, now, in the whole world I've only had to do with one place that was a volcanic vent of blue clay. That was the great De Beers Diamond Mine of Kimberley—what? So you see I got diamonds into my head. I rigged up a contraption to hold off those stinking beasts, and I spent a happy day there with a spud. This is what I got."

He opened his cigar-box, and tilting it over he poured about twenty or thirty rough stones, varying from the size of beans to that of chestnuts, on the table.

"Perhaps you think I should have told you then. Well, so I should, only I know there are a lot of traps for the unwary, and that stones may be of any size and yet of little value where color and consistency are clean off. Therefore, I brought them back, and on the first day at home I took one round to Spink's, and asked him to have it roughly cut and valued."

He took a pill-box from his pocket, and spilled out of it a beautiful glittering diamond, one of the finest stones that I have ever seen.

"There's the result," said he. "He prices the lot at a minimum of two hundred thousand pounds. Of course it is fair shares between us. I won't hear of anythin' else. Well, Challenger, what will you do with your fifty thousand?"

"If you really persist in your generous view," said the Professor, "I should found a private museum, which has long been one of my dreams."

"And you, Summerlee?"

"I would retire from teaching, and so find time for my final classification of the chalk fossils."

"I'll use my own," said Lord John Roxton, "in fitting a well-formed expedition and having another look at the dear old plateau. As to you, young fellah, you, of course, will spend yours in gettin' married."

"Not just yet," said I, with a rueful smile. "I think, if you will have me, that I would rather go with you."

Lord Roxton said nothing, but a brown hand was stretched out to me across the table.

CPSIA information can be obtained at www.ICGtesting.com
Printed in the USA
BVOW08s1834240216

437945BV00001B/70/P

9 781610 010290